Pink Shades of Words

Compiled by

Glorya Hidalgo
Fifty Shades of Pink

Pink Shades of Words

This is a work of fiction. Names, places, characters, and events are fictitious in every regard. Any similarities to actual events and persons, living or dead, are purely coincidental. Any trademarks, service marks, product names, or named features are assumed to be the property of their respective owners, and are used only for reference. There is no implied endorsement if any of these terms are used. Except for review purposes, the reproduction of this book in whole or part, electronically or mechanically, constitutes a copyright violation.

PINK SHADES OF WORDS
© 2014 GLORYA HIDALGO — FIFTY SHADES OF PINK
Cover Art Designer Kristen Karwan

For Sara
You are the strongest woman that I know and the big sister that I never had! Thank you for finding your breast cancer early so that I could continue to have you in my life!

Glorya Hidalgo
Fifty Shades of Pink team captain

Fifty Shades of Pink team participates in the Avon Breast Cancer Walk in beautiful Santa Barbara, CA.

You can donate to our team at
www.avonwalk.org/goto/50shadesofpink

Like us on Facebook
www.facebook.com/50shadesofpinkteam

Email:
glorya.hidalgo@gmail.com

Pink Shades of Words

A compilation of stories to raise awareness and money for

Fifty Shades of Pink
Avon Walk for Breast Cancer
Santa Barbara, CA

Contents

Ready to Wed	1
Forgetting	67
Max	99
Fate	144
Final Stage	172
Choices	186
Leap of Faith	207
Trying	288
Ruby and Finn	300
A Bend in the Road	305
More than a Friend Request	320
Songs of Dominance	416
Falling	433
Determined to Obey	439
Meeting Sin	471
Seduction & Temptation	481
Don't Close Your Eyes	512
Acknowledgements	553

Ready to Wed

J.L. Berg

Copyright © 2014 J.L. Berg
All rights reserved.

For Christine.
We love you.
Cancer can suck it.

Chapter One

Clare

"Where are my keys?" I shouted, running around the kitchen like a crazy person in search of my bright pink monogrammed key ring. It really shouldn't be that hard to miss.

"Why do you need keys?" asked Logan, my smug looking fiancé, as he casually leaned against the door frame.

"What do you mean? Aren't we leaving? Of course I need keys. Why are you just standing there? Start looking!" I commanded.

He didn't budge. He just continued his casual lean and grinned, looking cocky and gorgeous, before pulling his own set of keys out of his pocket.

"I don't really think we need both set of keys while we're away... do you?" he asked.

I just stared at him. Why was I so frantic and nervous? I'd spent the last twenty minutes looking for keys that I didn't need. I knew that. Logan was driving to the airport, so why did I need keys? Before the keys, I'd scrubbed down the entire kitchen from top to bottom after doing the same to all three bathrooms. Why? I have no freaking clue. Did I want the house to look nice just in case someone came to rob us? Because nothing says, "Welcome to our house, please take our television!" like clean bathrooms.

"You're right. I don't need my keys," I said calmly.

He left his post at the entryway and walked towards me, wrapping his arms around my waist. He pulled me closer to him and I sighed, settling into the warmth of his body instantly.

"Are you okay Clare? You've been wired ever since we started planning this a week ago. You know, we don't have to get married this weekend. We can postpone it. Like I've always said, I'll wait for you."

"No. I want to get married this weekend. It's just... there's a lot to do, and I feel like I'm going to forget something important," I answered.

"There are two things you need at that wedding," he said.

"Oh?"

"Mmmhmm... .me and a ring. The rest is just for show."

"Don't forget me!" Maddie said, barreling into the kitchen from the hallway. My overly excited five year old couldn't wait to hop on that plane and go to "the beach". She didn't even care what beach, only that we were going and she got to play in the sand. The fact that Logan and I were getting married was the icing on the cake. God, I was lucky. I gave Logan a once over, checking for signs of weakness, symptoms that he might be tired or sick.

Well, mostly lucky.

"You got all of your new meds?" I asked, looking at Logan with concern.

"Yes, there are only a few for now."

"Are you sure... about waiting?"

Logan had just been diagnosed with Hodgkin's disease, and in an effort to not put our lives on hold, we decided to get married as soon as possible. His doctors were optimistic, saying that since it was caught early, his likelihood of recovery was high, but I still worried. My first husband, Maddie's father, had died of cancer. I still remember every single day, every minute watching helplessly as he deteriorated in front of me. I had been useless, completely useless, and unable to stop it.

"I'm sure. It's only a couple weeks. The oncologist said it would be okay to delay treatment for two weeks. I want to enjoy our wedding and time away with you. I'll start the minute we get home. I promise."

I nodded, giving him a hint of a smile before turning to Maddie.

"Are you ready?" I asked brightly.

"Yes, yes, yes!" she beamed.

"Well, let's go!"

We loaded the car and headed to the airport for our two week long stay in St. Thomas. It had originally been our vacation for the summer... the first trip Logan and I would take together. He was my first ray of hope since Ethan died. He showed me love can exist after death, even when it seems impossible. When he proposed, we turned our vacation into an impromptu wedding, renting out a small resort and inviting our family and few friends. Logan still wouldn't tell me how much everything cost. He just smiled and started whistling every time I asked. I had a feeling it was a crap load. I knew he could afford it, but it didn't make me feel less guilty.

"When do Leah and Garrett fly in?" Logan asked.

Leah was my best friend and Maid of Honor. She was flying in with my brother, who was a groomsman for Logan. Leah and Garrett loved each other like brother and sister and always tried to hang out whenever they could. My brother's crazy work schedule didn't offer him much time off, so they decided to book their tickets together to give them some time to catch up.

"Um, I think they come in a few hours after us. Leah had to work late last night, so she wanted to take a later flight. Garrett is supposed to be picking her up around noon."

"Do they... I mean, have Garrett and Leah ever...?" he asked, skirting around the question.

"Eww... gross! No!"

He lifted a hand from the steering wheel in mock defense, "Just asking... didn't want to make assumptions. I've only met your brother a handful of times. I don't think I've ever met anyone who works more than he does... and I'm a doctor."

"I know. My brother, the workaholic. Who knew he'd move back home from college and we'd still never see him," I said with a shrug.

After checking our luggage, including the very precious garment bag that contained my wedding dress, we went through security. This was always a fun task with a child, and we of course got several glaring looks from the speedy businessmen. Once securely checked, we proceeded to our gate.

"I can't believe they wouldn't let me carry on my garment bag!" I said with a huff.

"Well, it was quite large," Logan said, pointing to our gate and taking a seat in our designated area. Maddie immediately reached into the backpack of activities we'd packed, pulled out a book and began reading... or at least pretended. Either way she was being quiet, and I thanked the heavens for the few minutes of peace. I loved her more than I ever thought possible, but man... she could talk. I guess I shouldn't be surprised considering who gave birth to her. I'm not known for being quiet, especially when I'm nervous. I babble a lot.

"It wasn't that large! Okay... it was, but crap. They let that dude in front of us bring his guitar," I pouted.

"Hey," Logan said, pulling my chin level so our eyes were locked. "It will be fine. Nothing could ruin this week, okay? By the end of this weekend, you will be officially and forever mine. I don't care if you're in a burlap sack, Clare. The only thing that matters is that you say those vows and bind yourself to me for eternity, got it?"

"Yes," I said, a bit breathless.

"Good." He gave me a quick wink before pulling Maddie on his lap. She'd only learned a few words so far, so he assisted by helping her sound out the rest. I just watched, loving the perfect picture the two of them made. I would have never guessed, walking into that emergency room several months ago when Maddie had fallen and given herself a concussion, that I would wind up here. Logan not only healed Maddie that day, he's been healing all of us ever since.

About thirty minutes later the announcement came that our flight was boarding, so we packed up Maddie's things and headed for the gate to check in. With Maddie bouncing up and down in his arms, Logan ran his free hand down my cheek, his eyes suddenly filled of emotion.

"Ready to go get married?" he asked.

"Absolutely."

Smiling, he grabbed my hand and we walked towards our future.

****

Logan

So many emotions hit me all at once when we boarded that plane to St. Thomas. The child in my arms was about to become my daughter. The woman I loved was about to become my wife.

A family. My family, finally.

It was something I'd always wanted, and here it was, all because I opened the right exam room door and found my future on the other side.

After a quick changeover in Charlotte, we were flying over water and headed for St. Thomas. Clare and Maddie had fallen asleep, both leaning their heads against my chest as I tried to read. I puffed out a small laugh and gave up, my awkward attempts at holding my e-reader with the two of them wedged against me proved fruitless. I tucked it in the front pocket of the seat in front of me, and rested my head against the seat, looking down at my two red-headed angels.

Maddie looked like a cherub plucked right out of heaven. Her strawberry blonde curls cascaded down her back in a fiery display, mimicking her mother's. Clare's red hair was deeper, more intense; closer to auburn but it still having that crimson glow to it that matched her personality. Sweet with just a touch of fire — that was my Clare. I never knew what I was going to get from one moment to the next, and that's what I loved about her. She kept me on my toes, loved me for who I was, and never let me be anything but myself.

I must have dozed off, because the next thing I knew I was being poked in the head by Maddie. *What did she have against my head?*

"You're awake!" she said brightly.

"Well, I am now, Princess!" I gave her side a pinch which caused her to giggle.

"Shhh! You'll wake up Mommy," I said, running my hand through Clare's hair as she rested against me. She really had been running around like mad the last week, so much so that I'd barely seen her. I knew planning the wedding start-to-finish inside one week had put a lot of pressure on her, so I tried not to take it personally. I just hoped that's all it was.

"So, Princess... what is the first thing you want to do when we get there?"

Figuring she'd say she wanted to go to the beach or swim in one of the many pools, her actual answer totally threw me for a loop.

"Ice cream. I want ice cream."

I silently laughed, being mindful of Clare.

"We fly all the way to St. Thomas and you want ice cream?" *Kids. Gotta love 'em.*

"Well, I've never been any other place but America. And ice cream is my favorite food. Is it different in different places?"

"Hmm... good point. I think we should check immediately, just to be sure."

She nodded, and I gave her a wink. She asked if she could watch a movie on the individual TV screens we had, and I said sure, letting her navigate the channels and pick her own movie. With one hand free now, I picked up my e-reader and started reading again, happy to have Clare warm and safe in my arms.

An entire kid's movie later, we were making our descent, and Maddie was plastered to the window looking out at the scenery below. It was quite the sight. Brilliant blue water contrasted with the deep green landscape. All I saw was my future. In a few days, on that island, I would marry Clare. I looked down at her as she began to stir and felt whole. Cancer or no... my life was perfect.

Chapter Two

Clare

"Where is it?" I asked again, as we watched the endless luggage go around the noisy carousel in baggage claim. Maddie was doing circles around Logan's legs which he did an excellent job of ignoring. He was settling into his Dad role nicely, I laughed silently to myself.

"I'm sure it's coming," he answered, although I could see even he was starting to doubt his words.

All of our bags had come through the carousel... all but one. My garment bag. The one the stupid perky blonde lady at the counter had made me check. The garment bag she had assured me would be fine. Where the hell was it? How could I get married without a dress?

Just when I had created the ultimate list of ways in which I was going to let the customer service reps have it, my garment bag appeared, like a beacon from heaven.

"There it is! Oh thank God!" I squealed, running to the carousel like a manic child, only to be immediately halted when I saw the huge gash in the side. My once mint condition ivory dress was now spilling out of the hole in the side and ripped to shreds.

I heard Logan curse right before the tears started to sting my eyes. What the hell was I supposed to do now? Taking charge, Logan grabbed the garment bag off the carousel before it made another long journey around the airport, and held it up for inspection. Yep, it was a total loss unless we wanted to change things up and have a themed wedding; if I wanted to go as the Bride of Chuckie, I was golden.

"Do you think it's fixable?" he asked gently.

"No," I moaned, before covering my face with my hands.

"Oh no Mommy, your pretty dress is all messed up!"

Logan patted her on the head and said it was okay to give Mommy a hug. She happily came to my side, offering her sympathy in the form of child-sized hugs. They helped for about five seconds until I saw that humongous gash again, and then the misery came rushing back.

Stupid airline. Stupid dress.

"I don't have a dress! What am I supposed to do without a dress? Do you think it's a sign? Maybe we aren't supposed to get married this week. Maybe this is one giant ivory colored sign that we are supposed to wait... go home, and get married later."

"Whoa... babe, you're babbling. Like, a lot." He gripped my shoulder and pulled me close. He smelled like aftershave and mint. Familiar and safe.

"Calm down. This is a wardrobe malfunction, not a cosmic sign from the universe, okay?"

I nodded, and pulled him closer, resting my head on his shoulder, knowing he was right. It was just the fact that with every step we took further away from home, away from that hospital and his doctors, I felt the panic growing and multiplying a bit more. I looked up at him and wondered, *Were we making the right choice in putting off his treatment?*

****

Logan

"Oh, thank fuck you're here!" I said, seeing Leah enter the hotel, with Garrett in tow.

"Well, it's nice to see you too. handsome," she answered with a wink and a sly grin. I helped them with their luggage and gave Garrett a friendly guy hug before turning back to Leah, my savior for the day.

"So, why are you so glad to see me? Not that I don't appreciate the welcome."

"Clare. She's freaking out. Her dress was trashed on the trip over here, and she is literally losing her shit. I don't know a thing about dresses. I don't have a clue on where to look, what she wants. And now she's got it in her head that this is some sort of sign that the entire wedding is doomed."

I started pacing the lobby because I really didn't know what else to do. I know weddings always had kinks, but ours was supposed to be low key. There were only a few guests, and yes… we threw it together in a few days and did it destination style, but still. Low key. *What happened to that?*

"Logan." I didn't answer, I just continued to pace, hoping an answer would magically appear to fix my freaked out bride.

"Logan, seriously. Look at me."

Leah sounded pretty damn serious, so I did as I was told and met her gaze. I'd learned to not mess with Leah. She could be kind of scary.

"Garrett, go take Logan out for drinks or something. I've got it from here."

"Wait, what?"

"You're dismissed. Didn't you hear me the first time?"

"Uh…"

"Go do dude stuff, and I will handle the distraught bride. I'm pretty sure I can find a wedding dress a lot faster than you can! We'll meet you for dinner!"

And just like that, Leah saved the day.

Chapter Three

Clare

"Okay, get up," Leah said, pulling my arm in a vain attempt to get my ass out of the lounge chair I was currently occupying.

"Nooo… I don't want to," I whined.

She looked at the little table next to my lounger and laughed.

"How many of those fruity cocktails have you had, Clare Bear?"

"Um… two, maybe?" I hiccupped a bit, and laughed. Okay, maybe a bit more than two.

"Was your plan to drink yourself a new wedding dress?"

I slumped back into my cozy lounge chair, enjoying the feel of the warm sun on my bare skin. After we arrived at the resort, a truly breathtaking place I might add, I dropped my ruined wedding dress in our suite and decided to take my sorrows poolside. The pool had sweeping, endless views of the ocean and the water seemed to disappear right into the blue horizon. Maddie was enjoying the kid's day program the resort offered, and I figured putting on my bikini and ordering a few drinks might improve my sour mood.

At least I was giggling and my mood felt a bit lighter. That was an improvement.

"No, but what am I supposed to do, Leah? Do you see a wedding shop here?" I asked, sweeping my hands in a grand gesture to point out the obvious. We were in paradise. There were bars, restaurants and tourist traps, but definitely no places to buy a wedding gown. I was screwed. Maybe I should just get married in that burlap sack Logan mentioned... or a bikini. He'd definitely like that a lot more than a sack.

"What are you grinning about?"

"What? Nothing."

"Shit, you're totally tossed."

"Am not."

"Are too."

"Nuh uh," I argued, but the words slurred and totally ruined my argument. I laughed.

"Oh, for fuck's sake, Clare!" she said, trying not to grin. I could see she was trying to be serious, but she was doing a terrible job of it because the corners of her mouth were struggling to stay turned down and she finally had to turn away.

"Come on, Leah! Have a drink with me! My wedding is ruined... let's get drunk! Well, I mean I'm already there... so you just need to catch up!"

She whipped her head around and planted her sundress clad body on the lounger next to mine. Her blonde hair and sun kissed legs looked right at home in this tropical location. I, on the other hand, with my freckled pale skin and red hair, looked like I hopped on the wrong plane. The only way I could stand the sun was slathering on four layers of sunscreen and wearing a huge floppy hat.

"You two are going to drive me insane by the end of the week. Listen to me, your wedding is not ruined. You had a setback, that's it. We are going to get a driver and I'm going to talk to the concierge and we are going to find you a dress, come hell or high water. Got it?"

Snorting and trying to mask my laughter, I nodded; Bossy Leah always cracked me up. I loved her to death and she always managed to take charge when needed, but when she took on her alter ego and started barking orders and taking charge, I couldn't help but grin. It reminded me of the little girl who stood up for me in that cafeteria so many years ago and instantly became my lifelong best friend.

"So, get your cute ass upstairs, change, and meet me in the lobby in fifteen minutes!"

"Yes, Ma'am!"

"And I'll get you some coffee."

"I like sugar!" I sung, as I started for the sliding door back into the hotel.

"Mmmhmm... I know. And for fuck's sakes, wrap a towel around that shit before your fiancé has to kill half the crew for hitting on you."

"Oh," I laughed. "Oops."

I grabbed a towel from the stack next to the door, and wrapped it around my scantily clad body. The last thing I saw was Leah shaking her head and laughing as I haphazardly made my way back to my hotel room.

****

"Drink it all," Leah said, shoving a huge cup of coffee in my hand as I walked out of the elevator fifteen minutes later. Dressed in jean shorts and a green tank top, I was ready for whatever adventure she'd mapped out for us. I tried to have faith, but I was really doubting that I'd be able to find a new dress with such limited time before the big day. I'd barely been able to find the first dress, having just enough time to visit two stores in a single afternoon. The dress I'd bought was off the rack, of course, and one of the few in my size. It was beautiful, well... not anymore.

"Yes, Ma'am!" I said again, snickering.

"Mommy is funny today!"

"Yep, sure is," Leah said, giving me a wry look.

While I was upstairs changing, Leah had picked up Maddie from the day camp and asked if she wanted to help us shop. Being the little diva she was, she naturally agreed.

"Let's go shopping, ladies!" Leah said cheerfully, and all of us, including my extra large cup of coffee with cream and sugar, headed out of the hotel and into the black rented sedan Leah had managed to obtain.

"The concierge gave me a couple places to check out, but based on everything she told me, there is one place I want to go to first."

I gave her a thumbs up and we were on our way.

"I think you should get a pink dress Mommy."

"Oh yeah? I'm not sure pink is my color baby girl."

She gave me a pointed look that could only be pulled off by a five year old and said, "Pink is everyone's color Mommy."

Put in my place by my own offspring. *Figures.*

"Well, if there is a pink dress... I promise I'll try it on." I gave Leah a wink, knowing full well I wouldn't have to keep my word. What kind of bridal shop had pink dresses?

I really should have kept my mouth shut, because as soon as we walked into the door of the beautifully decorated bridal salon Leah had chosen, in all its pink, glittery glory, was a dress that would have put Glenda the Good Witch to shame.

I think I almost went deaf from the squeals that emanated from my daughter.

"Mommy! You have to try this on!"

At least she said I just had to try it on. Based on the decibel level of that squeal, I figured she would have demanded I buy it on the spot.

No doubt hearing the noise from our grand entrance, a store clerk emerged and gave us a warm welcome. She was the nicest woman you could ask for when shopping for a wedding dress. A complete contrast to the stores I visited back home. They were all rush, rush… and highly annoyed I had come in at the last minute. Who gets married that quickly? *Um, lots of people.* Get over it. And no, I wasn't pregnant. But thanks for giving me the once over.

Was it a crime that I wanted to look good on my special day, even if it wasn't a year in the future?

The woman helping us, Maria, seemed to understand perfectly, having most likely helped plenty of women in similar situations. We weren't in Vegas, but with views and romance surrounding you at every turn in this place, impromptu weddings were likely to occur.

"What type of dress were you looking for?" she asked, which took me by surprise.

"Whatever you have off the rack, I guess."

"Oh darling… we have plenty. Tell me what you envision wearing the day you marry your special man, and I will see what I can do."

Maybe it was the alcohol, maybe I was overly emotional from everything that was happening… but I began to tear up. Leah threw an arm around me and gave me a gentle hug.

"See, I told you we would find you something special. Did you ever stop to think that maybe your dress getting trashed wasn't a sign that you weren't supposed to get married, but a sign that you weren't supposed to get married in that dress?"

I looked up at her confused.

"Clare, don't try and hide it. I know you hated that dress."

I tried to argue with her, but I couldn't. I really did hate that dress. It was, like I said, beautiful… with a sweeping matte satin train and fitted strapless bodice… but it wasn't me at all.

"When I see myself on that beach, marrying Logan, I see myself in vintage lace. Something simple — timeless and elegant, but not overdone."

Maria smiled, "I think I have just the thing."

****

Logan

"She's going to kill you, man," my soon to be brother in law said, shaking his head as I moved the last bag across the hall.

"I might kill myself first."

"They're not back yet. You could still change your mind. She'd never know."

I stopped in the middle of the hall, looking back and forth between the two doors and shook my head.

"No, I want to do this. I think we need a bit of tradition."

"Okay, but do me one favor?"

"Sure, what's that?"

"Let me be around when you tell her?" he said, before hitting me on the back and laughing. I groaned, hating myself already.

We didn't have to wait long. After finishing the task that would no doubt land me in the dog house, we headed downstairs to the bar and met the girls in the lobby, returning from their afternoon out. My eyes came to rest on Clare, and I felt my breath hitch. Even after months together, waking up each morning by her side, day after day, she still managed to steal my breath with just one glimpse.

She was glowing, full of joy, and no longer carrying that devastated expression she'd arrived with after finding her destroyed wedding dress.

Instantly, I was at her side. Bending down, I placed a lingering, tender kiss on her lips.

"I'm guessing it was a good trip?"

She smiled against my lips, and nodded.

"Leah, could you take Maddie to the pool for an hour or so, while I unpack with Logan?"

Her eyes had that look. That mischievous, want-to-fuck-you look. I was so screwed.

"Yep. On it. Come on, Short Stack!"

Leah picked up a giggling Maddie and headed upstairs to Leah's room to change. Maddie, deciding that since she was at the beach, a swim suit must be worn at all times. She was hopping up and down, ready to jump in. Leah kept tickling her, telling her to be patient. Garrett looked back at us, obviously trying to decide whether or not he wanted to be around for my bomb drop, and finally gave us a salute and hurried after Leah, catching her in the elevator just before it closed.

It was just her and me. She looked up with those seductive green eyes I adored and pulled my hand towards the elevator.

"So, about upstairs..." I started, but was interrupted the second the elevator doors closed. Clare pushed me against the wall with her free hand, holding her garment bag with the other and pressing her body against mine. She teased me with a light kiss, nipping at my bottom lip with her teeth, before taking charge in an all consuming kiss that left me dizzy.

My brain went haywire, and I lost the ability to think beyond her and how good her lips felt, how I wanted to take her right there in that elevator and if she didn't stop kissing me like that, I would.

I don't remember how, but somehow we made it out of the elevator when it came to our floor and to our suite. I swiped the keycard and we all but fell into the room. Immediately after closing the door, I had her pinned to it, running my hands down the curve of her ass to hook her legs around me. She wrapped both of her arms around my neck. I had no idea where the garment bag went and at that point I didn't fucking care. I said she could get married in a burlap sack, and I meant it.

Pinned securely to the wall, her hand went to the front of my shorts, palming my hard length through the fabric. Just that one touch from her could end me. God, what the hell was I thinking earlier? I needed to go across the hall and move everything back before she noticed.

Her eyes focused on me, a pleased smile spreading across her face, knowing she could bring so much pleasure with such a small gesture.

Just as I was about to reciprocate, dive my hand into the juncture of her thighs and feel that wet heat I loved, her eyes moved away from mine and focused on the room.

"Where are the rest of the suitcases?"

Fuck.

"Uhhh..."

"Logan, where are your suitcases?"

"Across the hall?" I don't know why I phrased it like a question. Like that would help.

"Across the hall? Why?"

"It doesn't matter. Forget it. I'll move them back." I moved in to kiss her, wanting to get back to the naughty fun we were having, but she turned her head, giving me an amused and slightly pissed look.

"*You* moved them? Why would you do that?"

I ran my hands up her shirt, still intent on distracting her. She slapped away my hand. I was not getting out of this.

"I thought it might be nice for the two of us to... you know, not be together until the wedding. A bit of tradition."

"Oh, I see."

Well, that wasn't so bad.

"And what is this exactly?" she asked, referring to the fact that I had her pressed against the door of our once shared suite, seconds away from stripping her naked and fucking her until she screamed my name so loud all the neighbors heard.

"I decided, after a bit of thinking, that it was a dumb idea… so I'm moving everything back."

She gave me a mischievous grin. A very different type of mischief though than what I witnessed in the lobby. Whatever she was thinking now, I had a feeling I wouldn't be enjoying it.

"No I think it's a great idea," she said, sliding her beautiful legs down to the ground, and giving my body a slight push off hers.

"You do?"

"Oh yeah. What is that saying? Distance makes the heart grow fonder?"

She sauntered away, bending down to pick up the garment bag she'd dropped in our mangled entrance minutes ago. She made a show of it too, sticking her ass up and bending down slowly.

How many days until we got married? Three?

I was so fucked.

Chapter Four

Clare

"Men are so dumb," Leah laughed, having just heard about my afternoon nookie that wasn't.

"I know! So, now, I'm holding him to it. If he thought it was such a great idea, then we'll do it. Separate rooms and no sex until our wedding night."

"That's mean," she said.

"Oh, no. What's mean is that I'm going to make it hell for him." I emphasized my point, perking up my boobs that were on full display in my very revealing teal dress I'd chosen for dinner.

"Okay, now that's just evil. Good job." She gave me a high five.

We continued to laugh and enjoy our relaxed time together. We didn't have a lot of it back home. One of us usually had to run off and we never had enough time. She worked full time as a nurse, and I had Maddie and now Logan. Our lives were chaotic, but we always made time for each other.

After an hour or so, everyone else joined us for dinner. We had a large party. My parents had flown in just a few hours ago, along with Logan's best friend Colin and his wife Ella who brought along their newborn son. We all ooh'ed and ahh'd over Colin's mini-me before settling down to eat. Maddie had spent the afternoon swimming with Leah, and when my parents arrived, she took them on a tour of the grounds, showing them where all of her favorite spots were. She'd only been here for a few hours longer than them, but she was the expert.

Naturally.

Logan sat down next to me, noticing my dress right away. His eyes widened and zeroed in on the cleavage billowing out. This was going to be fun.

"Nana, did you know that ice cream tastes even better on an island?" Maddie said to my mother, who had just taken her seat next to my father. Both were dressed casually and looked happy and relaxed. I was so glad to have them here.

"I didn't know that! You'll have to show me!"

"Logan took me right when we got off the plane and he got chocolate and I got mango. It was yummy!"

"So yummy, she got it all over her dress," Logan exclaimed, giving her a nudge which made her giggle.

Kids can never eat ice cream without making a royal mess. It's like they don't understand the concept of how to lick the ice cream. Only mash. *Lick the ice cream? Okay Mommy!* Five seconds later, the kid is covered in it from head to toe.

"You forgot to mention that I got chocolate, but I didn't actually get to eat any of it," Logan said, giving me a look.

"Your fault. You shouldn't have ordered chocolate. You should know better by now."

"I asked you if you wanted any and you said no!"

"Still your fault."

I love chocolate. A lot. Bordering on slightly obsessed? Maybe. He should know not to bring any around me. I've been stealing chocolate and desserts from him since our first date. Even before, actually.

All throughout dinner, I caught Logan staring at me. He was distracted and would have to be asked questions more than once before he could answer. My teal man-killing dress was working.

Was making my fiancé miserable days before our wedding mean? Maybe. But it was fun.

****

Logan

That dress. That god damn dress. Where the hell did she get it? And how soon could I peel it off of her? I knew what she was doing. I knew she was playing me... pushing all my buttons to punish me for moving out of our suite.

Men are dumb. We make stupid mistakes. A lot.

Even the smartest of us, no matter how many Ivy League degrees we may have nailed to our walls, are stupid as fuck when it comes to the opposite sex. I realized this about half a second too late — right around the time I had my fiancée pinned against a door, ready to devour her.

Tradition? A little time apart? *Fuck that.* I tried to move back in immediately, but no… the damage had already been done.

Clare had already initiated my punishment before I had formed the words of my apology. And now that punishment was right up in my face — two round perfect breasts surrounded by a teal dress that was probably illegal in some countries. She leaned forward laughing, and I got an even better view down that valley of sin.

Dying. I was dying.

Shifting slightly, hoping to not draw attention to my now very uncomfortable position, I tried to get back into the conversation that was taking place at the table. But all I could see was Clare; Her dark red hair, creamy smooth skin, and emerald green eyes that had held me prisoner since the moment I met her. A very willing prisoner, mind you. I had no plans of ever escaping.

She was my world. She had given me everything I'd ever wanted in life. If someone had asked the old me whether I thought one person could bring such happiness to your life, I would have laughed in their face. I'd spent a lifetime being screwed over by those who were supposed to love me, and finally when I found someone to love me back, I couldn't return those feelings. I'd decided love was something that was taught, learned from an early age and since my upbringing was less than warm and fuzzy, I'd missed out on those essential lessons needed to love another.

Meeting Clare had taught me otherwise. Her very presence showed me that I was so much more. Love was more than just a lesson or an acquired skill, and in a few days, she would be my wife. Mine to love and cherish forever.

She laughed again, the musical melody of her laugh bringing a smile to my face even though I had no idea what was being said. She lit up my entire world.

Clare's parents rose from their seats, thanking everyone for dinner and headed to bed. Apparently dinner was over. How long had I spaced out? Everyone else said their goodnight, and Clare, Maddie, and I headed upstairs to our suites. Plural.

God, I really was an ass.

"What's an ass?" Maddie asked as we exited the elevator on the top floor.

I looked at her, and quickly to Clare who was giving me a death stare. A slightly amused one, but a death stare nonetheless.

Great, I was thinking out loud now. Is this what happens when I went too long without touching Clare? *Would I go crazy?*

"Uhh... I said pass. Yeah, pass. I was thinking that we needed to get season passes for the amusement park when we got home."

"The season is just about to end," Clare said, arching her brow, almost as if she were challenging me.

"Well, for next year then. Never hurts to plan ahead, right?"

Maddie then launched into a ten minute conversation about what rides were her favorite and what order she would ride them and how much she loved cotton candy, especially the pink kind because pink was her favorite color. By the time we got her calmed down, she was dressed for bed and cuddling her favorite stuffed animal. We said goodnight and softly shut the door behind us.

It took about five seconds for Clare to burst out laughing.

"Season passes?"

"It was the only thing I could think of!" I said defensively. "Besides, I didn't hear you offering anything up."

"What were you muttering about anyway?" she asked, still snickering about my less than PG mumbling.

"I don't even remember. No sex is driving me bat shit crazy, Clare! You must take pity on me... for both of our sakes. Otherwise, I could be clinically insane by the time we take our vows, and then how would you know I actually mean them?"

"You're seriously asking for a pity lay?"

I sauntered over to her, grabbed her around the waist and pulled her body to mine with a bit of force, causing her to gasp in surprise. I let my lips hover over hers.

"I can assure you, a lay with me will never be pitiful."

I think her brain went offline for a moment or two, because her eyes glazed over and she licked her lips hungrily, causing me to groan. I bent down to finally take her perfect red lips, only to be stopped with a single finger. I guess her brain came back online. *Damn.*

"I think you have a room to go to," she said, her finger still holding court on my deprived lips. Her mouth was upturned in a slight smile, but her eyes still looked a bit unfocused, like she was fighting the desire as much as I was. Good, at least I knew this was affecting her as much as me.

I sighed, knowing she'd won the battle tonight, but only tonight. There was always tomorrow. We were going snorkeling, and she could never resist a shirtless Logan. The thought brought a smirk to my face as I turned and made my exit.

"Well, just in case you get lonely or cold… you know where to find me!" I said, before giving her one last panty dropping smile and exiting the room.

Clare — one, Logan — zero. That would have to change tomorrow.

Chapter Five

Clare

I'd never been snorkeling, but lounging outside on the sun-drenched beach next to my sexy as sin fiancé wasn't a bad way to spend an afternoon. I was becoming mesmerized by the way his dark blue swim trunks hung low on his hips. I could just make out the beginning of that "V" I so loved to trace with my tongue when we were alone. I licked my lips just thinking about it.

His hair was messy and yet completely put together. I have no idea how guys did that. I know, from living with him, he did little with it. He just ran his hands through it and *poof!* Magic hair! Me, on the other hand? When I woke up, it looked like a small woodland creature had taken residence in my red locks overnight. I had a thing for Logan's hair. It was one of the first things I noticed about him when we met, his gorgeous, just-fucked hair. And now, I knew from experience... it looked even better after a good roll in the sheets.

"You're staring at me," Logan said, his eyes still closed as he soaked up the sun.

"Well, there's a lot to stare at," I answered back.

"Well, anytime you want to transition from staring to touching, just let me know."

The corner of his mouth turned up into a half smirk, and I couldn't help but laugh. He was relentless. My little game of revenge had turned into an all-out war. Which one of us would cave first? I'd won round one last night, but then he showed up at my door this morning in a towel, water dripping off his perfect hair, running down his shoulders and broad chest, and I forgot how to speak. I stood there, momentarily stunned for God only knows how long, until I heard him say, "Hey, did you hear what I said?" Uh, no… how could I concentrate on anything else but those tiny beads of water dripping down his body?

He chuckled, "I said, do you have any toothpaste? I'm out."

I took one last look at up and down his scrumptious body, trying not to whimper as I walked away to retrieve the requested item. I almost caved, almost gave in right then and there. Had it not been for Maddie barreling out of her room asking for breakfast, I probably would have pulled him by the towel into the room and tackled him to the ground.

The shower trick was low. He knew how much I loved him in a towel. It reminded me of our first morning together. We'd woken up and showered together, and I finally felt like I had found home again.

Before I had a chance to come up with a witty comeback to his touching comment, our instructor showed up; he was a tanned young surfer dude with blonde hair and an accent to match his laid back style. We both stood to greet him, and he kindly shook our hands, but his eyes lingered on me, and Logan noticed.

"Nice to meet you, Derek. I'm Logan, and this is my *fiancée*, Clare. We're here for the week celebrating our upcoming wedding." It wasn't lost on me that he emphasized the word fiancée or immediately wrapped a possessive arm around my waist.

"Well, it's nice to meet you both. Very nice," he said, his eyes still trying to lock with mine. Not happening, dude.

"Well, who's ready to get wet?!" he said with enthusiasm. Logan's hand gripped my hip harder and I sighed.

Oh, this was going to be fun.

****

Logan

I hated snorkeling. If that guy looked at Clare one more time, I swore I was going to shove his air tube up his ass. Note to self, request old, gay instructor next time.

"Okay, guys… had a great time. Thanks for spending the afternoon with me," the douche said, before he narrowed in on Clare. "If you need any one-on-one time in the future, please be sure to ask for Derek."

Clare's eyes widened a bit before giving a polite nod. She said thank you, which was more politeness than I could offer up at the moment. It was all I could do to keep my mouth shut. It takes a special kind of asshole to flirt with your fiancé right in front of you days before your wedding. The asshole in question sauntered away, no doubt thinking Clare was checking him out as he did. She wasn't. She had turned to me, her eyes full of laughter.

"You're jealous. And mad."

"That was not fun."

"You're kind of hot when you're mad," she said, rising up on her tip toes to place a soft kiss on my mouth. Not giving her the chance to move away, I pulled her closer, deepening the kiss as I moved my tongue with hers. She moaned, making that sound I loved, and melted in my arms. I needed to pull away and stop before the semi I was now sporting went pro. Covering up a boner in swimming trunks was nearly impossible, and there was no way I was going to do so out in the open with our relatives and friends milling about.

I reluctantly pulled back, running my fingers down the side of her face, into her damp hair. The sun was hot, and her hair had already started to dry in waves against her back.

"Giving up so easily, Mr. Matthews?" she teased.

"Just trying to keep my sanity, Mrs. Matthews-to-be. If I keep going, I won't be able to stop, and then your family will end up getting quite the show."

She snorted out a laugh, giving me a playing slap on the chest.

"Come on, Casanova, let's go find Maddie. I think her day program will be wrapping up soon and I wanted to take her shopping."

I bent down to pick up our stuff which was still resting near the lounge chairs we had occupied earlier. As soon as I came back up, the world tilted, and my vision blurred. I grabbed the first thing I could find, the lounger, but I missed, or I think I did. All I know was I ended up on the sand, with the lounge chair upended next to me.

"Oh my God! Logan! Logan! Are you okay?"

Clare came rushing to my side, kneeling down to pull me into her lap. I was dizzy, so dizzy. I looked around, my vision returning back to normal a bit, but still a bit fuzzy. Clare's father and mother were rushing over to us.

"I'm fine. I'm okay," I said, trying to rise. "I just need some water."

She dove into her beach bag, retrieving a bottle of water, and handed it to me. I took a few sips and let the water slid down my throat.

"Mom, go to the hotel. Have the front desk get a car ready. We need to get him to the hospital."

"No," I said simply.

"What?" Clare looked at me suddenly, her eyes filled with horror.

"Babe, I'm fine. Just a bit of dizziness. It's passing."

"But, what if…"

"Laura, Tom… can you give us a minute?" I asked Clare's parents. They nodded, both still looking at me with concern. I understood. Everyone here had already lost someone to cancer. But I wasn't going anywhere, and they needed to stop walking on egg shells.

After Laura and Tom walked back to their spot on the beach, not too far away, I looked up at Clare. Her eyes brimmed with tears, and she looked half a second away from sobs.

"Babe, come here," I said softly, opening my arms so she could fill them. She came willingly like she always did. We sat in the sand, holding each other for a minute while I gathered my thoughts. She pulled back finally, meeting my gaze, waiting for answers.

I took another sip of water, trying to keep the dizziness at bay. "This has nothing to do with the cancer, okay? Remember, I have no symptoms yet. They caught it early."

"Then why did I just watch you almost pass out a minute ago?"

"It's the meds they put me on. That, combined with the heat. I haven't had enough to drink, so I got dehydrated. I should have been watching my fluids. I'm a damn doctor, you would think I'd know this… but we're usually the worst patients."

"Well, then why the hell are we still outside!" she demanded, immediately jumping to her feet and trying to pull me with her. I weighed a good deal more than her so it was like trying to lift a bear. I helped her, rising to my feet slowly so that I wouldn't get dizzy again.

We made our way inside, where she continued to fuss over me for the rest of the afternoon. After more water and a bit of food, I was back to normal, but I feared Clare was anything but.

Chapter Six

Logan

After a mid-afternoon nap, I was feeling like my old self again. The dizziness was completely gone, and I wanted nothing more than to find my gorgeous fiancé and spent the rest of the evening with her wrapped in my arms.

I knew she was supposed to be pool side with Leah and Maddie, so I threw on some board shorts, ran my hands through my hair and hurried out to the door in search of my family. I just about took out Leah in my attempt.

"Oh my God, Logan, would you slow down?" Leah said, catching her breath after having probably lost a year or two of her life from being scared out of her mind when I came barreling out of my hotel suite straight into her.

"Sorry! Was just in a hurry to get to... hey, aren't you supposed to be down at the pool with Clare and Maddie?" I asked suspiciously. I could see the straps of her bathing suit peeking out from under her cover up and a towel was tucked under her arm, but there was no Maddie or Clare anywhere.

"I was, but they never showed. I was on my way to investigate. Want to help?" she asked with an arched brow.

My answer was to turn and knock on Clare's door. It wasn't like her to blow off Leah without so much as a word. I know it was only a trip to the pool, but Clare was raised in the South and her manners were impeccable. I took her to a dinner party a week or so ago, not really explaining where we were going, and she about died when we showed up... without a hostess gift. A hostess gift? What the hell was that? Apparently it was a thing; A big thing to Clare. The next day she'd sent a card and a gift to apologize for her fiancé's oversight. Living in the South was a new and different world.

After a few moments, the door finally opened and Clare emerged, dressed in a pair of yoga pants and tank top. Definitely not pool attire.

"Oh. Hey, guys," she said, before turning around and walking back into the bedroom. Leah and I turned to each other confused, before walking into the suite together.

I looked around and everything was as neat as a pin. There were no clothes, no shoes... nothing. It looked like it did the first moment we walked in a few days ago. *What the hell was going on?*

Before I had a second longer to ponder, I heard soft sobs coming from Maddie's room. I immediately went to her, opening the bedroom door to find her curled up on her bed with her knees tucked under her chin. She was dressed in her hot pink Dora the Explorer bathing suit and a towel was lying next to her.

"Hey, Princess. What's the matter?"

Her eyes opened and focused on me and she briefly wiped away the tears before sitting up. I sat down next to her and she curled her body into mine. I loved when she did this. It was natural now. She didn't even have to think about it. When I put her to bed, or snuggled with her on the couch, she just melted into me. Such trust. I didn't know how in the world I ever deserved it, but I would spend the rest of my life trying to be a man who was worthy of it.

"Mommy says we have to go home."

My stomach fell to the floor and I couldn't breathe.

"What?" I managed to say, before looking up to see Leah's horrified face. She had stopped at the entry way, obviously not wanting to overwhelm Maddie... but still curious as to what had made our girl cry.

"I told her I didn't want to leave the beach. I told her I wanted to see her in her pretty dress."

"And what did she say?" I asked hesitantly.

"She said I would, but not yet. She said we had to get home. It wasn't safe staying here."

I took a deep breath. Clare was freaking out again. She was panicking and rushing home where she felt safe. Where she felt I was safe.

"It's okay Princess. We're not going anywhere okay? I'll fix it."

"Are you sure? Mommy said..."

"I know what she said, but I'll change her mind, okay?"

"Okay."

"Leah, can you take Maddie to the pool for a bit while I talk to Clare?"

"Sure thing!" she said brightly, trying to lighten the mood. "Come on, Short Stack," she said, holding out her hand to Maddie, "Let's go play in the water!"

Maddie held her hand out to Leah and gave a small giggle which was progress. Leah scooped her up and exited the bedroom. By the time they were leaving the suite, I could hear the two laughing. One girl down, one more to go.

****

Clare

There were times during Ethan's illness when I literally thought my chest was caving in. The doctors told me it was due to stress. Acute panic attacks, I guess. Sometimes there were just too many things to remember — what drugs he was supposed to take and when, what doctor's appointments to go to on what days, and what needed to be done... just in case. I kept my cool most of the time. I kept my brave face to show Ethan and the rest of the world. But there were times when I literally couldn't breathe... when it felt like there were so many thoughts in my head that if I had just one more, it would literally explode.

And that's when I would just shut down. I think it was for my own sanity. An off switch or something would engage and I would just shut down for a few hours until the breath returned to my lungs and my chest felt like it was back to its normal size.

As I was packing everything back into my suitcase the day before my wedding, I wondered how quickly we could get a flight back to Richmond. Listening to my daughter cry in the room next to me, I felt like I was moments away from that switch being flipped again.

He passed out. Right in front of me. The doctors told us he was going to be fine. We caught it early they said. A little bit of chemo and radiation and it should be fine, they said. I took a breath and stopped worrying after they told us that. He wasn't Ethan. There wasn't anything poisoning his brain, and he wasn't going to die on me. We would get through this. Right after we said our vows and celebrated our marriage.

But then he nearly passed out on that beach and I forgot how to breathe again. Every fear, every moment of agony came rushing back. I told myself I would fight for him… that I would be strong for us. But… Oh God, what if the doctors were wrong? What if he wasn't okay? What if he died, just like Ethan and I became a widow… again.

Neat folding turned into frantic packing. I started tossing everything in the suitcase without any sort of organization. TSA would just screw it all up right? I took one last look at my wedding dress, tucked away in its garment bag and put those sad thoughts behind me.

We needed to go home. Logan needed to go home. I would not lose another husband.

A knock on the door pulled my attention from thoughts and I saw Logan come into the bedroom. I had completely forgotten I had let him and Leah in a few minutes ago. I was so lost in myself I had barely registered opening the door.

"Hey, what is this I hear about us leaving?" he said, walking forward to take a seat on the bed next to me.

"We need to go home. I don't feel right being here. You need to be home, with your doctors and immediate care if you need it."

"And our wedding?" he asked.

I physically flinched at the reminder. By this time tomorrow, had things been different, Leah and my mother would be helping me into my wedding gown, making the final touches to my makeup. We would most likely be laughing as we watched Maddie twirl around in her dress, elated over her role as flower girl.

"We can wait. I just… I need you to be okay."

I looked up just then into the eyes of the man I'd fallen in love with; the man who had stolen my heart, and saw nothing but love. His steel gray eyes held mine and I could do nothing but stare back into their depths.

Without breaking eye contact, he took my hand in his, intertwining our fingers and bringing them to his heart.

"Do you feel that?"

I nodded, feeling the warm, solid beat of his heart below my fingertips.

"That's me telling you I'm right here, and I'm going to be right here forever, babe. I know you're scared. I know you're trying to be brave, but please don't run."

"I'm not running."

"Yes, you are. You're running back to where you feel safe. Whisking me back to my doctor, taking me to the hospital isn't going to change anything. We were just there. I passed out because I had a bit too much sun. Let it be that, okay? But please, stay here with me. Marry me tomorrow. Become my wife. Because nothing is going to make me stronger than having you by my side."

Before another second passed, I leaned forward, fusing my body to his and kissing him like it was my last dying wish. He instantly responded, flipping me so my back was flat against the mattress, as he hovered above me.

"Don't tease me, Clare," he warned. His eyes were already darker, and I could feel how much he wanted me. He gently rocked into the apex of my thighs just to remind me how hard and ready I'd made him.

"I'm not teasing."

That's all it took. He was on me in nanoseconds. His hands were everywhere, running up the inside of my thighs, pushing up my tank top to rip my bra from my body.

"Don't ever make me wait that long again," he said taking my breast in his hand, gently flicking the nipple with his thumb causing my toes to curl. "I think I almost went crazy."

"Oh God, yes," I moaned as his head descended on my breast, taking my taut peak into his mouth.

"Good, we agree. No sex is bad."

For the next several hours, he continued to remind me exactly how much I missed over the last few days.

Chapter Seven

Logan

The elevator door closed with a soft click, and I turned to my beautiful bride to be. The moment our eyes collided, she lost her cool and burst into a fit of laughter.

"It's thirty minutes after seven," she said, trying to cover her laughter with her hand. Her vintage engagement ring twinkled under the bright lights above.

"Uh huh," I confirmed.

"We're late for our own rehearsal."

I smirked, remembering twenty minutes earlier when a very happy and contented Clare was sprawled out on our bed. She'd been naked and sighing peacefully from the three orgasms she'd just screamed out under my expert touch. She stretched like a cat, looked over at the clock and froze.

"Oh shit!" she'd said. "We're going to be late!"

"Late for what?" I'd said, crawling up her body, more than ready for round two… or three. I'd lost count.

"Our rehearsal! We're getting married tomorrow!"

"Oh shit!" we'd both shouted in unison, as clothes went flying and buttons were snapped and hair was tamed.

We flew out of our hotel suite and made it to the elevator in record time. And now we couldn't hold in the laughter. We were late to our own rehearsal because we'd been too busy… getting busy upstairs.

"Oh God, I'm never going to be able to look your father in the eye again," I said.

"Oh my God, you don't think he'll know, do you?" she asked, completely mortified.

"Have you taken a look at us Clare? Your clothes look like they were thrown on while sharing a car with a bunch of clowns, and my hair? You can actually see Clare sized dents in it from where you were holding on for dear life."

She turned and took a good look in the floor to ceiling mirror of the elevator. Her eyes went wide as she took in her appearance. I thought she looked fucking hot, but I knew the exact reason she looked that way. She looked thoroughly used, and really damn happy about it. But I didn't exactly like the idea of my future father in law seeing her that way.

She started to quickly adjust her skirt and tank top, making it look more presentable. She grabbed her large mane of burgundy red hair and tied it in a bun at the nape of her neck. Within seconds, she went from sexy vixen to classy woman, and I loved both.

The elevator dinged, and as we exited, she gave me a knowing smile. Then she glanced up and suddenly looked horrified, "Fix your hair!" she whispered.

I laughed, but did as I was told, trying to smooth down my dark tresses without much luck. She always told me I had "just fucked" hair so I didn't know exactly what she wanted me to do with it. I ran my hands through it, and messed it up a bit and she seemed pleased.

As we walked outside to our ceremony site, we were greeted by just about everyone we knew.

"They're here!" Leah yelled, "Finally!" She gave us a look. One that said she knew exactly why we were late.

We were then rushed around and put in places and everything that happened after that was a blur. I always thought rehearsals were strange. It was like dry humping; Almost, but not the real thing. There was a nice dinner afterwards, and toasts were delivered, but no one actually got married and I definitely didn't get a wedding night. We were spending the night apart... Our wedding party had made sure of that.

Well, at least I'd taken care of us ahead of time.

"Why are you grinning like a moron?" Leah asked, smacking the back of my head.

"Just so damn happy," I shrugged.

"Gonna go puke now," she muttered, as we all made our way to the restaurant, having finished our practice run of tomorrow's nuptials.

"Oh, come on now, Leah. Don't you see yourself settling down one day? Finding that special someone who will make you go all mushy inside?" I grinned.

"Yep, just officially barfed a little in my mouth. And no, I will never settle down. There isn't a man in the world who could handle all this," she said, waving her hands up and down her body.

"You don't think my buddy Declan could handle all... that?" I waved my finger up and down, mimicking her motions.

"Shhh!! We do not speak his name!" she said.

"Is he like Voldemort?"

"No, Dr. Dork. But I would just prefer to not talk about that specific member of the male species. Ever."

I gave her a hard look, as she wrapped her hands across her chest.

"He didn't hurt you, did he?" Leah and I weren't as close as Clare and Leah were, but I'd come to be very fond of the crazy blonde walking next to me. Declan was a good friend of mine, we'd grown up together, but if he'd hurt her, I'd call him on it. I'd add a few other things to the list as well, like asking where the fuck was he? It was a day before my wedding day and he was nowhere to be seen. My best friend Colin, his wife and newborn son had all flew in today to be here. My mom, who until recently was estranged, was here. Everyone who mattered to me was here. Except Declan. He hadn't spoken to me since the day I told him I had cancer. It's not like I was going to give it to him... He knew that right?

Jackass.

"No, he didn't hurt me. We had a good time. A very, very... very good time."

"Seriously, don't need details," I said, raising my hands up in defense.

"But that's all it was. I would prefer to go on with my life not ever talking about Declan James again. It was one night, and that's it. No use talking about it anymore."

Her lips were saying one thing, but her body language was saying something entirely different. She looked edgy and pissed. Her arms wrapped around her chest, and her eyes narrowed in front of her like she was ready to shoot laser beams out of them at a moment's notice.

"Okaaay."

Women were weird. Like batshit crazy weird. And I was living with two of them now. My only prayer... and I didn't pray often... was that if Clare and I were blessed enough to have more children — for my sanity, please make it a boy.

****

Clare

"Grandma Cece!" Maddie exclaimed, giggling and running over to meet Logan's mother, who gladly caught my daughter in her arms, burying her head in her hair like she'd been counting down the minutes until their reunion.

"I missed you, Sweetheart!" Cece said, "Did you get bigger? You did, didn't you?"

Maddie laughed, and squirmed when Cece's fingers started tickling all the right spots, although, to be fair, there really wasn't a bad spot. Everywhere on Maddie was fair game when it came to tickling.

"She's eating like a horse, so it wouldn't surprise me if she's shot up about five feet since we were in New York," Logan said, coming up behind me. He wrapped his arms around my waist and placed a soft kiss on my bare shoulder.

His mother caught his sweet gesture and I saw the smile in her eyes.

"The other day, I ate all of my chicken nuggets, and I was still hungry. So, Logan gave me all of his and even his mashed potatoes. I love mashed potatoes. He even let me make a mashed potato snow man before I ate them."

Hearing my fiancé wasn't eating tugged at my nerves, but I promised I wouldn't nag him. He'd sworn he was fine, and things were okay. He'd said he was just getting used to the medicine and it would take time, but the part of me that had lost someone wanted to put him in a plastic bubble and force feed him just to make sure he was strong enough to take on anything.

I was marrying a doctor.

I had to keep reminding myself of that fact.

He wouldn't purposely hurt himself. Seeing the way he looked at Maddie and me, I knew he wouldn't risk his health. Not now. Not when he had so much to lose.

So I needed to do the impossible. I needed to trust fate, that cruel, twisted bitch who'd already taken so much from me. I needed to trust that he would fight this and would be here with me at the end, holding my hand, kissing my shoulder, just like he was today.

Because the alternative was just too hard to imagine.

After receiving a proper welcome from Maddie, Cece, or Cecelia as she was properly known, made her way around the room greeting everyone. She finally made her way back to us, and gave us both long, lingering hugs.

"I love you, Logan," she whispered as she held on to her son. So many years had been lost between them and I knew she was trying to make up for the time lost. For the time she'd wasted.

"I love you too, Mom."

Tears glistened her eyes, and she nodded, giving me a small smile. She cupped my chin briefly before being dragged off by Maddie once again. We said our hellos to her new husband, Richard, and made our way around the room, greeting our other guests that had made it in that day.

"Dude, vasecetomy. I'm telling you. Get one. Now," I heard Logan's best friend Colin say.

"It can't possibly be that bad, Colin. Millions of people have babies every day."

"I haven't slept in fucking days, Logan. Days. I swear that little monster is trying to make me slowly go insane. He's smart. Like freaky smart. I think he somehow knows when I'm about to fall asleep, because he'll pick that exact moment to scream bloody murder. My nerves are shot man."

I tried not to laugh. I really did.

"It will get easier, Colin. I promise," I said.

"I don't know, Clare. I think this is my punishment. I think this is what I get for trying to clone pure awesomeness — a baby demon."

Logan and I just stared blankly at him, completely unable to form words.

"What?" he said.

"I'm so telling your wife you just called your son a baby demon," Logan said.

"You wouldn't."

"Oh, I would. And you wouldn't be able to do a damn thing about it, because tomorrow's my wedding. That makes it like an unofficial holiday, so I guess I'm the unofficial king."

"What do you want?"

Colin must be really afraid of his wife if he was willing to strike up a bargain with Logan just to avoid the backlash. Of course, I'd seen Colin and Ella in action and part of me understood. They worked well together, but they were both very passionate. Colin was arrogant and full of himself and Ella was self-assured and independent. They both pretended not to need the other but they did. Badly.

"I want you to be the best damn best man in the history of best men. If there was an award for it, I'd want to see your face plastered on the top of a trophy. Got it?"

"Got it. Be awesome. I can do that."

"I have specifics."

"Of course you do," Colin sighed.

"When I need something, you're there. If Clare and I need to duck out for a few minutes... half an hour, you make excuses. If I need a good hiding spot, you find me one."

My eyebrows rose at this odd request. I gave him a look, and he grinned.

He leaned in, close to my ear and whispered, "Did you think I'd be able to wait all night to take my wife?"

Instant red flushed my face, and I turned away, trying to hide my obvious embarrassment. Colin was now grinning as well, and I pretty much wanted to die right then and there.

"Anything you want man, I'm there."

I was getting married tomorrow, and it was shaping up to be a very interesting day.

****

Logan

I had no idea she was going to speak, until she was tapping her fork against her wine glass to gather everyone's attention. We had decided not to give speeches. Too many emotions, and neither one of us wanted to break down in the middle of our rehearsal or reception. So, we were going to leave the speech making to everyone else, if they wanted. We still weren't sure we'd survive that so we weren't holding anyone to it. With lives like ours, celebrations went beyond champagne and fancy food. It was the ability to celebrate that was worth the celebration, and no one knew this better than the woman standing before me.

"Thank you all for coming. I know a lot of people say that at things like this, but I truly mean it. I know it was last minute and far away, but not a single one of you ever complained. Each one of you, the people who mean the most to us, happily took vacation days, did some last minute packing and hopped on planes to celebrate this special occasion, and it wouldn't be the same without you."

Clare briefly glanced down at me, giving me a faint smile. I took her delicate hand in mine, weaving our fingers together like I always did and smiled back.

"Life is full of unexpected surprises. Some good like the blessing of a child, and some not so good… like losing a loved one way too early."

She paused for a moment, gathering her thoughts and calming her emotions. I held on to her hand still, caressing her soft skin with the pad of my thumb.

"Logan is one of those surprises in life that takes your breath away, leaving you completely awestruck by the enormity of the gift. But sometimes, wonderful, sweet and even incredibly sexy gifts are hard to accept."

Our small group chuckled, and I looked up to give her a quick grin.

"How do you comprehend such an amazing blessing, when your life has already been filled with them? This was the question I struggled with. When you've already been given so much, can you really take more? Many of you don't know this, but before Ethan died, he wrote me a letter. I was supposed to open it when I was ready, but until recently I didn't know what I was supposed to be ready for. In that letter, Ethan gave me my answer. Life is too short to worry about the why, or the how or the what-ifs. Love is a risk, there are no guarantees. But in the end, it is always, always worth it."

Through my very unmanly blurry eyes, I looked around to find an entire room of matching tear stained faces staring back at us.

"I'm sorry to make all of you cry, but before all the craziness of tomorrow, I wanted you all to know how much of a gift Logan is to my life. He has taught me how to remember without being sad, how to live again, and most importantly, how to love again. I couldn't have picked a better man to love my daughter and complete our family."

Clare then quietly sat in her seat, and our eyes met. Everyone else in the room disappeared.

"Thank you for walking into that exam room, and for being brave enough to take on two redheads for a lifetime. I love you."

The small amount of space that separated us was suddenly too much. I reached out, wrapping my hand around the back of her head and pulled gently until our foreheads touched. Her brilliant green eyed gaze bore into me, seeing the deepest parts of my soul.

"I love you, Clare."

I closed the gap, kissing the lips of the angel who would soon become mine in every way.

Chapter Eight

Clare

"I look like a peacock," I said, staring at the scary reflection of myself in the hotel salon.

"A very cute peacock," Leah amended, before asking, "What exactly did you tell the woman to do?"

"I told her I wanted an updo. Something classy."

"Well… I'm not sure I'd say it's classy, but it's sure something." I could see her trying to hold back a laugh.

Just about the time I was about to disown her as my best friend and maid of honor for laughing at me in my hour of need, Maddie came bouncing over. She'd just had her hair done, and of course, her hair was gorgeous. A pile of perfectly curled red ringlets flowed down her back. It was pinned at the sides with tiny sparkly pins that matched her coral colored dress.

"Mommy! Look how pretty I am!" she exclaimed.

"Oh baby! You look beautiful!" She twirled around and both Leah and I clapped and "oohed" and "ahhed" at the right times. She loved every minute of it.

After a few minutes of undivided attention, where she showed us her perfect hair, sparkly pins and every single detail of her dress and matching shoes, she looked up and paused.

"Mommy! Your hair! You look just like that lady on TV!"

Confused, I asked, "What lady?"

"The one who sings those songs that Aunt Leah loves that you won't let me sing?"

Trying to think back and remember the many inappropriate songs Leah listened to, I remembered a conversation I'd had with her a few weeks ago, when Leah and I were watching the MTV Music Video awards.

"Lady Gaga?" I asked.

"Yep! That lady has hair just like you!"

I gave Leah a panicked look and the laugh that she'd been previously holding back suddenly burst out of her like a volcano and she doubled over.

"Hey baby, why don't you go find Grammy and see what her hair looks like?" I suggested, giving Leah a sideways evil glare.

"Okay, Mommy!" she said, skipping off in search of my mom.

"Oh my God. First, I'm going to kill you, and then I'm going to find someone to fix this bird's nest on top of my hair. No... scratch that. First, *you're* going to find someone to fix this... and *then* I'm going to kill you."

"Calm down, Clare-bear. It's going to be okay. I'm going to go find the manager, and we'll get this crazy disco stick disaster fixed and you'll be back to looking like you."

One hour, two hair stylists and several mimosas later... I had a brand new do. It was stunning. Leah had talked me out of an updo and we instead went with something more natural. Loose curls cascaded down my back and were pinned with small antique pearl clips that framed my face perfectly.

"You are a miracle worker, Leah." I said, staring at my own shocked expression in the mirror.

"Does this mean I've been forgiven?" she asked.

"What? Oh, yes. Definitely. You are redeemed. For another day."

"Well, good. Now, let's get you back to the bridal suite. We have a wedding dress to put on!" she practically squealed.

We all made our way back up to the suite, and it was my turn to laugh when Leah, having had one too many mimosas, pretended to be my own wacky version of secret service, jumping ahead to check around corners, and clear hallways to protect her "asset" from the men. She was taking her maid of honor role very seriously and we managed to arrive upstairs without being seen by anyone.

As we entered the suite, we were greeted by my mother and Cece who had an exuberant Maddie in her arms. She was telling her soon-to-be grandmother all about her adventures in the salon, and Cece was hanging on every word like it was the most important conversation in the world. Ella was in the corner rocking her little one, humming a soft lullaby. Her hair was curled and pinned to the side, just below her ear.

"Oh my, Sweetheart! You are a vision," my mother said.

"Mommy! What happened to your other hair?" Maddie asked, which all caused us to laugh.

"Well," I started, leaning down in front of her, "I decided I wasn't cool enough to have that hairdo, so we thought this might be more my style."

She gave me an appraising look, her eyes wandering up and down my long red locks, before she said, "You're right. It's much better."

I don't know if I was more relieved that she liked it or a little hurt that she agreed I wasn't cool enough. But either way, we were ready to move onto makeup, and that is where Leah came in. She was a wizard of all things cosmetic. She'd been doing my makeup for special events ever since we were old enough to have special events.

"Plant it right here" she said, pointing to an empty chair at the desk. It was a perfect spot, situated in front of a large mirror so I could watch as she did her work.

Half an hour later and with a little help from Ella, she was done. She'd done a beautiful job of making me look classy and sexy but not over the top. Just enough, with shimmery natural shadows and peach blush and gloss, and I looked radiant.

With Leah standing over my shoulder, our eyes locked and held in the mirror. I knew she was thinking about the last time she did my makeup for a major event — the day I married Ethan. Her lip quivered and my hand went up to my shoulder to grasp hers.

"I know," I said. It was all I had to say. I knew, like her, that we were all still grieving and always would be. I knew that this day was hard, even though there was so much joy. I knew this all because sometimes when a friendship goes beyond normal borders and you find a sister, rather than an ordinary friend, conversations aren't necessary.

"Well, let's get you married," Leah said, trying to steady her now shaky voice.

"Yes, let's do that," I agreed.

Both mothers gushed over my makeup, and complimented Leah on her fine job. She politely thanked them and we all made our way to my gown, which was still hanging in its bag by the closet.

"So Laura was telling me that your original dress was ruined?" Cece asked. She had obviously been caught up on the dress drama by my mom when they shared their hair appointments that morning. Both were sporting sophisticated updos that made them look regal and lovely. Their updos didn't resemble Lady Gaga at all.

"Yes, the airline ate it. But, it worked out well," I said, as I slid down the zipper and pulled the dress from its bag to a collective gasp.

"This one is much better."

"Oh my goodness, Clare," Cece said, at the same time my mother said, "Oh, sweetheart, you're going to be stunning!"

"Well, let's get it on me!" I exclaimed. The gown I'd chosen wasn't overly complicated which fit our outdoor wedding perfectly. It was vintage in style, with champagne satin underneath a beautiful lace overlay that flowed slightly behind me in an elegant train. A matching champagne colored satin bow completed the look and wrapped around my waist.

With everyone's help, minus Maddie who was jumping up and down shouting her Mommy was *the prettiest Mommy ever,* I was soon standing in front of the floor-length mirror in my gown.

"It's just…" Leah started.

"Perfect," I finished.

With teary eyes, Cece asked, "Do you have your something blue?"

Panic. Pure panic took over and I looked at everyone standing behind me with wide eyes.

"Oh my God. I completely forgot. Everything. The something old, the something new… I don't even have something blue! Is my marriage doomed?"

Leah's face curved into a smile and I seriously wanted to turn around and smack her for smiling in my time of need.

"Why are you smiling?" I nearly shouted.

"Logan knew you'd forget."

"What?"

"He knew you'd forget, with everything being so last minute and rushed. He knew this, so he took care of everything and asked me to deliver the goods to you."

"And you're just deciding to tell me now?" I asked.

"It was worth that face, that's for sure."

As I was silently chanting *I love my best friend, I love my best friend* in my head, Leah ushered me over to a plush chair where I sat down while she gathered whatever it was that Logan had planned.

She took a seat on the sofa adjacent to me and began.

"He wrote a letter. Do you want to read it, or shall I?"

Fearing I wouldn't make it through reading the letter myself, I gave her the go ahead, and she began.

"Clare,
Today you will become my wife, and I will give my sacred vow to always take care of you and Maddie. It is my honor and I will spend every day of my life trying to prove I'm worthy of the task. Ever since the day I met you, I've wanted to protect you from everything that may harm you, or cause you pain or stress. I know this impromptu wedding has been less than ideal, and if the circumstances were different, we would have had time to plan something different.

In all the craziness, I knew you would forget the small things. It is your nature to focus on everyone else's needs — Maddie's and mine... the guests. I knew you'd eventually realize the small traditional elements of the wedding you'd overlooked and by then it would be too late. So I took matters into my own hands and did them for you. This is my wedding gift to you — with a little help from Leah and our mothers.

For your something old — your grandmother's lace handkerchief. Your mother was gracious enough to pass this down to you, with the intention that we will one day pass it on to Maddie on her wedding day."

Leah handed me the lace handkerchief I'd always seen laying in my mother's cedar chest when I was growing up. I'd never been allowed to touch it, knowing it was delicate and old. I tried to hold back the tears as I felt it in my grasp for the first time. I glanced up and found my mom. She had the same teary eyed expression on her face, and I met her halfway, jumping from the chair to fall into her arms.

"I love you, sweetheart."

"I love you, too, Mama."

"Love that man with everything you have, for as long as you have, baby girl."

"I will, Mama."

With my handkerchief clutched between my fingers, I settled back into my chair and braced for whatever else Logan had in store for me.

"Are you ready?" Leah asked, and I just nodded.

"For your something new, I didn't need any assistance at all. I had everything I needed, because your something new is me! So, you'll have to wait until later to put me on. Our love is still young and new, and I will spend every day of my life making sure the love we feel for each other when we take our vows not only is the same but only grows stronger and deeper."

I laughed, and shook my head.

"Goofball," Leah said as we all laughed.

"Sweet goofball."

"For your something borrowed, I asked my mother to help out. As you know, my mother used to be quite the hoarder of labels and anything designer. But, when she met Richard, she gave it all up, keeping only a few things that had sentimental value to her. The pearl earrings she is lending you today is one of those pieces."

Cece came forward then and handed me a box.

"These were handed down to me by my mother, and were always very special to me. It would be an honor if you wore them on the day you married my son."

I simply nodded, the lump in my throat now reaching epic proportions. I wasn't going to survive the day. I really hoped whatever makeup Leah put on me was hurricane proof because I saw a lot of tears in my future.

She opened the box and enclosed where a beautiful set of pearl earring that matched my gown beautifully.

"Thank you, Cece," I said.

"From today on, you call me Mom."

We came together in a hug and silently thanked the man who had tamed the untamable woman and given Logan his mother back.

"Okay, Leah... how much more? I don't know if my makeup can handle more."

"Your makeup is just fine, and I will be there to touch it up if needed, so calm down. There's just one more thing and I think you're going to like it," she said with a wicked grin.

"For your something blue, I considered doing the blue garter thing, which is both traditional and sexy, but then I decided to take it one step further. So, I went shopping, and forgive me... my one step further went a little crazy. But picturing you in blue on our wedding night kind of drove me insane. Enjoy, and I'll see you soon. I love you, Logan."

I gave Leah a look, and asked, "Do I need to send my mother out of the room?"

"Oh please, Sweetheart. Like I didn't know why you two were late last night," my mother said with a flick of the wrist.

"Oh my God, I'm going to go in the corner and die now," I said, as Leah muffled a laugh.

"Oh, come on. It's only lingerie. It's not like your mom hasn't owned a thong or two," Leah said.

I gave her a hard look and motioned over to Maddie who was busy reading a book on the floor, completely oblivious to our conversation. Thank God.

"First of all — Maddie is right there. Second of all — gross."

"You know, you always use Maddie as an excuse, but ninety percent of the time, she's never paying attention when I'm talking, so it's a really lame excuse."

I opened my mouth to offer a rebuttal, but she was actually right. How did that happen? I wonder if Leah was more observant than I thought. *Nah.*

"So, let's see this lingerie!" Cece exclaimed and I tried not to think about the fact my mother and soon-to-be mother in law were getting excited over my wedding night lingerie.

Leah pulled out an elegantly wrapped package and waited and watched as I unwrapped it.

"Oh, hurry the hell up, Clare!" she huffed as I carefully opened the gift.

"The wrapping paper is pretty!"

"And you're going to take it home with you?" she asked.

"Well, no..."

"So, then... hurry! Otherwise, you're going to be late for your own wedding!"

"Okay, okay!"

I hurried up and had the box opened and was face to face with the most gorgeous undergarments I'd ever seen.

"These did not come from Victoria's Secret," I said.

"No. No, they did not," was all Leah could manage. I think I heard Ella say *holy shit* under her breath at the same time.

There must have been thousands of dollars of lingerie in there. A beautiful dark blue satin and lace corset with a matching blue thong lay amongst layers of tissue paper. White stockings with little blue bows and, of course, a blue garter was also in there.

"You know what this means?" Leah said.

"My fiancé has a shopping problem?"

"Nope, we've got to strip you down again and get you all sexified."

Awesome... putting on the lingerie I will wear on my wedding night...

with my mom and new mother-in-law.
    Great way to bond.

Chapter Nine

Logan

I was quickly discovering that being the groom on the day of a wedding was vastly different than being the bride. As Clare was being primped and pampered, going from appointment to appointment doing whatever it was that women did for these types of things, I was sitting in the bar with the guys.

"We really should have planned this day out a bit better," Colin said, taking a swig from his half empty beer.

"When I woke up this morning and realized I had an entire day with nothing to do, I thought we had it made. But dude, this is fucking boring. I'd rather be golfing."

I hated golfing. It was what rich people did to appear outdoorsy, and I'd been around it my entire life. My father was a huge golfer, and I had spent many summers caged up in a golf cart following him around while he tried to explain the virtues of the game.

"Golf is important Logan. I've made many important business deals over a good game of golf," he'd said. *Yeah, whatever.*

The fact that I'd rather be out hitting golf balls spoke volumes of the depth of my boredom.

"How long does it take to get ready for a wedding?" I asked.

"Really fucking long," Colin answered, "Don't you remember doing this same damn thing at my wedding? Those girls were gone for years getting ready. Damn if I couldn't tell the difference when she walked down the aisle either."

I gave him a look, the look I'd been giving him for years that told him he was crossing the line into his douchebag alter-ego. Colin and I had been best friends since college and I'd quickly learned he was cocky, self-assured and outspoken. Sometimes the combination of those got out of hand, and he went from being what women would classify as cute and cocky to instant jackass.

"No, man... I don't mean it like that. I just meant that she was already gorgeous. She could have spent an entire week getting herself pampered and ready to walk down that aisle, or she could have showed up in a paper sack, and I still would have thought she was the most beautiful woman in the world."

"Damn, Colin. I don't think I've ever heard you say something so poetic before in my entire life. Garrett — write this down," I said, motioning to my soon-to-be brother in law who was also nursing a beer next to us. "Colin just said something heartfelt and touchy-feely. I want evidence."

Garrett just shook his head and grinned.

"So, 'Colin the Wise', what last words of wisdom do you have for me before I take my vows?"

He gave me a doubtful look, "You seriously want me to give you advice… about marriage?"

"Well, it's not like we have anything else to do," I said, motioning to the rest of the bar which was completely empty except for the three of us. Make that four. I greeted my future father in law as he strolled in, taking a seat next to his son. He ordered a beer and then turned to our small group.

"Afternoon, gentlemen. What did I miss?" he asked.

"Colin was about to give me marriage advice," I answered, pointing to Colin who grinned like an asshole.

"This should be good," Mr. Finnegan, or Tom as he liked to be called, said. We all chuckled and agreed.

"Hey! For your information, I am a damn good husband. It's not easy, and it's not always hearts and flowers, but if you find the right woman, like Ella… it's worth it. Every damn minute. And if you're really lucky, she'll give you the greatest gift imaginable… a mini version of the two of you all mushed together. It's incredible."

"You had me," I said, clutching my chest, "right here… until you starting talking about mush, and then I got lost."

"Shut up Logan! You asked for wisdom and there it is. Work at it, every day. They may drive you crazy, run you ragged and send your mind spinning, but one look from Ella and I'm a goner. Still. She's it for me, and I will spend every day of my life reminding her that I'm the same for her."

"That was actually pretty good Colin. I'm mighty impressed," Tom said.

"Me, too. Who knew you were such a softy under all that crap," I joked. I knew he loved his wife. He'd loved her since the moment he saw her enter the crowded bar we'd be hanging out at all those years ago. He'd told me that night she was his future wife. I thought he was just drunk, but damned if he didn't do it.

"Well, I have a reputation to uphold. Can't let everyone know what lies beneath all this," he said, making a grand sweeping gesture over his physique. We all groaned, and I asked if he was finished.

"One more thing. Don't leave the toilet seat up. They hate that."

I shook my head and laughed and we all clanked our glasses together in a half-assed toast. I checked my watch and swore time had frozen. Not even an hour had passed.

Longest. Day. Ever.

"How about you, Mr. Finnegan," Colin said, "Got any advice for my boy Logan?"

He was silent for a moment, staring into the empty beer glass in front of him.

"Never go to bed angry and don't sweat the small stuff. You never know what tomorrow will bring, and life is too short to worry about things that don't matter. When I had my stroke, do you think I sat in that hospital bed worrying about whether the house chores would be done or the trash would be taken out? No, I thought about my wife and children and how much I wanted to fight so I could spend another day with them by side. You have a fight ahead of you Logan, don't waste breath on things that aren't worthy of it."

"Thank you," was all I could manage. I stuck out my hand for a handshake but he instead pulled me into a bear hug. I'd never had a loving father. I didn't know how to interact with one. Tom, along with Clare and the rest of her family, were showing me what it was like to have a family and a place to call home.

My future was bright and full of infinite possibilities because of her, and if the clock ever decided to move again, she would be my wife in just a few short hours. Nothing could keep me down. Not even cancer.

Chapter Ten

Clare

"Breathe, just breathe," I chanted. My heart was running a marathon in my chest and I was convinced it would soon explode from my ribs roadrunner style, headed straight for the altar to get to Logan first.

Now that I had that picture in my head, it was nearly as romantic as I had originally thought.

"Are you nervous?" Leah asked, standing beside me in her knee-length coral dress that accented her bronze skin and honey blonde hair perfectly.

"No, I'm ready. Like really ready. Why are we still back here?"

She snorted before answering. "Because you still have fifteen minutes before the ceremony is supposed to start. You have to allow the rest of the guests to be seated."

"What guests?" I asked impatiently. "The only guests that are here are family, and the wedding party. How can they not all be seated by now?" I huffed.

"Alright, Clare-bear, let's re-do your makeup and primp a little. We need to get your mind off the clock, otherwise you're going to explode."

I nodded in agreement. I really was going to explode. Logan was out there in his tan suit, probably standing at the altar with the deep blue ocean serving as a backdrop behind him. He was waiting for me, and I didn't want to make him wait anymore. I wanted to barrel down that aisle and hear the minister say *husband and wife* so I could scream to the world that he was all mine.

Leah dabbed, blotted and glossed my lips until she was satisfied, and then put all of her tools away in her little clutch bag that she'd stowed just inside the door we were about to walk out of. The wedding was not on the beach, but it was as close as we could get without having to make all our guests sink in the sand with their nice shoes on. The hotel had a beautiful garden patio with an almost surround view of the ocean. At the very edge was a grassy area where we'd set up chairs and a gorgeous flower covered altar. Nothing else was needed. The view took care of the rest.

Everyone else was either seated or being seated. It was just Leah, Ella, Maddie and me. We all grasped hands and tried not to cry.

"I love you guys," I said.

"We love you, too, babe," Ella said. "Thank you for loving Logan, and for bringing him back to us. You've completed him, and I've never seen him so full of life."

I pulled her into my arms and we hugged. I was so grateful Logan had friends that had cared for him through everything. Even in his darkest points when he pushed everyone away, Colin and Ella had stayed.

I kneeled down to my beautiful daughter who was just as excited as me, but when she jumped up and down, it was cute. Kids got off so easy.

"Are you excited baby?" I asked, and she gave me a huge nod, over exaggerating every movement.

"After you're married, can I call Logan my Daddy? Do you think Daddy would be mad?"

The tears I'd been trying to hold back let loose down my cheek and I pulled her into my arms.

"No, baby. I think Daddy would love that. Logan too. No one said you couldn't have two daddies, right?"

She pulled back and nodded, "Right. I can't wait to tell him!"

I turned to Leah who was holding back tears. She was my rock. She'd been with my almost every day of my life, for as long as I could remember. She'd been my protector, the sister I never had. and the shoulder I needed when everything fell apart.

"I wouldn't be here without you. You know that, right?" I said.

"You would have found your way eventually. I just gave you the push you needed to get you here quicker. The love you and Logan share isn't a coincidence. I'm convinced you would have found each other over and over until you realized you were destined for each other."

Squeezing her hand, I asked, "And what about you? You don't need to put your life on hold for me anymore. Start living again, Leah."

She gave a faint smile that didn't quite reach her eyes, "I will, Clare-bear. I am. Don't worry about me today."

After one last hug, the coordinator the hotel provided came by and gave us the go-ahead.

It was time.

Maddie went first, holding her little basket of flowers. She was very serious about her flower girl duties and held off on dropping any petals until the right time.

Ella went next, clutching her small bouquet of island flowers in her hand.

Before Leah was given her go-ahead, she turned around, gave me a quick wink and a kiss on the cheek, and she was gone.

"Didn't think you were going to walk down that aisle without your old man, did you?" my father said, coming to stand beside me at just the right time.

"I knew you'd make it," I said, giving him a sideways grin.

"I knew you three needed some girly time, so I hung back in the hallway. But now you're all mine. I love you, baby girl."

My lip quivered and every minute spent with my father in my childhood came roaring back. The skinned knees when he was teaching me to ride my bike, the yelling matches and frustration when I got behind the wheel for the first time, and that moment when he caught Ethan and I in the kitchen and realized I wasn't his little girl anymore.

"I love you too, Daddy."

He held out his arm and I took it and we were on our way, down the path toward Logan and my future.

****

Logan

"Breathe, just breathe," I silently chanted, as I caught my first glimpse of Clare walking down the path with her father.

She was a vision. Covered in lace that fit her like a glove, her dress blended old with new seamlessly. She had left her hair down and under the sun, it shimmered with the fiery red glow I loved. There was too much of her to take in at once, and my eyes were everywhere, trying to drink in every detail. I wanted to remember everything, sear it into my memory so I'd never forget the emotions that were welling up inside me.

"Marry Me" by Train was being strummed softly by a lone guitarist as she came towards me. Our eyes locked and everyone disappeared. I barely noticed when her father placed her hand in mine, still unable to believe this was my life. This woman was here. To marry me.

I heard a soft chuckle and I looked up briefly to see Tom shaking his head and taking his seat beside his wife.

The minister cleared his throat and Clare and I finally tore our eyes apart and turned our attention to him.

"I think we should begin, don't you?" he asked, and Clare and I both looked at each other and nodded. Apparently the world disappearing around us hadn't gone unnoticed.

"I do. I absolutely do," I said.

"I haven't gotten to that part yet," he laughed.

"Well, then hurry up," I joked, which earned a few laughs from the guests.

The minister welcomed everyone and began with a reading. It was a quote or a passage about love. I honestly didn't listen. It was something Clare and I had picked out and I remember it being beautiful. But seriously, how could I focus on anything when Clare was standing in front of me?

I did hear him say *vows*, and that's when I started to pay attention.

"Clare and Logan have chosen to recite their own vows, and will do so now." He turned to Clare and gave her the go ahead. She nodded, turned back to me and gave me that shy smile I'd fallen in love with.

"You once said you didn't think you were capable of love — that somehow that ability was lost on you. You were so afraid to let us in, scared that you wouldn't be able to give back what we could so freely offer. But I've never known anyone more capable of love than you Logan. It shines through in everything you do, and there is no one on this earth I would rather be binding myself to than you."

I didn't deserve her. Standing there, hearing her speak, I knew she was so much more than I deserved and exactly what I needed. She completed me in every way.

She took a deep breath and continued, "I promise to love you a little bit more each and every day. I promise to hold your hand, even when we're old and frail. I vow that no matter what life hands us, I will stand by your side, ready and willing to face the challenges that lie ahead. I will always try to make you laugh and promise to share my dessert with you — maybe." Her lip curved into a small smile, and she laughed which only made her more beautiful.

"But more than anything, Logan, I promise you will always have me. All of me. Everything I have is yours. You are my family, my future and my forever."

I wanted to kiss her. I'd never wanted to kiss her more, but before I had the chance, a throat was clearing again and it was my turn. My turn to pledge myself to this woman. For eternity, and I couldn't wait.

"I should have gone first. I should have gone first because I can barely speak after that. I've forgotten everything I was going to say. You rendered me speechless and I have been in a constant state of awe since the moment I looked into these mystically green eyes. You bewitch me, captivate me, and propel me to be a better person. I was an empty shell until you showed me what love was."

I had written vows, and memorized them. It had taken me days, and I done nothing this morning but pace my hotel room reciting them. And now, nothing. I was just a rambling, gushing mess of words. But, it wasn't pretty speeches and memorization that made a vow. It was what came from the heart, and suddenly forgetting my page-long vows didn't seem so bad.

"I promise to always make you pizza whenever you want. I will never leave the house without first kissing you goodbye and promising chocolate on my return. I will always put you and Maddie first in my life — you two are my life. I vow to spend every day of my life proving to you that the promises you just made to me were worth it — that we're worth it. I promise to always play the guitar for you when you have trouble falling asleep. I will never sweat the small stuff or allow the sun to set with anger in our bed." I gave Tom a meaningful look and he nodded. Repeating the words she said to me, I said, "You are my family, my future and my forever… and I will walk with you wherever this crazy road called life may take us."

Her hands tightened around mine and tiny tears trickled down her cheek. I reached up and gently wiped them away.

"Now that Clare and Logan have said their vows, they will now exchange rings. Rings are a symbolic representation of the love between a husband and wife. As a ring has no beginning or end, your lives are now joined in one unbroken circle, for love that is given comes back around again. May these rings you exchange today always remind you of the vows you have taken today and of the promises that have been made."

We had no ring bearer, so Colin and Leah served as our official keeper of the rings. Leah stepped forward and handed Clare my ring, and gave us a teary eyed wink.

Clare took the ring in her right hand and positioned it over my ring finger before saying, "With this ring, I give you my heart, soul and unending love. With this ring, I marry you."

She slipped the cool platinum band down my ring finger, and our eyes locked. It slid into place and I felt like a missing piece of my soul had just returned.

Colin tapped my shoulder and handed me the ring that I would place on Clare's finger. It was simple and handmade to match her antique wedding engagement ring. Repeating the same process, I took her left hand and positioned the ring and said, "With this ring, I give you my heart, soul and unending love. With this ring, I marry you."

Her eyes followed my movements as I slid her wedding ring down her slim finger.

"Now that they have recited vows and exchanged rings, I only have one thing left to do," the minister said and I grinned.

"You have made lifelong promises of love and faithfulness today, sealing yourselves to each other for all the days of your life. By the power vested in me, I now pronounce you husband and wife."

Turning to me, who was no doubt grinning like a fool, he said, "You may now kiss your bride."

He didn't have to tell me twice. I closed the small gap that separated us and kissed my wife. Our lips met and, like every time I kissed Clare, it felt like the first time. I wove my fingers into her hair and deepened our kiss, forgetting that there were about fifteen people around us, including my brand new mother- and father-in-law.

Better save some of that for later.

I reluctantly pulled away, just enough that our foreheads still touched, and I could feel her damp cheeks against mine.

Laughing slightly, our minister said, "May I introduce, for the first time, Mr. And Mrs. Logan Matthews!"

I liked the sound of that.

Chapter Eleven

Clare

I was really starting to regret the idea of a reception.

I loved my family and friends, but honestly... I wanted them all gone. Now.

Logan and I were married. *Finally.*

I wanted nothing more than just him and me and an endless amount of time to spend naked in a bed.

But I was the one who wanted a reception. Logan had said he didn't want anything after we said I do except me. Naked. I'd told him we needed to respect our family who'd flown out for the event, so he grumbled and agreed. We'd planned a small reception, opting out of many of the traditional things done at a larger wedding. Just a meal and cake was on the schedule for tonight, but I knew it would still be forever before we got out of here.

I hated that he was right all the time.

I didn't have a watch, but I was assuming it would be at least three hours before we could get out of here. After that, we had an entire week of vacation. We weren't calling it a honeymoon, because we had decided to include Maddie. The grandparents had all offered to take her for a week, but this had originally been our vacation, until we switched into our wedding celebration. We didn't want to kick her out of her own vacation. Plus, we were a new family and Logan was a new father. We not only needed time as a couple, but time as a family.

So, we were having a honeymoon, plus one. We could have a real honeymoon later. We still had our own bedroom and had activities planned for Maddie so we could have alone time when we needed it, but this felt right. We didn't know what our lives would be like in the next few months, and spending as much time together as possible sounded like the best option.

"I was right, wasn't I?" Logan whispered into my ear, returning with a glass of champagne from the bar.

"About what, dear husband?" I asked innocently.

"Mmm... say it again," he growled.

"Husband?"

"Yes." He wrapped his arms around my hips and pulled me forward. "I like that. *A lot.*"

"I can tell," I said, sliding my hand down his backside.

"Clare..." he warned.

"Yes, husband?"

"That's it. Meet me in the hallway, just over there," he said, pointing to my right, "In three minutes. Three minutes Clare."

I looked at him a bit amused. "Where are you going?"

"I'm going to cash in a favor."

Before I could ask him anymore, he was gone.

I didn't have a watch. How the hell was I supposed to tell when it'd been three minutes? I started counting in my head, *one-one-thousand, two-one-thousand...* and made my way around the small room, smiling and hugging as I continued to count in my head. I was just hoping no one asked me anything, otherwise I'd lose count. I was up to eight-nine.

"Honey, where did Logan run off to?" my mother asked, breaking my concentration.

Crap.

"Oh, um... I don't know. Probably to loosen up his tie, or check on the hotel room maybe?"

Had it been three minutes yet?

"Ah yes. We moved some of Maddie's things into our suite for the night, so she's all set. Are you two staying in the honeymoon suite?"

"Yes. I told Logan it wasn't necessary. We already had a room... two actually. But he insisted, so I relented."

"Well I'm sure it will be perfect."

"Yes, it will be," I said, just as I saw Logan dart his head in and search the room. His gaze settled on me and I knew my three minutes were up.

"I'll be right back, Mom," I said, not bothering to hear what she said after that. The look Logan had just given me was scorching and I had to hold myself back from running out of the room.

Without causing too much of a scene, and being sure I said hello to everyone as I passed, I made my way toward the exit. Just as I was about to make my disappearing act, I ran head first into a brick wall.

I heard a chuckle. "Looks like you're ditching your own party, Big Sis," Garrett said.

I blushed and bit my lip, glancing around in hopes no one had noticed.

"I was just going to…" I stumbled on my words, trying to think up an excuse.

Garrett gave me a knowing grin, his green eyes glowing with mischief. A perfect match set to my own. It was something we'd both inherited from my mother.

"It's cool, Clare. I don't want to know," he said, shaking his head and holding up his hands in defeat.

"I'm happy for you, Sis. You deserve it."

"Thank you Garrett. That means a lot. Maybe we'll be doing the same thing at your wedding a few years from now? I promise I'll let you go quietly into the hallway, too," I joked.

His eyes went glassy and he turned away.

"Yeah, maybe."

He gave me another quick hug and told me to make my getaway while I still could. I ducked into the hallway and was immediately grabbed around the waist and pushed against the wall.

"It's been more than three minutes," Logan growled.

"I don't have a watch," I answered, holding up my wrist which only had a small strand of pearls circling it.

"Come on," he said, taking my hand in his and pulling me towards a closed door down the hall.

"Where are we going?"

We reached the door, and he quietly opened it and we ducked inside. It was the grand ballroom, dark and unused, since Logan had rented out the entire hotel.

"I can't wait another minute, Clare. I need to have my hands on you. Seeing you in that dress… knowing that you're finally my wife. It's driving me insane."

He lifted me up and set me down on one of the round tables that were scattered around the room.

"What if someone comes in here?" I asked, biting my lip and totally loving the idea of doing something naughty.

"Believe me, no one's coming in here. Colin's making sure of that."

My eyes widened. "You don't mean he's out there," I said, pointing to the door, "standing watch?"

"What? No! Do you think I'd let that horn dog anywhere near here? He's paying off the staff."

"Oh," I said, smiling. "Well, how exactly are you going to get me out of this dress without me looking like a train wreck when we go back in?"

He flashed me a wolfish grin. "Who said I was going to take off the dress? I am definitely keeping the dress on. For now."

He stood between my legs and pulled me close, leaning down to kiss my lips. He was gentle at first, but became more urgent and heated. He fisted my hair and slanted my head so he could deepen the kiss. Moving down my neck, he kissed my collarbone and shoulder.

"Lie back," he commanded.

I did as I was told, and leaned back until my back hit the table top. His hands flitted down my curves, over my hips until he knelt and they found the hem of my dress. He lifted it and examined my champagne high heels.

"Nice." His eyes traveled to my legs. "Are these the stockings I bought for you?" he asked, his eyes quickly traveling up to meet mine in question.

"Yes," I answered.

He wrapped his fingers around my ankles and slowly started sliding his hands up until the found my hip and the lace top of the stockings where the blue garter was.

Logan stood, pushing my skirt up as he did.

"Christ. That's got to be the best money I've ever spent."

"And you haven't even seen all of it yet," I reminded him.

"Don't tempt me Clare. We need to keep you presentable for the family," he grinned.

Running his hands up my thighs, he paused. "I was just going to make you come because we don't have a lot of time. But seeing you like this, all spread out before me like a fucking platter? Now all I want to do is bury myself in you."

I pushed up to my elbows and gave him a challenging look.

"Then what's stopping you?"

He growled and suddenly I was in the air. My legs wrapped around his waist seconds before he pushed us against the wall opposite of where we'd come in.

My skirt was gathered around my hips, and I heard the telltale sound of Logan's zipper and belt. All my insides went tight in anticipation as his hand slid up my thigh to push aside my lacy blue thong.

"We're going to consummate our marriage in an empty ballroom, standing against a wall, with our family down the hall. You okay with that?"

I could feel him hard and ready against me, waiting for my answer.

"Yes, Logan. God, yes," I managed to say as he plunged into my slick core.

I muffled my cries and moans against his shoulder as he pumped in and out, filling me completely with every stroke.

"I love you. So fucking much," he said roughly, slamming into my body harder. I could feel the orgasm building in my belly, swirly and twirling in my body like a tornado. His eyes focused on mine and he must have seen it in my eyes, because he took my mouth seconds before I cried out my orgasm, muting the sounds with our kiss.

One hand snaked around my body and found my bare ass. As he braced us against the wall with the other, he pulled me closer. His strokes were fast and uncontrolled, and within seconds his eyes glazed over and he gave a guttural moan as he came.

Still panting and in our post-coital haze, both of us jumped when there was a knock on the door.

"Logan!" Colin whispered.

"What the fuck do you want, man?" He suddenly looked down to make sure I was covered in case Colin was dumb enough to walk in. I really hoped he wasn't.

"They're starting to notice you guys are gone. Might want to hurry things along," he laughed.

"All right, thanks."

We turned to each other and couldn't help but laugh a little.

"Guess we better go before we get busted with our pants down!" Logan said.

We laughed and redressed each other, and headed back to our reception, hoping to hell that we didn't look like we'd just been shagging down the hall.

****

Logan

Dinner passed in a blur. I think we had chicken, or pork?

There were so many people talking to us, I honestly didn't have a chance to eat anyway, so it could have been lasagna for all I know.

All I could think about, in between answering questions about our "honeymoon" and our decision to sell Clare's house and move into mine, was the time we'd spent in that ballroom.

Visions of Clare lying on that table flashed before my eyes. Her hair fanned out in every direction like a whimsical goddess. The touch of her skin as I held her and slid inside her for the first time as husband and wife. The look in her eyes as she came.

Then it hit me. I'd taken my wife for the first time in a dark ballroom, fully clothed, backed up against a wall. I was an animal. I looked over in her direction and took her hand. She caught my eye and smiled, a faint blush spreading across her face.

I should have waited. Taken her slowly and lovingly. Stripped her down and spent hours kissing every inch of her skin. Instead, I'd taken her fast and hard, slamming her and that stunning wedding gown into a wall.

I suddenly had this overwhelming desire to show her exactly how much I treasured, loved and adored her. Maybe it was the whole cancer thing or just the high of getting married, but I decided to be spontaneous.

Rising from my seat, I gently kissed her temple. "I'm going to run up to the room and grab something. I'll be right back."

She gave me a confused look but just nodded and said okay.

Within in fifteen minutes, I was walking back into the reception having completed my task.

Leah spotted me first, and her lips upturned into a smile.

"Hey, Superman, are you going to serenade me?"

Clare turned and saw my guitar slung over my shoulder and her eyes widened in surprise.

"No, I'm going to serenade my wife," I said with a grin.

The hotel staff was just about done setting up the impromptu stage, putting together a microphone and amp they had stored for larger weddings and business meetings.

All eyes were on me now as I set up, pulling my guitar out and taking a seat. I plugged everything in and then looked up to find Clare's green eyes staring back at me. I wasn't much of a performer. I played for myself, so I took a deep breath and tried to focus.

"I hadn't planned on entertaining everyone tonight, but one of

Clare's favorite things lately has been listening to me play the guitar. So, today… on our wedding day, I wanted to sing her something special."

It had been a song I'd been working on for a while now. I'd heard it on her iPod a few weeks ago and I knew she loved the band, but probably didn't know I knew.

I started strumming the opening of "I'm Yours" by The Script and her eyes sparked in recognition.

Leaning into the microphone, I sang each word like they were written for her.

When I finished, there wasn't a dry eye in the house. Except for Maddie who came bounding up to me and jumped in my lap the moment I set the guitar down.

"I liked that song. It's pretty." she said.

"It is. A pretty song for your pretty mommy."

Clare came up to us, her eyes still wet from tears and she kneeled down in front of us, completing our new little family.

"You married my Mommy."

"Yes, I did," I answered, grinning at Clare.

"Mommy said that means I can call you Daddy."

Clare smiled and my full attention turned to Maddie who was looking at me with her big brown eyes. I couldn't put words together fast enough so I just nodded.

"So, can I call you Daddy now?"

Still nodding, I choked out a yes and pulled her to me. She'd been my daughter since the moment I committed myself to Clare, but this? This was more than I ever expected. I never wanted to replace the father she lost, but I also didn't want to go through life being known as *Logan, the stepfather.*

Tears I couldn't contain anymore broke free and I felt Clare lean in to join us. I pulled my two girls closer, and thanked every deity known to man for bringing them into my life.

Chapter Twelve

Clare

After cake, which we very nicely fed to each other, and many well wishes later, we were set free. Maddie gave us hugs and said she was sorry she was leaving us to spend the night with Grandma and Grandpa. We laughed and told her it was okay and we'd survive one night without her.

As soon as we made our way up to the top floor and into our extravagant honeymoon suite, I gasped. He'd had the entire room covered in flickering candles and roses.

"You're crazy."

"Yes. Maybe a little," he said, "But only about you."

"This is over the top."

"I'm trying to make up for earlier."

"What do you mean?" I asked, confused.

He pulled me towards the bed, which was covered in red rose petals. There was a bucket of champagne chilling in the corner, and chocolate covered strawberries on the windowsill.

"I wanted every moment of today to be special for you. When we came together for the first time as husband and wife, I wanted you to know exactly how much I love you. I wanted to spend hours worshiping you and loving every part of you."

"So, you're worried that I'm going to look back and remember our first time as less than ideal?"

He cringed and nodded, "Yes, basically."

I pushed him down on the rose covered bed. He looked a bit startled but quickly grinned.

"The only thing that will make this night less than ideal is if you don't continue what you started in that ballroom and take me right now."

"Yes, Ma'am."

"Yes, what?" I asked, as he stood and slowly walked behind me.

"Yes, Mrs. Matthews," he whispered in my ear and began making quick work of the buttons and sash of my dress.

He rotated me around, brushing his hands around my waist as I turned until we were once again facing each other.

"You're so beautiful," he said. His fingers slipped under the fabric of my dress at the nape of my neck and gently began pulling. When his eyes collided with the lacy top of my blue corset, he sucked in a breath and his hand dug into my hip.

It really was a beautiful work of art. Sapphire blue and ivory colored lace, with tiny pearls scattered everywhere. The fact that it made my breasts look like a million bucks didn't hurt either. Garter belts and matching stockings finished the look.

After Leah had helped me out of my wedding dress and into this, I'd stood in front of the floor length mirror in awe. I didn't even care that both my mother and Logan's mother were behind me. I was freaking hot.

And by the looks my husband was giving me, I'd say he agreed.

"Jesus," he breathed, as the last of my gown hit the floor, and he eyes went everywhere, roaming over every inch of my body.

"Turn around. Slowly," he ordered. His voice had dropped to that sexy tone I loved, and my stomach clenched in anticipation.

I made a slow circle, placing my hands on my hips and pivoting seductively so he could see all of me.

Before I'd even made it all the way back around, Logan was throwing off his suit jacket, tugging at his tie and tossing it to the ground. His eyes were wild by the time he looked up and zeroed in on me. It was hot.

He undid his cufflinks, followed by the buttons of his shirt, letting it hang freely to the sides which exposed his chest and perfect abs. He smirked, knowing I was loving what was in front of me, and continued his slow strip tease. His shirt hit the floor, and then in a rush, he made quick work of everything else, leaving only him standing in front of me.

My husband was so sexy.

Logan stalked towards me, backing us up until my thighs hit the bed. He gently wrapped his arms around my waist and lifted me, placing me under him on the bed.

"I knew the moment I walked into that exam room, my life had changed. You gave me a reason… two reasons to live," he said, brushing his hand down my thigh, as he kissed my neck.

He did this for what seemed like hours — running his hands up and down my body, kissing me everywhere as he whispered endearments and promises in my ear. By the time his fingertips reached the waistband of my thong, I was practically writhing in need.

"Logan… I need…" I started.

"I know," he said, as he slipped his finger inside me and flicked my clit. My hips shot forward and I let out a low moan.

"I think my wife likes that," he chuckled, "Let's see what else she likes."

My thong slid down my thighs and joined my gown on the floor.

"Mmm… this is a good look for you," he said as he pushed my legs forward and apart, exposing me completely. "Yes, a very good look."

He scooted down the bed until he was kneeling in front of it, and I nearly whimpered as I waited, knowing what would come next.

"Wrap those legs around my head Clare."

I did as I was instructed, watching as his hands moved up and down my thighs as I wrapped them around his head. His eyes were darker, like clouds right before a storm.

I criss-crossed my heels at the nape of his neck and he didn't waste any time, making me cry out as his mouth made its first contact with my core.

He licked and worshiped me with his mouth and within minutes, I was climaxing, pulling at his hair as I screamed his name. "Oh Logan, yes!"

He crawled up my body, and I reveled in the feel of his skin brushing against mine.

"I love seeing you in this, but I think it's time for it to go," he said seductively, reaching down to separate my garter belt from my stockings with an expert flick of his wrist. He repeated the process on the other side and the slowly slid the stockings down my legs, stopping only to remove my shoes.

He returned, hovering over me, as he removed my corset, taking time to undo every tiny fastening with care. Apparently he didn't want to ruin this piece of clothing. It didn't stop him from tossing it in the growing pile on the floor however.

"Finally, nothing but you," he said, before leaning down to brush his lips over mine. He teased me, nipping, licking, and tasting me until I was whimpering beneath him.

"I need you, Logan," I begged.

"I know. I need you, too," he agreed, pulling our bodies closer until I could feel them almost joined.

"I love you, Clare. My wife, my lover, my soul."

"I love you, too, Logan," I said and then two became one.

Our heated breaths and murmured words couldn't drown out the overwhelming emotions that hung in the air. Logan was mine and I was his. Forever.

His body owned mine, pushing it closer and closer to climax and I felt it in the pit of my belly like an inferno.

"That's it, Clare… let go," he said, and I did. I screamed out my pleasure at the same time he groaned out his own.

We spent the rest of our wedding night entwined in each other, high on our love and intoxicated in the happiness of our marital bliss.

****

Logan

I awoke, bathed in ruby red curls and creamy soft skin. Clare's eyes were still closed and her breathing still even. She had an arm draped over my chest, and from this angle, I could see every glorious curve of her. I loved the way her waist curved in and flared out at her hip, and that perfect round ass she always complained about.

I didn't remember my life before her. I didn't want to. Every moment I'd spent before Clare and Maddie seemed like a blur; an endless blur of nothing to get me where I was today.

Laying in bed with my wife, with a daughter I couldn't wait to see, I now had a purpose. A calling in life.

I also had cancer.

Something that could tear me away from everything I held dear.

I would never tell her, but I was scared. Now that I had everything I'd ever wanted, I couldn't lose it. *I wouldn't*.

"Hey, you're awake," Clare said groggily.

I looked down on her sleepy face and smile. "Yeah."

"What are you thinking about?" she asked.

"How beautiful you are," I lied.

"Hmm… I sure hope that's not what you were thinking about with that face. Try again."

This woman knew me inside and out. It was the reason she knew I was lying about leaving her the night I tried to walk away. She could see it in my eyes I didn't want to leave, and kept calling me out on my bullshit.

"You're scared," she said. It wasn't a question.

"Yes. A little," I admitted.

She lifted her head and rested her chin on my chest.

"I would be a little surprised if you weren't. Despite what Leah may think, you are not Superman."

"I know. I just want to be strong for you."

"And you are. You will be. But being scared of what might happen is normal, Logan."

I nodded and kissed her head.

"So, what do we do now?" I asked.

"We live our lives like we planned. We spend a week with our daughter." The fact that she just called Maddie "our daughter" made me instantly grin.

"We go home and we begin fighting. And we fight until we win. And we will win Logan."

"And you're ready?" I asked, knowing everything she'd already gone through.

"I'm ready for anything, as long as you're there beside me, holding my hand."

"Forever," I vowed.

"Good," she grinned. "Well, Mr. Matthews, what do you want to do first?"

I paused for a moment, looking down at my naked wife. A million ideas came to mind, but there was only one that screaming at me.

"Honestly?" I asked.

"Of course."

"I want to go find our daughter and start living our life. I've never had a family and I'd really like to enjoy my new one."

She smiled, and lifted her head to kiss me, before pulling back.

"That is the best idea you've ever had. Let's go start our lives, Mr. Matthews."

And we did.

About the Author

J.L. Berg is the bestselling author of the Ready Series. Raised in California, she now resides in the beautiful state of Virginia. She's married to her high school sweetheart and they have two beautiful girls that drive them batty on a daily basis. When she's not writing, you will most likely find her curled up with her iPad reading, in a yoga studio or devouring anything chocolate.

J.L. Berg
Contemporary Romance Author
Website: www.jlberg.com
Facebook: www.facebook.com/authorjlberg
Twitter: @authorjlberg
Goodreads: www.goodreads.com/authorjlberg
Amazon: http://www.amazon.com/J.L.-Berg/e/B00E4LIA1C/ref=ntt_athr_dp_pel_1

Forgetting

J.L. Brooks

Copyright © 2014 J.L. Brooks
All rights reserved.

Chapter One
What Goes Up

    I loved this town. Despite the hordes of celebrities crawling around the quaint but luxurious village nestled within the Wasatch Mountains, Park City had a distinct charm I savored. Perhaps it was because it reminded me so much of home. The full moon illuminated the powder-covered giants looming all around. Soft yellow lights twinkled in a haze as soft snow flakes swirled in the howling breeze. While most of those here for the annual film festival partied far up in the extravagant log mansions owned by the uber-wealthy, I preferred the low-key rooms of the Washington School House.

    It was a renovated historic building, nothing frivolous, but absolutely elegant and right in the heart of town. Small enough that I could slip in and out unnoticed, it was my new favorite place to stay. I couldn't help but shiver a bit as the cold wind bit through the sheer tee-shirt I was wearing to smoke at the window. Shaking slightly, I took in one last drag before dropping the butt in a beer bottle and blowing the smoke away from the drapes. The crackling fire did little to warm my bones, yet I leaned in and held my hands against the flames as close as I could without harming myself. Watching the young man in my bed with the perfect features sleeping so peacefully, I gave him another moment in his dreams before I would violently crash them down.

    My fingertips danced along his shoulders, drawing a sweet smile as he rolled over and pulled me close.

    "Damn Stella, you were incredible tonight. Why aren't you sleeping?"

I pushed my fingers a little firmer in his skin to rouse him more.

"I don't sleep. In fact, I have things I need to do soon so I need you to get up. A driver is downstairs waiting that will take you to the airport."

Sitting up slightly, rubbing his face, I could see the confusion ripple across.

"Leave? I just got here. The festival is on for a few more days. I thought we would be seeing a few premiers."

I walked over towards the window again and cracked it wide, lighting up another cigarette and inhaling deeply. I normally didn't smoke this much, but I hated the awkward moments when I was forced to kick someone out of my room.

"The festival is going on for a few more days, but you my dear are leaving. If you choose not to, you must make other arrangements for the remainder of your stay and return to Los Angeles. You were here on a job, which was to be my arm candy. If your agent did not make that clear, I apologize and I suggest you get a new agent."

Joshua continued to reel from the rude awakening, looking hurt at his dismissal. I wanted to feel bad, but I was actually being nice. My kindness was feeling short lived, as occasionally these boys did not get the hint. One would think that the opportunity to bang a rock star would be enough, but sometimes they got a little too starry eyed, forcing me to live up to my nickname in certain circles. *Fly Trap*. I liked it so much I had a small tattoo of the carnivorous plant inked on the inside of my hipbone as a warning.

Without another word, he searched the room for his belongings and packed his suitcase. Standing quietly waiting for direction, his pitiful demeanor made me angry, not remorseful as it may someone else. I walked over to him and roughly grabbed his crotch with my left hand and his hair with my right. Jerking in reaction, he grunted yet did not fight.

"If you have any hope of making it in this world, don't ever let anything grab you by the balls the way that I am right now. Remember you are a fucking man and act like one. Now get the hell out of my room, I'm done with you."

I held the door open and ushered him out, but stopped him just before he crossed the threshold. Holding his chin gently, I kissed his quivering lips softly and whispered in his ear. "Goodbye Joshua."

Sadly, he was just the beginning. Nothing about the morning was unusual. This was the cycle I lived repeatedly. If I had the privilege of being anonymous it wouldn't be such a hassle, yet one careless image of me in a compromising position could damage my reputation in a way I couldn't afford. The agents knew I chewed these boys up and spit them out, yet not one had ever turned down my offer. Vida, my manager-slash-partner in crime, earned every penny making sure it all looked flawless, even when I wasn't sure what day it was. She was the savviest bitch I knew, and I trusted her with my life. Before sliding my keycard into her door, I pressed my ear against it to make sure she wasn't mid-coitus. Although I have purposely walked in on her a few times to scare the men she seduced for the night.

Hearing nothing, I gently pried the door open and saw her wave her hand at me as she lay sandwiched between two well muscled bodies.

"You are such a whore, I love it." I laughed quietly.

I slid myself up behind one of the men, who I knew would be handsome, Vida didn't slum. We had different taste, but often I would see them doing the walk of shame, or should I say pride. From what I had seen and heard, Vida was a fuck you never forgot nor denied. I tried my hardest not to laugh as I skimmed my hand across his naked chest and down to his groin, freezing when it grazed his erection. Knowing where it had been, I wiped my hand on his thigh, causing him to roll over. Opening his eyes to someone other than Vida, he jolted for a second and smiled broadly as he realized who I was. Fuck, he was gorgeous. If he hadn't just nailed my friend I would be half tempted to snag him for myself. Messy blond hair tousled perfectly against bronze skin and blinding white teeth. He looked familiar but I couldn't place him. As if reading my thoughts, Vida spoke up.

"He's Kai, the drummer for Mistaken Identity."

Raising my eyebrows, I pursed my lips. That's how I knew him. My band Protest had done a show with them a few months back and I had a fling with the lead singer Levi. Curious as to who was on the other side, a small part of me was really hoping it wasn't him. I couldn't imagine guys in the same band tagging a girl together, but then again, I had been known to do some weird shit with my crew.

"Who's over there?" I pointed to the body on the other side of Vida. Kai cringed a little and shrugged his shoulders.

With wide eyes, I mouthed, "seriously"?

He smirked and gave a devious grin. I could have had a lot more fun with him than I did the kid. As he pulled me closer into his arms, I shook my head.

"You should have waited; you could have had me instead."

I pouted my lips and tried to act contrite. Not giving in, he continued to squeeze me tighter against him, making his arousal known.

"No, no, no Don Juan. I don't do sloppy seconds."

Vida must have grown annoyed with our conversation and used her legs to shove Kai, kicking us both off the bed, with me landing on my back and he above me.

"Ow! What the fuck was that for?" I looked to Kai for an explanation but Vida rolled over and looked pissy from her perch.

"He was waiting for you, hoebag. He wouldn't fuck me."

Looking up, I stared at the handsome man skeptically for confirmation.

"Um, so why are you naked if you didn't do the nasty?"

He chuckled hard while keeping me pinned beneath him and smiled at Vida.

"Because she told me that you would be getting into bed with us and I better be ready. I thought she was talking shit but I couldn't risk the chance. Surely enough, here you are."

I smiled lazily and reached up my fingers to run through his hair.

"Good boy. Get your pant's on. You're coming with me."

"Yes, ma'am." He replied with pleasure.

****

For the next few hours, we created a song so loud and obnoxious Kai and I were asked to leave the hotel. Vida was none too pleased as she knew it would hit newsstands and tabloid magazines within a few hours. I was supposed to be snowboarding solo for the rest of the day, but plans changed slightly. Kai was dying to tackle the slopes and jumped at the chance to attempt my favorite run. Portuguese Gap was an exquisite double black diamond that never failed to get my heart pumping. With my tolerance to things that excited me growing dim, I was looking for ways to enhance the rush, and Kai was happy to join the party. Pushing far enough away from the crowd to avoid our actions being too obvious, I pulled the small vial necklace out of my jacket and twisted off the small plastic lid attached to a metal spoon. Holding my hand gently around it to prevent from blowing away the powder, I took a scoop and offered it up before taking two of my own and giving him one more.

Our teeth gritted unanimously between the cocaine and the rush of what we were about to do. Licking my finger, I coated it with a little more coke and rubbed it across his lips before kissing him deeply.

"Let's do this!"

Snapping our boots to the board, I went first and screamed loudly as I rushed down the side of the peak, sliding back and forth as the trees flew by me. Unable to see how far behind Kai was, I didn't care, the feeling of soaring through the air was all that mattered. My heart felt like it was about to burst from beating so hard, my bones wanted out of my body, I couldn't handle the rush, but I loved every second of it, because I felt alive.

I came to a place where I could stop and watch as Kai careened down the run with just as much enthusiasm as I'd had. His presence was unexpected but welcome. I knew that we had known each other for a grand total of about four hours, but our lifestyles gave us a sense of kinship not found elsewhere. He did not know me, but he got me. He did not have to ask questions because he already knew. There were no strings or awkwardness. We simply were, and it felt almost as good as the cocaine coursing through our veins.

He approached me with that same devilish grin, which he dropped quickly as he came to a stop. "Fuck, Stella. Your nose…"

As he reached into his pockets looking for something, I wiped my hand under my nostrils and looked at the thick crimson liquid soaking the fabric. My face was so numb I had failed to feel the blood pouring down. The sound of a bark breaking took my attention. Thinking it was a deer or animal in the woods, I glanced over and quickly realized I was wrong.

"Fuck, fuck, fuck… Three o'clock." I coiled my head towards Kai's chest and started to shake while pinching my nose.

I heard him growl loudly while rubbing my back. Reaching underneath his jacket, he ripped part of his tee-shirt off and wadded it into a rag for me to wipe my face.

"Damn it! Kai I'm sorry, you should go. You don't need to be a part of this. I can explain it later. High altitude, nose bleeds, shit happens all the time. Really it's cool."

"Stella, you're crazy if you think I am going to leave you like this. Let's get you down the mountain."

I looked up into his hazel eyes. His pupils were enlarged even against the glare of the snow and he smiled.

"Thank you."

He held my face gently and wiped a little where some blood must have smeared. Removing the cloth away, I looked at him with hope.

"Yes? No? Am I good?"

His hand took the cloth and pressed it again up to my nose.

"No, it's still going. Here, try this."

Kai ripped a little more from his shirt into two small balls of fabric and encouraged me to shove them into my nose as temporary plugs. It wasn't the most comfortable, but it had to do. Before going down, I sent Vida a text and told her that the paparazzi were on the hill, I had a nose bleed, and she needed to find out who it was and get it taken care of. Before she could respond, I shoved my phone in my pocket and refastened my boots.

I refused to look at the camera as I moved as quickly as I could past him. Hearing the motor of the snowmobile start up, I shouted over to Kai and pointed. I moved as fast as I could and became increasingly afraid. No one was out here to protect me. This wasn't like being somewhere I could go and hide. This asshole had a fucking snowmobile and was chasing us down like animals. *One day of peace, one day of fun. One day I want to be fucking normal again.* No sooner had the thought crossed my mind than I turned to see where Kai was but couldn't. I screamed his name, but could not hear back. The world went black.

Chapter Two
The Great Pretender

"I don't know what makes these rock stars think they are so damn invincible. They have the same flesh and blood as us normal folk. One day they are trashing a penthouse at some swanky hotel, next day they are in a hospital bed getting their asses wiped by people like us."

The woman's voice was harsh and full of sarcasm, although what it had to do with me I wasn't sure. At first it was muffled, but then it became a little clearer. I thought I'd heard my mom in the room earlier talking to someone, but it wasn't me. It had been seven hours since I'd woken up, if that's what you call it. The only reason I knew that was the radio playing soft classical music and the announcer stating the time every few songs. I wanted to scream but nothing would move, not even my eyelids. It wouldn't do much good, I could tell I was hooked up to a ventilator and there was a small tube running down my nose. Every time I swallowed the muscles in my throat constricted around it and I wanted to cough, but once again, zilch. I had so many questions. What happened, why was I here? I knew it was some hospital, and something was wrong.

I didn't want to believe this was permanent, to be able to hear everything around me but not respond. It had been less than half a day and I already wanted to die. I couldn't cry, couldn't do anything. I started to feel the fingers that touched me as they took my pulse and changed my bedding. The sheer embarrassment of soiling myself without any control was the worst. The only thing that made it any better was going back and thinking about the last thing I could remember. Yet that too was just as dismal.

My mom and I had just been in a fight. She'd received this great opportunity to take over a private practice in Mooresville, North Carolina. She found a house right on Lake Norris, and apparently, several famous racecar drivers lived nearby. However, it was my senior year. I wanted my mom to be happy. This is what she had been spending her whole life working toward, so I didn't have a choice. I had to go. We were moving in a few weeks. Summer was just beginning, and I couldn't remember leaving yet.

My heart was breaking thinking about all of my friends that would graduate together. Starting over somewhere new so late scared me. I would not have the teams I had played soccer and cheered with for years. No best friends. No boyfriend. I was alone.

All those things seem so trivial in the moment. I could not even breathe on my own. It was hard to tell if I was awake or asleep. I was praying this was a dream, but I knew it wasn't. The nurses should have been on their next rounds. Just then at six-fourteen, the door clicked and soft footing glided along the floor towards me. I felt a little jerking on the tube before the cool liquid poured down and into my stomach. I had not felt it before now. She pressed the stethoscope onto my inner elbow and the chill caused a shiver.

Canon in D Minor came on, the song that so many walk down the aisle to when they get married, and I felt the tears rush to the surface. Knowing that day would probably never come for me ripped at my gut. As the violins got stronger, the tears pooled and fell down the sides of my face, dripping into my ears. It was uncomfortable, yet for the first time that day, it was a sweet victory. I could actually feel something.

Throughout the night, I savored every nerve that began to come alive in my body. I still could not move, but I could feel. In the beginning, it came in slight twitches, and then eventually I was able to will a more forceful jerk. At ten-thirteen in the morning, my eyes finally opened. The light was blinding and I immediately shut them before slowly cracking them open. Taking my time to look around the room to assess my surroundings, my eyes widened in horror at the ink covered limbs covered in medical tape and heplocks. This wasn't my body. I didn't have tattoos. This was some horrible nightmare. Like the show the Twilight Zone. A really bizarre dream or hallucination.

I could close my eyes for only so long once I had opened them. I didn't understand. When the nurses would come in, I'd pretended to sleep. I wasn't ready to find out what kind of freak existence I had become conscious in. A sharp pain tore through my head, triggering some type of alarm. My heart rate must have elevated as a team rushed into the room.

"We have a response, she's waking up. Stella, can you hear me?" Loud snapping and shouting came from all around. My eyelids were ripped open with a bright beam of light shining down in them.

"Pupils dilating. We need to calm her down. Heart rate is too elevated, she's going to go into shock."

Shock? Why would I go into shock? Before I could think too much more, a warmth crept through my veins and over my confusion. The black abyss I had grown to know so well opened up and took me under once more.

****

I wasn't sure how much time had passed, but when I awoke I was no longer hooked to the ventilator, yet the NG tube was still in place. I willed my fingers to curl, and to my surprise, they did. I could move. Lifting my arms, I brought them closer to my face to inspect the designs etched into them. Once I got past the shock, I realized that the tattoos were beautiful. They had to be mine as colorful gladiolus flowers wrapped around in a bouquet of multicolored ink on one arm. Additional random depictions looked like they told a story I didn't remember. Angels and demons wrestled on the other arm amidst along with stars and other celestial objects.

Anger at my incoherency took over and I wanted out of the bed, away from the hospital and to find answers to why things were this way. Slowly pulling the tube out of my nose, I gagged as it slid out of my throat. Realizing I was hooked up to a monitor, I reached over to turn it off so it would not set off the alarm yet misjudged the distance and fell out of the bed onto the hard linoleum. Surely enough, the alarms sounded and several nurses came in and immediately moved me back into the bed. I could not pretend I wasn't awake any longer. A battery of questions came at me and once again, my head began to hurt. I could shake my head and nod, but had not tried to speak. The small bursts of motion were exhausting.

A doctor came in and quickly realized I was overwhelmed. Asking everyone to leave, he dimmed the lights and took a seat in the recliner to the left of the hospital bed. He introduced himself as Dr. Gleason, a neurologist at SLC University Hospital.

"I know you have a lot of questions, Stella, and we will answer them all to the best of our abilities. But you need to be patient. First we'll start with a few questions. Is that okay?"

I nodded my head, tired yet eager to find out what was going on.

"Okay, good. We will start out slowly." He said as he opened a small laptop and began typing while asking the basic questions of How old are you? Do you know what year it is? Do you know why you are here?

His face stilled for a moment as I tried to respond. I could feel my brain telling the muscles in my mouth to move, but nothing would come out. My eyebrows furrowed and jaw began to quiver in frustration at my inability to communicate. Dr. Gleason smiled and gently placed his hand over mine.

"It's okay, Stella. You are already showing remarkable progress. Sometimes certain motor skills take a bit to come back. I have noticed you move your arms, do you think you could tap on a button?"

Calming down a bit, my eyes widened when I saw him remove the screen from his laptop. Never before had I seen a personal touch screen, much less a laptop you could take apart. I hesitated and looked to him for confirmation that he wanted me to touch the screen that held multiple keys and buttons in the window.

"Stella, tell me what year it is."

I reached up to tap the screen, which responded to my fingertips with a slight vibration. I jerked back after the first one, but he encouraged me to continue. Slowly, my shaking hand pressed in the current year: 1997.

I did not have to see his face before knowing I gave the wrong answer. He remained silent and asked the next question. Where was I? Typing in *Ohio,* was also incorrect, as his badge read that we were in Salt Lake City. He stopped asking questions and put the screen back on the keyboard to type a few more things in before setting it down. In a practiced voice, he calmly gave me the news I was dreading, the truth.

"Stella, I know this may be hard to hear, but you are not seventeen. You are thirty-three years old. The year is two thousand thirteen. You were in a snowboarding accident. You hit a tree and suffered a major blow to your head. For the past two weeks, you have been in a coma. Do you remember any of that?"

Shaking my head furiously, the screams that had been contained finally found a way out and rattled my body as they moved, evoking the growls of the monsters that lived in my skull. Now I knew this was a dream. I was not in an accident. That was impossible. The tattoos on my body were not real. The anger once again caused a headache unlike anything I had experienced before. Grabbing my head, my hands prickled against the short stubbly growth and roughness of thick skin sewn together.

A large area of my head had been shaved. I had surgery. This was not a dream. I could feel the sutures with my fingertips.

"Make it stop." Graveled out of my throat towards the calm doctor. The first words I would speak would be a prayer of mercy. Knowing the pain I was in, he kindly injected more drugs into my IV line and let me slip into that thoughtless place.

****

My mother was at my side as my eyes cracked open once more to the nightmare I couldn't change. Time must have passed because she was different. Her hair was highlighted, whereas I remembered she always wore it in a chocolate brown hue. Her skin was sun kissed as if she had been gardening all day, a little too pink on the cheeks. Although she had aged, she was still the most beautiful woman I knew. Dr. Alessandra Brady once had a prestigious spot as the director of Neonatology at Columbus Children's Hospital. Her passion for working with infants ran deep, but as she grew older, she had longed to spend more time with my father in a less hectic environment.

Right now, she was not looking at me as a patient, but it did not stop her from checking every chart and monitor in my room. She was a bit demanding on the staff as they administered my medications. She watched like a hawk, and commented on everything. After I sobbed uncontrollably at her presence, she refused to leave my side. Within five hours, she had negotiated my release and transport to North Carolina. I said very little as everything whirled around me like a tornado. Although I had awakened, I was still merely an observer to a life I did not recognize.

Expecting to drive to an airport, I was confused when the elevator ascended to the top level of the hospital and a nurse wheeled me out to the hospital's helipad. Dr. Gleason opened the door for my mother, and then helped move me into a seat. I knew that the doctor would be traveling with us until I was admitted to the hospital in Charlotte. We traveled a short distance to a small airport where a jet was waiting for us. Inside the cabin, it was luxurious beyond belief. Even the doctor whistled while boarding and gave me a wink.

"I should have been a singer, not a doctor."

I glanced around while being strapped into a plush leather seat and was reclined back. My mother sat near me with Dr. Gleason, reviewing charts on computers and discussing my care without explaining his comment or either mentioning anything as to why we were on a private plane.

"We cannot determine how much damage has occurred. She has the ability to be vocal, yet she's choosing not to. It is most likely fear, as she believes it's almost twenty years ago and she's in Ohio. Something about that point in her life was a catalyst. Do you know what it could be?"

"I do." My mother whispered softly. "We moved that year. She was forced to leave her friends and the life she knew. It was really hard on her; she basically had to form a new identity. You know, we should really wait until she is asleep to discuss these things. I don't want her to be overwhelmed anymore than she already is."

Dr. Gleason agreed with her and they switched topics moving onto physical therapy, and cognitive testing, referrals and the best drug treatment options. Nothing made sense, so I did the only thing I could to be okay; I closed my eyes and pretended none of this was happening.

Chapter Three
Mother Knows Best

  I had finally come to terms with the fact I had been in an accident and suffered a brain injury. I retained all of my motor skills and resumed the ability to walk after several weeks of physical therapy. It may have been more difficult to accept if the damage had been worse. I could not change my situation, and tried to make the best of it. Initially, I refused to accept the diagnosis. One day, during a fit of rage, I cut off the rest of my hair. My father kept his clippers in the bathroom closet, which I found while learning where everything was. Because I was in a wheelchair, I was unable to see most mirrors. I tried to avoid them at all cost regardless, because I was terrified by my reflection. The bleached blond locks that still hung past my shoulders looked out of place with the massive area of hair missing from the surgery. Why they had not shave my head entirely I was still unsure.

  My mother had raced in as soon as she heard the distinct buzz of the clippers flicker on and drive through the handfuls of hair that fell all around me. With tears strewn down both of our faces, she gently took the clippers out of my hand and finished what I had started. Pouring a warm bath, she helped me move into the water and sat next to me, holding my hand as more tears poured down. As if I were a child, she washed my back and feet, behind my neck and knees. She knew I hated being so weak, as I had inherited her fierce nature.

  "Stella, I know this is hard, but trust me that it will be okay. You are home now, where I can take care of you. It will not be long before you are out in the world again, where you won't need anyone, including me."

She sounded so wistful, making me question her comment.

"You are my mother, I will always need you. Why would you say that?"

She stopped rubbing the soapy sponge across my back and dipped it into the water while collecting her thoughts.

"You are just a strong willed woman. I know you will thrive soon enough."

I could tell by her tone that there was something behind her hesitancy. I was in no position to prod, yet in that moment I resolved to find out exactly what kind of person I was before all of this occurred. I gave it a few days before approaching the topic. It would turn out that I would not need to bring it up; it would surface on its own. Two days later my mother was preparing to attend a homebirth. Being a partner in a small practice gave her control in a way a hospital never could. Despite her initial reservations, she had come to know the area's midwives and respect the decisions of the more holistic practices people preferred. Her lack of judgment made her trusted, so when she felt that more drastic measures should be taken, the townspeople were more willing to accept treatment.

I followed her into her office as she began to work on her computer and check her supplies. As she was typing away, I mindlessly pulled items out from the bag and organized them strategically with her standing by silently watching. Talking to myself, I listed them off while gently tucking each item back in. "Gloves, fetoscope, flashlight, suturing set, oxygen and ambu bag." It was only after the zipper was pulled did I stop and realize what I had done.

"Why are you crying, Mom?"

Growing a little frightened, my fears were put at ease as she wrapped me tightly in her arms.

"You are coming back Stella, you may not realize it, but this is huge."

Excitedly she grabbed my hand and dragged me into my room to redress.

"You are coming with me tonight, I might need you."

As her SUV bounded along the rural dirt roads, we arrived at the small home a few miles outside of town. It was quiet with the lights turned low. A petite blond woman named Rebecca greeted us at the door and hugged my mother warmly then turned to me wide eyed. I could tell she recognized me, yet did not approach me with the same familiarity. Readdressing my mother, her tone was dripping with concern.

"We have a stubborn one here, he's presenting breech and refusing to turn. I've already tried sifting with a reboza and we are looking at a standing birth."

My mother looked to me and offered an introduction.

"Rebecca, this is my daughter Stella. Stella, this is one of our midwives, Rebecca. She truly is gifted in what she does: I am merely here in case she needs assistance." Rebecca smiled and quickly pulled me into a hug as I outstretched my hand.

"I've heard so many wonderful things about you, Stella. It's nice to finally meet you!"

I hugged back and was interrupted by a woman howling in pain. Immediately I ran to her side and dropped to my knees. She stopped and looked spooked at my uninvited presence. Her husband was seated behind her as she was bent down on her hands and knees, breathing through the contractions. Panting heavily, I could see she was in distress. Rebecca and my mother both stood in the doorway, choosing not to intervene. The couple looked to them where they offered reassurance. The experience could only be described as autopilot. Without any recollection of how I had the knowledge, a deep part of me responded without effort.

"Let's drop your head towards the floor and rest on your elbows. I have an idea so we can try and get this little guy to turn, okay?"

Once again, they looked to those in the doorway and received confirmation to follow my direction.

"I need a few bags of frozen vegetables please."

Stifling a laugh, the women ran to the fridge to get my requested items. Feeling a bit of relief from the changed position, the mother, whose name I later learned was Jenny, raised a brow.

"Whada ya need with some frozen peas? I ain't hungry, darlin'".

Her southern twang was sweet with a touch of sarcasm. Her husband Dale rubbed her shoulders as she rocked back and forth, not even questioning what was taking place. Rebecca returned with the large plastic bowl containing the frozen bags. Grabbing one off the top, I tossed it to Dale and instructed him to help me hold them against her upper torso where the baby's head was.

"Babies do not like the cold, so we are going to use these to encourage him to where he needs to be. Once he flips, we will have you start walking to get him engaged in a better position, okay?"

"Whatever works, just get him out safely!"

Jenny's breathing increased as the contractions grew closer. I turned to Rebecca and asked how Jenny was progressed.

"Five centimeters. That was an hour ago. You get that baby flipped and she will most likely go pretty shortly after that."

My mother and Rebecca had their arms wrapped around each other as they watched me move synergistically with the family. A large blue tub with a plastic sheet covering it rested in the corner. Once I felt the baby start to move, a resounding burst of joy rippled through my body. I screamed, "Come on, baby! You can do it! You're almost here, move for your mama!"

Every one shouted together in an attempt to entice the little one to change direction. Guiding Jenny's head a little closer to the floor, we successfully encouraged the baby to turn. Immediately, Rebecca and my mother guided Jenny into the pool of water for the delivery. With adrenaline pumping, I raced out of the house and gripped the wood railing. More screaming and shouts of encouragement drifted through the home, pounding in my ears. A low bellowing noise hit my gut and I knew it was happening... a baby was being born.

With closed eyes, I dropped to the ground and began to weep. It was so beautiful and heartbreaking in the same breath; I wanted to scream as something new was rushing out of me. I could feel her inside, the woman I had become, whose body I inhabited. She was angry and bitter, fighting to the surface, but I had to fight back. The moon was full, lighting up the surroundings in a pale grey. At the bottom of the hill ran a small creek, iridescent with moonbeams bouncing off the surface. I knew I needed to calm down or else risk a debilitating headache. Walking quietly to the creek, I dipped my hands into the cool water and let it flow across my fingertips. Splashing my face a few times, the babbling brook soothed my nerves and slowed my heart rate.

I did not hear my mother walking towards me, it was only after she gently tapped my shoulder did I know she was there.

"I think you are ready to know a little more about who you are. Let's go make some tea. It's going to be a long night."

I took her outstretched and leaned into her shoulder as we said our goodbyes to the others and walked back to her truck. I could not contain the tears once my eyes fell upon the baby happily nursing at his mother's breast. Jenny and Dale both looked to me and smiled with gratitude. Rebecca walked out with us and opened the door for me.

"Welcome back Stella, we missed you."

I grinned back at her and offered a warm hug before climbing in. Trying to process everything that happened in just a few hours, the

FORGETTING

questions formed a list so long I was unsure where to begin. What kind of woman knows how to deliver babies yet is covered with tattoos? I thought I was a singer. When did I leave? Why did I leave?

My mother was quiet as she rummaged through the cupboards for her tea strainers and coffee mugs. A kettle shrilled on the gas stove top for a moment before she poured the steaming water over the herbs.

Holding the piping hot mug in my hands, I breathed in the lemon and ginger aroma in before stirring a few delicate cubes of sugar in.

"Does everyone here know me?" I queried softly.

She took a sip of her tea while tapping her foot against the stool in the kitchen nervously.

"Yes, they do. You lived here until you went away to college. You made many friends and adjusted well once you gave everyone a chance. Working with me helped because you were able to get to know folks a lot faster. Initially, you were angry about what you lost. But before the school year started, you found ways to get along."

I grinned knowing that I was happy here. She said I had made a lot of friends, so I asked if any of them were around still, as I had not talked to anyone outside of the hospital before tonight and was quite lonely. Her face dropped as she looked away.

"Stella, honey you stopped talking to people a ways back. When you left, you wanted nothing to do with this town and the gossip that came with it. If people see you and are somewhat surprised, it's not just because of the star you became, it's the person you were when you were here. No one ever expected you to step foot back in this town."

"Oh, I see. It's fine. Probably for the best since I don't remember anyone anyways. I just thought I would ask. So, my next question is what did I go to school for? Obviously not what I became."

Holding out my arms, I twisted them and laughed at the ink I had grown to know so well. My mother began to glow before answering.

"Honey, you were in Pre-Med. You earned a full scholarship to UNC Chapel Hill. You were close enough to home but it kept you so busy we didn't see you often. We were so proud of you, you did so well there."

We both sipped our tea solemnly for a bit. She was allowing me to absorb the information, and formulate new questions. It helped explain a little more about how I knew what to do tonight.

"Everything is past tense. Maybe someday I can make you proud again, because I have this feeling it's not something I did a lot of before the accident. I am not ready to know who she was, but I feel her. She lives in my bones, like a ghost haunting a house. Unwelcome, but thinks she belongs here. I suppose it makes sense, she doesn't have anywhere else to go. After all, I'm the ghost."

I stood from the island in the kitchen and placed my mug into the sink before turning around and hugging my mother. She held me close and rubbed my back.

"Baby girl, you are no ghost, this is who you were before the world failed you and your heart became stone. I never would have wished that this is what it would take to bring you back to me, but I won't deny the good lord has blessed me each day you have been here. I've waited so long just to see your sweet face, and tell you that I love you."

Breaking the embrace, I stood back and held onto her hands shaking. If I was such a cold person, I wasn't sure I wanted my memory back if all it would do is rip me away.

"Mama, if I go to sleep tonight and she's here when I wake up, know I am so sorry. I hope she knows that you love her. And whatever happened to her, wasn't her fault. I know people blame God, or their parents, things outside of themselves for what's wrong in life. But if she comes back, she needs to know she has a choice. She can keep being the person she was, or she can become the person she was always meant to be. If I ended up being as smart as you tell me, her heart must have been broken pretty bad to shut everyone and everything out. And if it's me that wakes up in the morning, and you know what made her that way, please don't tell me. Can you do that?"

Wiping away the tears, she nodded profusely. "Of course, Honey. I won't tell you anything you don't ask."

She kissed me goodnight, and I headed to my room. As I walked down the hall, I saw my father in the den watching a football game. He had been very reserved since I came home, nothing like how I remembered we had been. His emotional absence was the hardest thing to overcome. I stood in the doorway and waited to be invited in, which he did after muting the game. Sitting on the opposite couch, I said the only thing I could.

"Daddy, I don't know what I did to hurt you so you bad. I don't want to know. I told mama the same thing. I know when you see me, it's not as easy for you to look past things like she can. What ever happened, I hope you can find it in your heart to forgive me."

He said nothing for a few moments, making me believe I was being dismissed, as I leaned my arm over to stand, he motioned me to sit down.

"Stella, I should apologize to you. At the very least explain my feelings. I heard you and your mama having your heart to heart, so I know there's a lot of emotion right now. My feelings right now have nothing to do with forgiving you. Hell, I know you can't recall a thing past seventeen, and that must be scary. But when you left here, you took your mama's heart with you. Things were real rough for a while, I even thought we weren't gonna make it. But we did, and no matter how hard I try, I don't know what I will do if your memory comes back and you take off again. Your mama is thrilled to have you here, as am I. But I have to protect her, because we all know there are no guarantees. I understand you not wanting to know, and for now that's okay. But just because you don't remember, doesn't mean we have forgotten. You aren't the only one struggling here, and the truth will come out."

The conversation solidified my mother's overcompensation with affection. Rather than being wounded by his words, he merely confirmed what I already knew. Before walking out of the room, I held the doorpost for support, as my legs were still a bit unsteady.

"Daddy, you and I aren't that different you know. We're both afraid of the same thing."

I didn't wait for his response; I wanted nothing more than to crawl into my bed and sleep. An exhaustion I had not known before came over me as my body rested under the heavy quilts. There were no dreams, I had stopped having those too, or else simply could not remember them. When I closed my eyes I entered the only place I knew for certain would stay the same, nothing.

Chapter Four
The Sun Will Rise

Waking up long before dawn, an uncontrollable restlessness overcame me. I took great care not to wake anyone, including our Labrador retriever, Zoey. She slept soundly at the foot of my bed, only lifting her head for a moment as I slipped on my shoes and left the house. For the first time since I arrived, I dared to venture out on my own. The town was small and not likely to place me in any danger. Green hued lights illuminated from the street lamps made the dirt road leading into town a bit more visible. Crickets and frogs sang as I walked slowly towards the small brick buildings.

The older shops still held those open glass windows, where they elaborately decorated the displays. I passed a shoe store, an appliance repair facility and hardware store before my nose caught the delicate scent of fresh breads baking. My mother told me there was a French bakery in town that I had come to love, despite not knowing where it was. Once a week she would bring back crusty loaves of bread, and delicious pastries that I would devour almost immediately. I favored a tiny lemon tart with powdered sugar and candied lemon peel sprinkled on top. The chocolates were often too sweet, but I tried them anyway.

Around the corner, I spied the old metal sign hanging out from the doorway. It was a quaint building with flowers hanging from window containers, spilling out with various perennials. Small iron tables were scattered on the brick patio with chairs tilted against the edge for easy sweeping. Curious about the place, I crept closer to the shop and peeked into the windows as the workers busied themselves for the day. My mouth watered as I watched trays of desserts set out with care in the display cases and baskets on racks fill with steaming breads of all kinds. I pressed my hand to the cool glass for a moment to steady my legs when I felt a tap on my shoulder. Grabbing the wall to keep from falling, the man reached out to hold me in place.

He could tell I was frightened and stepped back a bit. "We open in an hour. But if you see something you want, I can get it for you. My treat."

Unable to speak, I simply shook my head and slid against the wall, moving away from the bakery and the stranger.

I rubbed my hand across my head nervously and remembered I forgot to wear a scarf. There was nothing to cover my ugly scars, not even the hair that had grown out a bit. Embarrassed, my chin dropped low.

"No thank you."

I was mortified beyond belief. Not only was he kind, he was beautiful. His olive skin was paled by black hair that curled out slightly from under the brim of his baseball cap. Even in the dark, I could tell his eyes were intense and captivating. Long lashes brushed his strong cheeks bones the brief moments he blinked. Patches of flour that transferred off his clothing dusted the black hooded jacket I was wearing in white, and the top of my head came just shy of his chin, which I noticed during the two seconds I had curved perfectly into his body.

We were at a standstill; I was too afraid to move but wanted to run. It was so quiet I could hear every labored breath coming from his chest. It was the ringing of the door from the inside of the bakery broke the awkwardness between us.

"Hey, Julian when you go to the store today, we need more baking soda. We have enough right now, but it's…" The man was loud until he noticed something was distracting the person he was speaking to. It was the break I needed to run, and for the first time since the accident, I did just that.

I could hear him yell at me to stop, but he did not chase after me. I ran past the hardware store, clear to the edge of town. It wasn't that much of a distance, but to someone who had spent weeks learning to walk again, it gave me hope. Holding onto the metal street lamp, I sat against the base and cried. Not out of despair, but relief. I grabbed my knees, and kissed them repeatedly, thankful for their strength and the physical therapist that pushed me to always try harder.

The imprints of white fingertips on my shoulders brought just as much excitement. It was first encounter with some one that made my heart flutter, and I knew his name. Julian. *Julian. Julian.* I said it over and over again just to hear the way it poured off my tongue and caressed my lips. I knew I would never stand a chance with someone like him, especially now; yet it did not keep my heart from pounding and consuming every thought. Creeping back into the house, everyone was still asleep and would be none the wiser to my morning adventure. Settling back into bed, Zoey crawled under the sheets and warmed my chilled limbs, as the thought of Julian heated my blood.

****

While I finally found rest, my mother opened my bedroom door to announce she was leaving. Her patient, Raina Moreau was having a difficult day and faced the possibility of being admitted to the hospital. Her white cell counts were really off, which was not a good sign.

"I am going to draw some blood samples Stella, you can come with me if you want, but I thought you might enjoy the rest. I know you do not sleep well, I am sorry to wake you, but I didn't want you to be startled."

Her hand brushed across my forehead and lingered over the scars, thick with hardened tissue and bumps from the staples. I turned away from her touch, remembering how his eyes traveled over the same places. Softly, she reached back up and touched my cheek.

"They are a testament to your will, do not be ashamed. In another month or so, no one will even be able to notice."

"I know mom, they just bother me. I don't feel pretty as it is, and those just add to it. I feel like a monster. Not just because of those, but the tattoos, everything. These are forever, they aren't going away."

I held my arms out. I had come to appreciate the artwork, but this wasn't the body I knew. If I knew what was behind them, I might have accepted them more. I wavered between acceptance and denial of my body almost hourly.

"You are no more a monster than I am the Queen of England, so hush. When I get back, we are going to the farmers market. You need to get out of the house so enjoy your nap."

I smiled and rubbed my mother's hand that rested on my shoulder.

"Yes, Mama. Real quick though. What's going on with Ms. Moreau? I hear you talk about her all the time, You're obviously very close, but I don't know what's wrong with her."

She held back her tears, but Holding back the tears, I could see my question drew a sadness from deep within my mother. "Raina is my best friend and she has Stage 4 breast cancer. She's had the mastectomy, and even several lymph nodes removed, but it was so aggressive when we found it, it took over everywhere. She has lesions on her brain from tumors. They interfere with her ability to walk. She barely can eat and is on morphine most of the time, but she's holding on. She is refusing chemo since the first two rounds only slowed the cancer down, right now she just wants to be comfortable, so that is what I do for her."

My nap would have to wait, as the distress my mother was experiencing was more than I could bear. Pulling her into my arms, I held tight as she let herself go. Knowing now what my mother was enduring in addition to taking care of me forced any self-pity I was experiencing to leave immediately. Her heart was in the blender and life was pressing the power button. As a physician, she developed a certain sort of detachment, which was professionally necessary. But this wasn't work. This was her best friend and child under her care, and she was damn sure to do everything in her power to make the best of it, despite knowing that for all the skill and knowledge she possessed, ultimately life and death was not dependent on her, but on the unseen forces of the almighty and his will.

Chapter Five
Intervention

My mother returned from Ms. Moreau's in high spirits. She said that they did not have to admit her today, somehow things were more stable and she was feeling better. In more ways than one, it was a good day for us both. I had showered and slipped into a soft cotton sundress with a mid-sleeve cardigan. Although it did not fully cover my arms, it was far too warm and the ink was not going anywhere. The top drawer of the dresser held a stack of bandannas my mother had sewn for me to cover my head. With the little bit of length that had grown out, they looked cute with the tiny corners of hair peeking out from above my ears and around my neckline. A costume pair of horn rimmed sunglasses was in a box labeled, *Halloween,* along with a strand of faux pearls.

There was also a felt poodle skirt in the box, which I passed over without question. However, the rest tied into a retro chic look as my mother called it. As we were preparing to leave, she approached me with a small metal tube and twisted the lid off.

"Pout your lips Stella."

I followed her direction and puckered them into the fish-like lips one makes when applying lipstick. As she pulled her hand away, I noticed she held a vibrant red hue.

"Go look, it's perfect."

Hesitantly, I walked into the bathroom to look at myself in the mirror. Barely touching the crimson stain on my full lips, I was in awe for the first time at the face looking back. It wasn't the girl I thought I was, yet it was not the monster whose body I held captive. It was a normal person about to enjoy a day at the market. My scars were hidden, and thought's of Julian brought a slight flush to my cheeks. If he were to see me like this, surely I would not be so afraid. Knowing he was most likely still at the bakery, my stomach dropped slightly.

"Let's go, Stella. We only have a little longer before the vendors leave. I want to make a nice dinner for us." With one last glance, I smiled and pulled down my shades while closing the door.

The sun was bright and delicious against my skin as we walked down the road into town holding baskets and produce nets. I listened to my mother ramble on about nothing and enjoyed the slight breeze flowing through the surrounding trees. This town was beautiful and I had barely seen any of it yet. It was the first farmers market of the season and everyone in town was anxious to get out and socialize. I trusted my mom not to put me in a situation that I couldn't handle, so I stayed close and smiled as she talked to everyone she passed.

I found myself doing most of the shopping while she chattered about. Taking the time to smell the crisp fruits and taste the fresh cheeses, every bite was an awakening of the senses. I scarcely heard the world around me, completely focused on each stop. She would grab my arm occasionally and turn me around to shake some one's hand before they went right back into the conversation. While I was trying a sample of homemade cinnamon apple butter, my mother grabbed my arm and squealed.

"Oh, Stella... try this tart, it's divine!"

She groaned unnecessarily as she reached over to put the half-eaten piece into my mouth. Within a few bites, my eyes closed and made the same exaggerated noises.

"I told you that you could have had anything you wanted. I'm glad you came back for it."

Frozen, I opened my eyes to an equally shocked expression on my mother's face. She looked past me with a half grin, half questioning look. I turned slowly to come eye to eye once again with a man who made me feel things I had never felt before, at least that I remembered. In the light, I could see his eyes were a dark hazel. Chocolate brown infused with spears of evergreen. A rough shadow of growth covered his chin and neck, trailing down onto his Adam's apple. The muscles of his shoulders and chest pushed against the snug sheer cotton tee shirt he wore with a black striped apron.

Looking back to my mother, she silently watched the interaction take place.

"You know each other?" She asked suspiciously.

Julian laughed and walked over to give my mother a big hug, causing my jaw to drop.

"No Sandy, not yet. We met briefly this morning when she was outside of the shop. I tried to say hi, but I think I scared her." He said with a chuckle.

"You were at the shop this morning?"

She walked closer to me, causing my flight instincts to rise again.

"I couldn't sleep, so I went for a walk. I smelled the bread. It was nice. That's all."

My mother laughed so heartily, I thought she had lost her mind. She walked back over to Julian and slid her arm familiarly around his waist. Patting his chest lightly, she offered an introduction.

"Julian, this is my daughter, Stella. Stella, this is Julian. Raina is his mother. He came back from New York when she was unable to take care of things any longer. This makes it, two years now?"

He smiled at my mother and squeezed back. It was indisputable the affection they held for one another. I wanted to be jealous of this stranger, yet it was hard to hate some one so handsome. He reached his hand out towards me, I took it lightly and shook back.

"Nice to meet you again Julian. I am sorry I took off like that. I get…"

My lip worried between my teeth trying to find the right words. He came to my rescue and put his hand up in the air.

"No need to explain Stella. I am a stranger after all. Hopefully that will change now."

Appreciative of his kindness, I grinned thinking about how much I would like that. My mother was practically ready to burst standing next to him as she held up our baskets up.

"Julian, you have to come to dinner tonight! It's been so long and I know you need the break. She will be okay. You know she worries about you working so hard. Please say yes. Besides, Jim will be thrilled to have another guy over to talk shop."

Knowing who my mother was referring to made me sad for Julian. Two years taking care of a parent and running the family business. I wondered what he did in New York. I wondered if I knew him when I was younger. After he agreed happily to the invitation, I was determined to know if we were acquaintances.

"Julian, how old are you?" I asked.

"Thirty four," he replied. "Why do you ask?"

FORGETTING

I shrugged my shoulders and took a basket from my mother.

"I was just wondering if we knew each other and you were just being nice because you know I don't remember anything. Because I know for a fact that you know who I am."

My mother looked guilty and peered up at Julian.

His expression was flat and unreadable. After a few moments of awkward silence, he smiled and shifted his hat.

"I know who you were, I don't know who you are now. It's a blank slate for both of us, don't you think?"

Happy with that answer, I nodded my head.

"See you tonight, Julian."

"See you, Stella."

As we walked away, my mother bumped my shoulder. "You have some explaining to do, missy! Why didn't you tell me you went into town this morning? It must have been before dawn."

"It was. I couldn't sleep, like always. I have been good on my feet for a bit, so I thought I would take a walk. Mama, I ran. I really ran. And it felt so good!"

She laughed loudly again. "Yeah, you were running away from a boy. I never thought that would be the thing to test your legs."

Playfully bumping her again, I felt the need to ask more questions before dinner.

"Julian said he knew me. How did we meet, do you know?"

Her tone became more serious with the question. "You met him at school. He just turned thirty-four, so you are not too far apart in age. Shortly after graduation, he joined the Marines and was deployed to Afghanistan. You used to write him letters and make care packages for him."

"So we were friends!" I said excitedly, and then remembered what she said earlier about leaving town without a thought.

"He's one of the people I stopped talking to, isn't he."

Nodding her head, she said nothing the rest of the way home. Feeling the mood sour, I stopped her from opening the door.

"He said it's a blank slate for both of us. Let us keep it that way okay? Tonight will be a good night. I am going to help you make dinner."

My words made her drop the basket and give me a strong embrace. I held back tightly. I found something that made my mother happy, and consequently, was making me happy too. If giving Julian a chance meant giving my mom so much joy, I would gladly move heaven and earth to keep it that way.

After hearing that Julian would be joining us for dinner, even my father's mood grew more buoyant. He placed the radio on a jazz station and danced with my mother in the kitchen while they cooked. The tomatoes simmered with the fresh herbs while pasta boiled next to it. My mother took the large slotted spoon from my hand and stirred while giving my father a look. His hand extended to mine and pulled me close for a dance. I remembered that when I was a little girl he would have me stand on his feet while he shuffled back and forth slowly to the music. I would cling to the back of his thighs with my little arms as mom swayed behind him. As a family, we moved in a soft rhythm.

Tears welled up and soaked his shirt as the music played. I felt his chest jerk under my cheeks and my mother came up behind us and held on as we shifted in circles. We danced until the song ended and laughed once we lifted our heads and wiped the tears away. The doorbell rang, drawing my attention. Butterflies collided in my gut knowing who was on the porch. On the other side of the screen door, Julian stood nervously wearing a brick red shirt and a pair of worn jeans. In his arms rested a large paper wrapped bouquet of gladiolus. Looking at my tattoos, he smiled brightly while handing them to me.

"I know they are your favorite, I hope you don't mind."

I smiled broadly while allowing the petals to tickle my nose. "They are beautiful, thank you. Please come in."

Julian opened the screen door and passed by me into the foyer, and then walked into the kitchen where my parents greeted him with hugs. A small bag hung from his arm with a brown cardboard box inside. Pulling it out, he handed it over to my mother who peeked inside immediately and shrieked.

"Sandy, that's dessert. She insisted." Julian playfully chastised my mother, while my dad patted his back with the same fondness my mother held.

"I hear Raina is having a good day, Julian. It's been a while since we've had you over. Like old times, eh?"

Watching in the doorway, the scene became overwhelming. The monster within reminded me I was merely a bystander to a life that was not mine. I set the flowers down on the sofa and walked onto the front porch, sitting in the swing and pushing off aggressively with my tiptoes. The citronella candles gave a sweet aroma to the cool air. Although the mosquitoes were not out yet, my mother had insisted on lighting them for ambiance. I heard the screen door creak open and wished for nothing more than to be left alone.

Julian came around to the front of the swing and leaned against the wooden rail.

"Mind if I join you?" He asked softly.

Simply shaking my head, I looked off into the distance. I hated feeling the way I did but I was unable to control it. He moved slowly and sat next to me without saying anything at first. We watched the sunset, listening to the sounds of frogs and crickets beginning their evening serenade. Once darkness gave way to the starlit sky, he turned to me and spoke.

"What's wrong, Stella?"

"What makes you think there is something wrong?" I replied shortly. I didn't need to ask, because my distress was palpable.

"Do you want me to leave? If I make you uncomfortable, I will."

Shaking my head, I rubbed my hands together nervously.

"No, you make my parents happy. Everything makes me uncomfortable, I just need to get used to it. If I could leave I would, but I have nowhere to go."

My voice was barely a whisper. Shaking from the cold, my teeth began to chatter. I tried to hide it, but he noticed and told me to wait as he retrieved a blanket from inside. Pulling it around us, he wrapped his arm around me and rubbed my shoulder briskly to warm me up.

"Now where were we? Oh yes. What's bothering Stella?"

The smell of him so near and the warmth of his body caused me to forget any animosity I'd had towards him to vanish. If we'd been friends in the past, it was clear he still cared about me because he could read me so well. Even my own mother was unable to decipher my moods from time to time.

"It's hard to explain. I feel like I am living a time warp. In my head I know that this is my real body, but in my heart I am someone else. Whoever I became was so unhappy. Every day I feel her inside just waiting to come out, and I am scared to death of the day that happens. My mom told me you and I used to be friends. But she also told me that I didn't have any friends left, which makes you one more person I hurt and I have no way of fixing it. So forgive me if I am distant, I'm just trying to prevent something bad from happening."

Julian's arms tightened around me.

"Stella, do you really feel that you are responsible for the things you don't remember?"

"In a way I do. It's like my dad told me last night, I might not remember, but you haven't forgotten. I am just protecting people. It's easier to stay away until my memory comes back. And then no one will have to worry about me."

I tried to hold in the sobs, yet they choked out in tiny bursts.

"Your dad told you that last night?"

Nodding my head, I wiped my nose to keep it from running onto Julian's shirt. His breathing increased and he appeared to grow angry.

"Julian, he's right. It's okay. He's just watching out for my mom. They won't tell me what I did. I told them I don't want to know, just like with you. Whatever I did to you, please don't tell me, because I am unable to atone for it. And if and when my memory comes back, just know in this moment, I am sorry for anything I ever did to you."

Julian's hand came up to my cheek and wiped away the tears as they fell towards my chin. Sniffling, I laughed and wiped my nose against my arm again.

"Stella, I was never angry at you. Hurt? Absolutely. I was devastated. I won't tell you why, but I will to tell you this: We were not just friends, you were my best friend, and I have missed you so much. When I saw you this morning, it took everything in me not to pull you into my arms. I didn't want to frighten you. But I knew you were scared, and that's why I didn't follow you."

I tried to smile, but could not stop the tremble in my lips. It was no wonder he made me feel so many different things. He knew me better than I knew myself.

"I'm still sorry, Julian." I uttered while more tears fell over his hand, which remained pressed against my cheeks. Pulling me close, my face rested upon his chest where I could hear his heart pounding furiously.

"I still love you Stella," he replied.

You can find J.L. Brooks at:

www.facebook.com/authorjlbrooks
@authorjlbrooks
authorjlbrooks@gmail.com
www.amazon.com/J-L-Brooks/e/B00FL2XIKG

Max

A Wilson Mooney Prequel

Gretchen de la O

Copyright © 2014 Gretchen de la O
All rights reserved.

Dedicated to my dear friend, Debbie

Chapter One

Max

"Come the fuck on, Max! Pull your shit together and get your ass back down there. You've got this, you are stronger than any of their bullshit," I growled, trying to talk myself back from the brink of hell. My heart pounded against my chest, my lungs collapsing, unable to fill with oxygen on their own. I gasped, struggling to breathe. Every fucking pore on my body burst wide open with enough sweat to give me chills, even as heat rolled across my flesh. My hair, black as night, was so dampened around my temples that when I ran my hands through either side it contoured back against my head. I twisted the bathroom faucet on and thrust my hands into the cold water, launching it at my face. I looked into the mirror, my skin soaked. My dark green eyes were cast far away in a place where I've recognized being before—a place where peace doesn't exist.

Why now? Why do I even let him get to me? One fucking sentence and I go into a tailspin?

I started seeing spots and shadows appear, bouncing across my vision. Thin, wiggling black lines floated and fell across my eyesight.

"Damn it!" I cursed. I was in too deep. A full-scale panic attack was quaking through my body and there was nothing I could do to control it. There was no way I could prevent the rapid-fire questions from endlessly barraging my mind. I was going to have to sit on the edge of the tub and breathe, or plant myself on the pot and wait until this shit passed.

"Max, you coming back downstairs?" Emily asked between the light raps of her knuckles against my bathroom door.

I pulled in a deep breath and found a way to string together a few coherent words.

"Yeah, Em, I'll be right down."

Another Gold-Vaughn dinner, and I had to sit there while nine people looked at me, eyes and lips drooping, like I was some helpless piece of shit. Everyone was swallowing their questions and comments. I just couldn't stay there any longer and watch them struggle with how to formulate their questions about Mallory's death and my future plans. Questions everyone wanted to ask, but I was done answering. When my father cleared his throat and blurted out that he expected me to join him at Goldstein Petroleum, I just couldn't take it any longer.

"Okay, your mom's bringing out her mixed-berry pie and your dad is trying to rally us to play pool, guys against girls," Emily Vaughn quipped through the solid oak door.

Yeah, that's my parents, when shit starts to go south, make it better by entertaining and feeding the masses.

Emily, one of my oldest friends, was beautiful enough; as a matter of fact she was a fucking knockout, with gorgeous, shoulder-length brown hair tufted in perfect layers of waves and curls. Her indigo blue eyes, layered with flecks of silvery grey, always caught every guy in the room checking her out. Her body was a scientific equation of perfection. But we'd grown up together since preschool. Her family and my family were tight and I'd always considered her more a sister than anything else; never girlfriend material. Besides, Emily and I didn't really share the same philosophy on social issues. She liked living the privileged life and wasn't afraid to make her status known in certain social circles. And me, well, that stuff didn't really matter to me. As long as she and I didn't talk politics or social issues, we were good.

"Sounds like my dad. I'll meet you down there, okay?" I huffed as my words struggled and got caught on the walls of my throat. I took a couple of deep breaths, looked around my bathroom, and snatched a hand towel conveniently left on the edge of the sink.

"Max, nobody noticed you left stressed out. Everyone is just talking."

I heard her slide her hand across the door before she knocked once more. "If you wanna talk—" she murmured.

"Em, I'm just—"

"Hey, I know, Max. You don't have to tell me…but I'm still here. I will always be here, ready to listen."

There was this part of me that wanted to open the bathroom door. I needed Emily to see what I'd been going through lately. Yet, if I could take everything I was and bury it someplace where nobody would find it, I'd do it in a fucking heart beat. I was tired of trying to be something I'm not. Tired of every waking minute being filled with doubt about who I am and what I am supposed to be. I was tired of waking up in cold sweats, begging the powers that be to forgive me for being such a fucking asshole. I decided to keep my bathroom door closed.

"I know. Thanks, Em."

Lately, the good days were starting to outweigh the shitty ones. But it never seemed to fail: when the dark, vacant hole calls my name late at night, or when I'm alone, I would rather find some place to run away to. If I could only keep the voice that haunts me stuffed in the closet I've conveniently called my past, my nights wouldn't seem so messed up. I would be able to move on with my life. Leave the vestiges of my past where they belong. Why does everything have to be so hard? Why can't I move beyond the selfish pain I've inflicted myself with?

Enough was enough. I couldn't do it anymore. I'd become an empty shell of who I always wanted to be. I was dead inside and lacked the fortitude to make something of myself. My entire life I'd struggled to maintain my textbook identity of being the good son, the best friend, the perfect brother, and the irresistible boyfriend.

I heard Emily mumble something before she shut my bedroom door and went back downstairs; maybe it was "asshole" under her breath. Who knows? I pulled open the bathroom door and shuffled to my dresser, finding a clean black t-shirt, folded perfectly, creased with crisp newness. It felt good to pull off the drenched wick-away shirt soaked with the results of my panic attack, and pull on my clean, refreshing, new plain black tee.

Emily was a perfect balance of her parents, Paul and Karen Vaughn. They were the types who would tell you their opinions, even if you didn't ask. Okay, well, more likely Mrs. Vaughn, after getting a couple glasses of red wine down her throat. Mr. Vaughn? Well, he took a backseat to Karen's sideshow, unless it was just the guys—then he'd have no problem growing some balls. His son, Jeff, who everyone knew was gay except his parents, was the exact same way. No balls when it came to Mrs. Vaughn.

Emily was pretty much the only person who was able to get my ass out of bed and to a shrink. Through those fucked-up days and months she busted my chops until I agreed to finish my last two years at

Michigan. On breaks, when I came home to Aspen and I couldn't pull myself out of bed, Emily would show up at my parents' house, barge into my room, and push me until I agreed to get the fuck up. Needless to say, I never missed an appointment with my shrink when I was home.

Through session after session of therapy, trying to rid my mind and body of the painful memories that had been dictating my future, I now know it runs deeper than the moment when Mallory decided to take her life our sophomore year at Michigan. I know this dark hole saturating my life was established well before the thoughtless acts of her poisoned and sickened mind. But it wasn't until the day my girlfriend decided to kill herself that the darkness came looking for me. I'm not going to lie—I was broken, lost, fucked up, and blaming myself for Mallory's death. If I would have paid more attention, if I'd just brought her home to meet my family…maybe she wouldn't have overdosed on pills.

But who the fuck am I kidding? I was brought into this world with preconceived, unrealistic ideas that I was going to follow in my father's footsteps as an oil tycoon. I couldn't be everything to everyone. I couldn't be the good son when I can't even stand being around my dad. I couldn't be perfect brother when I am always forced to be the mediator between my parents and my brother, Calvin. I couldn't be an attentive boyfriend when my girlfriend is 6 feet under in a cemetery in Michigan.

The therapy was supposed to help me understand my part in this whole drama of life. But no matter how many times I've sat across from shrink after fucking shrink, in office after office, I just never got over the belief that it was my words that drove her to do it. She swallowed enough sleeping pills to kill a horse because I didn't have the time or energy to invest in her. She was too needy, too insecure. And I wasn't interested in being someone's savior.

I pulled open the bedroom door a crack and peered out before I stepped into the hall, caught the door knob, and pulled my bedroom door shut. Invitation only, and tonight nobody was invited to hang out in my room. I've run, walked, climbed, fallen down, and descended these stairs my entire life. And yet tonight, for some reason, my legs caved with each step I took. Like I was heading to the lion's den. More questions, more pitying faces, more words that would try and make me feel okay about my future.

"Hey! There he is. About time you came back down. We're just about to play pool, guys against gals. You with my team or hers?" my dad announced, pointing to my older sister, Camille. His words were boisterous yet filled with complete insecurity. I knew it was his way of dealing with his grown son's fucked-up life.

"Dad, come on," Camille snapped.

"Frank!" my mom said as she came out with plates of pie.

"Oh, Nancy, Max knows I'm not serious. Isn't that right, son?" my dad asked as he accepted one of the plates from my mom. It was heaping with crushed berries and a buttery flakey crust. Mrs. Vaughn followed, handing her husband a plate equally overflowing with my mom's mouthwatering pie.

"Sure," I mumbled.

Karen Vaughn offered me the other slice. My stomach still in knots, I declined. I noticed the frown that captured my mom's face. Her shiny brown hair pulled back behind her ears, I could tell she was stressed out about my leaving the table earlier. I noticed the glossy layer that exaggerated her vivid green eyes and the deepening line that hung between her eyebrows when she was fighting back tears.

My father was the CEO of Goldstein Petroleum and it was my destiny to eventually take over for him—a decision that was never up for discussion. It was a one-sided conversation. I'd been groomed from a young age to fill my father's shoes, just like he did, and his father before him, and my grandfather before that. According to my father, GP was one of the last family-owned petroleum companies left in the United States, possibly even the world.

These fucked-up feelings of mine were not only built upon the groundwork of the expectations my father so carelessly spat under his breath every time we were together, but also by events beyond my control. I am shadowed by lofty dreams of becoming a reflection of my father, the great Frank Goldstein. He couldn't accept that I've always wanted to do something that made a difference in the world. If I was going to punch a clock at the end of the day, I needed to know that I'd done something to change a person's life. I didn't want to manage a group of people who stressed over bottom lines and argued for the wealthy so they could keep gorging on the souls of the less fortunate. I wanted to be someone who changed the world, one idea at a time; someone who conquered the fear of my father's wrath for not following in his footsteps.

My iPhone chimed with a text, pulling me from the negative thoughts pummeling my mind. It was from my brother, Calvin, who was across the room.

Bro U OK? U look like a ghost. Need excuse 2 leave? Dad's being a dick. Sorry.

I smiled. Calvin was one of my best friends. We had our childhood fights, our fucked-up arguments about girls, grades, and our parent's expectations. But ever since I went away to college, Cal and I had become really close. Granted, I spent most of my time being the buffer between him and my parents. Our dad thinks he's lazy, untrainable, unmotivated and will never make CEO material for GP. He and Cal are like oil and water. Our father won't even ask Cal to work for the company. He says Cal is better just staying out of the way as far as GP is concerned. I see that Cal is still trying to find himself. He lives by his own standards and doesn't let the disapproval of our parents affect him…that much. He does what he wants and that rubs Dad the wrong way.

I'm OK. Thx, I texted back. It wasn't long before everyone had a plate overflowing with dessert. While everyone's belly filled, mine still twisted in knots. Even the temptation of Mom's pie couldn't untangle the mess of anxiety that filled my stomach.

"Maxi, you sure you don't want some pie?" my mom asked as she wrapped her arms around my stomach. "Oh, dear, you're getting too thin; I can feel your ribs. You're not eating enough, Maxi."

She was the balance in the family. She was the giver, the pleaser, the one who would heal you with food and hugs.

"I'm fine, Ma. I'll gain all the weight back now that I'm home."

"You know you can stay with us as long as you need, honey," she whispered.

"Thanks, Ma," I answered.

It wasn't like I didn't want to stay and hang out, but I wanted to move on with my life. I earned a degree in education when I went back to the University of Michigan. I'd come to terms with Mallory's death, understanding she was sick beyond our relationship; that what she did wasn't because of me but because she needed help beyond what I was capable of giving her. It still stings sometimes when I try and see myself as boyfriend material, though. I mean, the last person who filled the role of my girlfriend decided to end our relationship, permanently.

It was Cal and Camille who said I should follow my passion of becoming a high school teacher. Maybe because they were the only people on the face of the earth who knew how it felt to live under the expectations of our father. So, with their encouragement I am doing what I want to do. I'm working to become a high school history teacher, something my father would never approve of. Don't get me wrong. He respects teachers, believes they are the salt of the earth, but he just didn't see *his son* doing that. He had my life all mapped out, with his thick fingers dragging the red sharpie across the route I was supposed to take. Struggling to make a living wage wasn't in the great plan he had marked out for his children. I had been so intent on being what my family expected me to be, I wasn't truly living my own life. So when my shrink told me I should tell my father that I graduated with honors with a degree in education, and that it would be good for me to take back the control of my life, I laughed in her face and decided I was done being shrunk. I no longer wanted to partake in her little psychology project.

I looked around at everyone happily finishing their pie and congregating in the great room to play some pool. I grabbed some empty plates from the dining room and made myself useful. The best part is nobody noticed as I slipped into the kitchen. Nobody except Emily.

"Hey, Max, are you going to come out and play some pool with me?" She placed the plates she was holding on the black granite island anchored between us.

"Did Jeff leave?" I asked, trying desperately to change the subject.

"Yeah, he said he had to get on the road before it got too dark. He said to say goodbye."

"Well, it was cool that he could make it over. He still friends with Michael?"

"I know what you are doing, Max. Stop trying to change the subject. Yes, Jeff and Michael are still a couple. And while you are still trying to avoid talking about what is going on with you, let me just add: no, my parents still don't know he practices *that* lifestyle," Emily declared as she walked around to my side of the granite island.

No more space between us, and nothing more than friends, Emily, as tiny as she was, pulled me into her arms and hugged me through the moment I wish I could just pretend didn't exist. I wrapped my arms around her too. Her warmth burned through my thin, black t-shirt, and her curly, brown hair tickled my cheek as I buried my face in the crook of her neck.

Chapter Two

Max

I was alone in the kitchen with Emily, vulnerable as fuck. Being wrapped in the warmth of someone who wasn't blood related really messed with my head. Emily rubbed her hands across my back, making my skin react to her touch. It was more than a healing or friendly hug. I couldn't help but pull her closer to my chest. She let out a slow hum as I tightened my arms around her. I wasn't meaning to make it more than what it was. I just wanted to feel comfortable in my skin again. Her aroma, pleasurable with sweet pears and refreshing cucumbers, tugged low in my gut.

I let out a breathy growl against her hair. Finally, I was somewhere else. The anxiety that thrust and pulsed through my veins a mere five minutes ago disappeared in her embrace. I could breathe and I could feel her breathe. I welcomed her movement as she shifted in my arms. Without thinking, I collected her curls in my fingers, pinned them behind her ear, and pushed my lips to the bend of where her jaw met her neck. I felt her head sway back and I accepted her invitation to drag my mouth down the side of her neck and against her collarbone. I pushed my hands to either side of her face, tangling my fingers into her hair, and kissed my way up her chin, finding the corner of her curvy lips. Needing to feel the comfort of her tongue tangling with mine, I bit her bottom lip gently, coercing her to open her mouth. And when she did, our kiss took me somewhere else. The warmth of her lips, the fervor of our kiss. She let me push further as my tongue, sultry and unrestrained, discovered the fuel to the fire raging in my belly. The charge had been ignited and I fell straight into the raw desire to forget all my pain. I pushed against her, trying to erase all the marks of loneliness seared across my soul.

"Max," Emily whispered as she began to wiggle away from me.

"Mmmm?" I hummed, forgetting we were in my parents' kitchen, still riding the wave of comfort she created in my body.

"I hear your dad calling us to go and play pool."

It wasn't until she mentioned my father that the sounds from the other room began to fill my ears. Instantly, the voices began to invade the peace I'd had for a moment. I let go of Emily, realizing who it was that I was finding comfort in. Talk about leading her on. Whether it was unintentional or not, she was a woman—a woman who would read more deeply into this than what it was: a moment of weakness. My heart exploded into a hammering palpitation.

Shit, shit, shit. What the fuck have I done? Son of a bitch, I have to fix this...now.

My throat went dry, and the words I needed to say created a clusterfuck in my head.

"Em, I am so sorry, I...ahhh. I shouldn't have done that. I don't like you...I mean, not that way. Not that you aren't...beautiful, but...Damn, it was an asshole thing to do. Please, forgive me," I stammered, trying to find the right words to say without offending her.

"Hey, stop, I get it. No worries, we both got carried away...that's all." Emily said as she took a couple of steps back.

"I've fucked this up. I shouldn't—"

Emily grabbed my face in her hands, looking at me. I noticed her usually clear, blue eyes were damp and clouded with disappointment, glistening with the pain or desire I'd just caused.

"Listen, Max, just stop. I should've known you were going to react that way. It's my own fault. You're a guy who hasn't been with anyone in two years, and you are lonely. I totally get it." She lowered her hands, and started for the great room. I snatched her arm and spun her around to face me.

"It wasn't like that. Kissing you the way I did wasn't coming from my need to get off. I wasn't trying to fuck away the shitty feelings I'm having. I felt comfortable, safe, even needed, and I confused your comfort for something it shouldn't or will never be. Em, you're like a sister to me."

"And that right there is why I should go." Emily pulled open the kitchen door. "I'm going to tell everyone that I don't feel well. I'll call you later."

I heard her give everyone the flimsy excuse that she was tired and that she was just going to call it a night. I heard my mom trying to argue but then surrender.

I took a deep breath and checked myself before I headed out to the great room. I couldn't help but feel the temperature in the room rise. Summers in Aspen weren't particularly hot, but they were warm nonetheless. Seeing how I was just hot and heavy with Emily in the kitchen, I prayed they had a couple of windows open in the great room.

"There you are. I started to think you were hiding so you wouldn't have to play pool. Finish all the dishes in there?" my father asked before tossing me a pool cue.

"Naw, I didn't get them done, but it's a start," I said.

"Thanks for starting them honey," my mom said as she kissed my cheek and headed toward the kitchen.

"Oh, come on, Nancy, we need you to play now that Emily left. You know Max is on your team. He's a gimme,"

"And what does a gimme mean, Frank?" my mom turned back around and headed toward him. Her evergreen eyes constricted.

My dad shrugged his shoulders and held his hands up in front of him.

"It means you ladies have just as good a chance as winning as us fellas. Max evens out the teams. That's all."

My father's words hovering around me began to morph into nothing more than white noise as images of Emily and our kiss fired through my head. Her lips, her taste—unexpectedly delicious. I wasn't supposed to kiss her…ever. I dragged my phone out, ready to call her to apologize for my indiscretions and thoughtless acts, but she'd only be down the driveway by now.

"Alright, boys, I'll play. But be warned, be careful underestimating my team. I have a mean serve," my mom proclaimed as she went over to Camille and Karen and slapped them a high five.

"Mom, sorry to tell you this but you serve in tennis, not pool," Calvin said with a chuckle.

"Well, that's what you think," she snapped.

"The only thing you should serve…is me," my dad tossed back jokingly.

"Excuse me? Mister who can't cook himself a grilled cheese sandwich," she came back at him.

"I can cook a grilled cheese," my dad answered as he tried to convince everyone in the room that he wasn't helpless in the kitchen.

"Ooh, I got it!" Camille shouted.

"What?" Dan asked.

"How about the losing team does dishes tonight, aaannnd makes dinner at the next Gold-Vaughn get-together," Camille sang as she started her rally, clapping and looking over at us.

"Okay, first thing, you father couldn't cook himself out of starvation, even if he was given all ingredients he needed measured out in front of him. And secondly, that man will not touch anything in my kitchen without my supervision," my mom teased.

"I don't know, I think the next get-together is Thanksgiving, and I don't want to risk having to eat food you cooked, Frank. No offense," Paul piped up.

"Oh, Paul, you guys lose this game and we'll be ordering takeout for Thanksgiving," Karen chortled.

"Fine, how about loser does dishes and massages the winner's feet?" Camille said. Her eyes narrowed.

"Deal!" everyone hollered except Cal and me.

There we go…how is this going to work out? Everyone has a spouse except me and Calvin, and I'm sure as hell not going to rub *his* feet or have him rub mine.

"Hey, listen, I'm not rubbing your feet and I'm not gonna let you rub mine, so we'll bet fifty bucks. How about that?" Calvin asked.

"Sure, Cal, fifty bucks," I said as we shook hands.

****

As my father, Dan, and Paul rubbed their wives feet, Cal was pulling fifty bucks out of his wallet. Yeah, the gals and I won on the technicality that Cal scratched the cue ball twice before hitting the eight ball into the left pocket on his next turn.

I almost cost us the game a couple of times myself. I just couldn't keep Emily out of my mind. Her face as I tried to explain away our kiss, how devastated she looked as she left. I'm a real fucking asshole.

"Cal, make yourself useful and start doing the dishes. Least you can do since you caused us to lose," my father bellowed as he massaged my mom's feet.

"No way, Dad. I wasn't the ass who bet a foot massage, I rolled with fifty bucks. Mom, you owe me big time," Cal said before he kissed her cheek. "Each loser for themselves," he hollered before he threw his hand in the air and waved 'bye.

"Drive safe, you'll be home late?" Mom asked.

"Ahhh, yes, and don't wait up," Cal flashed his mischievous smile before closing the door.

That was Cal's way of telling us that he had a new girl who would put out on the first date and he didn't plan on bringing her home to meet us.

"Alright you three, who's washing, who's drying, and who's putting away?" Karen asked, holding up dish towels.

"Max, you're taking Cal's place," my dad barked.

"No way, Dad, we won fair and square," I rebutted.

"Looks like it's just you, Paul, and Dan. Make sure you wear rubber gloves. You don't want to get dishpan hands," Camille quipped.

I pulled my phone out of my pocket. If I wasn't going to call and talk to Emily, then the least I owed her was a text apologizing for taking advantage of her sympathy. I lowered myself onto the couch and wedged my feet up onto the coffee table. I tapped out some words explaining my fault in creating the debacle we had in the kitchen and sent it on its way.

Karen and Paul said their goodbyes, making their rounds to everyone like they did every time we were together. It was a ritual that had become as normal as breathing. I shook Paul's hand, mumbling our goodbyes and nodding before kissing his wife on the cheek.

Karen pressed her hands to either side of my arms, locking me in her grasp. With three glasses of wine in her, I prepared for the words that were going to spew thoughtlessly out of her mouth. Tradition at its greatest.

"Max, sweetheart, it's nice to see you moving on from that girl's tragedy and finally happy again." Her words poignant and hard to swallow, I nodded and watched her meander out the front door. There was nothing I could say in response so I smiled—enough of a response to satisfy her observation.

My phone vibrated in my pocket. Emily had texted me back.
WTF???

I didn't understand her response until I looked at what I'd sent her. Sadly enough the wrath of auto-correct made me look like a babbling idiot.

U OK? Sorry I kicked u. I didit 2 lead u on. Duck it, plz Calvin me later!

Great, I probably should have called.

Chapter Three

Max

Waking up with Emily on my brain and morning wood in my boxers was fucked up on so many levels. I'd texted her back late the previous night, attempting to explain how auto-correct screwed up my apology. I tried to stay awake, but my eyelids took over my vision and decided to close up shop around midnight. I knew first thing in the morning that I was going to look like an asshole. I pulled my phone off the nightstand, checking for her response. Nothing. *Damn.*

"Maxi, breakfast," my mom sang from downstairs. She finally had all her kids under one roof again and she was going to make up for all the time we hadn't been together. She'd made me breakfast every morning since I'd been home.

"Okay, Ma, I'll be right down," I answered just as melodically. Arguing wasn't an option, and who was I to argue over warm breakfast every morning?

I stretched out across my bed, constricting and releasing every muscle, before I got up, went to the bathroom, and made my way downstairs.

I pushed my way into the dining room to find the table all set with plates for five. I noticed Cal's place wasn't set.

"Cal's not home?" I asked.

My father, already sitting at the head of the table reading the diminutive local section of *Aspen Times,* folded the paper up, exaggerating his long, flowing gestures before wedging it under the edge of his plate. His eyes pinned me and his cheeks flushed red, mirroring the burning scarlet across the edges of his ears.

"Nope, your brother chose to stay out all night, spending it with God knows who, doing God knows what."

"Now, Frank, the kids have lives outside of ours, as hard as that is to admit. Calvin called me last night and said he was going to be at Jeremy's today. Camille? Dan? Come sit."

Funny how everyone obeyed.

"Now, who wants waffles with sliced strawberries?"

My mom fed us, because that's what she does, making sure each and every person had enough so they'd have to unbutton their pants and roll away from the table.

"Hon, thanks for breakfast. I've gotta run to the office. Max, you coming down later?" my dad asked as he stood and patted his belly.

"Uh, I wasn't planning on it. A couple buddies of mine are coming into town for a day or two—"

"Oh, no problem. Dan, you ready to go?" my dad asked.

"Yep. Bye, sweetheart," he said as he kissed my sister and hopped up, ready to go.

Dan Finch was my father's golden boy when it came to GP. If Dad asked him to jump, he'd ask how high. He was given a job at the company before he even asked my sister to marry him. He'd become my father's right hand man, and even though Dan was as qualified as anyone else to take over as CEO in the company, my dad operated in the old ways of doing things—handshakes and promises. It was a family-owned business, and it had to be a Goldstein who'd take over Goldstein Petroleum. My father truly believes that one day I'll wake up and take up the helm at GP. Maybe that was why he was beginning to lighten up on pressuring me...just a little. If he couldn't force me, maybe, just maybe, he'd find a way to persuade me. As for my mother, God graced her with mountains of patience. She has fielded many heated discussions and venomous words between my father and me about GP. We'd go round and round and he'd push until I'd be totally pissed. Then he'd give just one more dig to reel me over the edge. When he'd try and pull that shit on Cal, my little brother would make himself as scarce as possible, disappearing for days on end. I found out later that he'd always call our mom and tell her where he was.

Camille, who is a good couple of years older than me, is married and out of the house. My father, being from that old-world mentality, believed that her place was making a home for Dan and the children they're supposed to have some day. I know it pisses Camille off, but when our dad is employing her husband and paying him enough so she doesn't have to work, she finds that rocking the boat isn't worth it.

Camille and Dan bought a house last year, right down the hill. They live close enough to drop in whenever Camille sees fit, and now that I'm home she's decided to make my mental state her new cause. I'd just mentioned to her the night before that I would like to find a teaching gig out in California, and that next morning she shows up at the breakfast table with a page full of student teaching internships all over the state of California. At least she waited until Dan and our father left.

"Max, look what I found on the internet. All I did was search available student teaching internships in California. There are literally hundreds all over the state." Her pale lips curled up into a protective smile and I noticed she was looking at me the way she used to when we were kids. It was that same look she'd give me when Dad would ride me for not taking out the garbage, or sliding by with a B on a math test. She leaned forward and dropped the page onto the dining room table, scrunching her nose before pinning her brown hair behind her ears. She started to scan the list.

"How many in the San Francisco Area? I would rather go North than South," I said as I leaned over her shoulder, looking at the list of schools.

"Well, let's see, there's two, six, eight, ten, fourteen, fifteen, it looks like there are fifteen available positions in the Bay Area. Ten in public schools, K through twelve, and five private. Hey here's one that looks interesting," she said as she scooped up the page and read me the write-up for a position at an all-girls, private boarding school. "The most prestigious boarding school on the West Coast, Wesley Academy for Girls, in Danville, California, is looking for well-qualified applicants for our student teaching position. Competitive salary, summers off, room and board negotiable. Inquiries for the position accepted by email only. A cover letter, copy of transcripts, proof of credential, resume, and letters of recommendation required, no exceptions. Interviews will be held August 1st and 2nd. Max, this looks really good. I think you should apply," Camille said as she pointed to the listing.

"I don't know, Cam, a private school for girls?"

"It's a boarding school Max. Whether it's girls or boys, who gives a shit? They are willing to give you room and board. Why not try it? If you aren't happy or don't like it, you can come home. You won't be tied into an apartment lease or anything."

"Are there any others?" I asked.

"None that looked as appealing as this one. Heck, Max, just give it a try," she insisted.

"What are you two talking about?" Mom asked as she came into the dining room wiping her hands dry with a dish towel.

"Max is looking at a teaching position in California," Camille spouted as she took the paper I was looking at and pointed to the listing. "I told him to go for it."

"California, Maxi?" my mom asked. Her deep green eyes glazed over with tears.

"Ma, don't get all misty. Come on, we've talked about this, I need to do this," I said as I stood up and pulled her into a hug. She was my biggest supporter. She was the one who told me I could do anything I set my mind to. She got my dad to back off enough so I could live my life. Her tiny arms wrapped around my chest as her hands locked behind my back. She squeezed me tight, a sign that she was trying really hard to let me go.

"I just want to make sure you're okay, Maxi," she sniffled.

"Ma, I'm fine. And you know I'll come back for every holiday, I promise," I said, struggling to convince myself of the words that were coming out of my mouth so easily.

"You'd better, no excuses. Do you hear me?" she demanded as she let go and attempted to snap me with the dish towel.

"No excuses, I hear you…loud and clear," I said.

I leaned over and kissed the top of her head. I knew it was either I'd leave and come back for holidays or I would become the son who lived in town and never came by.

****

It'd been a couple of weeks since Camille made me send my resume to Wesley. I had to assume it wasn't going to work out. There had to be hundreds of people applying for the same job—people from California who had a leg up on me. They were there and I was here, in Aspen. So, I made a deal with myself: if I didn't hear from Wesley in the next couple of days, I was going to write them off and start applying to public schools up and down the coast in California.

I pulled the rolling chair out from my desk, plopped down, and turned on my laptop. The desk was cold against my fingers as I drummed them in succession, waiting for the log-in screen to come up.

"Knock, knock," my mom sung.

"Come on in, Ma," I hollered as she twisted the knob and made her way into my room. Her delicate, thin frame didn't look strong enough to carry the bulky pile of t-shirts she brought up to me.

"Here are your t-shirts, honey."

I hopped up and grabbed them from her, giving her hands the freedom to snatch up the leftover clothes from yesterday.

"Ma, come on, you don't have to do that. I can do my own laundry."

"Well, Maxi, I know, but I don't mind. Your father will be home in another thirty minutes and I could really use your help with the barbeque," she said as she tried to convince me with her smile.

"Why do you need so much chicken?"

"Well, your father has some clients coming over," she answered back quickly before she trailed her hand down the back of my head and neck. "You need to call Bill's and schedule a haircut, sweetie."

She tucked the cluster of my dirty clothes in the crook of her elbow.

"I know, Ma, and yeah, I'll come down and help you. God knows I need the distraction."

She stopped scouring my room for more dirty clothes.

"You still haven't heard from that teaching position out in California?" she asked before she spotted a dirty pair of socks rolled up next to my bed.

"Nope."

"Honey, don't be discouraged, you never know, maybe it wasn't supposed to be that school. There are plenty of other schools worthy of a Goldstein." She bent down, kissed the top of my head, then snatched up the socks from the floor. "Now, I could really use your help downstairs, Maxi." She walked out, trailing with a grumble, "I don't know how many times I need to say it, your father needs to give me at least a three-day notice before he invites people over for dinner. We're going to have a full house; Camille, Dan, and your brother are coming too."

"Okay, I'll be right down." I knew she really didn't need my help but was taking the moment to check in with me. She liked to trap me in the kitchen and just talk. As long as our hands were busy, she knew our mouths would be voluntary with information. It made her happy to chat and it only took about ten years to finally figure out her strategy. But once I got it, I played into her hand every time.

Chapter Four

Max

Things with Emily were okay for a while. We cleared up the kissing mistake, and were hanging out from time to time. I could feel it had changed for us, but I figured we could get through it and go back to the friendship we had. Then one day she just showed up at my house with a knock on my bedroom door before it swung open.

"Hey, Em. What are you doing here?" I questioned.

"Your mom called me, said you wanted to talk," she whispered.

"What? I never told her that. I never talked to her about what happened," I blurted.

Emily stood frozen in the doorway of my bedroom wringing her hands together. Her eyes marked on her fingers before she met my gaze.

"Max, come on, you hear our parents talk about us, don't you? You have to feel something for me. You can't stand here in front of me and tell me you didn't feel that kiss was something more than a mistake."

Emily was right in front of me by then, the heat radiating from her breath pressing against my skin, her hands trembling as she wrapped them around my neck. This was going exactly where I didn't want it to since I screwed up and kissed her.

I pulled her arms from around my neck and held them firm in my grip.

"Emily, you are one of my best friends. A best friend I don't want to have a romantic relationship with. I am so sorry I misled you. I wish I could take that kiss back, but I can't."

"I don't know if our friendship can ever be the same. Don't you love me, Max?" she cried.

"Yeah, Em, I do love you…as one of my best friends, but that's all."

She pulled her wrists loose from my grip, cocked her hand back, and slapped me across my face.

"That's for leading me on," she spat.

Then, as I recovered and looked at her, she slapped me again. "And that's for being such an asshole." She turned around and walked out.

After she left that day, things changed for us. She never came by anymore or even talked to me. I guess things really weren't going to be the same between us. The whole thing just got too tense. I hadn't talked to Emily in over a month. Her mom and my mom were going back and forth with theories and questions, words I'd overhear over coffee in the kitchen or phone calls my mom put on speaker. I couldn't tell anyone what I did. It was totally fucked up and entirely my fault. I'd never meant to lead her on. Things were starting to go south with my dad too. I just needed to get away.

Every day I checked my email, but day after day nothing came from Wesley Academy in California. I was starting to think it was a dream filled with bullshit ideas, nothing more than wishful thinking. Who'd hire a guy to work at an all-girl's high school, let alone a twenty-one-year-old kid?

That was it. I decided to research some of the other schools I'd put off in hopes of getting the private school. It was already the end of July and most schools were looking like they'd filled all their positions from out of state. I clicked on links for school districts up and down the California coast, central valley, and even southern California. I was desperate. Dates of submission had all passed. Only a few extended their dates of submission and most of them were schools in huge cities with gang problems.

I had to face the fact that, even though I needed to get out of Aspen and spread my wings, I might be destined to be there for the long haul, cooped up and pinned to the destiny everyone but me saw as something positive. Don't get me wrong or look at me like I was some piece-of-shit spoiled brat. I was at a snapping point—Emily was done with me, my friends were all working and moving away, and my dad was done with the excuses I'd been giving him about joining him at GP. I was getting restless and, sooner or later, something had to give.

"Hey, honey, something came in the mail for you today. From Wesley," my mom chimed with a swell in her throat.

"Is it a thick envelope? Heavy? Does it look like something important? Here, just let me see," I said as I swirled my rollie chair around, hopped up, and met her halfway.

She handed the huge manila envelope to me. It was thick, heavy enough to have registration papers. This could be it...my ticket out. I held it, just feeling its weight and texture.

"Well, open it!" my mom snapped.

I pushed my finger into the corner. It was as exciting and nerve-wracking as my acceptance to the University of Michigan. Everything I needed hinged on the words typed across the letterhead.

I ripped it open, slipped my fingers around the stack of loose papers and glossy brochure, and pulled. I curled my lower lip between my teeth and gnawed the fleshy part of my lip until it was raw. This was it. This was my moment of clarity. Either I was going to California or staying in Aspen and living in my dad's shadow.

I let the envelope fall to the ground. I pulled the top letter off the stack of papers and dropped the rest of it onto my desk. My eyes were burning. The font scrolling across the paper was fancy enough to mean something important. I scanned the sentences looking for words like congratulations, next round, even the date I was supposed to be there for my interview.

Dear Mr. Maximillain Goldstein,

We would like to extend an invitation to visit Wesley Academy for Girls... (blah, blah, blah) *our internship program is world renowned...*(words, words, words) *the program will be for an entire year.* I kept scanning the letter. *We are the one of the only schools that offers this type of extensive training and dedication to our student intern program.* (blah, blah, blah and words, words, words)...then there it was, the words I wanted to read.

We are requesting an in-person interview with you on August 1st at 9:30 a.m.

I skimmed to the bottom of the page.

Sincerely, Dean McCallous, Principal of Wesley Academy for Girls.

"Sooooo?" My mom stood waiting to hear the news.

"I got an interview. They want me there August 1st. I got the interview!" I laughed, pulling my mom into my arms.

"I'm so happy for you," she said. Her eyes filled with tears. "Honey, August 1st is only a couple days away."

"I know. I'd better book a flight and get ready to go."

"You could ask your father to use the plane."

"Ahhh no, Ma, I don't think so. I don't want Dad to know anything until I know that I have the internship. Please, just don't say anything."

"Maxi, this is your thing, your business. I just want you to think about your father and his feelings too. That's all I'm going to say."

"I understand and thanks for keeping it between us, Ma."

She smiled at me and, with that, she turned on her heels and left my room.

I knew this was bittersweet for her. I knew she looked at this as losing me to the West Coast. But for me, everything was right again. The stars aligned and the Gods were smiling on me. Finally.

****

I didn't want to use any services affiliated with GP, so I asked Cal to drive me to the airport in my car.

"So how far away from Tahoe is this girly school of yours? If it isn't too far, heck I can come crash with you and hit the slopes. I've heard people talk about how nice the skiing is there," Calvin rambled. This was his way of settling into the fact that I was going away…again.

"I'm not sure. I think it's about three or four hours," I answered. I really didn't know much about skiing in Tahoe. Even though snow skiing is a big part of our lives, right then skiing was the last thing I was thinking about. I know Cal just motor-mouths when he is either avoiding an issue or doesn't want to deal with his feelings.

"What time do you have to check in again? Did you get a rental car in California? When are you coming home? If you move out there, I volunteer to drive your B-mer out to you," Cal rapid fired as he drove us down to the Aspen Airport.

"Oh geez man. Come on, bro, you're starting to sound like Mom. I have to be there two hours before my flight. I have a hotel room near the school. I rented a car from Budget, I think they gave me a Ford Focus, and I will be flying back in a couple of days. Anything else? Are you done with the fifty questions?"

I noticed Cal's shoulders drop slightly lower as he let out a deep breath. "A Ford Focus?" he leered.

"Yeah. Hey, Cal, I'm sorry. Look, if I get this internship, you'll have to come down and stay with me. Find out if Tahoe even compares to Colorado's skiing. And sure, you can bring the Z4 out to me." I punched Cal in the arm. "Out-of-state license plate." I pointed to the car next to us with California plates.

"Yeah, just don't forget that if you're in California next time you play that game, Colorado will end up being the out-of-state plate, asshole."

Calvin pulled up to the curb and that was the first moment it really sunk in that I could be in California for more than just a school year. That if the whole job thing worked out, I could be calling California my home state.

Chapter Five

Max

Two Years Later...
When I decided to take the student teaching internship at Wesley, I did it for two reasons. One, it meant I'd be far enough from home to keep myself an arm's length away from my father; and two, I was still close enough to feel the sting of his wrath. I wasn't a sadist in the least, but it motivated me to be the best teacher I could be, because it kept me aware of what I would be going back to if this teaching gig didn't work out.

I went home for holiday breaks and the summer and tides changed slightly for the better. My dad softened on his determination to get me to work for him at GP. However; there was never a visit without a couple digs about the choices I had made. I'd come home and, I swear, I would gain fifteen pounds. Mom kept me fed and always reminded me when I need a haircut. Cal started making himself a little scarcer than he was before. I guess he and Dad had been fighting a lot, and without me as a buffer, it'd been tough. Camille and Dan were fine; same old same old. Dan was still busting his ass for my father, working for a position he would never get, and Camille, well, she was still determined to be mother hen when I came home. And Emily? Well she came around and we talked again about our misunderstood kiss. She was dating the son of the owner of Aspen Snow Park and Resort. Our kiss became old news; all it took was some time and a new interest.

When I found out that Wesley had decided to hire me on permanently I was determined to get my own place. I came back to

California after the Fourth of July and started looking. I appreciated the on-campus housing my first year, but I was ready to have my privacy, something that campus living didn't offer. Let's just say everyone knew your business.

A year into it now…I know that I made the right choice. I loved California and my job. There was something innately rewarding in seeing the light go on in the heads of those girls. Sure, it's a school where the entitled are plentiful and money flows like rivers through their hands. Plastic is treasured and the attitudes are about as big as the task of keeping the boundaries drawn. I thought I was going to be nothing more than a babysitter who just happened to know a thing or two about government and history. I was surprised to realize that there were just enough students who truly cared about their education.

I found an apartment about ten minutes away from campus, and moved in a couple weeks before school started. A week later, I received my class assignment: Government and U.S. History. It was a lot better than the World History I was originally hired to teach. I never expected Mr. Foust to retire one week before school was about to start. I guess Dean McCallous pissed him off, so instead of hanging around for another year or two, he took his retirement a few years earlier than planned. When Dean McCallous called me into her office, she told me that I was the only logical choice because I'd trained under Foust last year and I knew how he worked. Plus I was the only one who could read his writing. It wasn't that bad…his writing, that is.

I showed up the day before school started, figuring I'd organize the classroom the way I wanted it. I relished the fact that it was going to be the first time in that room without having Mr. Foust hanging around critiquing my job as a young whippersnapper with my "newfangled" style of teaching. It never seemed to fail, when I would take over his class, he'd always leave through the back door grumbling something about "back in my day" under his breath. But I knew I would survive that first year on my own…a room filled with senior girls who were all worried about what Ivy League school their daddies were going to bribe them into.

I noticed the class schedule and roster on my desk. Dean McCallous must have left it for me. Perfect opportunity to find out what type of students I was going to encounter. All the personalities of twenty eight students ranging from the self-centered to the self-reliant. But as I ran my finger down the list of princess's names, my eye caught one that didn't have the delicate taste of letters that rolled off your tongue or the snap of brazen femininity like the other ones ending in an "a" or "e" sound. I immediately assumed it was a misprint or a mistake: Wilson Mooney. Falling in line when it came to the Briannas and Britneys of the world, maybe Wilson would have something more to offer than belonging. Maybe the girl's names ending in an "s," "a," "y," or "e" weren't what drove this girl's parents to choose something so intently different than most. Wilson...*what would possess someone to name their daughter Wilson?*

I noticed an asterisk and a check mark by her name. When a student had both marks next to their name, it indicated that they were a financial burden to the school. The checkmark represented the student's enrollment in the work-to-learn program established by the board of directors. The asterisk indicated that the student was receiving a sizable scholarship. Not that it was important, but I hadn't had any students the previous year who had any financial aid whatsoever. It left me curious about what job she'd been assigned to work off her education. Did she have to sweep the halls, mop the science lab's floor? What job could she do around this pristine campus that would warrant paying off a tuition that's over fifty thousand dollars a year? Personally, I felt like it was one way Wesley used humiliation to devalue a student who wasn't really supposed to be there in the first place. Let's face it, Wesley is a school for the elite and privileged. Not for a wannabe who's hanging around begging for scraps and nibbling on the leftovers. Never would I ever condone it...but calling a spade a spade kept the *haves* and the *have-nots* in total perspective. I wondered if this Wilson girl was someone who was working hard to keep herself in school. Or maybe she was a total fuck-up that Wesley kept there to prove they are compassionate. Either way, it would be interesting to put a face to the name.

I pulled out the chair behind my desk, sat down, and wrote out each name across the small rectangular box in my grade book. Cindy Browler, Jacky Burlington, Joanie Emerson, and so on, until I got to Wilson Mooney. Still, I was at a loss as to why someone would name their daughter Wilson.

The door slid across the floor as my pen scribed the last student's name, Bonnie Wente. I didn't look up immediately, knowing it was most likely the twelfth-grade English Lit teacher, Theresa Clouser, coming in to tell me about the blow-up Dean McCallous had with Bill Foust. If there was one person who tended to perpetuate the drama blow by blow, it was Theresa. She was the one person you could go to and find out about everything happening on campus. Who was sleeping with who, who hated who, whose husband was having an affair with the babysitter, even down to the reasons why someone missed a day of work. So when I heard someone clear their throat, I didn't expect to look up and see such a beautiful girl.

"Oh…I'm sorry, I thought this was Mr. Faust's Government class?" she offered as she turned quickly to leave. "Oh. My. God…I'm in the wrong place," she mumbled under her breath. I stood up, letting the pen I was using drop with a thud on the desk.

"No, you're not in the wrong place. This is Mr. Foust's—I mean—this is the right place. Mr. Foust quit—well, um, retired suddenly," I said as I fumbled my way from behind the desk, slamming my thigh firmly into the corner. I bit my bottom lip and pulled in a quick breath. The girl noticed.

She was very pretty, in a natural kind of way. Her wavy blonde hair bounced across her shoulders and her indigo blue eyes capped her delicate yet more mature features. There was something very familiar about her, like I'd seen her before, but I couldn't place her.

She cast her eyes down at the floor. I could tell she wanted to say something. She swallowed with an exaggerated gulp. It was as if words that needed to be said got caught up in the back of her throat.

"I'm Wilson," she mumbled. Her cheeks pushed a shade darker. Not offering her hand, she shoved them in her pockets.

"Oh, right, Wilson. I'm Max, umm, Mr. Goldstein. I think I have you, I mean, you are going to be in my government class," I felt my heart begin to speed in my chest. My hands tied up with each other as I tried to make my words make sense. I thumbed through my roster to show her…that she was mine, my student. It was Wilson, the girl with the name that didn't belong to any debutants or princesses.

"Well, my guidance counselor told me it would be a good idea to introduce myself, and to tell you that I've been assigned to erase your whiteboards this year; so…hi." She kept looking everywhere but into my eyes—down at her feet, over my shoulder, across the room, but eventually her intense blue eyes glistened with a slight radiance as she looked at me.

"Hi, Wilson. And I appreciate your help…with my, uh, boards," I said with a slight nod of my head.

There was an awkward moment of silence between us; she fiddled with the edge of her khaki shorts. I took a deep breath, pulling her scent of coconut and flowers through my nose and down into my lungs. I was captivated by her and the delicate curl of her blonde hair as it danced on her shoulders. Her exaggerated smile obliterated every lonely place I'd tried to avoid for the last three years. Who was this girl?

She pulled a wide grin across her face before she bit her bottom lip between her gorgeous, white teeth. I felt her eyes as they tapped across my thrashing heart.

"Well, 'bye,'" she uttered before she turned away.

"Hey, wait!" I blasted, causing her to spin back around.

Everything that made my body react became primitive. I wanted to recognize where these feelings were coming from. How could I get twisted for someone I didn't know beyond an introduction? There was something in her eyes, her tone, the way she carried herself against the air in the room.

What am I doing? I can't look at her this way...but there is something different about her...something entirely different.

I could feel the swirl build in my gut, an excitement that had nothing to do with the fact that this girl was going to be my student. My eyes instinctively raked over her chest. Her breasts, flawlessly round, were pulling her sweater just enough for me to notice her nipples were unleashed against the dark blue cardigan. *Damn, shit, stop! I can't look at her like this...I can't look at her at all.* I dropped my sight to the floor before I decided to look toward my classroom door. I was desperate to have someone come in and save me from where my mind was tilting me...into images of inappropriate behavior with this girl named Wilson.

"So, I'll see you tomorrow, in class and after school, to do my boards...I mean erase my whiteboards," I spluttered.

She nodded. A genuine smile broke across her face, and as if walking on a cloud, she turned and floated out the door.

Chapter Six

Wilson

There I stood at the entry to my government class, the same classroom I had visited a couple of days ago. My eyes burned from staring at this drop-dead-gorgeous guy leaning against the front of his desk. My throat ran dry and my head got a little swimmy and my heart started to flood my bloodstream with tingling endorphins. His arms were folded against his chest, his ankles crossed. Casual in his demeanor, he started instructing everyone to take a seat. The door was wide open, propped against the vacant wall behind it. Clearly, my whole reason for coming to fourth period had totally changed.

Mr. Goldstein had taken over for Mr. Faust. I can't say I was terribly upset by it. Mr. Faust had been there for over twenty-five years. Teaching had carved every deep line around his mouth, every craterous pox mark across his rosy, bulbous nose exaggerated by his puffy jowl and droopy eyelids. The guy's skin was riddled with patches of spider-webbed red splotches and milky brown age spots. Let's just say he wasn't too easy on the eyes.

Now, Max. Or Mr. Goldstein? He was really nice on the eyes, and if I was going to enjoy learning about government, then at least I'd have a reason to show up to his room every day. Looking at him made everything better, even having some of the bitchiest girls in the school sitting in my class didn't seem to matter so much.

When he tracked his thin, long fingers through the edge of his thick, black hair, all the girls swooned; I swear I heard a unified sigh erupt simultaneously. It was the tiny, almost unnoticeable acts like running his hand through his hair or curling a half smile across his lips before catching it between his teeth that drove all the girls crazy. It could have been that he was also one of the youngest teachers on campus. Most of the other teachers were already past the prime of student gawking. This guy was barely out of college. My heart thundered in my chest and my legs shivered as if it was 30 below zero. *Come on, Wilson, it's the first day, 179 more to go.*

He turned and noticed I was still there, just standing outside the door. His emerald eyes twinkled with every breath he took, his lips shaped round enough to catch between his pearly white teeth with his heart-stopping smirk. He smiled, and the eyes couldn't help but follow suit.

"Well, Miss Mooney, are you going to join us?" he asked as he leaned in my direction lifting his body off his desk. His hair tumbled across his perfect forehead before he swished it out of the way. Laughter busted out, filling the room with snide-ass remarks and whoops.

My breath caught in my throat when I tried to speak. He didn't give me a chance to answer before he slipped past me, went out into the hall and pulled the beige metal door closed. The scent of Crew for Men found its way into my nose as his sweater brushed across my exposed skin, causing a shiver to radiate down my spine. Right at that moment, nobody else was in the class with us. Whether he knew it or not, this guy was hot. Purely physical, I know, but when he came up behind me, just close enough for me to feel his energy, and told me to find a seat, I must have turned every shade of red. All the nerves on the surface of my skin exploded with goose bumps. I struggled to convince myself for the next fifty-five minutes to focus...*focus, focus, focus. Damn, the only seat left...front row, right in front of his desk. Focus, focus, focus, Wilson.* I pushed myself into the seat and dropped my backpack next to my leg. I folded my hands and fiddled with a pencil that someone left from the other class. Finally finding my groove, I tapped the eraser against the desk.

Mr. Goldstein paced back and forth while he spoke, pushing both hands through his onyx black hair every once in a while. His long white sleeves were folded and pushed up past his elbows. I noticed no rings on his fingers. Score one for me.

"Well hello, ladies. This is twelfth-grade government. It is a required class to graduate. If you are not a senior you are in the wrong place." He stood waiting for a moment, expecting someone—anyone—to get up and walk out. Nobody did. "Alright, that's that. I would like to introduce myself and tell you a little about who I am before we go around the room and do introductions." He stopped and leaned against the front of his desk, which happened to be right in front of me. His eyes met mine and he pushed a panty-melting smile at me. My face rushed crimson.

"I'm Mr. Goldstein. This is my first year teaching on my own. Last year I student taught under Mr. Faust, in this very room. I grew up in Colorado, earned my degree from Michigan, and decided to come out west to set roots in Northern California."

"Are you married?" a voice interrupted from the back of the room.

Mr. Goldstein leaned forward with a chuckle, shifting his weight onto the balls of his feet before rocking back against the desk again. His eye gleamed with embarrassment and his lips strained to a formidable smile.

"Ahhh, no, I am not married. But I am excited about this class." He pushed his fingers through his sharp black hair, pulling it away from his sea-green eyes.

"How about a girlfriend?" another voice from the back interjected.

"No, I don't have a girlfriend either."

His complexion flushed a shade of red. He shifted and pushed his sleeves back up above his elbows. A couple of girls vocalized their excitement while the rest of us silently swooned over the fact that we actually believed we had a chance with this exquisite gift God put before us. Everyone could feel the shift in the room—a shift that he had to hear and we embraced.

"How about we focus on this class, government, and talk about some of the expectations I have for this year. Government doesn't have to be boring or rote. I plan to make it exciting once again. But first, how about we go around the room, say your name, and one thing you are excited about this year."

Voices became murmurs that tainted my ears as I watched him look interested in what every other girl had to say, telling him their name, plus some hollow ideas they thought he'd want to hear, hoping to impress him with the idiotic, self-centered plans they made for when they'd leave high school. Every girl tried to one-up the next, everyone trying to impress him with sentences strung together with bullshit stories of acceptance letters expected from Stanford, Harvard, and Yale. Their voices dripped with entitlement; egotistical, self-absorbed ideas that they had what the Ivy League schools wanted. Unfortunately, most of those girls really would be accepted to those schools. It wasn't what was in their head the schools were after but the fatty checks their rich daddies funneled to their programs, building new wings, science and research centers, even libraries and social halls. Let's face it: I was nothing more than a charity case, a means to the end of making Wesley Academy for Girls look good on paper. I was nothing more than a prop that made them look like they gave a shit about the average person receiving a proper education.

"Thank you, Hilary, for sharing. Alright, next," Mr. Goldstein said.

I didn't realize it was my turn to talk about myself. Mr. Goldstein waved his hands in front of my face, taking notice that I was somewhere else. He actually leaned down trying to make eye contact with me. Oh, I felt so foolish! Dissolving from my pot of self pity, it wasn't until I heard my name being screeched from Jacky Burlington, that I realized everyone was waiting for me to say my name and where I wanted to go to college next year.

"Wilson, earth to Wilson, it's your turn! Geesh, wake up already. You won't hack it in Harvard if you keep spacing out."

The room burst into laughter and snarky remarks. Embarrassed to every shade of red, blood pooled and settled in my cheeks. It was Joanie Emerson, my best friend who stuck up for me.

"Shut up, Jacky. At least Wilson will get in to Harvard on her grades, not her daddy's promises."

Jacky huffed before she turned to Cindy Browler and mumbled something under her breath.

"Ladies, please, when you walk through my door, we are to treat each other with respect. Alright, let's continue." Max thrust his hand out toward me, waiting for me to drone out the same drivel that every girl before me delivered.

"My name is Wilson Mooney, and I—" the bell broke my words. *Whew, saved.*

Chairs scraped across the floor, voices cackling and murmuring, as everyone began to shuffle out of the room.

"Um, Miss Burlington and Miss Emerson, don't leave. I want to talk to you. The rest of you, we will finish up tomorrow. Enjoy the rest of your day."

I took my time collecting my backpack. I wanted to hear what he had to say, hoping beyond all hope he was going to ream Jacky for being such a bitch. He watched me as I messed with some zippers. Jacky waited next to his desk, huffing and pouting every couple of seconds because Mr. Goldstein was waiting for Joanie to join them.

"Ladies, it is the first day of school. Let's not start out on the wrong foot. We have a long year, and I will not tolerate disrespect in my class. Do you both understand me?"

They both nodded. Jacky, with her smarmy attitude, let out a sharp "tsk" under her breath before asking if she could leave.

"Yeah, I'm sorry Mr. Goldstein," Joanie answered quickly before she tossed her backpack over one shoulder and left without looking back at Jacky.

I glanced at Mr. Goldstein and his eyes met mine, filled with apologetic sympathy. I looked down at the floor before hurrying to catch up to Joanie.

Great, what did that look mean? I have to go to his classroom after school today and clean his whiteboards. The last thing I need from him is a courtesy look flooded with pity.

Chapter Seven

Max

I was totally sideswiped by Wilson. I didn't expect to be so affected by her. I shouldn't be enamored with one of my students, ever, let alone on the first day of school. I'd been around beautiful women all my life, women with way more life experience than this girl. But there was something about Wilson; something that got to me. When her scent floated in the air, I fought to inhale every particle. When she spoke, I strained to listen, and when she moved I ached to touch her.

I lost my train of thought as her aroma pulled and tugged at me below my belt. Jacky cleared her throat, pulling me from the trance Wilson put me under. *Damn.* It was the first day of school and I was already longing to keep her smell permanently planted in my nose. *What in the hell are you doing? You can't get all caught up in her. This isn't who you are. Damn it, Max, you need to stay professional. Pull your shit together. You're her teacher. She's your student, for Pete's sake.*

The bell rang and the next class began to shuffle in, a perfect excuse to keep my mind busy and preoccupied with teaching. So why couldn't I stop counting the minutes until she'd come back into my classroom and clean my whiteboards?

I can't be here when she comes back. I'll have to preoccupy myself with things I need to get done. That's it! I'll save all my prep work until after school. I'll do my copying, grading, and correlating while Wilson is in my room. It will be so much better that way.

I never looked at my watch once or chased the clock on the wall. So when the bell rang, the twenty students from my sixth period class got up and randomly began to shuffle out into the hall, racing to get to their next class. I had it all worked out in my head that I would make myself busy and unavailable when Wilson came into my room after seventh period. I was pretty sure I was strong enough to handle anything she could throw my way. Besides, I had a whole fifty minutes to prepare. Maybe it was a request that Mr. Faust set up with Dean McCallous, seeing he was about to retire in a year or two; whatever the reason, I didn't have to teach a seventh period. Thank you, Mr. Faust.

I decided to call my brother, Cal, who was still "stuck" in Aspen. I knew calling him would give him the opportunity to remind me, again, that he was still willing to deliver my Z4 out to California…no charge. I let out a slight chuckle before I dialed his number, tapped the speaker button, and propped my phone on the desk next to me. I pulled out the next day's work to determine what I was going to assign as class work and homework. Yep, that's me, the second day of school and I was the asshole who gave out homework.

By the third ring, Cal picked up.

"Hey, bro, what's up?"

"Hi, Cal. Nothin' much, just checking in," I answered.

"How was the first day teaching on your own?" Calvin asked.

"Not too bad. A couple little glitches, but other than that, pretty good." I wasn't about to admit the glitch had to do with a girl named Wilson, and the feelings she stirred in my gut. "When I called Dad yesterday, he mentioned something about you starting a new job tomorrow?"

"Yeah, he talked to the head guy over at Syncorp or Sycorp, something like that. I guess they need someone to reprogram their warning system."

"Warning system? What, like for a fire and natural disaster?" I asked.

"No, Max, hackers, thugs, and cyber-thieves."

"That sounds like a pretty cool gig," I added.

"Yeah, if you like building code and working with html all day. Come on, Max, you know me, I'm happiest outside, not poured into a suit and tie."

"I hear you. Hey, how's that girl you were dating? Clara?" I clipped, hoping to change the subject.

"You mean Clarisse. Yeah, I guess she's fine," Calvin answered matter-of-factly.

"What happened? I thought you were all into her?"

"Yeah, well, I guess half the male population in Aspen was into her too. Turns out she's a slut and I don't play cleanup."

"Only sloppy seconds," I joked.

"No, bro, I'm not even one for sloppy seconds—"

"So your new quest is, what? Deflowering virgins?"

"Not necessarily, but I'm getting a little choosier lately. No chicks coming off breakups. That used to work for me, but not anymore."

"That's funny coming from you, my brother the man-whore."

"Really? Man-whore? Look, I'm just not interested in investing in these heartbroken, little 'hos anymore."

"Whoa, Cal. Come on, man."

"Come on nothing, I'll respect a girl who doesn't spread her legs for every Tom, Dick, and Harry."

I heard my classroom door slam shut then. When I looked up, I saw Wilson. She'd come early to clean my whiteboards.

Heat collected in my cheeks. The idea that she could have heard any part of Cal's and my conversation worried me.

"I can come back," Wilson mouthed as she shuffled backward toward the door, her arms folded across her midsection.

"No, you're fine, please come in," I whispered as I snatched my iPhone off the desk and took it off speaker phone. "Hey, Cal, listen, I need to call you back. A student just came in."

He didn't argue, just gave me a grunt and hung up.

"I'll come back and do your boards later, if you need time," she said as she hung her thumbs on the edges of her pockets and raised her shoulders just enough to indicate she felt bad.

"No, I'm done. It was my brother. We were just talking about…nothing really," I professed.

She stood there and stared at me. Her smile curved to a slight frown and her clear-as-spring blue eyes constricted as she scrunched up her nose.

"I kinda need to get right there…to clear the whiteboards," she hinted as she pointed at me.

"Right. Here, let me get out of your way," I asserted, trying not to stammer my words.

The muscles in her jaw tensed. She tossed a slight smile my way before she danced her fingers along the edge of the aluminum pen tray that housed my dry-erase markers and a huge eraser.

I wanted to just watch her erase. *Damn, this is so, totally wrong.* I forced myself to drop my eyes down to my desk. There sat my grade book, wide open. *That's it, I'll just act like I have stuff I need to do. I could write due dates on assignments for the next week. Yeah, that's what I'll do; anything to keep me from watching her drag my erasers across the whiteboards.* I pulled out my chair, sat down, and started searching for a pen or pencil, anything that worked.

"Umm, excuse me, Mr. Goldstein, I'm not sure what you want me to erase and what you want to keep." Her voice was shaky. She caught her bottom lip between her perfectly white teeth before jutting out her hip enough to make her upper body sway back and forth, tapping the eraser against her thigh. Her mannerisms mimicked those of someone who was confident in her abilities but uncomfortable in having to wait for me to make my choices.

Everything in my body started popping off. My head was fuzzy, my heart hustled to a quickened pace, even my hands were part of this siege, pushing perspiration across my palms. My skin glowed hot, and every exposed part of my skin grew sensitive to the air she exhaled.

Damn, I have to get out of here. I pulled in a breath and let it out really slowly. It's quite possible I sounded and looked like I was irritated.

"Erase everything," I spat as I gestured to both whiteboards, snatched my worksheet from my desk, and left. "I'll be back, I need to make copies," I said as I walked out the door without looking back.

In my head I hoped that when I got back, she'd be gone. That she'd just erase both whiteboards and be on her way to another classroom. But in my heart, I wanted her to be waiting for me. I wish making copies would have taken longer, but it didn't. It took a whole ten minutes. Ten minutes of twisted fucked-up thoughts about how I was ever going to survive nine months of seeing her five days a week. Scenarios flashed in my head—ignoring her as she came into my classroom, moments where I was able to swallow my raw and totally ridiculous desire to be close to her. Maybe she'd spare me the torture and transfer out of the school. Truthfully, I didn't want her to go; I just really liked my job. I was just going to have to find a way to deal with it.

By the time I got back to my classroom, Wilson had already left. My heart plummeted into my stomach and every excuse and lame-ass story of why I shouldn't feel this way about a student swam through my head. Being torn between guilt and desire sucked. I tossed the stack of copied and collated pages onto my desk, turned around, and walked out. *Damn.* I didn't even look to see if she'd finished cleaning my whiteboards.

****

It'd been eight weeks and two days since Wilson sauntered into my classroom, the longest, hardest, and yet most exhilarating couple of months I'd had in a long time—quite possibly in my entire life. She'd smile at the perfect times and frown when called for. She was something different, something unique apart from the same old worn out idea that money and power is the answer to everything. Watching her interact with other girls in the class was like experiencing the first rain in spring.

Every Monday through Friday, I couldn't wait for fifth period. The bell would ring and, without fail, my eyes would dart to the door. My blood would speed and I'd realize I was holding my breath until she crossed the threshold. There was a calm before the storm raging throughout my body. I kept a secret language I hoped she'd decipher one day—the brush of my fingers across the back of her chair, the times I'd call on her to answer, the moments she'd ask for help and I'd lean in close enough to inhale her scent, feel her energy.

I was completely aware that my feelings were inappropriate. I knew if society had the powers to dive into my mind, they'd find themselves swimming amongst buried desires of a guy who wanted to be something more to his student then her teacher. They'd see a guy who tried to fight these feelings every day, battling the desire to make her see me as something more than a potential opportunity. That I really wasn't a creepy guy who just wanted to take advantage of her, but a boy who simply was starting to fall for a girl.

Unfortunately, I was becoming nothing more than a worried man barreling down a road toward a destination I couldn't come back from. What if Wilson's actions were nothing more than her normal energy she has with every guy? Or worse, what if I finally took a step in the direction of letting my feelings known and she didn't feel the same way? Risking my career for an improbable chance with her seemed irresponsible, even stupid. I was in too deep. I was fully aware that I needed to reign in the feelings I was having and put a cap on the attention I was paying her. But on the flip side of the coin, what if she did…feel something for me? What if she'd been fighting back the same feelings burning deep in her belly?

Either way, the worst part of the whole thing was the weekends. They were my hell. From Friday after Wilson finished cleaning my whiteboards to Sunday night before I went to bed. I'd try and keep myself busy, diving into work, finding places to go that would devour the time fast enough so Monday could show up right on time. I'd gotten pretty good at finding things to eat up those useless days I called the weekend.

The fifth period bell rang and I noticed the same ritual as always beginning to bubble in my gut. Waiting for Wilson to show up I nearly stopped breathing. As the students shuffled in I looked up, waiting to see her walk through the door, but I was interrupted by my phone chiming. It was a text from Calvin.

TGIF Bro! Hey, Ma said Ur coming home next weekend?

I was thinking about going back home for a weekend. I figured it would be something else I could do to burn up time, and use it as an excuse to surprise Cal. But it looked like Mom had mentioned it to him. So much for keeping it on the down low!

Yeah, I was thinkin of coming out. Maybe meeting up w/some friends to go skiing. How's mom? I texted back.

What day? She's Fine. Excited UR coming. His reply was quick and to the point.

Good. Thinkin fly out Fri. Skiing with friends on Sat. Leave Sun. UR home right?

YEP. OK. C U next weekend. And that was the end of our conversation. Looked like it was time to start looking up prices for plane tickets home.

When I glanced up from my text, looking to see who was pouring into my class, my eyes locked on Wilson, who'd just sauntered through the door as the second bell rang. My breath hitched and the muscles in my jaw ran taut as my throat struggled to swallow the knot she put there every time I looked at her...*God, I hope nobody noticed.*

Chapter Eight

Wilson

Every day I looked for signs that Mr. Max Goldstein might be interested in me beyond a teacher-student relationship. I'd been coming to government and cleaning his whiteboards for over two months, and I still couldn't figure out what he thought of me. Was it totally ridiculous to think that there could be more there? That maybe the feelings I had for him were enough for both of us? I'd done everything I could think of without coming right out and saying it. — sauntered past, swayed my hips, made him laugh, asked him questions, batted my eyes, and even passed notes hoping he'd take them. I'd worn perfume, tied my hair up off my shoulders. Hell, I even let a couple buttons loose on my top once, all with little or no success.

The second bell rang right as Joanie, my best friend, and I were meandering in. It was Friday, and on Fridays we had a tradition of free-choice seats. So Joanie and I chose the back seats, middle row. I figured if we were going to commentate on his class or talk about my infatuation with him, the last row would be the place to do it. Joanie was the only person in the entire world who knew I had the *hots* for Max Goldstein. Okay, so maybe it was more than the "hots." I had it bad. And she was the one who kept me grounded in my infatuation. Let's just say he was the highlight of my senior year. Period.

"Alright ladies, find a seat, please, that was the bell. We have a lot to cover today. We are going to be continuing our discussion regarding the fiscal impact and responsibility of the governmental agency, Health and

Human Services."

Mr. Goldstein commanded the room. I loved the way he'd walk back and forth, his blue-and-gray sweater vest over his white button-up shirt creasing and pulling as he talked with his arms. His collar was tucked and peeking out just enough to give his shiny black hair a place to dance. His voice ebbed and flowed with his words and straightened with his conviction. Yeah, he was passionate, enthusiastic, and I liked—no I loved—it. His eyes, mossy green and as vivid as a beacon, illuminated the passion in his soul.

"You know, Mr. Goldstein, my dad says that human agency thingy is nothing more than a soup kitchen for lazy people," Bonnie Wente piped up, interrupting my totally perfect vision of Mr. Goldstein.

"Well, Bonnie..." he started.

"The only thing that agency helps are people who want to live off the government and have a bunch of babies. That's what my dad told me," another voice piped up through the low grumbling mix of "oohs" and "aaahs."

"Hey, hey, hey, ladies, come on," Mr. Goldstein interrupted.

The banter continued, even when he worked to control the dynamics of the group. Some of the girls popped off about the poor living in our country, while others talked about starting a foundation for poor people. Once everyone stopped talking at the same time and the room unexpectedly turned quiet, I cleared my throat. Instantly, it felt like everyone was looking at me, eyes piercing through me as though they wanted to know what it was like to want or need. Having no desire to accommodate their silent request, I smiled and turned around to Joanie. I wasn't about to enter into a pointless discussion with girls who had no idea what it's like to go without. They had no clue what the real picture of life looked like.

"Wilson, you have something to add?" Mr. Goldstein piped up. I could feel the blood rush to my cheeks. How was I going to come across sounding educated when every girl around me was more worried about what outfit they were going to wear to the parties that weekend?

"I just don't see the correlation between thinking this agency is all about the parasitic relationship of the poor and this country, when clearly it has other branches such as children's welfare, and rights for the elderly," I said. I could feel everyone's eyes marking me for a target, but oddly enough they all sat silent.

"You're right, Wilson. The Health and Human Services provide support to more than just socially disadvantaged individuals. It isn't just designed to serve the poor or lower middle class. It's designed to serve the masses. Social Security is a big part of the HHS. They have services for the elderly, children who have lost one or both parents either by death or disability...I am glad you pointed that out. Thank you." His eyes sparkled with excitement, his smile contagious.

"I just remember my grandparents telling me that Social Security really helped them a lot." The room fell silent again as Mr. Goldstein and I shared a moment of connection. Finally someone saw things the way I did, and didn't worry about their new cars, clothes, or their next vacation. We connected, deeper than the surface level.

The silence broke into little snippets and, snide remarks filled the room again until the bell rang.

The classroom cleared quickly with a couple whoops and hollers about the weekend, while others still felt they needed to take a dig at our social programs and how the wealthy support the country. It was a sign of capitalism at its worst. Swirl in their selfish display of entitlement and, voila, our generation at its best. Yeah, sadly enough my generation seems to be the first one that will most likely end up being supported by their parents. But hey, if your parents have it, why not spend it?

"Wilson, I have to jet over to Spanish before sixth period. I'll see you later," Joanie said as she flipped her backpack over her shoulder, her long, brown hair tangling and tucking under the shoulder strap.

Struggling to fit my books and folder into my backpack, I looked up and discovered I was the last person in class...alone, with Mr. Goldstein. His eyes crested mine before dropping back down to his task at hand.

"Pretty heated discussion, you think?" he said as he fiddled with papers from the top of his desk and worked them into organized piles.

"Aah, yeah, that was pretty interesting," I answered while literally fighting to shove my government textbook into my backpack.

"Need some help?" he asked as he looked up. His furrowed eyebrows gave a home to the random pieces of sharp hair that fell across his forehead. He dropped the papers onto his desk and came over to help. *How attentive!* His hands, large and commanding, grabbed the edges of my backpack and held them open, his aroma filling every square inch I breathed. His arm and shoulder pushed delicately but just enough against my body. The connection nearly made me combust. I could hear him breathe, taste his scent, and feel his intention as he looked at me.

"You want to give it another try?" he breathed. His eyes, danced with mine, his lips bent to a smile and the butterflies that hovered in my gut spread their wings.

Already frazzled from the class discussion and now with Mr. Goldstein in my space, I couldn't find the words to respond. I was afraid if I opened my mouth the butterflies that were in full migration patterns around my body would fly out, so I just nodded.

I tried to wedge the last book into my overflowing backpack. With just a little more force at a better angle I'd be able to push the book down and zip the damn thing up. That's when, without any warning, Mr. Goldstein took his large, strong, gorgeous hand, put it over mine, and pushed the book down into my backpack.

O.M.G. He....was...touching...me!

"There you go," he said as he tapped the top of my hand and let his lengthy, nimble fingers linger just long enough against my forearm. He looked at me, his face inches from mine. Our eyes met and, for a glimmer of a moment, I begged him wordlessly to give me a sign, some hope that he felt something more for me than just being his student. A lifetime could have strolled by and I wouldn't have cared. He was looking at me and that was all that mattered.

The classroom door flew open then and students from his next period began to shuffle in. He turned away and headed back to his desk.

"You need a pass to your next class, Wilson?" he asked in a matter-of-fact tone. I looked up at the clock and saw that I had less than two minutes. I wanted to say yes, I wanted to say thank you—and every other word that filled my mind about him—but I couldn't find my voice. I shook my head, heaved my backpack up over one shoulder and gave him the best smile I could muster.

"See you after school then," he blurted as I rushed out the door.

I didn't know how much more I could take—being so close to him and not being able to tell him how I felt, or even whether he liked me or not. I guess I should have been happy, at least I would get thirty minutes of uninterrupted time in the same room with him after school. A smile crept over my face as the wind pushed back my hair. The sun danced in my eyes and I thought about him in his classroom.

Yeah, that's right, Max Goldstein; I will see you...after school.

Want more of Wilson and Max?

Visit Gretchen de la O at:

www.gretchendelao.com

www.facebook.com/booksbygretchendelao
www.twitter.com/GretchendelaO
www.pinterest.com/delaogk
www.youtube.com/delaogk
www.amazon.com/author/gretchendelao
www.goodreads.com/gdelao

*Purchase the
Wilson Mooney Series at
The following online retailers:*
www.amazon.com
www.barnesandnoble.com
www.smashwords.com

Edited by: Tiffany Barkman Grayson (2014)

Dani Hart

Fate

The Life of Arie Series, Short Story

Dani Hart

Copyright © 2014 Dani Hart
All rights reserved.

Chapter One

Being an orphan was never easy on anyone, but I was fortunate that I loved my group home mom, Jenny. She raised me after I showed up at the orphanage when I was just two years old, and I secretly wondered why she didn't adopt me, but I took what time I could get with her. She had visibly aged over the years. She was a tall, heavyset woman now in her sixties with slightly graying hair and a thin smile. Her eyes were a beautiful hazel that resembled a rare genuine amber stone.

Orphans dreamed of two things: being adopted or turning eighteen. I should have been elated that day, but my eighteenth birthday came with trepidation and sadness. I would be leaving Jenny, and I would be on my own. Plus, I had learned the other day that the elderly couple who visited me almost every day since I was ten had passed away. It had all happened so fast. First, Grandma Alice passed, and then, within a week, Grandpa Joe. I imagined his heart was so broken when Alice passed on that it gave out so he could join her in whatever place was awaiting us after this life.

They were sweet and tried to adopt me, but the State said they were too old and in failing health. It broke all our hearts when they were denied, because we had become a little family during the visits, but even after the rejection, they still treated me like their own. They bought me clothes and toys and spent every minute they could with me. It was unorthodox, but Jenny understood and loved them as much as I did. She had been an orphan and respected the bond we had formed. Her experience was quite different than mine, but she also grew up in a different time.

FATE

I sat on the edge of my bed, staring at the blank white walls. I had to restore my room back to a sterile blank slate for the next child in line. Our orphanage had a waiting list. It was depressing that there were that many kids without homes, all for various reasons. I made friends easily, so I was leaving behind a big piece of my heart when I walked out of those doors. It was funny, because I was offered emancipation when I was sixteen, which most kids would die for, but I turned it down. I didn't want to be on my own, and my pseudo parents had grown very ill over the past few years, so I didn't want to be a burden on them, although they tried to convince me it would be fine.

I missed them.

A quiet knock alerted me to Jenny's presence in the doorway.

"Are you ready to go, Ariana?" she asked cautiously.

When I looked up, the tears I was holding back trickled down my cheeks.

"Oh, sweetie," she said as she rushed over, sat down on the bed, and pulled me in tight to her side. "You're going to be great, and you know you can visit anytime, which I would love."

She pulled away to put my dark chestnut brown strands into a mock ponytail, something that seemed so motherly. "Jenny, can I ask you a question?"

"Of course."

I was nervous. I had wanted to ask her this question since shortly after my adoption was denied. "Why didn't you adopt me?" I muttered under my breath. She grabbed me into her arms and rocked me.

"I wanted to, sweetie, but I couldn't. I did my best with you here, though. Don't you think?"

"Yes, you did. Thank you." I wanted to press her for more, but if she wanted to tell me, she would have.

"Do you have everything?"

"I do." I had donated a lot of items to the other kids here, so I was leaving with only a few suitcases full of clothes, memories, and a box full of canvases I had painted. I loved painting. Jenny caught on to my talent right away. She told Alice and Joe, and they paid for private art lessons for me a few times a week here. My last lesson was a few weeks ago right before they passed.

"You know, they are leaving a beautiful piece of them with you. You won't be alone. They will be with you in their house."

They had left their estate to me because they didn't have any other family, so I was moving into their house. They also owned a little mom and pop bookstore in town that was now mine. I wasn't stupid, but I didn't know the first thing about running a business. Jenny said she would help me get on my feet with it, something she didn't have to do on her free time. She was truly a special person.

"I'll drive you over. I was just going home for the day."

"Thanks."

We stood up and grabbed what little things I had and loaded them into the back of her car. The drive from the orphanage to their... I mean, *my* house was majestic. It was so beautiful on the outskirts of town. Magnificent towering trees filled the roadsides, and enchanting wildflowers sprouted randomly out of the ground in an array of hues. Every so often I would see a break in the trees where a little driveway led to a hidden house.

I twisted my hair nervously, thinking about the isolation out here. I was so used to being around an abundance of people that this was a stark contrast to that. There was literally no one around me for at least a mile. We turned down a dirt driveway, and a large two-story house came into view. The same type of trees on the roadside hugged the house closely.

"It's beautiful," I said, stunned.

"It really is. They had a lot of money, Ari. You are very lucky. Most orphans that come of age struggle to just get by. It's awful. I'm so glad you won't have to go through that. Not that I would've let that happen." She winked.

"I know," I responded sadly.

She parked in the gravel driveway in front of the main door. There was a charming patio with two old-fashioned rocking chairs. I could picture Alice and Joe rocking as they drank their morning coffee. A pang of sadness stabbed at my heart, and a tear fell that I quickly wiped away. This would have been a wonderful place to grow up. It was the first time I was seeing its beauty. Due to legal issues, the State wouldn't let me visit. I knew it was to protect me and for my own well-being, but I still hated not being able to see where they lived. Until now.

"Let me help you get settled in," Jenny insisted.

"No, it's okay. Go home to Leo. You will be helping me enough with the store."

"Are you sure, sweetie?" She placed her hand on mine.

"Yes. Thank you, Jenny."

She leaned over and gave me a parting hug. I loved the way she smelled. It was like running through a garden full of roses.

"I love you," she said.

"I love you, too."

I got out of the car and emptied out the contents of the trunk and hauled them onto the front porch. As soon as I had everything unloaded, I waved goodbye to her. Watching her leave was unnerving. I was in the middle of nowhere in a place I had never been and was expected to accept it as my new home.

I sighed as I turned and stared at the door like it would magically open, and a monster would grab me and pull me in. I was being silly. This house had to be filled with amazing memories, knowing how good Alice and Joe were. I fished the house keys out of my jeans pocket, unlocked the door, and pushed it open hesitantly.

The air was stale from the lack of inhabitance, but I could still faintly smell the natural fragrance of Alice and Joe. It was a sweet smell, much like most seniors seem to develop in older age. I shoved the door open wider and carried my bags into the house and locked the door behind me. Instead of immediately exploring my new living quarters, which was massive in comparison to my little room and community bathroom at the orphanage, I closed my eyes and relied on my other senses to get a feel for the house. It felt warm and inviting, and even though the windows were closed, I could hear the faint sounds of nature singing outside.

I stood like that for a few minutes and then walked around the downstairs first. There was a decent size living room with the usual furniture — a leather couch and recliner, a coffee table, and a full book shelf. It was open to a spacious kitchen that looked like it had been renovated recently. It had a beautiful light marble countertop and white-washed cabinetry. I was almost afraid to look in the refrigerator, but I couldn't resist. I was pleasantly surprised to find it was empty and freshly cleaned. In fact, everything was clean. Someone had taken the time to clean the house. Who would do that? They didn't have any living relatives.

I closed the fridge door and marveled at the glass windows that lined the back wall overlooking a picturesque view of a meadow just below the horizon line. The yard was fenced in by the same large trees, and the grass was perfectly manicured. Inside by the breakfast nook, there was an oversized bay window. What an incredible place to eat breakfast every morning!

I went out the French door onto the back porch, which was furnished with two rocking chairs identical to the ones out front. I smiled. It was obvious they loved to spend time together. I hoped one day to have a love that strong, one like theirs that transcended death. It was early afternoon, and the way the sun hit the meadow was too enticing to resist, so I made my way down.

It was even more breathtaking up close. There were beautiful flowers in a perfect little circle. They boasted every color of the rainbow, including every shade in between. They were wild and fit right in with the rugged scenery. I was curious as to why they only grew in this perfect little circle so purposely.

I lay down and closed my eyes to shield them from the mid-afternoon sun. The sound of buzzing bees and fluttering wings filled the meadow along with a distant trickling of water. I would have to see where that was coming from when I was done soaking in the rays.

The warm sun baked my skin gently. I had to be careful with my fair skin, or I would turn into a third degree burn victim in no time. It almost happened once when I was younger. I didn't know any better, and the orphanage had taken us to the beach for the day. I forgot about sunscreen and regretted it for a week after. No amount of aloe vera and aspirin could alleviate the pain I had suffered.

A noise startled me. I sat up and looked around. I squinted in front of me to see someone walking down a path I hadn't noticed or explored yet. My curiosity got the best of me, so I jumped up and followed the path. Probably not the smartest thing to do, being I lived alone and there was no one around for miles, but for some strange reason, I didn't feel like I was in danger.

I tried to walk quietly, but the dead leaves on the ground cracked under the pressure of my bare feet. I paused, but I didn't see any sign of the person anymore. I was slightly disappointed. I was looking forward to meeting the neighbors. I kept walking until I ran into a magnificent creek. It was a relatively small creek, maybe ten feet wide. Just on the other side, down the way a bit, there was a deer lapping up some water. It completely ignored my intrusion.

"Hi."

Chills ran down my spine as a voice whispered into my ear, the man's breath warm on my neck. When I spun around, I was confronted with heavenly beauty and amber eyes that spoke to my soul. He had sandy blonde hair that hit his shoulders and a gentle chiseled face that looked a little bit older than me. He wasn't wearing a shirt, and the afternoon sun added a glow to his dewy sun-kissed bare chest. It was strong and defined and delightfully inviting. I was tempted to touch it to see if he was real.

He chuckled. "Are you going to say something?"

His voice was the icing on the cake, and I wanted to lick every inch of him. I blushed at my foreign thoughts. I had never entertained the idea of having a boyfriend at the orphanage. I stayed focused on school and art and eventually moving out, but the prospect was very inviting as he stood in front of me. "Hi," I said shyly.

"You're new around here."

"Yes. I just moved into the Hadley house."

"Oh. I'm sorry for your loss. They were very sweet," he said.

"So you knew them?"

"Yes. Quite well, in fact. I live in the next house down the road. I run by here every day and occasionally helped them with yard work."

"That's very nice of you."

"Are you family?" he asked.

Conversation with him was so natural. I was at ease around him, and I didn't even know his name yet. "Yes. Well, no… it's complicated." I bowed my head as I thought about them and how much they were missed.

"My name is Tivon," he smiled proudly.

"That's an unusual name."

"It means nature-lover." He winked.

My knees weakened. He had a dazzling smile. "My name is Ariana. I'm not sure what it means."

"It means holy one," he informed me.

"That's amazing that you know that. I am far from holy, though." I had never prayed or attended a church. I wasn't anti-God or religion, but living in a State-run facility it was never practiced. I believed there was a greater force at work in our lives that we would never be able to see, so I guess I had faith above anything else.

"You would be surprised what you conceal deep within you."

Such a weird thing for a complete stranger to say to me, but somehow I hung on every word that he spoke. He was ethereal.

"I have to go now, but I would love to sit and talk with you more. Will you meet me here again tomorrow?" he asked confidently.

"Sure." I could feel my cheeks redden with heat.

He leaned in close and teased my cheek with his lips for a moment suspended in time and then kissed it with his soft lips. It took my breath away.

"It was nice meeting you, Ariana," he whispered into my ear and then dashed away down the path.

I stared in the direction he went for a few minutes trying to regain my composure and strength. His touch had weakened me and left me giddy. I wanted more. I instantly knew I wanted to spend every second I could with him. I turned back to the creek and noticed the deer staring at me. It was an odd feeling to be watched by such a skittish creature.

When it started walking through the creek to me, I almost ran away, but instead, I was transfixed. It was a female and absolutely stunning. She came right up to me and stopped only a foot away. She stood a little shorter than my five foot four inch stature, so she arched her head up to look at me. I stood deathly still. I wasn't sure what to do, and I was shaking a little bit, but I was curious. She took another step forward and nudged her muzzle into my side, begging for affection. I obliged and petted her head like she was a household pet. She made quiet noises of enjoyment. I was in complete awe. I had never heard of deer being so friendly. After she got what she needed, she turned and disappeared into the forest.

This place was truly magical, and I was never more grateful for the beautiful gift that Alice and Joe gave me. They had transplanted me from a world of isolation into a fairy tale life. I would do my best never to disappoint their legacy and endeavor to make them proud. Jenny was right. They were with me. I could feel their presence, and it made me feel less alone.

Chapter Two

I spent a lot of time walking around the house and taking inventory of the lives I never got to be a part of. The walls were adorned with beautiful photos of them at different stages of their lives. From the looks of it, they had been together since they were in high school. They never told me how they met, but I'd bet it was romantic. They didn't tell me much about themselves. It wasn't that they were private; it just never came up. I guess I could have inquired, but I hated being nosey, and I didn't want to give them an excuse to disappear.

Another question I never asked of Jenny was how I came to be at the orphanage and if she met my parents. I wanted to know, but I was afraid I wouldn't like the answer; instead, I imagined that something out of their control happened, and they didn't have a choice but to give me up. I liked that dream. It gave me hope that one day they would come back for me. I still hoped.

I knew the first thing I needed to do was clean out their personal belongings, such as clothes. I would donate them, but I wanted to hold on to the photographs and other items that would keep them close to me. I left the ones on the walls untouched, but placed the others into a box and marked it *Hadley's,* and I piled the donation bags by the front door. I hadn't located the entrance to the attic yet, so I went through all the closets in the house, including the linen closets. The house was expansive, but only had two master bedrooms with adjoining bathrooms. It made me think it was a custom-made home, because that seemed like an odd layout.

I found the cut out for the ceiling in the master bedroom closet that

Alice and Joe had occupied. It was completely inaccessible without a pull to open it. In fact, it looked like they painted over it, so it must have gone unused. I released a frustrated sigh. This was going to take some work. I went down into the garage and located a ladder and hauled it up to the closet. I also grabbed a cement spatula to shimmy in the cracks. It was not an easy task. I cut around the perimeter and then used the spatula to pry it open enough to get my fingers in the cracks to pull it down.

With a little effort, it un-jammed and opened, and down with it, came a cloud of dust. I coughed and fanned it away. It was safe to assume there wasn't an attic light. At least not one that worked.

I thought I saw a flashlight in the garage, so I climbed down to retrieve it. It turned out I was right, and it actually worked, which was a plus for me. I had no idea where to find the battery stash. I turned it on and looked around the attic from the ladder before I got the nerve to go up. Light filtered in through a small window on the far edge. It still wasn't much, but better than just the flashlight.

I hauled the box up the ladder and then pulled myself up. I shined the flashlight around to discover a fairly empty space. The attic was unfinished, so exposed rafters and insulation made up the floor. I had to be really careful where I stepped, so I didn't accidentally fall through. If I got hurt no one would know. Shivers crept through me at the thought.

I spotted one box in the corner by the window. There was a piece of plywood lying haphazardly underneath it. I pulled the box over to the window and opened it. I felt slightly guilty going through things that didn't belong to me. *So dumb.* They were dead, and technically everything was mine now according to the will, which still hadn't really sunk in. Less than eight hours ago I had nothing but the orphanage, and now I had a house, a car, and a bookstore. Talk about surreal.

The box contained canvas artwork and a few books. My jaw dropped when I took out the first piece of art. It was breathtaking. The landscape reflected a world out of fairy tales. There were lush oversized glossy foliage, soaring trees, and the most incredible blue flowers that almost looked like butterflies the way their blooms were shaped. The artist had also made it seem like they manifested into butterflies with the loose brush strokes leading up to butterflies swarming just above them. Whoever painted this had a raw talent beyond lessons. It was natural and from the heart. I searched for a signature, but couldn't find one.

The other oil paintings were different, but of equally amazing landscapes. I was awestruck by the imagination of the creator and a little jealous. I was good, but I didn't come close to this kind of talent. After I was done admiring the artwork, I scooped out the books. One was a leather bound journal, another an old book filled with children's fairytales, and the last one was a child's book called *The Spirits of Nature*.

The corners were worn, and the binding was tattered. It was a pity, because it looked like a beautiful book from the cover. The figures were wispy and almost blended into the landscape in the background. I would have loved a book like this as a child, just for its artistic quality. I opened it and paged through it quickly, admiring the pictures and skipping the words. Good picture books didn't need words to tell a story that the artwork could. There was an expressive inscription printed on the last page.

My Dearest Alice,

This book was mine and my mother's before that, all the way back to your great great-grandmother and maybe further. It was discovered in the forest that surrounds our house, and it has been in the family ever since. I hope you find your way within the pages of the world as we have.

Love, Mother

Wow!

In that one inscription I had learned that this book was ancient and that her family had lived on this plot of land for over a hundred years. I marveled at the history of the world I was now living in. I wondered if Alice wanted to adopt me to keep the legacy going. No matter what her reasons, she was a remarkable person, and I would honor her in any way I could. I looked for publisher information, but there was nothing. It was a shame that a book so aesthetic was so beat up. I carefully placed it back into the box and made a mental note to go the library to research the book to see if I could locate more.

I exchanged one box for the other and lugged the canvases down the ladder. I had a feeling Alice painted these, and I wanted them showcased around the house. They were too beautiful to be holed up in the dark. I took the books and placed them on the book shelf and stacked the canvases by the fireplace until I figured out where to put them. I had already put my minimal personal belongings away, so I decided to make a cup of tea, which I had found hidden in one of the ceramic jars on the counter. They had a perfect view of the sunset from their rocking chairs out back. At some point, I would need to go out for dinner since the house was stripped of anything edible.

As I sat in the rocker I imagined Alice sitting here with her own cup of tea, watching the same brilliant colors dance across the sky as the sun made its descent behind the horizon. It was winter, but the weather was always so mild here that you would never be able to tell. There was a calm warm breeze that added to the magic of the moment. I closed my eyes and focused on the sounds of the natural setting.

The orphanage was in a busy part of town, so the sounds most frequently heard were honking horns, people talking, and emergency vehicles. I had never heard the sound of a cricket rubbing its legs together or a frog croaking for attention. Well I had, but not in person. It was amazing to hear the natural music of the world. I could also hear the water trickling over the rocks in the creek that wasn't far away, and the rustling of the leaves on the trees from the swaying of the wind.

If heaven existed, I was in it.

The only thing missing was someone to share it with, but I had faith I wouldn't be alone forever. I was only eighteen and had a new life to look forward to. I smiled to myself. I was content. I had finally found peace.

All the noises of the forest ceased, and the breeze froze. I opened my eyes curiously. The leaves had stopped moving, and the night was stationary as if I had pressed *Pause* on a remote. The only thing moving was me in the rocker.

Eerie chills chased each other across my bare arms. I wasn't sure what I should do. Should I sit still and blend in, or should I rush into the house and lock the door?

As I was leaning forward to go inside, I caught sight of a shadow at the forest line not too far from me. I held my breath and squinted to get a better look. Before I knew it, I was face to face with it. I was scared to move or breathe. The panic started to rise in my throat as I realized I was helpless out here.

We both stood paralyzed. I felt like we were in a staring competition or a game of freeze, only I felt like my life depended on winning. Then, as quickly as the shadow had appeared, it disappeared, and the world came back to life. I looked around frantically and then stumbled quickly into the house and secured the lock. My heart was racing a million miles a minute as I sprinted around the house and made sure all the windows were closed and the doors were locked.

I had no idea what just happened, but I was definitely going to be introducing myself to the neighbors tomorrow. While this place was straight out of a fairy tale, the reality was that I was alone and defenseless. I couldn't be naïve. I needed to start making friends here and quickly.

Chapter Three

Sleeping in a new bed in a foreign place, and after the night's disturbing encounter, was hard to say at the least. I even skipped dinner, which I now regretted as my stomach growled angrily. I was starving.

The phone on the end table rang. It was the first phone call of many that I had to tell the caller the Hadleys had passed away. I sucked in a deep breath and picked it up. "Hadley house," I said awkwardly. I was so used to answering the phone at the orphanage in a similar manner that it was a hard habit to break, but one of many I would work on.

"Hi, is this Ariana?" the female voice asked.

"Yes?" I questioned curiously.

"Hi. My name is Sierra. I live in the next house over. My mom said I should call and introduce myself."

She sounded caring and sincere. "Hi," was all I could respond with. I was a pretty social person, but I wasn't sure what else to say.

"Have you eaten breakfast yet? My mom wanted to invite you over."

"No. I was just thinking about it, though. That would be nice. Thank you."

"We are the first house up the road from you."

"Okay. I will be there in a little bit. I just need to shower."

"Great. See you soon," she said cheerfully as she disconnected.

I hung up and rolled out of bed. My eyes were still heavy from the restless sleep, and my head hurt. I needed coffee and a shower, but since I didn't have coffee yet, I jumped into the shower. It was the nicest shower I had ever been in. The bathroom was miraculous. The tiles were a natural marble stone, and the cabinets were a deep cherry wood. There was an oversized vintage bath tub and a shower large enough for a small family. I gaped at my dumb luck. Too bad it came with the loss of two astounding people.

After my quick shower, I threw my long wet hair up into a tight bun to save time and threw on a pair of jeans and a comfy, nice button down shirt. I wanted to look nice, but still casual. I was nervous and excited to be meeting my neighbors, and it sounded like Sierra was close to my age, so the prospect of making a new friend so close by made me smile. I took a quick look into the mirror and approved of my appearance, so I rushed down the stairs and outside. I looked at the car, but then decided to walk. It was a lovely morning, and I was really starting to feel right at home among the natural beauty of my surroundings. I had always felt slightly out of place in the middle of town, but never really understood why. Now I did. Every part of me felt like it was finally home. I took in a deep breath of the dewy morning and reveled in its purity as I walked the mile up the road.

When I came to their driveway, I hesitated for a moment. Tivon stood halfway up it. I was slightly disappointed that this time he was wearing a shirt. He seemed to float toward me. He had such a graceful walk, and the way his hips moved made my thoughts swirl like a tornado.

"Hi again," he said softly.

His voice was like melted butter trickling down the side of a mouthwatering biscuit. "Hi. Do you live here?" I asked.

He looked up at the house and then back at me. "No. I was just walking. The path crosses here." He tightened his lips into a sexy smile.

The amber in eyes sparkled in the glistening sun. They had me hypnotized. Jenny's eyes were a similar color and one I had not seen again until now.

I blurted out, "Your eyes are beautiful." I bowed my head in my own embarrassment as he laughed soulfully. Everything this man did made me warm inside.

"Why, thank you. Are you visiting the Grants?" he inquired.

"Yes. They invited me over for breakfast. Do you know them?"

"Sort of." He winked.

He was oddly mysterious. "I should go. They are waiting for me." I didn't want to leave. I wanted him to breathe down my neck again. I wanted him to touch me again even if it was just for a second.

"I'll see you later then," he said confidently as he jogged down the path.

"Bye," I whispered and swooned at the way his body moved. I hoped I would see him again soon. I walked up to the Grant house and knocked.

An angelic girl my age with a friendly face, rosy cheeks against milky skin, long wavy blonde hair, and a body blessed with a petite frame answered the door.

"Ariana," she shouted as she hugged me warmly. "It's so nice to finally meet you. Alice and Joe never stopped talking about you."

A gorgeous woman appeared behind her.

"They were never at a loss for words about how much they loved and adored you. Please, come in, Ariana. I'm Sierra's mom, Violet."

I followed Sierra into the house. As I passed by Violet, I said, "It's nice to meet you. Thank you for having me." She reached out with a comforting touch and squeezed my arm.

"I'm sorry for your loss."

She was paying me her condolences. It was strange since I wasn't related to the Hadley's, but I appreciated it since I loved them like they were. "Thank you," I said as I shuffled passed her after Sierra.

Breakfast could only be described as a feast. Violet had made homemade French toast that was absolutely delectable, veggie egg scrambler, and pastries. We also had fresh-squeezed orange juice.

Her husband, Lark, was perfectly handsome and sweet. He made me feel at ease immediately. They were a beautiful family and I was humbled to be welcomed into a small piece of perfection. After breakfast we spent time exchanging memories of Alice and Joe. It was nice to hear that they were just as humble outside of the orphanage. They were truly loved and missed by the Grants.

Sierra and I hit it off right away. She walked me down the driveway to the road and gave me a huge hug.

"I hope you like it here. I'm just glad I have someone's house to escape to now." She giggled.

"Come over anytime," I replied politely. "It's kind of lonely in that house by myself, so the company would be nice."

"It's going to be so much fun, Ariana." She skipped excitedly. "We just moved here last year, so I haven't made many friends, being out of high school and all."

"Are you in college?" I asked.

"Not yet, but I plan on going next semester. Just to the local junior college. What about you?"

"Well, I have the bookstore to run now, so probably not. At least not right away." I had planned on going straight to college out of high school, but I didn't, and now I couldn't. I wasn't really sad about it. I love painting, and those would have been the only classes I would have looked forward to anyway.

"If you need any help at the store, just let me know. I would love to have a part-time job to keep me busy."

"Okay. I will. My friend Jenny is going to help me get things running again, so I'll let you know if I need someone. That would be fun." I was genuinely happy to have a friend now. She was so nice and easy to be around. Our friendship came so naturally. It was like everything out here was meant for me.

"I'll see you later," I said as I started back down the road.

"Bye." She waved.

It was past noon now, and the sun felt good on my skin. It felt like it was feeding my soul with some much needed energy. I admired the wildflowers on my way home. I wasn't in a rush to get home today. I wasn't in a rush to do anything. I felt an unfamiliar giddiness rising in my chest that made me feel like breaking out into song and jumping around like a silly little girl. I felt wonderful. I didn't know why, but I also wasn't going to question it. As I touched the flowers my fingers tingled. I threw off my sandals and let the earth beneath my toes tickle them to life. I had never felt things so intensely before. I laughed as I jumped into a bed of flowers and spun around watching their petals fly with the force of the breeze I was creating. They swirled around me, grazing my skin as they flew up and fell back to the ground. It felt otherworldly.

Before I knew it, I was in my back yard at the meadow where the circle of flowers grew. I knew who I was when I stood in this spot. I felt every part of me buzzing with vitality, and I wasn't alone. I felt his presence before I turned and faced him, breathless. He stepped into the circle and locked eyes with me long enough to make my body twitch with excitement. I had thought about my first kiss many times, but had never imagined it could be this magical, although I hoped it would be.

Without saying a word, his eyes bore deep into my soul, and he reached out and stroked my cheek, burning sparks into my skin like rubbing two sticks together. His fingers tightened gently and pulled my lips close to his. I closed my eyes and enjoyed his sweet hot breath only centimeters from me.

After a moment of hesitation, his lips met mine, shocking them to life for the first time. I pressed back hungrily like a starving beast finding food after hibernation. I wrapped my arms around his neck, securing my hold on him. His hand crept from my cheek to the back of my neck, sending tingles jumping down my spine. He kissed me with the passion of a hundred lives. The world around us faded, and it was just the two of us swirling around in a world of fantasy and fiction trapped in the pages of a dream world.

He laid me on the ground carefully and made love to me underneath the watchful eye of the setting sun. I could have never painted a scene as amazing as this one. He was gentle, sensual, passionate, and above all, careful. With every tender kiss, he cemented his hold on my heart. I barely knew him, but what I did know was I had just fallen in love for the first time.

He laid his head on my stomach as we watched the twinkling stars and the playful lightning bugs. He exposed my stomach and kissed it lightly, a gesture I found oddly comforting. He then placed his hand on my belly and a magnificent light glowed, and a warm tingling feeling manifested. It tickled and made me squirm. The feeling and light were gone as soon as he lifted his hand. I wasn't sure what I had just witnessed nor was I sure of anything that had happened since I came to the Hadley house, but I felt safe here with Tivon, and that's all that mattered.

Chapter Four

Tivon and I spent every moment we could together after that day. He didn't tell me much about his life or family, but instead, he talked about his love for nature. We went on a lot of walks in the forest, and he taught me how to listen to the music of the world. It was beautiful. If you listened closely enough, the world moved in unison, creating an orchestra of perfectly played notes. We were always in some sort of embrace, whether it be as carefree as holding hands or a moment of blistering passion.

He disappeared for days at a time, which finally piqued my curiosity. Although when he came back he always gave me his undivided attention, I was passively curious of his whereabouts. He did everything around the house and yard, and he practically lived here, spending most nights with me. It felt nice not being alone after all. That first lonely night here was a distant memory.

One night as we lay in bed, I mustered up the courage to ask him about his disappearing acts. I snuggled into his side, but my heart was racing. I was nervous to ask him because he never offered it up, so I was afraid that what he was going to tell me would be bad, or at the very least, something I would not like. I had to know though. My tell-all nervous habit of playing with my hair kicked in.

"Is there something wrong, Ari?" Tivon asked.

"What gave it away?" I responded with a question.

"Well, judging by the way you are chewing on your hair, you're either very hungry or nervous, and since we just ate a huge meal, I am going with the latter." He smirked.

"Ugh, you know me too well. Yes, Teve…"

He arched one of his eyebrows curiously.

"Yes, I nicknamed you Teve. Do you not like it?" I asked, piling on my stress.

He laughed. "I love it, Ari. You can call me whatever you want," he said as he kissed my head. "Now tell me what's bothering you so much."

I stayed hidden in his arm. "Where do you go when you leave?" My heart kicked into high gear, as if that was possible. It was already in overdrive.

"Would you mind if I showed you one day, rather than tell you right now? I think it would make more sense."

He was being mysteriously vague, but my intuition told me to trust him. "I would like that," I said as I sat up and kissed him.

The next day he was gone again. He left a sweet note with one of the flowers from the meadow on his vacant pillow. I loved his simple gestures to make me feel special, but it hardly filled the void I felt when he was away.

Over the months, I started to feel weak and sick. I spent a lot of time sleeping. It never occurred to me that I could be pregnant, which was dumb. But when I started showing, I knew. I was excited to tell Teve. He had been gone for longer than normal, and I was getting anxious. I was also starting to feel lonely, something I hadn't felt since I first moved here. I called Sierra to come over. I stared at my growing belly in the mirror and placed my hand where Teve had put his hand the first time we made love. I heard Sierra's knock at the door, so I went down to meet her. At this point, she usually just let herself in, but always knocked first, just in case Teve and I were in a compromising position.

"Hey, girl. Tivon's not back yet?"

"No," I responded sadly. "He's never been gone for this long."

"Don't you know where he lives?" she inquired.

"No. Is that weird?" I went and sat down on the couch.

"A little," she said as she plopped down next to me.

We sat in a comfortable silence for a moment. I played with my hair nervously. I was eighteen, pregnant, and alone. I didn't want to be judged, but Sierra had never given me a reason to think she was anything but supportive.

"I'm pregnant," I whispered with my eyes closed. When the silence lingered, I slowly opened one of my eyes to a squint to see her reaction. I couldn't gauge it. After what seemed like forever, she spoke up.

"I'm not sure what to say, Ari. How do you feel about it?"

How did I feel about it? I was excited that I was procreating with Teve, but I just entered the world of freedom and independent decision-making and was essentially alone. "I don't know. I mean, I love Teve, and he said he wanted to marry me, but he's been gone for so long, and the idea of raising a baby by myself scares me."

"First of all, you aren't alone. You have my parents and me. And don't forget about Jenny. As far as Tivon, you know how much he loves you, and so do I. He would never leave you alone if he didn't have a good reason. He'll be back, Ari."

I smiled at her innocent confidence. Deep down I knew I wasn't alone and never would be. I had formed such a great bond with her family and spent a lot of time with them when Teve was gone. They treated me like one of their own. Plus, Jenny spent a lot of time at the bookstore. She retired from the orphanage shortly after I left. She said it was lonely without me, so she worked with me instead.

Sierra left to go to class shortly after we talked. It was early spring, and classes had started a few weeks ago. It was just barely April, but it felt like late spring, and the flowers were already blooming.

I went outside to our circle in the meadow, rubbing my belly along the way. I missed Teve so much. We nicknamed our spot the butterfly circle because an unusual amount of butterflies frequented it. It was serene and captivating to watch hundreds of butterflies of varying colors and sizes interacting with each other.

The sun was mildly warm as I lay down in the circle with my eyes closed, imagining the first time Teve and I were together. I never asked him about the glow radiating from his hand as he touched my belly, but now I believed it had something to do with the little gift growing inside me. I was starting to feel sleepy. A nap out here was tempting as I started to drift off, but then a hot feeling on my stomach alarmed me. I shot my eyes open and froze at the sight of a dark shadow standing over me. My belly was glowing brightly as a hand hovered just above it. I screamed out when a sharp pain traveled through the light inside of me. I was paralyzed and could only whimper from the inflicting torture. *Please don't hurt my baby.* I closed my eyes as tears rolled down my cheeks while I imagined the worst for my baby and me.

Then, the feeling was suddenly gone, so I opened my eyes to see two shadows in some sort of battle. It was hard to tell what was happening with the sun blinding me and the figures being shadows, but it looked like something was trying to help me.

I wasn't paralyzed anymore, so I jumped up and ran for the house.

Something tripped me, and I fell to the ground hard, hitting my cheek on the grass and momentarily blurring my vision. The two shadows were still rolling around by the butterfly circle. *Who tripped me?* I was terrified when I saw a half dozen or more shadows approaching me. I scurried to my feet as fast as humanly possible and continued charging for the house. I looked back briefly to see them take chase after me. When I reached the house, I slammed into the door and threw it open, launching myself in and kicking it closed as they reached me. I jumped up and locked it and backed up, hoping the door would keep them out. I held my breath in fear until I was satisfied that they couldn't enter.

I allowed myself a moment of contemplation as I bent over my knees, panting and hacking from the sudden burst of exercise. When I looked up, it was as if nothing had happened. The shadows were gone, and the sun was still shining brightly. Hesitantly, I approached the glass door to scan the yard closer.

They were gone, but *who* were they? More importantly, *what* were they? I frantically pulled up my shirt and grabbed my belly as I searched for any physical damage. Everything seemed fine, but I had no idea what things were like internally. I was terrified at the prospect that my baby could be hurt. I needed Teve.

****

As the months progressed, my belly continued to grow, which was the reassurance I needed that our baby was okay. Teve was still missing, so I kept myself busy at the bookstore with Jenny and at the Grants. I had spent a lot of time trying to track down that faery book without success, but I was able to find a printing company that was willing to reproduce it. I only had a dozen printed, because I didn't want to over-produce it. It was a special book, and the few that had the pleasure of taking it home would never know how valuable it really was.

I decided on a home birth with the encouragement of Jenny. She knew a midwife who could safely deliver the baby. The idea of being in the comfort of my own home was all I needed to be convinced. I had no reason to think anything would go wrong.

Jenny and I were stocking books from the latest shipment. The store was thriving, so we had been ordering more.

I squealed as I opened a box and saw the faery books on top. Jenny ran over.

"Ari, are you okay?" she asked frantically.

I grabbed one of the books and excitedly waved it in front of her. "Look what just came? I need to label these as limited edition and put them in the window."

"It's beautiful," she commented as she took the book. "But the next time you make that sound, it better be because you're in labor. You about gave me a heart attack."

I started laughing. She was more uptight as the days came closer to my due date than I was. I felt fabulous my whole pregnancy and was confident the birth would be perfect. Jenny marveled that I didn't have any of the negative side effects that pregnant woman complain about. I never felt tired or nauseous. In fact, I almost had too much energy. I was truly fortunate. I was having the perfect pregnancy and was looking forward to a perfect life with my perfect little baby. Sadly, Teve would miss all of it, but I knew he was out there somewhere thinking about us. I could feel it.

I put one of the faery books in the window with a limited edition sign. I was excited to share such a beautiful piece of art with some of the diehard readers out there. A few faces popped in my head that made me smile until an uncomfortable cramp captured my attention.

"Ow," I said to myself. As quiet as I was, Jenny still came running.

"What's wrong?"

I had to laugh through the pain. She treated me like her own and I loved it. "It's just a cramp. I'm fine."

"What kind of cramp? Like I have to go to the bathroom type cramp or I am having a baby type cramp?" she spat out quickly.

"Um, I don't know. I guess it could be a contraction. It's only a few days from my due date, so it's a good possibility, right?"

"Let's keep track of them and then we can decide if you're in labor. Just take it easy."

"Okay." I wasn't nervous about the delivery until now. The contraction brought reality forth, and I had to admit, I was a little afraid.

A few minutes later, I had another contraction and then again a few minutes after that. Jenny decided it was a good idea to call the midwife and close up and go back to the house, so we did. On the drive home the contractions were getting closer together rapidly. "Is this normal?" I asked Jenny.

"Nothing is normal when it comes to child birth. Every birth is unique. It just looks like you'll be having a quick labor." She smiled reassuringly.

I laid my head back on the headrest and relaxed for the rest of the short drive home. Well, relaxed in between contractions. They were getting stronger, too. When we got to the house, I could barely walk. Jenny helped me wobble into the TV room where we had a makeshift bedroom, so I wouldn't have to climb the stairs when it was time. We also had a little bassinet.

I crawled onto the floor mattress, rolled on my side and closed my eyes, trying to imagine what I was having. It didn't matter either way. I just wanted it to be healthy. The contractions were painful and coming only a minute apart now. I tried to breathe through them like Jenny taught me, but I didn't expect this kind of pain. It hurt like hell, and at times, I thought I was going to pass out.

The midwife arrived quickly, followed by Sierra and her parents. They politely waited in the living room on the other side of the house to give me privacy. Sierra stayed by my side, taking the place of Tivon. God, how I missed him.

"You're doing great, Ari," Sierra whispered as she held a damp cloth on my forehead.

"I miss Tivon," I whined softly.

"I know."

The midwife and Jenny were positioned and ready for my baby to be born.

"It's time to push," said the midwife, Penny. She was a happy little old lady, much older than Jenny, and shared the same eye color. It was such a rare color, yet three people I knew had it. That amber was so rich and intense I was a little jealous I didn't share it.

While the pushing was minimal, it was far from painless, but thankfully quick. When I heard the cry, I was overcome with the joy I hear every new mother talk about it. It was hard to put into words.

"It's a girl," Jenny said joyfully as she wrapped her in a blanket and handed her to me.

She was beautiful. She had my blue eyes and Tivon's olive skin. I never thought I could be in love again after Teve disappeared, but I was wrong. This was a deep, unconditional love that penetrated further than the surface of my heart. It reached down into my soul. I kissed her forehead softly and whispered, "I love you, my little Arie."

Sierra's eyes bugged out. "You named her Arie? Aw, I love that."

"I think Tivon would like our daughter to have my name, but I think I'll just call her Arie." I couldn't take my eyes off of her. She was so quiet and observant already as she watched me talk. Penny cleaned up and left Jenny with a set of instructions should anything come up. Violet and Lark joined us a little while later and played a round of pass the baby. Arie was new to this world, but managed to bring a renewed joy to everyone's hearts, something I believed she would continue to do for the rest of her life.

Epilogue

Arie's birthday was not only special because it was hers, but because she was born on the Autumnal Equinox of the northern hemisphere where night and day are equal. It only happens twice a year. For us it was September 23rd this year, and in the southern hemisphere, it would occur around the same time in March. Arie was unique in every way possible.

It had been a few weeks since her birth and we had moved back upstairs. I had her bassinet set up right next to my bed. She was an amazing baby. She rarely cried and always seemed to be happy. Every time I looked at her I thought of Tivon, and tonight was no exception. Before I climbed into bed, I watched her sleep for a few minutes. I couldn't get enough of her pulsating lips as if she was sucking on her pacifier. I stealthily kissed her cheek and deftly crawled into bed and drifted to sleep.

I walked through the meadow to the butterfly circle where hundreds of fireflies were twisting around a figure under the shade of the night sky. I couldn't see the figure clearly, but I knew it was him. I could feel him. How I had missed his touch, his warmth, his beauty. I wanted to tell him we had a baby girl. I wanted him to smell her sweet scent and see how much she looked like him. More importantly, I wanted her to know him. He reached his hand through the veil of the fireflies. I came closer and touched my hand to his. The energy flowing through us brought me to tears. I couldn't hear him, but I knew he still loved me by the tingles he sent shooting through me.

He slipped a ring onto my finger as he started to fade. I didn't want him to go. My heart was breaking all over again. Suddenly, the fireflies twisted manically around him, and he was lost in their whirlwind. They floated into the sky and disappeared in the light of the full moon taking him with them. I fell to the ground and pounded it as tears filled my world. Once I gained control, I focused on the ring he had placed on my wedding finger. We were supposed to get married just before he disappeared. It was beautiful. It was a snow white oval-shaped opal encircled by diamonds. The opal was glowing softly, or was it the moon's reflection? It was hard to tell. I was too weak to walk back to the house, so I spread out on the grass and let the moon absorb my sorrow and the wind dry my tears. At some point, the twinkling stars lulled me to sleep.

I woke up on the grass filled with sheer panic. The sun was just beginning to ascend over the horizon. I ran up to the house and darted up the stairs. Arie was still sleeping soundly. My racing heart began to slow down as relief washed over me that she was safe. I tried to wrap my mind around what I had experienced. I went to sleep in bed, had what I thought was a dream, but then woke up on the grass where I fell asleep in my dream. Was I sleepwalking, or did that really happen? Then I remembered the ring and found it adorning my finger. I rubbed it just to make sure it was real. I fell back on the bed. *It was real.* I was blissfully in shock. Tivon was trying to communicate with me.

Little did I know when I met him that I would enter a world outside of reality where dreams were real and love superseded invisible barriers between them. I no longer felt alone. I felt him with us in everything we did and everywhere we went, but especially in the butterfly circle where I brought Arie every day, telling her stories about her daddy and her amazing new life.

Arie's story begins...
Reality: The Life of Arie **Series, Book 1**
Available Now

About the Author

DANI HART graduated from the University of Southern California with a degree in Theatre and a concentration in screenwriting and resides in Southern California with her family. To learn about her other projects visit her website www.danihartbooks.com.

Acknowledgement

A special thank you to Glorya Hidalgo for inviting me to be a part of this amazing cause. I am honored that a little piece of my heart is alongside so many talented authors.

Final Stage

Jade C. Jamison

Copyright © 2014 Jade C. Jamison
All rights reserved.

Ruth Manning had always tried to live her life by following all the rules. She had been, for the most part, a dutiful wife, mother, daughter, and employee. Save for a few minor slip-ups along the way, she had succeeded, which is why her boss found her behavior so unorthodox that Friday afternoon in October.

Ruth tapped on the big wooden door just enough to get Mr. Potter's attention. She heard his baritone voice answer, "Come in," and she turned the doorknob, entering one slow step at a time.

Mr. Potter was working on some papers at his desk. His hand, still holding the pen, rested on the side of his head where his hair was starting to thin and his scalp had started peeking through. Ruth cleared her throat, being as quiet as she could. Mr. Potter raised his eyebrows, impatiently urging Ruth to speak.

"Mr. Potter, I'd like to take next week off."

His eyebrows slowly furrowed. "Ruth, you know company policy states that you must give me one week's notice before requesting more than a day off."

"I'm aware of that, sir. But I really need to take some time … for myself."

Mr. Potter looked down at his report. In the twenty years he had known Ruth, she had never made outrageous requests for time off. He took a deep breath and asked, "Is there something going on that you'd like to talk about?" He suspected that maybe she was getting a divorce or visiting her daughter out of state who desperately needed her mother.

She pursed her lips. She knew she should give him a reason, but she wasn't ready to talk about it. "I just need some time, sir."

Mr. Potter knew Ruth had more than two weeks of vacation time saved up. He sighed. "All right. Take the week."

"Thank you," she said, handing him the piece of paper recording her request for leave.

Mr. Potter signed the appropriate place on the form and handed it back to Ruth. "Just be sure to give me more notice next time, and don't tell anyone else about this. If it gets out that you receive special favors, then everyone else will expect them."

She nodded. "Thank you, Mr. Potter." She knew there would be no next time. She left work at the end of the day, still looking sharp in her professional suit, a slate gray jacket and skirt that she wore with a white blouse and sensible low-heeled shoes. Today felt like a normal day, but it was not. Ruth felt grateful that Mr. Potter hadn't remembered she had been gone yesterday afternoon for a doctor's appointment or he might have asked more questions that she wasn't ready to answer.

At home that weekend, she pretended everything was normal. It wasn't difficult because Jim was absorbed in football — both pro and college — constantly flipping channels from one game to the next, occasionally getting up to grab a sandwich, a soda, or go to the bathroom. She spent most of her time in the sunroom, tending to her plants and trying not to remember.

"Ruth, you have Inflammatory Breast Cancer."

The words she tried to ignore echoed in her ears. Other words like "metastasized" and "stage four" kept the rhythm going, and finally she went for a long walk, hoping to clear her head. The walk around the neighborhood didn't help though, and when she walked in the front door she simply stared at herself in the mirror near the front door in the entryway. She *looked* healthy. Her blue eyes were still clear and bright; her skin, though it had more lines every year, still looked vibrant and smooth with only a few spots that were easily hidden under her pale foundation; her hair, though gray and wiry, still appeared bright and shiny. Her mouth drew down into a frown, her nose red from the cool air of the walk.

She turned away from the mirror, unable to look at herself anymore. She couldn't believe the doctor knew what he was talking about. Surely he had confused her results with someone else's and his office would call next week, his nurse laughing sheepishly that they had made such a stupid mistake.

****

On Monday morning she got out of bed and got ready, even though she wasn't going to work. She hadn't told Jim that she'd taken the week off. She didn't want to tell him what the doctor had said. She wasn't ready yet.

Their morning routine went just like any other morning. She arose before he did and took her shower. By the time he got up, she was already in the kitchen. He said, "Good morning," and poured a cup of coffee, then sat at the table, glancing through the newspaper. She sat next to him, jotting down her regular "to do" list, but her "to dos" today were just for show. She didn't really intend to buy milk on the way home or return the shoes she'd bought two weeks ago that didn't fit properly. "Hmm," he muttered. "Looks like City Council finally authorized the downtown road repair. You might have to take a different route to work starting next month."

"Oh," she nodded, knowing that he would need no more response than that. She finished her coffee and rinsed the cup, placing it in the dishwasher as Jim folded his paper and left it beside his cup on the table.

He rose and kissed her on the cheek. "See you tonight," he said and walked out the door.

She took his cup and plate from the table, rinsed and put them in the dishwasher, and sighed. She turned off the light, grabbed her purse, and walked out the door, locking it as she left. She watched Jim's black sedan drive down the street as she got into her blue one and backed out of the driveway.

She started driving her regular route to work, realizing that it would be pretty stupid to eat up a week of vacation; she'd been saving up her time, hoping to talk Jim into taking a Caribbean cruise next summer. She'd always wanted to be on a big ship in the ocean — she loved the smell of the salty air, the warm breeze, the sun shining brightly without a shadow to cast down on her. She imagined a week spent doing nothing — traveling to various ports, maybe catching a show, swimming in the afternoon, gambling a little, eating well. Now, though, she might never have the chance.

It *was* stupid — she had the maximum amount of sick leave she could accrue — one hundred and fifty days and not an hour more. But taking sick leave would mean she was *sick*, and she refused to believe she was.

Instead of turning off the highway and heading toward the drab brick county building as she would have any other workday, she kept driving north, finally taking a turnoff five exits down the road.

"Call me on Monday so we can schedule your chemotherapy and set a

potential date for your surgery."

Surgery? She'd never had surgery before — not for gall bladder problems (like her mother had), not for appendix problems (like her daughter Mary Anne), not for hernia problems (like Jim); not for a hysterectomy (like her sister); she'd never even had a c-section when her children were born. But this surgery was just the beginning.

"Ruth, what you have is rare. It's treatable, but we're looking at surgery, chemotherapy, and *radiation. You're still young enough and healthy enough to withstand with rigors of..."*

Chemotherapy and radiation would mean it was *real*. She wasn't ready for it to be real.

She'd never gone to the mall during the week, so she wasn't sure what time the doors opened. She sat in her car waiting, leaving the engine running with the heater on. The warmth on her toes helped her relax some, but she gripped the wheel, her face turning down in a grimace. "How can I be dying when it feels like I haven't even lived?" She shook her head and rested it on the steering wheel.

****

She and Jim lay quietly in bed. His larger hand was holding her smaller, seemingly fragile one, and her soft brown hair spread out over his firm chest, her head resting in the crook of his arm. His voice was soft and gentle.

"Where should we live when we get married?" he asked.

She interlaced her fingers through his and batted her eyelashes, trying to stay awake. "I thought we would live here, didn't you?"

"I don't know. There aren't many job opportunities here. Not much chance of being a stable breadwinner for our family."

She sighed, stirring under the warm covers but reluctant to sit up. "Where do you want to live?"

He cleared his throat, and she heard a seriousness in his voice that she hadn't heard before. "I was thinking of enlisting in the army."

Her eyes widened and she sat up, holding the sheet to her chest. "The army? Do you want to get yourself killed?"

"People are talking draft, Ruth. Would you rather I enlist freely or be drafted and sent to Vietnam?"

She swung her legs over the edge of the bed, not wanting to look at him. She loved him so much; she didn't want to think that he could fly overseas and die. She felt his warm hands on her shoulders, and she looked over and met his brown eyes. "I don't want you to get killed."

His full lips turned slightly up, almost into a smile. "I'm not going to have a choice. And I've done my research. The army will help me care for you and our family."

She knew she couldn't argue. She loved Jim and would marry him, follow him anywhere he took her.

She bent over and picked up her dress off the floor. Her parents would be expecting her soon. She hurriedly dressed and let him kiss her sweetly before wrapping up tightly in her wool coat. "Let me drive you home."

"Jim, you'd better not. Then they'd know."

"They're going to find out soon enough." He grinned, his brown eyes flashing. "Or would you rather elope?"

She playfully slapped his arm. "I guess I'd better talk to them." She slipped her feet in her shoes. "You can drop me off a block away from home, okay?"

But she hadn't noticed until they got outside that the snow had started coming down heavily; her breath flew out of her mouth like smoke, and she realized the temperature had dropped at least ten degrees since she'd come over. The snow quickly accumulated on her shoulders as she waited for Jim to unlock the car door. She stepped in, shuddering the whole mile to her house. Jim had turned the heater on, but it was blowing cold air on her feet.

Jim didn't stop a block away but pulled right in front of her two-story white house. All the lights were on. She knew that meant that everyone else was home from various activities and ready to sit down to dinner. Jim leaned over toward her in the seat. "You sure you don't want me to come in? No better time than the present to ask your parents..."

Ruth sighed. He was right. She'd put it off long enough. She was a senior in high school and would turn eighteen right before graduating; she would soon be an adult. Her parents knew she and Jim went out to the movies every weekend. They just didn't know she spent a couple of hours with him every afternoon. "How about on Saturday? They'll be expecting you then."

He nodded and smiled. "Okay."

She kissed him one last time before rushing up the sidewalk, sliding, almost skating, so that she wouldn't slip and fall. She heard his car slowly pull back onto the street as she walked in the front door. She hurried to the dining room where her parents, sister, and three brothers sat already eating. Her mother stood. "Ruth, I'm glad you're here. Why don't you help me with dessert?"

Ruth, flushed and barely warming up, met downcast eyes from the family except from her father, whose eyes seemed cold but communicated nothing. Her mother clipped to the kitchen, and Ruth hustled around the table to catch up. Her mother got some strawberries and whipped topping out of the refrigerator; Ruth grabbed dessert plates out of the cabinet. She said nothing.

Her mother placed shortcakes on each plate before finally saying, "Ruth, have you been over at Jimmy Manning's house every day after school this whole year?"

Ruth's pupils widened. "Um, yes."

Her mother cleared her throat, grabbing several spoons from the silverware drawer. "And what exactly have you been doing for two or three hours every afternoon after school?"

Ruth drew in a deep breath. She paused, then finally said, "Talking."

Her mother began spooning the dripping strawberries carefully onto each cake. "Talking. About what?"

Ruth felt the muscles in her shoulders tense. "Marriage."

Her mother gently laid the spoon back in the strawberry mixture. She looked at Ruth and inhaled deeply. "Ruth, you haven't finished school yet. What makes you think you're ready for marriage?"

"I love him, mom."

Her mother picked up the spoon again. "How can you be so sure?"

"I just know."

Her mother finished putting the strawberries on the cakes and reached for the whipped topping. Ruth saw her jaw clench. She didn't look at Ruth as she dropped a large dollop of topping over each cake oozing with strawberries. She said, "I certainly hope the two of you have not fornicated. You know what the Good Book says about that." Ruth remained silent. "A sin is a sin, Ruth." Her mother set the spoon down and began placing the lids back on the strawberries and topping. "I suppose if you have, then you'd better marry that boy. Better than burning in a lake of fire."

Ruth could barely sleep that night, but she knew she'd made the right decision about marrying Jim. She would wear white, and no one would know any better…

****

The foot traffic in the mall was light and quiet. Only a few shoppers roamed around, and Ruth walked quietly, listening to the soft clicks of women in heels and jazzy music lilting in the echoing cavern of the mall. She smelled the faint sweet odor of caramel popcorn and thought of finding the shop peddling it, but she didn't look very hard. She wandered in and out of clothing stores, halfheartedly pushing blouses aside but buying nothing. Finally, she sat on a large carved wooden bench in the middle of the walkway, surrounded by rubber plants. She looked up at the bright skylight above her as her thoughts drifted back, a tear slowly falling down her cheek.

She remembered raising babies as an army wife while she and Jim slowly drifted apart. Jim had told her he loved her, but he didn't seem to *like* her very much. He spent a lot of time away, and when Jimmy Jr. and Mary Anne went to high school, Ruth found herself wondering what to do. She'd never gone to college, never pursued a career. She felt fairly useless. Her children no longer needed her help with homework or rides to school; they rarely sought her advice anymore. Her house could only get so clean. She felt trapped by her home. Should she go to school? Should she find a job? Should she leave and begin life over? She shook her head; even though her family had little use for her, she felt obliged to stay. Her parents would not approve, and how could she live with herself if her children felt abandoned? She needed *something*, though, and spent several weeks at the library and Job Service, putting together the first resume of her life.

Eventually, she obtained an entry-level position with the county clerk. The job was simple enough; other workers filled out forms, and she typed them into the computer. She'd never seen a computer before, and she loved watching the blinking yellow box respond to her fingers hitting the keys, filling the black screen with the words she typed. The blanks on the forms corresponded to the blanks in the computer, so the job was easy for her. She also answered the phones and helped customers on occasion, but her main duty was typing.

She loved the job at first. She felt fulfilled by having a place to go during the day and earning extra money that she could spend on whatever she felt like. But most evenings at home she still felt alone — the kids were participating in school activities, and if Jim was home, he was parked in front of the television. She redecorated the house with her money, but even that didn't take much time or energy. She went to church every Sunday but felt like she was just putting in time. She soon found herself in another unfulfilling rut.

Around that time, Pete Johnson started working in the office. Pete was about eight years her junior. Ruth had taken on further job duties and received a promotion, and Mr. Potter hired Pete to take over her old job. Ruth was in charge of training Pete. He had light brown hair and green eyes, with a smile that lit up his entire face. He had a sarcastic sense of humor and managed to make Ruth laugh easily.

Because Ruth and Pete still managed the data-entry part of the job, they spent more time with each other than with any other employees in the office. They began going to lunch every day, enjoying each other's company. One Tuesday afternoon, Pete said, "Hey, Ruthie, there's a new French restaurant a few blocks away I've been wanting to check out. How's that sound for lunch?"

They'd usually gone to fast-food places or delis, somewhere they knew they'd be fed in an hour or less, but lunch at a real restaurant sounded pleasant. "Why not?"

Ruth had never had French food, so she wasn't sure what to order. Pete recommended the Coq au Vin, and they sat sipping iced tea while waiting for their order. "So, Ruth, tell me more about you. I mean … I've heard all about the kids and your husband, but tell me about *you*."

She blushed. "Like what?"

"What are your dreams? What do you *really* want to do with your life?" Ruth felt as though Pete had been looking in her head. She didn't know what she wanted to do; she only knew she didn't feel fully satisfied. Unlike her husband, Pete seemed to care about Ruth on the inside, what she wanted for herself, rather than what he wanted from her.

"I don't really know. I almost feel like I'm starting fresh." She took a sip of her tea. Before a frown formed on her brow, she asked, "What about you?"

He grinned. "I told you I was saving up for law school, and I'm definitely going to do it. I think in about a year, I should have enough."

"Why don't you take out student loans?"

"Are you kidding? I just finished paying off the ones from my Bachelor's degree. I don't want to do that again."

"But wouldn't you make enough money as a lawyer to pay them off quickly?"

He smiled again, his dimples carving large arcs in his cheeks. "I guess so. But then I wouldn't be sitting here talking with you."

She blushed again. If she didn't know better, Pete was *hitting* on her. But she must be imagining it; She was too old for him. And she was married. He was young and good-looking and could find any woman he wanted. She sipped more tea and finally allowed her eyes to meet his again. They were open and honest. She *was* imagining it. Still, her right finger gently pulled back a lock of her brown hair as she wondered if her new moisturizer was really hiding the fine lines she'd started noticing around her eyes. She smiled and Pete smiled back. His eyes drifted to her lips and back to her eyes. She wasn't imagining it. She forced herself to swallow. "I guess you're right."

His smile faded. "What are you doing after work?"

She felt her smile fade too as goosebumps formed all over her body. "I was planning to go shopping." She inhaled deeply. "Why?"

"Because I think I'd like to spend more time with you."

That afternoon at work, she felt young and desirable. Pete never said what he had in mind, but her imagination ran wild. She felt guilty, having done nothing, but she decided she would do whatever he suggested. Thoughts of eternal fire slowly dissolved in her mind as she thought instead of the fire that burned within her, wishing it to be quenched by Pete's lips. Jim had had plenty of affairs during their marriage — this much she knew. So one little indiscretion she could justify in her mind.

Pete came by her desk about an hour before it was time to leave work. He asked, "Do you trust me?"

"Yes."

After work, he drove her to a hotel just a few blocks from work and made her feel like she was twenty again. She could feel what he must have seen.

They continued seeing each other this way for about three months. After the first week, they started going to Pete's apartment. He had a roommate who was never there in the afternoon, and they had the place to themselves. One afternoon as she lay in his arms, she thought seriously about leaving Jim. Jimmy, Jr. was a senior in high school, Mary Anne had left for college, and she and Jim hardly ever spoke anymore. She knew she'd be able to carve out a happy niche with Pete. He made her feel happy and alive. She sat on her elbow, ready to tell him what she was thinking.

Before she could speak, though, he lifted his hand and pushed her hair to the side. "I want to tell you something," he said. She took a deep breath, not liking the sound of his voice. "I was accepted into law school. I'll be leaving next month."

Her heart felt as though he had taken it into his hand and crushed it.

"Oh." But maybe… "Where is it?"

"It's in New York."

Ruth looked down at his sparsely hairy chest. "Would you want some company?"

Pete smiled. "My nose will be buried in books." He saw something in her eyes, and his smiled faded. "Ruthie, you can't leave your family. You and I both know that."

She didn't know that, but she knew she was being rejected. "I guess I can't." She slowly slid out of bed and quietly got dressed.

"We've had fun, haven't we?"

She nodded, not wanting him to know that tears were streaming down her face. She took a deep breath and whispered, "Yes." But now she was wondering why she had done it in the first place. The thought of going back to Jim's cold bed made her shudder.

****

Later, she sat on a picnic bench, eating a chocolate ice cream cone and watching the crisp brown leaves drift past her feet, hearing an occasional one scrape across the sidewalk as though it was reluctant to leave the park. The sun still shone high over the treetops; it was cool outside but pleasant enough that her sweater kept her warm. She barely tasted or even felt the creamy glide of the ice cream as it slid down her throat. After a while, she grew irritated with the breeze. The leaves started blowing into her lap, her hair. She threw the bottom part of the soggy cone into the trash and felt warm tears streaming down her face.

"Ruth, I don't want you to give up hope. This cancer does have a high mortality rate, but you have a chance. You'll have to undergo chemotherapy first. We have to kill the cancer before we go in surgically…"

She reached into her purse and found the picture of her grandson, a fine young man who would be going to high school himself in about a year. Time had simply refused to stop, and she looked at the picture of him when he was three years old, the one she'd had in her wallet for more than a decade. The colors had faded slightly, but nothing could remove the feeling she got every time she looked at Charlie's picture. He had a bit of the devil in his eyes just like his daddy, Jim, Jr. But Charlie touched a spot in Ruth's heart that her children never did. Her own children, though she'd loved them and through no fault of their own, made her feel anxious and inadequate. Charlie made Ruth feel loved simply because of who she was, made her feel appreciated. She saw in his eyes the unconditional love of a child she'd expected but been unable to find as a young mother. She felt relaxed and happy with Charlie. Charlie, though young, seemed to understand her more than anyone else on the planet.

****

"Grandma, how come your cookies taste so good?"

Ruth looked down at little Charlie. She sat in the chair and stroked his cheek. "Didn't you know it's because I made them with all the love in the world?"

Charlie grinned. "But mom makes cookies with love, too."

She smiled back. "Yes, but grandma's love is always extra special." She couldn't explain it to him but knew she didn't need to when he wrapped his small stick-like arms around her waist. She hugged him tightly, breathing in the smell of his hair. She kissed him on the forehead. "Do you want another?"

He nodded. "And then let's go watch cartoons."

She stood up, reaching for another cookie. "It's a deal."

****

She walked to the car and reached for a tissue, rubbing it under her eyes. She realized that Charlie wasn't the only person who had ever loved her completely in her life. Ruth was simply at a point in her life, when Charlie had come along, where she could accept that sort of love, could recognize that it was love. She'd felt, as a mother, that her children's love was based on a fulfillment of needs like food and shelter. She hadn't realized that children are so dependent upon their nurturer that they tell their mother they love her when she's giving them a baloney sandwich or tucking them in bed at night. It's not that they loved her because of those acts, but because those acts had defined her as that person not only in the children's minds, but in her own as well. Looking back, Ruth realized that Charlie was merely her realization of letting go, of finally accepting herself, good and bad.

And maybe she needed to forgive Jim, too. He had spent the last several decades trying to be a good husband, to earn a solid living, to give her what she needed. He'd just forgotten that she needed him most. And maybe she needed to tell him rather than feel alone. He would be home from work soon. She would tell him now — first, that she loved him, that she needed him; second, that she needed him especially now.

She turned the key in the ignition and slowly eased the car into the dimly lit street back toward the freeway. She was going to call the family together for a large dinner this weekend. She had a lot to share with them. But first she wanted to hug her husband and mend what she could — then she'd do the same with her children.

She pulled in and parked next to Jim's car in the driveway. She felt her heart swell as she stepped out and walked toward the front door. The doctor had said she might die, but for the first time in a long time, Ruth Manning believed that she might really live.

More About the Author

FB: www.facebook.com/JadeCJamison
Twitter: @JadeCJamison
website: www.jadecjamison.com
Goodreads:https://www.goodreads.com/author/show/4876604.Jade_C_Jamison?from_search=true
Amazon: http://www.amazon.com/Jade-C.-Jamison/e/B004XO696S/ref=ntt_athr_dp_pel_1

Choices

Sloan Johnson

Copyright © 2014 Sloan Johnson
All rights reserved.

Chapter One

We turned off the highway into an industrial area. If I wasn't sitting directly behind the girl I've grown to love like a sister since our freshman year of college, my heart would be racing in panic. I'm wearing a short, bright red dress that accentuates both my long legs and ample cleavage. We're heading to a party Stacey begged me to go to, and driving deeper into what might have, at some point decades ago, been a thriving hub of commerce. I can't help but notice the number of factories with broken or boarded windows as she guides her bright blue Ford down the dark streets.

"Are you sure your GPS is right?" I ask, leaning between the front seats. "This doesn't look right at all."

"Yes, Mel. It's not my first time coming down here," she assures me. "You used to be laid back, what happened to you?"

My current emotional state has nothing to do with whether or not I'm uptight, and everything to do with the fact that I'm not a fan of putting myself at risk. I've worked too hard for everything in my life to allow one careless move to derail my life.

Tyler reaches between the seats, giving my knee a reassuring squeeze. "I'm fine," I mouth to him when he turns to look at me. And I am. Mostly.

"Nothing *happened* to me. Do you seriously not think there's something sketchy about this setting?" As I ask the question, Stacey turns into a parking lot. The car fills with damp, hot air the moment she rolls down her window to speak to the parking attendant.

"This lot's full," he says flatly. "Go down one driveway and they'll show you where to park."

The latest development heightens my anxiety. Now, we're being told we'll have to walk back to the party. Having Tyler with us does nothing to make me feel safer. When you get right down to it, he's the least likely of the three of us to be able to hold his own should anything happen. He is every stereotype of the gay best friend personified.

To my surprise, there are three attendants working at the property adjacent to where the party is being held: one at the street, one directing people where to park, and a third escorting party-goers down the path between the buildings.

****

"I'm gonna tap that ass," a stout black man states as he brushes his body against mine, his meaty hand reaching for the curve of my hip. I feint to the left to keep him from touching me.

I resist the urge to rip his nasty hand off at the wrist. Men making lewd comments about my body is nothing new, it's what I deal with every night at work, but never has someone offended me as much as this guy with his approach.

"You think so, but I can assure you, you're wrong," I say politely, giving him an insincere smile as I size him up the same way he's doing to me. The difference is, I have no desire to even think about what he looks like without his clothes, but I'm reasonably certain he's already picturing round two of what he would like to do to me. "You see, if you want to tap *anything*, you'd be well served to learn that women prefer a man who doesn't treat her like a walking vagina the moment he is in her presence. Maybe come up with a genuine compliment. One that *doesn't* have to do with tapping, fucking, screwing, or anything of that nature."

Stacey's eyes are wide as she watches me put this creep in his place, not bothering to intervene. Once she has paid our cover charge, she pulls me away from the glass counter. "Damn, Mel! I'm not sure whether to be proud of you for the way you stood up to him or scared for what the rest of the night is going to hold for you."

With words like spa and ballroom used to describe the party venue, I was expecting something completely the opposite of where we are. The walls are lined with videos available for rent, and I'm not talking about the latest Hollywood blockbusters. In the center aisle, four metal shelves displayed the most pathetic assortment of toys I've seen in my life. Stacey's going to owe me big time for this bait and switch.

Perhaps my expectations are skewed thanks to my time spent at *Artemis,* but this is nothing like what I had expected. The atmosphere is almost clinical with white walls and worn linoleum floors.

When we round one corner, we're greeted by walls lined with booths for viewing porn in relative privacy, compared to the theater setting of the room I only caught a glimpse of when we first arrived. Although I know what the holes drilled in the divider walls are meant for, I try to push the mental images from my mind. The thought of random sex acts performed for those to see through a hole in the wall churns my stomach.

Through the next door, we're led to the "spa" area. What has been hyped to sound like a grand palace of debauchery made of marble is closer to a high school locker room, with the constant clanking of metal doors closing as people make their way to the communal shower lined with mildewed ceramic tiles.

With every step, I'm wishing I was back on the plush leather sofa in Xavier's basement. I'd be alone, which is what I had been hoping to escape by coming out, but I wouldn't feel out of place the way I do here.

"You look fine." Stacey giggles when she sees me yanking on the hem of my dress. I *know* I look fine, but right about now, I feel overdressed. The flyer might have advertised this as a semi-formal affair, but it appears that most of the attendees missed that little detail. The women are strutting around the room in outfits ranging from tight jeans and ill-fitting, bedazzled t-shirts all the way down to nearly nothing. As for the men, well it appears a couple of them made an effort to look good tonight, but most of them look like they had been heading for a night at the sports bar and made a quick detour.

The night goes further downhill as we enter the "ballroom." The round banquet tables are chipped and bare, each adorned with a cheap arrangement of fake flowers and confetti. In one corner, there are two stripper poles on an elevated stage, currently occupied by women who have no business dancing the way they are. And the music...I feel like I've stepped into a high school dance from 1992.

When I turn to ask Stacey a question, I notice three rooms along another wall, with men crowding the open door to see what's going on inside the room at the end. They begin adjusting themselves as a woman screams in pleasure, ending my curiosity as to what's going on in there.

After an hour of cheap porn on the big screen, desperate women flaunting what they think they have, and tacky come-ons, I decide it's time for things to change. "Give me your keys," I demand, holding my hand out to Stacey. There's a liquor store down the street and if I'm going to be subjected to this crap for another four hours, I have no intention of doing so sober.

"You're not leaving," Stacey protests. She's sitting on the lap of an attractive man. Under different circumstances, I would be slightly jealous of her because he is one of the few men here worth a second glance.

"I'm not leaving, but I am going to get something to drink. You didn't tell me I was getting dressed up to sit in a room that makes my grandparents' anniversary party seem like a wild time."

"I'll go with you," Tyler says, springing out of his chair. I feel bad for the boy. It's obvious to me that he's been lured here under false pretenses as well.

The bad thing about needing a booze run is that we have to wade through the sea of horny, middle aged men of every race and size. None of whom seem to have learned the fine art of seduction. Then again, seeing as we're all in an adult theater that caters to the carnal cravings of life, should I expect anything less?

"A girl like you is going to get eaten alive in here." A velvety voice laughs as we reach the edge of the crowd. "Follow me."

I look up and realize that Stacey hadn't snagged the only beautiful man in the building. His midnight black eyes could be intimidating on another face, but dimples almost masked by his well-groomed goatee soften his face. Looking at him, I know instinctively that he isn't a threat. When he reaches for my hand, I allow him to take it, noting the stark contrast of my light ivory skin against the espresso tone of his.

"Seriously, you shouldn't be walking around here alone. Not tonight," he scolds me. I look behind me to see if I had unknowingly gotten separated from Tyler, only to see him one step behind me looking slightly offended by the stranger's comment.

"In case you hadn't noticed, I'm not alone." I reach my free hand back to Tyler, pulling him to my other side. "And I'm not a naïve child who needs to be protected."

Xavier used to treat me the same way, as if I was going to get myself in trouble if left to my own devices. I know my doe eyes and all-American looks give the appearance of something other than a strong-willed, intelligent, independent woman, but it still pisses me off when people make assumptions based on my looks.

"Never said you were, sugar. And you might as well be alone. Do you really think he's going to ward off the horny creeps in there if they decide to make a pass at you?" The stranger leans forward, offering a brilliant smile to Tyler. "No offense. You just strike me as much more of a lover than a fighter."

Tyler shrugs, playing off the unintentionally hurtful comments. "None taken. I'm all for a good cat fight, but yeah, those guys are something else." He lets out a low whistle, looking back as we reach a side door to the building.

Proving that chivalry is not dead, even in the musky bowels of this industrial hell, the stranger holds the door as we exit. "Please tell me you're not leaving already," the stranger pleads once we're outside, free from the chaos inside.

"Does it matter to you if I am?" I ask, flinching at the bitchy tone I hear cross my lips.

"Of course it matters." He laughs. "You're different from the rest of them, and I was hoping to get to talk to you tonight."

The fact that the stranger is the first person tonight who hasn't commented on my tits or ass, within sixty seconds of entering my field of vision, is not lost on me. That knowledge puts me off a bit. *Why* hasn't he commented on my looks? Not to sound conceited, but I know I'm good looking. Certainly better than most of the women here, who are either young, desperate and trying too hard, or old, worn out and trying to recapture their younger, wilder days.

"Oh honey, I'm not sure you could handle me," I say, patting him on the cheek. Tyler tugs on my arm, silently pleading with me to shut up. "But if it makes you feel better, no, I'm not leaving. I just need something to liven the night a bit."

"Well, then I guess I'll see you when you get back." The stranger leans down, placing a chaste kiss on my cheek. He releases my hand after a quick squeeze.

"You can count on it," I say, feeling more alive than I have in a long time.

Chapter Two

"What the hell was that?" Tyler hisses as we stumble across the gravel parking lot in the dark. Between him in his skinnier than skinny jeans and me in a dress so tight it looks spray-painted on, we're quite the pair trying to climb through a hole in the chain link fence without embarrassing ourselves.

"What was I supposed to do, ignore him?" I ask defensively. I'm already berating myself as I realize what a bad idea it was to come here tonight.

I'm not supposed to be in Chicago right now. As far as Xavier knows, I'm buried under a mountain of research working on my thesis, over a hundred miles north of here. Instead, I let Stacey talk me into taking a night off to "relax my brain" and unwind.

We could have done that anywhere, but no, she insisted that we come down to what she raved was going to be a night to remember. It's definitely turning out to be every bit of that, but not in the way she promised. I've already seen things I'm fairly certain I'll never be able to scrub from my mind, and the night is still young.

"How about tell him that you have a man at home who's going to kick his ass into the next millennium if he finds out he touched you?" Tyler narrows his eyes as we stand on opposite sides of the car. It's freezing outside, but I'm too stunned by Tyler's acerbic tone to move.

"I haven't done anything wrong," I justify, more to myself than anything. I'm a grown woman with no intentions of crossing the line tonight or any other night.

The thing that scares me is the way my heart raced as we were escorted from the building by Mr. Dark and Mysterious. The way my skin sizzled under his touch. The loss my body felt with every step I took away from him. Xavier *is* a good man. We've been together since my sophomore year at the University of Wisconsin, and he recently bought the house of my dreams as an early graduation present.

After four years together, things with Xavier are familiar. Tonight has already shown me how much I miss the days when he made me feel this way.

"Not yet," Tyler mumbles as I unlock the car. He reaches for my hand before I can turn over the ignition, taking the keys from me. "I'm serious, Mel. X is going to have a shit fit if he finds out you were flirting with someone. That scares me."

Tyler is my world. We've been friends since the third grade when my family moved from Minneapolis to a farming community outside Madison. He was the one who didn't pick on me for being the tall, knock-kneed girl with glasses. At one point, he was the man I was going to marry. Of course, that all changed the day I caught him glancing down the hall trying to catch a glimpse of my older brother as he got out of the shower. Talk about an awkward moment!

"Tyler, there's nothing to be scared of," I assure him. *There just happen to be some things that even you don't understand about me.*

I reach for the silver chain around my neck, worrying the heart pendant between my fingers. It's the only piece of jewelry I've ever received from Xavier and it means more to me than the biggest diamond ever could. Tonight, feeling the cold metal in my hand doesn't fill me with the same joy it normally does, it's a reminder of what my choices tonight could be putting on the line.

"You say that, but I've seen how he is with you. I've seen you back away from him when he confronts you about talking to study partners." I put the car in reverse as Tyler continues what has become a frequent topic of conversation between us since Xavier handed me the keys to our new home. "You've even admitted there was a time when he wasn't thrilled that you and I are friends. Seriously, there's no way he didn't know that I'm batting for the boys, but I was a perceived threat because I have a penis."

"Ewww," I squeal with a shudder. "Do *not* talk about your junk, it's seriously disturbing."

We pull into a strip mall and I wish the mystery man had offered to ride with us. He might be an unknown, but I didn't get a creeper vibe from him. My hand rests on the door handle, willing myself to pull. I can do this. There's something about the group of men lingering around the liquor store entrance that puts me on edge. Out of the corner of my eye, I see Tyler shaking his head. He's one of only two people besides me who knows what happened that night. What he doesn't understand is that I am over the fear that used to plague me. The sinking feeling in my stomach isn't because of what happened to me, it's because this feels like some sort of cosmic reminder of where I'm supposed to be.

"Mel, it's okay. Look, there's a security guard right inside the door." He points to the portly man sitting on a bar stool reading a magazine. If my hesitation was fueled by memories of the night I was attacked, I'm not sure I would feel reassured by his presence. "Do you want me to run in and you can lock the doors as soon as I get out of the car?"

I shake my head, unable to say anything for fear of what will come out of my mouth. If I tell him that the only thing I want to do is retrieve Stacey and get home, where I told Xavier I would be all night, he's going to berate me for feeling guilty for having my own life.

"No, I'll be fine." I open the door and slowly step out, taking time to make sure I'm steady on my four-inch heels. As we make our way through the group of men, I feel them undressing me with their eyes. This is why I spend most of my life in jeans and t-shirts when I'm not working. At work, it's a different story, because I get paid well and know that Braydon only hires the most competent bouncers to make sure no one crosses the line.

We make our way to the back of the store, quickly selecting two six-packs. The cashier barely looks our way as he rings up our purchases and we're on our way out the door. I ignore the cat-calls as I unlock the car, knowing that my big mouth will get me in trouble if I say anything.

Chapter Three

"You came back." I nearly fall on my ass when the mystery man walks out of the shadows. He reaches for the plastic bag in my hand and I pull it closer to my body. Despite the way I reacted to him earlier, I have to be smart.

"I told you I would be back," I snip, turning away from him. I need to put space between us because I'm starting to have those feelings again. I hate the fact that my body and my mind aren't on the same page right now.

"Why are you running away?" Mystery man asks. I hear his boots hitting the concrete, his pace quickening as mine does the same.

"Not running, just trying to get back in to my friend." Tyler opens the door, ushering me inside. He wraps his arm around my waist as we make our way through the retail area, stopping briefly to show a security guard our wristbands.

I want to vomit as we travel deeper into the building. There is now a video playing in one of the semi-private rooms and five middle-aged men are all enjoying themselves right there in the hall. Tyler presses my body against his side as we avert our eyes from that particular scene.

"I might have to kill Stacey." He laughs in my ear as we hold up our arms to show a second bouncer that we're here for the party.

I look back and see that the mystery man is nowhere to be found. I should be happy about that since he's a complication I don't need in my life, but I'm not. There's something about him I want to know.

It takes me a minute to find Stacey in the ballroom. She's now sitting at the bar with a different man standing between her legs. I can't tell if he's attractive or not because his face is buried in the crook of her neck, but his body isn't bad at all. Maybe a bit short for my tastes, but that doesn't matter seeing as I'm not the one he's trying to seduce.

I watch as she wraps her legs around his waist, and he maneuvers his way through the crowd. As much as I don't want to know what's about to happen, I follow, needing to make sure Stacey is okay.

"Stacey Jane," I yell when I see him carrying her into a room lit only by a single red light bulb. She winks over his shoulder just before they disappear. Before I can reach her, a group of men gathers for the show she and her new friend are about to put on.

"You're a hard woman to pin down," the mystery man says as he falls in line beside me. I don't acknowledge him because right now I need to figure out how to break through a swarm of horny perverts to keep my friend from making one of the biggest mistakes of her life.

His hand wraps around my wrist, and I'm jerked back. I fight back the panic threatening to cloud my senses. Whipping around, I momentarily forget about Stacey as my body begins to shake.

He holds up his hands in surrender the moment he realizes that I'm on the verge of a full-blown freak out. "Hey," he says quietly. "I didn't mean to scare you. I promise, I just want to talk."

"I...I have to go." I look from the exit to the side rooms, wanting to run away but needing to stop Stacey. I can't let her do this. It's one thing to go home from a party with a different guy every week, but she can't degrade herself this way while allowing complete strangers to jerk off to the live show.

"I'm going with you," he informs me. I think about telling him to get lost, but until he surprised me, I would have welcomed his touch. And looking at the growing crowd, I have a feeling I'm going to need his help. "Never took you for the type of girl who likes to watch." He chuckles as I begin pushing my way through the sweaty men.

"Shut up," I yell over my shoulder. "My friend is in there being an idiot."

"Has she been drinking?" he asks, one hand resting at the small of my back while the other pushes men to the side.

"No."

"Is she on drugs?"

"No."

"Then why are you charging in there?" I can't believe he thinks I *wouldn't* be trying to stop her. What kind of friend would I be if I didn't?

"Because she's a college student, not some trashy whore."

Standing at the threshold of the door, I feel like my argument is flimsy at best. Stacey is laid out on a plastic bench, her skirt hiked up to her waist. She's nearly panting as the man she walked in with buries his face between her legs, fucking her with his tongue.

"Oh god, yes!" she screams as his fingers begin working quick circles around her clit. I need to stop this. Why won't anyone stop this?

I'm so stunned that she's allowing a man she doesn't know to give her oral sex that it takes a moment to register another man standing near her head. This one is taller than the first one. His body is sculpted, complete with that sinfully sexy V that would disappear into his pants if he was wearing any. Stacey's fingers wrap around the base of his shaft as she begins stroking him in time to the rhythm between her legs.

I need to stop this. But I can't. If I allow myself to forget that this is Stacey, it's erotic as hell. I shift, clenching my legs together to ease my arousal. I can*not* be getting turned on watching my friend fooling around with two men.

"I thought you were going to stop her," the mystery man whispers in my ear. I should find out his name if he's going to hang around, but that would require turning around. It would also give him the impression that I'm interested in him and I'm not. I can't be. Xavier will be home tomorrow and I would never cheat on him.

"Christ, princess!" The man between her legs groans as his cock plunges deep inside her body. "You're so fucking tight!"

I take a step forward, needing to stop her before this goes any further. The whole scene is wrong on so many levels. Before I can call out to her, I'm being pulled back. I spin on my heel, ready to tell the mystery man to get lost, but his midnight black eyes aren't the ones staring down at me.

"Xavier," I cry, seeing nothing but unadulterated rage boring into me from his sapphire eyes.

Chapter Four

Xavier throws his jacket over my shoulders as he pulls me out of the ballroom. He doesn't say another word to me as he storms through the building, shoving past anyone who dares stand in his way.

"Please, let me go," I beg him, not wanting someone to get the wrong impression and call the police. "I'm sorry! Please, Xavier, talk to me!"

We're almost to the door when I hear Stacey screeching at people to get out of the way. I lose my footing when I look back and see her racing to me. "Let her go, you pompous ass!" she yells from across the room.

"Stay out of this, Stacey," Xavier warns her, never breaking stride. With the force he uses to push the door open, I'm surprised his hand doesn't go through the solid pane of glass. Outside, he spins me around so my backside is resting on the hood of his illegally parked Mustang.

"How did you know?" I sob, a chill coursing through my body despite the warm late summer night.

When Xavier slams his fist against the hood of the car, I jump. Never before have I been scared of him, but I've also never pushed him to this point. It's not the fact that my mind is still seared with the memory of what he did to the three men who jumped me the night we met that keeps me from being the source of his anger. My driving force is, or was until tonight, the respect I feel for him. From the very beginning, he has made his motivations clear when telling me what he expected of me and I obeyed. Until tonight.

"Does it matter how I found out?" he screams, the muscles in his neck corded so tightly they threaten to break through his skin. "You *lied* to me and you have the audacity to question how I knew where to find you? That's rich, Melanie."

He begins pacing in front of me, running his hands over his normally perfectly styled blond hair. Tonight, it's a disheveled mess reminiscent of the way he looks first thing in the morning. The tie around his neck is loose, the top button of his dress shirt open.

"Xavier, please listen to me!" I shriek, emotions threatening to buckle my knees. He stops in his tracks, glaring at me with arms crossed tightly against his chest. "I'm sorry I didn't tell you I was going out tonight. Stacey asked me to come with her and I've been so stressed between work and school that I let her convince me it would be okay."

"So it was better for you to lie to me than tell me you wanted to go out?" he asks incredulously. I push the sight of Stacey storming across the parking lot to the back of my mind. Right now, I need to give Xavier my complete attention. Anything less would be yet another sign of disrespect. "I can put up with many things, Melanie, but what you did tonight…I'm not sure there's anything you can say that will make it okay."

"I'm so, so sorry!" I make no attempt to wipe away the tears streaming down my face. "I didn't want to deceive you, I think…"

I didn't think and that's the problem. I thought about what I wanted to do but I didn't think about the consequences of my actions.

"Xavier Ross, you're an asshole!" Stacey screeches as she slaps his arm away when he reaches for me. "What gives you the right to barge in here and yank her out like you're her father and she's the disobedient teenager?"

"Stacey, I told you to stay out of this. Unless you'd like me to call Braydon and tell him about the state you were in when I got here, I would suggest you shut up." His gaze never leaves mine as he speaks.

"I don't give a shit if you tell him or not! He knows we're not exclusive and he also knows that I'm a grown woman capable of making my own decisions," she screams, drawing more of a crowd to see what's going on.

"Clearly, you're the epitome of responsible choices." Xavier huffs, motioning to the building. I purse my lips, stifling the laugh that threatens to escape. I don't want to do anything to draw attention back to my own transgressions so I enjoy the silence as Stacey tries to think of a witty comeback.

"Fuck you, Xavier!" She pushes past him, wrapping her fingers around my upper arm. "Let's go, Mel. Tonight is a girls' night, and he can kiss my ass. You're twenty-four, not twelve. It's time you stop letting him dictate your life for you."

I teeter precariously on my heels, the rope in a game of tug-of-war as my friend and my very angry boyfriend try to sway me to their side.

While I appreciate what Stacey is saying, she doesn't understand how things are for Xavier and me. Part of what makes us work is the fact that I trust him to never abuse the control I've given him over certain aspects of my life. It's screwed up, but giving him that has allowed me freedom as I've never known before. It has allowed me to focus on my own goals, leaving the more mundane decisions to him.

"Stacey, I think I need to go," I say softly. "I'll call you tomorrow."

Most of our audience has grown bored with the drama and headed back inside. The sight of my mystery man leaning against the building, one leg bent with his foot resting against the cinderblock doesn't evoke the same stirring it did earlier. Now, seeing the way he's assessing the situation consumes me with guilt. Guilt for not flatly refusing his advances from the moment we met. Guilt for the way he made me feel.

"Whatever," Stacey groans, dramatically throwing her hands in the air and rolling her eyes. "One of these days, you're going to wake up and wonder what in the hell happened to you. When you do, *this* is what happened. You're letting him strip you away and when he gets bored, he'll leave you lost and broken. Who's going to be the one to put the pieces back together then?"

I sit on the hood of the car, slack jawed as Stacey walks away, shaking her head and more than likely mumbling to herself about what a fool I am. She doesn't understand and never will.

"We're going home," Xavier declares, leading me to the passenger side of his car. I slide into the seat, knowing better than to protest or continue trying to justify my actions.

I stare out the window, watching as the lights of the city give way to suffocating darkness once we're on country roads.

Chapter Five

It's after two in the morning by the time we get home. I take a moment to appreciate single-story house with its perfectly manicured lawn. I would have been happy in something older, smaller and more modest, but Xavier insisted that if we were going to move in together, he wanted me to have a home I could be proud of. And he found it. Without asking for my input until after closing, Xavier chose a house that I can envision living in for years to come. "Inside," Xavier says, the first word he has uttered since getting behind the wheel.

Head bowed, I follow him into the foyer, the light hardwood floors cold as I slip out of my heels. I stand in place, hands clasped behind my back as I await his next command. His dress shoes disappear out of my line of sight. I'm desperate to reach out to him, but I stay strong, knowing my only hope is to patiently wait for him to speak.

"Meet me in the living room," he instructs me. His voice is distant and cold. I would give anything to hear the heated anger from hours earlier. At least then, I knew what to expect.

As I plod across the plush carpeting in the living room, I reach over my shoulder, freeing the single button at the back of my dress. The fabric slides down my stomach as I continue walking. I place my dress, neatly folded, over the back of the leather couch.

The camel-colored upholstery has a naturally faded look to it, giving the illusion of being rustic and well-loved from the moment it was delivered. This couch was the first place Xavier and I made love the day we moved in. It's where he sends me every evening after dinner to wait for him. Tonight, it feels as if he has sent me here to receive my sentence for violating the single most important tenet of our relationship.

I step out of my black silk thong and slide the matching bra down my arms, stacking them on top of the dress. As I kneel in front of the couch, my hand drifts to the pendant resting just beneath the hollow of my neck.

"Without trust, there is nothing," Xavier says, standing before me. He reaches down, tipping my head upward. "You've given me your trust, which is everything. This heart is a symbol of my love for you. I cherish your gift every moment of every day and promise that I will do everything I can to keep from hurting you. You, Melanie Elaine Erickson, are the world to me. I love you."

Xavier moves behind me, gathering my hair to the side. "Hold this," he breathes into my ear. I reach up, holding my long brown waves as his hands brush against my shoulders. The metal of the pendant is cold against my bare skin. Once clasps the chain behind my neck, he holds a small mirror in front of me.

"It's beautiful, thank you." I sigh, my eyes fixed on the silver heart with one emerald and one sapphire in the center. The union of two souls represented by each of our birthstones.

The sound of Xavier clearing his throat brings me back into the present. My hands drop to my sides, my eyes cast downward. This is the moment of truth.

"What were you thinking tonight?" he asks, taking a seat in front of me. More than anything, I want to rest my head on his knees, feel him stroking my hair as he tells me we'll be okay. From the shattered tone of his voice, I think we both need the reassurance but doubt either of us can give it.

Somewhere along the way, I lost sight of what motivated me. I fell into the comfort of our daily routines as his career took off. After a brief adjustment period, I grew to love rushing home after class to make dinner for him. I didn't see it as degrading to be solely responsible for the household chores. I didn't resent him for tasking me with setting out an outfit for him as he showered every morning, even if I didn't have to be up at the crack of dawn. I lived to serve him.

Since June, he's been traveling almost non-stop from one conference to the next or meeting with college students hoping for an elusive internship with his medical technology firm. His absence left a bigger hole in my life than I could have imagined. In recent weeks, it has gotten to the point that I roam around, lost, when he's not here. That feeling left me questioning everything about myself.

Now that I think about it, I know *that* is the real reason I went to the party tonight. I needed to prove to myself that I still exist, that I am still capable of making decisions on my own. That I'm not so dependent on Xavier Ross that I would crumble if I lost him.

"I'm sorry," I begin, wishing I could look into his eyes. It's not protocol or anything like that keeping them fixed on the pile of the white carpet between my knees and his feet. It's shame and regret. "I think I did it to prove that I could."

He grips my chin firmly between his thumb and forefinger, pulling my face to meet his. "Prove to whom?"

"To myself. Stacey was right tonight, sometimes I feel as if you're stripping away pieces of me. I don't like the way I feel when you're not home." He brushes tears from my cheeks with his thumb as I continue pouring my heart out to him, every fear that has been weighing on me.

"You don't trust me." It's not a question, but a somber statement.

"I do trust you, more than anything," I promise him, shuffling closer, needing to feel more of his body connected to mine.

"No, you don't." I cock my head to the side, trying to figure out why he feels this way. My decision had nothing to do with trust. If there's one thing I *am* sure of, it's Xavier's love for me. That's unwavering. "When I gave you that necklace, I told you it was a sign of my devotion to you. You asked me if it was a collar and I told you it was not, that I would never do that to you because you're not my slave. I promised I would never take away your free will. And you didn't trust me enough to tell me that you were going out."

Xavier continues speaking, but my mind drifts again to a happier time...

"I don't love you for your servitude or submission when we're playing. I love you because you challenge me. I love you because you're smart and sarcastic and beautiful. I don't ever want to see that light in your eyes dim, don't want you to feel bound to me if you should decide to leave. It would kill me, but it's because I love you so much that I would let you walk away."

Xavier leans forward, gently kissing my forehead. We stay connected this way, his hands resting on my shoulders. "Without trust, we have nothing," he whispers, sliding his hands around to the back of my neck.

My body quakes as I'm overcome with sobs. I don't want to believe that my one decision is leading him to such a drastic measure. The moment he releases the clasp, I feel as emotionally bare as I am physically.

"I'm sorry too, Melanie. I'm sorry for whatever happened that made you feel as if you couldn't come to me with these concerns. I need some time..."

Xavier releases me as he stands. Without another word, he walks out of the room. I collapse over the seat of the couch, not even trying to hold back the wails coming from my mouth.

The night I received the pendant, Xavier asked me to only remove the chain if it was required medically. Beyond that, he informed me, my bare neck would be a sign to him that our relationship had come to an end.

I lie naked on the floor, bawling until exhaustion overcomes me sometime after dawn. I'm covered in a chenille blanket when I wake and I know without having to get up that this really is the end.

Chapter Six

"Daddy! There's a woman at the door, but she's not saying anything!" My cheeks flood with embarrassment as a little boy's voice slices the early morning air.

I can't help but wonder how long I've been standing here, lost in another time. It's been six years since I walked out this very door, but the pain in my heart is as raw today as it was then.

"Melanie?" My eyes shift from the three year old at my feet to the only man I've ever loved.

"Hello, Xavier," I bite out, hoping I sound professional. "I'm here to help with Alyssa."

****

I knew it was a bad idea to take this assignment, but I couldn't think of a way to ask to be relieved that would have been plausible. Sometimes, there's nothing to do but stare into the eyes of those who we've hurt and live with the choices we've made. And sometimes, that includes walking back into the life you could have had to help him heal from another broken heart.

Facebook: https://www.facebook.com/authorsloanjohnson
Twitter: https://twitter.com/authorsloanj
Goodreads: https://www.goodreads.com/author/show/7162059.Sloan_Johnson
Amazon: http://amazon.com/author/sloanjohnson
Website: http://authorsloanjohnson.com

Leap of Faith

Sometimes… you have to go with it.

Shayne McClendon

Copyright © 2014 Shayne McClendon
All rights reserved.

Prologue

It was the last play of their season, and the final touchdown of Tucker Irvin's career.

Putting him back on the field as the starting quarterback hadn't been enough to take them to the Super Bowl, but he'd managed to save the last few games from the over-confident rookie.

The young man for whom team management had unceremoniously benched him to promote.

The powers-that-be finally tired of their shiny new toy — drafted for a ridiculous sum out of Oklahoma State — after ten back-to-back losses. They put Tuck in for the last six games.

His offensive line knew Tuck well after years of working together. When he rejoined them on the field, they celebrated with utter brutality. Sportscasters would be talking about this game and his teammates for a long time.

During the last huddle, they unanimously determined that *he* had to carry the ball over the line. As Tuck crossed into the end zone, he felt at peace. He was certain that his decision to retire was the right one despite his devotion to his team and the sport.

Yeah, his knees felt like they were made of pudding and his shoulder wouldn't handle lifting anything heavier than a pencil for a while, but it had been worth every ice pack and cortisone shot to go out on top.

He spiked the ball and ran for the stands to make his last Lambo Leap… the best one in all his twenty years on the field.

Powering up on nothing but adrenaline, Tucker cleared the side and was groped, hugged, and kissed by the people who'd meant so much to his career. They screamed his name.

A woman was directly beneath his facemask.

She stared at him with huge golden eyes shining from a heart-shaped face. Wrapped in enough clothes to qualify her as the Michelin man, he watched two beads of sweat drop from his body and land on a tiny patch of bare skin at her throat.

He smiled and shouted over the noise, "Give me your name!"

"Sasha." Nothing else.

"Last name?"

"Fowler." Definitely not happy to admit it.

"Sasha Fowler?" She nodded and he raked a gloved hand down the side of her body and lightly squeezed her butt. "Meet me outside the locker room after the game. Nice to meet you."

They shook hands with the Giants' players and many said a few words about his career, his leadership, and his last game as they passed.

He gave a couple of post-game interviews despite the fact that he could feel the sweat freezing on his hair in the sub-zero temperatures. The questions ranged from what he was going to do now that he was retiring to how he felt about the fact that they hadn't made it to the playoffs.

Tuck laughed. "Even though it wasn't enough in the end, I feel good. We turned the season around. I have to thank my line for that. They kept me on my feet tonight; didn't let a single damn sack complete, and blocked me for the best touchdown of my career."

Running a towel over his head, he gave the female sportscaster a winning smile. "As for what I'm going to do now? I don't have the full plan yet, but I know that for the next few weeks I'm going to relax and take a step back. Take my time deciding on the rest of my life. I hope it's as fulfilling as the first half has been."

Several members of the offensive line hauled him off the field to the sound of fans chanting his name. These guys had been part of his inner circle for more than ten years; one had started the same year he did. They'd stuck with the same team throughout their career despite bad seasons, lackluster coaching, and poor management decisions.

Tucker wondered when Grady Teutonico would make the choice to retire.

"Dude, you looking to get pneumonia to start retirement right? We aren't one of those spoiled Florida teams. A couple words and get the hell inside to dry off."

"You're right, Dad."

Grady punched him in the arm and Tuck thanked God it wasn't his throwing arm because he might have cried like a little girl. The big man didn't understand *pulling* his punches. His bright white smile faded in the cocoa of his skin.

"Don't have a fucking clue what I'm going to do without you here. I got nothing else."

"You are so full of shit, Grady. What happened to your dream of becoming a coach? You're one of the best offensive linemen in the league. Any team will snap you up and you can stop getting beat the fuck up every season."

He nodded and pulled his dreads behind his head and secured them there. "We'll see. I pretty much fucked up my personal life so football is it."

A messy and highly public divorce three years before had ended with Grady in rehab and his kids in foster care after his ex-wife took her life. She left a note blaming him and it took another court battle to regain custody of his kids from her sister. He hadn't been the same since and Tucker didn't remember the last time he'd seen his best friend genuinely happy.

He locked their forearms and pulled him close. "Take some time off. Hang with me while I muddle through — bring the kids. Get your fucking feet under you."

Grady nodded. "I'll think about it. Thanks, man."

The two of them were suddenly bathed in champagne by the entire team. They laughed and roughhoused with the younger guys before they hit the showers.

The doctor checked him out afterward with a huge smile.

Dressing in a dark gray Brooks Brothers suit with a green tie that matched his eyes, Tuck pulled on the Rolex he bought himself for his twentieth high school reunion. As he exited the locker room, he was stopped by coaches and support staff.

Almost two hours after the end of the game, he walked down the hall toward the parking lot. Once he left the stadium, he'd be officially retired. It was permanent. He couldn't keep putting his body through hell day after day and expect to live with any quality of life by the time he hit sixty.

In a couple of days, he'd come back to clean out his locker. Maybe he'd ask one of the assistants to box it up and ship it to him. No way was Tuck risking coming back until the temptation to keep playing was gone.

It's time to see what life after football is really like.

The exit to staff parking was mobbed so he signed autographs and posed for photos. He waved goodbye to the fans, the best in the league in his opinion, and headed in the direction of his Hummer.

He realized that he'd scanned their faces for Sasha Fowler but she hadn't shown. He was disappointed. Her eyes were gorgeous and she'd been familiar to him for some reason.

Climbing into the driver's seat, Tuck contemplated hanging out with the rest of the team for a few hours and getting into some trouble. It was still early.

He just wasn't in the mood. Instead of driving in the direction of the bar district the team frequented, he went the other way toward the highway.

As the anti-environmental vehicle he'd received as part of an endorsement deal idled at the light, he glanced over at the side road that lead to the fan parking lot.

A Range Rover was parked on the shoulder under the bright lights. The driver was jacking the vehicle up with a tiny flashlight between their teeth. The person crouched and started loosening the lug nuts. Apparently unable to remove one, the driver stood on the T-bar, jumping up and down but making no progress.

Tuck went through the light and made a U-turn. He parked behind the Rover, pulled on thick leather gloves, and grabbed his heavy jacket.

Green Bay weather was no joke. The wind was howling and the temperature would drop another twenty degrees by morning.

Approaching the back of the vehicle, he said loudly, "May I be of some assistance?"

The driver screamed, their supporting hand slipped off the side of the SUV, and the person fell. He jumped forward to catch the smaller figure.

Wrapped in a hat, scarf, and heavy jacket, it was hard to determine gender... until he saw the eyes.

"Well, well... Sasha Fowler."

Chapter One

"Oh lord, you already groped me once tonight, let me up. Shit." Chuckling, Tuck set her on her feet. "I've got this. Continue on your merry way, please."

She climbed back on the iron bar and used renewed energy to get the lug nuts to loosen.

Tuck watched her with a grin for a moment before he stepped forward, lifted her to the ground by her waist, and grabbed the T-bar in both hands. Putting his power behind it, he got it to turn and dropped the metal to tug the wheel away.

He set the spare into position, reattached the lug nuts, and removed the jack. As the car lowered, it was obvious to both of them that the spare tire was *also* flat.

As he watched, Sasha stomped several feet away in the snow and gave the most furious blood-curdling scream he'd ever heard. It was impressive actually.

She clenched her fists, took a deep breath, and took out her cell phone. It was obvious that she was on the phone with the rental company's roadside assistance service.

"Yes, I called earlier. It's been changed but the spare is no good." There was a pause. "Because you said no one could come out for three *hours*. I'm in Green Bay, ma'am. It's below freezing. I can't wait three hours. Please… *please* send someone to tow the car. No, I don't know the area, I've never been here."

She listened for almost a minute, rubbing her temple. "Listen, can you help me?" Another pause. "Yes, I realize the roads are icy… I'm sure you're getting lots of calls." She sighed. "I understand."

Sasha glanced at Tuck and clenched her jaw. "No, ma'am. I don't know anyone here." The person on the other end rambled for almost a minute and Miss Fowler's patience was running out. "It's after midnight and I'm stranded because of the rental I got from *your* company. Is there someone else I can call?"

Tuck watched her pat her pockets as if she was looking for something. She walked unsteadily back to the driver's door, opened it, and reached into the console. Strangely, she removed a small bottle of orange juice. She took off the cap, tilted it back, and realized it was frozen solid.

As he watched, her eyes went wide and something that resembled panic crossed her face.

Opening the back driver's side door, she yanked a computer bag closer and rummaged through an outside pocket. Her hands shook badly as she removed two packets of honey and tried to open one. She dropped the honey and her phone before hitting her knees in the snow.

Tuck crouched worriedly in front of her. She whispered, "Diabetic… please… I need sugar."

He ripped the first packet of honey open and held it between her lips, squeezing the liquid on her tongue. Before she could say anything, he repeated the process with the second packet.

Not caring if he pissed her off, he picked her up and carried her to his truck. He dropped her rather roughly on the passenger seat. The Hummer was still running and warm.

Walking back to her rental, he threw the tire and iron in the rear. Scanning the interior, he gathered her luggage and purse, found her phone on the ice, and threw everything in his backseat.

Slipping into the driver's seat, he called stadium security.

"Hey, Gary, it's Tucker. I need a favor."

He explained the problem, asked them to tow the rental inside the gates, and told them where he hid the keys. Assured the stadium employees would secure the SUV, he turned around on the road and headed toward the nearest hospital.

Twenty minutes later, he parked and grabbed her purse before carrying her through the front doors of the emergency room.

The nurse at the desk glanced up in surprise. "Aren't you…?"

"Yes, I am… this is Sasha Fowler. She's diabetic and her blood sugar hit bottom. She's had two packets of honey and lost consciousness about four minutes ago."

There was a flurry of activity as another nurse rushed out of the triage area. He followed her to a room and placed Sasha on the bed. He stood out of the way while they started an IV and took her vitals. His relief was palpable when she came around with a groan a few minutes later.

Leaning over the bed, he gave her a smile. "Hey there, how you feeling?"

****

Looking up into the face of Tuck Irvin, Sasha sighed in frustration.

Nothing about this trip had gone as planned and she was exhausted just thinking about the hours of questions her father would ask and the list of *should haves* he would give her.

"I'm your new agent, Mr. Irvin." His green eyes widened in surprise. "My dad is Collin Fowler. He's retiring at the end of the year. I'm supposed to take over your representation. I'm sorry to meet you under such bizarre conditions."

"Well, shit." Tucker laughed and held out his hand. "Pleased to meet you, Sasha. I think under the circumstances, you can call me Tuck. I can't believe Collie's retiring. He's been my agent since I was drafted a hundred years ago."

"Maybe not a *hundred*…" She smiled and he took the subtle compliment with class.

"I've met your brothers several times but never had the pleasure of meeting you. Allow me to apologize for my earlier behavior." He shrugged and she saw the boyish charm that made so many women fall willingly under his spell.

"I just returned after several years in England." She chose her words carefully but she could tell by his face that she hadn't been careful enough.

"I can't believe I didn't recognize you. You're Sasha *Baxter*… you married the rugby player."

"No, I'm Sasha *Fowler*. Peter and I have been divorced for over a year and we were separated for three before that. It was kept quiet."

"I'm sorry. Again. *Fuck me.*"

Tucker was obviously replaying the media footage of Collie's only daughter in his mind. Unfortunately, there had been far too much of it for far too long.

"I considered it. No need to apologize." The meaning of what she said hit him after a slight delay and he grinned. "Don't look so smug. I've been celibate for a long damn time." She winked at him. "Besides, I'm thirty-four and way too old for you."

A look of confusion crossed his face. "I'll be forty-one this year."

"Yes, I'm aware. Your ladyloves are typically fifteen years younger than you and often more." Seeming to disregard his presence, she sat up and motioned to a passing nurse. "I'd like to be discharged. I'll schedule an appointment with my endocrinologist in the morning."

The nurse opened her mouth to argue and Sasha held up her hand.

"I've had diabetes all my life. I know the risks and why I had an attack — I travelled all day, I missed eating, and dealing with the stress of breaking down and the extreme cold. I'm fine now. Please let the doctor on call know I'd like to be released. I'll sign whatever you need me to."

She gave the woman a huge smile and the nurse backed out of the room. Being careful of the IV, she swung her legs over the side and rubbed her temples.

"What happened with Peter? You guys seemed so, I don't know, perfect."

"Nosy much?" Tuck had the good manners to look embarrassed but Sasha just couldn't find it in her to care what anyone thought about her. "I caught him in bed with a blonde supermodel ten years younger than me a month after my miscarriage. Took all the romance right out of things." She knew her laugh was filled with the bitterness she'd tried so hard to let go.

"Jesus. I'm sorry."

She shrugged. "I suspected for months. The second he found out I was pregnant he was... how shall I put this delicately... not *inclined* to come near me?" She stood as the ER doctor entered the room and saw immediately that he planned to argue her decision.

"Doctor, do you have my release paperwork? Don't shake your head. I need get to my hotel and eat. I have meetings beginning at noon tomorrow. I want to leave. Right now."

The nurse stared at the arm she held out and Sasha lifted her brows. The woman wore bright scrubs that were overwhelming in the fluorescent lighting. She looked at the doctor expectantly and he nodded for the nurse to proceed with a small frown.

The IV was removed in moments and a bandage placed over the small hole.

Sasha could feel Tucker staring at her as she gathered her things.

She pretended to be unaffected by it but she didn't lie to herself.

The mere presence of the man made her feel overheated.

To compensate, she located her phone and dialed her father's number. She didn't realize she paced the room and would have laughed to discover it was a habit every time she spoke to her father.

"Dad. You... what? You *saw* that?" She turned to face Tuck and glared. "*Lovely*." He began to rant and the tension headache started at the back of her neck and worked its way forward.

Then he started talking about her ex-husband.

"Are you fucking kidding me? Peter has no right to call you and tattle. I don't give a *shit* if we still represent him. No, I will not speak to him." Her pacing was faster now. "Dad, I divorced him. I had a valid reason. There is no relationship with him."

She listened for a few seconds but there would be no reasoning with her father. Instead, she cut him off. "I'm at the hotel. I need to eat and I'll talk to you in the morning. You tell that lying, cheating fuck where I am and I will cause the biggest scene you've ever seen in your life. There will be no spin control for the lunacy I'll unleash on him."

The nurse appeared and she rapidly signed the paperwork presented on a clipboard. When she was gone, Sasha threw everything into her purse, shrugged on her jacket, and ground out furiously, "Do what you want. I know for a fact you and Mom didn't speak for weeks over this. I call her next." Closing the phone, she stormed from the room.

Tuck Irvin was right behind her. "You alright?"

"No, I'm not alright. You've done enough, but can you *please* take me to my hotel?"

"Of course."

He opened his passenger door and closed it gently behind her when she was settled. They didn't speak as he drove and for that, she was grateful.

Under the hotel entrance, he handed the keys to a valet and grabbed her luggage. The man at the front desk blatantly checked her out as she approached and it was almost too much.

"Really?" The name badge on his chest pronounced him the night manager. His name was Roger. "Roger, my name is Sasha Fowler. I need to check in. I'm exhausted and not at my best."

Sniffing, Roger typed rapidly on his unseen keyboard and presented her with her room key a few minutes later. "Enjoy your stay, Miss Fowler."

She nodded but said nothing as she spotted the bank of elevators.

Tuck got in behind her and she met his eyes.

"I'm seeing you up, Sasha. You've had quite the day and you're exhausted."

Twelve floors later, she stepped into a hallway that looked like hundreds of others she'd been in and suddenly felt like screaming.

This was not what she wanted. This has never been what she wanted.

Keying the electronic lock, she stepped just inside the room and held the door. Tucker moved past her to put her luggage on the dresser.

By the time he turned back, Sasha had removed her overcoat and was pulling the black turtleneck over her head. He took a step back and his legs hit the king size bed.

Saying nothing, she removed her boots, stripped the black suede pants from her legs, and faced him in her lace bra and boy shorts. Reaching up, she unpinned her hair and let it fall around her upper body.

Hands on her hips, she stared at him.

"You're stunning... you were hiding a lot under all those layers." He frowned. "Are you sure, Sasha? Why are you changing your mind?"

"Does it matter? We're not shooting for happily ever after. You wanted to use me and I'm in the frame of mind to use you. Looks like all signs point to yes."

With that, she reached behind her, unhooked her bra, and released her breasts. Hooking her thumbs in her panties, she pushed them down and kicked them away.

"Your move, Tuck."

Chapter Two

Tucker wasn't sure he was breathing. His eyes traveled from her pretty feet, over a trimmed patch of red curls above her *mons*, a slightly rounded tummy, to full breasts with pink nipples. Her hair was a river of auburn that stood out against flawless ivory skin. She was toned but not muscular, about five-seven, with amber eyes he thought he might drown in.

His examination of her body from bottom to top took less than three seconds. Then he made quick work of his winter gear, pulled away his suit and boxers methodically as Sasha stared at him hungrily. When he was completely naked, she tackled him to the bed.

"You were due a sack." They were the last words she said for almost half an hour.

Shoving at him until he rolled over on his stomach, Sasha *massaged* him. She went deep into the tissue better than anyone he'd ever known and concentrated on the heaviest muscle groups of his back and legs. She didn't neglect his ass or his feet.

She treated every inch of his body to the same attention and he was moaning after the first ten seconds. After two minutes, he knew he could postpone his standing appointment for an after-game massage tomorrow.

Standing at the end of the bed, she nudged him to his back and smiled. He imagined the look of euphoria on his face was obvious.

From the tips of his toes, she worked her way up his body. She straddled his hips as she worked his hands, arms, shoulders, and neck. Backing up, she worked his chest and abdominals.

When she took his cock more than halfway into her mouth, his entire upper body arched off the bed. The kneading of every muscle in focused silence hadn't prepared him for her switch to something so sexual.

His hands went into her hair and he watched her suck him differently than any woman ever had. This wasn't foreplay to Sasha. She didn't look as though she was trying to appear seductive or get him more turned on.

She enjoyed the act itself.

That turned him on more than anything else could have. Most women rushed blowjobs, doing it only because they were checking it off a task list on their way to orgasm. Some women actually seemed to hate everything about giving oral but did it anyway.

Not this woman. Sasha sucked him hard and didn't rush. Several times, she stopped him from coming when she felt him tightening.

No part of his groin was neglected. Her fist stroked the portion of the shaft she couldn't take in her mouth while her other hand worked his balls as firmly as he'd ever done himself. Every so often, she released them to pet his thighs or abs.

Her suction remained steady and she alternated by carefully using her teeth on the upstroke. Her tongue never stopped moving, coiling around the head and following the ridge.

Tucker gripped her hair in his fists and dug his heels into the bed.

When she stopped him from coming a third time, he was reduced to begging. "Please, Sasha. I can't stand it. Please let me come."

Magnificent amber eyes lifted to meet his. She didn't look away as she reached beneath his sac with one finger while maintaining the pressure on his balls. It pressed his perineum, massaging in small circles, as she increased the speed and depth of sucking him.

Then he was coming and it was unlike any orgasm in his life alone or with a partner. It felt stronger than he thought possible and stole his ability to think.

"Yes. Fuck *yes*, Sasha. That feels so fucking good."

She used the strong muscles of her throat to milk him, her fingers continued their massage, and never had he been *emptied* so completely.

At the last moment, she pulled back to watch the last stream of semen hit his lower abs. Tucker watched as she licked it away. It gave him a full body shiver. There was a small smile on her face as she returned to clean every inch of his balls and cock. When the process was done to her satisfaction, she kissed the head and crawled up to lie down beside him on her stomach.

"Feel better? I know I do."

Her voice was smug and he turned his head to look at her. He couldn't hide the awe in her performance or the embarrassment that he was completely… for the first time in his sexual history… *flaccid*.

"You're like a mythical creature. My god, I can't see straight."

Tuck felt like he was truly looking at her for the first time. Her lips were red and swollen from sucking him and her cheeks were flushed. Her amber eyes were the color of warm whiskey and he'd never wanted to fuck someone more in his life.

Impossible for the time being. Holy shit.

There was no doubt that she knew *exactly* what effect she'd had on him. Her smile grew bigger and she leaned over to kiss his lips lightly. "I'm going to shower and let you recuperate."

She bounded off the bed, grabbed a clip from her purse, and pulled her hair into a haphazard bun. He watched her ass as she walked into the bathroom.

Between the massage and the blowjob, Tuck was more relaxed than he could ever remember being.

****

When Sasha left the bathroom wrapped in a towel ten minutes later, she found Tuck Irvin, one of the best quarterbacks in NFL history, soundly asleep in her bed.

With a small chuckle, she turned off all but one lamp, climbed in beside him, and pulled the blankets over their bodies. They'd both had a long day.

Sleep wasn't an insult; it was proof of a job well done.

Sasha drifted to sleep with the sound of Tuck's deep breathing. It was soothing to a woman who hadn't had a man in her bed in three years.

Several hours later, she woke clutching the sheets.

Glancing down the length of her body, she was met with the image of Tuck settled comfortably between her legs, tracing his tongue lazily back and forth over her clit.

Two strong fingers stroked steadily in and out of her body, and before she realized how close she was to an orgasm, she was coming hard and fast.

His green eyes watched her and after he brought her back down to earth, he winked. She started to lift, prepared to accept him fully. She was surprised when he held her down with his arm across her pelvis.

"No. My work here isn't done."

Tuck licked her from her pussy to her clit with the flat of his tongue and she collapsed against the pillows, watching him eat her. The man took his time, seeming to enjoy giving as much as she was enjoying receiving.

A first for her, if she was being honest about past lovers.

His fingers never slowed and he curled them, stroking over her G-spot. Her eyes lost focus as another orgasm built. It didn't completely surprise her when he prevented her from coming by stopping all movements.

Rapid pants escaped her lips and she whispered, "I'll beg sooner than you did, Tuck."

"You don't have to beg for a fucking thing, Sasha."

He resumed his attention to her pussy and she was shocked to realize her entire body was vibrating. Everything about him seemed focused on driving her up and over the edge of climax. He licked her clit, nibbled it with his teeth, and sucked it between his lips.

It stole her breath.

"So good... don't stop." He didn't until she crashed from a third climax ten minutes later. When she trusted herself to speak, she asked, "Where did you learn to do that?"

"I dated a girl in college who wasn't sure of her sexual orientation. Though she eventually chose females as holding the greater sexual attraction, she left me with a new appreciation for eating pussy. I watched another woman go down on her and realized I didn't know a fucking thing."

She laughed. "You certainly corrected it."

"I'm quick at learning things I really want to know."

Sasha cupped her breasts, pinched and rolled her nipples as she stared at him. "I really want you to suck these for me, Tuck. Please come up here."

The green of his eyes darkened and she watched a sexual flush spread over his cheeks. He slowly pulled his fingers from her body and sucked her essence from them. He moaned and lifted her ass in his huge hands, bringing her closer to his mouth. He fucked into her with his tongue several times before lowering her to the bed and crawling up her body.

His lips settled over hers with a murmured, "Taste."

The flavor of her sexuality blended with the warm richness of Tucker's mouth and she groaned. His hands circled her, fisting her hair and gripping her ass as he kissed her differently than any man had before.

She felt consumed and all she could think was *more*.

Their first kiss went on and on. Her hands explored any part of his body she could reach and his hold on her didn't loosen. His fingers curled around the bend of her ass and stroked into her pussy from beneath her. Her gasp was swallowed as he deepened the kiss yet again.

When he broke it, he continued to hold her immobile as he bent to take a pebbled nipple to the roof of his mouth. Her scalp tingled where he gripped her hair. She flexed around his fingers and his suckling was telegraphing strong signals to her womb.

He took turns with each breast, going back and forth between them. He licked and sucked, scraped the peaks with his teeth. When they were fully swollen and distended, he grabbed a condom from the side table.

He slipped his fingers from her pussy, rolled the latex over his shaft, and notched himself at the entrance of her body. He drove to the root in one stroke and the tight walls worked to stretch to him.

"So wet and hot. Fuck, you feel incredible."

Tucker painted her lips with the moisture on his fingertips and licked across her mouth before settling into another deep kiss. He didn't move, didn't rush to fuck her now that he had the opportunity. His shaft throbbed as he ransacked her mental processes.

It was the single most intimate sexual experience of her life.

Sasha took his face in her hands and he lifted slightly to stare into her eyes. They stayed like that for a long moment and she swore she saw the same fascination on his face that must have shown on her own.

"Fuck me hard, Tucker."

Without breaking eye contact, he brought his knees higher and rested her ass against his upper thighs. Slipping his arms under her, he withdrew and stroked carefully to the hilt. She said nothing because the next thrust was deeper, harder.

Soon enough, he was driving down into her body with brutal force and her mind zoned into the moment to absorb every detail. His shaggy blonde hair was darker with sweat. Muscle definition in his arms and torso were sharp despite the soft lighting.

He was present, in the moment with her, and it opened a part of her she closed after too many hurts. A part of her she didn't want to open for this man.

He was a fantastic lover, but a horrible gamble.

"Stop thinking." Tucker's words snapped her back into reality and he glared at her. "I can practically see your thoughts, Sasha."

"I'm sorry."

"Don't be fucking sorry. Be *here*. We'll think more tomorrow."

She nodded and he increased his efforts, dropping his mouth over hers, and forcing her to take his breath and give it back. There was no control left inside her and when her orgasm started, he broke the kiss with a growl.

"Yes. Come for me."

Stopping would have been impossible and her upper body lifted from the bed with the force of pleasure that crashed over her. She knew she cried his name but would have been shocked at the emotion she betrayed when she did.

Before the peak could subside, he said, "Again."

Eyes on hers, holding her hard, he worked to drive her up a second time. She was incoherent with sexual joy she'd delivered but never personally experienced.

He reached around to hold the nape of her neck and pulled her with him as he went back on his heels. Large palms braced her shoulders as he pounded into her from below, moving nothing but his hips into her body.

Sasha clawed him with her short nails and bit his shoulder. One hand trailed down and squeezed her ass before slapping it sharply. When he held her jaw still and kissed her aggressively, eating at her mouth, she came.

Her pussy milked his cock like a fist as he lowered her to the bed and stroked into her deep and slow. It dragged out her orgasm and when he joined her, she watched his face contort in release.

"Best orgasm of my fucking *life*."

His words came through gritted teeth. He slowed his movements but didn't stop, exhaling roughly as both of them went limp.

They were quiet for a long time before Tuck said into the bend of her neck, "I have to see you again." She smiled against his chest but didn't respond. Lifting his face, he met her gaze directly. "Sasha, I'm serious."

He pressed his hips snuggly into the cradle of her body and as she tried to think of what she should say, a familiar sensation washed over her. His eyes widened.

"Are you alright?"

"Tuck, I… I need sugar. Right now."

Chapter Three

Tucker pulled carefully from her body and leapt from the bed. He discarded the condom while he dialed room service.

Sasha stared at the ceiling and smiled when he told them to get it to the room in ten minutes for a hundred dollar tip. He ordered an assortment since he was unsure what she liked. He also told them to send up several packets of honey and a carafe of orange juice.

When he hung up, he rummaged in the outer pocket of her bag and found another two pouches of honey. Opening them both, he crawled up beside her and held them to her mouth.

She held the sticky sweetness in her mouth for a long time to let as much of the sugars enter her blood stream through the soft tissues of her gums as possible. When she swallowed, he stretched out beside her, and pulled the blankets over her body.

"You're too cold. I completely forgot you hadn't eaten."

She shook her head carefully. "I know better. I just… I wanted you and I forgot about food. You're much better looking in person, Tuck."

"So are you. I can't believe I didn't recognize you. You're better known in the States."

"Not for anything good. My first two boyfriends were idiot clients of my father's just like Peter. He was older and my dad pushed him at me hard but my mom never liked him. She said I'd regret it and I sure as hell do."

Tucker stroked her hair away from her face and kissed her forehead as room service arrived. Shrugging on a hotel robe and picking up his wallet, he guided the cart in and gave the man two hundreds on top of the total.

He was obviously a fan. "The first hundred is for getting here so fast. The second is to forget I was here. Understood?" The man nodded slowly and Tuck asked if he wanted an autograph with a smile. He signed the back of his order pad. "Have a great night."

The moment the door closed, he poured Sasha a glass of orange juice and set it on the bedside table. Bending, he moved her higher on the bed and handed her the glass. She was shaking and he cupped his hands around hers so she could drink.

He made her a plate of several different foods and sat while she ate. "You've got to be starving, Tuck. Tell me you ordered food for yourself?" He nodded with a smile. "I'll be okay. I normally don't have drops but traveling messes me up. I'm careful and usually have more snacks."

Tucker pulled the cart along the bed and sat on the edge as he cut into a thick steak. "Weak is the last word I'd use to describe you, Sasha." He gave her a shrug. "You're fucking awesome. I can't believe Baxter let you get away."

"My dad loved him, I didn't. We were only married a couple of years and most of that he was traveling. I didn't intend to get pregnant. I kept having major sugar fluctuations from dealing with his bullshit and lost the baby. It bothered me more than I thought it would."

"I'm sorry. I can't imagine."

She chewed carefully as she looked at a man expressing more understanding than most would have thought possible about a woman's trauma following a miscarriage. "Thank you, Tucker."

"I'm glad we met. Glad you're back in the States."

"I stayed in England because my dad wanted me there to represent the company. When I realized he wasn't interested in me doing anything but getting back with Peter, I quit. He begged me to come back and said there were three people he was switching to me to handle. I don't think this is what he had in mind, Tuck."

"Maybe not, but you still need to agree to see me again." He didn't push but nodded at her food. "You should eat more." He finished his own food and put the dishes back on the rolling table.

"I don't eat much, just more often." She added her own dishes and felt much better. Gritting her teeth, she checked her blood sugar. The readings weren't great but they were better.

She leaned back on the pillows and stared at the beautiful athlete, the man to whom half the women in the country probably had in mind as they masturbated. It was surreal to be here with him like this.

"Thank you for everything tonight, Tuck. If you hadn't come along when you did, I'd have gone into diabetic shock alone."

He kissed her forward before he pushed the cart into the hall. Shutting off the lamp, he climbed in bed beside her and tugged her to his chest.

"Tuck…"

"Hush, Sasha. Get some sleep."

Surprisingly, she did just that.

The next morning, Tuck woke her gently. The night before seemed like a dream until she rolled over and he found himself staring into her eyes.

Her eyes drifted over his body, dressed in slacks and dress shirt, mostly unbuttoned. A small sigh slipped from between her lips.

His grin made a little crinkle form between her eyes. "You said you have meetings starting at noon and we've got to get a regular meal in you before then. It's nine now, and though I'm all for stripping down and getting back in that bed with you, I'm going to make it your call."

Kicking her foot in a mini tantrum, she rolled over and pushed back the covers. Getting gracefully to her feet, she stretched and padded sleepily to the bathroom. A few moments later, he heard the beep of her blood sugar monitor.

Tuck wanted his dick somewhere in Sasha's body but knew she had work to do; play would have to wait until later. Rubbing his hands down his face, he finished getting dressed and turned on the television.

Flipping through the channels looking for ESPN, he thought he caught a quick flash of his own face and went back. There was a celebrity gossip show on and Sasha's picture filled the screen. It was a photo from a few years ago. Her hair was shorter and she was sporting a fake smile.

When a picture of Tuck in uniform appeared next to her, he turned up the volume, a sense of dread forming in his gut. The leading story was Tuck's last game, last touchdown, and last grope of a previously unknown woman in the stands.

The newscaster was excited to relate, "The woman has now been identified as Sasha Fowler-Baxter, ex-wife of international rugby star Peter Baxter."

A picture of Baxter appeared, Sasha's photo positioned between the two athletes. The implication was obvious and total bullshit.

"Details of the Fowler-Baxter divorce were kept from the public, though there were rumors of infidelity. Peter Baxter has repeatedly made it clear he wants his ex-wife back."

Running her hand through professionally straightened hair, the woman tried to assume a thoughtful expression. "One can only wonder how the four-time World Cup winner will react to reports from our sources that Sasha was brought to the hospital by Tucker Irvin after last night's game. Once she was released, he took her to a local hotel."

A front view of the hotel they were standing in showed on the screen and Tuck gritted his teeth.

A clip of the man who checked Sasha in the night before appeared. "She checked in late looking out of it and Irvin was carrying her bags. They went up together and he never came back down. So, you know."

Tuck leaned close to the television and growled. "You are fucking toast, little man."

"I take it our little rendezvous is blown?"

Chapter Four

Sasha stood behind him. She wore a towel while she dried her hair. Her phone vibrated on the bedside table and she approached it with a blank expression.

Tucker watched her scroll through text messages. Her entire demeanor changed. She chose a contact and put the phone to her ear.

"Who the hell do you think you are? *None of your goddamn business*, that's who I'm fucking. We are no longer married, you hypocrite. I will fuck who I want, when I want, as many times as I want and there isn't a goddamn thing you can do about it."

The man was screaming obscenities on the other end of the line and it made Tucker want to reach through the phone and choke the fucker out.

"Fine... you want to know? He is a *hundred times* better than you. So many explosive orgasms I *lost fucking count*, you asshole."

She ended the call and stormed into the bathroom, slammed the door, then opened it one second later. "I'm sorry. I shouldn't have..."

Tucker cut off Sasha's words with his mouth and carried her to the bed. Dropping to his knees, he ripped away the towel and buried his face between her legs.

He held her still with one hand while the other unbuttoned his shirt and pants. By the time he had his cock sheathed in a condom, she was coming, one hand fisted hard in his hair, the other in the sheets.

"Oh my god! *Tucker*... now."

He sucked her clit a final time, causing a chill to chase its way up her body, then stood and drove to her womb. She shoved the clothes away with her hands and feet and when he was free of the restrictions, he shoved her further up the bed, taking her hard and fast.

"I've wanted you since I opened my eyes. To bury myself in your beautiful pussy... to feel you come. I needed to taste you... to fuck you."

His strokes were fierce and she writhed, met his thrusts, her fingers digging into the muscles of his ass to pull him a little deeper, a little harder, inside her.

"Please don't stop. Don't stop. I'm coming!" She screamed his name and he fucked her harder. The motion of Tucker's hips was incredible and her torso met his with a sharp slap as the climax took over.

Then Tuck was squeezing her breasts as he came high and hot with a shout that echoed through the room. "You make me come so goddamn *hard*, Sasha. My body doesn't want to stop... it wants to keep going. Keep moving so I don't go soft. Take me... take everything I can give you."

He pulled out and threw the condom on the floor as he found the last one. Rolling it on, he pressed back inside, desperate to keep from softening before he could have her again. Pumping his hips into the slick heat sent a shiver racing up his spine.

"I want you on your knees, Sasha. Get on your fucking knees."

He withdrew and flipped her to her stomach, driving deep as he pulled her over his cock. Settling on his heels, he wrapped his arms around her and lifted her back to his chest. They were slippery with sweat and breathing hard.

His voice was barely recognizable as he ground out, "Ride me, Sasha."

Sasha impaled herself on his shaft and he lost his breath for a moment. Tucker held her hips, pulled her down with each thrust to increase the force. He kissed and bit along her shoulder and neck as he thrust into her body from underneath.

"It's too good... too much."

He ignored her. His touch was everywhere and she whimpered softly. He took her hand and slid it down to her folds. He pressed gently against her fingers, circling them over her clit. Sasha's head dropped back on his shoulder.

"I could fuck you forever. You feel incredible, Sasha." The tremors traveled from her body to his. "I love the way your pussy wraps so tight around my cock."

She turned her face and he kissed her. It changed everything. Her kiss tasted of warm, vibrant female with a hint of the toothpaste she'd used. Every inch of her smelled good and tasted better.

Suddenly, the moment slowed down and Tucker took in the layers of sensation this woman caused. The fact that they'd been fucking for more than an hour registered in a hazy part of his brain that would realize later it was a personal record.

The room smelled like sex, a blend of both of them that made him feel primal and powerful. He felt drops of sweat sliding down his back and legs. His hair was soaked with it. Their muscles vibrated from the physical exertion.

Tucker broke the kiss and stared into the warmest eyes he'd ever seen. The expression in them was something he'd never seen... but he could stare into them for the rest of his life.

"I know you need to come, Sasha. I can't wait to feel it. Let go. It's alright. Let go."

She lifted her hand and raked her fingers through his damp hair as her eyes drifted closed. His thrusts were deep and steady. Holding her across her body, he caressed her breast and lightly stroked her clit. With a sharp gasp, the walls of her pussy tightened around his cock like a fist.

This time she sighed his name.

Tuck kept moving until she went limp, and then let himself come. This time, he gave her everything he had, and he knew he'd need recovery time before he took her again.

He cupped her chin and lifted her face to his, kissing her as their orgasms ran their course.

"Thank you, Tucker." Her damp hair stuck to both of them as he lowered them to their sides on the bed.

He whispered, "No, Sasha... thank you."

For a long time, they stayed that way. His body cradling hers so their breathing could return to normal. They didn't speak and that was good because he had no idea what would have come out of his mouth.

Eventually, he knew he'd have to take care of the condom and pulled carefully from her snug warmth. Relieved that his legs agreed to support his weight, he led her to the bathroom tugged her into the shower.

They washed one another, kissed often, and Tucker marveled at the extreme physical and emotional bond he'd formed with a woman he barely knew.

Love had never been a big part of his life. He'd heard the words but never really believed them. For two decades, he'd focused on playing a game and having a good time. That part of his life was over now.

Something told him the next stage was going to begin a bit differently than he imagined.

****

After their shower, Tuck dressed and sat to watch Sasha dry her hair. She tilted her head to look at him in confusion.

"What are you doing?"

"I'm waiting for you. We're going out together. I'm not going first and looking like the conquering man-whore people are slapping on the back then leaving you to follow and deal with questions that imply you're *cheating* on your ex-husband. We walk out together like adults. I'm proud of our time together, and I won't let you be torn apart by the media because of it."

She stared at him and he realized it was probably the first time she hadn't had to deal with fallout alone. No matter where things went with Sasha, Tucker wasn't going to treat her the way the other assholes in her life had. She deserved better and she was damn well going to get it.

"Okay. Give me ten minutes." Her voice was cautious.

He watched her move around. She slipped into a gorgeous bra and panty set in pale gray. Then she tested her blood sugar and jotted the number in a small book before putting everything away in the leather case.

Sasha brushed out her hair, bent over to brush the underside, and flipped her head back. He went immediately hard as he watched it cascade down her back. She twisted it into a simple chignon at the base of her neck before stepping into a dark gray pantsuit.

After she stepped into her heels, he expected her to apply makeup. She didn't do more than apply moisturizer, lip balm, and follow that with a pale lipstick.

The woman was done. He called downstairs to the valet and asked them to have his SUV waiting.

She moved into the main space and started gathering her stuff. Dumping her Coach bag on the bed, she removed items she no longer needed. In a small pile, she put her essentials and added a bag that contained honey and another bottle of orange juice.

Seeing a woman straighten up a hotel room was a first for Tucker. When she finished, she picked up her purse and winter wear, and waited for him to join her.

"You look beautiful, Sasha."

"Thank you."

"You're riding with me. I assume you're my noon meeting?" She nodded with a smile. "Excellent, we can make it a lunch meeting then figure out what else you have to do today."

He held the door open and she stepped into the hall. As they rode the elevator down to the lobby, she started to shake. This time, he knew it wasn't her blood sugar dropping.

Stepping closer, he said quietly, "Nonchalant. You don't owe anyone a fucking explanation and we're going to pretend we haven't seen the story. Just smile, Sasha. Keep your hand on my arm like this. It's all about body language."

Then he tilted her chin up and gave her a soft kiss as the doors opened.

There were reporters near the front desk and he waved as he gently pulled Sasha with him through the lobby. Hotel guests took out camera phones. He thanked those fans who complimented his game or career but he didn't slow down.

If they hadn't been wearing sunglasses, the camera flashes just outside the hotel might have disoriented them. He pretended not to hear the questions asked.

His Hummer idled at the front of the curved drive and the valet staff ensured no one could get close to it. Tuck handed the valet a huge tip and both men's eyes went wide.

"Parking fee and extra for clearing the way. I'll be bringing her back later… remember me, alright?" They nodded with huge grins. "Have a good day."

He handed Sasha up into his vehicle and closed her door, smiling and waving to the reporters and fans as he jumped up in the driver's seat.

"See? Easy." Her smile was brilliant. "I'm taking you for food because we're not going to have a repeat of yesterday." Her eyes widened and he chuckled as he put it in gear and got moving.

Chapter Five

They had lunch at one of his favorite steak places and he started the process of actually getting to know Sasha while she went over business. In her portfolio, she withdrew several proposals from charities and apparel lines.

He didn't care about any of it.

"Pick what charities are important to you. I trust you. If you think the endorsement deals are something I should do, I'll do them… tell me when and where. What's your favorite color?"

****

Sasha hesitated, not understanding why he *wanted* to get to know her, why he seemed interested. It wasn't typical behavior with women he was linked to sexually. Anyone with a television or access to a computer knew that about him.

"Tuck, I live in California. You live here." He just stared at her and she sighed. "Green. Green is my favorite color."

"Why do you work with your father when you hate it?" She glanced up at him. "What is it you really want to do, Sasha?"

"How…?" Taking a moment to gather her thoughts, she said, "I don't *hate* what I do."

"You're lying. You hate dealing with a bunch of spoiled, self-proclaimed demi-gods with egos and bank accounts to match. You find the whole process of spinning their publicity to be another way of over-indulging them. You do not enjoy the spotlight and go out of your way to avoid it."

"I don't hate people with money. I'm one of them."

"You've come out of three high-profile relationships and don't even wear earrings. Your style is professional, not enticing. You're beautiful and extremely intelligent, yet you're doing a job you wouldn't have chosen for yourself." He shrugged. "I'm curious about what you *would* have chosen."

There was a long pause as she decided what to admit. "I paint."

Tucker grinned. "I can see you doing that. What do you paint?"

"Everything and anything. I've always done it, since I was little." Sasha looked at her hands folded in her lap. "I don't wear jewelry because I forget about it when I paint. Since I paint a lot, I simply haven't gotten in the habit of jewelry."

Glancing up at him, she added quietly, "You read me so well considering we've only known one another for five minutes."

Tuck leaned toward her over the secluded table they'd requested. "We've spent almost fifteen hours together, learning one another *very* well, Sasha. I'm an open book since I've lived in the public eye for twenty years."

He grimaced. "Not that all of that press was good but I'm used to it. You've only been in the media's crosshairs during highly publicized relationships where you try to remain unknown. When they end, you disappear off the grid."

She didn't know how to reply to the strangely respectful and insightful man sitting in front of her. He'd always been a good-time man. Life was a party and he had an endless supply of pretty young starlets to be his *plus one*.

"Why are you so curious about me, Tucker?"

Sitting back, a strange expression crossed his face. "I have no idea. You know, I've lived a shallow, self-absorbed life. Sure, I give to charity until it hurts, but that's because someone told me at the beginning it would be great for my image. I've spent half my life in a bubble, Sasha; focused on winning games and having a good time. I guess I'm wondering what to do with myself now."

"Your life doesn't have to change. You have more time to party now."

"Ouch. That stung a little." He stared at her and she could see him making the connections she was gently providing him. "You'll never have anything to do with me long-term. Will you, Sasha?" She shook her head slowly. "Fuck. So honest."

"You're a wicked temptation, Tucker. Good looking, charming, and *incredible* in bed." He smiled and she returned it. "If you want to hook up whenever you're in California, I wouldn't be able to resist. Honestly."

"I sense a *but* coming."

"You aren't the right man for me. When you earn your living playing a game, it's hard to see the big picture the rest of the world deals with. It's hard to grow up when every wish is fulfilled and every woman is willing."

She sat back and folded her hands on her crossed legs. "Though I understand why men remain perpetual Peter Pans, I'm tired of playing to it, making excuses for it, and being hurt by it. I don't belong in a world of excess and parties. Really, I never did and I hated every time my stupid choices landed me there."

"What if I could prove I didn't want that life anymore?"

"Tuck, suddenly you don't want today what you wanted yesterday? I must give better blowjobs than I thought." He sucked air sharply through his teeth and she grinned. "You're experiencing sexual afterglow. It'll wear off."

"I think you're wrong."

Changing the subject, Sasha got back on a business track. He paid the check and guided her from the restaurant a few minutes later.

Tuck was her primary reason to be in Green Bay so he took her from meeting to meeting, arranging his local endorsement deals and charity appearances. The reporters followed them.

The gossip magazines would overflow with stories of their "relationship" the next day. Their faces would be plastered everywhere.

In the end, it would be yet another famous athlete she was linked to in the press and she would still go home alone.

Around five o'clock, he stopped to pick up a bag of Italian food, stopped at the drug store, and drove back to her hotel. After dropping the keys in the valet's hand with another tip, he entered the lobby with the bag in one hand, hers in his other.

Approaching the front desk, he requested to speak to the night manager.

The moment the man appeared, he blushed red, and looked around for reporters. One was skulking behind the column at the end of the desk. Tucker leaned one elbow on the granite surface.

"I see you remember us. You are the single most unprofessional employee I've ever seen. You work in a hotel, where many people… not just myself and Miss Fowler… expect you to conduct yourself with a sense of decorum, to respect our privacy, and not make salacious comments to the press about things you don't fucking know."

"Sir, your language…"

Tucker stood to his full height and gave the man a stare that had shaken seasoned football players for two decades. "I wasn't *done*. You will lose your job and likely not find work in another hotel. I can see you're just waiting to give your next statement without an ounce of shame. My attorney will be in touch so I suggest you choose your words carefully."

He turned and guided Sasha to the elevators. She didn't speak but smiled as they rode up together and entered the room.

Inside, he placed their food on the table, pulled her to him, and backed her against the wall. While he stole her sanity with his kiss, he undressed them and rolled on a condom. Tucker followed her down to the bed and she sighed as he entered her in one thrust.

Their cell phones rang sometimes but they ignored them.

Tuck fucked her for a long time before he made her eat and gave her a chance to catch her breath. They showered together again and she thought he would leave, but he didn't.

Over the next couple of hours, he took her on every surface and in every position until she was wiped out mentally, physically, and emotionally. He tucked them into bed and she passed out. At four in the morning, he made love to her again, slow and easy.

It was so beautiful she felt like crying… but she didn't.

When he fell back to sleep with his arm and leg thrown over her, she watched him sleep. It was impossible to ignore how beautiful he was.

Life was never simple.

Years ago, she'd given up on finding the kind of happiness he made her want. She wished she were the type who could stay with Tuck despite her fears about history repeating itself. That she wouldn't freak out when he wasn't with her, wondering who was keeping him company.

Everything she'd told him was true. He *was* tempting and she worried she might have grown attached to him already. How it was possible in such a short time, Sasha wasn't sure.

She knew she had to nip it in the bud before it got worse.

****

The sun shone through the window the next morning. Tuck opened his eyes and found himself alone in bed. He could still smell Sasha on his skin, as well as the combined scents of their last time. It was highly erotic and not something he was used to.

There was a note on the pillow beside him.

"Tuck... I didn't want to disturb you. You know, that's not the whole truth. I hope, when you examine our time together, you'll find it was as wonderful as I do and understand why this is all it can be.

"Thank you for coming to my rescue. I'd also like to thank you for being magnificent in bed. I've never felt so good in my life. You are a leader among men in many areas, it seems.

"I wish you all the best in your retirement. You've had an outstanding career and your body has earned a break. I'm going to have someone else assigned as your agent. I'm experiencing momentary weakness watching you sleep so I'm heading home today to remove the temptation of coming back to you. Goodbye, Tuck. ~Sasha."

Tuck read the note then got out of bed, taking in the hotel room. All evidence of Sasha was gone. He was floored. A woman like Sasha didn't run.

For the first time, Tuck found himself alone the morning after... and it hadn't been his choice. He showered, dressed, and headed downstairs.

When the valet brought his Hummer, he asked about Sasha.

"She left before dawn, sir. We had a car pick her up in the parking garage. She... looked upset, Mr. Irvin." Tuck nodded and gave the man another huge tip. "You don't have to tip me, sir. I won't say a word to anyone. You can count on me."

Tucker took the young man in more fully. There was no doubt he worked hard and had respect for others. His nametag said *David*. He was well groomed and articulate. "You happy with your job here? At the hotel I mean?"

David smiled with a small shrug. "It's alright. I don't mind it."

"How would you like to work with my personal assistant? It wouldn't be glamorous and you'd still have to hustle."

His dark brown eyes lit up. "I'd be honored."

"Excellent. I have a good feeling about you. My assistant has been begging for someone who can help her out." He withdrew a business card and wrote Christy's contact email on the back. "I'll let her know to expect your call in the next few days."

"Thank you, Mr. Irvin."

With a nod, he slid into his SUV and pulled away from the hotel with a wave. By the time he was halfway to his estate, he had to grin.

Sasha forgot one important thing about him. The one thing that set him apart as a quarterback for so many years.

Tuck never fucking quit.

If he wanted something, he went after it hard until he had it. Though this was the first time in his life that drive had applied to a woman, he wasn't going to question it.

He would go on the *offense*, drive after drive, until her defense *fell apart*.

Chapter Six

Arriving at her beach house in California later that afternoon, Sasha found it stocked as she'd instructed. She made herself a protein shake and went to shower.

She needed to give herself a little pep talk. Leaving Tucker at the hotel had been harder than she would have imagined and she hated how vulnerable she felt. She didn't handle vulnerable well.

He had a much stronger effect on her than she cared to think about.

"You're an idiot, Sasha. The man is *famous* for his sexual escapades. How do you think it would have ended if you hadn't left?"

Talking to herself as she stripped, she stared at her view of the Pacific. Climbing under the hot spray from multiple jets, she stood there for a long time, letting the hard streams massage the soreness and tension from her body.

The soreness was the result of hours upon hours of porn level sex with a body that was unused to the activity. The tension came from leaving Tucker in Green Bay.

With a sigh, she performed her usual rituals before drying off and crashing in her bed naked. She needed a nap and hoped she'd actually be able to slow her thoughts down to make it possible.

Surprisingly, she fell asleep quickly.

Hours later, she put on yoga clothes and headed out on her deck. She almost dropped her phone when a text came in from Tuck.

"Not cute, Sasha. I'll be in California in a few days. Plan on seeing me."

She didn't respond since she had no clue how to respond to that. Curling up in a padded chair, she stared at the ocean, lost in thought. The thought of what he could do to her heart scared her to death. There was no denying the pleasure she felt about seeing him again. Every cell in her body focused so intently on him she could almost feel his touch.

Sasha shook herself into the moment with a mental slap.

"Oh my god... you did not fall for that man in less than two days! No way. You'd be an idiot to do that!" Realizing she was talking aloud when she was the only one around made her feel worse. "The cats are coming. You keep this shit up and you'll be old and bitter with a houseful of cats. You need to snap the fuck out of it."

She went to work out and pushed herself harder than usual. Looking at her body in the mirrored wall, she sighed. She wasn't as tight as she used to be.

The treadmill, elliptical, Pilates, and yoga... none of them worked as well as they once had. It was going to come down to a personal trainer. Mix things up and see if she'd get better results.

After she rinsed in the shower, she dressed in loose cotton sleep pants, a tank top, and pulled her hair into a wild bun on top of her head. Her studio was off her bedroom, a sun-filled room with three walls of windows that faced the beach.

"What are you doing? I'm bored. Thinking about our time together."

Before she could question her need to interact with him, she replied. *"Just worked out and I'm going to go paint. Don't torture me."*

A minute later, her phone buzzed again. *"Torture? Here I was thinking you enjoyed yourself. My ego is shattered... LOL."*

Grinning, she sat in a thickly padded chair near the window. *"Don't fish for compliments... they jump in the boat. Why don't you go out?"*

The tone of his next text startled her. *"YOU are not HERE to go out with, Sasha. I can't believe you didn't say goodbye."*

"Tuck, you don't have to put up with boredom or loneliness... you have people, baby! Like H&R Block. I hate goodbyes."

"You called me baby... in a text. Does that mean we're going steady?"

The man was diabolical. He knew that wasn't how she meant it. *"Going steady? Um... I don't know if people do that anymore."* Thinking for a moment, she added, *"We're friends with benefits, I guess."*

"Sasha, I don't want people. I want YOU. I don't want to be your friend with benefits."

She frowned at her phone screen. Of *course* he wanted a friend with benefits! All men wanted a damn friend with benefits.

How was she having this conversation... via text no less? *"Tuck, I don't know what that means. You barely know me."*

Tucker was not done shocking her. *"I want to spend next weekend with you. Send me your address."*

The weekend... *in four days*? Was he insane? She had no defenses against him yet. *"That is a horrible idea, Tuck."* To have him in her house, at the beach, able to touch him in warm weather. Holy shit that sounded good.

He called her on her shit, *"Don't be a chicken. Send me your address."*

"Tuck, you are being unreasonable. Honestly... bad idea." She ignored the sweat gathering on her back and under her arms. The moisture between her legs wasn't sweat.

"It's a great idea and you know it. I NEED to touch you. You NEED me to touch you. Send. Me. Your. Address." When she didn't reply immediately, he sent another message. *"Think about every moment we were together in Green Bay and send me your fucking address."*

She did it. The moment Sasha hit 'send' she about had a panic attack.

"You won't regret it. I'll see you in a few days." Sasha knew she *would* regret it. Another taste of him would only make it worse in the end.

Still, the chance to see him... to touch him... to have his body on her again? She'd deal with the pain after. The memories would have to be worth it.

Standing at the window, Sasha hugged her waist with her arms. For a long time, she just stood there thinking. She knew she couldn't get away from the subject her hands itched to sketch. Mentally kicking herself, she pulled out a wide blank canvas that wasn't very tall. Setting it up on the easel, she grabbed her charcoals and let her hands move where they wanted to go.

In the middle of the night, she stepped back and stared at the fruition of labor.

The bottom of the canvas was the mattress. It was Tuck as he'd looked when she left the bed. A sleeping Greek god unaware that she was sneaking away like a coward.

It was the best human subject piece she'd done in years. Her anger and embarrassment after her divorce leaked into her work. The pieces she painted since then were dark and turbulent.

This one filled her with peace. Though it might end up being short-lived peace, she decided to take it, to hold it to her, and enjoy it.

Releasing a deep breath, she stood and went to make herself a snack. After she cleaned up the kitchen, she climbed naked between cool sheets and listened to the ocean outside her window.

At four in the morning, she woke in the midst of climax with her hand between her legs. She cursed her subconscious and struggled to find sleep again.

She gave up before dawn and walked into her office to catch up on any correspondence she'd missed. There was an email from her father asking when she planned to return to work. She'd forwarded the contracts and other documents on Tuck's behalf; He wanted to know why she didn't bring them herself.

The only response she could give him without lying was that she wanted and needed time off. When he tried calling, she ignored it and went to shower.

She turned off the jets and heard the doorbell ring. Quickly wrapping a robe around her wet body, she ran through the house to answer it. The plate glass windows along the front showed a Towncar leaving the driveway.

Tuck stood staring at her. He wore cotton cargo pants, a t-shirt, sunglasses, and sneakers. He was holding a small duffle bag.

Oh my sweet lord... he is so fucking beautiful.

Sasha moved in a daze to the front door and unlocked it with a million questions on her lips. She didn't get a chance to ask a single one.

Chapter Seven

Tuck lifted her, slammed and locked the door, and dropped his bag on the floor of her foyer.

Putting her against the nearest wall, he kissed her so possessively, she felt physically marked by it. Claimed as *his* so completely that she knew this was going to be the man who would ultimately shred her heart.

To hell with it.

Her arms locked around him and she slid her fingers through his hair. Their foreheads touched as he took several deep breaths.

"Fuck, you smell good. I couldn't wait. Knowing where you were kept me up all night. Knowing I could kiss you, touch you… if I got on a fucking plane." He kissed her again and moved her higher on the wall so she could wrap her legs around his waist.

He didn't hesitate to press his body into hers and she gasped softly at the intimate contact. That fast, she was ready for him.

I will take every second with him and chastise myself for it later.

Tuck's kiss was gentler this time. He made love to her mouth until she started moving against him. Sliding his hands under her ass, he lifted her easily.

"Which way?"

She motioned toward her bedroom and used the time to touch him. She didn't think she'd ever tire of touching him.

In her bedroom, he set her on her feet beside the bed. Stripping his t-shirt over his head, she stared in newfound amazement at the sculpted expanse of his chest and shoulders.

Large hands, always so steady on the football field, shook slightly as he reached for the buckle of his belt. Sasha put her hands over his and moved them away, taking their place. He took condoms from his wallet and dropped them on her bedside table.

He toed off his shoes and she flowed gracefully to one knee to remove his socks and pull the rest of his clothes away. Running her palms up the backs of his legs, he locked them but not before she felt the vibration of the thick muscle.

Leaning forward, she kissed his thigh and he groaned, his hands fisting in her hair.

"I can't bear it, Sasha… I *cannot* bear it. I need you too fucking much."

She nodded and stood so Tuck could untie her robe and push it away.

"More beautiful than my brain allowed me to remember…" He sat on the edge of her bed, gathered her between his knees, and rested his head on her sternum. Their skin was warm where they touched. "You haven't said a single word. Are you okay?"

"I can't believe you're here, Tuck. I'm glad you came." She cupped his face, raised it, and kissed him, doing her best to hide the intensity of her emotions.

He licked against her lips and tongue with his own. When he couldn't wait anymore, he wrapped his arms around her and flipped her around to land on the bed. Warm palms stroked down her body, plumped her breasts, thumbs flicking over the puckered nipples. When he moved as if to lower his shoulders between her legs, she grabbed his biceps.

"I can't bear it, Tuck… please. Now."

Staring at her for a long moment, he nodded and reached for a condom. He moved over her, settled into the cradle of her body, and notched the head of his cock at the entrance of her pussy.

"I missed you, Sasha…" Tucker surged forward and she arched into him with a long moan. His forehead on her shoulder, he whispered, "Fuck… I need a minute."

Sasha lifted his face and saw the tension that furrowed his brow. His green eyes were dark with passion. "Fuck me, Tucker… we'll go slower next time."

Without looking away, he settled more firmly over her body, his weight on his elbows. When he pulled back, she tugged her lower lip between her teeth. The return stroke made her body respond as if they'd been lovers for years.

Her eyes drifted closed and she pulled him to her for a kiss. "Drop lower, Tuck."

"I'm too heavy…"

"I need you closer."

He moved his hands over her head, into her hair, and put his face against her neck. Tucker pulled back, using shorter and harder thrusts. Tremors started in her torso and spread out over her arms and legs. Small kisses planted from her shoulder to her ear made her arch for more like a cat.

She wrapped around him completely. "You feel amazing."

Without any warning, she came after a few minutes, the vibration of her body harder as she tightened on the length of his dick. Lifting his face, he stared into her eyes as he moved only his hips and watched her come.

The climax happened in slow motion and she didn't believe she'd ever felt a moment so fully. "Come with me, Tuck…"

He didn't look away. Several harder thrusts that felt almost too good and he released the insane tension she'd sensed. It went on for a long time and when he pumped the last of his come into the condom, they went still.

"I feel so much better." Adjusting their position, he sank to the core of her and she sighed. "I want to crawl in your body with you… this is as close as I can get to that. Does that sound insane?" She shook her head.

"I'm sorry I left without saying goodbye, Tucker."

"I missed the way you smell. The way you taste… how it feels to have you wrapped around my cock. What you look like when you're about to come. How smug I feel when you do because I have to focus every moment with you. No half-assed measures, no bullshit."

Strong fingers stroked her hair back from her face. "I know you're mature and too good for a man like me, Sasha… but I want you *any-fucking-way*. I have a golf tournament in two days in Phoenix. I can't get out of it but after that, I'm coming back. We're going to work out our hang-ups and shit until we come up with a workable plan."

Sasha couldn't think with him so deep inside her. Every thought fled as she stared into his eyes. Eyes that looked at her differently than any other man had. Anything she said would give her away; He'd know how vulnerable she was in regards to him.

She was afraid, but she'd be damned if she let him see it. She nodded and he smiled.

Reaching for another condom, he pulled from her body long enough to re-sheath his cock. Then he was moving slow and deep as his hands roamed her skin.

"I'm going to take you again and then we'll shower." Her response was a deep kiss and it struck her that she'd never kissed a man so often during sex. Lifting his head, he stroked his fingers along the side of her face. "You have the most gorgeous eyes. They're lighter now… like honey."

Just like that, Sasha accepted the fact that she was in love with a man she'd known for three days.

You are such an idiot.

Then she was lost in the sensation of his touch, his attention, and there was no more thinking.

Chapter Eight

For two days, they walked on the beach, ate meals naked, and made love constantly. Tucker admitted his lack of experience in conversation with a woman but Sasha didn't judge him.

He eventually took her in almost every room of her house.

On the morning he had to leave for the golf tournament, he found her studio. Coming in from the living room to grab his forgotten watch, he turned the knob, and had it open before he realized what room he was entering.

Sasha mumbled behind him, "*Fuck*."

His eyes found her sketch of him on the easel near the bank of windows. Walking slowly across the room, he approached the canvas with his mind buzzing. The detail was incredible. He wasn't educated about art but even he knew she was talented. Several paintings decorated the rooms in her house and when pressed she shyly admitted to being the artist.

The fact that he immediately recognized the moment was not lost on him. No one had ever drawn him before, and that Sasha had done so from memory spoke of an emotional element she'd been hiding.

She rushed to play it off and downgrade the significance. "As an *artist*, I have to sketch or paint what comes to…"

Tuck turned and took her in his arms.

"Hush." He kissed her. He wanted her to feel the turbulence inside him. Only when she was moaning did he lift his mouth from hers. "You've avoided talking about what's happening between us. You're more affected by all of this than you're admitting to *either* of us."

She opened her mouth to deny it and he kissed her again.

"Be prepared when I get back. We need to talk. You're not avoiding me anymore."

"Tucker…"

"Sasha. Stop it. Do you think you're alone in how you feel?" A small frown appeared between her eyes. "This is new for me, too."

"You aren't good for me."

His arms tightened around her. "Don't judge me based on the assholes in your past and I won't judge you by the casual relationships in mine. This is different and you *know* it."

Their kiss went on for a long time. At her ear, he whispered, "I won't lie to you and I won't hurt you. Give me a chance to prove that. Say you will." She nodded and even though he could feel her hesitation, he counted it as a win.

She walked him to the front door. A car was waiting to take him to LAX. As he picked up his bag and slipped sunglasses over his eyes, he took in her body language. Dressed in a tank top and shorts, her arms were crossed tightly over her chest her tension obvious. Sasha tugged her plump lower lip between her teeth.

"Come here." She stepped into his arms. "You know I'm coming back, right?" He felt her small nod against his chest and chuckled. "Rest up, honey. You're going to need it."

After one more scorching kiss, he walked outside and got in the car. He rolled down the window and watched as a slight breeze in the open door swirled her hair around her torso.

"I'll see you in a couple of days, Sasha."

"Okay. Travel safe."

"I'll call you when I land." She nodded and he sat back as the car pulled away. That woman was about to have her entire world shaken up and Tucker couldn't wait to get started.

****

Sasha watched until the car disappeared at the top of the drive then closed the door. Walking through the house to her studio, she stood in front of her sketch.

There was no doubt that it was good. It was also filled with her emotional attachment to Tucker Irvin. She sighed heavily and thought about their last conversation.

"I *want* to believe you, Tucker."

Every cell in her body wanted him... *craved* him. The thoughts and feelings bombarding her peace of mind were unfamiliar and confusing. He'd been gone for less than ten minutes and she missed him already.

When her phone rang, she took it from her pocket, and grimaced when she realized it was her father. After a small pause, she answered.

"Dad, I told you I needed time off. What's so urgent?"

She listened as he launched into an overly loud speech about his retirement and how much had to be done before he felt comfortable leaving his children in charge.

Pressing her fingers to her temple, she interrupted. "Oh my god, stop. I'll come in this afternoon."

"Why can't you come in now?"

Her father's resemblance to a spoiled child struck her again. He wanted everything his way and tended to throw tantrums when he didn't get it. Too many years spent around over-indulged athletes had taken its toll. How her mother tolerated him was a mystery to her children.

"I'm at the beach house, not the condo. I said I'd be there, Dad." Without another word, she hung up and ignored it when he called her back.

For a couple of hours, Sasha straightened her house and made a grocery list after eating a diabetic-friendly breakfast. Her blood sugar was off and she took an insulin pill. If she couldn't get it regulated, she'd have to return to shots.

Every time she saw a text from Tucker come through on her phone, she replied without questioning the way they were acting like teenagers in their first relationship.

It was hard to remember the last time she'd smiled so much.

She showered and dressed, anxious to get the *office visit of great urgency* over with so she could get back to painting. Deciding on a black skirt suit with a silk top that mirrored her eye color, she stepped into matching high heels.

Slinging her bag over her shoulder, she walked down the short flight of stairs to her garage. The sight of her 1967 Karmann Ghia convertible filled her with anticipation and she settled happily behind the wheel.

It had only been driven a few times in the years she'd been in England, mostly when she came here on vacation without Peter to get some distance from his stupidity. In the years they were together, Peter never knew the location of her beach house. He hadn't been allowed to invade her sanctuary.

Her personal interactions with professional athletes were turbulent and short-lived. The media coverage lasted much longer than the relationships.

The first was a soccer player who had a complete meltdown during the World Cup. That night, Benson smacked her around and she'd had no choice but to kick his ass. Since the entire incident took place in the hallway of the hotel, it was captured on someone's cell phone.

After losing the playoffs, her hockey player second boyfriend actually told the press that he blamed Sasha's presence at the games for their losses. The fact that he'd developed a reputation for choking long before they started dating hadn't crossed Jakofski's mind.

Peter had been a mistake from the very beginning but her father continually put them together until she caved under the dual pressure.

She hadn't asked for a dime from any of her relationships but attorneys for Benson and Jakofski had worried about her giving interviews to the press. She signed non-disclosure agreements and received checks for a couple of million after their breakups.

With Peter, she took their townhouse in London. For keeping her silence about the miscarriage and his incessant philandering, his lawyer took her NDA and made sure Sasha received three million for pain and suffering.

She had money from her parents but it was her *relationship money* that had purchased her house and restored her car to factory spec. Wise investments in small business instead of property and the stock market meant she still had a healthy financial portfolio.

Raising the garage door, she put her hair in a bun and slipped on her shades. Heading in the direction of the city, the top was down and the sun was shining. A few miles from the office, she stopped at her favorite French bakery and loaded up on pastries for the staff.

Less than two hours after leaving her house on the beach, Sasha pulled into the parking garage. Stepping from the elevator, staff greeted her with smiles and hugs. When she handed them the three huge boxes of baked goods, they complained about their waistlines with happy sighs.

More than her tendency to spoil the employees of their agency, she knew they missed the calming effect she had on her father and brothers. She was the youngest, and being the only girl caused the Fowler men to tone it down. Sasha had been a surprise child for her parents; her youngest brother was already ten when she was born.

Her corner office was cheerful and bright when she opened the blinds and plugged in her laptop. Her assistant entered a moment later with mail and urgent messages. Kelly caught her up on the office drama and told her Collie wanted to see her when he got back to the office.

Collie Fowler was a man's man. Big, loud, and always the life of the party, he'd been a sports agent before anyone even knew what that meant.

His work in the seventies and eighties changed the way athletes were compensated for putting their bodies on the line game after game. Most of his clients were football and basketball players, but his reputation brought him business from all over the world.

Collie Junior — they called him CJ — was like their dad in many ways. He was brash and balls to the wall in regards to the company. Where it really counted, the two men couldn't be more different. Seventeen years older than Sasha, he'd been more of a dad than her actual father, who had been off traveling more than he was home.

CJ had been married to the same woman for almost thirty years. They had three kids whom Sasha loved hanging out with because they were only a few years younger than she was. As her oldest brother, was extremely protective, and had gone toe to toe with their father over the men Collie thought were right for her.

Nathan, her middle brother, was thirteen years older. He was a sweet and gentle human being. Very young female clients typically ended up in his charge because he put them at ease without making them feel intimidated like Collie or CJ often unknowingly did. She adored him but wondered when he'd get over his divorce. His son was spoiled rotten to compensate for Nate's perpetual sadness over what he'd lost.

Aaron was the youngest. Sasha loved him, but couldn't quite forgive the fact that he still hung out with her ex-husband. It infuriated her mother and oldest brothers as well.

With three failed marriages behind him, he showed no sign of growing up in the near future. They butted heads constantly — usually over Peter. Aaron liked to tell her she was overly emotional, and she liked to remind him that he wouldn't recognize an emotion if it bit him on the ass.

Just as she answered the last of her emails, CJ poked his head around her door.

"Sassy girl! Don't you look pretty as a damn picture?" Sasha stood and ran around her desk. He caught her up and swung her around. "You've lost weight. How you feeling? Mom said you had an attack...

ended up in a hospital in Green Bay."

She searched his face and he smiled.

"Honey, you are a grown-ass woman. If you want to hole up in a hotel with Tuck Irvin, I think you're smart enough to figure it all out. I'm serious though... how are you feeling?"

"CJ, I've missed you. Do you have a few minutes to talk?"

He closed the door behind him and led her to the small seating area in her office. They sat side by side, angled toward one another with him holding her hand.

Taking a deep breath, she met his eyes. "Peter is calling, emailing, and texting constantly. I don't want to work here anymore." Saying nothing because he had always been able to read her, CJ knew there was more. "I think I'm truly in love with a man for the first time in my life... and I've only known him a few days." She swallowed hard. "I look like a tramp in the media."

Her brother's brows shot up. "Good lord, those are some heavy damn subjects. Let me break them down one at a time. First, I'll have a conversation with Aaron and Dad. I know they aren't leaving you alone about your ex and you're too sweet to tattle. Then I'm going to have a discussion with Peter. That shit is going to stop."

CJ patted the top of her hand. "I also know you hate it here and I don't know why the fuck you stick around." It was Sasha's turn to weather the shock of his words and he grinned. "I wish you'd focus on your painting. Dad's been pimping you out to hot single athletes for years and that isn't what you need in your life."

"Jesus, CJ... that one stung."

"You know it's true. Assigning you to Benson and Jakofski at the start of their careers assured him they'd stick with us when they shot up in earning potential. As for Peter, well, that was Aaron and Dad looking to settle him down. I didn't like it then and I like it less now."

He stroked her hair back from her face. "You've given enough. You're a private, talented woman with plenty of resources to do what you want. Don't waste any more time."

Sasha's eyes filled with tears and she knew how fortunate she was to have him in her life.

"As for Tucker, he's a good man at the end of his career. I know what you're worried about. Only time will tell, but most men *do* grow up eventually." He glanced away for a moment before meeting her eyes again. His voice was cautious when he asked, "Did Lana ever tell you I cheated on her?"

Sasha's mouth dropped open. "No, CJ... not you."

He nodded and looked out the window. "Yeah... me. I was so fucking full of myself. Ten years into our marriage and bored with being a husband and dad. I was a *man among men* and all that bullshit. I bought into my own publicity and nearly lost the best part of who I was."

One big hand rubbed across the back of his neck. "She forgave me but it took her *years* to trust me again. It was a long time before I could make love to her without knowing she cried silently the moment that she thought I was asleep. I hated myself. I've never screwed up again."

"I never even knew you guys had a rough patch."

He nodded. "She swore me to secrecy. It was a condition of her taking me back — that no one could ever know that she hadn't been enough. I took my beautiful, brilliant wife and turned her into a woman filled with self-doubt about her looks and her sexuality."

Nothing could have shocked her more than seeing tears slide down CJ's face. "I'm fifty now. I look back on those couple of months as the most shame-filled of my life. To this day, every so often, I see her think about it and know it still hurts her." His eyes, so like her own, closed briefly. "I did that to the only woman I have ever loved."

Reaching out, he cupped the side of her face. "Love is a leap of faith, Sasha. You step out with no guarantees, no safety net, and no backup plan. You do your best and hope the other person does, too. It wouldn't surprise me if the first time you really fell in love, it hit you like a freight train. I say run with it."

Sasha hugged him fiercely. "I don't think you could possibly know how much I love you, CJ. Will you be mad if I leave the company?"

"Nope... but the staff will. We torture the shit out of them when you aren't here." He grinned and stroked her cheek with the back of his knuckles. "I'll let you get back to work. I've missed you being close. Lana and the brats ask about you constantly."

"How is everyone?"

"Joel just finished his residency so we'll start seeing him again. Erin intends to come on board as one of our lawyers. I told her she is insane and to talk to you first. I can't wait to tell them you're back. Are you staying at the beach house?" Sasha nodded. "Good, we'll make plans."

After one more hug, he was gone.

She returned to work and an hour later Aaron burst through the door. "Sassafras! How you doing? Dad should be back in a couple of hours. I need to eat, wanna grab food with me?"

A quick glance at her watch reminded her she needed to eat. She picked up her bag with a nod. They took the elevator down with Aaron rambling about one of his clients. Once they left the building, they walked a block to her favorite Irish bar and restaurant.

She settled into the booth across from Aaron and tried to decide what meal would suit her current mood. Suddenly, someone scooted in to sit beside her. Glancing up, she met Peter's eyes briefly and glared at her brother across the table.

"I will *never* forgive you for this, Aaron. You had no right." His eyes widened but he didn't say anything. Looking at her ex-husband, she hissed, "Let me out of this booth right now."

Peter shook his head and leaned closer. His thick cockney accent flavored his words. Once upon a time, she'd found it charming. "Love, we need to talk. You made your point. Stop being difficult." She tried to shove him out so she could leave but he didn't budge.

"I'm not letting you leave… I said we need to talk."

Chapter Nine

Aaron used his voice meant to calm her down. "Sasha, he just wanted to talk to you for a minute. Can't you sit still and talk for just a minute? Come on now, be reasonable." He reached across for her hand and Sasha snatched it from him. "Sasha, don't be mad."

His *calm down* voice had exactly the opposite effect on her.

Glancing around the restaurant, she spotted Ben behind the bar and called his name. The mountain of a man approached the table and smiled at Sasha.

"How ye doin', lass? Haven't seen ye in here in a good long while."

Ben was six-seven with long dark red hair and a trimmed beard. His gray eyes were always merry. His gentle giant demeanor was at odds with the numerous tattoos that weren't concealed by his snug black t-shirt.

"I'm sorry to bother you, but I'd like to get out of this booth, Ben. Right now, please."

Ben glanced between the two men and smiled dangerously. "Aaron, ye helpin' a man keep yer sister where she don' care ta be?" He gave her brother a *tsk tsk*. "Gents, we can go easy 'bout this or we can go hard." He shrugged as if he didn't care what they chose. "Either way, ye're lettin' Miss Sasha out or I'll be makin' ye let her out."

Peter sneered and pointed his finger at the big man. "This is no business of yours, boy."

Ben grabbed the hand and twisted, tugging gently but continually until Peter had no choice but to follow where his stressed hand was being led.

Her ex-husband yelled, "Do you know who the *fuck* I am?"

"Aye, I know who ye are. Don' much care, boyo. When a lady says she don' wanna be sittin' and talkin', ye move yer arse out the goddamn way!" He easily held Peter away as Sasha scrambled from the booth.

"Thank you, Ben. I'm sorry for the trouble."

He shook Peter by the neck. "No trouble at'all, lass. Ye come next time an' I'll have the girls make yer favorite, yeah?"

Picking up her bag, Sasha nodded and left the bar at a fast pace. She was just outside when Aaron caught up to her.

"Sasha! Why are you being so fucking crazy?"

Whirling on her brother, she shoved him with both hands in the center of his chest. "You have *no idea* what you're talking about as usual, Aaron. When are you going to grow up?"

She turned to go and Peter stood there, rubbing his wrist.

"Leave me *alone*, Peter. You weren't this concerned when I left."

"I'm not leavin', Sasha. You belong to me. No one else is gonna touch you."

"Ah. I see. It's about wanting to piss all over what you consider your territory. It's none of your *business*, Peter. We're divorced, damn it. You fucking *cheated* on me for the umpteenth time, in our bed, a month after my miscarriage." She shook her head. "What should I think about you? *I can't stand you.* Leave me alone."

She went to move past him and he grabbed her arm, gripping painfully hard as he tried to kiss her.

"Aaron, do something, Christ!" She couldn't get any distance between them.

"Peter, let her go. Come on, you need to cool down. You can't manhandle my sister, dude." He grabbed Peter's shoulder and the back of the other man's fist came up to crack him full force in the temple. Aaron dropped like a stone.

Sasha was shaken so hard that her teeth clacked together as Peter yelled in her face. "You are *mine*. No one leaves me! It was humiliatin' and now you're fuckin' somebody else? I don't think so, darlin' wife."

He had her wedged between his body and the concrete wall, his mouth over hers, trying to press his tongue between her lips. He forced her mouth open while he ground his pelvis into hers.

Fury unlike anything she'd never known boiled up inside her. She kneed him in the dick as hard she could and he yelped as he wrapped a hand around her throat.

"You're gonna fuckin' *learn*."

The pain at the back of her scalp was awful but she would fight until she passed out. Bringing up one hand, she reached between his legs to grip his balls. With no hesitation, she tightened her fist and twisted. Part of her relished his scream.

"Take your hands off me, Peter."

Instead, he wrapped both hands around her neck and squeezed. "You bitch. You always were a fuckin' *bitch*, Sasha."

Then he went flying to the side and Sasha gasped, hauling air into her lungs gratefully. She slid down the wall and landed on her ass. A huge form crouched in front of her and she smiled at Ben.

"Thank you... once again."

For a long moment, he didn't say anything. "Don' like men who mistreat women. Yer brother not know the score?" She shook her head. "Ye okay?" To her complete humiliation, she started crying. He helped her to her feet and hugged her tight. "There, there, lass. It's alright now."

The ambulance arrived and the paramedics checked her out as she tried to stop the sadness bubbling up inside. Aaron sat groggily a few feet away holding an ice pack against his temple.

Peter was still out and being loaded on a gurney. It looked like he had a broken nose as well as two black eyes and a swollen jaw. His well-known vanity was going to suffer when he saw the result of Ben's huge hands.

Brushing aside the paramedics, Sasha grabbed her bag. She wanted to get her laptop and go home. Enough was enough. The moment she stood, she knew she was about to have another repeat of her first night in Green Bay.

As she started to fall, her youngest brother shouted, "She's diabetic!"

Chapter Ten

Sasha woke up in the emergency room of the nearest hospital and rubbed her head. It was pounding and her throat was killing her.

Aaron sat in a chair beside the bed with their mother standing in front of him. She didn't raise her voice but her children knew when she was truly angry.

"Your sister comes before your drinking buddy. That piece of shit better not come within a mile of my daughter or I will personally hire someone to castrate him and sauté his cock with wine and wild mushrooms."

That's an image I didn't need in my head. Thanks, Mom.

"You tricked your own sister into a situation that could have ended up far worse. We're not going to talk for a little while. Grow the fuck up, son."

Glancing at Sasha, he saw she was awake. "I'm so sorry. Please forgive me."

"I love you but I'm pissed. You need to let me cool off, Aaron."

The brother she'd always thought didn't have a bone in his body that could feel shame stood and kissed her cheek. "I'll make this up to you. I won't let you down again."

Then he left.

Deirdre Fowler hurried to her side and cupped her cheeks with cool hands. "I should have called a family meeting. I let your father bully you. I let your brother think it was fine that he hung out with your despicable ex-husband. I didn't protect you and I'm sorry."

"I'm okay, Mom."

There was a sudden commotion and Tucker slid to a stop at the opening of the small room. He came around the bed, smoothed her hair back, and kissed the corner of her mouth. He wore cargo shorts, a polo, and sunglasses were pushed back on his head.

He smelled like sunshine and coconut.

"I got here as fast as I could. Came off the course and it was on every TV in the clubhouse. Someone caught the whole thing." He kissed her lips lightly.

"I'm sorry you had to leave the tournament."

"You'll have to go everywhere with me so I know you're eating." He stroked his fingertips through her hair. "I almost had a coronary trying to get here. Other than that, I'm good." His face went hard. "He's going to pay, Sasha. I'm going to pound that motherfucker into nothing the moment he's out on bail. He had no right to hurt you."

Lifting her hand, she grabbed his. "Look at me, Tuck." He was practically vibrating with tension. "I'm fine. The only reason I'm sitting here is my sugar… again." She heard his growl and smiled. "Promise me you won't go looking for trouble."

"I promise not to do anything that will get me in trouble." His wink was not reassuring.

Narrowing her eyes, she said, "I sense a loophole. I get a call to bail you out of jail and I'm going to be annoyed."

Tuck chuckled. "I'd never make you go down to a jail for me. That's why I have an attorney. Aw, don't give me that face." He leaned over to kiss her. "I promise unless he doesn't back off. Is that better?"

"Better."

Tucker traced his fingers over what she assumed were bruises on her throat. His eyes lifted to hers. "Did he act like that when you were married?"

"No, not physically."

"How then?"

"I can't put my finger on what it was. He had a way of trying to intimidate. Nothing like how he was today." Glancing up, she met her mother's eyes. "Tuck… this is my mom, Deirdre Fowler. Mom, this is Tucker Irvin."

He stood and turned. "Ma'am, I apologize. I didn't see you there. It's nice to meet you."

"Likewise, Tucker."

The police showed up a few minutes later to take her statement. Both officers asked for Tuck's autograph, which he gave them.

He sat holding her hand while her mother worked on her phone. As the sun was beginning to set, three big men burst into the room. After a second take, Tucker recognized her father and older brothers. They all shook hands.

Her father glanced at Sasha. "How you holding up?" She stared at her father and brothers for a moment then burst into tears and covered her face. Collie smiled reassuringly. "Don't worry, honey, we can put a good spin on it…"

Chapter Eleven

Tuck's mouth dropped open in shock as Sasha cried harder.

CJ shoved his father around by his shoulder. "Dad, what the *fuck* did you just say to her?"

"What…?"

"There isn't going to be any *spin*. Peter is off our roster and Sasha — your *daughter*, goddamn it — is pressing charges for assault. Either Aaron grows up or I will personally fire his ass. As for you, Dad… you are *done* spinning Sasha's life. You sent her own brother the signal that it was fine to help her piece of shit ex get back in her good graces."

"Everyone makes mistakes, CJ. You know Peter has never acted like this before."

Unable to contain himself, Tucker stood and leaned over Sasha's bed. "He was *choking her out* on a city street. Are you fucking kidding me, Collie?"

"There's a conflict of interest for you, Tucker. You both want the same woman."

He didn't blink as he took in his long-time sports agent. "She isn't a chew toy. She's a human being. You don't decide who gets to be in her life. No one gets to decide but Sasha. It isn't about who wants *her*… it's about what *she* wants. How can you not understand that?"

"You're blowing this out of proportion. That *bartender*…"

"Enough!" Even Sasha was shocked at her mother's scream. "Not one more word, Collie. That bartender *saved her life*." Deirdre moved to stand between her husband and her daughter. "While you have done nothing but try to use her. If you'd been born a rodent, you would have eaten your young."

"DeeDee, don't be like that."

She shook her head slowly. "All this time, I fooled myself into believing it was the job. That no matter what you did for business... it wasn't who you *were*. I was so wrong." Standing to her full height, she whispered, "Get out, Collie."

"DeeDee..."

"I'm serious. You've proven that you don't care about the situation other than how it affects your client. Your daughter deserves to have people around her who have her best interests at heart. You aren't one of those people, Collie. I don't know that you ever were." She wiped angrily at the tears that slid down her cheeks. "Get out."

A deep frown slowly spread over Collie's face. For a long time, he stared at his wife's face then glanced past her to Sasha. He tilted his head to the side.

Tucker swore it was as if he was seeing the women in his family for the first time. Without a word, he nodded and left the room.

Deirdre kissed her daughter and walked to the bathroom across the hall.

Sasha's brothers looked at one another in shock. CJ raked his fingers through his hair and murmured, "Seriously... what is *wrong* with our family?" He stepped out in the hall and Nathan followed so they could talk privately.

Wiping her face, Sasha took a deep breath. "I am so tired of this shit."

Bending over Sasha's body, he whispered at her ear, "Everything is going to be alright." He gently stroked her arm. "By the way, I can see down your shirt from this angle. Very pretty bra, Sasha."

Unable to help herself, she laughed and he stroked her hair back from her face with a smile. "You know, we've got to stop spending so much time in hospitals."

"I'll work on it." She traced her finger over the bridge of his nose to his lips. "Thanks for being here today. You didn't have to do that, you know."

"Shut up, Sasha." He kissed her and she opened instantly. A throat clearing made him pull back, but he gave another light kiss before he stood. "Mrs. Fowler."

"Tuck." Her smile was genuinely amused. "I brought a bag for you, Sasha. Your clothes were dirty and your blouse ripped. Don't get me started on the condition of your stockings. The nurse is coming with the release forms."

"Thanks, Mom." She sat up and rubbed her neck. Opening the bag, she rolled her eyes. "Seriously?" Deirdre grinned. "The photos should be fucking *precious*."

"I thought so, too."

Tuck peered over Sasha's shoulder and laughed loudly. A Green Bay jersey bearing his name and number sat folded on top of a pair of jeans and sneakers. He winked at her mom.

"Hustle, darling. I looked through your log and if you don't get your sugar under control, you're going back on shots. As soon as you're done, we need to get some actual food in your system."

Ignoring the well-meaning lecture, Sasha stood and asked them to push the door closed. She stripped to her bra and panties without glancing in Tucker's direction and was dressed in the new clothes in under a minute. He tried not to stare.

Fail.

As she was tying her laces, her brothers returned. They found her outfit hysterical. In sneakers, she was the same height as her mom while Tucker and her brothers towered over her.

"Shut up. I mean it."

"I'm buying you a Green Bay onesie." Nathan couldn't stop laughing at the image he put in his own head. "Pigtails and a teddy bear…"

"I hate you," she told him with a grin.

"You *love* me and I love seeing you smile." He gave her a smacking kiss on her cheek. "Now, you need to eat and you know I can always eat so… move your ass, sis."

The nurse brought her paperwork and she quickly signed several pages.

CJ handed her the big bag that held her laptop and wrapped his arm around her shoulder. "Sasha?" She looked at him expectantly and he gave her a brilliant smile. "You're fired."

She hugged him hard and against his neck murmured, "Thank you."

He kissed the top of her head and handed her off to Tucker, who took her hand. Ten minutes later, they were driving away from the hospital and on their way to the Irish pub. All of them wanted to thank Ben for his help. His menu didn't hurt.

Sasha settled on the seat beside him and Tucker gave her a squeeze. She smiled at him and the rest of her family but he knew she was still

upset, no matter how well she was hiding it.
There was no sign of Collie.

Chapter Twelve

After her brothers and Tucker shook Ben's hand, she and her mother took turns hugging the big man. He blushed at their effusive thanks.

"Sit, lass. I'll bring ye some food to hold ye over." He gently nudged her into her chair between Tucker and CJ. "Might I say, yer grip had boyo screamin' like a wee girl." With a wink, he walked to the kitchen and it was Sasha's turn to blush.

"Speaking of that, what happened to the self-defense lessons I gave you? You used to be able to flip me." Nathan volunteered at a local women's shelter where he taught courses in personal protection.

"I admit that I went blank at first. I was shocked that he would attack me a block from the office in broad daylight. I just wanted to get away and everything you showed me went right out of my head. I may need a refresher."

Her gentle brother winked across the table. "No need, sweetheart. I'll happily pound him for you. He can deal with someone his own fucking size." He fist bumped CJ and Tucker.

"Dial it down before someone gets hurt or arrested. I'm fine and I'm pressing charges." She smiled. "Even though you're technically the most deadly, I need you to continue being the most *rational* of my brothers, Nathan."

His dramatic sigh made the others laugh. "Fine. I'll expect you at the house on Saturday."

"My muscles are sore already."

****

Food arrived and they chatted while they ate. From his position facing the door, Tucker saw Collie enter the bar and approach Ben. The two men spoke quietly for a minute and Sasha's father settled heavily on a stool. A glass of bourbon was in his hand soon after.

Tucker leaned over and whispered in Sasha's ear, "Your father is here. I'd like the chance to talk to him as someone outside your family."

Her eyes located Collie at the bar and she tugged her lip between her teeth. Everything about his body language spoke of a man who was tired. Meeting his eyes, she nodded.

Dropping a kiss on her lips, he stood and went to join his agent. Collie looked up in surprise before glancing around the bar and seeing his family. A pained expression crossed his face and he turned back to stare into the glass.

"I honestly never knew what to do with her, how to treat her, or how to just be... nice to her. I was too abrupt. When she was really little, I made Sasha cry a lot. Then she just stopped reacting to me at all; started going to CJ or Nathan when she needed help or advice. I'm close to my boys, but I never bridged the gap with my only daughter."

He grimaced. "I forced her into one relationship after another over the years, putting powerful men in her way whether she wanted them or not. She pretended and I realize now that she did that to make me proud." Silence stretched between them. "She refused to do it with you, Tucker."

"What do you mean?"

"When she got back to California, she told me she knew exactly why I sent her to meet you and said she wanted nothing to do with your representation." The older man met Tucker's gaze directly. "Do you want to know why?"

Tuck wanted to know why more than anything at that moment.

"She said you were different; that you could break her heart and it wasn't worth the humiliation. Nothing I said changed her mind."

"Did you know Peter was here?"

Collie sighed. "I helped Aaron set her up. I never thought he'd put his hands on her and I didn't know she lost her baby. I didn't know how bad the cheating was or that she was in deep mourning the last time she caught him." His eyes closed. "I thought she was being difficult. I was thinking like her boss, not her father."

"I've known you twenty years, Collie. You're one of the few people

I've trusted over the course of my career." He sat up straight and put his shoulders back. "There will be no more games with Sasha. She is *mine*. Let me show her what her life can be like what it *should* be like."

"I respect you on and off the field, Tucker. I think you'll be good for her." Collie took a long pull of his drink. "You cheat on her and it will break her. She'll never get over it."

"I won't." Tuck ran his fingers over her hairline. "She's the last for me."

Finishing the bourbon, Collie said, "Now I need to get my head out of my own ass and fix things with the only woman I've ever loved. She'll leave me over this, no matter how much she loves me. I lose her, I lose the only part of myself I can stand anymore."

Tucker stood and clapped his agent on the back. "Then you better get to it. Take her on vacation and lose your fucking phone. You've got it good from what I've seen… don't fuck it up."

Collie chuckled and followed him back to the table. Everyone was quiet.

"CJ… I'll be officially retired in thirty days. You and Nathan run things now. I'm taking your mother on vacation for the next month. If you need me, call her phone." Their mother was shocked into silence. Collie handed his oldest son his cell phone and gently tugged Deirdre from her chair. "We need to talk, DeeDee."

When she was standing at his side, he leaned down and cupped Sasha's face in his hands. "I love you, princess. I suck at showing it and I know that. I reacted badly today and so many days before. I'm sorry." Her tears slid over his hands. "Forget the company and be happy." He kissed her forehead and both her eyes before pulling her into a strong hug.

Then he took his wife's hand and led her outside.

The siblings sat stunned for almost a minute. Tuck pointed at one of the televisions and they all looked up to watch the footage of Sasha's run-in with her ex on national news.

"Oh my god…" she said quietly and then laughed without a trace of humor. "Cell phone video quality has really come a long way, huh?" The men tried to pull her from her instant funk but it was no use. She pressed the heels of her palms against her eyes. "Here we fucking go *again*. I'm so *sick* of this shit."

In the pit of Tucker's stomach, he knew what was going to happen before it did. Sasha sat up, wiped her face, and turned to him.

"I can't do this, Tucker. I'm sorry. I just can't. Please understand."

She ran her fingers through his hair and pulled him to her for a careful kiss. "We can't see each other anymore. Don't call me. Don't text me."

"Sasha…"

"No. I am *tired*, Tucker. As you said, it is *my* choice who I have in my life. *Mine*. I will not choose the path that leads to more bullshit." She picked up her bag. "I need you to give me space because I'm asking for it."

There it was. The one thing he could do for her that no other man ever had. He could respect her wishes, give her the space she thought she wanted, and hope to god it ended up being the right decision. If it didn't, he'd fuck her until she caved in.

With a firm *option B* in his mind, he nodded carefully. "Alright. If that's what you really want. I'll see you around, pretty girl." He stood up, kissed the top of her head, and left.

He was disappointed — but not surprised — when she didn't follow.

CJ and Nathan started talking at the same time.

"What are you doing, Sasha? It's obvious how much you like him."

"Don't do this because of the fucking news, sis."

"You're going to regret this decision. Think it through."

"Why is today so filled with drama? Fuck."

She went around the table and hugged each of them. "I'm going to get my car from the office and head home. I love you guys very much."

"Let me drive you…"

"No. I'll walk. I need to." She slipped her sunglasses in place and stepped outside. As she headed in the direction of the office, she said aloud, "Don't hate me, Tucker. Please don't hate me."

Chapter Thirteen

Three months later…

After her workout, Sasha made her shake and turned on the television for background noise while she straightened her studio.

Tucker's *voice* froze her in place.

Turning, she stared at the image of him on one of her favorite morning talk shows. He was wearing a tailored suit, a tie that matched his eyes, and appeared relaxed as he answered questions.

"How are you enjoying LA, Tucker?" The female host she normally liked and respected seemed a bit too enamored with her guest. Sasha propped her hand on her hip in annoyance.

"Soaking up the sunshine. I like it out here. The pace is pretty relaxed."

The male host laughed. "Unless you're on the freeway."

"Very true. I listen to music and keep my head down. My driver this time around doesn't seem to ruffle at all under the pressure. He would have been great to have in the huddle."

Sasha found herself examining his every feature while they bantered back and forth. His hair was a little longer. It curled at the ends and she thought it looked good on him. He looked good period.

Tilting her head, she watched his eyes. Though he smiled and interacted with his usual charm, she thought he seemed tense.

The blonde leaned closer. In a voice Sasha found overly seductive, she asked, "So, Tucker. You've developed a reputation over the years as something of a lady's man. Anyone special in your life right now?"

Tucker rubbed his big palm on his thigh. "I wish I hadn't developed that reputation. It cost me the woman who could have been my other half. I still think she is even though we haven't talked."

"Does this other half have a name? She sounds fascinating."

"She's a private person." He glanced out into the audience and took a deep breath. "You go through your life and figure every day is a fresh start, a clean slate, you know? Sure, we all make mistakes but you think you have time to make up for it."

He shook his head. "Until you get a chance for something great and your past jumps up and bites you on the ass." Tucker smiled at his hosts and shrugged.

They stared at him, unsure how to respond to a heavier topic than they planned on. Eventually, the male said, "Making good choices is so important." Then they moved on to his charity and glossed over the too-serious content.

Sasha didn't realize she was crying until tears dropped on the skin of her crossed arms. She wiped her face and stared at the man she dreamed about almost every night.

There was no way Tucker was hung up on her.

"What are your plans while you're in Cali, Tucker?"

He stared directly into the camera and said, "I plan to spend some time at the beach."

Instantly, Sasha's body went rogue. Every moment he'd spent with her at the beach house flooded into her brain, destroying the defenses she'd erected against them. Her hands itched to touch him, her lips tingled with the need to kiss him, and her pussy ached for him to fill her.

There were pleasantries and then the show ended. She watched him until the credits rolled then shut off the TV. Still, she stared at the black screen.

Her phone rang and she jumped. Relieved and intensely sad that it was her mother, she answered.

"Honey, are you alright?"

Clearing her throat, she controlled her breathing. "Of course. Why wouldn't I be alright?"

"You sound funny."

"No. I'm fine. Are *you* alright?"

"Wonderful, dear. Your father and I were wondering if you'd like to drive into the city for lunch. We haven't seen you in weeks. Say you will."

Since their trip to Hawaii, family life had been drastically different for the Fowlers. Collie laughed more now that he was retired and PDA was common between them. If any of her brothers brought up business, he quickly changed the subject and asked about their lives.

Their marriage had never been stronger.

Their children had never been more confused.

"Sure, Mom. What time do you want to meet?"

"Let's meet at the office. You know the staff so loves the chance to see you."

"Two o'clock sound good?" Her mother agreed and they ended the call. She ran her hands over her face and quickly gathered her hair into a messy bun.

The ocean caught her eye and she moved to the window. Sasha wasn't sure how long she stood there with her arms wrapped around her waist.

She knew she spent the time thinking about Tucker.

****

After a long shower, she thought about spending more time on her hair but she didn't; A quick pass of the hairdryer and she called it done. For some reason, she tossed around the idea of applying some makeup then realized she wasn't motivated. Lip-gloss was sufficient.

She also considered dressing up as she always had when making an appearance at the agency and changed her mind. A linen sundress and heeled sandals were more fitting. Gathering the leather slouch bag that just might qualify as the perfect purse for her laptop and sketch supplies, she walked to her car.

The day was far too beautiful to keep the top up. Shades blocked the glare and a huge clip kept her hair from flying everywhere. An accident on the freeway made her glad she left a bit earlier than usual.

She would have been too late to grab pastry. Tucking everything into the passenger seat, she made it with a few minutes to spare. Both of her parents hated when their kids were late.

Surprisingly, she was excited to be heading into the office. Since the explosion in the media over her very public confrontation with Peter, she'd avoided the city completely.

The day of his court appearance, he'd taken her aside to apologize. No press, no ulterior motive. That was when he told her about his increasingly dangerous addiction to prescription medication.

"I got hurt and they gave me pills. I never stopped taking them. It doesn't change what I did but I wanted to tell you face to face that I'm sorry."

He received community service and probation. He was banned from visiting or working in the United States for three years. His new agent enrolled him in anger management classes, sent him through rehab, and seemed to have much greater control over him than Collie ever had.

Only time would tell, but she felt as though they could be civil if they encountered one another.

Driving beneath the agency, she nodded at the waving parking attendant and took her usual spot near the elevator. The doors slid open on the executive floor and staff happy to see her swarmed from seemingly everywhere.

CJ worked his way through almost a dozen employees with a grin. "Hey there, little sister. Mm, spoiling us again." He turned a fierce glare on the people around him and growled, "One fucking chocolate croissant. Just save me *one*."

They laughed and his assistant nodded.

His big hands cupped her shoulders. "You look incredible. How's your sugar?"

"Finally back on track. I'm down to one pill in the morning."

"Glad to hear that. You resemble a super classy beach bunny. You realize redheads aren't meant for too much sun, right?"

"I dip myself in a vat of sunscreen, CJ. Are you kidding?" She glanced around. "Where are Mom and Dad?"

He winked. "They run late for everything now. Too busy making out." Sasha pretended to choke down a gag and he laughed loudly. "I see it daily. I don't freak out as much." Wrapping his arm around her shoulder, he led her to his office.

Collie and Deirdre broke apart like teenagers. Taking in their daughter, they both gave her big smiles as they came to greet her.

"Well aren't you pretty as a picture?" Her dad hugged her hard and tilted up her chin. "You look wonderful. Why do I think you're a little sad?" She shook her head. "Hmm... we'll see. Look at our girl, DeeDee."

She stood still while her mother fussed over her outfit. "I love this more relaxed you. Are you relaxed?"

Sasha laughed. "Sure. I spend my days painting. Very relaxing."

"Anyone interesting in your life?"

"I... no, Mom. I don't need that right now." Deirdre stared at her and Sasha wondered how much she could see.

"No one... you're sure, honey?" Controlling her breathing and trying to slow her heart rate, she nodded. "Have you eaten today?"

"Mom, is everything okay? You're acting strange."

Her mother stomped her foot. "Answer the question, darling."

Eyes wide, she replied, "Yes. I ate a meal and two small snacks before I left the house." Her family was looking at her oddly. "What's going on?"

Far too cheerfully, her mother said, "Let's take you around the office before we go. You know how the staff loves when you visit." Reaching behind her head, she removed the clip holding back her hair. "You know, I thought you were lovely as a child. That was nothing compared to you as a grown woman. I love you, Sasha. You know that, don't you?"

"I love you, too. Are you sure you're alright?"

"I just want to make sure you know… and remember."

Linking arms, Deirdre led the way out of the office and big smiles and several hugs greeted Sasha from the administrative and accounting staff.

CJ stared down his PA. "You saved me one? The chocolate kind?" She nodded seriously.

Sasha chatted and laughed with the people she'd worked with for years. Some of them, she'd known since she was a little girl. She was surprised to find that she missed the atmosphere of the agency. Several asked if she was coming back and she shook her head.

Bumping shoulders, Nathan said, "You wouldn't even come back part time? Once a week? You're the only sane person in our family, Sasha. Look at their *faces*."

It was impossible not to laugh as a bunch of adults gave her boo-boo lips.

"We'll wear her down. Don't worry everyone. Pastry is an inalienable right."

"You know, you *can* buy it yourself." Hand on her hip, she raised her brow suspiciously.

Nathan clasped his hand over his heart and whispered, "But… you bring it with *love*, Sasha! The perfect mix!" He grabbed her shoulders and gave her a little shake. "The perfect mix filled with love, woman!"

Her mom tugged her away with a grin. "We'll beg properly later. Over wine." As they passed the conference room door, Deirdre stopped and turned to her. "Sasha…" She smoothed a strand of hair away from her face. "You know how I adore you, don't you?"

"Of course, and I love you, too."

"I have your best interests at heart."

"I know you do, Mom. What is it?"

"Remember that." Reaching out, her mother opened one side of the large double door. As it swung wide, it wasn't the luxurious appointments of the high-end conference room where they signed multi-million dollar contracts that held her attention.

Tucker Irvin stood just inside and he looked fucking *delicious*.

Chapter Fourteen

Sasha took a step forward before she narrowed her eyes on Tucker.

"It's good to see you again, Sasha. I have a few things I need to go over with you."

Glancing at her mother beside her and her father just behind them, she frowned. "What's going on? Did I just get set up... *again*?"

Deirdre rolled her eyes. "Don't be dramatic, dear. If you recall, you're Tucker's agent."

"I no longer work for the company..."

"Actually... that isn't one-hundred-percent accurate," CJ said behind her. She glared at him and he shrugged. "We never put the paperwork through. You still represent him. I filled in for the last three months but you know how many clients I have. He's not getting what he deserves from this agency so... he's your only client."

"I can't believe you were part of this." The butterflies in her stomach and dampness between her legs told her clearly that she wasn't ready to see Tucker.

CJ leaned close and kissed the tip of Sasha's nose. At her ear, he whispered, "You're miserable and I'm tired of it. I thought you'd shake it off and you haven't. That means you give a shit. What kind of brother would I be if I didn't help you get what you didn't realize you wanted?"

"Can everyone give us a few minutes?" Tucker spoke to her family but didn't taken his eyes off her face. "I need to speak to Sasha."

"Of course, take your time. Sasha, we'll have lunch after you young people chat." Deirdre guided her dad and brothers from the room and closed the door behind them with a smile.

Alone with her personal kryptonite... oh shit.

She took a deep breath and clasped her hands. "Tuck, what's going on?" Her feet were rooted to the expensive carpet near the door. Part of her considered running.

As if he read her mind, he smiled. "Don't do it, Sasha."

He wore slacks and a dress shirt unbuttoned at the collar. The jacket and tie he'd worn to the set of the morning talk show currently hung over the back of a chair. His hands were on his hips and the rolled up sleeves exposed powerful forearms.

"What are you doing here, Tucker?" Sasha took a step back as he took a step forward.

"You look fantastic." His gaze roamed down her body before settling back on her eyes. "Great dress and I love the heels. Come here, Sasha."

Caught retreating again, she paused. "Tuck, let me assign another agent for you. We can't maintain professionalism like this." She took several steps around the end of the conference table and he paced her. "You're being ridiculous. There's no reason for you to chase me around the room. You don't chase women. They fall, weeping in gratitude, at your feet."

Moving suddenly, he covered the distance between them, and she lost her balance an instant before he wrapped his arms around her snugly.

"Tuck..."

Pivoting sharply, he pressed her to the nearest wall beside the enormous wall mounted television. He didn't trap her but he was *close* and he smelled so *good*.

"I'm finding I much prefer people who *don't* fall at my feet. I have no interest in *chasing women*... simply in catching *one* woman." His fingers squeezed her hand before tracing up her wrist and arm to her shoulder. "I'll chase you as long as I think I have a chance."

"This isn't a game, Tucker."

"No. It's my *life*, Sasha." For one moment, she caught a glimpse of her own emotional state reflected in the green of his eyes. "This is far more important than any game. I take it seriously and you should, too."

A strong hand slid along the back of her neck as he kissed her. Nothing could have prepared her for the instant, visceral reaction her body had to him.

Her breasts arched against his chest and her hips ground against him. He devoured her mouth and left her without the ability or will to think clearly. One hand slid over her hip and he pulled her against him forcefully, pivoting his hips into the cradle of her thighs. The hard ridge of his cock pressed against the cleft of her and she moaned into his mouth.

"I do not fucking *want* anyone else and I haven't since the night I met you. I want you under me, over me, screaming my name. My mouth waters for the taste of you. My cock throbs every time I think about you. I've never felt like this for anyone and it scares the hell out of me... but I'm not fucking running and by god, you're not running either."

Tuck cupped her face in his hands and made love to her mouth until she whimpered. Her mind was in a turmoil of need unlike anything she'd ever experienced. Sasha's hand moved to the back of his head and her fingers stroked through his hair.

"We don't know each other. This is crazy, Tucker."

He lifted his mouth and laid his forehead against her with his eyes closed. Leaning back, he smoothed the curls from around her face.

"I know you hold your head up even when you're hurting inside. I know you're afraid to trust me and worry about being humiliated again. I know it will take a long time for me to prove I *won't* hurt you and you *can* trust me. I also know I'm fucking *in love* with you, Sasha."

Her lips parted in surprise and he kissed her again, licking into her mouth and stroking along her tongue. His hands moved to her back, gently kneading as he pulled her closer.

Sasha went willingly and Tuck groaned against her lips. Her hands moved over him in a desperate need to memorize the body that was already strangely familiar. She pulled his shirt from his slacks and unbuttoned it, sliding her palms along his chest and around his sides.

Raking her nails down his back, she stroked them around to the front. In moments, she unbuckled his belt, unfastened his pants, and pushed the clothing off his hips.

Tuck responded by sliding her sundress up her torso and quickly whipping it away. Not quickly enough, their clothing was scattered over the carpet and their arms were tightly wrapped around one another.

"We're buck-ass naked in the conference room of Dad's company."

"Don't care. Do not fucking care."

Tucker lifted her, held her against the wall, and slid smoothly into her embarrassingly wet pussy in one stroke. Her arms and legs gripped him tightly as he started to move.

"You're so wet and hot. I have fucking *missed* you, Sasha."

Hard hands braced her as he powered deep and all she could do was hold on for dear life. Every stroke was more intense as he stared into her eyes. When it was too much, she brought his face to her for a kiss. He gave her what she wanted but broke it quickly.

"You won't run from me that way either." She shook her head and a lock of her hair stuck to skin that was already slick with sweat.

The first climax rolled over her like a train but Tuck never slowed the movement of his hips against her. He kept going, kept moving, and dragged out her pleasure. When he felt her begin to relax, he positioned his elbows under her knees and somehow fucked her even harder.

"More, Sasha."

He changed the angle, plunging to her womb again and again. She did everything she could to shield her heart from what he was making her feel. She needed to protect herself.

Then she was coming again and still he stared at her, fucked her, *loved* her. There was no denying it. No pretending he was just infatuated. No brushing off how he felt about her as just another conquest in a long line.

Tuck Irvin *loved* her.

Sasha wanted this man with every part of her mind, heart, and body. The orgasm was harder this time — than any other time before — and she felt her pussy tighten like a vice around his cock. He almost lost control but reined it in. When her sheath loosened, he exhaled hard and she smiled.

"I love you, Tucker."

At her words, he lost control. The force of the semen leaving the head of his cock was unlike anything she'd ever felt. Her pregnancy was the result of a condom that broke, so it took her a moment to realize why this particular experience was different.

Tuck's rhythm stumbled to a stop and he reached up with both hands to hold her face. "Don't freak out. It happened and I'm sorry but I don't care." His smile reminded her of a child's face at Christmas. "You love me?"

Tamping down the baby panic — that wasn't as extreme as she would have thought — she raked her fingers through his damp hair. "I've never been in love and I'm afraid."

"Let's be afraid together. That's better than being afraid and alone." Tuck's smile was warm and she laughed softly until he held her still for his kiss.

It was his way of sealing the deal.

He carefully gathered her close and carried her to the sofa on the other side of the room. As he settled over her, sinking to her womb, he wrapped his arms around her back.

"I can't leave your body yet. I need to stay connected to you." She nodded and wrapped her bare feet around his ass, pulling him flat to her chest. He rested his head beside her, his mouth near her ear as he stroked his palm up and down her side. "Sasha, I won't hurt you."

Her hands smoothed his hair and stroked over his face. "Stay with me? Let's see if this works?"

Tucker nodded and started to thrust gently inside her. "It'll work." He nuzzled her neck and nibbled along her shoulder. When he lifted his head, he was grinning and she traced the dimples. "I hope no one was especially hungry. We have three months to make up for. Celibacy sucks."

The sound of her laughter faded into a low moan as Tucker got to work.

Epilogue

Five years later...

In a move that *still* had celebrity gossips talking, Tucker proposed to Sasha within days of them getting back together. They were married in a simple morning wedding at the beach with their family in attendance.

Later that night, they were married again in an extravagant production that included some of the biggest names in the sports world. Her parents had insisted. As their only daughter, the big wedding was part of the package.

For months, Tucker spent every moment they weren't sleeping trying to get his wife pregnant and they were rewarded for their efforts when she gave birth to a beautiful son they named Connor. Her tears as she held her baby were two-fold and her husband understood.

Despite the complications the first time and the increased risk to her body to carry a second child, Sasha wanted to try to have one more child before she had her tubes tied. She was on bed rest for the majority of her pregnancy but didn't complain because she wanted to remain calm.

Tucker almost lost her during labor.

Their extended family spoiled their children rotten and he was thankful every single day that Sasha survived bringing them into the world.

Connor was a little hellion and if he did something wrong, he used his dimples to get him out of trouble. The response always received a heavy sigh from his mother and she often pointed at Tucker silently.

Paige allowed her family to dress her up despite showing all signs at almost three of being just like her mother. She preferred to play on the beach and spent hours every day drawing and coloring.

The doting grandparents picked them up for the weekend and laughed as Sasha shooed them gently to the car. As the car disappeared up the drive, she took off running for their bedroom.

Tucker tackled her gently to the bed and made short work of their clothes. Only when he slid deep inside her body did he release the breath he'd been holding.

"Finally. I've missed you."

"We had sex this *morning*."

"It was *quiet* sex. *Kids-are-in-the-house* sex. Not the loud, sweaty kind you know you prefer."

"Me?"

"You are so dirty…"

Their laughter filled the brightly lit room as Tucker Irvin made love to his agent. No one got the kinds of benefits from the agency that he did. Later, he'd whine until she gave him one of her famous massages and turned him into a pile of goo.

Sasha's smiling face as she came was everything and he slowed down to drag out the moment. "I love you so fucking much."

"I love you, Tucker."

He rolled to his back and watched her rise above him. "Ride me, Sasha. Let me touch you."

Her hands on his shoulders, Sasha set a lazy rhythm, staring into his face as his hands moved over her body. He pulled her closer and took a pebbled nipple in his mouth. Switching back and forth, he sucked and licked her breasts until she couldn't bear to hold back her orgasm.

Throwing her head back, Sasha came around him and Tuck's hands gripped her too hard as he tried to hold back.

"Come with me. I want to feel you coating my pussy." Her hands fisted in his hair, her eyes glazed with passion as her climax washed over her in waves.

Everything about making love to her was hell on his control. Tuck thrust upward hard as she powered down and he came growling her name, his hands too rough on her hips as the sensation of release wrapped tightly in her body stole his breath.

Sasha's eyes stayed on his. "I want all of it… give me every drop, Tuck."

"Every drop belongs to you." He barely recognized the sound of his voice. When both of them were spent, she stretched out on his chest and he rubbed her back. They were quiet for so long that he thought she'd fallen asleep. Her words out of nowhere made him grin.

"Tucker, that is nowhere near as dirty as what I plan to do to you later."

They treated themselves to a rare nap and then she kept her promise.

On the other side of the world, Nathan Fowler stepped from the back of the car and looked around. He'd never been to Austria and it was beautiful.

Movement from the side of the small cottage caught his eye and he turned to watch a woman running up a narrow wooded path. She stopped a few feet away and wiped her face with a towel.

She was beautiful. She had pin-straight black hair, huge almond-shaped black eyes, and skin the color of caramel. Her body was narrow and ridiculously fit.

Nearing fifty, Nathan had gotten very good at pegging the ages of women far too young for him. This woman was no older than twenty.

"You must be Mr. Fowler." Her voice was tinged with a touch of England while her ancestry was most definitely rooted in India. "I am Saleia Andou."

The young woman he was here to sign to the agency. The sports magazines were going to eat her up. He shook her hand and gave her his business card.

She glanced over his shoulder and her smile turned brilliant. "*Maman*, this is Mr. Fowler."

Nathan turned and almost stumbled. An older version of his new client held out her hand. She wore a flowing cotton gown in pale green. Her feet were bare.

"Monsieur Fowler. What a pleasure to finally meet you. I am Saleia's mother, Nessa."

He took her hand and then the delicate scent of almonds and jasmine washed over him and he lightly squeezed the soft fingers in his.

"Mrs. Andou, thank you for agreeing to change the date."

Shockingly, he found himself thinking about tracing his tongue up her neck. She called to him on a primal level he had never felt in his life. Nathan couldn't recall a single woman who had ever inspired him to bow over her hand.

When he did just that, her eyes widened in surprise and, if he wasn't mistaken, pleasure.

"Call me Nessa. I am not a missus."

"Excellent." The meaning was not lost on either of them but he gave her a professional, reassuring smile. "Where can we talk?"

"I… this way, please." Nessa led the way into the house and he found himself staring at the sway of her full hips.

Since his divorce, he'd been numb to women. He was not numb to this one. Right now, thousands of miles from home, with a woman he'd known less than ten minutes, every sexual instinct came roaring back to life.

More than three hours spent going over contracts in the comfortable warmth of their tiny kitchen had him close to crawling out of his skin. The way she moved, spoke, and thought drew him. Then she laughed and that was when Nathan knew…

This woman was going to be his.

"Leap of Faith" is the first story in a new series. I hope you enjoyed it! Subscribe to my website www.alwaysthegoodgirl.com for free stories and information about upcoming releases.

The Barter System
Some people will go to great lengths to get their research…

Riya O'Connell requests applications from men around the country willing to participate in the research she needs for her dissertation on Male Sexuality. She narrows down her thousands of submissions to eight men. In return, Riya will give them… whatever they want.

Ultimately, Riya discovers where her heart truly belongs… and gets an education she didn't plan on.

Yes to Everything
Life at the top isn't all glitz and glamour.

Brooke Kincaid's life takes a turn for the better when she's asked to join a country band. In a single moment, her struggle to care for her younger siblings is a thing of the past.

Fame and fortune have a price. Brooke embraces the realization of her dreams only to have happiness ripped away in one act of brutal violence. Starting again takes courage but love has a way of finding its way home.

About the Author

Shayne McClendon is an indie author who has received rave reviews for her premiere novel "The Barter System." Other projects recently released are "In the Service of Women," "Yes to Everything," "Damaged," "Being Delightful," "The Hermit," "Hudson" - the second book set in "The Barter System" world, and many more.

Writer, mom, and hermit… Shayne listens to the voices in her head because their ideas are awesome. Those around her have learned not to question the crazy. Coffee consumption is too high, amount of sleep is too low, but the words always feel just right.

She currently lives in Oklahoma wrangling teenagers, opening doors for her pets, and running her content writing company. She dreams of peace, quiet, travel, and always having a viable internet connection.

You can contact her by email at shayne@alwaysthegoodgirl.com, stop by her Facebook page, or visit her website and subscribe for your free story!

Shayne McClendon's work is available at all major e-book retailers. Print editions of her work are available on her website.

Also by Shayne McClendon

The Barter System
Yes to Everything
Damaged
In the Service of Women
Obsession - Endurance
A Little Bit Country — Volume One
Being Delightful
The Hermit
The Great Outdoors Collection
Love of the Game Collection
Gravity
Roadside Assistance

Compilations
Just a Little Kilted — *with Alexandra Andersen*
Just a Little Crazy — *with Alexandra Andersen*
All the Better To — *with Christopher Southers*

Trying

Book Five of the *This* Series

J.B. McGee

Copyright © 2014 J.B. McGee
All rights reserved.

Prologue

Bradley

Rolling over, I wrap my arms around my gorgeous wife. "Gabby Girl," I mumble, nibbling on the soft lobe. "Wake up."

Grumbling something inaudible, she moves her body a little closer to mine. Pushing myself against her, I hope it will be the only cue she needs to become aroused in more than one way. "Sleeping," she whispers, denting my hopes.

Moving my hands to her front, I cup her breasts in my palms. "You're beautiful in the morning. Grumpy and all."

"Not in the mood right now, Bradley."

"You're never in the mood anymore. I thought the honeymoon period was supposed to last at least a year." I chuckle, only partially joking. "It's been six months." I huff, the irritation beginning to ooze from my tone. "In the last month, we've had sex twice. What's wrong? Is it me?"

Gabby slowly rolls over into my arms, her big hazel eyes locking with mine. "It's not you. I love you."

Pleading, I beg, "Then show me."

"I can't." A tear trickles from her eye. "It's hard to describe how I feel."

Sighing, I stare at the ceiling. "You've always been great at shutting me out. Should've known that wouldn't change when we got married."

"It's not shutting you out. If I knew how to tell you, I would."

Trying unsuccessfully to not become furious with frustration and hurt, my eyebrows furrow. "Do you regret marrying me?"

Rubbing my chest, she kisses my cheek. "Not at all. How many times do I have to tell you that I love you?"

The sting of her kiss lingers. Yet, its venom is something I crave, longing for more. "Loving someone and being in love are two totally different things, Gabby."

****

Gabby

"Ouch, that hurt," I growl, scooting out of his arms. "I'm very well aware of the different types of love." The reality is that I love him so much it hurts. It hurts that my body and my brain aren't in sync. Trying to find the words to explain this is so hard. There's a part of me that hopes going for my yearly gynecological exam will shed some light on the situation. "I can't help the way I feel, and your pressure is only making it worse."

Hearing the rustle of the covers, and the bed shifting, I know that Bradley has rolled over. Now our backs are facing each other. The air is thick, nearly suffocating me. The distance between our bodies is symbolic of the distance between our souls. Our connection is broken, and I'm pretty sure are our hearts are, too. "Sue me for trying to make love to my wife. I've never pressured you to have sex before, I won't start now," he says, defeated.

Just like that, everything shatters. The small tear that fell earlier has grown into a puddle. Wrapping my arms around my chest, I am determined to not let the heaving in my chest be heard, or the sniffles for that matter.

Six months ago I became Mrs. Bradley Banks. Going into the wedding, nearly all we, *I*, could think about was being together, making love for the first time. Things haven't been easy. It's hard for me to wrap my mind around how I can love him so much. Yet, the desire to do anything other than cuddle left my body as quickly as that magical day ended.

Chapter One

Gabby

"Gabby. So good to see you," Dr. Gibbons says, warmly.

Holding the paper drape around my bare body, I stand, embracing her. "Good to see you, too." A grin overtakes my beaming face.

Shaking her head, she laughs, as she washes her hands. "How have you been? How's married life?"

"Good," I sigh, sitting on the exam table.

"Go ahead and lie back." Rubbing her palms together, she says, "Sorry, can't seem to warm up today. So married life?"

As many exams as I've had, getting used to the awkward small talk has never happened. "Married life could be better," I whisper, my voice cracking.

"Oh no. What's wrong?"

Swallowing, it occurs to me that this is a conversation I should be having with my mother. The irony that her former doctor is listening while doing my breast exam isn't lost on me. "You know we waited to have sex until after we got married."

"Yeah. I was so proud of you when you came in to get your birth control pills last year."

"Well, the first few months were okay. Now, sex is the last thing I want. Bradley thinks it's him. It's not, though." Biting my lip, I try to find the words again to describe these feelings, but it's so hard. "It's like I'm complacent with snuggling, and that's it."

When she finishes my breast exam, she brings in the nurse, and they start to prepare for the lower portion of the exam. As she puts the gloves on her hands, she turns her head a bit. "That's a side effect of the birth control."

"What?"

"It's not you. It's the medicine."

"Well, that's not exactly how I'd hoped they'd prevent pregnancy."

She laughs, "We can try a progesterone only contraceptive, also called the mini-pill. It may help."

"Okay. I trust you. At this point, I'm desperate. He thinks I don't love him...that I regret marrying him," I whisper.

Shaking her head, she reassures me, "Well, tell him it's not your fault, or his, and to be patient with us as we work things out."

"Relax," she instructs me, tapping my legs that are now in the stirrups. "Come down just a tad."

After adjusting my position, I take a deep breath and do my best to relax my legs as the cold, metal speculum is inserted into my vagina. The Pap smear is done first, then she inserts several fingers, feeling to my left, which causes intense pain. "Ouch!"

"That hurts?"

Inhaling, holding my breath, I breathe, "Yeah," through clenched teeth.

"That shouldn't hurt. How about over here?" She asks, moving to the right side.

"Uh huh," is all I'm able to mutter.

"All right, try to relax." She continues to nudge around my insides.

"What's wrong?" I inquire.

Glancing to the nurse, Dr. Gibbons nods towards the door. "Not sure. We're going to bring the ultrasound machine in and have a look around in a minute." Pulling the speculum out, she puts it in a container, then removes her gloves, tossing them into the trash. "Your ovaries are very sensitive. Just want to have a look around, especially since you're on the pill. Anything else going on that is different with you?"

"My back has been hurting a lot lately, lower back," I say, pointing to the base of my spine. "Thought maybe it was sitting in all those uncomfortable chairs in classes."

"Your mother had endometriosis. That can be a symptom. Let's do this ultrasound first, though."

"Okay."

A tapping on the door prompts us both to say, "Come in," simultaneously. The ultrasound machine barely fits through the opening.

Dr. Gibbons taps my legs again. "Feet up, knees out, and scoot down to the bottom of the table for me." After replacing her gloves, she grabs a probe that resembles a penis, even down to the rubber covering it. She squirts jelly onto it. "Would you rather I put it in, or you?"

"Um. You can do it." Something about sticking that into myself just doesn't do much for my already frazzled nerves.

Dr. Gibbons chuckles. "Okay, here we go." Turning the screen so I can see, she explains what the grayscale pictures are. "This is your uterus. Everything looks good." The wand moves towards my left, and the intense pain is back. This time, it's as if I'm being stabbed. Immediately, it causes me to squeeze everything below my waist, prompting her to tap my thighs. "Relax as much as you can, okay?"

"Uh huh." I let my knees fall a little, wishing at this point Bradley were with me. If he were, I'd squeeze his hand until his knuckles were white to alleviate the pain.

"Your ovaries aren't looking so good." I never knew how a few words could suddenly change my life. "I'm afraid it may be now or never," Dr. Gibbons says, stoically. Those words freeze time as she finishes the rest of the ultrasound.

Shaking my head to snap myself out of my trance, I gulp, as the words echo in my mind and out of my mouth simultaneously. "Excuse me? Now or never what?"

Pulling the rubber gloves off her hands, she pushes the pedal to open the lid to the stainless steel trash can, all the while discarding her waste.

"If you want a family, it's now or never," she calmly replies. Nodding towards my naked body only covered with a drape, she continues, "Why don't you get dressed, and then we can talk."

The rippling and crunching of the paper clenched between my fingers rings out in the room like fingernails on a chalkboard. Releasing it, I push myself up and carefully climb down the one small step to retrieve my clothes. It only takes me a second to replace them. The wool on my chest is rhythmically moving up and down in tempo, the beat pounding through my ears. Touching my face, I feel to see if it's hot. My skin is scorching, like I've been standing in the sun for hours, and it must be as scarlet as my sweater. Then, frightening thoughts start to overtake any physical discomfort I'm currently experiencing. *I'm not finished with college. There's no way that I'll ever finish school if I have a baby now, but having no children was never a part of my plan, either.*

Mom's words then enter the internal conversation. Important

conversations, rather lessons, she shared before she passed away. They were words she would have said to me gradually, had cancer not robbed her of her life. This particular one replays vividly. She breathlessly whispered, "You'll fall into lust first. You'll think you love the boy, that he's worthy of everything you have."

Tears pricked the backs of my eyes, my chin quivered. Not at the thought of a boy loving me. It was watching my mother's eyes, her strength, and the realization of how unfair life had already been to me in such a short period of time, of how unfair life had been to her. My mouth opened as if to speak, but it was impossible to form words.

She took my hand in hers. "Gabby, you have to promise me that you will at the very least save yourself for marriage. Please give me the peace of mind of knowing that."

Her body was weak, and the guilt for causing her to even have to make the statement, to have to ask such a question, immediately caused regret to set in the pit of my stomach.

The familiar feeling quickly returns, as I sit in the only chair in the room. Wrapping my arms around my waist, I squeeze trying to dull the ache.

She had responded, "I just want you to reach all your goals, and I don't want to see a boy or a baby get in the way of them." Her lip quivered as she continued. "And you may love him. But no boy is worthy until they have married you. Promise me you'll wait."

My head automatically moved up and down as I swallowed back the tears, trying to be as strong as she was. "I promise."

"Gabriella, I don't want you to not be able to finish school, reach your dreams because you made a poor decision… because you got pregnant too soon."

My body shuddered. It's not like there anyone had ever been interested in me. It wasn't the thought of waiting until marriage to have sex, but rather the knowledge that it was the last promise I would ever get to make to my mother. I'm thankful for a moment I was able to keep it. At least part of it. The waiting until marriage was hard, but not unbearable. Then there's finishing school.

A voice, her voice, pops in my head. "Bradley won't let you fail. You will finish school. You can't control your body, but you can control your mind."

There's a quick knock, and the knob starts the move. "Are you dressed, Gabby?"

Clearing my throat, I whisper, "Yes, ma'am."

Dr. Gibbons pushes through the door, and sits on the stool. Wasting no time, she immediately says, "Gabby, I'm concerned about the number of cysts the ultrasound showed on your ovaries. Have you heard of Poly Cystic Ovarian Syndrome or PCOS?"

Shaking my head, "No," I mumble.

"It's a leading cause of infertility. Typically, it also causes insulin resistance. I'd like to do some blood work and a glucose tolerance test to see if you're experiencing that."

This is all too much. The words swarm around in my head, bouncing off the sides and crashing into each other. Certain ones echo with each hit. "And if we wait to have children? I'm not ready."

"I'm telling you that you're not guaranteed right now. I'm telling you that I think it's going to be a long, hard road." Closing her eyes for a moment, she purses her lips together. "The more you wait, the harder it's going to be I'm afraid."

Nodding, I take a moment to gather my wandering thoughts. "When will the blood work be scheduled? What's your plan?"

"Hopefully within a week or so. Takes some time to get the glucose tolerance test and have it read. Let's wait to get these results back, but I can speak with fairly certain terms that this is what we're dealing with. You should go ahead and be thinking about what you want to do."

Nodding, I whisper, "Thank you." Why is it customary and polite to say thank you even in the wake of bad news? I'm not thankful for this.

Chapter Two

As my feet cross the threshold into my dream house, it's as if my heart exited my body, remaining on the huge front porch. When Bradley turns to face me, the heaviness in my chest cavity aches with emptiness. The color leaves his face as quickly as the tear falls from my eye, splashing onto the floor.

"Hey, hey. What's wrong?" His brows furrow. In an instant, his arms are entwined around my waist, pulling me into his solid chest. Inhaling, I try to speak, but it's impossible. Instead of the intense pain that I should be feeling, the only thing that is overwhelming is the numbness. "Gabby. Talk to me. What is it?"

Using the backs of my hands, I swipe the tears, swallow, and take a deep breath. "I went to the doctor today."

"Yeah. Just your yearly, right?"

Nodding, I glance away. "Right. Things weren't normal, though." Walking further into the house, I toss my things on the foyer table. "She said that the likelihood we'd ever be able to have a family is very slim."

A flash of what I think may be relief washes over his beautiful face, blue eyes sparkling with something...maybe hope. Taking a step back, Bradley's head bobs. "You scared the heck out of me. I thought you were going to say she found a mass in your breast, or something. You know, with your mom's history and all." Moving closer, he brushes the new tear from my face. "That bit about the family is hogwash, and just plain wrong."

"Hogwash?" A small laugh escapes. "She's the doctor. She would know."

"Hogwash because even if you're not able to have a baby, we will have a family. And what makes her say that?" He shakes his head. "You're not one to just take what someone says at face value, either. We'll get a second opinion."

Shaking my head, I vehemently refuse that notion. "I don't want another opinion. She *is* the one who found Mom's breast cancer before she relocated here to Atlanta. If I don't trust her, then we've got a serious problem."

Turning on his heel, Bradley heads for the kitchen, and automatically, I follow. Opening the built-in wine cooler, he pulls a bottle, "White." Grabbing another, he holds it up and asks, "Or red?" That smile is dazzling and gorgeous, and it's clear he's trying to fix the situation. Before I'm able to answer, he repeats his movements, "We have the Villa Raiano Fiano di Arellino." Then he holds the red up, continuing, "Or we have the Giacomo Conerno Barolo Monfortino."

A giggle escapes, and a smile wins over the frown. "Such long names. We got those on our honeymoon for a special occasion." Sadness, regret, and fear quickly return. Hanging my head, I mutter, "This isn't a special occasion."

"It is. When we took vows, we took them for better or worse, and in sickness or health." Placing the two bottles on the counter, he walks back to me, taking my hands in his. "It was a ceremony of commitment, and that's what we're about to do again. I'm vowing that we're in this together. Whatever it is that she thinks is going to be so difficult won't be as hard because we have each other." Tears begin to flow freely, and he kisses them away this time. "We're going to drink one of those bottles of wine tonight. We're going to save the other for a day after you have our baby when you can enjoy it with me. Right now, though, we're going to make plenty of incredible memories trying."

About the Author

J.B. McGee was born and raised in Aiken, South Carolina. She is the mother of two beautiful children and a stay at home mom/entrepreneur. She finished her Bachelor of Arts degree in Early Childhood Education at the University of South Carolina-Aiken in 2006. During her time studying children's literature, a professor had encouraged her to become a writer.

In 2011, it was discovered that both of her children and her husband have Mitochondrial Disease, a disease that has no cure or treatments. Being a writer allows J.B. to remain close to her family, work on raising awareness for this disease and to lose herself in the stories that she creates for her fans.

J.B. McGee and her family now reside in Buford, Georgia. She is an Amazon Top 100 bestselling author. She is represented by Stacey Donaghy at Donaghy Literary Group.

Please follow J.B. on Twitter and Facebook to stay up to date on the latest teasers, giveaways, and new releases.

Other Books by J.B. McGee

Broken (This #1) — Now Available
Mending (This #2) — Now Available
Conspiring (This #2.5) — Now Available
Forgiven (This #3) — Now Available
Falling (This #4) — Coming in 2014
Trying (This #5) — Coming in 2014
Blinded (This #6) — Coming in 2014
Skipping Stones (Standalone) — Now Available
Saving Alex (Standalone companion to Skipping Stones) — Coming in 2014
Let Me Testify — Now Available
50 Ways to Market YOUR Online Business — Now Available

Ruby and Finn

This is a Point of View excerpt from the novel:
The Legend of Ruby and Finn (release Fall 2014)

Maggi Myers

Copyright © 2014 Maggi Myers
All rights reserved.

RUBY

I can feel a hundred pair of eyes bore into my back, encouraging my feet to make haste across the slick asphalt.

"Godammit," I mutter under my breath, scanning the rows of cars for my ancient Civic. All I want is to go home and open the bottle Malbec that started this whole fiasco. I should know better than to let my guard down, even for a minute. The unavoidable truth is even most simple trip to the store is a lesson humility, when you're me. My name is Ruby Dolan, and I'm a social pariah. Scratch that, I'm not the pariah, my father is. Unfortunately, in the court of public opinion, I'm guilty by way of tragic DNA. The bitter January wind freezes my tears in their tracks, stinging my face almost as badly as my pride. I can't say I was shocked to find our family portrait splashed across the latest edition of The Weekly Buzz, but finding it clutched in the hands of the lady in line ahead of me was a bit discerning. Even more so when she rather loudly stated "Hey, isn't that you?" Every person in hearing distance swiveled their heads to catch the commotion she caused. "That is you. You're Eddie Dolan's daughter." A statement like that used to fill my heart with family pride. That time past the moment my father was arrested for embezzling money from his clients. The second the judge let him out on bail he ran with the money, leaving me and my mom to deal with his mess. He ruined everything, that selfish...

"*Fuck!*" I shout. I can see tomorrow's headline:

Humiliated Daughter of Disgraced Investment Banker Eddie Dolan, Found Wandering Parking Lot of Giant Foods from Suspected Mental Breakdown.

"Where the fuck are you Gertrude?" Oh God, I've lost my mind *and* my car.

"Ma'am?" A voice calls from behind me. "Are you okay?" I take a deep breath and turn around. A policeman idles in his cruiser a few feet away, watching me with concern. Fan-fucking-tastic.

"Fine, officer. Just peachy." I say, and renew my hike to find good-ole Gertie. I can hear the ice crunch beneath the tires of the police car, as he creeps along behind me. Really? Can't a girl lick her wounds in peace?

"Are you sure? You look lost."

I am lost. Just not in the way that he's referring. When my father was arrested, the world I thought I knew was dragged away with him.

"I can't find my car," I say. I keep my eyes fixed on the frozen ground, willing it to open and swallow me whole.

"I can help," he says. His intention is to help me find my car, I know this. Still, the words permeate my defenses, sending a fresh wave of tears to crystalize on my cheeks. What I would have given to have just one person help me when my father's lies were unearthed, but everyone I knew ran for the hills when he did.

The soft click of a car door, brings my focus back to present. I turn back and find Officer Friendly walking around to the passenger side of his cruiser. "Come on, get in. It's freezing out here."

"Thank you, officer," I say as I duck my head inside the warm cabin of the car. He nods his head and give me a quick smile before closing the door.

When he slides into the driver's seat a moment later, he extends his hand to me "Mike Finnegan, but you can call me Finn." His features come into focus under the dome light. He's handsome, very boy next door, but with a set of steel grey eyes that almost don't match the rest of his face, for their intensity.

"Ruby," I say as I shake his hand. His grip is warm against my chilly skin, and I sigh of relief slips from my mouth before I can let go.

"Well Ruby, what kind of car are we looking for?" He smiles at me, and I find myself smiling back.

"She's a white 1998 Honda Civic."

"Getrude?" He laughs. I cringe, realizing he heard me shouting for her like crazy person.

"Yep. Cantankerous old lady name for a cantankerous old car."

We coast up and down a few aisles before finding her parked outside the other entrance to the store. Note to self: The next time you brave the grocery store, map out your exit strategy from the ensuing angry mob.

A rush of arctic air whips through my hair when I open the car door. "Thank you, Officer Finnegan," I offer before I close the door behind me. Before I can take a step toward my car, the window rolls down and those grey eyes peer at me from across the front seat.

"Finn," He insists, with an easy smile.

"Sorry. Thank you, *Finn*."

"Hey, Ruby?" He calls once more. On a wary sigh, I lift my eyes to his. "Whoever made you cry, isn't worth your tears." I nod my head, afraid I'll blubber if I try to speak. He's right, my sorrow isn't worthy of the man who broke my heart. He never considered his choices impact on me when he was spinning his web of deceit, and I can't sever the tie to him by divorcing him like my mother did. He is my father. No matter of disownment can rectify that. If nothing else, this night has taught me that no matter how much you try to disassociate yourself from the past, you can never out run it.

"Goodnight, Finn," is all the answer I can summon.

"'Night, Ruby."

If things were different, I could really see myself liking Finn. He's handsome and really good at the whole white-knight thing. Even if I let myself like him, I doubt he'd stick around past the shock of my last name. What a joke: The cop and the crook's daughter. Yeah, that would never work.

...TO BE CONTINUED

www.maggimyers.com
www.facebook.com/author.maggi.myers
@Magnolia_B_My
www.goodreads.com/author/show/6549512.Maggi_Myers

A Bend in the Road

Tess Oliver

Copyright © 2014 Tess Oliver
All rights reserved.

"A Bend in the Road" is dedicated to my mom, Jutta Eva Walker, a true romantic who was never without a book on her lap or a smile on her face. She survived and escaped the horrors of Hitler's Germany, but she couldn't beat breast cancer. Let's find a cure.

I glanced up in the rearview and the faded blue bruise stared back at me, mocking me, reminding me that I'd made an embarrassingly bad choice. Decent radio stations had vanished along with the chunks of tract homes, gas stations and mini marts. I pushed the CD button and turned up the volume.

The sky was a crystal blue and the smell of manure and garlic drifted through the miniature vents on my very miniature car assuring me that Aunt Gail's house was just a few miles away. Four years of college and another year of slogging through job searches and interviews had kept me from visiting my favorite aunt. But as my carefully planned, carefully controlled life had unraveled over the past year, I'd realized how badly I needed to see her.

Aunt Gail had always been a free spirit, a never take life seriously type of person, the complete and polar opposite of my mom . . .and of me. From as early as third grade, I'd had my life planned and organized right down from my Hello Kitty pencil box to the college I would attend and the type of man I would marry. But last summer, when my perfectly methodical and predictable mom announced in an almost humorous fashion that she was leaving my dad, it knocked me off my path. That one bend in the road led to a series of wrong turns from which I was still reeling.

A highway sign was my marker for the unpaved road leading to my Aunt's farm. The sign was still tilted at a precarious angle from when Ryder Stevens, a neighbor boy, and I had taken a joy ride in his dad's tractor. Ryder had given me my first real kiss, and if my uncle had not decided one blistering hot August day to sneak out to his barn for a midday beer, Ryder would have been my first *everything*. Ryder had been one of those dreamy boys who never said much but who could still talk any girl out of her jeans, and I had been no exception. My teenage hormones would spin out of control whenever he was near, and even though he'd never fit into my perfectly tailored scheme of life, he'd been impossible to resist.

Titus, Uncle Robbie's massive black shepherd, looked the same but moved a little slower as he trotted out from the farmhouse to greet my car. After the long drive, it felt good to stand. "Hey, Buddy." His plush fur smelled like hay as I leaned down and hugged his wriggling body. In the distance I could see Aunt Gail with a red kerchief on her head strolling in from the field with a basket resting on her hip.

She saw me and lowered the basket to the ground. "Janie!" We both ran.

We threw our arms around each other and hopped around in a circle, laughing and crying. It had been too long. We finally stopped long enough to catch our breaths and Aunt Gail took a step back. Some of the creases around her mouth and eyes had deepened and some of the auburn hair had been replaced with streaks of gray but she was still radiant.

"My little Janie." She reached up and brushed back a strand of my hair and her smile sagged. "Ooh, that man, I could take him out back and—"

I took hold of her hand. It felt warm and slightly calloused. "Aunt Gail, it's fine. He's out of my life for good, and I would rather not be reminded of my stupidity."

She nodded and kissed my cheek. "I won't mention it again." She took my hand and led me back to the basket, which was brimming with smooth red tomatoes. She sighed. "We've had tomatoes coming out of our ears." We picked up the basket together and carried it back toward the house. Aunt Gail laughed as she said, "I've been serving Robbie tomatoes for breakfast, lunch, and dinner, and even though he doesn't complain much, I fear if I put one more tomato dish in front of the man, he's going to run from the house screaming. I'm planning to box some of these up and drop them off on neighbor's porches. But not Fran down at the end of the road...she's having the same tomato abundance problem as me." She paused, then smiled. "Although it might be kind of funny to leave her a box! Anyhow, enough about tomatoes. Come inside for a sandwich and you can tell me everything that has happened in the last four years."

Aunt Gail's kitchen had a breathtaking view of the entire farm. A weak breeze bent the tender tips of the grass that ran along the border of the fields. The air lingered with the fragrance of freshly picked vegetables and a hint of garlic. The neighboring land had been used for growing garlic for years and the entire valley had always smelled a bit like an Italian restaurant, but it had never been an overwhelming smell, just enough aroma to keep you perpetually hungry.

"Where's Uncle Robbie?"

Aunt Gail reached into the refrigerator and pulled out two premade sandwiches. "He had to haul the tractor into town for some repairs. And, of course, I remembered too late that I needed some cheddar cheese." She grinned at me. "I'm making your favorite tonight-- mac and cheese, or at least I was planning to. I forgot to remind him about the cheese, and he never remembers to take his cell phone with him." She lowered the plates to the table and we sat.

"I could drive into town later and pick up some cheese."

"That would be great. Are you sure?"

"Uh, mac and cheese? I think I can make the sacrifice."

She looked over at me and some of sparkle faded from her eyes. "So, Janie, tell me what happened. You sounded so distraught on the phone."

"I'm sorry if I worried you, Aunt Gail. Everything just sort of went to crap all at once." My voice wavered a bit so I stopped to take a bite of sandwich, hoping to squelch an eruption of emotion. I swallowed and took a breath as Aunt Gail waited patiently for me to continue. She had always been a much better listener than my mom, who would start in with her advice and lectures before I could even get three words out. "The company I was working for had to lay people off, and since I was as the bottom of the heap, I was the first to go. Almost immediately, Trey started acting differently toward me. He'd always seen us as this future power couple climbing the ranks together, sweeping up tons of money and prestige on our rise to glory and success. But then, suddenly, I was jobless… and, in his eyes, worthless." I swallowed to relieve the thickness in my throat.

Aunt Gail reached across and patted my hand. "What an awful man."

"He really is, but it took me a year to realize it, and I feel so ashamed."

"No," Aunt Gail protested. "You were young and—"

"Trey fit perfectly into my plan. He was successful, ambitious and handsome." I gave a small grimace. "Although now I cringe just thinking about him."

"Good. You should. He sounds truly monstrous."

"The final blow came when a friend of mine needed to find a home for a stray kitten. I haven't had a pet since I left home for college, and I was sorely in need of a little furry friend. Trey exploded with rage telling me I had some nerve bringing a cat into his home without his permission." My jaw clenched tightly just thinking about the fit he'd thrown. "Up until that point, I'd paid for half of that overpriced, cramped apartment, but once I was jobless, it became *his* home. I told him he was a selfish prick, and," the words stuck in my throat, "he threw the glass he'd been holding." I could sense Aunt Gail tense with anger as I spoke. "I have no idea if he'd truly meant to hit me, but we were through. I walked straight into the bedroom and packed."

"I'm sure it was heartbreaking for you, but I'm glad you left."

"You know something, it wasn't all that heartbreaking. In fact, it was kind of freeing. Not even sure how I ended up with him in the first place."

Aunt Gail sipped some iced tea. "The plan, remember? Maybe it's time for you to veer away from that plan. Which reminds me, your mom called me just before she left on her cruise." She looked at me over the brim of her glass. "She has never sounded happier."

Aunt Gail knew how to get her *point* across without ever really *pointing* it out.

I picked up my sandwich. "I guess she's finally learned how to *veer*." A horse whinnied in the distance. "Oh my gosh, was that Queenie? How is she?"

"That sounded like Charger." Aunt Gail rolled her eyes. "Your uncle bought himself a new gelding, and that horse is the most ornery, challenging animal I've ever met. I told Robbie he should have named him Widow Maker because that is what he's going to make me. Ryder's been coming over to work him, but I don't know if he'll ever be broke enough for Robbie to ride." She picked a piece of lettuce off her sandwich and dropped it onto the plate. "I sort of hope not."

"Ryder? I'd forgotten all about him."

Aunt Gail's brow arched at my obvious lie.

"He got married, didn't he?"

She waved her hand. "That was over faster than a summer thunderstorm. They were never suited for each other. I think Ryder just married her to placate his father, who was sick with cancer at the time. After his father died, he got a quick divorce and left town for awhile. Ended up in some trouble with the law-- a bar brawl or something, I think, but he's back now and he's been fixing up the farm."

I chewed a bit faster as she spoke, as if some of my teen hormones had resurfaced with just the mention of his name.

Aunt Gail grinned at me. "And he is still a tall drink of water, that one. But he never got serious with anyone again. Or at least not that I know of. "She stood and carried her dishes to the sink. "Speaking of Queenie," Aunt Gail could snap to a different subject without taking a new breath, "she's been standing out in the pasture with the other horses all day. She'd probably appreciate you taking her out for a little ride-- if you're up for it."

"I'm *so* up for it I can't even tell you." For the first time in months, I heard happiness in my tone. "But first, I'll go into town to get that cheese."

Town was really two parallel lines of outdated, quaint shops bordering a thinly paved stretch of road called Main, but it was the kind of place that made you feel at home even if you were from out of town. I pulled my car into one of the three spots in front of Bert's Market and Sundries and hopped out. It was one of those stores that had a little bit of everything.

Bert's beard had thickened along with his waist. He glanced up from his cash register and then his face popped up with a bright smile. "Janie Morris, you're back. It's about time."

I waved. "Hey Bert, Aunt Gail sent me in for some cheddar cheese."

"Straight back and to your left."

I grabbed a package of cheese that looked as if it had been on the shelf for a good long while and returned to the check stand. The bell on the door rang behind me, and Bert nodded a silent greeting to the customer.

"Don't think I've seen you around these parts since you were a teenager," Bert said.

"I know, it's terrible of me, but I went off to college and got too busy. But, now I've found my way back, and I'm glad." And it couldn't have been more true. All through college I'd convinced myself that I could only be happy in the bustling world of business and finance. Now I had my reservations.

Bert's mustache had grown completely gray, and it twitched as he spoke. "That'll be five, eighty-five."

I reached into my pocked and pulled out the five dollar bill Aunt Gail had given me. "I have another dollar in my—" A large hand reached from behind me and a dollar bill fluttered to the counter.

I turned around. His shoulders had filled out, his arms had thickened with muscles and he'd added some tattoos, but his gaze was as familiar and unsettling as always.

Ryder stared down at me from a dark curtain of lashes, and I was instantly transported back to my teen years when one glance from those cool blue eyes could set my skin on fire. "You're back, J.J." It was the nickname he'd given me and hearing it now made me smile. He paid Bert for the gallon of milk he held.

Bert bagged the cheese and handed it to me with a wink.

"I'm visiting my aunt for a few weeks." We walked outside. The black jeep he'd driven in high school, the very same jeep where we'd had more than one major kissing session, was parked next to my car.

"You drove all the way up here in a lawnmower?"

I lifted my chin. "Bob is not a lawnmower. He's a Smart Car."

His lazy smile, the smile that was one of his major weapons in charming a girl out of thinking straight, appeared. "You named it Bob?"

I shrugged. I was acting cool and smooth as whipped cream on the outside but for some silly reason my insides were churning like butter. "It seemed to fit."

That infectious gaze of his drew me in just like it always had. He stood there so cool and confident and familiar, the same boy who could sweet talk me into anything, it felt as if I'd never left. "Well, I guess I'll see you around."

"Yeah," I said a little too loudly. "See you around." I slid back into my puny car and had to make a conscious effort to slow down my breathing and the slight tremble in my hands. He backed his jeep out of the parking spot, and I watched him drive off as the tiny, annoyingly logical voice in my head reminded me that he was the last thing I needed right now.

****

Queenie snorted softly as I buckled the bridle. She'd whinnied as soon as she saw me walking toward her in the field and I'd been overly pleased that she remembered me. I led her out of the barn to the garden bench that I'd always used to climb onto her wide, sloped back. It had seemed too hot and sticky for jeans and boots so I hadn't changed. I slipped off my sandals and hiked my dress up to mid thigh.

Queenie stood as still as a sentry as I climbed onto her bare back. For the first ten years of her horsey life, Queenie had pulled a wagon around an amusement park, and Uncle Robbie said that the experience had made her the best trail horse in the world. He'd insisted that a meteor could come crashing down to Earth next to where she was grazing and Queenie would likely just flick her tail in irritation from having her lunch interrupted. Aside from several dull rides on rental horses, my only riding experiences had been on Aunt Gail's farm, and Queenie had given me the confidence to learn quickly.

It was just an hour or so before dusk and the shadowy sunlight made the stretch of fields and pastures looked endless. Birds were diving into the tall weeds along the side of the road hunting for their last meals before the settling darkness would banish them back to the safety of the trees. A rhythmic hammering in the distance pricked Queenie's ears forward, and she picked up her heavy feet and plodded faster down the dirt path.

Ryder's house came into view as we reached the top of the road. Again, the stupid rational voice in my head spoke up, telling me to turn around. For years, I'd stuck to my plan and listened to that sensible voice, and it had ended badly. I squeezed my legs against Queenie's sides and prodded her forward.

Fresh, unpainted wood lay in stacks along the front of the house. Harold and Chuck, Ryder's two giant dogs, heard us approach and lifted their big heads. Apparently Queenie and I were not exciting enough for more than a tail wag and short bark.

Ryder stood up from behind the balustrades on his newly built porch. He reached up to wipe the sweat from his forehead with the back of his hand and then he scrubbed back his dark hair.

"Looks nice." I was surprised but relieved to hear the confidence in my tone. Even though I was still feeling a blush all the way down to my toes, I was done behaving like a red cheeked school girl.

Ryder glanced around at his handiwork. "Thanks. It's taken a hell of a lot longer than I'd expected." He walked down the newly built steps. "Hey, Queenie." He reached up and patted the mare's neck. His gaze drifted along my bare legs. Then his long lashes lifted as he looked up at me. His throat moved as he swallowed hard and words seemed to be stuck in his throat at first. "You are a sight, Janie. A man could spend his whole damn day just looking at you."

I smiled down at him. "And you're still a smooth talker."

"Yeah, it's always worked for me." A wicked smiled turned up the side of his mouth. "Talked you right out of your jeans in your aunt's barn, a day that is scorched into my brain forever. Never did get over the disappointment of your uncle coming across that yard and stopping us."

"It's a good thing he's a loud sneezer, or we never would have heard him coming."

He smiled up at me. "Want to come inside and see what I've done to the kitchen?"

"Sure." I slid my leg around and he reached up to grab my waist. He brushed my body against his as he lowered me slowly to the ground. Taking reins from my hand, he walked Queenie over to a patch of grass and she dropped her head to graze.

Ryder looked down at my bare feet. "I'm not great at keeping track of nails." Without warning he swept me into his arms. I laughed and threw my arms around his neck.

"Remember when you got stuck in the middle of the river and you were too afraid to cross the rocks—"

"And you lifted me into your arms? Ryder Stevens, there isn't a girl on this planet who could forget being swept up in your arms." I looked at him and his nearness made me forget my words for a second and when I spoke they came out as a whisper. "Of course I remember." I rested my head against his hard shoulder. He carried me up the porch steps and I pushed the screen door open with my foot.

Reluctantly, he lowered my feet to the floor. In the kitchen, the smell of cut pine mingled with fresh paint. I reached up and ran my hand over the new wood. "It's beautiful, Ryder. You made all this cabinetry by yourself?" I looked over my shoulder to where he was leaning against the adjacent kitchen counter, watching me in a way that sent waves of heat through me.

"Yep. But this took me a hell of a lot longer than I'd expected too." He looked around. "At the rate I'm going and with having to stop for planting and harvesting, I figure I'll be ninety six by the time I get the whole house remodeled."

"And then the kitchen and porch will be old and you'll have to start all over again."

He laughed. "I hadn't thought of that."

I tucked my hair behind my ear only to remember too late about the ugly bruise. He closed the distance between us with two heated steps. Anger flickered in his eyes as he raised his hand, his calloused fingertips grazing the bruised skin lightly.

"It was an accident," I said quickly. "I've left him."

His jaw twitched beneath the dark stubble as he lowered his hand. He looked at me. "What an asshole. God, J. J., if you were mine, I'd stand in front of a moving train just to protect you."

The truth was, even when we were just two teens having a good time in each other's company, I'd always felt incredibly safe with Ryder.

His gaze drifted down to my lips, and I closed my eyes in anticipation of a long, hard kiss. The ring of a phone broke the charged silence that had swept in around us. He pulled his phone out of his pocket.

"Hey, Robbie. Yep, I'll be there in a few." He slid the phone back into his pocket. "Your uncle's record of interrupting us remains unchallenged. Mind if I walk back to your aunt's with you and Queenie? I've got to ride your uncle's crazy horse."

"Sure," I said with a good measure of disappointment. "I should be getting back anyhow."

He led me out to the porch and sat down on the steps to pull off his work boots and pull on his cowboy boots. "I don't have the heart to tell your uncle, but I don't know if this horse will ever be tame enough for him to ride." He stood and whistled. His two dogs jumped up and trotted lazily behind.

In the city, the summer heat never seemed to leave, as if the closely set buildings and crush of people kept it trapped, but out in the wide open, the hot summer air shifted easily to a cool, comforting breeze. It pushed the hem of my dress up higher on my thighs and I made several futile attempts to push it back down. The entire process seemed to amuse Ryder.

"What's so funny?"

"Who are you hiding those silky thighs from? I've already seen them-- more than once if I recall."

It seemed I'd blushed more often in the past few hours than I had in the past four years. "Now how would you remember this particular pair of silky thighs, when you've seen so many?"

He laughed. "My reputation has always been greatly exaggerated." He walked alongside of Queenie and looked up at me. "And even if I have seen more than my share of thighs, I'd never forget yours."

****

Aunt Gail and Uncle Robbie had gone to bed and aside from the usual chorus of crickets, the occasional snort of a sleepy horse and the settling walls of the old house, a peaceful quiet had fallen over the farm.

Ryder had ridden Charger for one long, harrowing hour during which I'd traded off between gasping in horror and holding my breath in angst. He'd managed to remain in the saddle and Aunt Gail had rewarded him with macaroni and cheese when he was done. More than once, the toe of his boot had tapped my bare calf under the table and even that small, harmless flirtation had left me with an insatiable urge to be in his arms.

Just as I went to slide of my dress and get into bed, something small smacked the bedroom window. It was a sound I'd heard before, and my heart raced ahead as I hurried to the window and pushed it open.

Ryder stared up at me from the front yard. "Hey J. J., come out and play." It was the same line he'd always used and it had always worked. I pulled on my sandals and, just like I had as a teenager, I tiptoed down the stairs and out the front door.

I ran up to him and he wrapped me in his strong arms. He gazed down at me. "There was no way I was going to sleep tonight knowing my favorite pair of lips—" He reached down, and I gasped as his calloused fingertips reached under the hem of my dress and slid along the skin of my leg. "—And silky thighs were just five hundred yards down the road." He dropped his arms and grabbed hold of my hand. I was certain he would lead me back to his house, but instead we headed into Uncle Robbie's barn.

I looked at him questioningly.

"I told you it's been etched in my brain. I don't think I can ever go easily to my grave until we finish what we started here." I followed him obediently up to the hayloft. A soft quilt and bottle of wine waited for us. A half moon provided just enough light and cast a warm glow through the open loft window.

"I don't remember the blanket or the wine last time," I said.

"Well, back then my dad would have had my hide if I'd been walking around with a bottle of wine, and I keenly remember getting straw stuck in places it shouldn't have been." He pulled me into his arms. "Let me make love to you, Janie." It was the same thing he'd said that afternoon when we were two overheated teens and it felt just as right this time.

I lifted my face to his and felt his arms wrap tightly around me as his mouth came down over mine, making my knees weak. I clutched his shirt to keep from sinking to the ground. His hands smoothed down over my back, and he inched the hem of my dress up. He pulled his mouth away from mine just long enough to lift my dress up and over my head, then gazed down at me with a hunger that made me nearly melt into a heated puddle.

Ryder reached forward and undid the clasp on my bra and slid it from my shoulders. I pushed off my sandals and stepped back into his arms in just my panties, pressing my nearly naked body against his. I could feel his heart beating wildly as he held me against him. His hands ran over my bare skin as he pushed my panties down. My arms circled his neck and I pulled his mouth down to mine.

"I've never wanted anything so badly," I whispered. My fingers reached down and grabbed the end of his t-shirt and I clumsily pushed it up over his head. I pressed my hardened nipples against his heated skin as my tongue moved along his throat.

"God, J. J., I've been waiting for this for four damn years." He led me to the quilt. It was soft and warm beneath my skin as I stretched back and watched him take off his jeans. He was even more beautiful naked. He knelt down next to me, his gaze drifting over my naked body." I can't stop looking at you." He leaned over me and kissed my breasts, softly at first and then his tongue circled my taut nipples and I inhaled deeply, pushing up against his mouth. His hands caressed my stomach moved down to the moist warmth between my legs. I arched my hips eagerly toward his touch as his fingers slid inside of me.

A soft mewl floated from my lips and disappeared into the cool air of the loft. I ached for him. My fingers slid along the long hot length of him, and he groaned as I ran my thumb over the smooth, slick tip.

He reached for his jeans and pulled a condom out of the pocket. He pushed my thighs open as he knelt down between my legs. Leaning over me, he slid one hand beneath my bottom and he kissed me again as he slipped inside of me, slowly at first and then with the urgency I'd longed for. His mouth devoured mine as he thrust deeper, and I curled my legs around his waist, pulling him harder against me, not wanting him to stop... ever.

Our bodies fit together perfectly, and we moved in rhythm as if we'd been made for each other. I could not get enough of him. I wanted him to go deeper and harder. My fingers clutched his shoulders as he rocked against me, leaving me wanting more with each thrust. My legs gripped him tightly and I cried out as shuddering waves of heat and pleasure coursed through me. His movements became frenzied as he ground his body against mine. A low groan rolled up from his throat and his fingers clamped around my arms as he came.

He collapsed down over me and rolled onto his side, bringing me along with him. His fingers tenderly brushed the fading bruise on my cheek. "I think you should stay here, with me."

I snuggled against him and it dawned on me that the only time I'd ever been truly happy was when I was here in the country, away from the stress of the city, and in Ryder's arms. My 'predetermined' path had always led me to the wrong place, and it had taken a few bends in the road to help me find my way home. I lifted my head and kissed him. "Thank you, Ryder."

His arms wrapped around me. "For what?"

"For waiting. For still being here when I finally came to my senses."

Facebook: https://www.facebook.com/tessoliverauthor
Twitter: https://twitter.com/Tess_Oliver
website: http://www.tessoliver.com/
Blog: http://tessoliverauthor.blogspot.com/
Goodreads: https://www.goodreads.com/tessoliver

More than a Friend Request

Julie Prestsater

Copyright © 2014 Julie Prestsater
All rights reserved.

Chapter One

1 New Friend Request

Hannah tapped her phone like she'd done many times before to view the new friend request on her FaceSpace page. But little could have been done to prepare her for what she was about to see.

Adam Cooper would like to be friends.

Accept or Decline.

Adam Cooper wanted to be her friend. *Her friend*. After fifteen years, he wanted to be *her* friend. On FaceSpace of all places. No phone calls, no emails, no old-fashioned snail mail. He used a social network to initiate contact after what seemed like a lifetime apart. What? Were they fourteen?

Her head spun as she steadied herself long enough to plant herself in a chair at her kitchen table. Thankfully, it was a Saturday morning or else she may have gotten the request at work and wouldn't have been able to hide this near hyperventilation. Maybe it was cardiac arrest because her heart was sure beating faster than ever.

Hannah stared at the screen of her phone that she gripped tightly in both her hands.

Adam Cooper.

Like any other woman with a FaceSpace page, she'd spent many nights trolling the pages searching ex-boyfriends, old flames, and all those who could've been. She'd come across Jason, who was her first kiss in fourth grade. She was genuinely happy for him when she discovered he was married with four children, two boys and two girls who were just as gorgeous as their parents.

MORE THAN A FRIEND REQUEST

When she located Luke, Hannah actually sent him a friend request. When they had ended their three month relationship after he moved to a different school in junior high, they remained in contact for years. Sometime in high school, they had lost touch but she'd always wondered what happened to him. Now, on occasion, they'd meet after work for drinks. On a platonic level, of course, since he came out to her. Talk about a waste of a good man. For women, anyway. For a man, he was quite the catch. He was stunning, well groomed, and well dressed. She guessed that should have been her first clue. At any rate, she was happy for him and his partner, David. They seemed more than content with the life they'd made together, with their catering business and a pair of his and his matching Old English Sheepdogs.

Hannah's high school sweetheart had tried to friend her, but she ignored the request. There was no way in hell she was going to talk to that jerk online or any other place for that matter. You'd think after all this time, she would've gotten over how Ryan had cheated on her with one of her close friends, yet she hadn't. And to top it off, she had no interest in reading more about how they were still together since they'd married right after graduation since she was knocked up. Fortunately for her, Ryan's FaceSpace was private, so it saved her the grief of snooping and seeing just how happy they were.

But Adam. She had searched for him on FaceSpace many times. On occasions when she was lonely and feeling needy. Sometimes after watching a chick flick and getting caught up in happily ever afters. Or when she'd had one too many beers, and she'd thought about the one who got away. She thought about him all right. There hadn't been a day since she met him all those years ago that she hadn't let her mind wander with thoughts of him, his warm smile, and the tenderness of his touch.

And now there he was — wanting to be her friend. Wow. Hannah still stared at the screen, making no attempt to accept or deny the request. She just looked at his name on the screen, and sat while her belly did back flips with all the anxiousness that came with seeing his name in print. The more she looked at it, it was like she could feel his gentle hands on her. The way he would take her face in the palms of both his hands and hold her still while he gazed into her eyes — silently expressing his love and desire. She'd never once felt that kind of love again. It had been fifteen years since she'd last seen him, and she could almost feel the taste of his lips on hers. Sweet, warm, and delicious.

Tears filled Hannah's eyes. Her face got hot, and she could feel her palms getting clammy. Why now Adam? Why now?

She tried hard not to think about their past but knowing he was trying to get in contact with her caused all the memories to come crashing back like the break of waves in the ocean, one after another, without any relief. There was no stopping the images of his gorgeous face from popping up in her mind. They'd always been there, so vivid as if he were standing right in front of her.

Hannah clicked her phone off, blacking out the screen and set it down on the table. She needed a cup of coffee. Maybe a vanilla latte would ease her mind, and her stomach, for awhile. On second thought, she was going to need a little more than some caffeine to do the trick. She decided the caffeine alone would make her mind race even more. She settled on toasting a bagel, and then slathered the thing with gobs of raspberry cream cheese. She was going to need coffee and sweets to deal with this.

She took her breakfast back to the table and started with a sip of her latte. She couldn't resist any longer. She turned on her phone and brought up the FaceSpace app. Yup, she hadn't dreamed up the whole thing. It was still there. A friend request from Adam Cooper. She placed it face down on her placemat, and dug into the bagel.

With each bite, she thought about Adam. She could picture the first time she met Adam clearly, like she'd just seen him moments before. Her college roommate, Leila, had been dating Adam's brother for months. There were many nights when the two girls would stay up talking about how exciting it would be for the roomies to date brothers, twins in fact. The more they talked about it, the more nervous she got. Hannah didn't have much luck in the boyfriend department. She could count the number of boyfriends she'd had on one hand, and she didn't even need to use all her fingers. Yet, her roommate was about to set her up on a blind date. Well, not entirely blind. She knew what he'd look like since she'd seen his brother almost every day for the last several months.

When the day finally came to meet him, Hannah was a nervous wreck so Leila talked her into a shot of tequila to calm her nerves. And when Adam finally walked into her dorm room, she regretted not taking more than one. Saying the guy was hot would have been the biggest understatement of all time. He was on fire. A real scorcher. His brother did *not* do him justice. They were definitely not identical twins.

Adam was close to six feet tall, and had a strong build. He had thick dark wavy hair. It was longer on top, short on the sides and in the back. It didn't look gelled or anything. It was a perfect effortless mess she immediately wanted to run her fingers through. She had laughed out loud when she thought about how she hoped she'd get the chance to tug on his locks in a night of passion. When he'd asked her what was so funny, she waved him off in embarrassment. He had caught her stare with a raised brow, and she got lost in his almond-shaped hazel eyes. In those first few minutes, they seemed to be paralyzed in the moment, staring each other down. They just smiled like fools, even when his brother and Leila tried to spark conversation.

At dinner, they sat side by side and when their thighs brushed against each other, they both flinched like they had just touched their tongues to a nine volt battery. Hannah had never felt such an instant connection with anyone in her life. She was sure that the feeling was mutual. She knew he was feeling something too. Why else would he have responded to her touch in such a way?

When she finished her bagel, she turned her phone over and clicked it on again. This time, she tapped on his name, bringing up his profile page. She tapped on his face to enlarge the photo. There were those eyes. He was wearing sunglasses in the picture, but she could still see through the tint to make out those long lashes and his sexy stare. He was grinning, like he'd been caught doing something he wasn't supposed to. His angular face was still thin, and he was tan. She could imagine him surfing one early morning and then spending the rest of the day on the beach playing volleyball and reading a book. The passing years had been kind to him. If Hannah didn't already know his age, she would have thought he was younger, maybe in his late twenties even.

She backed out of the screen and tapped again to bring up his personal information. She scrolled down the list of attributes till she found the one she was looking for. Single. Thank god. He was single. How could that be? How could a man like him still be single? She was still single, but she was a woman and it was a lot more difficult to find the right man. But he was Adam. He could have had any woman he wanted.

Hannah licked her lips as she read more. It was like feeding a hunger that she had suppressed for way too long. She needed more and she was going to get it. She rushed to her office and powered up her desktop computer. The screen of her cell phone was way too small to investigate Adam Cooper.

She scanned all the things she knew about him. His hometown, high school, college, and degrees. She snickered when she saw that he admitted to liking Britney Spears. She knew that about him, but she would have never thought he'd put it out there for the world to see. She paid close attention to the things she didn't know, things that were new since she'd seen him last. She choked up a bit when she took note that they shared some of the same favorites like the book A Thousand Splendid Suns and the movie The Holiday with Kate Winslet and Jude Law. She could picture snuggling up to Adam on her sofa and watching the flick together. She could also imagine blasting Britney and dancing all over the house with him. He'd always been fun and care free like that.

She glanced at the top of her screen, to the icon telling her she still had a new friend request. She was well aware of it. Her entire body, mind, and soul was on full alert, yet she had no idea how she was going to respond.

****

Adam stared at the screen of his laptop waiting for a notification. Surely, she'd gotten the request already. Every damn person in the world had smartphones these days. And they all chimed when something like a friend request on FaceSpace came through. So what was taking her so long?

Maybe she was one of the few people on the planet that didn't have 100% access 100% of the time. But he doubted it. He knew Hannah, and he knew her well. She was a social butterfly and he knew she probably set her phone settings to update every two minutes, even if it did drain her battery at warp speed.

He'd finally grown a pair and sent her the request and now it was utterly painful to wait. Adam had been debating on whether to send the thing in the first place. He only recently signed up on the site because his baby sister had just moved an hour and a half away and she wanted to stay in touch. It was a short drive, but his sibling made it seem like she was going to be on the other side of the world. He knew her frequent weeknight visits would stop, but he also knew they'd talk all the time. Even so, she practically begged her big brother to sign up so she could share all her thoughts and photos with him whenever she wanted. Now he was second guessing his decision to sign up on the site, even for his sister. He knew that once he did, he would start looking for Hannah. Something he'd been trying to avoid since the last time they saw each other after his graduation.

Had it really been fifteen years? How did he let all this time pass without one single word? Not even a damn email? How easy would it have been for him to send her a measly email for crying out loud? It's not like he didn't know her address. Or where she worked. Or what she'd been up to for a decade. He may not have searched for her on FaceSpace but he'd Googled her many times. He'd always been touched that she had become a high school counselor. He could see her making such an impact in her students' lives. He would have loved to have a counselor like her when he was kid. He wouldn't have ditched so much, that's for sure. He would have wanted to spend as much time with her as possible.

He was surprised they hadn't run into each other in all these years. They lived so close to one another. There had been many times he thought he had spotted her at a grocery store or at a movie theater and was disappointed when it wasn't her. He secretly wished he'd bump into her, giving them the chance to reconnect. Rather than using a social network like he was now. God, he was such an idiot.

Adam refreshed the page, thinking maybe he'd missed something and Hannah had accepted his friend request. However, there was no such luck. She had yet to respond. Maybe she wasn't going to.

That couldn't be. She was probably pacing the floors at her house, trying to decide what to do. She was probably doing the same exact thing as him. Reminiscing. Just seeing her face on the thumbnail photo on the site sent him reeling. His breath hitched and he felt his chest tighten. It had been quite some time since he'd seen her, but she still had the same effect on him.

Adam remembered the first time they met. When his brother, Aaron, and his brother's girlfriend set up the blind date, he was furious. He had no intention of keeping some ugly roommate company so his brother could get laid. That just wasn't in his plan. Sure, he wanted to meet someone. He was pleased that his brother had found what he thought was love, although Adam wasn't sure non-stop sexual encounters everywhere and anywhere at all times of the day were considered love, but hey, who was he to judge. He liked Leila. She was nice and she put a smile on his brother's face so he had no reason to complain. But…and there was always a but…he really didn't want to be set up. Especially with Leila's roommate. If things went south, and he was sure they would, he was going to have to deal with some sort of fallout from his brother and his girl. No thank you.

Things changed though. From the second he walked into Leila's dorm room and spotted Hannah, he was toast. A total goner. He'd heard of people falling head over heels before but he didn't think he'd ever experience it. The way she had smiled at him, with such a sweet innocence about her made his heart melt. After her big smile, her eyes caught his attention next. They were big brown eyes he could get lost in. She had insanely long lashes that made her eyes open up to him even more. And all that hair. Wow, she had thick, wavy brown hair that fell passed her shoulders. She could have been one of those models for commercials that he had seen advertising hair products.

In the midst of devouring all her beauty, he could sense immediately how nervous she was. She had what looked like a napkin in her hand and she was twisting it around her fingers, something that he'd come to find out was her trademark way of fidgeting whenever she was anxious about something. Thinking back on that first night made Adam smile. He wished he could have a do-over of the last fifteen years to include the woman he fell so hard for and ultimately, and so stupidly, let go. He ran his fingers through his own thick hair contemplating that last thought. Well, he wouldn't redo them all. He had one thing to be grateful for during his time away from Hannah.

But now, he wanted nothing more than to see her again. To hear her voice. To have her in his arms. He clicked on her name again so her profile would show up. It still showed a pending request. He had the option to take it back but he wasn't that much of a wimp. He stared at the screen and gazed into her big eyes that were looking back at him. He felt like she could see him through the fiber optic lines of the internet. He knew it was crazy, but she could always see him, or through him. He smiled at her, imagining her smiling right back. She was absolutely glowing in her photo and Adam wondered what — or who — made her look so happy. She looked perfect. Her face had filled out a bit and she had grown into a gorgeous woman. He couldn't wait to see the rest of her.

If only she'd respond to his friend request. Maybe that was a bad idea. Maybe he should've just called her. But that seemed too aggressive. After all that time, he couldn't just pick up a phone and say, "Hi, it's Adam. Remember me? Wanna go to dinner?" No, that wouldn't work. At least this way, if Hannah was interested in seeing or talking to him again, she'd accept him as her friend first. And then he could figure out how he was going to pursue it further. Or if he even could. Hannah's profile was blocked and Adam had no idea if she was single, what her interests were, or anything else of a personal nature. Maybe that's why he had tried to friend her. Seeing her picture wasn't enough. He wanted to know more and the only way he was going to find out anything was if he could see her page. If only she had left it unblocked, then he could have stalked her in private. That would have been enough, right? No, Adam knew reading about Hannah wasn't enough. Nothing would be enough until she was his again.

Adam threw up his hands with a loud sigh. Patience was not a strong suit for him and all this waiting was driving him mad.

"What's up, Dad?"

Adam looked up at his mini-me, standing in the door way with a bowl of cereal in his hands. "Nothing, just getting a little testy in my old age."

The young man walked over and said through a mouthful of cereal. "You got that right. Eleven, Dad, really? I can't believe I have to be home so early. Any chance we can get that curfew extended?"

"Listen, Danny, you're only thirteen not eighteen so let's just leave it alone before you don't go anywhere at all." Adam felt guilty for being so harsh with his son, but he was a little irritated at the moment and they'd beat that conversation to death the night before.

Danny plopped himself down on the desk and peeked at the screen. Adam made no attempt to hide what he was looking at.

"So her name is Hannah Jones?" Danny wiggled his brows at his dad.

"What's that supposed to mean?"

Danny leaned in again to get a better view at the image of Hannah on the screen. "Well, I've seen her picture in your wallet for as long as I can remember, and always wondered about her."

"Oh," was all Adam could think to say.

"Is she my mother?" Danny asked softly, lowering his eyes to meet his dad's.

The solemn look on Danny's face hurt Adam to his core. He had talked to his son about his mom so many times and explained why he didn't have any pictures of her. While the truth wasn't pretty, he always prided himself on being completely honest with his child. There were never any secrets between the two. At least none that he kept. "No, she's not. I'm sorry, bud."

"Then who is she?" This time he sounded only curious and the color flooded back to his cheeks.

"She's a girl I knew in college." He looked back at her picture with one corner of his mouth rising in a half smile.

Danny patted his dad on the shoulder. "By the goofy look on your face, I'd guess she was more than just someone you knew. Old girlfriend? The one who got away?" He hung his air quotes over the last two questions.

"How did you get to be so smart?" Adam asked. "Wait, I know, you probably got your wit from the same place you got your amazing good looks." He sat back in his chair and pretended to brush dust of his shoulder.

The two chuckled before Danny questioned him some more. "So what happened? Why did she get away?"

Adam ran his fingers through his hair and tugged at the ends in frustration. "I blew it, kid. I just blew it."

"Is she married? Does she have any kids? Where does she live? What does she do? " The questions just started flying out of his mouth.

Adam was taken aback by his son's inquisitiveness. Just minutes ago he was going crazy waiting for a friend notification on his computer. Now, he was being interrogated by his teenage son. "Let's see. She lives around here. She's a high school counselor. And I have no idea if she's married or if she has kids."

"So how are you gonna find out?"

"Well." Adam paused. Sure, he'd always been honest but did he really have to spill his guts about his love life, or lack thereof? "I haven't spoken to her in fifteen years and I just sent her a friend request a couple of hours ago. Now, I'm just waiting to see if she even acknowledges me."

Danny nodded his head in approval. "Friend request. Good thinking, old man. So what happens when she friends you back?"

"I don't know." He leaned forward to rest his elbows on his desk and stared at Hannah's photo again.

"Well, you're gonna get her back, right? Assuming she's available."

Adam raised a brow at his son. "I'd sure as hell like to try, but I can't do that until she at least accepts my plea for friendship."

It was as if it was on cue. The speakers of Adam's computer chimed and they both looked. Their eyes shot from the screen to each other. Adam looked terrified while Danny was as giddy as a kid in a candy store.

"Well, it looks like you're going to get your chance, Dad. Now start typing."

Chapter Two

Hannah did it. After wearing a path in her hardwood floors, she finally just clicked on her phone and tapped the button to accept Adam's friend request. She did the whole thing so quickly it was like tearing off a Band-Aid. She stared at the screen which screamed back at her. **You are now friends with Adam Cooper**.

She grabbed for her house phone, not wanting to take her eyes off her cell. "Leila, oh my goodness, you're never gonna guess what I just did."

Her friend sounded groggy, and all she said was, "Hannah, what time is it?"

This was an extremely important moment in Hannah's life, and she needed her best friend to be conscious for it. "Lei, wake your ass up. Splash some water on your face and call me back."

"Nah, I'm good, Hannah. What's going on?" her friend asked with a groan.

"Good, you're awake. Like I said before, you're never gonna guess what I just did."

"What did you do?"

"This morning I got a new friend request on FaceSpace, and I accepted it," Hannah explained, leaving out the most important detail.

"From who?"

"Um, Adam." Hannah wondered how her best friend would react. When things went wrong between her and Adam, Leila was ready to feed him to the wolves.

"Adam, who?" she barked.

"Adam Cooper."

"Adam Cooper? Hannahlynn Marie, are you crazy?"

She just had to call her out by her first and middle name. This wasn't going to be good, Hannah thought.

"No I'm not crazy. I'm curious." Although, she did think she was more than crazy, she was certifiably insane for what she had just started.

"Well, curiosity killed the cat." Leila slammed the phone down and Hannah flinched at the loud noise that erupted in her ear. She'd give her friend time to cool off before trying to talk to her again. She didn't have to get that angry. So she and Adam were cyber friends. What was the big deal? It's not like they had even talked yet.

Hannah was just about to cozy up with a hot romance novel and a strawberry banana smoothie when her phone alerted her of a new message. She expected to see a text message from Leila yelling at her in all capital letters. What she didn't expect to see was a new FaceSpace message… from Adam.

Don't know what to say after 15 years. So I'll start here: Hi, Hannah.

She almost spit the smoothie right out of her mouth as she read the message. She read it over and over again, dissecting every one of the fourteen words written. At least he had acknowledged it had been a long time. And that it was awkward to say the least. He hadn't a clue where to start either. And just like that, with that tiny message, he started to warm her heart all over again. He was just as uncertain as she was and he wasn't afraid to show it. That was one of the things she admired most about him, his honesty. No matter how brutal it was sometimes.

Hannah powered down her electronic reader, picked up her phone and smoothie and shuffled back to her home office in her slippers. If she was going to write anything back to him, she needed to get comfortable and she needed a keyboard. She knew whatever she decided to write back was probably going to come after several drafts.

When she finally logged into FaceSpace and retrieved her messages, she noticed she was shivering. It wasn't even cold out, yet she was shaking like she was on the sinking Titanic. She sat back in the leather chair and rocked back and forth, while she chewed on her straw. By the day's end, the straw would be in shreds if she didn't get a hold of herself. She had already destroyed two paper towels. When she realized the mess she'd made, she brushed off the evidence of her nervousness into a wastebasket.

She tried calming her thoughts long enough to come up with

something to write back, but her head seemed to be crowded with thoughts and all she heard was noise. She turned on her favorite playlist which she called *Mellow*. It was a combination of slow songs by Lady Antebellum, Jay Sean, Puddle of Mud, and Bruno Mars. Listening to these songs and belting out the ballads one by one usually soothed her soul. She took deep breaths and even considered doing some yoga and Pilates stretches before writing back, but she just couldn't wait.

Or maybe she should wait. Maybe she should play hard to get and ignore the message for a few days. No. She couldn't do that. They weren't the type to play games. Instead, she started typing away.

In her first draft, she wrote: *Hi Adam. Wow, it took you fifteen years to come up with HI*. She thought better of it and deleted that message. Then she wrote: *Whatever*, which didn't look very good either so she backspaced over that one too. After several more takes, she finally decided on: **Well, it's as good a place to start as any. Hi yourself, Adam. Nice to hear from you**. And then she added a smiley face at the end, because that was just her nature.

She didn't have to wait long. His response was almost immediate.

Truth?

Always.

I wish I hadn't waited this long.

She thought for a moment before responding: **Truth?**

Always.

Me too.

There was a pause before the computer chimed with another reply from Adam: ;-)

Hannah smiled at the computer winky emoticon as a lone tear slid down her cheek. She'd been waiting for this moment for so long. She'd never imagined they'd meet again for the first time on a computer, but she'd take it. Had she known it would be this easy, she would have tried harder to find him long ago.

As she traced back over their small exchange, another message came through.

So you're a counselor. That must be pretty rewarding.

I see you've done your research. But yeah, it is. Saving one misguided youth at a time.

You know me, always thorough.

She chuckled when she read that. She remembered just how thorough he could be. He'd always taken his time with her, making sure to touch and kiss every inch of her body from the top of her head all the way down to the tips of her pinky toes. And she took pleasure in every second of it.

You still there?

Yes.

Thinking?

Yes.

About?

Your thoroughness. She couldn't believe she was teasing him, but it was Adam. She couldn't lie.

Haven't forgotten that huh? lol

Never.

Glad to know we can still be honest with each other.

That won't ever change. No matter how much time has passed.

Hannah knew that was true. She could always tell him how she felt without having to worry about sounding needy or feeling like she was suffocating him. She'd always been completely upfront with him, and he was too.

You can still make me smile. He chimed in first, again.

Well, I may need ice for my cheeks. I haven't stopped smiling since I got your first message.

Good to know. You weren't nervous?

Hell yes, I was nervous. Still am. You?

I was a wreck up until a few minutes ago.

I calmed down after our initial hellos. I'm good now.

Same here.

She had no idea what to say next. As much as she wanted to tell him to come over so she could see his beautiful eyes in person, or so she could wrap her arms and legs around him and hug him like a koala bear, she didn't. There was honesty and there was up front and open, but she wasn't willing to put herself out there entirely. Not just yet anyway. So she added, **What are you doing these days?**

Working, hiking, reading. Surfing when I can.

And by work, you mean?

Hannah knew quite well what he did. While he was MIA from FaceSpace, he wasn't completely off the map. His name had popped up several times in any quick internet search she tried. She just didn't know the specifics.

Yes, Hannah. I finished medical school. I have my own practice.

Congrats.

She typed that with a lump in her throat. She was completely happy for him. And proud. But his goal of becoming a doctor came at a cost, and she wasn't thinking financially. It cost them their relationship.

What kind?

Pediatrics.

Could the man be any more endearing? Hannah thought for sure he would have gone into surgery of some sort. He had always talked about getting into cardiology. It surprised her that he'd decided to treat children, but she couldn't deny that it touched her more than she wanted it to.

That's great. Very happy for you.

Thanks.

Anytime :D

Speaking of that. Interested in getting together some time?

Of course she was interested. There was one problem though. She wasn't ready. She enjoyed chatting with him online. She'd had more fun typing back and forth with him in the last twenty minutes than she'd had in years. She just wasn't ready to take it any further. Hannah was fully aware what would happen if they saw each other again. It wouldn't be long before they were back in each other's arms and in each other's lives, but for how long? She wasn't sure if she could handle the heartbreak all over again.

This she could be honest with him about.

I'd really like to see you again. But not just yet.

The operative word is YET. So that means we will meet again.

Maybe.

Well, it's not a no, so I'll take it. Gotta run, Hannah. Talk to you soon.

TTYL.

****

"You were smooth, Dad," Danny told him when he sat back and exhaled a long sigh of relief.

Adam felt like a weight had been lifted from his shoulders. They spoke to each other like no time had passed them by at all. It was more than he could have hoped for and he knew it was just the beginning.

"Thanks, bud," he said. "And thanks for sticking by me. What do you think about all this? Are you okay with me dating again?"

His son was easily pleased and he doubted Danny would have any reservations, but this would be new, to both of them, and he needed his son to be okay with it. It had been just the two of them for so long. He couldn't be entirely certain how his kid would react.

"*Again*?" he questioned in a sarcastic tone. "Have you *ever* dated anyone? I'd say it's about time. A man has needs you know."

He looked at his boy and his eyes nearly popped out of his head. "Needs, Daniel? Dating a woman isn't all about needs. You should know better. I didn't raise you to treat a girl with such a lack of respect."

"I know, Dad. I was just joking with you. I'm totally for you finding someone. You've spent the last thirteen years of your life making sure I'm happy. You deserve to be happy too."

Adam looked at him, grateful for the fine young man he'd raised on his own — with the help of his parents and siblings. But they weren't around all the time. They didn't live with them. He had done it almost completely on his own. And he was damn proud. "I'm happy, bud. I've got a good looking son who's very smart and obviously takes after his old man. What more could I want?" He chuckled as he mussed up Danny's hair.

"Hannah."

"Maybe."

"I can't wait to meet her," Danny said while he rubbed his hands together mischievously.

Adam smiled. "Yeah, I know the feeling."

Later that evening, Adam received a phone call from his twin, Aaron.

"What the hell where you thinking, bro?" Aaron asked him.

Adam checked his phone again to see that the person on the other end of the line was in fact his brother and not the wrong number. It was. "What are you talking about?"

"You're talking to Hannah again." The anger in his brother's tone irritated him.

"How did you know?" He immediately got on the defensive. He knew he was going to catch some grief for making contact with her but he was hoping that they would have reconnected and maybe even started dating before anyone had the chance to weigh in on the issue and ruin it. Apparently, his luck had run out before it even started.

"Lei called me. Can you believe that? She hasn't talked to me in over thirteen years, never accepted any of my calls or returned any. But she calls me now to cuss me out because you're trying to get in Hannah's pants again." His brother was the dramatic one. He brought new meaning to the term hyperbole.

"We both know I'm not trying to get into Hannah's pants. I haven't even talked to her. We've only chatted online. That's it. And it's none of Leila's business. You can tell her I said that." It frustrated him to no end that she had already intervened by calling Aaron. If she was willing to do that, she was probably filling Hannah's head with trash about him. Or maybe Hannah had told her to mind her own business and that's why she had to resort to calling his brother. He decided he liked the second scenario better.

"Okay, forget about Lei. This is me talking." Aaron paused. "You weren't there after you stopped seeing each other. I was. She was devastated. I'm the asshole twin and it even broke my heart to see how much you hurt her. Just don't do it again is all I'm going to say. I really hope it all works out this time."

It pained Adam to hear his brother talk about how hurt Hannah had been. Aaron never once told him how she was doing after their split. And he had always ensured Adam that he didn't share anything about him with Leila. Ignorance was bliss at the time. Now, he was the one feeling like an asshole.

"I hope you mean that, bro."

"Of course I do."

Adam took in a long slow breath before admitting, "Good, because I have every intention of trying to get her back. If she'll have me."

"Call me crazy, but I doubt that will be a problem."

Just hearing his brother's confident words made Adam feel so much better. The tone of his voice earlier and the thought of Leila's call had him rattled. The more he thought about it though, he came to the realization that not even Leila and her terrible attitude and meddling could keep him away from Hannah.

Adam crawled into bed with his electronic reader and bowl of kettle corn. He needed something to take his mind off Hannah. It hadn't even been twenty four hours and he already wanted to message her again. He remembered her sassiness when they chatted earlier. He could only imagine what she was thinking when she spoke of him being thorough. Just the thought of all the times he had tasted her from head to toe made him hard.

His mind traveled into the past to a time they went camping on the beach. The memories were so vivid that he could actually smell the salt of the ocean and feel the grit of the sand in his teeth. It was dark out and after roasting marshmallows and walking along the water, they had decided to return to their tent. It wasn't too chilly out so they left the rain flap off the top of their tent so they could view the stars through the window netting. That was their plan anyway. Instead, only she was able to look at the twinkling sky as he had devoured every millimeter of her bare skin. She ran her soft hands through his hair and she had squeezed his shoulders. She had let soft whimpers escape instead of unleashing the shouts she sometimes roared at his apartment, so as not to disturb other campers. Adam had taken the time to please her in every way possible. He had taken her up and over the point of no return before he even parted her legs. But when he finally did, to kiss her core and explore her with only his fingers and his mouth, she let go again. That night, he didn't even take care of his own needs. He was pleased enough to take care of Hannah. When she had curled up to him with her naked bottom in his lap, he wanted her, but he also just wanted to hold her tightly in his arms and never let the moment go. Now, fifteen years later, he was grateful that they had experienced times like those. He hoped Hannah's memories were just as loving as his. He hoped more than anything that her memories weren't tainted by their split.

Adam shook his head to clear his thoughts and powered on his reader. He scanned all the reading suggestions on his home page before settling on the latest John Grisham novel. There was just something he found compelling about a good book about lawyers. Maybe it was because of his own career. He had no interest in reading medical fiction. There were plenty of books about people dying from cancer, and there were too many to count with a medical examiner as the main character, but he wasn't interested. He wanted to be wrapped up in the suspense and mystery of the law.

On second thought, he wanted to be wrapped up in his sheets with Hannah.

Adam groaned. He really needed to get his mind off this woman or he'd never get any reading done. He wouldn't be able to sleep either. And he was going to have to take care of the situation growing in his boxers if she invaded his thoughts any longer.

Fortunately, Danny got home early and was able to occupy his dad's time. Adam got out of bed when he heard the door and went downstairs to meet his son. They opted to throw in a movie and chow down on the kettle corn Adam had made earlier. When they finally agreed on an action film, they relaxed in the family room with their feet on the leather ottoman and a tub of licorice in between them. They watched in silence as cars blew up on the fifty-two inch plasma screen and endless amounts of gunfire blared through the speakers of their surround sound system. When they finished the first batch of popcorn, Danny ran to the kitchen to make some more, and Adam refilled their Dr Pepper.

This scene wasn't uncommon at the Cooper household. Adam loved spending time with his son. It would have been cliché to say his son was like his best friend, but it would have been accurate. It wasn't like Adam was trying to be a cool dad or anything. He didn't let Danny get away with much and was fairly tough on the young man, but they had a great relationship. They had a mutual respect that allowed them to get along unusually well for a parent and a teenager.

Adam looked over at his son who had a large mason jar full of soda between his legs, popcorn spilling out his mouth, and a handful of red vines. Then, he watched as his son took one of the ropes and bit the ends off each side before sloshing it in his drink. He lifted the cup to his lips and took a swig, using the licorice as a straw. Adam chuckled inside. He could do this for the rest of his life and be totally content.

Only one thing could make it better.

And this time, he was determined to make it work.

Chapter Three

Sunday morning, Adam woke up to the sound of football. He looked at the clock and couldn't believe he slept in past ten. His eyes burned and he had a headache. And even worse, his teeth felt like felt. Did he really forget to brush his teeth last night after all that junk they ate? He smiled. One would think since he was a doctor, a pediatrician even, he'd feed his son healthier food. But first and foremost, he was a dad and a man. And today they were going to order pizza and wings and watch some pigskin. Maybe later they'd get around to showering and getting dressed.

****

During halftime of the morning game, Adam heard an alert come through on his phone. He picked it up and was pleasantly surprised to see a message from Hannah.

Afternoon game today. U ready?

Adam shook his head with a chuckle. God, he missed this woman. How could he have forgotten her love for football? She was just as insane as he was when it came to their beloved Lonestars.

Do you really have to ask? How about you?

U kidding me? I even watched all the pregame shows.

You're awesome.

Flattery will get you everywhere. Lol.

Hmm. He'd have to keep that in mind. He headed to his office to fire up the desktop. Danny could text all day on his phone, but he was not that savvy. His hands started cramping up and he hated straining his eyes on the little screen. It was one thing to send a text message to his son to tell him he'd be home late, it was another to actually have a conversation. For that, he needed a full keyboard that would accommodate his large fingers, and a large flat screen monitor that wouldn't kill his vision.

Have you been to a game yet?

They had always talked about making the trek across the country to see a game live, but he'd never made it. He wondered if she had.

Nope. Just a few more San Diego games. Preseason sucks though. Starters rarely play more than a series.

I love it when you talk football.

Haha. Well, I better let you go. Halftime is almost over.

Already? He wasn't ready to cut their conversation so short. Was he really going to say it? He was thinking it. He'd rather miss the game and stay on the computer, chatting with her on FaceSpace.

All right. When will I talk to you again?

That sounded desperate. But he didn't care. He hated not knowing when he'd talk to her next.

Maybe sometime during the week. Late though. Definitely over the weekend. How does that sound?

Good. I'll be looking for you online. Have fun watching the Stars.

You too.

Adam went back to the family room with a smile on his face, and spent the rest of the day snacking and watching football with his son. Every once in awhile, he'd check his phone on the off chance she sent him another message.

****

She stared at her phone with a silly grin. It was unbelievable how giddy he made her feel with so few words. With just a little chitchat about football, she felt complete and happy.

She started watching the Lonestars' game alone with a bucket of buffalo wings. She made a mess and had sauce all over her face and hands, but she didn't care. She loved her Sundays during football season when she'd stay in her jammies all day and watch game after game, snacking on junk food and drinking disgusting amounts of soda. Whenever her brother came over, they'd polish off a twelve pack of beer, but that didn't happen often — which was a good thing because she always had a terrible headache the next day at work.

Sometime during the game, she thought about the first professional football game she'd been too. She remembered thinking as they pulled into the parking lot three hours before the game, it was better than going to Disneyland when she was a kid. Tailgating was interesting considering they were the few people decked out in navy blue jerseys and stars on their hats. She had laughed when people walked by shouting, "Lonestars suck!" She knew better than to say anything back. For one, she'd let the final score speak for itself. And two, it was preseason. It's not like the game mattered for anything.

Once inside the stadium, Hannah almost came to tears. It was massive and overwhelming. She'd always wanted to attend a game but it had just never happened. Adam surprised her with tickets claiming it was a birthday gift, although her birthday was still months away. When the game got underway, she sat at the edge of the seat only for a moment before she was on her feet, yelling at the refs and the coaches for what she considered bonehead calls. She flipped the bird at some hecklers. It was all in fun.

She could feel the roar of the crowd and the sound of crashing helmets and pads all the way down to her toes. The whole thing was so exciting that she didn't want to leave. She remembered being sad when the game was over, even if it was just a preseason game and the starters only played for one drive. It was long enough for her to use her new camera to take some amazing photos of her favorite players. She had gone out and bought a new camera with the highest amount of megapixels and strongest zoom. She knew she couldn't take a telephoto lens in the stadium without a press pass or she may have been tempted to splurge even more.

A Lonestar touchdown brought her back to reality. She couldn't resist picking up her phone and sending Adam a message.

Nothing like a good punt return for a touchdown to get the heart pumping.

She laughed as she hit send. She didn't know how long she could keep it up. Sooner rather than later she was going to cave and agree to meet up with the man. She already couldn't keep her hands off her phone. She needed something more.

Tell me about it. That kid has some speed.

She texted back a smiley face and put her phone on the coffee table. If it was more than an arm's length away, maybe she wouldn't send him another message. She smiled again, thinking that it wasn't likely to work.

Her phone buzzed on the table.

I know you're not ready to see me but how about a phone call? You game?

She thought about it for a good five minutes before she sent him a reply. She thought long about how hearing his voice would either make her melt or break her heart all over again. She could almost hear his words like a broken record stuttering the same sentences over and over again. *Hannah, I'm sorry but we need to break up. I can't start medical school while we're in a relationship. It wouldn't be fair to you and it wouldn't be fair to me. I've worked so hard to get accepted to a good school. I can't let anything get in the way of my goals.* The words rang through her mind as clear as the day he spoke them.

When she heard his voice again, would it be tainted with memories of the last time she had spoken to him? She couldn't see how she could talk to him and not want to cry over all the lost time they had over the years. What she needed was to forget about the past. She needed to move past that, if she was going to try having him in her life again, whether it be a small role as an acquaintance or as a… something more. Maybe hearing him speak again would give her a chance to create a new memory. One that didn't break her heart.

When she was ready, she finally messaged back.

Sure, if our boys win, you can have my number.

She may as well have said an emphatic, YES. Their team was up by twenty points going into the fourth quarter. But hey, on any given Sunday, anything was possible.

Sounds like a plan. I'll call you later tonight. Around 11ish.

Even after fifteen years, things seemed very familiar between her and Adam. Back when they were together, when they weren't staying over at each other's places, they often went to bed with their phones to their ears talking and laughing throughout the night until either of them was almost asleep. When Adam told her he'd call her so late, Hannah felt a mixture of excitement and unease. She couldn't figure out which one was stronger.

Like many other Lonestars games, it was a nail biter to the end. Even with their enormous lead, the defense managed to allow the win to come down to a field goal. Luckily for Hannah, their opponent shanked it to the left, and their team won. She still had about six hours before Adam would call her and she didn't know what she was going to do to pass the time without pulling out her hair, strand by strand. There was always the Sunday night game, but she knew she wouldn't be able to focus on the game like she had before. There would be no yelling at the TV as if anything she said would change the outcome. There would be no flipping channels to see red zone action. That night, she'd be going nuts.

She decided to eat an early dinner. She warmed up left over wings and pizza in the microwave and searched in the refrigerator for a beer. She found an amber lager from a local brewery in the back and took out a bottle opener. She couldn't watch football with a glass of wine in her hand. That was just as wimpy as some of the new rules the league had been initiating lately.

When the game finished, she hopped in the shower. She liked a hot shower and the glass fogged in no time. She wrote Adam's name in the steam with her finger and smiled. She had no idea why she felt compelled to do that. The thought just came to her and she acted on it. She had seen his name quite a few times in the last two days. Sometimes she still couldn't believe it. She took her time washing her hair. While the conditioner sat in her locks to moisturize, she slowly and meticulously shaved her legs. She laughed when she thought that she was glad she wasn't seeing him tonight. With her legs all smooth and silky, she doubted she'd be able to stay out of bed with him. Then, she thought about how terrible it would be to sleep with him the first time she saw him again. No, that wasn't going to happen. She couldn't let it.

By the time she got out of the shower, and completed her nightly routine of exfoliating her face and applying night creams, eye gels, and moisturizers, it was close to eleven. She picked out a silver silk chemise to sleep in. Normally, she slept in some knit boy shorts and a tank, but she felt the need to be sexy that night. It's not like Adam could have seen her, she was just in that kind of mood.

Just before eleven, Hannah's phone went off. One new message. From Adam.

Looks like we all won tonight. What's your number, Hannah?

She sent him the number for her home. She thought that would be safe. She wasn't ready to have constant access to him just yet through their cells. She needed to maintain some amount of self control and she didn't know if she could keep herself from sending the occasional text message because it would be so easy to do so.

It felt like she just hit send when she heard her phone ring.

The caller ID showed: Cooper, Dr. Adam. Wow. A doctor calling her house.

"Hello," she answered, bringing her comforter up to her chin.

The voice on the other end of the line was deep and smooth. "Hello,

Hannah."

And just like that, she lost it. Tears pooled in her eyes and her throat tightened. She wanted more than anything for this to work. She was just having a hard time trying to find the words. Sending messages on FaceSpace was one thing, but actually speaking to Adam Cooper was another. It was his voice singing in her ear. It was really him. All he did was say her name and she wanted him there with her, with his arms wrapped around her making her feel special and safe, the way he had done in the past. How she could want that so badly frightened her. How could she possibly just forget that he had left her and never looked back? But somehow, that didn't seem to matter to her. Not now, when he was that close.

"Hannah, are you there?" Adam called out to her.

She took a deep breath and began talking. "Yes, I'm here. This is just a little more difficult than I thought it would be."

"I'm sorry." He paused. "I really am. If this is too much for you, I'll understand. I'll be really disappointed, but I get it if you don't want to talk to me after all."

Hannah chuckled through her tears. "Are you kidding me? I can't begin to tell you how many times I've thought of this moment. You're not going to get off the hook that easy. So don't you go hanging up just yet."

"Good. I'm not going anywhere. So, how are you?"

She thought about it for a second or two. "Actually, I'm doing okay. Great, really. I have no complaints. You?"

"I'm good. Busy, but good."

There was an awkward silence for a few beats before Hannah chimed in. "I'm really happy to hear your plans worked out for you. I never had any doubts that you'd be a doctor. That has to be so exciting."

"Thank you. It wasn't easy. I hit a few bumps in the road but we… I made it. Sometimes when I'm at work, I look around and still can't believe it's all mine. It seems like a dream."

Hannah's mind raced when she heard him say, "we". He did say *we*, didn't he? She wasn't imagining it, right? She felt a bit deflated. She thought he was a single man. And if he wasn't, what was he doing calling her?

Her voice was shaky. "That's great."

"So … good game tonight, huh?"

She was thankful for something to talk about. "Yeah, but I wouldn't mind just kicking the shit out of a team every once in awhile. These down to the wire games are going to cost me a lot of money on manicures every week." She looked at her hands, noticing only her thumb had fallen victim to her nerves.

"You're still very funny, Hannah. I'm glad you still have that sense of humor of yours."

"I'm still the same person, Adam."

"Just more beautiful. In your profile pic, you look gorgeous."

"Why thank you. You look pretty darn good yourself."

"You wanna get a better look?" Before she had a chance to answer, he continued, "Just dinner. During the week. No pressure. Just two friends catching a bite to eat after work. What do you say?"

The sound of his deep voice combined with his easy going words caused Hannah to drop her guard. How bad could it be? She did want to get a better look. More than she wanted to win the lotto. More than she wanted her next breath of air. Speaking to him was not going to be enough. It never was going to be. And she knew that. She had to see him.

"Why not? You already got me on the phone. Let's do dinner."

Chapter Four

He nearly fell out of his bed with excitement after Hannah accepted his invitation to dinner. He wasn't sure what she'd say but he had to at least ask. Now that she'd said yes, what the hell was he going to do? Where was he going to take her? He knew that dinner would need to be casual. Someplace that was friendly and easy going. He couldn't take her somewhere with candlelit tables and menus without prices. First, she just wasn't that kind of woman. And secondly, she wasn't ready for him to be romantic with her. She needed to feel safe with him before that happened. He knew her all too well which was evidence enough that they belonged together.

"You okay? Did I hear something break?" Hannah screeched into the phone.

He had to get a hold of himself. He was acting like a girl. "Yeah, I'm fine. My book just fell of my bed."

"Oh. Listen, I've gotta get up early for work so I'm going to cut this short."

He couldn't help being disappointed that she was getting off the phone with him so soon. She was right though. He needed his sleep. Neither of them had ever been morning people. He thought it was ironic that they both picked careers with early morning wake up calls.

"No problem, you know how irritable I get if I don't sleep."

"Still hate to wake up in the morning?"

"Yup, it's gotten worse in my old age. I've even thought about opening the office at eleven, but then I'd have to stay open until seven or eight and that's out of the question."

"Ha, I wish school started at eleven. The kids probably do too."

"I'll send you a message with details about dinner, okay?" Adam threw it out there.

He could hear her yawn through the receiver. "Okay, sounds good. I'll look forward to it."

"Good night, Hannah."

"Good night, Adam."

****

Hannah went to sleep with a goofy smile spread across her face. She was feeling so many ups and downs since she had reconnected with Adam in the last few days but overall, she was happy to speak with him again.

As she headed into work, she prepared herself for Leila to kill any kind of happiness that was brewing in her life. She only talked to her best friend once the day before and she cut the conversation short, blaming it on her football rituals. Leila never called on Sunday or Monday nights during football season, there was no reason for her to start now.

Once the first bell rang and students scattered toward their classes, the assistant principal sauntered into her office and shut the door.

"Spill it," Leila demanded. There were times when Hannah regretted choosing to work at the same school as her friend, and it just happened to be one of those days. "Come on. Tell me. Have you seen the bastard yet? Did you sleep with him already?"

"Lei, you need to relax. We're at work and …"

The other woman, dressed in a light gray blazer and pencil skirt, sat down across from her and interrupted. "Don't start that crap with me, Hannah. I can't believe you're seeing him. Just like that. Have you forgotten how many months you spent crying over that self-absorbed ass?"

She raised her hand to stop Leila, but her friend didn't waiver. "Let me remind you. He left you. He was too much of a coward to go to medical school and love you at the same time. He chose his career over your happiness and he always will. How can you forget?"

Hannah took a deep breath and gathered her thoughts. Leila had finally stopped badgering her and she wanted to make sure she said what she needed to before she started in again.

"I didn't forget. How could I? You've taken every opportunity for the last fifteen years to remind me of how broken I was when he left.

Since you screwed up everything with Aaron because, let me remind you, you weren't ready for a husband and kids, you haven't let me have any peace. It's like since you're miserable because Aaron would have given it all to you and you passed it up, you want me to be just as miserable as you."

"Now wait a minute," Leila tried to get a word in.

"No, I let you talk. Now you listen to me. When Adam left, I was broken. He hurt me. And now he wants to talk to me again. I don't know what he wants but I'm willing to find out. I've never loved another man the way I loved him. And despite his choice to move on without me, I've still never found another man who has loved me like he did. I'm sorry if me talking to him again brings back bad memories for you, but maybe now you'll try and talk to Aaron too. We both know you two need to talk as much as me and Adam."

Leila didn't say another word. She stood, opened the door, and walked out, tossing her long straight black hair over her shoulder in a big "eff you" to her friend.

"Well, I'm glad we were able to have that conversation," Hannah murmured to herself.

Hannah scanned her desk for anything she might have forgotten to toss in her tote. She'd already packed her lunch bag, an educational journal that featured an article about improving graduation rates, and a book a student had recommended to her. Just as she was about to grab her keys, she felt her phone vibrate in her bag. She stopped, set everything down again, and searched for her phone.

A new FaceSpace message from Adam.

Meet me at Giovanni's for pizza and the game. Plz! :-)

Cute. Hannah giggled at the little emoticon and sent him a message back telling him she'd be there before kickoff.

It seemed like a better time than any to go ahead and meet this man again. Who knew? Maybe they'd meet, take one look at each other, and feel nothing. That wasn't something she'd ever considered until now, but it was very possible. Expecting all the emotions and longing to still be there after so much time, was starting to sound more and more ridiculous the closer she got to the pizza joint.

When she finally arrived at Giovanni's at close to five o'clock, Adam was already there. She wondered if he was a regular. She'd been there a million times and had never run into him. But now, they were both in the same place at the same time. Finally.

She saw him almost immediately. He was seated at a table facing a big screen TV, with a basket of garlic bread and two beers in front of him.

As she approached, Hannah got a little lightheaded just looking at him. When he stood to greet her, she almost fainted. He was wearing a black striped dress shirt which he cuffed so she could see his strong forearms. His black pants and shiny black shoes made him look so professional. This look was so different from his FaceSpace profile photo where he was dressed so casual. But even in his big boy clothes, she still saw his easy going demeanor in his beautiful eyes as he smiled at her.

It seemed to take a lifetime to walk the short distance from the door to his table. While the place was packed with the Monday Night Football crowd, it was like no one else existed.

Hannah finally stood before Adam and she had no idea what to say. He reached for her, brushing a strand of hair away from her face and tucking it behind her ear. A gentle smile spread across his lips as she looked up into his hazel eyes. There was a still silence until he cupped her face in the palms of his hands and lowered his lips to hers.

She didn't turn away. She didn't push him back. She stood on her tip toes and allowed him to press his mouth to hers in a kiss that she had longed to have for what seemed like an eternity. His lips were gentle on hers at first. Then, he opened his mouth to her and she did the same. She was the first to brush her tongue against his. He responded by deepening the kiss allowing their tongues to dance together with such passion that it would have never ended had it not been for the whistles and cat calls from the other patrons of Giovanni's.

Hannah had forgotten where they were at. She lowered her feet flat to the ground, and rested her hands on Adam's hips. He tore his lips from hers and scooped her up in a tight embrace. He bent down to nuzzle his face in her hair and planted a few pecks against her neck. She relaxed in his arms and wished to god that they were somewhere else a lot less public.

****

"Hi, Hannah," he whispered in her ear. He pulled back, his hands still wrapped in her hair, and said, "I'm sorry. I didn't plan on doing that." He really hadn't. But she took his breath away. She waltzed in with her usual glow. Her silky, wavy hair was down passed her shoulders. She wore an innocent smile that seemed so effortless to her. He loved her casual, yet sexy style. Her tight jeans with heels and a shimmery sweater thing made him ache for her. So when she got within his reach, he couldn't resist taking her in his arms and kissing her like he'd imagined every night for the past fifteen years. He couldn't remember a night that he'd gone to sleep without thinking of this very moment. Of kissing his Hannah again.

She giggled in his arms. "Don't apologize. I was kind of hoping you would. You wanna get out of here?"

"Excuse me?" Did he hear her correctly?

"Umm. Why don't we watch the game somewhere a little more private?"

Yes, he heard her loud and clear. "Let's go."

He grabbed her by the hand and led her out of the restaurant. She quickly rattled off to him to follow her in his own car. He sure as hell didn't argue. He wasn't sure about how this would turn out but he wasn't about to stop to think about it.

It was a short ride to her house in a neighborhood known for its old lush trees and historic homes. He tried to pay attention to all the turns and street names so he could retrace his steps in the future but one thing kept weighing on his mind. He needed to tell Hannah about Danny. But when? He figured sooner rather than later would be best.

He couldn't believe that she didn't know he had a son, but then again, why would she? The only contact she would have had with him would have been through Aaron, but he had completely been cut off by Leila when they parted ways. Sure they'd had friends in common but all of those relationships had fizzled by the end of his first year of medical school. He hadn't met Danny's mom until his second year of school and he wasn't born until after Aaron and Lei's split. When he found out that he was having a baby, he made sure Aaron wouldn't breathe a word of it to Leila or Hannah. It was something he had always wanted to tell her himself. She deserved that much from him.

She pulled her car into the garage and left it open. She got out and waited for him to park on the street. As he walked up the drive way, he had to remember to breathe. He couldn't believe he was just a few steps away from kissing the woman he loved.

Adam strutted toward her and enveloped her in his arms. He lifted her off her feet and spun her around. She squealed and he laughed. They had always been very playful, and he was happy to be able to still have that with her.

He set her back on her feet and left a kiss to her forehead. She then took his hand and he followed her inside. He scanned the small house quickly and felt at home. It was decorated very simply. It didn't scream that a woman lived there with frilly pink things and lots of cats. He chuckled inside at the thought.

It was comfortable enough that he could walk around in his socks and throw his feet on a table. He thought of how easily they could sit in front of the tube and eat in the family room, and not have to eat at a formal dining room table. He loved the hard wood floors and the white Wainscoting. She'd done well for herself and he was proud of her.

"Nice place, Hannah. It's very you."

"Thanks, I think."

He grinned. "It was a compliment. I really like it." He walked toward her where she was leaning against a sofa. He stopped in front of her and threaded his fingers through the tips of her hair. "This seems unreal. I can't begin to tell you how happy I am to finally see you."

"I'm pretty sure I know how you feel," she said, tugging on the pockets of his pants. He lurched forward till their bodies brushed against each other.

It was these little things that made him confident that this just might work. The way she still looked at him. The giggles she let out while he held her. The tugging of his pockets. Those were the things that were so characteristically Hannah. She'd always hooked her index fingers on his pockets and pulled him close to her. She'd hold on and yank him closer till their bodies smashed together. For the most part, it had been her way to let him know she was in the mood for a little loving. He wondered if that was what she was trying to say to him. Well, he was in her house and if that wasn't a clue, what was?

He leaned forward and she met him the rest of the way for a kiss that rocked his world. He was instantly hard as their lips pressed together. He squeezed her hips and brought her body smashing up against his. He opened his mouth slightly and teased her with a little nibble on her bottom lip. He felt her smile against his kiss and he couldn't help but chuckle.

"Come with me," she told him.

He followed her to what he assumed was her bedroom.

Hannah was wide-eyed and gazing at him. Her mouth was puffy from their kisses and he wanted nothing more than to finish what they started but he couldn't. Not yet. Not until he told her about Danny.

There was no way he could make love to her if she wasn't willing to accept his son. What if she wanted nothing to do with him after she found out? It would be so much more difficult to walk away once they'd slept together.

While his body was telling him to strip Hannah naked and have his way with her, his heart wouldn't allow it.

"Are you sure this is what you want?"

She smiled at him. "I think that's obvious. Don't you?"

Adam laced his fingers through Hannah's. "I do. Believe me, I do." He paused. "But first, I think we should talk. A lot has happened since we last spoke." He really didn't want to relive that last conversation yet he was determined to tell her about his life.

"You're probably right," she said, releasing his hands. "Get undressed."

He put his hands on his hips. "You gotta be kidding, right?"

Adam watched as she kicked off her shoes and began unbuttoning her jeans.

"No. I'm not. We should have done this last time and maybe we wouldn't have wasted almost half our lives not speaking to each other." She had a point. One night they'd gotten into a fight and they were both tempted to walk out the door before they were finished. Adam couldn't even remember what the stupid argument was about, but he remembered the pact they'd made. They had decided that before they had any serious talks, they'd get undressed and talk in bed. Walking out would be a lot less likely if they were in their underwear. But their last night together, Adam had done little to prepare her for the conversation so they had kept their clothes on, and when he was finished breaking up with her, he just left. He didn't stick around to talk about his decision. He knew that if he did, he would've never been able to follow through with it.

She was absolutely serious. She was down to her undies and a camisole and he hoped she didn't notice the swell in his pants. He couldn't help it. She had the most perfect legs and her pink lace panties were making it hard for him to think.

"Well, Adam, you better take it off, mister, or we're gonna be here all night doing nothing but staring at each other. And that thing isn't gonna go down with me just looking at it." She gestured below his waist.

He ran his fingers though his hair with a chuckle. "Fine." Adam, reluctantly, pulled his shirt from his waistband and unbuttoned it. He kicked off his shoes and slid his socks off. He unbuckled his belt and allowed his pants to fall to the floor. There he stood in his black boxer briefs. He looked down at himself and laughed. "I can't believe we're doing this."

Hannah chuckled too. "Neither can I."

Adam reached out to touch her shoulder and she took his hand and kissed his palm. He then watched as she flipped back her comforter and slid onto her bed moving to the far side. She patted the space next to her, and he followed her.

"So shoot. What's on your mind?"

He couldn't believe how easy she was making this. How could she not be mad at him? How could she be letting him off the hook this easy? So he told her what he was thinking.

"Hannah, this doesn't seem right. How can you be so nonchalant about seeing me again? You're acting like not a day has passed since the last time we saw each other. You don't have anything to say to me?"

He gazed into her beautiful eyes that seemed to study him. "What do you want me to say? For a long time, I practiced how I'd cuss you out and tell you I hated you. But then, I'd feel like shit for even thinking that. Then, I thought about how I wanted to find you and tell you that we could work it out. I wouldn't be the needy girlfriend while you were in med school and I'd give you all the space you needed. But then I thought about what you'd said and how even though we'd say we were going to be cool with not spending so much time together, we really wouldn't and then your grades would really suffer. You were right. There's no way we would've been able to stay away from each other." As they both stretched out side by side in Hannah's bed, facing each other, Adam didn't know what to make of Hannah's words. She continued, "So I followed that old saying. I loved you so much, I let you go. Without a fight. If it was meant to be, I knew you'd come back to me someday. I just didn't think it would take this long."

"Aha," Adam grunted. He was touched by her confession and a frog was lodged in his throat. After a pause, he said, "You are a very wise woman."

She placed her hand on his side. "So what took you so long?"

Adam stared into her big brown eyes and tried to send her signals to remain calm and understanding after what he was about to tell her. Her eyes seemed to plead with him to just tell her what was on his mind and get it over with.

And so he did.

"Hannah, I have a son."

Chapter Five

Hannah yanked her hand back as if she'd just been stung by something. He had a son. She didn't know what to make of that. She sat up in her bed, pulled the sheet up over her, gathering it in her fists at her breasts. Adam sat up slowly but didn't say anything.

She looked into his eyes and saw the worry. She didn't mean to make him so nervous but she was at a loss for words. He reached out for her hands and took one in his. She felt his warmth and started to feel a wave of calm come over her.

He must have sensed that she wasn't going to say anything, not yet anyway, so Adam started talking. "Danny is thirteen. He's in eighth grade and he's a great kid. I just really wanted to tell you about him before anything happened between us."

Adam rubbed his thumb over the back of her hand. She was stunned by this revelation and so many things were going through her head. She had no idea where to begin. "Hannah, are you okay?" He reached out and squeezed her shoulder with his free hand.

"Yeah, I'm okay. Just in shock." She looked up into his eyes trying to find the right words, if there were any. "Let's start with some basics." She paused. "Who's Danny's mom?"

She felt Adam tense at the mention of his son's mother. "Her name is Amber. I met her during med school. She was in my cohort of first years."

Hannah had so many questions come to her that couldn't wait, so she interrupted him. "Where is she now? Did you marry her? Did you love her? Are you still in love with her?"

He ran his fingers through his hair and took a deep breath. "No, I didn't marry her. I'm not in love with her and I never was. I may have loved her at one time because she gave me Danny but that's it. She left us when Danny was only three months old. We haven't seen her since so I'm not sure where she is."

"She left her baby boy?" Hannah didn't have kids but she couldn't imagine ever leaving one. What kind of woman would abandon her newborn son?

"Yes. She never wanted to have children. Not while being in medical school anyway. Danny wasn't planned by any means. I wasn't ready for him any more than she was, but we made do. My parents and Aaron really helped me out so I could finish school. And Angie helped as she got older. I think we've done all right."

"So you've raised him all on your own, since he was a baby?"

"Yes, I have."

She didn't think she could ever love him more than she had in the past, but she was proven wrong. Her heart overflowed with love and compassion for him. She could see in his eyes how much he loved his son and she was in total awe of the man he'd become, raising a child all on his own.

"You're amazing, Adam Cooper." She pushed on his chest till he was flat on his back. She spread out, lying on her side, till her face was across from his. She pressed her lips briefly to his before snuggling against him. She rested her cheek on his chest and draped one of her arms across his belly. "So tell me about Danny. I want to know all about him, if you don't mind sharing."

She got comfortable as Adam wrapped his arms around her. She felt a tingling sensation run through her body when she felt his lips press to her temple.

She listened to him as he combed his fingers through her hair. "Well. He's a really cool kid. He's handsome, just like his dad." They both chuckled. "He gets good grades, likes playing football, and is starting to go out with his friends a lot. This is new territory for us and we don't always agree on what I think is okay for a thirteen year old to do and what time he should come home. Curfew is a hot topic at our house right now."

"Sounds like fun," she said, looking up at him. He caught her gaze and grinned.

"Loads." They snuggled together again before he continued. "What I love about Danny is that he has a really good heart. He could have grown up to be an angry kid or a little emotionally off considering he grew up without a mom, but he's perfect. He really is."

"Well, sometimes you don't miss what you've never had. You probably more than made up for him not having two parents. I'd say that's a big testament to what a great dad you've been." She kissed his chest just above his nipple. "Does he ever ask about his mom?"

"No. Well he hadn't until he saw your page on FaceSpace."

She propped herself up on her elbow to get a good look at him. "Why did he see my page? He knows about me?"

"He asked me if you were his mom. He shocked me when he asked, but it made sense. From his point of view anyway. He's very perceptive. I didn't even realize he noticed but he did."

"Noticed what?"

"He noticed a picture of you that I have in my wallet. He said he knew about it for as long as he could remember and thought maybe you were his mother. I told him you weren't and explained to him a little bit about you."

Wow. She didn't know what to think about that one. Adam's son had wondered if she was his mom. If they'd stayed together like they should have, she could've been. She felt a pang of sadness about what could've been but quickly shrugged it off.

"Why would he think I was his mom? Doesn't he have any pictures of his own?"

He ran his fingertips up and down her arm. "It's not like we dated long and took pictures together. She took the only photos I had of her. The ones from the day he was born. It still pisses me off that I don't have those pictures. It's not like how it is now, with digital cameras or cell phones to capture every moment."

"I'm sorry." She could hear the frustration in his voice.

"It sucks but it makes sense that he'd ask about you, you know?"

"And how does he feel about me? Or feel about you talking to me again?" Now that Adam had a child, her thoughts had changed. It wasn't about just her and him anymore. They had a young boy to consider. She wasn't naïve. She knew it didn't matter how much Adam liked, or loved, her. If his son didn't like her, or want her around, her relationship with Adam was doomed.

"He thinks it's cool. He told me that I've spent too long making sure he's happy and I deserve happiness of my own. See, I told you, gotta love his heart." Adam's eyes glossed over as he talked about his son.

"Sounds like he's a lot like his daddy." She leaned forward to kiss

Adam again. His lips were soft against hers, and she thought she could stay like this for the rest of her life.

"You know, I never meant to stay away so long."

"What was your plan then?"

"I thought I'd get situated with my classes, get into a routine that I knew worked, and then I'd try to contact you and see if you were willing to take me back. I just needed to know that I could do it on my own. Back then, I wasn't so sure I could do it and I was afraid to let you see me fail."

Hannah couldn't believe what she was hearing. She had never once doubted that he would be a success in medical school and as a doctor. She knew that it was going to take an insane amount of dedication and hard work, but she believed in him and she knew he could do it.

She shook her head at him. "Well that's just crazy talk. I never had any doubts that you'd do just fine." She rested her head back on his chest. "But what happened? Once you were settled, why didn't you come back for me?"

He trailed his fingers up and down her back, and she prepared herself to hear about what had kept them apart.

"Thanks for believing in me, Hannah, but I got off to a pretty rocky start. Classes were overwhelming and I was having trouble keeping up. It took me a lot longer than I expected to get into a groove where I could actually take a moment to relax every once and awhile. By that time, I convinced myself it was too late. I just figured you'd moved on and I didn't want to disrupt you after so much time had passed."

"So disrupting me after fifteen years seemed like a better idea?" She shook her head again.

Hannah could feel his body shudder underneath her with a slight chuckle. "Crazy right?"

"Very. So what changed your mind? Why now?"

"I ran out of excuses to stay away. I always wanted to call you, to see you. But then I had Danny and making sure he was taken care of was my first priority. As he got older, I tried meeting other women but I always compared them to you and they were never good enough. It made me think I should stop trying to find your replacement and just find you instead. But mostly, I just think I was ready, and was really hoping you'd be too."

He always had a way of saying all the right things. She knew exactly how he felt. She did the same thing with every man she'd met since she and Adam had parted ways. They didn't smell like him. They didn't make her laugh like he did. They didn't know a punt from a kickoff. But most of all, none of them came close to making her feel the way he did.

Like always, whenever she was in his arms, her entire body was oversensitive to his touch and her girl parts tightened. There was no way she could resist him any longer.

"Well, this must be your lucky day, big guy, because I've been ready since the day I met you."

She scooted closer and brought herself face to face with him. She brushed her hand through his hair before she lowered her lips to his. He met her with a hunger that excited her. She kissed him frantically, like she couldn't get enough of him. She kissed his forehead, both sides of his face, his chin, and then back to his lips. She nipped at his bottom lip and sucked on it playfully. Then she felt his tongue enter her mouth and tangle with hers. The kiss got deeper and more passionate until they were out of breath.

Adam held her tightly and flipped her around so he was on top of her. Then he sat up and she was in awe of the view of his chiseled physique. He was almost forty and he still had the most amazing body she'd ever seen. His shoulders were broad, and his chest was lightly dusted with dark hair. Just looking at his muscular pecs, strong arms, and well defined abs made her feel drunk with desire.

He bent down to plant a peck on her forehead before he gathered the bottom of her camisole in his hands and tugged it up her body and over her head. She reached around to her back and unhooked her bra. He slid each strap off her shoulders and tossed it aside. Her breasts freed and Adam didn't wait one second to pay them attention.

He lowered his head and kissed her between her breasts as he cupped each one in the palm of his hands. He then dragged his tongue to the left and sucked hard on her pebbled nipple. She let out a whimper as he caused her a pleasure she'd dreamed of for so long. He moved his way to the right taking in the other breast with even more passion. Hannah grasped the back of his head and tugged on his hair as he nibbled on each of her erect nipples.

Kiss by kiss, he trailed his way down to the top edge of her panties. He slid his index fingers into the waistband at her hips and lowered them until she was able to kick them off at her feet. His fingers felt like they were branding every inch of her body with such an intense heat she was close to catching fire.

He nipped at her waist and traced his tongue down to her center. She was primed and ready for him and she was sure that he would take note the moment his mouth came down on her. The sensation of his warm wet mouth on her sex was more than she could handle at the moment. She loved what he was doing to her but when her first orgasm rocked her, she wanted it to be with him. With him inside her. He sucked on just the right spot causing a hitch in her breath so she tugged on his hair to bring him upward.

Adam took the hint and pressed his lips to hers again. This time their tongues found each other instantly. A moan escaped from both of them when Hannah wrapped her legs around his waist and thrust herself against the swell in his boxers. Only one thin piece of material separated them and she wanted nothing more than to shed him of his last article of clothing. She'd waited too long for this moment and she couldn't wait a second more.

Hannah ran her hands down Adam's back and hooked her fingers into the waistband of his boxers and tugged them down.

****

He couldn't believe this was really happening. He'd thought about this night for as long as he could remember. He had memorized every part of her body and when he finally saw her naked again, it was as familiar as it had been many years before. Her full breasts, her curvy hips, and ultra soft skin. He could have kissed every inch of her again and again, if she'd let him.

As much as her appearance hadn't changed, neither had her horniness. While he had always took pleasure in kissing, licking, and sucking on every bit of her from head to toe, she couldn't ever get to the main event fast enough.

Adam was so close to burying himself inside of Hannah, but he had to stop suddenly. "Baby, are you sure this is what you want?"

She didn't say anything. Instead she lifted her hips to him and he worked in short strokes till he was buried deep inside of her. She wrapped around him like she was made for him. He had to take his time with each thrust. He wasn't interested in finishing before he had a chance to get started. This was their first time together and he wanted it to last as long as possible.

Slowly, their hips met each other stroke for stroke. He sucked on her neck and she grasped his behind. He could feel her nails dig into his skin and it was all he could do to keep from finishing right then. He slowed the pace, kissing her gently, until they both went up and over together. She shuddered underneath him as he placed soft kisses to her eyes, to her chin, and again to her lips.

Finally, Adam gazed into her eyes. She was beautiful and she was his, again. His throat tightened, but he managed to get the words out anyway. "I love you, Hannah. I always have."

She cupped his face in both of her hands and pressed her lips to his. She looked at him with tear filled eyes. "And I love you, Adam. Then, now, always."

****

Adam hated that he had to leave her after their first night together. But he wasn't some bachelor without responsibilities. They both knew that their relationship was not only about them. He had Danny to consider every step of the way.

When Hannah asked about where Danny was that evening, Adam explained that his son spent some Monday nights with friends watching football and that he had to be home by ten, she understood that he needed to leave. Danny was thirteen and old enough to be left home alone, but there was no way Adam would leave him by himself overnight.

Adam had the rest of his life with Hannah. It wouldn't be long before they slept in each other's arms every night.

Danny beat his dad home and when Adam walked in the door, his son pounced on him with questions, or more like teasing.

"Hot date tonight, Dad?"

Adam made his way to the fridge and pulled out a bottle of water. He drained almost half the bottle before he answered. He wasn't sure if he was really that thirsty or if he was just trying to buy time. "Something like that," was all he could think of to say.

"Did you see Hannah?" His son's happy interest made him smile.

"I did." He couldn't hide his excitement. He stood before his son grinning like a little kid.

Danny took a bottle of Gatorade from the fridge and hopped on the counter to take a seat. In between swigs, he continued to question his dad. "Looks like you had a good time. When do I get to meet her?"

That was one thing Adam hadn't thought about yet. While he was confident things would continue to go well with Hannah, he wasn't sure when he wanted her to meet his boy.

"I don't know, bud. I haven't gotten that far yet."

"Come on, Dad. Afraid I'll embarrass you? Afraid she'll want to dump you once she meets me?"

He couldn't tell if Danny was serious or just playing. "I'd never be embarrassed by you, kid. And if she wanted to dump me after she met you, then she's not the person I thought she was. If anything, she'll want me more because of you. You're a bonus. Like a puppy."

Danny barked and they both chuckled.

"At least talk to her and see if she wants to meet me. I really want to see her in real life. Not just a two inch picture on a screen." His son hopped off the counter and opened the pantry to get a box of Oreos.

"Listen, bud, I'm sure I'll get a chance to introduce you soon. But let's not rush it. This is still very new. Don't forget that tonight is the first time I've seen her in fifteen years."

Danny seemed to understand. He hugged and kissed his dad good night and trotted up to his room. Adam finished his water, checked all the locks, turned off the lights and went to his room as well.

When he was finally in bed, he took out his phone to text Hannah.

I miss you already

Same here

Didn't want to leave you tonight. Wish you were here with me.

Me too.

Can I call you tomorrow?

Of course.

Hannah, I love you.

I love you too.

Chapter Six

Hannah thought she would have been more upset when Adam left her bed after they'd made love. Surprisingly, she was feeling just fine. Sure, it would have been better if he was able to stay. She would have loved to snuggle up to him the rest of the night and wake up in his arms but she was content with what they'd shared.

Things had changed since they were first a couple. They had both grown up. In her younger, less confident mind of long ago, it would have hurt her if he just got up and left with a *wham bam thank you ma'am*. She'd matured over the years and was much more able to see the big picture.

It was getting late and she really needed to get some sleep, but the wheels kept turning in her head.

Her heart warmed when she thought of Danny. She was anxious to meet him. She could just picture a miniature version of Adam. She wondered how much they resembled each other. Did they have the same eyes? Same hair? Same smile? Would he be tall like his dad?

She thought of Danny's mom. She still couldn't get over how his mother was able to leave him behind. What could she have possibly been thinking? Of course, raising a child was difficult. And even more so if you're in medical school, but abandoning your child? No way. That should have never been a consideration. If she ever met the woman, she'd be tempted to smack her.

****

Hannah sat at her desk the next afternoon, daydreaming — or

fantasizing — about the previous night's events. She tried to hide her giddiness when Leila walked in with her lunch.

Her friend, and boss, set a Diet Coke on her desk and took out two salads. They did that often. One of the girls brought lunch for the other and vice versa. Sometimes neither of them brought anything and they were forced to eat in the cafeteria, which was hit or miss. The food was either delicious or downright disgusting. Hannah was grateful to her friend for stopping through a drive-thru for a grilled chicken salad with raspberry balsamic dressing for each of them.

"Why thank you," Hannah told her, as she popped off the lid and began dumping the dressing and croutons on the bed of lettuce.

"No problem. You know I got you." Leila stuck out her hand to do a fist bump.

Hannah chuckled. "It looks like you're in a better mood today." She raised her brows at her friend. "What's the catch?"

With Leila there was always a catch. She was one of the moodiest people she had ever known, but also the kindest and most loyal.

"I figured it would just be best not to argue with you. I know it's not going to make a difference, so I may as well be supportive."

Hmm… that was too easy, Hannah thought.

"Plus, I'd rather know what's happening and get to hear all your stories."

There's the Leila she knew. She wanted the dirt, and she knew she wasn't going to get it if she was acting like a brat.

"Gee thanks. So the only reason you're being nice is because you want the juicy gossip." Hannah paused to take a bite of her lunch. "This has nothing to do with you wanting to know about Aaron too?"

Leila stopped chewing and practically spit her food out of her mouth. "Just because you and Adam are talking again doesn't mean I have to talk to his brother. I think it'll be better if I don't get involved. Other than the juicy gossip, of course."

Hannah had to decide what she wanted to tell Leila about what had happened between her and Adam the night before. She really had to consider whether or not to tell her the truth about Adam's son. She had no idea how Leila would react.

After some chitchat about the week's activities at school, Hannah finally decided it was best to tell her closest friend everything she came to find out about Adam, and all that had happened between them.

"Lei, there is something I need to tell you."

"Shoot," she replied before gulping her soda.

"I saw Adam last night." Hannah rubbed her hands together with worry. She couldn't believe how easy it was to be thrilled and nervous at the same time.

Leila continued chomping on her salad. "I knew that," she said, through a mouthful of food.

"How did you know?"

"I tried calling you several times last night, and you never answered. Even if you were watching Monday Night Football, you'd still answer my calls. Or at least call me back during a time out. So tell me what happened?"

"Well." She paused. "We had an interesting conversation. Adam told me some things about him that neither one of us knew." That was one thing Hannah was sure of. Leila couldn't have known about Danny. She would have told her long ago if she had. She'd never keep something that big from her, and Hannah surely couldn't keep that kind of secret either.

Leila looked at the blank stare on her friends face and said, "Just tell me already. What happened?"

"Adam... Adam... he... he... he has a son."

"What?" she shouted.

Hannah put her index finger to her mouth to shush her friend. "Yeah, you heard me. Adam has a son. He's thirteen and his name is Danny."

She watched as Leila whipped her cell phone from her pocket. She immediately began tapping frantically on the keyboard.

"What are you doing, Lei?"

"I'm texting that son of a bitch."

"You cannot text Adam. I didn't tell him I was going to tell you about Danny."

"I'm not texting Adam."

"Then who are you texting?" Hannah was confused.

"Aaron!"

"Why on earth are you texting Aaron?"

"Because I can't believe he didn't tell me something so important. How can he not tell me that his brother had a son considering my best friend has been pining away for him for the last half of her life?"

Hannah stared at her friend, speechless. She watched her slide her cell phone shut with such force it felt like she was shaking the whole office. Damn. She felt bad for Aaron knowing he was going to catch a wrath of shit because he held on to that little — well not so little — secret.

Leila was about to take a drink of her soda when her cell vibrated. She watched her read the text.

"What does it say?"

Leila turned the phone around for Hannah to see.

It read: HOW COULD I TELL YOU IF YOU WOULDN'T TALK TO ME??

She almost laughed at her friend who was so annoyed, but she couldn't bring herself to let out the giggle.

Leila looked at her sternly. "Now is there anything else that you wanted tell me?"

She needed to tell her friend. She knew she couldn't keep something so big from her and she was dying to tell someone. She had to tell her just like she told her so many times before about everything she shared with Adam. It was just something she needed to do. That's what friends were for, right? She could tell her anything. She could tell her all about how she kissed him the moment she saw him. She could tell her all about how her body still tingled with the slightest feel of his touch. She should tell her about how he still looked into her eyes and she felt the same love that she felt so many years ago. She *could* tell her everything.

So she looked at the woman sharing lunch with her and said, "I slept with him."

Leila had a blank look on her face and Hannah wondered what she was thinking.

She watched as Leila's face went from complete anger at Aaron for not telling her about Adam's son to a look of sadness. Tears welled up in Leila's eyes and Hannah wondered what she had said to make her so sad.

"Lei, are you okay? Why are you so upset?" She put her hand on her friend's.

"I'm just happy for you, Hannah. I know this is what you've always wanted. You're finally getting your happily ever after. You were right. I'm really sad about Aaron. Knowing you and Adam are getting back together makes me think about him. I know it's not possible for us so it just makes me sad."

"Honey, you don't know it's not possible for you and Aaron to reconnect. If you want him back as much as I wanted Adam, things are always possible." Hannah truly believed that.

"I don't know. You've always wanted to get back together with Adam. I've never even tried to contact Aaron since I broke up with him. He tried to talk to me and I just blew him off. He probably hates me."

Leila planted her hands on her knees. "You know what? Don't

worry about me. I'll be fine. Let's concentrate on your happiness. So when do you get to meet the little tyke? Should we go shopping for a toy?"

"Lei, he's not a little kid anymore. He's a teenager. He's thirteen."

"Well then, should you give him an iPod or something?"

Hannah laughed. "Now you're sounding like a crazy person. I'm not trying to buy him off with electronics. Give me a break here."

"Well, you're going to meet him, right?"

"I'm pretty sure I will eventually. I really don't know when though. We didn't get that far."

"Too busy getting naked?"

Hannah felt her cheeks get hot. "Something like that."

"Okay, well let me know when it happens. I want to hear everything. Please don't hold back for me, Hannah. Please tell me everything just like you would with anybody else. I can handle it. I really can."

"Don't worry. I'll tell you all the dirty details." She hoped making light of everything would make Leila feel better. She had no idea that all of this was going to bring up unresolved feelings for Aaron. She'd always thought Leila was over it. She sure put on a good act. Until now.

Leila stood up, straightened out her pant suit, and left Hannah's office.

Hannah was putting all their stuff away from lunch when she got a text from Adam. They had moved beyond FaceSpace messages and she'd broken down and given him her cell phone number. It's not like she was trying to hold back anymore. She did sleep with him.

Thinking of you

Hannah smiled and texted back.

Thinking of you too.

What are you doing after work?

Nothing much

How about we grab a cup of coffee? I'm free. Danny has football practice till 6.

I'd love to.

****

Adam watched her as she breezed through the door, sunglasses covering her eyes, and her hair pulled back into a messy ponytail. She put a smile on his face, and a twitch in his pants, without saying a word or a touch. Just looking at her made him want to ravage her right there in the coffee shop and it didn't matter who watched.

"You're looking at me like you want to eat me," she whispered in his ear when she reached him and he bent to kiss her.

"Thank you for the idea." He encircled her with his arms for a moment before he let her sit down.

She placed her bag on one empty chair and sat in another. "As if you needed my help. I know what you were thinking." Her sexy grin made him wish he'd asked her to meet at her place or his. But then again, if he wanted more from her than just sex, public places were probably a good call. It's not like he didn't want her underneath him, over him, and any which way he could have her. He just thought it would be nice to talk more first.

"I got you a vanilla latte, although you might want some more cream. This place has some strong stuff," he said, before taking a sip of his own black coffee. He didn't do frilly drinks with whipped cream and ice. If he was going to have a girlie drink, it was going to be one with plenty of alcohol.

She took a drink and made a face. "You're right. I'll be up for two weeks if I don't water it down a bit." She stood. "Be right back." He studied her movements. She walked with pure confidence. Her bottom in those tight jeans made him want to send her back to the counter for sugar or something just so he could enjoy the view again.

"So Danny plays football?" she asked when she got back to the table. She took another drink and nodded this time. It must be okay.

"Yes. It's flag football. He plays for his school." He kind of figured she'd want to talk about his son some more. They really hadn't talked much about him the other night. Not that he was complaining.

"Is he good? Will he play in high school?" The warm look of interest in her eyes made his heart squeeze. He knew she was going to fall in love with Danny once she met him.

"Yeah. He is pretty good." He smiled, thinking of his boy. "He's quick on his feet, and has a good sense of the game."

"What position does he play?"

He laughed. "This is just junior high ball. They kinda move all over. But if I had to guess where he'd be a star, I'd say corner. He's fast, good with his hands, and he can read his opponents really well."

She put her hand on his, and he ran circles on the back of her hand with his thumb. The slightest touch of her soft skin made his gut tighten.

"I bet he's tall like his daddy," she said, smiling up at him with those doe-like eyes.

He nodded. "He's a big boy. He hasn't caught me yet, but it wouldn't surprise me if he did by the time he graduates high school. I feel like he grows an inch or two every year. Just when I think we're done shopping for clothes and shoes, he's outgrown them and we need to get more."

Adam noticed her watch him intensely as he spoke of his son. He wondered if he was scaring her off yet. She was quiet all of a sudden and it was making him nervous.

"Hannah, are you okay? Is this weird for you?"

She shook her head, as if to clear her thoughts, and gave him a smile. "I'm fine. And yes, it's weird. In a good way. I love the expression on your face when you talk about Danny. It's endearing."

He winked at her. "Really, maybe I should talk about him some more."

She relaxed into the back of her chair with a quick laugh. "You're too much."

There were a few things he wanted to know about her too. And he thought right now was as good as any to fire away. "Hannah, how have things been over the years? You know about my biggies. Do you have any of your own?"

"Well, I don't have any kids, if that's what you're asking."

He shook his head. "Any relationships?" She had said she didn't love anyone like him but that didn't mean she didn't love anyone just a little. And although she hadn't been his in fifteen years, the thought of her being anyone else's made his body stiffen with unease. He couldn't say he'd be angry, but it sure as hell wouldn't make him happy either.

"I've dated. But when I told you the other night, there hadn't been anyone. I meant it. I think the longest relationship I had was six months and that was totally pushing it. It should've been over in half the time, but I was starting to think I wasn't going to get any better offers. How about you? Anyone else other than Danny's mom?"

"No, not really. A few dates here and there, but nothing that ever lasted. I was too wrapped up in Danny. I didn't want to bring just anyone home to meet him. I didn't want women coming and going. It's been important to me that he learn respect for women even though his mother had such disrespect for him."

****

"Do you actually say that to him? About his mom?" She'd been around enough kids to know it was never good when one parent trash talked another. But she didn't need her counseling credential to know that. It seemed like common sense.

"No, no. I've never said one bad thing about Danny's mom to him. I wouldn't do that to the kid. But, I'm sure he's old enough now to form his own opinions."

Hannah nodded. "I bet he is." She watched as Adam looked down at his coffee and then brought his eyes back up to glance at her. "What's on your mind?" She knew that look. He had something to say and didn't know how.

"Danny really wants to meet you." He took in a deep breath and exhaled slowly.

"I'd love to meet him. But the look on your face tells me you're not so sure." She knew him well. She still couldn't believe that it felt like such little time had passed between them now that he was here.

He took his hand out from beneath hers and held it. "I can't wait for you to meet Danny, but I don't want to rush it. We need to be sure this is going to work out for us. Right now, it's new and feels good but what if something happens in a week or a month, and you decide it's not what you expected or wanted? I can't bring you into Danny's life without caution. He already had one woman leave him without a second glance. He's a growing boy with a huge heart. I can't let that happen to him again."

"Come here," she said, leaning toward him and tipping her chin. A grin spread slowly across his face and when his mouth reached hers, she kissed him gently. She closed her eyes, and with their lips joined together, she let her heart and soul pour through. It was like fireworks were bursting from different pressure points all throughout her body. When she was sure he felt it too, she backed away from him slowly. "Adam, I'm not going anywhere, honey. Danny could be the devil child, which I'm sure he's not, and I'd still be here listening to your stories, holding your hand, kissing your lips, and sleeping in your bed. I'm scared and nervous about meeting Danny, but I'm ready whenever you are. I love you so much, and I'm sure I will love him too."

She saw the tears in his eyes. She didn't mean for him to get all emotional but she needed him to know she was here to stay. She didn't wait all this time for him to just let him slip away, again. There had been many guys her friends had fixed her up with and none of them would do. Leila would get pissed at her saying she wasn't trying hard enough.

But with Adam, she never had to try at all. It was as natural as breathing. Even when she thought about Adam with other women, she wasn't even motivated to sleep with someone. She knew he was a man, and probably had sex on a regular basis but it did little to fuel her desire to jump into bed with another man. She hadn't told him that yet. She wasn't hiding it. That it had been fifteen years since she'd made love. She thought maybe he would notice, but the other night, he had her slick with desire and ready for him.

****

Adam had to take a minute to breathe before he spoke again. The things she said to him made him believe her. There was no reason he shouldn't. What did he ever do to deserve her? He had to be the luckiest man alive to let go of his one true love and then get her back. Did that kind of thing really happen outside of a movie?

He looked into her big eyes, and took a deep breath before he spoke. "Thank you so much, honey. You always seem to know exactly what to say."

"They're not just empty words. When I say something, especially to you, I mean it with all my heart."

He knew that. There was never a doubt in his mind. She wasn't the type of woman to just tell you the shit you wanted to hear. "Oh, I know. I could feel everything you said, right here." He touched his chest. When his hand fell, he looked at her with a raised brow. "Why are you nervous, honey? About meeting Danny?"

She let out a soft chuckle and raised her hands, palms up. "Why wouldn't I be? He's your son, Adam. And if he doesn't like me, I'm tossed out like yesterday's garbage. I couldn't be with someone who my kid didn't adore, and I know you couldn't either."

He laughed off her worry. He knew Danny was going to love her. In fact, he thought Danny already did. He saw the sweet expression on his son's face when he saw Hannah's picture, and when he talked to him about her. Adam thought his son was really happy for his dear old dad.

"He's going to love you, or adore you as you said. I don't doubt that for a minute." Adam stood and held out his hand to his one and only love. "Come on."

Hannah stood, grabbed her purse, and let him guide her out of the coffee shop.

What was he thinking? Well, he had known what he was thinking, but it hadn't been his plan. When he felt her kiss and listened to her assurances, he was confident he didn't have to wait to let Hannah meet Danny. It still made him nervous, but he couldn't keep sneaking away from work to see her before Danny got home, or going to bed early so they could talk. He needed to find some kind of balance and making her part of his and Danny's life sooner than he expected was going to do just that.

When they were on the street, he turned to her and put his hands on her shoulders. "Come with me to watch the end of Danny's practice and then I'll introduce you."

"Just a minute ago, you were unsure and now you want me to meet him. Now?" Her eyes were wide and she was smiling with nervousness.

"Yes, what do you think?" They didn't have time to talk if they were going to catch Danny before the practice was over.

She gave him one last look in the eye and said, "Let's go for it."

Chapter Seven

He gave her quick directions and told her to call him if she got lost. She wouldn't though. She knew exactly where she was going. The thought made her stomach do cartwheels. She couldn't believe how close they'd been all these years and never ran into each other. She supposed they didn't live in a small town so she shouldn't be surprised. Even at work, she could go months without seeing people, and she worked in the office. She guessed they could chalk it up to the large city they lived in and fate. Maybe they just weren't destined to meet again until now.

She saw a small convenience store on the way and made a quick decision to pull in. She couldn't meet his son for the first time empty handed. She thought of Leila's suggestion of buying him a toy and laughed. On her way inside the store, she took out her cell and sent a quick message to her best friend telling her where she was going. She was crazy nervous and thought she might need a drink when she got home.

Hannah raced through the store, grabbing a giant bottle of orange Gatorade, a package of beef jerky, and some licorice. That would do it. On her way out, she heard her phone chime. It was Leila wishing her luck. Her friend had stopped pouring salt on old wounds and had finally given in to the idea of Hannah and Adam getting back together. After hearing Leila talk about Aaron, Hannah knew that it had to be hard for her. If the roles were reversed, she knew her heart would ache knowing her friend was going to be happily back together with her lost love's twin brother. The only difference is, is that Leila gave him up. She could have punched her through the wall when Lei broke up with Aaron. She couldn't believe her friend would give up something she so desperately wanted.

Ten minutes later, she pulled into the parking lot at the junior high. Adam was waiting for her near the sidewalk, and he looked nervous. He ran his fingers through his thick messy hair several times as she made her way to him and she thought he might have changed his mind.

"Did you get lost?"

She gestured to her bags. "No, I stopped to get Danny some snacks for after practice."

He smiled and he bent down to kiss her. "I love you."

"Yeah, yeah. Don't think your sweet talk is gonna get your hands on this food," she joked with him as he took her hand. They walked through the school till they came to a wide open field. She could see the boys in formation on either side of the ball. Some wore the yellow mesh covers to differentiate the teams. She scanned them quickly, wondering which one was Danny. They reached some lunch tables and took a seat. Hannah set down her purse and the bag of snacks, and focused her attention back on the players.

Adam took one of her hands in his and held it on his thigh. "Don't worry, Hannah. Everything will be fine."

She stared at the group of boys as they ran another play. One kid stood out with his tall lean body, and thick jet black hair. He intercepted the ball and ran for a few yards before someone pulled his flag. He didn't spike the ball or drop it, he ran it back and gave it to the coach who put it back down where he spotted it. That had to be Danny. What a great sport. Hannah watched him as they ran a few more plays, each time he was in a different position, and each time he kicked ass. She loved watching football, but she had never watched anyone she knew who was good. Her brother played, but only because their dad wanted him to and he was terrible.

When the coach blew a whistle, the boys jogged to the sidelines. She looked at her watch.

"Water break," Adam told her. "Did you spot him yet?"

She looked up and noticed a big smile on his face. "Sure did."

"I thought you would."

They looked back at the players and she noticed someone get Danny's attention and point in their direction. He ran over to his coach and then started jogging toward them. This was it. She was going to meet Adam's son. He was adorable. She couldn't believe how tall he was. He would pass up his dad, for sure. His hair was just as dark and wavy as his dads, but shorter.

Time sped up as he got closer. She thought she might faint. When Adam stood, she did too.

"Hey, I don't have much time," Danny said as he jogged toward them. "I just wanted to say hi real quick."

He reached up and gave his dad a hug and her heart melted. "Hey, Dad." And then he turned to her and put his arms around her. "Hey, Hannah." She was in complete shock, in a good way, and she didn't know what to do. She quickly hugged him back and a swell of emotions rose through her chest.

Danny released her. "Sorry, didn't mean to get you sweaty." And then he jogged back to his team, leaving Hannah and Adam speechless. They watched him in silence as he turned back with a giant smile and thumbs up.

Hannah sat back down while a tear slipped down her cheek. With just one hello and a quick sweaty embrace, she was toast. She loved this kid as if he were her own. She couldn't believe how he'd come over and treated her as if he'd known her forever. With that one sweet gesture, he'd calmed her nerves and made her feel so welcome.

"He's perfect," she said, just barely above a whisper. Adam hooked an arm around her shoulder and pulled her closer to him.

"He is, isn't he?"

She watched the team get back to their plays, and studied Danny as he followed his coach's directions and played with a smile on his face. He did have a huge heart. He was definitely something special.

****

Adam nearly came apart when his son hugged Hannah. He never expected it, but he wasn't surprised. The look on Hannah's face was priceless. He watched in awe as her nerves melted away and her eyes welled up with tears. He knew the look in her eyes. She was going to fall in love with Danny faster than he thought. Danny had that way with people.

Adam rubbed his hand up and down Hannah's arm until she wiped the last of her tears away and he felt her relax. "You okay?"

She looked up at him and kissed his cheek. He smiled at her touch. "Yeah, I'm okay now. Just needed a minute." She let out a sigh with a loud, "Woo!" Adam laughed. "That was amazing. I didn't know what I was going to feel. It was like he knocked the wind out of me. He just walked up and got. Right. In. Here." She punctuated her words with a tap at her heart.

"I know the feeling. He still does that to me and I've known him since he was born."

They both looked up at the sound of a whistle. Practice was over. Adam wasn't sure what was going to happen next, but he was feeling pretty confident that everything would be just right.

They watched as the players gathered gear and put it away in a metal storage container near a locker room. The coach excused the team and some walked in groups out of the gates while others met their parents. Some even met up with girls, and Adam wondered if his son ever chatted with the ladies after practice. If he was anything like his dad was at his age, he knew damn straight he was taking any chance he could to do just that.

Danny said his goodbyes to his teammates and made his way to his dad and Hannah.

"Hey, guys," Danny said, without a care in the world as if it were any other day. As if he hadn't just met the woman who he'd envisioned as his mother for almost his entire life. "Thanks for coming, Hannah."

"You're welcome. I'm glad I could make it." Her voice was a little high pitched at first, but then it settled. "I brought you some after practice snacks. I bet you worked up an appetite." She held out the small plastic bag to him, and he took it.

Danny took a peek inside and did a goofy little happy dance. "Dad, I like her. I think we're going to get along just great." He reached in, grabbed the bottle of Gatorade, untwisted the cap, and took a long swig, draining half the bottle. He went for the licorice next. He yanked open the package and took a bite from one. While he chewed, he asked, "So what's for dinner? Pizza? Hannah, wanna come over and watch the game? Dad's recording it."

Adam gave Hannah a questioning look, and she nodded.

"Sounds good, if it's okay with your dad." They started to walk slowly to the exit.

"Of course it is." He held out a hand to his boy. "Hey, bud, give me a piece of licorice."

"You're crazy, old man. I just worked hard and need the calories. I wouldn't want you to mess up your girlish figure."

Hannah laughed. "I already told him to get his own. He's been eyeballin' them since we got here."

Ha. She hadn't forgotten his love of sweets, especially Red Vines.

"Punks. I'm gonna buy a tub, and I'm not sharing with either of you."

The three of them strolled to the parking lot, joking and chatting away while Danny shared his licorice with Hannah and his dad.

Adam couldn't help but smile. Someone should probably be pinching him because it felt an awful lot like a dream. He had his son. He had his love. And the three of them were all together. Talking away, and messing around. Just like a family. It may have taken too many years for it to finally happen, but it was worth the wait.

Chapter Eight

The next month flew by with Adam and Hannah falling into a solid routine. After that first dinner watching Thursday Night Football, Hannah had become a consistent fixture in the Cooper household. Adam was starting to think he needed to do something to make sure not only was her presence consistent, but it was also permanent. He could truly picture waking up to her gorgeous face for the rest of his life. The few times she had slept over, it was pure bliss. They had to wait for nights when Danny stayed at a friend's, and those times weren't enough for him. He wanted her in his bed every night.

Even without her having slumber parties at their house, she was still there at least two nights a week. He'd prefer more but he didn't want to push her. She was adamant about making time for Leila. She had told him Lei was ready to have a meltdown when she heard they were back together. It didn't surprise him at all. Leila and Aaron belonged together as much as he belonged with Hannah. Maybe there was something he could do about that. That is, if Lei put her bitch act aside and let him. It would take a lot for her to admit she was wrong whereas Adam had gladly worn the asshole badge. He would've done anything to get Hannah back.

Danny walked into the kitchen where his dad was drinking a cup of black coffee, and eating a piece of whole wheat toast with a generous amount of fake butter. He considered the fake butter spread and whole grains a compromise so he could eat fat and carbs in the form of pizza and wings during football games.

"Dad, can I go to the movies tonight?" he asked, as he poured a glass of milk.

"With who?" was always Adam's first question.

"The usual. Sean and Billy." Danny sat next to his dad at the table with a cold Pop Tart. The kid didn't even toast the things. He ate them straight out the box. Adam made a face at his son's choice of breakfast. He passed him a banana. "What? You're the one who buys these things."

Adam gave him a look, and Danny flashed him a smile. "I'll remember that the next time we go to the store."

"So, can I go?" he asked again, crumbs falling from his mouth as he spoke. Adam had a great kid. Now if only he could get him to eat with his mouth closed and not talk with his mouth full. His mom had reminded him that he was the same way until he got his first girlfriend. Then it was all about brushing his teeth and taking showers three times a day, not to mention the bathing in cologne. Their phone had yet to start ringing off the hook with calls from squealing teenage girls, and he'd gladly put off that time for as long as possible. But, he wouldn't mind food staying in his boy's mouth.

"Who's taking you and what time will you be home?"

Danny frowned at the twenty questions but he didn't expect anything less from his dad. "Billy's sister is taking us and Sean's mom is picking us up. Just like always. I'll be home by 11."

"What are you going to do until then? You don't have practice today." Adam was sure the boys didn't play the last day of school before vacation. Danny was going to be off for a full week for Thanksgiving. He thought he might take a few extra days off himself so they could do something together. Nothing big, maybe just some quick day trips. He knew Hannah would be off too, with her school schedule, so he'd hoped the three of them could agree on something.

"We're going to Billy's." Danny shoved the last of his fruit in his mouth. "I gotta go or I'm gonna be late. We good?"

"Yeah. Just keep your phone on. Take your charger if you need to. If I want to talk to you, I don't want to hear the 'my battery died excuse.'" He hadn't heard it yet but it didn't stop him from reminding the kid.

"Thanks, Dad." He leaned down for a hug. "I'll see you tonight."

"Be careful," Adam called out as his son made his way to the door.

Danny turned back around. "Dad." Adam raised his chin to him. "I think you should invite Hannah to Thanksgiving dinner. It'd be cool, don't ya think?"

Adam smiled. "Yeah, bud. I think it's a great idea."

****

Hannah sat at her desk thinking about the two new men in her life. She was giddy as all get out and sometimes felt like a smiling idiot. But what else could people expect from a girl whose dreams were coming true? Well, to be honest, she'd never dreamed of Danny, but she still felt like he was part of them the whole time. It was often she thought back to the first time she met him at his football practice and now was one of those times. His sweet hug was something she'd never forget. She had been a ball of nerves, and Adam looked just as freaked as she was even though he wouldn't admit it. But Danny swooped in and saved the day.

She had dinner with them that night. Hannah stopped to get dessert on the way over and when she got there, everything seemed to fall into place. Danny was getting paper plates and napkins out of a cabinet when she walked into the kitchen. He greeted her like they had been lifelong friends. And for the rest of the night, the three of them sat on a couch in front of a big screen plasma TV watching football, eating pizza, wings, and licorice. During the fourth quarter, she got up and made root beer floats. She served the guys their ice cream drinks and sat down, again, between them. She asked Danny for a piece of licorice and used it as a straw. A silly grin came over his face, and Adam shook his head. She wasn't sure what that had been about but it looked like a cute inside joke. When the game was over, Danny helped clean up and then he said goodnight to both Adam and Hannah like it was part of some nightly routine.

And it had become routine. Somewhat. A few nights a week, she had dinner with the guys but didn't stay too late. They had only been to her house once. It made sense for her to go to Adam's so Danny could do homework or go to sleep whenever he wanted. She made sure that he was always comfortable with anything they did. He was an easy going kid so it didn't take much to please him.

She laughed herself out of her daze when the bell rang signaling lunch time was over for the students. Her stomach growled reminding her to take out her food and chow down while she had the chance. The office was quiet today, probably because so many kids had left for vacation early.

Leila peeked her head in. "Want some company?"

Hannah rolled her eyes. "I don't know why you ask. It's not like you'd leave if I said no."

"Bitch," her boss called her.

Hannah raised a brow. "You better watch it, sister, or I'll file a grievance."

Both women laughed at the thought. "So how's the instant family coming along?"

"Same as when you asked yesterday." Hannah was getting tired of her negativity but she didn't say anything. She knew she didn't mean anything by it. It was just her way of dealing with Hannah's sudden happiness and the heartbreak she felt over Aaron. "Hey, I was thinking …"

Leila cut her off. "You should try not to think. The last time you did that we ended up in Vegas, bar hopping in that one casino at two dollar drink night."

"Hey, don't hate. That was a perfect night. Who knew there were like ten bars in that casino? We never had to leave. It was safe. And cheap."

Leila took the last bite of her sandwich through a smile. "Okay, fine. Tell me your bright idea."

"Come over for dinner tomorrow night. I'd like you to meet Adam." She paused. "Well, you know him. But you can meet Danny too."

"Is Adam okay with that?" she asked as if she couldn't believe he would be.

"Yes, I told him." She reached out and covered her friend's hand with her own. "Adam knows you're my best friend and we come as a package deal. Of course, he wants to get to know you again."

Leila sighed, but a smile swept across her face. She got up and stood in the doorway of Hannah's office. "Fine. What should I bring?"

****

Hannah had thought about making lasagna, salad, and some toasted cheese bread but the weather took a turn toward summer in November and she had no interest in turning her oven on. Adam talked her into having a good old BBQ with hamburgers and hot dogs. It was less work for her and little clean up so she thought it was a fantastic idea.

The guys came over early to help her set up. The way they all moved throughout the house with such ease made her feel like they were just any ordinary family, and that made her feel good. The guys brought in the groceries as Hannah started putting things away. Danny took out the trash as it filled and Adam headed outside to get the grill going.

"Is there anything I can help you with," Danny asked when he came back from another round of trash duty.

Hannah looked around. She was about to start slicing tomatoes for the hamburgers. "Hmm. You wanna make the dip. If I do it, I'll eat it all before everyone gets here."

"Sure thing, but I might do the same. I could eat the whole bowl of chips with dip by myself." They both laughed and settled in to work. She thought about all the things they had in common. They both loved football, used licorice as a straw, and now she knew they could both polish off a round of chips and dip on their own. Hannah was definitely going to enjoy spending more time with this young man, along with his sexy father.

They both mumbled the words of some pop song coming from the radio as she sliced and he mixed. When the song was over, Danny asked her, "Hannah, can I ask you a question?"

She turned around to look at him. "Sure. Ask away."

"It's about a girl."

Oh goodness. Hannah felt lightheaded. She talked to kids all day long and new exactly what was happening with some teenage couples these days and she wasn't so sure she wanted to talk about this kind of stuff with her boyfriend's son. She let out a slow breath to gain her composure. "I'm a girl." She laughed, nervously. "Maybe I can help."

"I'd ask dad, but then he'll go all birds and the bees on me and I don't want to have sex with Mandy, I just want to talk to her." Danny spoke fast, and with his hands. It was too darn cute.

"That's funny." She felt a wave of calm settle over her now that she knew they weren't venturing out of PG areas. "So what do you wanna ask?"

"Mandy has been my friend since we were in elementary school and just recently I started having different kinds of feelings for her. We talk at school but always in a crowd. I'd kinda like to talk to her on my own, but I don't know how."

Hannah raised her hands to her chest, tilting her head to the side, melting at the puppy love look in Danny's eyes. It was adorable.

"Hannah."

"Oh, yeah. It's kinda tricky at your age. You're not old enough to drive and ask her out, but it's not like you're going to go to her house to play on the swings either." Hannah thought for a moment. "Does she live near school?"

"Yeah, just a few blocks away."

"Why not ask her if you can walk her home? If you do that, she'll know you're interested and it will give you two a chance to talk."

He seemed to be considering her idea. "Why didn't I think of that?" He smiled. "I'm gonna try it."

"Cool. And I can take you to the movies too, if it's okay with your dad and her parents. Maybe it won't be so embarrassing."

He raised his brows at her. "I don't know, Hannah. You should have seen your face when I was telling you about her. I thought you were going to cry. You might scare her away."

She loved that he joked with her. "You got a point. Maybe you should ask your dad instead."

Adam walked in just as Danny had come over and threw an arm around her shoulder and squeezed. "Ask your dad, what?"

"Nothing," Hannah and Danny said in unison.

Danny leaned down and whispered, "Thank you." And she winked at him.

****

Adam studied his girlfriend and son. He knew he missed something but they seemed to share a moment and he wasn't going to take that away from them. It made his heart overflow with happiness knowing they were able to get along so well without him.

"You guys all ready for the fireworks?" he asked, thinking about the guest list.

Hannah shook her head. "I still can't believe you talked me into this. It may be more like gunfire."

Danny looked back and forth from his dad to Hannah. "Why? Who's gonna flip? Leila or Uncle Aaron?"

"Both," they said together.

At the time, it seemed like a brilliant plan. From what Hannah had told him, Leila was still in love with his brother and she was one drunken chick flick night away from rehab. And he knew Aaron still harbored insane feelings of love for the girl so why not get them back together. He was so crazy in love he wanted everyone to feel what he was feeling.

There was a knock at the door before it opened. He guessed it was Leila. His brother and sister wouldn't just walk right in. "Too late to cancel. Let's just go with it," he mumbled as she came into the kitchen.

Adam went to her and put his big arms around her. "Nice to see you again, Leila. It's been too long."

"Same to you, big guy. You been juicing or what? Look at those guns," she joked, squeezing one of his biceps.

"I see you haven't lost your wicked sense of humor. That's great." He looked over at Hannah, thinking they all might just get a big kick out of his plans when his brother arrived. Or not. But, he could hope. "I'd like you to meet my son." He gestured to the miniature version of himself. "This is Danny."

He reached out and gave her one of his signature squeezes. "Hi, Leila. Nice to meet you. I've heard a lot about you."

"You two telling old stories again?" She looked over at the two adults in the room with a smile.

Danny shook his head. "No, my uncle told me some stories."

The room was silent as a graveyard, which was fitting because Adam was about to kill his son.

"Well, uh oh. That couldn't have been good." Leila looked to her friend with a sneer.

"No, it was all good. You're just as pretty as he described you. And funny too. They were all good stories, I promise." He turned to his dad. "Wanna go start the food?"

"Sure." That sounded like a brilliant idea. The sooner he could escape Leila's wrath, the better. His son may be a genius or a total fool. The verdict would be out until Aaron showed up.

Chapter Nine

"Oh my gosh, where did you find that kid?" Leila said as soon as the sliding door closed.

Hannah shook her head with a smile, and watched the two men in her life through the glass window. "He's something else, huh."

Leila dabbed at the corner of her eye. "He kinda made me cry. His story was almost believable."

Hannah reached out to her friend and hooked an arm around her. "Don't do that. If he said those things, he meant them. It's okay to think Aaron might have good things to say about you. I'm sure his feelings for you are just as strong as the ones you still have for him."

Her friend rested her head on her shoulder. "I doubt that, but it was nice to hear he still has nice memories of me. Or that he even spoke of me at all."

Just then, the door bell rang. "I'll be right back."

"Who else did you invite?"

Hannah walked to the door, and called over her shoulder. "Just a few more guests."

She swung the door open, and was greeted with two crazy smiles.

"Hannah, it's you. It's really you." Adam's sister, Angie, threw her arms around her and swayed from side to side. "It's been way too long. I've missed you so much. You know I didn't talk to my idiotic brother for a month after you broke up. But that's all over now, because look at you. You're here. We're here. We're just one big happy family."

Hannah couldn't help but laugh inside. She was just as thrilled to see Angie and cracked up that time had done little to slow her down. She was still as wild as the last time she'd seen her. Her dark hair was set in a high pony tail that whipped in every direction as she spoke like it was her last five minutes on earth. She was only thirteen the last time she'd seen her and she still had that youthful way about her.

"Come on in," Hannah told her. Angie came in, and Aaron stepped inside after her.

"Hi, Hannah." Another hug. "It really is wonderful to see you," he said softly into her hair.

"Same here." She was starting to get choked up. "I really missed your whole family. I lost more than just your brother when we split."

He stepped back and looked at her. "None of that matters now. Like Ang said, we're one big happy family."

She turned on the balls of her feet and headed back to the kitchen as Aaron followed her with a twelve pack in his hands. *Remember that,* she thought.

When Hannah and her two guests rounded the corner and Leila looked up with a chip hanging halfway out her mouth, Hannah's stomach dropped to the floor. She could see her friend try to chew quickly, and she could also see the tears from before starting to come back.

"Hannah," she said, her lower lip quivering. "How could you do this to me?"

"Oh, stop," Angie said. "Don't be a brat and come here and give me a hug. So you're here and my brother's here. It's not the end of the world. You'd have to see him sooner or later with those two love birds back together. If you ask me, you two may as well start shacking up again instead of looking at each other like you wanna cry." Angie came around the counter and enveloped Leila in a bear hug. Hannah was beginning to understand where Danny got his trademark hugs from.

Leila couldn't stop looking at Aaron, and he couldn't tear his eyes away from her. The only thing that broke their stare was Adam and Danny coming inside with a tray full of steaming cheeseburgers and hot dogs.

"Cool," Danny said, with a silly grin. "We're all here. Let's eat." He went to his aunt first and chuckled as they swayed back and forth in each others' arms. He kissed her on the forehead before he went to his uncle. He gave Aaron one of those handshake chest bumping bro hugs. She thought it was cute.

Adam greeted his siblings and everyone started piling their plates with food. She tried to listen to Angie and Leila's whispers.

"Just talk to him," Angie said. "You know you want him back. I can see it in your weepy, longing, eyes." She was right. Anyone would be blind not to see it. And Aaron looked the same, but with a little more edge. It was different. Hannah saw determination in his green eyes.

"Let's head outside once you have your plates ready. Danny and Hannah set the table out there and it looks real nice. The weather is great and the cooler is full of drinks." Adam pointed toward the door.

One by one, they followed him outside. It was a little awkward at first, but little by little the conversations started to flow. Hannah noticed that both Aaron and Leila sat at opposite ends of the table.

"You ready to take on the rest of the family at Thanksgiving?" Angie asked her.

"Of course. I can't wait to see everyone," Hannah said, between bites of a hot dog smothered in ketchup and sweet relish.

Angie took a drink of her beer. "My mom is thrilled. She can't wait to get her hands on you."

Lei leaned over and whispered to Hannah. "That's nice. She probably hates me."

Her words were louder than she probably intended them to be. Angie overheard. "That's not true, Lei. My mom loves you too. We all do." She eyed her big brother and gave him a shove under the table.

****

"Can I get everyone's attention?" Aaron called out. The chatter and the sounds of crunching chips silenced. Everyone's focus shot toward Adam's twin.

Oh, no, Adam thought. What is my brother up to?

Aaron stood, holding his beer in a shaking hand. "I just want to welcome Hannah back to the family. It's great to all be together again, with the addition of my nephew, Danny. Many years ago, I didn't think it was ever going to be possible for us to be in the same room again, let alone share a meal with one another. It makes me grateful for my family, friends, and for... forgiveness. I was right there with a front row view of the heartbreak both Hannah and Adam suffered as they split up. But as they've grown and matured, both accomplishing their goals along the way, they have realized their love is way bigger than the mistakes they made or the bad timing of the past. I'd like to wish you both a long and happy future together." His voice hitched at the end and he took a quick drink of his beer. Adam stood to shake his brother's hand and thank him for the kind words. Aaron bent down and kissed Hannah on the cheek.

Adam looked at the beautiful woman sitting next to him and saw her wet eyes. If he hadn't tried so hard to hold them back, he'd be right there with her. He wasn't expecting his twin to make a toast. But he was glad that he did. He was confident in his relationship with Hannah, and it made it even better that his family felt the same way.

"I'm not done yet," his brother said, as they all started to chat again. There was instant silence again. Now, Adam was thinking, *Oh shit*. Instead of *oh no*. "When I first heard Adam was getting back his girl, I have to admit, I was jealous. I once lost my true love, the one who made my heart beat a little faster whenever she was around. And then, today, when I saw her again for the first time in years, I realized I don't need to be jealous because we can have exactly what my brother and Hannah have. There's no reason why we shouldn't."

Adam watched his brother close the distance between him and Leila. *Good for him*, he thought. Things were going to work out for both of them. He just knew it.

Aaron held out a hand to Leila and she looked stunned, but she stood anyway. "I wasn't sure if you still loved me, but the look on your face when you saw me told me everything I needed to know. I've been dying to see that look again, and if it wasn't for these two," he gestured back to the couple who were enjoying the show on the edge of their seats, "I might not have seen it again. Now that we're both here, there's no way I'm going to let you go again. I love you, Leila. Always have. Always will." Aaron lowered himself until he stood before her on bended knee, and then he pulled something out of his pocket. "Leila Anne, will you marry me?"

****

Hannah's hand shot up to her mouth in shock, as did Leila's.

The only sounds to be heard were that of birds and cars traveling nearby. Hannah held her breath as she waited for her friend's reaction.

Slowly, Leila's hands moved until they cupped both sides of Aaron's face. Tears slid down her cheeks. "Aaron, we haven't seen each other in a decade. Who knows if we'll get along? We don't know anything about each other anymore."

He took her left hand off his cheek and held it in his. "I know I love you." He paused. "Lei, do you love me?"

"Of course, I do. I've never stopped loving you."

"Then, that's all that matters. Marry me, so we don't ever have to spend another day apart."

Hannah's eyes flooded with tears as she watched her best friend nod her head and as Aaron placed a ring on her finger. This had to be the best BBQ she'd ever had. Aaron jumped to his feet, engulfed Leila in a tight embrace, and kissed her.

Adam looked back at Hannah. "That was awesome."

She nodded and he dipped his head to kiss her.

"Well, Auntie Ang, I guess it's you next. Looks like we gotta find your long lost man," Danny said, with a low chuckle.

"Who says I ever lost mine?" Angie fluttered her brows at her nephew.

That caught her brothers' attention. Hannah laughed as the both glared at Angie and said, "Excuse me."

****

Everyone took turns giving the newly engaged couple their best wishes and offering their congratulations. When dinner was over, Aaron and Leila couldn't split fast enough. Aaron tossed Angie his keys and told her he'd pick up his car, eventually. Hannah would be shocked if she saw Leila at work on Monday. Something this big required a few days off. They had years to catch up on and if she remembered the old days, a lot of that catching up would be done in bed, or on the floor, in the kitchen, and any other place with a surface. She laughed at all the memories of Leila coming back to their place and sharing her wild sexcapades. She had a few of her own but she wasn't the detail sharing type like her friend was.

Angie helped Hannah in the kitchen while the guys cleaned up outside. When the girls were finished, Hannah got them each a glass of lemonade and they relaxed on her soft cozy couch.

"I'm so happy for them," Angie said. "It's all coming together. I can't wait to hear my mom's reaction. She's going to flip. In a good way, of course. She's been worried about those two boneheads for what seems like forever. She'll probably say she can die in peace now knowing both her boys found happiness."

Hannah smiled at the thought. She was more than thrilled they found happiness too. Sometimes, it still felt so surreal to look up and see Adam's gorgeous face. Leila was going to feel the same thing. She and her friend had to be the luckiest women in the world. "How did he come up with that proposal? Does he just carry around an engagement ring in his back pocket on the off chance he might want to ask a girl to marry him?"

Adam came in the room, and plopped himself next to her. He reached his arm around her and gathered her close. "He's had the ring since before they broke up and has always kept it. I kinda tipped him off that she might be here today. I had no idea he'd bring it with him."

"You dog, I thought we were keeping it a secret."

"From Leila, sure. We knew she wouldn't come. But, I knew my brother would. He's been dying to see her," he confessed.

"Hey, buddy. Wanna go see a movie with your lonely old aunt?" she asked Danny when he came in. "I bet we can find a good action movie. Something with that Chris Evans dude."

"You don't like action movies, Auntie Ang." He rolled his eyes.

"I do if it has Chris Evans in it. I could watch the movie on mute and the thing would be even better." Hannah laughed, and Angie turned to her. "Hey, don't you laugh. I know you agree."

"Hey." Hannah put her hands up in surrender. "I didn't say you're wrong."

Adam cuddled Hannah even closer. "Get outta here, Ang, before you corrupt my woman."

They all laughed together.

"Can I go with my crazy aunt, Dad? Do you mind, Hannah?" It threw her for a loop that Danny would ask her as well. There went those heart strings tugging at her again.

Adam looked a Hannah, and she nodded with a smile that reached all the way to her eyes. "Go ahead, bud. Have a good time." He stood, took out his wallet, and handed Danny a few bills.

"Thank you for all your help today, Danny," Hannah said when he said goodbye to her.

He squeezed her tight. "And thanks for your help." She grinned thinking about a girl named Mandy who caught the boy's eye. She was another lucky girl and she didn't even know it yet.

Chapter Ten

Adam let out a loud groan when he finally shut the door. "I thought they'd never leave," he said, pressing his body against Hannah's and backing her against a wall.

"Did you ask Angie to take Danny?" she whimpered as he sprinkled kisses on her throat and collarbone. He'd been eying her exposed chest all day and felt like a vampire who wanted to tear into her skin. All this talk of love, forever, and lost time made him want to take advantage of every moment they had together until Danny came home in the morning. There would be little talking and a lot of what he was doing right now, and then some.

"No, I'd never do that," he said against her soft skin. "But I love her for it. I love my son too, but I've been dying to do this all day." He tore his lips away from her neck and backed away. He checked that he'd locked the front door and then grabbed her hand and tugged her down the hall. "I smell like charcoal. Wanna shower?"

Hannah was sexy as hell when she raised her brow to him. She always tried to play innocent with him but they both knew better. Either way, act or not, his pants were getting tighter by the second. "Well, if we have to," she teased him.

He opened the shower door and turned on the water. Then, he undressed her, pulling her little floral print dress over her head. She wore lavender laced panties and a matching bra. She was beautiful. She worked at the buttons of his shirt as he studied her silky skin from head to toe. Then, she placed her hands on his bare shoulders before sliding it off. The touch of her hands on him made his dick throb even more.

Hannah's fingertips grazed his waist when she reached for his fly. The pressure of her hands so close made him moan in anticipation. She pushed his cargo shorts and boxer briefs down at once until they fell to his feet. He stood there with it all hanging out and she reached for him.

"Not yet," he said, trying to hold on for as long as possible. He turned her around, brushed her hair aside and let his fingers drag down her skin to the clasp of her bra. He unhooked it with one hand, the straps loosened and he slid them down, peppering her shoulders with kisses along the way. Finally, he reached his hands down the front of her panties and uncovered the rest of her sexy body. He tapped on her bottom and she tiptoed into the shower as he followed her.

As much as he wanted to make up for lost time, he also wanted to take his time. He had always loved devouring every part of Hannah's body. It was one of the things he missed most about not being with her. He enjoyed watching the pleasure pour over her face as she let him touch her, kiss her, love her. And he was going to do that, right now.

Adam started with a soft kiss on her mouth, as the warm water showered down on them. He teased her mouth open with the tip of his tongue. She nibbled on his bottom lip and the ache in his gut got tighter. He moved from her mouth, dragging his tongue down the length of her neck, shoulders and along her arm. He raised her hand and sucked on the inside of her wrist. The whimper in her throat let him know she was enjoying this just as much as she had in the past. He kissed, sucked, and licked each of her arms from her wrists to her elbows. He pushed against her, backing her into the marble stone of the shower to keep her from falling. Her legs were wobbly and he wasn't anywhere near done with his feast.

****

Holy, Jesus. He was going to make her faint. Thank god, he pinned her against the wall or else she would have slid to the tile floor like dripping paint. Did this man suck on Tootsie Pops all day for practice? He was an expert with his mouth, and she was enjoying every wet second of it.

Her breasts were his next area of focus. He rolled one nipple between his thumb and index finger while his mouth worked miracles on the other. He gave the same attention to both the girls. The touch of his hands caressing her breasts softly in one moment, and rough in the next made her cry out in ecstasy. Hannah was fairly certain she wasn't going to make it through the rest of his seduction. She knew his routine and he was only half way through.

She combed her fingers through his hair as her breathing became more rapid and his head slid down the front of her body, lapping up her skin from her breasts down to her core. He nipped at her hips, dragging his teeth from one to the other.

"Adam," she cried out, when he reached behind her knee and placed it on one of his shoulders. He held it there, kissing her inner thigh from her knee to her hip. "You gotta stop. I'm gonna go and you haven't even touched me yet."

"Oh, baby." His words were warm on her skin. "I've been touching you, everywhere. I just haven't gotten to the best part." She could feel his breath on her sex just before Adam slid his tongue inside her.

Her breath caught, and she whimpered, moaned, cursed, and cried out again as he worked his magic.

When Adam finished his sultry seduction, and she could barely stand, they quickly washed and conditioned their hair and took turns soaping each other up. Hannah washed the front of him, and when he was clear of suds, Hannah ran her hands from his chest to his abs and around his waist to his back before getting a firm grip on his tight ass. Then, she slowly dropped to her knees and began her own seduction.

****

Hannah woke up the next morning tangled in sheets and sandwiched between Adam's arms and legs. She glanced over at the clock. It was almost ten. She hadn't slept in like this in years. She smiled thinking of the man who cuddled her. In his arms, she could sleep forever. She tried to squeeze out from under his leg and arm without waking him, but her body stopped her. She ached all over. Their long hard night flashed before her and she knew exactly why she was sore. She hadn't had a workout like that in... fifteen years. But she would sure have fun getting back into shape.

She noticed a smile spread across Adam's lips. "Good morning," she said.

"Best ever." He pulled her closer.

"It's already late. We should get up and get ready so we can pick up Danny." She closed her eyes, enjoying the back rub Adam had started giving her.

"He's gonna stay another night with Angie. We're all on vacation, remember?"

"What should we do then?" she asked, studying the angles of his sexy face. She loved it when he hadn't shaved for a few days. The scruff on his face was sexy as all hell, and she could still feel it all over her body.

He finally opened his eyes. "Let's take advantage of the weather some more and go to the beach."

"Sounds like a great idea. Who would've thought it would be in the nineties in November? Although, it'll be a lot cooler at the beach."

He kissed her forehead. "That's okay. We can just take some blankets, or chairs, and kick back with a book. Maybe pack a picnic."

"That sounds perfect," she told him. She thought about all the times she had woken up at the crack of dawn to go surfing with him. She wouldn't surf, of course. But she'd bring a bag of books and when she wasn't watching him, she'd enjoy a good romance. When he was finished, he'd change his clothes and park himself right next to her with a novel of his own. They could spend all day like that. Reading, holding hands — and stolen kisses between chapters. Sometimes she'd jump on his board and pretend like she was surfing. He'd stand behind her and they'd ride the fake waves together. She had loved their long walks in the sand as the sun came down and the times he'd carry her on his back as the wind whipped her hair around. Just the idea that they could experience that again excited her to no end.

****

Hours later, they sat on the beach, side by side, soaking in the sun. The weather was perfect. It wasn't warm enough to get into the water, but it was just right to lounge around and enjoy the relaxing sound of the ocean.

"I missed this," Adam said, turning his head to look at the stunning woman next to him. He stole glances at her turquoise bikini that peeked out of her light cardigan, wishing the sun would blast down some intense heat so she'd have to take her clothes off.

She smiled up at him with her big brown eyes. "So did I. I'm so happy we're finally here, together. I've waited so long for us. For this. For *a lot* of things." She looked out at the waves but he could see a blush come over her.

He leaned a shoulder into hers. "What's that all about?"

"What?" Her cheeks got even brighter.

"You said you waited for a lot of things. And you're face lit up like a Christmas tree. Tell me why." She glanced up at him, and he could tell she was hiding something. "I love this shy blushing thing, but you know how impatient I am. So tell me or I'm dumping you in the water."

She took in a long breath and let out an immense sigh. "When I said I've waited for this," she flipped her finger back and forth between the two of them, "I meant I had waited for *it* too. Like, I mean I *really* waited."

He stared at her for a few seconds before a smile curved his lips. "You mean, you waited for me? To make love again? You haven't been with anyone else in fifteen years?"

She shook her head, and leaned into him, tipping her chin to invite his lips to hers. He met her halfway and softly kissed her. A breeze kicked in as he peeled his lips away. He studied her with a smile. Her sun-kissed skin took his breath away as her hair whirled in the wind. He couldn't believe it. His Hannah had waited for him. He'd been the only man to make love to her, ever. And if he had his way, he'd be the only one to, ever again.

Chapter Eleven

Hannah spilled the beans at Thanksgiving dinner when everyone took turns talking about what they were grateful for. Adam's parents were grateful for the recent happiness of their sons. Leila and Aaron were grateful to Adam for requesting Hannah's friendship on FaceSpace and to Hannah for accepting it. Angie was grateful to have her two big sisters back. Adam and Danny both said they were grateful for having her in their lives. It was really sweet.

But when it was Hannah's turn to say her piece, she had knocked their socks off. "I'm grateful to the eBay gods for allowing me to win a bid on three tickets to see the Texas versus Arizona game a week from Sunday."

Everyone had looked at her strangely until her words sank in. "Are you serious?" Adam had asked. She just smiled wildly. Her hair had felt like it was standing on end, she was so excited.

The next question came from Danny. "Who are you taking?"

"You, silly," she had told him. Adam cleared his throat. "And you too."

That is how they ended up flying from LAX to Phoenix, and renting a car to the stadium. With such little time to plan, they were pushing it. They only allowed themselves two hours to get to the game after they arrived. Thankfully, they didn't have any luggage, so they didn't have to deal with baggage claim. This was a quick trip. Fly there and back in the same day.

They were hoping to get there early enough to see some pre-game drills and snap a few pictures before the chaos of the game struck. The look on Danny's face was that of complete awe as they entered the stadium. Hannah remembered feeling the same way when Adam took her to her first game. A giant-sized screen hung in each of the end zones, the roof was open, and the turf was greener than any grass she had seen in her lifetime.

She noticed that Danny walked slowly, his head turning in from side to side, up and down, taking in the massive stadium from every direction.

"This is so cool," he said on his way down to their seats.

They watched both teams warm up. When she bought the tickets she thought they'd be close enough to take good pictures. While the seats were awesome, on the bottom level even, the players were still quite a distance away. As the seats filled, Hannah was surprised by the number of stars she saw. She wasn't the only one who'd be cheering on her favorite team. The Lonestars drew fans in every city.

It was chilly out and by the end of the game, Hannah was frozen and she was pissed off. Her cherished team had given up their lead in the fourth quarter and lost. Her hands hurt from clapping during the good times, and her throat was sore from shouting during the bad. Sure, she got dirty looks from the Heat fans but she didn't care. Now, they all had to do the walk of shame out of the Heat's stadium with their Lonestar gear on.

Before they left, Hannah stopped them. "Excuse me," she said, tapping the woman, who sat behind them, on the leg. "Can you please take a picture of us?"

The woman took Hannah's cell phone and snapped the picture. Hannah stood between the two guys, her arms around each of their waists and their arms around her. So what if her team lost, this felt pretty damn good.

****

Adam adored Hannah for the surprise she'd given them that day. When she made the announcement at Thanksgiving dinner, he had thought she was joking but that bright smile of hers let him know she was totally serious. He'd only wished their trip could have been longer. Instead they were on their way back to the airport and flying home that night.

He didn't know what his boy was more excited about — the game or the flight. He'd never been on a plane before and here he was about to board another one for the second time in less than twenty four hours.

"This must be how rich people live," Danny said. "Renting town cars, flying back and forth from city to city to catch a game or a concert. Pretty cool."

"Don't get used to it. You're gonna need to go to college and get a really good job to keep a lifestyle like this. For us, it's a once every five years kinda thing."

"You're a doctor, Dad. It's not like we're broke."

He laughed at his son's reasoning. "We would be if we did this all the time."

"You've got a point." He seemed to mull that over for a bit. "Thanks for everything, Hannah. I had a great time today."

Hannah turned around to look at her boyfriend's teenage son in the back seat. "You're welcome. I thought it was pretty great too. Although, next time, we're going big or we're going home."

"What does that mean?" Danny asked her. Adam knew exactly what she meant. She'd been dying to get to Texas for as long as he'd known her. He still couldn't believe he'd found a woman who loved his dear team as much as he did. Or who loved football at all.

"It means, we're going to Texas, kid, so you better git yer boots, spurs, and cowboy hat ready." He loved how she slipped into a Texas drawl for that one. She was not only beautiful, she was cute as hell.

****

Hannah and Danny waited near the entrance to the airport while he turned in the keys to the rental car at a kiosk. He'd just finished signing off his credit card receipt and turned around to head back to them, when she came into view. She did a double take and smiled. His chest tightened and he thought he might be having a heart attack. The doctor in him took over and told him to breathe. It wasn't his heart. Maybe a mild anxiety attack, but what should he expect? It was Amber. Danny's mom. He thought about ignoring her, but she was already walking toward him and he didn't think he could get away.

Amber was in his face before he could think of anything to do. Out of the corner of his eye, he could see Hannah on full alert. Danny was looking his way, but he showed no signs of interest. "Hi, Adam, how are you?" she said, as if she hadn't left him with an infant over thirteen years ago.

"I'm fine, but now's not a good time. If you'd like to chat, call me.

Or don't. But you can easily find my number on the internet. I gotta go." He tried to walk away, but she caught his arm.

"I haven't seen you in years. Can you just take a few minutes to talk? Tell me about Daniel," she pressed, looking up at him with creases between her brows.

"Daniel? I've never heard anyone call me that but my teachers on the first day of school." Their son was standing right next to him, along with Hannah. Adam was about to pass out. "Hi, I'm Danny." He stuck out a hand to greet her.

"Hi, Danny, I'm Amber. Your mom."

Danny pulled his hand back as if he'd just touched something hot. "Oh," was all his poor kid could say.

"I'm sorry we're meeting this way, but I'm going to call your dad. I'd like to get in touch with you and really talk. I'll see you soon." She patted *his* son on the arm and turned to him. "I mean it, Adam. I'll be in touch." And that was that. She left again, and left him stunned in the middle of the airport parking lot.

His world felt like it was falling apart. He wanted to take back those last few minutes and throw them away. Have a redo. Something. *That did not just happen*, he thought. But, it had. Amber was back, and she said she'd be in touch.

"Hey." Hannah's voice startled him. "Both of you breathe. Let's get inside and find our gate."

He put a hand on his son's shoulder and the other on Hannah's. By the time they got to the gate, boarding had already started. He sat between the two of them in stunned silence. Danny was pretty much the same. A blank stare shone on his face. His little boy, the one whose smile you could see from the sun just an hour ago, was deflated.

Hannah elbowed him in the side. "Snap out of it," she whispered, "for Danny's sake."

He nodded. He understood exactly what she meant. He just didn't know how to deal with it.

"Hey, bud. I know you're probably a little confused right now. Maybe angry, or maybe even a little happy. I don't know. But whatever you're feeling or thinking, I'm here, kid. We can talk about it. Now. When we get home. Whenever you want."

But his mini-me didn't say a thing. He just nodded.

Chapter Twelve

Hannah didn't know why she went to work the morning after the game. After that hideous return flight home from Arizona. After that horrible meeting with Danny's mom. It was pure torture to watch the lively, happy-go-lucky kid she knew transform into a sad little boy. She wanted to punch that women in the face for doing that to him. She could barely keep her thoughts straight long enough to get any work done, but she figured it would be better to go to work then stay at home all day thinking about what might happen next.

Leila didn't wait until lunch to waltz into her office and shut the door. "How are you?" she said, before she even sat down.

"News travels fast, huh." Hannah shredded a napkin to pieces at her desk. The bits were so small it looked like someone had sprinkled confetti all over her office.

"The twins just talked and Aaron called me." She put her hand on Hannah's, and it temporarily stopped her from making more of a mess.

"How is he? I haven't talked to him since he dropped me off last night. I feel so bad for the both of them. You should've seen Danny. He was so lost."

"Aaron seemed to think he was okay. A bit nervous waiting for the baby mama to call."

Hannah rolled her neck in circles, trying to relax. "I hope she calls soon and gets it over with."

****

She couldn't wait for the final bell to ring. She let Leila know she'd be leaving early rather than staying after school as contracted, and jumped in her car to head to Adam's office. He asked her to meet him there. He didn't want to make any phone calls from home, in front of Danny so he was opting to keep it business like.

Apparently, Amber had contacted him around lunchtime and said she'd like to discuss visitation. That seemed insane to Hannah. Why would she want to see him now? What if they had never seen her at the airport? Would she have still tried to reach him? She doubted it, and couldn't believe the woman would make an issue of it now. The boy was thirteen years old, and had lived a happy life so far. Why would she want to interrupt it? It's not like she didn't know about him, which is the case with some fathers who never knew their children. This woman carried Danny around in her belly for nine months, and gave birth to him. She knew about him, all right. She just didn't know him.

The waiting room was empty when she walked in and the office manager greeted her and asked if she could get her anything to drink. She politely declined and thanked her for the offer before she went back to Adam's office. He stood when she walked in the door and enveloped her in his arms. She held him, rubbing his back, until he was ready to let her go.

"Hi, honey."

"Hey, how are you doing?" She sat at his conference table and he pulled a chair next to her.

He held one of her hands in his and kissed her fingers. "I've been better."

"I'm sorry you're going through this. I'm sorry Danny is too. I know this is hard on both of you. Just let me know what I can do to help. I'd do anything for you guys."

He reached his hand out and touched her cheek with his fingertips. "Thank you, Hannah. I'm so glad you're here. She called me this afternoon and I told her I'd call her back after my last appointment. I don't want to make that call alone. Do you mind staying? I have no idea what she's going to say and I think I'll handle it better if you're with me."

"Of course, babe. Have you thought of what she might ask? So you can prepare yourself?" She felt his hand squeeze hers tighter.

"I think she's going to ask to see Danny."

****

Adam filled her in on the legal agreement he had with the mother of his child. Amber would have to go to court if she wanted to see Danny. He had sole physical and legal custody and she had waived her rights to visitation when he was a baby. Adam could make it difficult for her if wanted to, but he thought better of it. He didn't want to put his son through any more heartache than he'd experienced the night before. What if Danny wanted to see his mom? The thought had occurred to him, but his boy wasn't ready to talk about it yet. He hated leaving him this morning, but he had a full schedule and didn't want to cancel all his patients. Angie had picked Danny up that morning and promised him a fun day of playing hooky from school. But even his aunt couldn't snap the kid out of his funk.

"Well, here it goes." Adam dialed the number and put the call on speaker. He wasn't hiding anything from Hannah. He wanted her to be there with him through it all.

"Hello, Adam, thank you for calling." She sounded so matter-of-fact, he wanted to slug something. This was a life changing call and she came across like she was on the line with the cable company.

"Sure. What can I help you with?" He felt Hannah's hand rubbing circles on his back. Some of the tension dissipated but not much.

There was a pause that seemed to go on forever.

"I'd like to see Daniel... I mean, Danny. I can't believe he's fourteen already and I haven't seen him since he was a baby."

Neither can I, Adam wanted to say. "He's actually thirteen. Why now?"

"Look. To be honest, if I hadn't seen him yesterday, we probably wouldn't be having this conversation. But I did see him, and now I'd like to talk to him. Get to know him. That is, if he'd like to get to know me too. I'm not stupid. I know I have little in the right's department and I wouldn't force myself on him. The ball's in his court. If he'd like to know his mom, then here's his chance."

She acted as if it was a game and she was a prize Danny could win. It disgusted him. And it hurt him. He had raised an amazing son, and while he had no interest in having her in their lives, it would've been nice for his mom to truly want him. But she didn't.

He looked over at Hannah and she wore the same look of frustration that he felt.

"Okay. I'll talk with Danny and get back to you."

"Will you, Adam? Will you really talk to him?" She questioned him as if he was lying.

"Of course I will." He placed the handset back to the receiver and put his head in his hands. He had been combing his fingers through his hair all day. By the time this nightmare was over, he was sure to be bald.

"It's not as bad as I thought it would be." Hannah's voice was soothing to his ears. "It's actually pretty good. At least you know she's not going to take you back to court."

"There was no sincerity to her words. It was like she really didn't care either way."

Hannah sighed. "Yeah, I heard that too."

"So what do I tell Danny?" He turned his face to one side so he could look at her.

She put her warm hand on the side of his face. "You tell him the truth and let him decide."

****

He drove home thinking about how he was going to approach this with his son. He thought of what Hannah had said and decided she was right. But it would have to wait until the morning. Danny was out with Angie and he wouldn't be back until late. He invited Hannah over to kill the time with him. He didn't want to be alone with his thoughts. He should've felt better knowing Amber wasn't interested in a lasting relationship with her son, but he didn't. Instead, he felt horrible for Danny. He had never really shown any interest in knowing his mother until the day he saw Hannah's face on the computer. He looked almost hopeful. And now that his biological mother was back in the picture, he knew Danny had little to hope for with that awful woman.

He was surprised to see Danny sitting on the couch shoveling cereal in his mouth when he got home.

"I thought you weren't going to be back until late tonight."

"I changed my mind. I just wanted to come home and talk about Amber. I sent you a text. I'm ready now." He set his bowl on the coffee table and scooted over to one side of the couch.

Adam pulled his phone out of his pocket. Sure enough, there was a text message from Danny and a few missed calls from his sister. He remembered putting his phone on silent earlier and forgot to turn in back on.

"Okay, let's talk."

"Have you talked to her yet?"

"Yes, I have."

"What did she say?"

Adam's heart rate sped up to full throttle and he ran his fingers through his hair several times before he could speak. "She said she'd like to get to know you." His son starting shaking his head. "But she said it's up to you. If you'd like to talk to her, great. But if you don't, she's not going to force you."

He watched as his son seemed to mull over the idea in his head. Danny stood and took out his cell phone. It looked like maybe he was staring at a picture on the screen, but he couldn't be sure.

"Look, Dad. You need to get rid of her. I don't want to see her. I don't want her to come over. I don't want to talk to her. I thought maybe I'd like her around but I don't." He held up his phone for his dad to see. "I already have a mom. I don't need another one."

Chapter Thirteen

Hannah sat in her car, tears spilling down her face like warm, salty waterfalls. It couldn't be happening. She was losing Adam all over again. And not only the man she'd loved for almost her whole existence but she was losing his son who she'd come to love as her own.

She had stopped to get dinner on the way to Adam's. When she got there, the door was open so she had let herself in. The house was quiet until she had heard Danny's raised voice. It was something she'd never forget. *Look, Dad. You need to get rid of her. I don't want to see her. I don't want her to come over. I don't want to talk to her. I thought maybe I'd like her around but I don't. I already have a mom. I don't need another one.*

He didn't want to see her anymore or talk to her. She'd always known he had a mother already. She would have never tried to take her place. Maybe she should have been clear about that from the beginning. But she never felt like she had to. Up until the night before, Danny's biological mother was like a ghost. Nonexistent. But now that she was back in their lives, the little man didn't want anything to do with her.

Hannah's heart ached with the loss. She frantically wiped her tears, started her car, and drove away, far away. She glanced in her rear view mirror and said goodbye to the life she loved and never thought she'd have to give up. Again.

****

Adam's throat tightened. He choked up at the photo he saw on Danny's phone and what it obviously meant to him. It was the picture from the night before. The one Hannah had asked someone to take of the three of them. On their way out of the park, Danny had asked her to send it to him. He hadn't given it a second thought until his son showed it to him again.

"I know I just met Hannah a few months ago, but I feel like I've known her my whole life. Since the day she met me, she's treated me like her own kid. And she wanted me. If you would've tried to get back together with her when I was born, I'm sure she would've wanted me back then too. Too me, she's more like a mom than that other lady could ever be."

He had no words to describe the joy his son gave him. He never ceased to amaze him with his big heart and kindness. This kid was special. He reached out to his boy and held him. He could feel Danny shaking and sniffling in his arms. He knew his son was crying. It was about time. This conversation was probably long overdue. He had no idea what he'd been afraid of. He should have trusted that his son could handle a talk about his mom. And now, at thirteen, he was plenty old enough to make his own decisions when it came to his biological mother. If he didn't want to see her, then Adam wasn't going to make him. He couldn't agree more. It would've been different if she had actually been sincere about wanting to see Danny. But after their talk, he was sure she wasn't really interested. She was probably more curious than anything.

He released his son and took a step back from him. "You okay, bud?"

"Yeah, I'm okay. I was thinking. I don't want to be mean to Amber so you can give her my email address if she wants it? I'm not sure I'll respond. Something tells me she won't use it anyway. So I'll think about that when and if she ever does."

"I can do that."

Danny got his bowl of cereal and walked over to the kitchen. "Hey, where's Hannah? I thought she might come over tonight."

How could he have forgotten? She should have been there already. She said she was stopping to pick up dinner but it had been a long time since he'd left her at the office. "I'll call her."

Adam took out his cell and dialed her number. He waited ring after ring until her voice mail picked up. "Hey, honey. Where are you? I'm a little worried. Call me." He tried her again, just to be sure. But again, she didn't answer. He called her at home, and there was no answer there either. He was really starting to worry. Terrible things like car accidents, muggings, organ failure went through his mind. He needed to stop expecting the worst and calm down.

"Is she on her way?" Danny came back into the room with a handful of licorice.

"I don't know. She's not answering." Adam eyeballed his cell, almost willing it to ring.

"Try Uncle Aaron. Maybe Leila knows something. Don't get your boxers in a bunch. I'm sure she's fine. She probably stopped for dessert." Danny sat on the couch, put his feet up and reached for the remote control.

Adam called his brother.

"What the hell is going on?" Aaron shouted.

"What are you talking about? I was just calling to see if Leila has heard from Hannah. She was supposed to come over but she's not here yet and I'm worried."

He heard his brother groan. "She did go over, Adam. She heard Danny say something about not wanting her in his life because he already had a mother. Leila is on her way over to see her now. She's a mess. Please tell me this is a misunderstanding."

Dammit, he thought. It was a total misunderstanding. And he had to fix it. He couldn't imagine what Hannah was feeling right now. Instead of her being there with them, having dinner like a real family, she was probably at home crying her eyes out. How could she believe Danny would say something like that about her? How could she not know his son loved her like a mother? "Yeah, bro. A total misunderstanding." He filled his brother in on what was said and asked him to come over and stay with Danny while he went to see Hannah and straighten things out.

****

Hannah was sitting on her bed rehashing the horror story once again when Adam rushed through the door. At first, she wondered how he got in. Then it dawned on her that she'd given him a key weeks ago.

"Leila, you can go now. You can go to my house if you want. Aaron's there with Danny." He was breathing heavy and his forehead was furrowed between his brows.

Her friend stood but she caught her arm. "Don't. Stay."

"Well, if you want your friend to see me naked then, by all means, she can stay." He kicked off his shoes, and bent down to pull off his socks. She thought he was joking until he went for the buttons of his shirt.

"What are you doing?" Hannah asked. Leila was silent as she tried to pull away from her grasp.

"We're going to get undressed and talk. Actually, I'm going to talk and you're going to listen. Listen to everything this time. Not just a piece of a conversation." He pulled off his shirt and reached for his belt.

"I better go," Leila said, breaking free. "I'll call you later." She was out of the room before Hannah could even blink.

"Take it off, Hannah."

"You're crazy."

He took the few steps needed to be in front of her. "If you don't start getting undressed, I'm going to take off your clothes for you. We need to talk and you know the drill so stop being stubborn and just do it."

Fine, she thought. She got to her feet, and little by little she shed her clothes down to her undies and bra and climbed into her bed. Tears still streaked her cheeks even though she tried to remain strong.

Adam followed her with only a pair of charcoal gray boxer briefs with a thick black band around his waistline. "First, you have to disregard everything you heard tonight." She tried to speak but he put an index finger to her lips to hush her. "You had to be there to understand what he was talking about."

"I was there, Adam. I could understand just fine." She could barely manage to get the words out. Her throat felt like someone was choking her.

"Did you see the picture he held up when he said he already had a mom?"

"What picture? No, I didn't see a picture." She was completely confused now.

Tears filled Adam's eyes. He reached for his cell phone on the nightstand. He tapped on the screen and showed it to her. "He showed me this. He meant *you*. He doesn't want to see or talk to his biological mother at all. He considers you his mom."

His words overwhelmed her. She never thought she could love Adam or Danny more than in that moment. "Me," she squeaked. Her trembling lips smiled as she looked at Adam through blurry, tear filled eyes.

"Yeah, you."

Chapter Fourteen

The nightmare was finally over, and Adam couldn't wait to move forward with his new family. He knew Hannah was the one. He knew it since the day he met her in that hideous dorm room of hers with posters of boy bands and flower scented candles. Her wild hair and big brown eyes captured his heart and he had never once stopped thinking of her or wanting her since. Now she was his. And he and Danny were ready to do something more to make sure that she knew she was part of their family.

Adam invited his parents, sister, and brother over for lunch, along with Hannah's brother. She had lost her parents long ago and her sibling was the only family she had. He had met with Steven recently to ask for his blessing. He wished he could have asked her father, but asking her brother was just as fitting. He was thrilled with the news and said he wouldn't miss the gathering for anything.

Everything was in full swing when Hannah and Leila arrived. Her friend had taken her out for a spa day. He wasn't quite sure what that entailed. All he knew was that when she came back home from one of those, she smelled delicious and her skin felt like silk. Not that she didn't on every other day.

Hannah and Leila worked the crowd, exchanging hellos and hugs.

Adam glanced over at his son who looked like he was about to burst with excitement. He nodded and Danny winked. They were ready.

"Can I get everyone to gather in the family room?"

****

Hannah looked up from a mouthful of chips and salsa when she heard Adam's request. She quickly finished her bite and grabbed a napkin to wipe her mouth. She made her way to the family room and saw Danny standing front and center with Adam.

"Come on over here, honey."

She shuffled around her brother and Angie and stood with them. She felt him take her hand. *This is it*, she thought.

"I want to thank everyone for coming today. It was important to me and Danny that you all be here to share this. We're very big on family here and it just wouldn't feel right to take this next step without you. So thank you." He turned to her, and slowly lowered to one knee. She stared into his eyes, filled with love and knew that he could see the same in hers. It was like they were mirrors reflecting back all the emotions they felt for each other and always would.

"Let's see if I can do this better than my brother." She let out a short laugh, as did their family. "Hannah, I've waited almost half my life to have you in my arms again. There hasn't been a day that has gone by that I didn't think of you, wish you were here with me, and love you with all my soul. You're a part of me. You're a part of my son. I love you and I look forward to spending the rest of my days walking on the beach with you. Watching football with you. And even sipping Dr Pepper out of a licorice straw with you. Hannah, will you marry me?" He held up a rather large square-cut diamond ring in a platinum setting and slipped it on her finger. It was beautiful.

"Yes, Adam. Yes a million times. I love you," she said as she knelt down next to him and kissed every part of his face. She heard cheers and sniffles as she kissed her man, the one who got away, and found his way back to her.

She heard Danny clear his throat with a dramatic effect. She smiled against Adam's lips, blushing.

"We're not done yet, Dad."

"Oh, sorry, bud. I got a little carried away." He rose to his feet and held out a hand to Hannah, who got up and stood next to him.

"It's my turn," Danny said, looking at Hannah. She stared at him with the same smile she always had when she thought of him. He made her just as happy as his dad. "When Dad asked me if I would mind if he asked you to marry him, it felt like waking up on Christmas morning. I was really happy. Then I asked him, if I could ask you to be my mom." His smile reached all the way to his glassy eyes. "When I was growing up, I would always look at the picture my dad kept of you hidden in his wallet. I would dream that you were my mom and someday you'd come back for me. And then that dream became real. You're here, and I'd like nothing more than to call you my mother, for real. So what do you say, can I call you mom?"

Her heart was overflowing with every happy emotion one could ever think of. He held out a necklace to her. It was an open circle made of white gold with three names engraved on it. Adam. Hannah. Danny. In between each of the names were their birthstones. It couldn't have been more perfect.

She cupped his cheeks in both her hands. "Honey, I'd be honored to be your mother, for real. I've considered you my son from the moment your dad told me about you. You're stuck with me. With both of us." She hugged him so tight she had to remind herself to let him go so he could breathe. He helped her put the necklace on. She reached for it, hanging on her chest and brought it to her lips. She faced him again. "I love you." This had to be the best day of her life. She couldn't imagine anything topping it.

But then, Danny did it again. He topped it. With only five, quickly spoken words. "I love you too, Mom."

Epilogue

Angie could barely take all the romance lingering in the air. Her big brothers had soaked up all the happiness in the world, while she was feeling lonely and heartbroken.

First, Aaron and Leila got married. Thankfully, they eloped to Vegas. She claimed to be busy with work, so she flew in for the ceremony, gambled a bit with the girls, and then flew right back home while the rest of the family made a vacation out of it. But Adam and Hannah's wedding? Yeah, that was proving to be a pain in the ass... and her heart.

What had she been thinking when she started fooling around with him? Well, she hadn't been thinking. That was the problem. She had been tipsy and horny, a bad combination when a sexy-as-sin man was around. It didn't matter that he should've been off limits to her. Maybe that had been part of the appeal. Or maybe it had been the lust she felt when he racked his teeth across his bottom lip. Whatever it was, the years that passed should have tamed her fluttering heart. If not the years, then her sober, clear head should have done the trick.

But there he was, standing opposite of her, on the other side of the alter looking like a freaking sex God in a slim fitted grey suit that caused his flexed muscles to show nicely through the material. Angie took in the delicious sight of him from head to toe, her stare lingering on the clean-shaven outline of his jaw, then down to his strong hands that he held together in front of his hot body. It was going to be one long day if she couldn't hold it together.

"Family and friends... Thank you very much for joining us here today for the marriage of Adam and Hannah. They are so happy that you could be here today," the minister said, snapping her attention to where it should be — on her brother and her soon-to-be sister-in-law.

Hannah was an absolute beauty wearing white shimmering lace. She looked like an angel in her sheath dress that hugged her curves from the top of her strapless gown to the floor where the small train puddled at her feet. Yet, Angie had a hard time focusing on the gorgeous bride. Instead, she was preoccupied with Hannah's brother.

Years before, Angie and Steven had shared one night of hot, slippery sex. They vowed that it would only be a one-time deal. How could it be more? She was away at school while he stayed in town taking a never-ending array of courses at a community college. She had goals and plans for her future, while he lived by the seat of his pants, taking on any new adventure that came his way.

"I, Adam, take you, Hannah, to be my wife, my constant friend, my faithful partner and my love from this day forward. In the presence of our family and friends, I offer you my solemn vow to be your faithful partner in sickness and in health, in good times and in bad, and in joy as well as in sorrow." The tears in her brother's eyes only brought tears to her own. The love that Adam and Hannah shared was beautiful, passionate, and complete. Angie could only hope to have that some day.

When it was Hannah's turn, she repeated the same vows, finishing them with, "I promise to love you unconditionally, to support you in your goals, to honor and respect you, to laugh with you and cry with you, and to cherish you for as long as we both shall live." Each word she spoke was shaky with emotion. Every time Hannah got choked up, barely getting the words out, Angie's heart squeezed a little more.

The happy couple exchanged rings as Angie watched in awe, wiping the tears that slowly meandered down her cheeks. She couldn't help stealing glances at Steven. He smiled proudly as her brother put a wedding band on his sister's finger. Then, she caught him looking over at her too. She wondered if he thought of her like she did him. The look in his eyes told her that he had. He had definitely thought of her, but to what extent?

Did he think of the nights they had spent together? Holding her tightly in the warmth of his arms? Did he think about the times he told her he wanted to be with her forever? That one time would never be enough? Did he remember when they had called it quits? When he told her he was sick of keeping their relationship a secret because of their siblings? She could recall that day with the blink of her eye.

"Who cares if Hannah and Adam aren't together anymore? Or Leila and Aaron? They don't have anything to do with us?" he had told her. But Angie couldn't see how things could work when their families couldn't stand hearing each other's names much less be near each other.

Things were different though. Leila and Aaron were married. Hannah and Adam were in the midst of saying I do. What was stopping Angie and Steven from getting together now? That was a question Angie needed to ask, but she was terrified to hear the answer.

Look for Angie's complete story — *In a Relationship* — in the Summer of 2014 where Julie will be sure to include more of Adam, Hannah, and Danny.

About the Author

Julie is a high school teacher by day, and a writer by night. She writes both young adult and adult romances. When she's not writing, she can be found out and about with her family, reading, and watching football. As a reading intervention teacher, she prides herself on matching her students with great books to encourage them to become life-long readers.

Julie has written five young adult books which are all available now:
The Double Threat Series
So I'm A Double Threat
Double Threat My Bleep
Double Time
Double Threats Forever
You Act So White

Julie has also written five adult romance novels:
Without You
More Than A Friend Request
Against The Wall
Between The Sheets (Against The Wall #2)
Straddling The Edge (Against The Wall #3)
Playing Chase (Against The Wall #4)

Songs of Dominance
Monica

C.D. Reiss

Copyright © 2014 C.D. Reiss
All rights reserved.

JONATHAN

I brushed my thumb against her nipple, bending it, then I leaned down to suck it. She wove her fingers in my hair. I tasted the water of the shower on her, the tinge of soap on my tongue. Steam still fogged the room.

"Jonathan," she whispered. "I'll miss the plane."

"No, you won't." I picked her up and sat her on the vanity.

I drew my tongue down her belly, flat and tight, stopping at the navel bar she still wore for me, then down between her legs. I bent one of her knees and put it over my shoulder, giving my mouth access to her.

"I haven't packed yet," she said, but I knew I had her. I opened her lips with my thumbs and licked her clit slowly, tip to hole and back again, tasting the fresh, clean skin and clear, rushing fluids.

"Pack fast," I said. She'd be gone for a week. I wanted her before she left.

"I have to pack the Theramin and it's oh, God," she moaned when I sucked her, hitching her other leg over my shoulder. "Delicate. Jesus, what is with you lately?"

I stood up and wiped my mouth with my hand. She sat spread eagled on the bathroom vanity, wet and ready. She was mine, and I loved her.

"What's with me lately?" I was in my underwear, which I didn't bother taking off as I pulled my dick out. "Maybe I'm bored."

"You could work again."

"I could."

I slid in nice and easy.

There was a feeling, as I fucked her on the vanity, that something wasn't quite right. Something was missing. She was wet. I was hard. Her tits bounced when I thrust and there was enough nudity between us to get my dick inside her.

But her arms, I didn't know where they were going next. She moved in unexpected ways. I put my arms around her, holding her together and I leaned in close to kiss her, dragging my stubble on her cheek and the sensitive part of her neck. She whispered, *ouch.*

I felt suddenly powerful. I'd been fucking her for months with this borrowed thing in my chest, but when she said ouch, I wanted to more than fuck her. I wanted to tear her apart.

I lost my shit at the thought of it, coming in her the way I'd been since the hospital, without control or intent; just because I was ready.

Monica came a second after I started, and we gripped each other, quivering. The steam had barely cleared the mirrors when I kissed her shoulder and realized I had a problem in my arms.

****

I stretched out in the sun with my chest to the sky and felt that thing beating. The July heat baked me, muggy and sticky, sharing sweat with a stranger's tissue, grateful to be alive, yet in a state of constant bewilderment, thinking how the fuck was I pulled from death for this? I pondered it too often, and for too long.

"Hey," she said, stepping into my sunlight. She wore a pale blue dress and clunky bracelets. "I'm going."

I patted a place for her to sit next to me.

"I can't," she said. "Lil's waiting."

I flipped my sunglasses up so I could look her in the eye and with that gaze, let her know I was entitled to a minute of her time.

"Goddess."

"I'll call you when I land." She bent to kiss me, and when her lips hit mine I held her head there an extra few seconds. She smiled and trotted away.

I had a problem. She was going to Caracas for three days to open two shows with some madhouse band, and I wasn't going with her by doctor's orders. Not yet.

The impulsive side of me wanted to follow her, and let the team of highly-paid specialists kiss my ass, but I stayed behind. There was no need to rush. Three more days wouldn't change anything.

When I'd met Monica, I'd known what I was. Who I was. I knew what I was made of and I knew how to get what I wanted. I'd still been in love with my idea of my ex wife, but my goddess had cured me of that.

I thought being happy was what had made me demand control in the bedroom, but I was wrong, or at least only partly right. All the soul-searching in the world had led me to a false conclusion.

I'd been dominant because I knew myself, and in knowing myself, I had the confidence to bind and hit and hurt, because I'd know when to stop.

We got home from the hospital, Monica and I, and eventually made love again. Still, I wasn't myself. I was mostly me and partly someone else. An alien piece of meat had been lodged in me. I didn't know what it would do. Would it beat right for me, or for the person it was meant for? Would it skip a beat at the sight of some strange woman? Would it break over a different past or a lost present? I kept dreaming it jumped out of me like a frog on a frying pan, slapping to the kitchen floor with a *splat*, beating on the tiles, squirting yellow plasma. Once, I dreamed it bounced out of me and landed in the pool, swimming with my sister, Sheila in a trail of curly red blood. And I laughed, in my dream, but when I woke up, I ran to the bathroom mirror to make sure I had a scar instead of a hole.

I'd felt like a foreigner in my own skin, dragging around a sack of muscle and bone held together with medicine. Even after the doctor appointments dwindled and life returned to something that looked like normal, I still hadn't adjusted to being two people in one body, and my wife knew it. She was drifting away like a bottle bobbing in the surf, tide by tide. She wasn't Jessica. She'd never leave, at least not for someone else. But she'd leave with distraction and indifference. And at the thought of the lost intimacy, I felt a blade of ice cold rage so thick I had no room for a reaction or an emotion. My head was clear. The anger had pushed out all the clutter. She was mine to lose, but she was mine.

Three days.

MONICA

I missed two things.

I missed my freedom, and I missed slavery.

I got myself caught in a nether region where I couldn't come and go as I pleased, and I didn't feel protected.

I was being unfair and I knew it. What man could be expected to keep up Jonathan's intensity for any length of time? No human could continue to be a raging lion after having their heart ripped out.

So, though we burdened each other with many things, I never burdened him with my longing for my dominant Jonathan. That man was gone. I loved the man who replaced him. He was everything I almost lost in that fucking nightmare of a hospital. He was funny and thoughtful. Gracious and wise. He was still the best lover I'd ever laid my hands on.

"Hello?" His voice was thick with sleep. The sun was just coming up over Caracas, tainting the sky brown.

"I'm coming back early," I said as I walked across the tarmac toward the Gulfstream. Jacques waved. His temp copilot for the day took my rolling suitcase and stowed it underneath.

"Really?" Jonathan sounded as awake as a gallon of coffee. "I have something for you."

"But I have to go right into the studio," I said. "Jerry wants me to work on *Forever* for this sampler idea he's—"

"I'm sorry?"

"I'll walk in the door the same time as if I'd stayed here. I just wanted you to know what I was doing with your plane."

"Well, thank you."

"Don't be mad."

"Goddess," he said, and I heard something in his voice I hadn't heard in half a year. It stopped me on the steps up to the fuselage door.

"Yes." I was shocked at the small sound of my own voice.

"I don't give a fuck about the plane."

"It'll be fast. I'll be home by lunch."

"Text me where you're going to be."

"Why?"

"What?"

Fuck. I promised myself I'd never forget what Jessica did to him, yet here I was, serial-bailing on him and giving attitude about it.

"It's the same place as always," I said, backpedalling as I snapped my seatbelt on.

****

I ate a lunch of chicken fingers and a half a radicchio salad in the engineering room. I shot the shit with Jerry and Deshawn. We talked about promoting the sampler, getting beer thrown at me in Caracas as a sign of respect, the roaches in the hotel, the excellent food. Half an hour later, we were back to work. Executives drifted in and out to hear me. Eddie even showed up for fifteen minutes.

The phone had been face down on the baby grand piano; the sheen of it let me know when the glass lit up with a call or text. But I wouldn't pick it up. I was in the middle of something. Only when I was done did I check it.

—*I want to see you*—

The text had come ten minutes earlier, when I was in the middle of recording *Forever*. It was based on a poem I'd written while Jonathan was in the hospital, and I was so angry I imagined myself in an eternal, raging battle with death.

I couldn't take a text. We were trying to get the last two words right. *Forever fuck*. It had to sound like a powerful curse, but be muddled, and on key, and gravelly and transcendent, all at the same time. My feet hurt and the foam egg carton pattern on the walls seemed inverted, my brain and eyes were so exhausted.

I couldn't possibly take a text, even from my husband.

—*Where are you?*—

Ten minutes later.

—*You were supposed to be out two hours ago*—

I scrolled through his texts. Jerry and the sound team packed up. I was going to have to deal with this. I had my career. He knew what it entailed. He didn't have the right to harass me while I was recording.

I took a deep breath and called him from outside.

"Hi," I said. The parking lot behind the studio smelled like sweaty asshole and stale cigarettes.

"You're out?" Jonathan asked.

"Just finished up."

"I have a surprise for you when you get home."

Home. A house in the hills that already had too many painful memories. Medications. Falls. Fights. He'd been sick and pissed. I loved him. I'd never leave him. But some days, I felt like we were coming apart at the seams.

"The guys were going to dinner. I'm a little hungry."

He paused. The silence seemed eternal, and though I imagined him staring into space with the phone at his ear, when I heard a car door slam I knew he hadn't been inactive.

"Jonathan, it's—"

"Stay there."

"Not tonight, I—"

"This sounds to me like you're telling me no." The calm, arrogant dominance in his voice was like a slap in the ass because I hadn't heard it in six months. "For the sake of clarity, goddess, when it comes to me, that's not in your vocabulary. I don't hear it."

I said "Yes, Sir" with all the sarcasm of a spoiled adolescent, and immediately regretted it. Luckily, my husband had already hung up the phone.

JONATHAN

This shit stopped tonight.

I parked in the back and went into the building. There were a couple of doors ajar, behind which I could hear the laughter and mumblings of men. I heard her behind the third, her voice humming, piano strings getting hammered one by one, slowly.

I slipped into the engineering room and looked at her through the window.

She sat at the keyboard, scribbling something onto a notebook, then considering the keys again, back straight, neck as long and white as a swan's, ebony hair braided and twisted to the top of her head. A goddess. She'd waited. I don't know what would have happened with us if she hadn't.

The engineering booth was empty and dark, and I watched her like a movie. I saw her bite a fingernail. Close her eyes. Tap a finger, then suddenly burst out with a word in one long note. It was *you*. She hit three keys, then three different keys, sang the word again, in a different register, and wrote it down.

It was as if I hadn't seen the length of her neck in months, nor the delicacy of her wrists. I knew every inch of her skin, every curve of her body, yet, that day, when she'd said *no* to me, I anticipated the prospect of showing her why that wasn't going to wash any longer with no little delight.

I went back into the hall, closing the engineering room door behind me.

MONICA

His scent cut through the dank musk of the studio before the sound of the door closing reached my ears.

"Hi," I said without looking up from my notes. "Can we meet with those guys? Jerry wants to lay out a plan for Wednesday."

His fingertips grazed the back of my neck, and I shuddered, closing my eyes halfway.

"No," he whispered.

"I'll meet you at home later, if you want."

"Stand up."

I looked up. He stood over me, hand at the back of my neck, face broaching no arguments. I don't know what my expression said, but my mind went utterly dark for a second.

I stood, reaching for my bag.

He gently took it from me and laid it back down. I started to object but didn't get past the first syllable before he had his fingers to my lips.

"Unbutton your shirt," he said. We gazed deeply at each other for longer than usual, and I knew even before my fingers touched my shirt, that he wasn't interested in a standard, sweet, encounter.

He brushed his thumb over my lips, across my jaw, and lodged it under my chin, forcing me to look at the dusty fluorescent lights.

I undid my buttons in a businesslike fashion while he spoke.

"I haven't told you this in a long time, so I want to remind you. You are mine. Any time. Any place. Without questions. You get on your knees when I say. You spread your legs when I say. You open your mouth and take whatever I put in it. Do you understand?"

He must have felt me swallow against the heel of his hand. He was back. I didn't know when or how, but this wasn't sick Jonathan getting pissed at his handful of pills. This wasn't the guy who let me top him, or the man who made love to me fearfully and gently. That man was a good husband. Difficult, because he felt like his body wasn't his own, but a good life mate by any standard.

For as long as I'd been married, I hadn't felt safe.

Until then, staring at the ceiling, unprepared to hear the voice of my king again. Then, my insides vibrated like a piano string and I shut my eyes tight against tears.

"Yes, sir," I said.

"Pull your pants down."

I worried about the door. Was it open? And the door to the engineering room. Anyone could walk in.

This was a simple matter of trust, which I'd forgotten how to do. *Trust him. You're safe with him.*

I opened my pants and wiggled them down. I wore lace and garters, which felt scratchy and uncomfortable under jeans, but I wore it because I promised I would, even if I'd promised a different man.

He slipped his finger under the straps. His touch had gone electric, exactly right, like when we first met. I felt it through layers of skin and muscle, to my bones.

"All the way off."

I stepped out of my pants.

"Why are you crying, goddess?"

"I don't know."

"What's your safe word?"

I blurted a laugh to the ceiling. "Fuck. I forgot."

"Do you want a new one?" He slid his finger under my bra, pushing it up, releasing my breasts. The nipples were hard candies, ready for him.

"Yes, sir."

"Your choice."

"*Invictus.*"

He pinched a nipple and pulled it to the point of delicious pain. "Out of the night that covers me, black as the pit from pole to pole, I thank whatever gods may be, for my unconquerable soul."

"Jonathan..." His name was a prayer.

"Turn around."

I faced the piano, putting my back to him. He slid his hand over my neck and around my shirt collar, pulling it down my arms, drawing his hands over my skin.

"I'm going to ask you something," he said, pulling my long sleeves halfway off. He twisted the sleeves around my arms, wrapping them around and tying them tightly at the elbows.

His pause long enough for me to say, "sir?"

"Are you happy?" he asked. I heard the distinct clack of his belt buckle.

I didn't answer. He slid his belt out of his pants with a *whook*.

"I asked you a question."

"Yes, sir."

"Is that the answer?" He gripped the back of my neck

"It's confirmation that I heard you."

With a sharp push, he pinned my face to the shiny black of the piano.

"Are you happy?" he repeated.

"Can you be more specific?"

"Sure." With a thwack that was as hard as it was unexpected, he slapped my ass with his belt. I screamed.

"Too hard?"

"No, sir." It was. A fierce burn was settling where he'd hit me, and I already wanted more. I wanted him to tear me apart. In the second, the breath's worth of time it took for my body to register pain, I cracked. I didn't want to go to dinner with Jerry and the guys and I didn't want to go home. I wanted to hurt, and hurt deep. I wanted to feel pain, and safety, and surrender; to lose myself and my own will. I'd forgotten how much I needed it, but like a woman waking from a dreamless sleep, the reality of who I was came back to me. I swore I wouldn't say my safe word until I was near death.

"Behave, then, before I gag you." He whacked me again, and again. I grunted, but didn't cry out, even when he hit the sensitive area at the backs of my thighs.

"Now," his breath rasped with effort. "Tell me, goddess, are you happy?" his last stroke was so hard it felt like a blowtorch on my ass. He took the hair on the back of my head in his fist and brought his face close to mine. "To avoid misunderstandings. Are you *happily married*?"

I swallowed.

He put his belt down in front of my face and squeezed my ass. The pain was overwhelming. I could barely see through it, nor could I form words past the gushing arousal between my legs.

"Answer me," he said. "And the truth. Are you happy?"

He was foggy through my tears, but his voice was clear enough to focus on.

"No," I said. "I'm not."

As much as I broke down into tears and hitched sobs, he seemed unfazed by the news. As if he'd already known. And as if he didn't give a shit about my happiness. He brought his hand over my burning cheeks, lacing a finger in the crack, down to my opening.

I was soaked. Dripping. Gushing readiness for him. I wished he'd asked me for the truth after he fucked me, because how could he now? I tell him I'm miserable and expect a body-ripping, passionate screw? Crazy, magical thinking.

He slipped a finger inside me. I'd fucked him a few hundred times in the past six months, but that finger cruelly jamming into me, with the palm laying against my scalding ass, was the best thing I'd had in half a year.

"Thank you for telling me the truth," he said. "But you're wet. And crying."

"I'm sorry, sir."

"Poor goddess." He pulled his finger out and slipped it to the hard nodule of my clit. My eyes shut. My mouth opened. My cunt was awake with anticipation as he continued. "Even in love, you need pain."

"I love you," I whispered.

He drew his hand back and slapped my ass with full force. I bit back a cry. "Don't talk," he growled. "There's been wholly too much talking between us."

I nodded.

He folded the belt in two and said, "Open your mouth." When I did, he put the belt in it. "Bite."

I bit the leather. It was still warm from hitting me. Had he ever been this cruel and hard? Had he ever been this *dominant*? I couldn't remember. I couldn't think.

Then Jonathan put his hands on my hips, and let his cock touch where I was wet. I bit the belt as if I wanted to swallow it. He didn't ask for permission to jam his dick into me in one fell stroke, making me grunt into the tanned skin. He didn't ask if my happiness was required. He just fucked me. He fucked me like I wasn't even there, slapping himself against my burning ass cheeks, a frame of pain for the pleasure between my legs. He pulled my cheeks apart, stretching them, pain everywhere, and drove into me with everything he had, using me mercilessly. I lost myself in him, in the hurt, the rising tide of my emotions. I'd told him I was unhappy, and the weight of the misery fell off me, leaving an empty place for him to fill with his cock and his searing belt.

I grunted with every thrust. It was coming. The rush of pleasure. My grunts turned to squeals, and he slowed to barely moving.

"I didn't say you could come."

I hadn't had to ask permission for an orgasm in six months. I hadn't even thought of it.

He removed the belt.

"I'm sorry, sir," I gasped. "May I come?"

"When?"

"Now?" I paused for a hitched breath. "And later, if it pleases you."

"No." He slowed, letting me feel every inch of him. He opened my cheeks again, right where my legs met my ass and I was red and sore, getting his whole length in.

I choked out a half sob, half moan.

"No," he said, slapping my ass. "The answer is still no."

"I don't think I can stop it."

He pulled out. I gasped. But as much as I expected him to continue fucking me, I didn't expect what he did next, quickly guiding himself to my asshole and mercilessly pushing forward.

"No!" I shouted.

He yanked my head back by the hair. "What?"

I couldn't repeat it. Safeword or no, he'd stop. "Nothing."

He pushed the rest of his cock in my ass without preamble, my soft weeping turned into face-soaking sobs. "God, oh God, it hurts."

"Pain is the point, isn't it?"

"Yes, sir."

"Your ass is mine, whether I warn you or not. Do you understand?"

"Yes."

He yanked my hair again, pulling back until I faced him. "Yes, what?"

"Yes, sir."

The first few strokes were murder. I felt torn apart, ripped from the inside. We'd done some gentle, well-lubricated anal in the past few months. But not like this. Not as a beating.

"You've been a bitch, goddess. That's over. From now on, you step when I say walk. You eat when I feed you. You come when I allow it. If I so much as look at your knees, you get on them and open your fucking mouth."

I grunted. He reached around me and put his palm to my throat. He pulled me back, and though I felt like I was falling, I trusted him and put weight on my aching legs, shifting back. He sat on the piano bench, and with my back to his front and his cock in my ass, I sat into him.

"Spread your legs." Not giving me a chance to even obey, he yanked my legs apart, squeezing my ass cheeks together, tightening me around his cock. I bit back a cry of pain. "All the way. I want your cunt out."

I spread my knees, on tiptoes to the floor, fighting for balance. My elbows were still tied behind my back, and when it looked like I'd fall, he pulled me upright.

"Reach back," he said. "Spread those gorgeous cheeks apart."

I did, fighting the constraints of my knotted shirt, cursing the stinging skin on my ass as much as I blessed it.

"Now, come down, all the way. All the way. That's it. Bury me in you." He reached around and slipped his middle finger in my cunt, gathering wetness, and dragging it to my clit. "You're not coming until I say. And you're going to hold back by concentrating on one thing, and one thing only."

"What, sir?" I groaned, the pleasure in my clit pushing against the pain behind it.

"Pleasing me. So, fuck. And fuck hard. Go."

I moved up his length, and back down, his shaft sliding against my anus, friction hot against the dry muscle.

"Faster."

His cock beat my insides, shredded me, while his fingers took my hole three at a time and the heel of his hand kept a constant pressure on my clit.

"Come on, goddess. I'm not pleased."

I grabbed my cheeks wider, slammed down on him harder, knees aching, arms on fire, ass beyond pain. Yet the pleasure between my legs grew, pressing against the agony and winning.

"That's good," he growled. "Very good."

"Thank you." I gasped, relieved, relaxed now because he was content. I heard his breaths getting shorter. I was close, but I didn't care. I wanted him to have what he wanted. I wanted him to be satisfied. I beat down on his cock, mindless of what I was doing to myself.

"I'm going to come," he said.

"Thank you," I squeaked, more tears streaming.

"Come with me."

"Yes. Oh, yes."

He grunted, but it was more than a grunt, and in the second before I lost myself in pleasure I noted how vocal he was. More than ever. He released, truly, fully, losing control, pulling my hair until I thought he'd tear it out. I was washed away in it, the pleasure of his hand on my clit, the torture in my ass as my orgasm clenched it around his cock in an undulating rhythm. I came forever, lost in it, in him, his satisfaction, in the pain. I was gone, my identity washed away in complete submission to his pleasure and his will; without ambition or desire of my own, simply enslaved, caged, collared. Nothing. No one. Not a feeling of dissatisfaction in my belly, only humility and a feeling of complete, overwhelming gratitude.

"Goddess?" he whispered when I stopped twitching.

I tried to answer, but I was blubbering. I took a few breaths to calm down. "Yes, sir?"

"Are you okay?"

"Thank you."

He untied me. I put my aching arms on my knees and he pushed me gently forward, his dick slipping out of my ass. I sucked in a breath.

He pulled me into his lap and kissed the tears running down my cheeks. I held him and wept fully. The emotional release poured out of me as he rubbed my back and kissed my face and neck. My awareness of the world around me, my body, the chair, the room, the building, the time of day, was brought about by the softness of his lips and the way he whispered my name, *goddess, goddess, goddess.*

"I haven't been what you need," he said softly.

"You couldn't be. I understand."

"That's over now."

"Thank you."

He put his hands on my cheeks and brushed my lashes with his thumbs. I let my eyes flutter closed.

"You can't leave me until I destroy you."

"If you destroy me, I'll never leave."

"Regularly." He took out a monogrammed hankie and held it up. "Blow."

I blew my nose. He pinched and wiped for me, as if I were a child.

He kissed my lips, taking them against his, owning them with tenderness and confidence. I let his tongue into my mouth, its soothing warmth, exploring me as if for the first time. The tenderness with which he kissed me was in such contrast to the beating I'd just received, that I broke down in tears again. He held me and rocked me in the soundproof studio for what seemed like hours, saying sweet things in my ear. I felt so good, so calm, so loved.

"You'd better cancel dinner," he said. "You're going to need some serious after care."

"You think the guys would notice if I ate standing up?"

"Come home, and I'll feed you in bed."

"Yes, Jonathan. Yes to everything."

"And you shall have everything."

THE END

Author's Note

I finished this series with *Sing*. I gave these two a happily ever after and moved on.

But my readers felt I'd left some stuff out. Many thought the conclusion was too open-ended. What did Monica and Jonathan decide to do about children? How were they coping with Jonathan's shortened lifespan? Questions remained about Kevin, Brad, Eileen… on and on.

So, I will produce a Coda, but I cannot do it right now. The series is complete. I need to move on. The emotional space these two beasts take up makes it impossible for me to work on anything else. So unless I can cover Jonathan and Monica's story within the scope of the Drazen Sisters stories, I'll make a brief return to *Songs of Submission* after *Songs of Corruption* is complete. Just enough to write a Coda.

We're looking at the last quarter of 2014.

FACEBOOK: https://www.facebook.com/CDReiss.writer
TWITTER: https://twitter.com/CDReisswriter
GOODREADS:
https://www.goodreads.com/author/show/6896405.C_D_Reiss
PINTEREST: http://www.pinterest.com/cdreiss/
Last - Mailing list - http://bit.ly/18bj9oD

Falling

Julie Richman

©2014 Julie Richman
All rights reserved.

Lying on the rough, worn carpet of the dorm room floor, textbooks and notebooks finally pushed out of the way, Mia rolled on her side and looked at Schooner. She took a deep breath. This was it, the project was done for the night, their teammates had just left, and finally, they were alone.

Anxious. Scared. Wanting. Mia tried to identify the emotions bombarding her from all angles, as she self-coached inside her head, "Stay cool. Act like this is normal for you. Like you do this with guys all the time." But the truth was, she didn't do this with guys, ever. And she certainly didn't do it with the hottest guy in the entire freshman class - none other than Mr. Tennis God himself, tall, blonde hair, blue eyed, gorgeous Schooner Moore.

Earlier in the day on a mountaintop, Mia thought he was going to kiss her when he pulled her snugly against his chest after their snowball fight. But he didn't, he didn't kiss her and that left her wondering if he wasn't feeling what she was feeling, or maybe he was really in love with his absent girlfriend, CJ.

Had she was just imagined this "thing" between them? Did they really have a moment like she thought they had? Or was it in her head? Mia was fully aware, at sixteen, she didn't have enough experience to really know. This was where being so much younger than her college classmates definitely left her at a huge disadvantage.

He was dating the hottest girl in the freshman class and Mia knew she couldn't compete with that - not with her curly brown hair and her glasses. How could 5'1" compete with a long, lean goddess that had a sheath of silky, straight blonde hair that swished and flowed across her back when she walked?

****

Funny, off-beat girls don't get the guy, the goddesses always do.

Even knowing that, she silently begged no one, please let him feel what I feel, please let that "moment" that I think happened, be real.

Silent and very still, Schooner was looking at her intently. Slowly, the corners of his mouth pulled up into a smile that lit his eyes. It was what Mia had come to know as his "real" smile. Reaching out, he took one of her long curls between his fingers and began playing with it.

"C'mere," he gently pulled her head down onto his chest, as he continued to play with her curls.

He seemed so calm and in control and Mia could hear her own crazy heartbeat pounding in her ears. It was deafening.

Snuggling her face into his chest, Mia smiled to herself, *I'm not imagining this. He feels it, too. Yes! I'm not alone. I didn't just make this up in my own head. This isn't just some little girl fantasy.*

Stealing a glance at his beautiful face, Mia was shocked to see that the look in his pale sapphire blue eyes mirrored her own emotions, and that overwhelmed her. Feeling the blood rush to her cheeks, she knew that she was blushing.

He rubbed her arm, as if to calm her down, but she still couldn't breathe. Hiding her face in his chest, she hoped he wouldn't notice her flushed cheeks and figure out that she didn't know what the hell she was doing. She wasn't experienced like the other girls he'd been with, girls like CJ. Those girls knew how to give him what he wanted. What he needed. Mia didn't have a clue about what she was supposed to be doing and even if she did, she knew she'd be too scared to do it.

Schooner's arms tightened around her and he kissed the top of her head. There it was again, that gesture that began the other night when he called her 'Baby Girl'. He had kissed her on the top of her head then, too. There was something so personal and sweet about it, she thought. It wasn't that crazy groping thing most boys did. It was warm and intimate. It was real. And it was theirs. Every time she felt his lips in her hair, she melted just a little bit more.

****

Mia looked up at him and he rubbed the tip of his nose against hers. Another unexpected gesture. She giggled, and he smiled at her, that beautiful smile - his real smile.

"I think you've figured it out already?"

"Figured out what?" *He's clearly giving me too much credit for knowing how all this stuff works*, she thought.

"That I'm crazy about you."

Feeling the heat rising in her cheeks again, she didn't want Schooner to see it and buried her face back into his chest. *Did he just say that? Really say that? Holy shit. Am I really not in this all alone?*

"Mia, look at me."

Taking a deep breath, she looked up at him, excited, fearful.

Schooner looked into her eyes and in that moment, she knew, with absolute certainty, that his words were sincere. His eyes weren't lying. It was the look he had given her on the mountaintop earlier in the day, when she thought for a split second that he was going to kiss her.

Tracing her cheekbone with his fingertips, he smiled and pushed her long curls from her face as he brought his lips down to hers, "Really, really crazy about you, Mia. I want to be with you all the time. I never want to leave you at the end of the day."

"Then don't," Her heart was soaring in that bold moment.

Every night when he'd left her dorm room, she would throw herself down on the bed and grab her pillow alongside of her, wondering what it would feel like to have her head on his chest, to feel his fingers combing through her hair. And now she could feel his lips smiling against hers at her words.

Kiss me, Schooner, she willed. *Kiss me. I. Just. Want. To. Be. Yours.*

****

As if reading her mind, he took her face in his hands and softly kissed her. An "mmmm" involuntarily escaped from her throat as she felt his kiss everywhere. On her lips. In the tightening of her nipples. The tense ache gripping her between her legs.

Opening her mouth, she invited him in to begin his unhurried exploration. She loved the way his tongue felt, slowly caressing hers, then coaxing it. Wanting him deeper in her mouth, she threaded her fingers through his thick, soft hair, molding her body to his.

I want you, I want you, I want you, her voice shouted inside her head, too shy to outwardly verbalize her feelings.

With legs tangled and bodies molded, he pulled her on top of him. The length of him felt so good beneath her. Smiling up at her, with his right hand threaded through her curls, he pulled her toward him, kissing and biting her lips. Reciprocating, she could feel the ache his kisses were causing as every muscle south of her belly button tensed and released and tensed again. His left hand slowly made its way down her back, settling on her bottom, where he pressed her down onto his hardening cock. Mia could hear her own sharp intake of air and his grip on her head simultaneously tightened, as his tongue fully claimed her mouth.

Pulling away, he took a deep breath, a slow smile lighting his face. Reaching up, he grabbed the blanket off of her bed and draped it around them.

Mia settled her head back onto Schooner's chest, trying to catch her breath and slow down the crazy beating of her heart. He kissed the top of her head again and she smiled. There was such a sweetness to that gesture,. A caring. And she loved it.

"Oh, Baby Girl," he sighed, "you have no idea of what you do to me."

"It's smoochal," she smiled.

And they both laughed.

Snuggling her face deeper into his chest to find her spot, Mia wanted to forever commit to memory the feeling of what Schooner's muscular chest felt like against her cheek. As he wrapped his arms around her tightly, she silently prayed as she drifted into a fitful sleep, *"Please let him be mine. I don't want to fall alone. Please don't let me fall alone."*

Julie A. Richman
Website: www.juliearichman.com
Facebook: www.facebook.com/AuthorJulieARichman
Twitter: @JulieARichman
Email: julie@juliearichman.com

Searching for Moore
Moore to Lose
Moore than Forever - 2014
Bad Son Rising - 2014

Determined to Obey
A Dark Duet Spinoff

C.J. Roberts

Copyright © 2014 Neurotica Books, LLC.
All rights reserved.

Dedication

I would like to thank Gloya Hidalgo and everyone working with 50 Shades of Pink to raise money and awareness for breast cancer research. Your dedication to the cause is a beautiful thing and I feel blessed to be able to contribute toward making Shades of Words a success.

I would also like to thank anyone reading this. You've done a good thing and hopefully gotten off in the process. That's a good day!

Warning #1: Heed the warning.
Warning #2: 18+ This book contains very disturbing situations, dubious consent, strong language, and graphic violence.
Seriously, it does.

Preface
PLEASE READ
A note from the Author

The character "Kid" appears in both *Captive in the Dark* and *Seduced in the Dark*.

I've taken pains to limit possible spoilers, but given that Kid is introduced during a pivotal scene, a few were unavoidable.

This short story takes place in Mexico and follows Kid and his girlfriend Nancy after they are taken hostage by a group of men led by Caleb, the hero/antagonist of *Captive*.

Unbeknownst to Kid or Nancy, they are taken to the mansion of Felipe Villanueva, an eccentric crime boss with a taste for the taboo.

Wrongfully accused by Nancy of the attempted rape and subsequent assault of Caleb's escaped captive, "Kitten", Kid is tortured by his captors.

We join Kid in the dungeon, where he is about to meet Felipe and his companion Celia for the first time…

Kid is eight years old. He's scared. His eyes look everywhere at once but he can't see her. She should be there—on the bench—waiting. He wasn't gone very long, he thinks, but can't be sure. How big is the park? Where is she? Where is his mama? Tears spring from his eyes like jack from his box, sudden and fierce. He cries out in panic. "Mama!"

No answer.

An old man turns to look at him. His dad constantly tells him to stay away from strangers and from strange men especially.

He starts running but has no idea where it is he wants to go. He just has to keep moving, searching, calling out—whatever it takes to find her. If he stops moving, he'll fall down and start crying—his dad says there's never been a problem solved by crying.

He thinks about going back to the skate ramp to see if the boys he met left, but he knows they did. He only came back because they were leaving. He can't remember where his mom parked the car. What if it's gone? He brushes the thought away—his mother would never leave him.

"Kid!" His mother yells. He knows it's her without having to lay eyes on her. Relief slams into him so fast he isn't ready. His knees buckle and land on the soft grass at the same time his butt hits on his ankles, and he cries. He cries loud and hard, until his throat burns and his stomach cramps.

His mother lands on her knees in front of him. He screams as his narrow arms are crushed within his mother's grip—she's never hurt him before. She lets him go and rubs his arms like she never meant to hurt him. Her hands inspect him, checking and rechecking imagined wounds. She's out of breath—she's crying too.

"Oh Kid, oh God, thank God! I thought I'd lost you." She says between sobs and messy kisses. Satisfied he isn't hurt, she runs her fingers through his sweaty, blond hair—presses her nose to his scalp and inhales. She wipes tears

from his crystal blue eyes and stares into them in the way only a mother can — like he's the only thing that has ever mattered — like she'd die for him — like she'd kill.

Kid soaks in his mother's love like a flower absorbs light, by turning toward it. He allows himself to cry within the cocoon of her embrace because there are indeed some problems that can be solved by crying. He knows there will be consequences for running off and yet it seems unimportant. His mother loves him, keeps him safe, and that's all that matters.

"Don't cry, baby." She sings the words into his ear and rocks him.

"Don't cry."

****

"Don't cry." Delicate fingers dragged through Kid's hair.

Kid leaned into the touch. "I'm sorry," he whispered. "I was all alone." His throat felt dry, like he hadn't had a drink in days. He couldn't wait to get home and enjoy a large glass of juice. "I love you, Mama."

"Shhh, *pobresito*."

Kid knew that word. It meant 'poor baby' or something like that. He frowned; his mama didn't speak Spanish. A prickle of awareness penetrated the thick soup of his consciousness — he was dreaming and it was very important he not wake. He burrowed deeper into the twelve years' old memory of his mother's arms.

"Don't leave me," Kid whispered. His chest hurt. Vaguely, he understood there was more hurt yet to be catalogued, knew he'd been hurting for a while. He shook his head and whined. *Don't open your eyes.*

A man spoke. Kid began shivering. Bad things happened whenever he heard a man's voice. Realization crept over him like quicksand sucking him down into his body, and into the present. He was no longer eight years' old. His parents were long dead and he'd watched the rest of his family get murdered two days ago. He and Nancy had been taken as hostages and tortured. Nancy betrayed him.

Kid couldn't suppress his dry sobs.

"I don't know anything!" he yelled. The words were barely audible. He'd screamed himself hoarse. At first he'd thought Caleb's absence had been a good thing, but Kid had quickly learned the men they'd been left with were just as vile. Despite his fear, he attempted to open his eyes. He couldn't.

Kid replayed Nancy's betrayal in his mind. Though he had been in the room, watching, listening to Nancy assign her own misdeeds to him, he couldn't believe she'd sold him out. Now that his eyes were swollen shut, he could believe it. Kid was angered by the ridiculousness of it all. He would never have hurt that girl—the one their captors called Kitten. He would never have held her down while Abe and Joker tried to rape her. He would never have stood by while she fought them off and was beaten unconscious. Nancy had!

In sleeping with Nancy, Kid had been sleeping with a woman he never actually knew. The betrayal still cut him deeply, yet he understood why Nancy had thrown her sins in his direction. She wanted to live, even if it meant telling their captors how Kitten had ended up at the house, about the ransom, and about the meet Tiny had set up. She'd also sold out Hog and the rest of the guys before they were done with her. Kid wouldn't be surprised if he were the only surviving member of the Night Devils. *Fucking Nancy.*

By the time they dragged Nancy away and left Kid bound, bruised, and bleeding, he had no desire to stop them—not that he could have.

"What is your name?" asked the man. He had a thick Spanish accent. Kid didn't recognize the man's voice, nor did he know the woman whose fingers still sifted through his tangled hair.

"Kid." He didn't know if they could hear him. He mostly mouthed the word. "Water? Please?"

"Did you rape the girl?"

"No." Kid clenched his jaw. If they were going to kill him, he wished they'd get on with it. He couldn't take any more questions. "Where am I?"

"You're still in Mexico. I have many homes, but this is my favorite. I'm a little disappointed they brought you here to be honest. Torture is often necessary, but I prefer not to sully my home. Are you certain you're not a rapist?" His words were spoken with all the gentleness of a hammer striking a nail.

"No," Kid pleaded. "I keep...I keep telling you. Please." He sobbed, but he was too dehydrated to produce tears. He'd always loved the club's rides into Mexico. The food was incredible, the women eager, and bouncers never carded him. Every month for the last two years he and the rest of the Night Devils had come into Mexico to hang for a week, pick up their drugs, and head back across the border. Not this time. This time, Tiny had fucked with the plan and it had cost them everything.

"Felipe," said the woman. She sounded genuinely concerned as she continued on in Spanish.

Felipe laughed. "My Celia has taken a liking to you, Boy. What do you think of that?"

"Water," Kid said forcefully. All he could think about now that he wasn't being punched or kicked was the debilitating dryness in his mouth. When something wet touched his lip, he found energy he didn't know he still possessed. He lifted his head, swallowing greedily until the bottle was empty. "More! More please."

"It will make you sick," said Felipe.

"I don't care," Kid replied. Desperation laced his voice.

"I care." Felipe's tone had gone from amused to authoritative.

Kid shut his mouth and nodded. He had no interest in pissing off the first people who'd shown him a shred of kindness since he'd arrived. "I'm sorry. Thank you." He let his head fall back against the wooden beam he was shackled to.

"Kid," said Felipe. "What is it you want most?" He pressed a warm, thick finger to Kid's lips before he could speak. "Out of life, I mean."

Kid's adrenaline began to spike. Whenever anyone spoke to him about living, it was a prelude to threatening to kill him. "You gonna kill me now?" He tried to sound unafraid. Death had to be better than the torture.

Abruptly, feminine lips pressed gently against Kid's own. He pulled away in shock. Felipe's laugh came out as a bemused rumble. "I can, if you wish it. Though, I was going to suggest the opposite. Would you like to live instead? Would you like to get out of this room?"

Kid licked his dry lips. He was exhausted. He was hurting. He had no reason to lie, even if he had no cause to believe he would be set free. In fact, confession sounded like mercy. "I want to go home." His eyes burned without tears.

Celia, pressed against Kid's side, made an empathetic sound. "Where is home?" Her voice soothed him somewhat. She lifted a bottle to his lips—one sip and nothing more.

"With my parents," Kid whined before he could stop himself. Gentle hands seduced him into a trance-like calm. "They're dead," he whispered. He suspected his latest interrogators might be surprised by his answer, but it was true nonetheless. He was only twenty. Other men his age were in college, or working, or *something.* Meanwhile, he was tied up underground and pleading for his life. Down to his marrow, he knew his life would have turned out better if his parents had lived.

Celia whispered her condolences while continuing to stroke Kid's hair. He found her presence oddly comforting considering she made no move to free him. Then again, she hadn't kicked him in the ribs either.

And maybe it just made his burdens marginally more bearable to share thoughts and emotions he'd kept stored inside for too long. His uncle Tiny had never been one for sharing or caring, even if it was his own brother who died—even if it was Kid's father.

"It happened five years ago, on their anniversary." He shifted closer to Celia. His mother had been a loving woman, always hugging and kissing him. He'd loved it as a boy, hated it as a teen, and ached for it since she'd died.

"I should have gotten a clue when I had to use my key to get in the house. Mama was usually home. She used to make me a sandwich, ask about my day, shit like that." His stomach growled. "She wasn't there. I remember the house felt weird. Empty. Turned out dad had come home early to take her to lunch—they never came back."

"Celia, give the boy more water," Felipe said softly.

Kid drank the few sips offered to him and only just stopped himself from begging for more. His stomach was beginning to cramp. "Why are you being nice to me?"

Felipe laughed. "I'm not being nice, Boy. I'm deciding what to do with you. The men who brought you have gone for a while. Your female companion has been found responsible and her fate is out of my hands. That leaves me with you."

Kid shook within Celia's arms. "If you already knew I didn't do it, why did you ask me?"

"I had to know if they'd broken you."

"Is Nancy dead?" He didn't want her to be dead. No matter what Nancy had done, she'd paid already. They'd all fucking paid.

"She's alive. Though, like you, she probably wishes for death. The two of you have angered a very dangerous man." Felipe was matter-of-fact.

"Caleb, you mean." Kid's stomach cramped a little more. He hadn't seen or heard Caleb since he'd been taken hostage. He had no interest in a reunion. He recalled with too much clarity their introduction.

Kid and Nancy didn't resist as they were led into the living room. Kid spared a glance for his friend as he passed. Abe was dying a slow, agonizing death.

Kid heard his uncle cry out with pain and his head snapped in his uncle's direction. He gasped. Tiny lay face down on the floor, arms tied behind him, and his back painfully arched. Caleb straddled Tiny's back in a standing position while holding Tiny's long hair in his fist.

"Jair," Caleb spat. "Knife."

Tiny screamed. Kid screamed. Even Nancy went to her knees and begged Caleb to stop. It was too late. Kid watched as Caleb slit his uncle's throat and kept hacking through muscle, bone, and sinew. The more everyone screamed the more incensed Caleb seemed to become.

"I warned you!" Caleb yelled over the screams. "I warned you what would happen if you hid her from me." Blood arched through the air and covered Caleb's hand, his arm, his chest, and even parts of the wall. "I warned you," Caleb sucked air harshly into his lungs and spoke through bloodstained spattered lips. "I warned you not to hurt her."

Tiny's head came away from his body.

As the men around him cheered, Kid stared at his uncle's blood as it pooled around his body and crept outward. Some of it soaked into Kid's socks. It was still warm.

Nancy's scream and the sharp tip of Caleb's knife under his chin brought Kid's attention into focus. He saw his imminent death in Caleb's eyes. Something warm dripped down his neck. He closed his eyes and tried not to swallow, or breathe, or even move. Caleb's breath touched his face.

"Kid," Caleb said lowly. "I'm going to take you both with me and when Kitten wakes up..." Caleb shut his eyes, seeking composure. He pressed the knife at Kid's throat deeper. "She's going to tell me what happened. Understand?" He ran his blood slick fingers over Kid's face.

Felipe sighed. "Yes, Caleb is a dangerous man. Unfortunately, he is not the only man angered by this situation. Tell me—because I sense something else is in play—why do you suspect Caleb reacted so...passionately? Could it be he has affection for his captive? I'm curious." He reached out and ran his thumb across Kid's bottom lip. He chuckled when Kid pulled away. "I'm an extraordinarily curious man...Kid."

Kid felt numb. His uncle was dead. Abe was bleeding out. Joker was gonna burn. Kid didn't want to think about his and Nancy's fate. As Caleb walked past with the girl cradled against his chest, Kid saw the mirror of his own pain reflected on the face of the other man.

Caleb kissed her forehead softly, tenderly, as though he weren't the same man who'd just decapitated someone with a knife only minutes prior. "Don't worry, Kitten, I promise I'm going to make it better."

"She ran away from him," Kid managed to say. "Tiny said we were helping her escape."

"For a price," Felipe accused.

Tiny walked to the door and made sure it was locked before he addressed the club. "I hope you assholes are ready to make some serious money. That girl is worth a hundred grand once we get her to Chihuahua."

Hog was the first to speak. "What the fuck, Tiny? You go out for a beer last night and come back with some girl? Who the hell is she?" He said the last in an angry whisper.

Kid kept his mouth shut, as usual, while the other guys murmured in agreement with Hog. Kid was just as curious as everyone else, but Tiny was his only real family so he tried not to piss the man off. Maybe the girl just needed a ride and was willing to pay a lot to get there. Kid shook his head at his own stupidity. No one paid a hundred grand for a damn ride.

"What are you?" Tiny admonished. "You a bunch of pussies now? I took a ride over to the bar after I hooked up last night, and the bartender let me drink. So, he's bringing in crates and I'm sitting there, having a beer and minding my own damn business, when this half-naked girl runs in screaming for us to lock the door." Tiny instantly commanded attention. "Her and the bartender are shouting back and forth. Apparently, the girl was being chased by some guy named Caleb who's been keeping her locked up for weeks. Dude! She didn't even know she was in Mexico! How fucked is that!"

Hog sat up straight and lifted his hand. "Wait, wait, wait. You're telling me that girl has people looking for her? And you want to take her with us to pick up our shit? Are you crazy, man? Have you lost your goddamn mind?!"

"I'm not done!" Tiny shouted and Hog went silent. "The bartender freaks and leaves me there with this girl. She won't stop crying and asking me to take her to the cops, which is stupid because the guy who took her could easily bribe the cops. I'm in the middle of telling her this when the fucking guy starts pounding on the door. Girl hides under the bar and I cover her with the crates the bartender brought in. Then, bang! The door gets busted in."

"Fuck!" exclaimed Joker. "Man! I wish I'da been there!"

"Right?" Tiny laughed. He started pacing as he became engrossed in his story. "So in walks this pretty boy—no offense, Kid."

"Fuck you." Kid rolled his eyes and pretended the words didn't cut deep. The guys frequently liked to remind him of his 'cock sucking lips' and 'pretty' face. It had been old for a long time.

Tiny laughed and kept talking. "He's already blown through the door, so I know the damn shotgun he's carrying is loaded. I play it cool and pour myself a beer." He grins. "Right away he asks about the girl, and I tell him I ain't seen her. We go through this whole thing, sizing up each other's peckers, and then I pull my gun out. This fucking guy...he doesn't even flinch. He tells me he's willing to pay if I bring him the girl—he's staying in that old plantation. And then he leaves, just like that. He even showed me his back like he didn't give a shit if I shot him."

"Man! What? Serious?" Joker was enjoying himself immensely. "What are we waitin' on? Let's just give her back, let him pay us off. I ain't ready to head out yet."

Tiny scoffed. "Yeah right, that guy would just as soon kill us after we gave up the girl. Witnesses, stupid. Besides, I already made us a deal. Her friend's willing to meet us in Chihuahua and pay. I told her no cops or we'd kill the girl. All we have to do is get there." Tiny opened his arms wide and grinned. "A hundred thousand fuckin' dollars, guys. That's double our usual take."

"We ain't in the kidnapping business, Tiny!" Hog stood abruptly, nose to nose with Tiny. "Cut that fucking girl loose and let's get out of here before anyone comes lookin'."

Someone had come looking alright. Kid regretted not leaving with Hog when the club split in half over the issue. Then he regretted thinking such a thing. Tiny may not have been a great man, but he'd saved Kid from ending up in foster care. He'd said there was no way he was going to let his brother's son live with strangers.

"I didn't care about the money," Kid sobbed. "Uncle Mike...Tiny." Kid called him by his road name because Tiny had always insisted Mike was his slave name. The name he'd had before he started riding and discovered freedom. Tiny lived—*had lived*—for the road; all the guys did. They ran just enough cocaine and pot out of Mexico into the U.S. every month to support their lifestyle: ride all day, drink and fuck all night. Kid had found it all so seductive after his parents died. It wasn't seductive any more. "I couldn't leave Tiny. He was my family."

"Hmm," was all Felipe had to say on the subject. "You didn't know with whom you were dealing."

Kid shook his head. He *still* didn't know. "Are you going to kill us? Me? Nancy?" Kid was only slightly surprised to discover he suddenly didn't care too much. Everyone he had ever loved was dead and anyone he'd ever cared for had betrayed him. What did he have left? *Who* did he have left?

"You haven't answered my question yet. What is it you want most? Death? Revenge? Your freedom?" Felipe seemed amused.

Kid took the time to consider the odd man's questions. Part of him wanted all those things—wanted them desperately. But the voice in his head didn't respond with words of vengeance, and Kid held no illusions about being granted any freedom aside from death. Instead, he thought about his grief spreading inside him like a cancer and eating away everything that was good in him. He thought of his mother's worshipful eyes on him and how he'd never lived up to that look. Yes, he wanted revenge. Yes, he imagined cutting his captors open and literally ripping their guts out. But even as he had the thoughts, he knew how false they rang. The voice in his head screamed his answer loud enough to silence any errant thoughts of revenge. He knew his truth.

"I can't have what I want most," he whispered. He still couldn't open his eyes. It made his yearning easier to confess. "There's no one left to love me." His physical pain abated somewhat to make room for the pain of emotional wounds ripping open. When Celia shifted him, he readily took comfort in her awkward embrace. Even with his arms bound behind him and his shoulders screaming with pain, he felt better being held. No one had held him in a long time. No one had stroked his hair and told him everything was going to be okay.

"Loyal *and* sentimental," Felipe said. "There may be hope for you yet." Felipe paced, his shoes making shuffling sounds along the concrete floor. Celia said a bunch of things in Spanish and Felipe replied in kind before returning to English. "You're quite handsome under all those bruises, aren't you boy?"

Kid hadn't thought much about his nudity, but he did after Felipe's comment. It was hardly the first time someone had mentioned Kid's appearance. As far back as he could remember, he'd been complimented on his near-platinum blond hair and striking blue eyes. Kid had his father's strong build, but he'd come out looking like his mama from day one. The girls had always gone crazy for him —and a few men too. His dad had always poked fun at his pouty lips and inability to grow more than sparse facial hair, but he'd also been sure to warn him about perverts. More than a few times, some asshole had tried to grab his dick in a men's room and had to be reminded what the word no meant. Regardless, he'd never thought of his looks as a bad thing, not until he found himself helpless. He forced himself to remain languid in Celia's embrace as he began to cry in the hopes it would solve his problems—no matter what his dad had taught him.

"The way I see it," Felipe began, "your options are limited. I can't let you go, but I have no use for a hostage." Kid sucked in a breath and huddled closer to Celia as Felipe continued. "You've trifled with some serious people, boy. They're the kind who buy and sell beautiful creatures...like Kitten, whom your friends have ruined, and occasionally, blond-haired and blue-eyed boys...like *you*."

"Please," Kid pleaded. "Just—"

Felipe cut Kid off. "However! Let me finish, boy. Occasionally, masters find it difficult to part with their slaves." He sighed and said something to Celia that sounded endearing to Kid's ears. Felipe laughed at her response. "So difficult, in fact, that they keep them for themselves and spoil them rotten." Celia's tinkling laughter fluttered the hair that had fallen in Kid's eyes.

"What does that mean?" Kid asked, hesitant. Nothing Felipe had said so far made him feel at ease.

"It *means*, Celia has asked me to consider you," Felipe snapped. "Don't interrupt. I have no time in my life for insolent pets. No matter how beautiful they are. Understand?"

Kid nodded.

"Good. Your options are these: find it within yourself to submit to Celia *and* to me...or die." He knelt beside Kid, purposely crowding him against Celia and the beam at his back. "You see? I'm not a nice man, Boy, but I *can* be fair. I'll spare your life, and in return you'll surrender it to me, as Celia did many years ago." He pulled away and stood.

Kid tensed. A feminine hand fondled his exposed junk. "What are you doing? Not there." He was still sore from the punches he'd taken—not even his balls had been spared. Kid struggled despite knowing the futility of his attempts.

"Shhh, *no llores pobresito.* Don't cry," whispered Celia. Kid felt marginally comforted by Celia's feminine presence. He sighed as her fingers continued to stroke his hair. Fleetingly, he thought if a knife were to be slipped into his side at that moment it would be an okay death because he wouldn't be alone. Then he remembered the way his friends had died and knew no such death awaited him.

"I'll do whatever you want. You don't have to hurt me." The hand on Kid's dick persisted. Slow, gentle, enticing, Celia continued to stroke his flesh. Too worried about what they'd do to him if he let desire take hold, he couldn't get hard.

"You're not doing what Celia wants," Felipe teased. "Is she treating you too kindly?"

On silent cue, Celia squeezed.

"Stop!" Kid hissed. "Please...I can't." What the hell were they doing to him? Anger began to outweigh the fear he felt. His captors had taken everything from him—his last remaining family, his friends, and Nancy. Did they have to humiliate him?

"Celia, the boy would rather take his chances with the others." Felipe spoke as though he hadn't a care in the world, save for his own amusement.

Celia's touches became soft once more. She pressed her lips to Kid's ear. "Come with me. Come for me." Her phrases were clipped, her English obviously limited.

Kid clung to the meager promise in Celia's words. He suspected she might be leading him into a trap. He knew more than he cared to know about what his captors were capable of doing. However, he also knew they'd get what they wanted out of him one way or the other. If the slight possibility existed he could walk out of his situation alive—he had to take it.

"Yes," Kid whispered. He turned his body toward Celia as much as he was able and settled his head on her narrow shoulder. Celia was a slave, apparently had been for years, and she seemed okay. Kid tried to hold on to that thought as she continued touching him. Through swollen eyelids, he could barely see Celia's hand attempting to inspire his erection. Embarrassment stirred. He usually had problems hiding his passion, not stoking it. Kid mumbled something about his pain and the difficulty it presented.

"Focus on the pleasure and the pain goes away," said Felipe.

Kid startled, forcing his eyes uncomfortably wide when strong, masculine hands pulled his knees up and apart. "What are you—" Celia's arm curved around his head to cover his mouth. Kid heeded the warning and cut himself off from further protest. Maybe the guy was going to fuck him, he thought. The idea terrified him, disgusted him, but perhaps it wouldn't hurt if he went along? Some guys liked being fucked, so it couldn't be all bad, right? Kid buried his nose in Celia's neck. He pressed a series of pleading kisses against her soft flesh.

Celia coddled him briefly but quickly left him so she could stand. "Open your eyes," she said firmly.

Kid forced himself to obey, though he could only do so partially. He stared up into the faces of his new captors. He'd been expecting…well, he wasn't sure what he'd been expecting, but not the two he saw. Felipe looked to be in his late forties or early fifties. He had dark salt and pepper hair and a five-o'-clock shadow that would have taken Kid a month to grow. He met Kid's eyes with a smile that bespoke his confidence. Kid raised a muddled brow when he noticed Felipe was wearing a flamingo-pink suit.

Celia was, in a word, stunning. Kid surmised she was older than his own twenty years, but likely in her twenties somewhere. Her dark hair was pinned away from her face to reveal dark eyes rimmed with dark lashes, an aristocratic nose, and full red lips. He gauged her height at a measly five feet. He was equally taken aback by her flimsy attire—

nothing but a tiny pink tube dress. Kid unwittingly called to mind the kiss they shared and her possessive touch upon his flesh. He felt a trill of unwanted pleasure, then guilt for wanting more.

Felipe had been smart to not let her come alone; Kid could have easily overpowered her, even in his weakened state. He was just desperate enough to have tried.

"Like what you see?" Felipe raised a brow and tilted his head toward Celia.

Kid averted his eyes. "I guess," he murmured. He wasn't going to admit to another man, a lunatic, that he thought his girlfriend—or *slave*—was ridiculously hot.

Felipe patted Kid on the head, chuckling. "Smart boy." Celia made an impatient sound. Both men looked toward her. Felipe tsked. "Celia only deals in absolutes. If I were you, I'd answer her properly."

Kid must have telegraphed his confusion because Felipe clarified. "Yes, Celia. Or no, Celia." Felipe winked and stood.

Celia wasted no time in pulling her slight pink dress down toward her waist to expose her small breasts and raspberry-colored nipples. She tugged on the modest peaks until they tightened. "You like me?" she asked.

Like a wild animal being coaxed with food, Kid could neither deny his desire nor abandon his instincts. The nicer the carrot, the more brutal the stick—and Celia was one hell of a carrot. He licked his lips, wishing they weren't so dry. He looked at Felipe before he answered, cautious. "Yes, Celia?" He relaxed some when they smiled.

"Good boy," Celia said, as though mimicking Felipe. She went to take a step forward. Felipe put his arm out to stop her.

Felipe addressed Kid with a deadly seriousness. "Hurt her, and I will take my time gutting you."

Kid shut his eyes and balled his body against the beam at his back before he remembered his options: Obey or suffer. He resumed his unprotected pose.

"Felipe!" Celia admonished. Amusement twisted one side of her mouth into a half smile before she straddled Kid's hips and sat in the cradle of his spread knees. Her bare pussy rested against Kid's barely thickening cock. "Please?"

Felipe kissed her upturned lips. "I know, my dear. I promised."

Celia thanked Felipe in Spanish then refocused her attention on Kid once again. She rocked her hips back and forth, tiny thrusts that rubbed her clit against his cock. She ignored his aggrieved whimpers as her slight weight reignited his pain. She only seemed to care that his cock was getting hard. If she showed any concern, it was that she kept her rhythm steady and predictable so Kid could brace slightly when she pushed back against his balls.

At length, Kid found himself lost in Celia's rhythm. His head rubbed in time against the beam behind him until he felt drunk, unsteady, and somewhat adrift on sensation. His thoughts scattered and to his obscure delight, his pain began to lessen. It didn't disappear, but it somehow served to make him focus on his pleasure. He decided the pain was worth it. He could do anything if it meant the pain would stop. He allowed himself a tiny thrust of his own. His cock pulsed. Maybe they'd give him water. He thrust harder. Maybe they'd feed him. He heard himself sigh as he slid across Celia's wet pussy. Maybe she'd let him sleep in her bed. Maybe she would let him inside her and he could come. Kid whimpered. Loud.

Celia leaned forward. Her breath quickened and her chest felt slightly tacky with burgeoning sweat as it made contact with the side of Kid's face. Her hard nipples dragged against his neck. Kid was too far gone to contemplate sucking on Celia's tits. He was too out of his mind to acknowledge she was sucking Felipe's dick as he stood to the right and behind his shoulder. He even ignored the drool that dribbled on him as Celia gagged on Felipe's cock. It was enough that Kid's pain was nearly non-existent.

Celia said things Kid didn't understand or take notice of until a masculine hand gripped his hair. "She wants to know if you like this." Felipe grinned. He pulled Celia's mouth back toward his cock.

"Yes, Celia," Kid said without hesitation. He didn't care if he was looking up at an exposed Felipe when he said it. He was so close to the end. Oblivion waited if he could just get there. He struggled with keeping his hooded gaze on Felipe.

"Good boy." Felipe continued to hold him in place. Kid could barely hold himself together. The urge to come was overwhelming. Thoughts of his own cooperation shamed him, excited him, destroyed and remade him. All the while, he stared up into calculating green eyes.

A few minutes later Felipe pulled away from Celia's mouth and moved behind her. He pushed Celia forward until she and Kid were resting one another's heads on each other's shoulders. He reclaimed his hold in Kid's hair, pushed into Celia, and came.

Shock assailed Kid, lust quick on its heels. Above him, Celia cried out. She rocked her hips hard and fast, milking the cock inside her.

Semen oozed out of her and landed on his cock. That was all it took for his sore balls to tighten sharply. Pain, not pleasure, hit him hard with every shot of come pushed onto his own stomach.

Kid passed out before shame could find him.

****

Much later, after being washed, shaved from the nose down, fed, and given an opportunity to rest in a bed more lavish than any he'd ever slept in before, Kid learned the nature of what was expected of him.

His body would be meant for pleasure, though not his own. Kid's circumstances were terrifying in the extreme, but less so than death—at least he hoped. Felipe had alluded to selling him if Kid's submission left anything to be desired.

Upon hearing the threat, Kid opted to surrender to the lesser of two evils. No matter what Felipe and Celia might put him through, it couldn't possibly compare to the horrors of his imagination or the terrible things he'd already witnessed. Instead, with each blind and tremulous step he traversed he felt his old life slipping away and he hadn't the strength or will to fight it.

Celia spoke her words with authority. "Put him on his knees and lock his wrists to his ankles." As Felipe translated, an intimate crowd applauded.

Kid froze. Whatever he'd feared might happen, he had taken solace in believing no one but Felipe and Celia would witness his shame. His new situation was far more grotesque. Shock kept him from struggling against the strong hands that guided his submission. Blindfolded, gagged, and surrounded by strangers, Kid nearly considered their hold on him a mercy.

"Take the gag out of his mouth," Celia ordered. She ran her fingers through his shoulder-length hair, easing him into a false sense of security before she fisted the gold strands and snapped his head back.

"Fuck!" Kid yelled. He hadn't been expecting pain. He chided himself for always trusting the wrong people. Celia and Felipe were one and the same. She held him easily in her tight fist.

"Does it hurt, Slave?" she mocked. Laughter could be heard in the room.

Kid fell silent. Behind his back, his fists clenched and his arms strained against the restraints he wore. Celia pulled harder, wrenching his head back in such a way to completely expose his throat.

"Yes...Celia," he finally whispered.

Gradually, the soft music that had been playing began to fade until the room was stark in its silence. It drew the moment into sharper focus, each sound lending itself to an action. The room itself seemed a living thing, breathing, vibrating, and hungry.

"Very good, Slave." Felipe's voice was scarcely above a whisper when he translated Celia's words. Celia released Kid's hair and he audibly sighed in relief. She stroked the gold strands for a few seconds. Her audience seemed to sigh in approval as they listened to Kid's ragged breaths.

Kid felt unhurried, seductive fingers caress his face, neck, and shoulders. As in the dungeon, Celia took her time attempting to coax him into desiring her. It was sort of working. He could smell Celia's perfume and feel the heat of her proximity against his bare skin. An image of her tight, raspberry-colored nipples perched on small pale breasts invaded his thoughts. If he leaned closer, he could take one in his mouth. Celia pulled away and he nearly fell on his face leaning after her.

Kid listened intently to every sound. There were whispers and stifled giggles. He jerked when the room erupted in laughter. "Damn it, Felipe," said a man in a thick Texas drawl, "You are a lucky bastard. Go on, honey—you teach that boy a lesson."

Kid licked sweat off his upper lip.

"Put your face on the ground and lift your ass in the air," she said. Kid flinched and didn't move to obey, even after Felipe translated. The crowd hissed in disapproval.

"No?" inquired Celia.

"Please," Kid said with a whimper. And it was most definitely a whimper. "I've had enough. No more."

"Enough? I've barely started," simpered Celia. "And of course..." Kid waited with bated breath. "You forgot to say: Please, *Celia*."

Kid felt a blow across his chest before Felipe finished translating. It stung like a motherfucker. He groaned, biting hard on his lip as he attempted to rub his chest against his knees by doubling over. Whatever she used on him felt like a belt or a lot of belts together.

Celia swished the object in the air and brought it back down across Kid's back. His groan was loud and open-mouthed. "Will you obey me?"

"Yes, Celia," Kid spat through gritted teeth. The crowd applauded.

"Prove it," Celia purred. "Lift your ass."

Kid would swear he had ice in his lungs. He teetered on his knees before he finally managed the head-down-ass-up position Celia demanded. The crowd murmured their excitement.

Celia dragged long leather strands across the bare expanse of Kid's flesh. Naked and tightly bound, he had no choice but to accept what was about to happen to him. His breathing hastened, sounded ragged, and each breath moved his entire body. The tips of the flogger kissed his balls. He hissed, writhing against the carpet.

"Do you like that, Slave?"

"No, Celia."

Another tap. "That's not polite. Shall I hit you harder? Like a man?" The audience was positively giddy over the idea.

"No! No, Celia. I'm sorry. I'm sorry," Kid pleaded. He sobbed into the carpet after a series of fierce blows struck him across his ass.

"How was that, Slave? Hard enough?"

"Yes, Celia!"

"You're doing so well, Slave. Just a little more and I'll reward you," Celia crooned.

"Th-thank you, Celia." Kid could hardly breathe, let alone speak, but he struggled to get the words out anyway. His humiliation was momentarily usurped by his keen desire to keep Celia happy if for no other reason than he disliked pain. Though the strange desire to return to Celia's room and her bed also existed. He wanted to be held again.

The sound of the flogger slapping against naked flesh echoed throughout the room, punctuated by Kid's pained growl. Again and again the flogger fell against his increasingly-warming skin. With each stroke, he lost more and more of his bearing, until at last his muscles stopped bracing for the blows and he ceased to temper the sounds pouring out of him.

Abruptly, Celia stopped.

Kid, rigid with apprehension, attempted to ball himself up. He wanted to crawl so deep inside himself he would disappear. All he succeeded in doing was building the collective lust of his voyeuristic audience.

"Push him back. I want him sitting on his heels," Celia directed.

Kid's face was wet with tears now that he was hydrated enough to have them. He sobbed harshly when Celia bade him to open his legs, but he complied.

"You've been such a good boy. I think you've earned a gift." Celia trailed the flogger leisurely across Kid's cock and balls. His breath stopped all together and didn't return until after Celia had made a few passes with the soft leather.

Little by little, Kid's cock began to fill, growing hard despite the resurgence of his shame. Despite an audience. Despite his fear. He groaned, lustily, when she palmed his freshly shaved and highly sensitive sac. His cock found its way into her other hand.

Kid marveled at the way his pain simmered the more his pleasure mounted. Sensations, both painful and intensely pleasurable, radiated outward through his body. Celia's gentle hands and tenderly spoken whispers became his entire world, one where his mind felt disconnected from his body. He wanted to stay there forever. Forward and back, his hips worked to keep his delicate flesh in Celia's hands.

"Greedy slave," Celia whispered into his ear. She brushed her nipples against Kid's chest. "Would you like to suck on one?"

Kid nodded. "Yes, Celia."

Celia took her hands away and teased his mouth by pressing a plump nipple to Kid's lips. "Suck."

Kid opened his mouth. He moaned, loud and unabashed. His cock jerked in midair. His pain forgotten, he latched on and suckled Celia in long, hungry pulls that had her gasping and pulling his mouth closer.

"Yes!" Celia cried, "Suck harder."

Kid required no translation. He obliged, drunk on sensations he couldn't name. He only pulled his mouth away to breathe or switch breasts.

There was a loud pop when Celia pulled away. She placed a hand on Kid's head to hold him steady. "Now, suck this." The crowd, momentarily forgotten by Kid, rippled with palpable anticipation.

Kid, sensing something foreign, reared back and turned his head. "No, Celia. Please, no." Celia didn't bother to respond. She raised the flogger and struck him across the chest with so much force there was a collective wince in the room.

"Suck it!" Celia repeated. Kid opened his mouth and let Celia fuck it with what he knew instantly to be an enormous rubber dick.

He couldn't help but imagine what everyone else could see—a pretty boy sucking the cock of a girl half his size. Adding to his embarrassment, they snickered whenever he choked. Kid sobbed around the cock in his mouth, but he was almost sure he wept for the wrong reasons. He was enjoying it. Not what she was doing to him, not the rubber phallus in his mouth, but the way Celia commanded the entirety of his attention, the way she had him believing she deserved to have him like this. Without fully understanding how or why, he was fucking loving it. His surrender, more than anything else, crushed him.

By the time Celia gave the order to cut him loose so he could fuck her, Kid didn't give two goddamns about doing it on the carpet in front of a room full of strangers. Blindly, he reached for her and tossed her to the ground with brutish force. He reveled in her abandoned cries, in the way she spread her legs and opened her arms to invite him close. She made no attempts at all to stop or guide him. She gave him everything. Everything! And she'd been right—Kid *was* greedy. His hips tilted back for only a moment. He thrust forward into Celia's pussy. They both whimpered as he rutted against her.

He sought Celia's nipple instinctively. He suckled in rough, bruising pulls. His hips moved like a piston. He was violent in his need to come, and he would fight anyone who attempted to stop him.

Before long, Kid let out a sound best reserved for a dying animal, thrust one final time, and came. As the crowd applauded and cheered, Kid hid within Celia's arms from thoughts of who he'd become.

****

Four months later, Kid no longer bothered with petty emotions like shame. Felipe and Celia had broken him of it over several debauched encounters designed to show him he had no choice other than to accept his own lust. Kid had become wanton.

"Please, Celia," Kid panted. He shook with need. He pulled on his tethers, secure in the knowledge they would hold him tight and keep him from touching. He only wished they could keep his hips from thrusting. Above him, Celia's breasts, slick and shiny with sweat, bounced hypnotically. "Please let me come."

Celia rode them both hard, thrusting her ass against Felipe behind her and her pussy down Kid's cock. Both men groaned as their cocks struggled for purchase within Celia's body. The bed beat a staccato rhythm against the wall like a metronome keeping their lust in sync. Celia was insatiable. She would fuck for hours if Felipe let her, and sometimes he did.

"Please!" Kid implored. He felt hot, suffocated, and overstimulated.

"No coming," Celia said. Sweat dripped down her neck onto Kid's chest.

"Fuck!" Kid shouted angrily. He forced himself to change his rhythm to stave off the inevitable. He knew this game. Celia was setting him up for failure. He'd come without being given permission and Celia would punish him. Celia had seen to it by tying him down, sucking his dick, and then riding him while Felipe fucked her in the ass. Even when Kid stopped moving, he could feel Felipe rubbing him through Celia's tight, wet walls.

"Language, Boy," Felipe grunted. "Celia isn't going to let you come." Felipe slowed and swiveled his hips in such a way that both Celia and Kid groaned. "You're her distraction." He thrust. "Without you…" Thrust. "She couldn't take me." Thrust. Thrust. Thrust.

Celia collapsed on Kid's chest in a wet heap. Her hair clung to his arm and shoulder as she panted hot in his ear. "Ugh. Ugh. Ugh."

Kid had failed his mistress. He let himself feel ashamed of that, if nothing else. He'd been so caught up in his own pleasure that he'd forgotten his responsibility toward Celia, and Celia's toward her master, Felipe. "I'm sorry, Celia," Kid said through clenched teeth. He wouldn't come. No matter what.

Celia pushed herself up to grip Kid's jaw. Her nails dug into his chin. She licked his lips until he opened to her kiss. She pulled back and groaned. She stared into Kid's eyes. "If you come…" she said as she laughed at the pained sound he made, "I'll beg him to fuck you instead."

Kid's eyes widened, but he knew better than to show preference one way or the other. He might as well sit on Felipe's cock if he were going to succumb to that type of stupidity. Kid also knew it would happen one day, eventually, but he was in no hurry. Sharing Celia and knowing he could not compete with Felipe was difficult enough, rolling over for him would be worse.

"Filthy little mouths, both of you. She never used to say things like that before you came, Boy." Felipe smiled and kept pounding his lovers into blissful submission as Celia asked Felipe's forgiveness.

Felipe's hands cupped Celia's breasts to pull her backward onto his chest, and Kid's jealousy roared to life. He wanted to be the one pulling on her pebbled nipples. He wanted to be the one sliding a hand down her belly and rubbing her clit fast and hard.

Kid felt Celia's muscles tighten, a prelude to orgasm. He rebelled against the vision of his own cock pushing against Felipe's as they flooded Celia with come. Every thrust brought it back. He wanted to scream when Celia hastily pulled off. Kid fixated on the sight of her bright pink lips quivering, and her hungry little hole contracting around the ghost of his cock. Felipe's fingers filled her void, sliding inside to keep her coming. Kid couldn't tear his eyes away, not from Celia's juices sliding toward her asshole, not from Felipe's balls slamming against her, and not from the semen running back out.

Kid could no longer control himself. He cursed them. He bucked wildly, pulling on the satin ropes that held him spread out on the bed. His hard cock was red and leaking precum onto his stomach. "Please! Just touch my fucking dick. I'll come. Please. Please!"

Celia and Felipe laughed pitilessly as they fell to one side of the bed. Celia reached out and lazily pinched one of Kid's nipples to make him hiss. "Shhh," she sang. "You know better than that."

Kid knew the emotional high Celia was riding and he wanted it for himself. Suffering provided a high unlike any other—once it ended. Over the course of the last four months, he'd endured pain and debilitating pleasure in equal parts—but always, he found peace afterward. The moments he spent wrung out in Celia's arms after he'd done well made him feel safe, cared for, and even loved.

"I'm sorry, Celia." Kid did his best to conceal his anger.

"Mmm." Celia purred beneath Felipe's fingers. "What do you think, Felipe? Should we let him come?"

Felipe's laughter shook the bed. "He's nearly as spoiled as you are." He met Kid's glare with a wink. "Besides, he just tried to threaten me." Kid's mouth dropped open. Felipe continued, "He uses foul language, forgets his mistress's pleasure, and I know it didn't escape your notice he tried to get loose. We shouldn't have to tie him down! Isn't that right, Boy?"

Kid wanted to punch something. He was being punished after all. And worse, he deserved it. "Yes, Felipe. I'm sorry."

"Tell me why." Felipe reached across Celia's body to place his hand on Kid's thigh. One finger rubbed along Kid's rigid cock. Felipe was fond of this forced intimacy, never taking it further than the threat of making his claim on Kid reality. Kid had come to suspect it was his fear that Felipe enjoyed. Or perhaps it was that Kid remained hard.

Kid swallowed despite his lack of spit. He pulled air into his lungs slowly, purposely timing each breath to keep from panting but only succeeding in heightening his own tension. His cock bounced gently against his own stomach with every wave of arousal. He recited the words he knew by rote. "I'm your slave."

"Yes. You are." Felipe's fingers curled around Kid's hot length.

Kid began to pant. Felipe's large hand felt like a claim, like a brand being burned into his mind. It occurred to Kid that Felipe had never abstained from fucking him, he'd just never wanted to. The moment Felipe decided otherwise, Kid knew he would have to obey.

Felipe stroked Kid's cock once–twice—and Kid moaned his pleasure to the ceiling as he coated Felipe's hand with come.

****

Six months later, Kid no longer needed to be tied. There had been another series of debauched acts to teach him control. Without control, there would be no pleasure, and Kid couldn't breathe without pleasure.

Kid held tight to the ring dangling from the ceiling and kept his bare feet on the floor through sheer force of will. He didn't brace for the paddle. He let his body absorb the dull thud—accept the pain Felipe doled out.

"*Gracias*, Felipe," Kid groaned. Between his spread legs, Celia sucked his cock.

"I can stop," Felipe offered. He ran a hot, open palm across Kid's pink ass. "Or Celia and I can both keep going."

Kid didn't hesitate. "Please, Felipe. Don't stop."

"Good boy," he said.

Kid felt no shame over the joy the compliment brought him. He wanted to be good for his master and mistress. He craved their approval and lived for the pleasure they wrung out of him. He felt safe with them, sure they would never hurt him, never break him. So long as Kid obeyed, the outside world couldn't touch him.

He could hold on forever.

****

Sometimes Felipe would go away on business and leave Celia and Kid to their own devices. Never alone, but with a few hands to make sure Kid didn't lapse into disobedience or try to escape.

Celia was much softer whenever she and Kid were alone.

As they lay next to each other in the dark one night, Kid whispered to Celia. "What's gonna happen to us, Celia? Will we ever be free?"

Celia hugged him tight. "I don't want to be free."

Kid nodded. "You love him."

"I do." Celia kissed and stroked his hair just the way he liked.

Kid sighed. He couldn't begrudge Celia her feelings toward Felipe when Kid had also come to have feelings for his captors. Though Kid had begun to suspect he loved Celia, he couldn't deny he felt something toward Felipe too. Kid hated to admit it, but Felipe was…compelling. "Do you think you'll ever love *me*?"

Celia tilted Kid's chin up. She smiled, kissed his lips. "I do," she whispered.

He wasn't foolish enough to believe she meant she loved him, but it was enough that one day she might. Kid blushed. Celia liked it when he was shy, and sometimes he pretended he was—but not this time. The moment they shared had nothing to do with making him suck strap-on dildos or masturbate for Celia's amusement. He'd given up getting shy over things like that. This was different; he was showing her how to hurt him most. "Thank you."

Celia kissed him, savored him.

****

On the anniversary of his captivity, Felipe informed Kid he'd like to celebrate by having another one of his raunchy parties. Kid would do anything for his mistress and master, but he dreaded having to perform in front of strangers. Of course, it wasn't the first time and wouldn't be the last.

As Celia prepared him for the party, Kid speculated on the choices that had led him to toward his new life with Celia and Felipe. After his parents died, he'd made a slew of self-destructive choices. Hell, even before then if he were honest. He'd been willful toward his parents and the weight of that guilt rested heavy on his shoulders after they passed.

Unable to please his parents, Kid had done his best to be an obedient son to his uncle, a man who had never wanted children. The guilt Kid had felt, coupled with his crushing loneliness, had made it easy to drop out of school at fifteen, learn to ride a Harley, and follow Tiny. Kid had quickly discovered soft drugs, something Tiny encouraged, going so far as to push him toward selling them for easy cash. From there, Kid's decision to join the Night Devil's on their monthly runs into Mexico had been a foregone conclusion.

Kid supposed he had always tried to please someone: his parents, his uncle, and now Celia and Felipe. His parents had loved him unconditionally, but it was a love he'd lost. His uncle had felt responsible for him, but Kid had understood his uncle's love was reserved for his lifestyle. If Kid had been too young to ride a motorcycle, Tiny would have let the state raise Kid. With Celia and Felipe, Kid knew he was wanted, if for no other reason than they wouldn't let him leave. Somehow, they'd given him the structure and affection he'd been missing in his life and Kid knew exactly how to please them because they never left him to wonder. His world had become simple: obey or be punished. Kid decided simplicity offered its own peace.

Pulled abruptly from his thoughts, Kid grunted as Celia rubbed flavored oil all over his cock and balls. He was sore after a tryst they'd had earlier but continued to eagerly anticipate release. Which, of course, had been Celia's intention all along. *Little bitch.* Kid smirked. At least he could still mouth off in his head.

Yes, there were times when Kid felt like a traitor for not holding on to his anger, but he always let it go. Felipe could behave like a civilized man and Kid had come to think of him fondly, but he also knew Felipe could turn. Kid never forgot he'd been brought to Felipe's house as a prisoner. The dungeon was his. Celia was his. The *rules* were his. Kid had realized early on that there was no point in being angry when the only person to suffer was him. For all the crappy choices Kid had made, letting his anger go always felt right.

Celia reached between Kid's thighs to secure a strap to the back of his loin cloth. Kid hated the outfit but didn't protest. Just as he didn't protest the clamps adorning his nipples or the flavored oil Celia rubbed all over his body. After all, Celia wore something similar.

Celia stood and circled Kid until she looked up at him. She smiled. "So beautiful." She traced Kid's bottom lip with her fingertip and he licked it.

"It tastes like honey," he said.

Celia's smile broadened. "I wanted you to taste sweet."

Kid chuckled and it sounded exactly like he felt—bewitched. "Yes, Celia."

Celia's smile faltered. "Tonight will be hard." She ran her hands along Kid's bound arms. She seemed to be soothing herself rather than Kid.

"It always is, Celia." Kid tried his best to be comforting. Celia had been unusually emotional that day. It made him uneasy.

She tugged on his arm until he went down to his knees before she wrapped him in a hug. "No one will hurt you," Celia said softly. "I promise." Celia's English had improved significantly since Kid arrived. He felt grateful to Felipe for suggesting Celia and Kid practice English and Spanish together. Kid was damn near fluent—getting spanked by a ruler was one hell of a motivator.

Kid made a feeble attempt at smiling. Celia was in no position to make promises, but the gesture was sweet nonetheless. *"Gracias,* Celia."

"De nada, Kid." They kissed for long minutes.

DETERMINED TO OBEY

Her behavior prompted Kid to be more suspicious than nervous. "What's going on, Celia? Why are you both acting so strange?" His mind quickly filled with all sorts of awful scenarios. "Is he sick of me?" Kid felt dizzy with fear. "Is he going to sell me? He wouldn't do that, would he, just separate us?" He didn't dare imagine what he would do if Felipe tried.

Celia laughed. Hard. She placed a fervent peck against Kid's lips. "I feel better now. Thank you, Kid."

Together they walked through the mansion and into the dining room. Kid was shocked to discover the room was empty save for Felipe and a few of the staff. Felipe smiled when his gaze landed on Celia and Kid.

"Look at the both of you." Felipe gestured for them to turn in place and they obliged. "Like Pocahontas and John Smith. I love that story."

Kid couldn't help but laugh. Felipe said the strangest damn things. "I thought there was going to be a party?"

Felipe grinned. "I said there was going to be a celebration. Please sit." Kid took his place on Felipe's left and lowered himself to the floor as usual. "In a chair, Boy." Felipe ruffled Kid's hair affectionately.

Kid did as he was told with some trepidation. "Please," he said. For the first time in months it had nothing to do with coming. "Tell me what's going on?"

"Kid!" Celia hissed from across the table.

Kid met her eyes. He swallowed. "I'm sorry, Felipe." In a much smaller voice, "I'm sorry, Celia."

"It's not a problem." Felipe smiled. "Just this once."

Once the first course was served, Felipe surprised Kid by asking him a series of questions about his past and his childhood in particular. Kid obliged by recounting a story he'd heard hundreds of times.

Kid had been born Andrew William Benson. His dad had been William, but everyone called him Wild Bill, after the gunslinger. His dad liked to call him The Kid, after another famous outlaw. His mother told him he used to carry two cap guns in his diaper. Felipe seemed to genuinely appreciate the detail.

"Do you shoot well?" Felipe asked.

"Nah," Kid smiled as he polished off his main course. "My mama never liked guns. After she died, I never wanted to carry one. It used to drive Tiny crazy cuz it meant he had to watch out for me."

Kid fell silent.

"Do you miss him?" Felipe inquired.

Kid gave a shallow nod. "Sometimes." He was glad to have the moment broken by the dessert course.

Felipe didn't let it stay broken. "When you miss him, do you ever think about revenge?"

Kid looked toward Celia. Her head was down. She intently pushed her dessert around her plate. Kid returned his attention to Felipe. "No. I don't ever think about things like that. What would be the point?"

Felipe smiled. "So it's a matter of opportunity then. Would you go searching for revenge if you were free?"

The four courses Kid had eaten so far threatened to come up his throat. "Felipe?" Kid asked a million questions with his eyes but couldn't manage a single one out loud.

"You're free, Kid." Celia's broken voice drifted across the table.

Kid shut his eyes tight. The silver fork between his fingers squeaked under the pressure of his intense grip. "Why?" The question burst out of him. He was beyond angry.

"Isn't that what you want, Boy?" Felipe asked. "Haven't you been here long enough?"

Kid let go of his fork and covered his face with his hands. In his experience, the worst days of his life began typically. Kid's parents had gone out for lunch and never returned. His uncle had gone out for a beer and returned with a death sentence. The normality of the events leading up to each catastrophe had always sat heavy in his gut. He'd become wary of ever feeling safe and secure. Wary of the happiness those things might bring him. Terrified of what might happen if he ever found himself completely alone.

Terrified of *this* fucking moment.

"Boy. Look at me," Felipe said.

Kid called upon every lesson Felipe and Celia had taught him. He met the other man's eyes without sobs or protests. He sat quiet and patient as *this* world crumbled around him too.

"Do you remember what I asked you when we met in the dungeon?"

Kid answered steadily. "You asked me what I wanted most in the world."

"Do you remember what you said?"

Kid didn't dare look at Celia. Felipe had a fondness for poetry and Kid had to hand it to him, this shit was poetic. Felipe had somehow found a way for Kid to provide his own send off and break his own fucking heart in the process. "I said…" He wiped at a tear that had somehow escaped. "I said I couldn't have what I want most," he whispered. "There's no one left to love me."

Felipe smiled. "Yes. That's what you said. Do you still feel like there's no one left to love you?"

Kid shrugged. "I guess."

"Truly? Because I'd wager you're wrong."

Kid couldn't take much more. "What are you saying?" He glanced first at Felipe, then Celia. Hope clogged his throat.

Celia had tears in her eyes. "He's saying you're free, Kid."

"I'm also saying you can have everything you want…if you stay."

"Fuck!" Kid exclaimed. "Why the fuck didn't you just say *that*? I thought you were getting rid of me! I'm over here choking down my dinner so at least I have something in my stomach when you toss me out. I'm wondering how I'm going to live without you guys and the whole damn time you never said I could stay?"

Felipe laughed heartily. "Language, Boy. Such a filthy mouth."

Celia wiped her eyes and grinned across the table. "We'll just have to remind him of his manners."

Kid laughed. "Yeah, I guess you better."

About the Author

CJ Roberts is the *USA Today* Bestselling Author of *Epilogue: The Dark Duet*. She is an independent writer who favors dark and erotic stories with taboo twists. Her work has been called sexy and disturbing in the same sentence.

She also stalks her reviewers… What? Caleb had to come from somewhere!

She was born and raised in Southern California. Following high school, she joined the U.S. Air Force, served ten years and traveled the world.

She is married to an amazing and talented man who never stops impressing her; they have two beautiful daughters.

Books and Stories by CJ Roberts
Captive in the Dark (The Dark Duet, Book 1)
Seduced in the Dark (The Dark Duet, Book 2)
Epilogue (The Dark Duet, Book 3)

Stories by Jennifer Roberts
High Stakes Nikki (Sexy Shorts)
Manwich (Sexy Shorts)
Seducing Sunshine (Sexy Shorts)

Books with contributions from Jennifer Roberts
Sin City: Six Scintillating Stories (Anthology)
High Stakes Nikki
Some Like it Bi (Anthology)
Seducing Sunshine

Meeting Sin

*A POV from "Savor Us Volume 2: Wrecking Me"
Full Length Novel Coming Summer 2014*

Emily Snow

Copyright © 2014 Emily Snow
All rights reserved.

Zoe

"My dad's going to be pissed, I just know he will be," I said for at least the fifth time since walking into the coffee shop and sitting down for lunch. I glanced at my turkey panini. It smelled amazing, but so far I hadn't been able to force myself to take a bite. "I can't do it."

"Don't say that." My best friend Norah rested her elbows on the edge of the table, pressed her Cupid's bow lips to her straw, and practically inhaled the remainder of her iced vanilla latte. "Grow a pair and tell him you're sick of the violin. That if you play Bach one more time, you're going to break the damn thing over his head."

"It's not that—"

"Guess where Sinjin Fields is staying?" Norah's question was so sudden—a complete turn from the conversation about leaving college for a short break—that it took me a moment to process what she said. Sinjin Fields? The name sounded familiar, but I wasn't sure why. I shook my head and lifted my shoulders, earning a dramatic eye roll from Norah. "Good god, Zoe, don't you read? It was on OMG."

That didn't answer my question, but judging from the gleam in her dark eyes, and the grin playing at the corners of her lips, that was her plan.

"Of course I read," I argued. "Just not those type of things." Norah knew I was on a dystopian kick. Over the last few months, I'd gone through everything from *Anthem* to *The Handmaid's Tale*. She called it depressing, but I couldn't tear myself away.

Maybe it was all the angst.

Norah, on the other hand, veered toward entertainment nonfiction—if it was about a celebrity, she'd read it in a heartbeat. She swore she had been that way since well before we met three years ago, when I slammed into the back of her car. Her sturdier, older model Jeep had decimated my new Hyundai, but the friendship that ensued over the swapping of insurance information was a fair trade.

Even if that friendship *did* include listening to an incredibly detailed report on celebrity's lives at least a few times each month.

Norah tapped her short, shamrock green-painted fingernails together. "Everyone dies in the books you read." When I opened my mouth to protest, she quickly continued, "Okay, maybe I should backtrack. Do you even know who I'm talking about, Zoe?"

Did I know 90 percent of the stars she mentioned? I fussed with a packet of artificial sweetener and shot her a sheepish grin. "Nope. Which is probably why I can't guess where he's staying."

"Sinjin's the drummer for Your Toxic Sequel," she replied, releasing a deep sigh.

"Ahh, I see." Admittedly, I leaned more towards pop music, but I'd listened to Your Toxic Sequel before—in fact, they were on the workout playlist I reserved for ass-kicking cardio days. I tried to picture the band's drummer, but the only person I saw when I closed my eyes was Lucas, the muscular, sexy, over-the-top front man "Alright, so spill it. Where's he staying?"

Norah leaned in close to me. "Melody's House," she whispered as if sharing a secret that hadn't been broadcasted all over the world by now.

One thing I was very familiar with was Melody's House. It was the rehab that my father and several of his associates founded years ago—the center in Malibu that I would be heading to as soon as lunch was over. It was no surprise I hadn't heard about a rocker being one of the current residents, though. Not only did many famous faces pass through the halls of Melody's House, but also, my dad made it a point not to bring his work home. All our dinner table discussions revolved around music.

Which, given how I've felt for the past six months, was frustrating.

"He checked in last week," Norah informed me, running a napkin over her mouth carefully so as not to ruin her bright red lipstick.

"Then, hopefully he gets the help he needs." It was a lame response, but I was being honest. Even though the center was, literally, my father's life, I didn't wish the problems that led to rehab on my worst enemy. "So … you're telling me this *because*?"

"Because it made you stop freaking out for a few minutes. You asked me to come here saying you were starving and yet we have *this*." She pointed to my side of the table, from the coffee cup to my sandwich, both of which were untouched.

My lip quirked into a half-smile. "And now I'm back to worrying, but thank you for the distraction."

Norah fussed with the tip of her straw, looking like she wanted to say something else, but then she blew her blunt bangs out of her eyes and checked her watch. "Alright, it's five 'til one, and I've got to go back to work." She stood and dusted scone crumbs from the front of her fitted pinstripe shirt. As she tossed a tip down on the table, she crooked an eyebrow.

"You can do it, Zoe."

"I know, I know. Grow a pair."

She winked. "You better."

A few minutes after Norah left, I followed behind her, waving goodbye to my favorite barista as the glass door clanged together behind me. It was unusually warm for February, even for Los Angeles, and I shoved the sleeves of my V-neck sweater up to my elbows on the way to my black Jetta.

"Grow a pair," I repeated while I cranked the car and eased out into the street.

But as I made the fifty-minute drive from downtown to my dad's center in Malibu, I restarted my inner debate about what to say to him. There was always the truth—that I could barely look at my violin without feeling sick to my stomach, or that I was sick of the music college that I worked so hard to get into two years ago. The more I thought about it, though, the more screwed up it seemed, especially since I was driving to see my dad to pick up a check he wrote for tuition.

Lifting my brown eyes up to the rearview mirror, I gave myself a disgusted glare. "Someday you'll stop being such a wimp," I said as I pulled my car up to the rehab's security gate.

Five minutes later, I opened the French doors and stepped into the casual, beach-themed entrance hall that smelled like the inside of a Bath & Body Works. I had made up my mind, even if it did make me feel like crap. A variety of conflicting emotions rushed through me as I crept down the wide hallway to my father's office, smiling and waving politely at the staff along the away.

I walked through his assistant Suze's tiny office, which was right outside of his, but she stopped me the moment I grabbed the doorknob. "Dr. Whitlow is with a patient," she said in a clipped, professional voice. I lifted my eyebrow, and she relaxed in her blue balance ball chair. "Sorry, Zoe. I know you probably have things to do, but he just told me to ask you to wait a little while."

"It's fine, Suze. I'm just going to—" I racked my brain for something to do while I waited for Dad to become available, but since I had no idea how long that would be, I finally shook my head. "I'm going to get some air. I'll check back in fifteen minutes."

If I hadn't already snuffed out the urge to have a heart-to-heart with my father, this would have done it for me. Having too much time to talk myself out of following through with my plans had always been one of my biggest downfalls.

Suze nodded, her lips pulled into a sympathetic expression that somewhat resembled a smile. "If it ends sooner, I'll text you."

As I ducked out of the office, I could hear the open therapy session taking place across the hall. Not wanting to listen in because the thought of invading their privacy made me feel sleazy, I walked as fast as possible until I was surrounded by foliage and silence. I pulled my phone out of my purse and checked my messages as I followed the large stone path to the center of the garden. There was one text, from Norah, and reading it made me smile.

1:45 PM: *Be strong, Zoe!*

I was so immersed in typing a response that I didn't realize somebody else was sitting on the garden bench.

Until I sat down on his lap.

"My first groupie. Nice," he said sarcastically.

As I jumped up, my phone clattered to the ground. I scrambled to pick it up, feeling every inch of my body ignite in embarrassment.

"Those motherfuckers break easily," the man drawled. "So you're screwed unless one of your visitors brings you a replacement."

Visitors? Did he think I was a patient here? Instead of automatically correcting him, I bit my tongue and began examining the iPhone screen for cracks. When I found none, I flashed my intact phone at the man.

"It's okay but thanks for your concern." Despite that concern being fueled by blatant sarcasm. At last, I met his gaze, and I took a step back. I had seen this man before— light brown hair, a smaller nose with a slightly snubbed tip set in a narrow face that looked like it hadn't been shaved in days, and dark circles beneath his eyes. There were a multitude of tattoos covering his thin arms and peeking out from beneath the crew neck of his plain brown tee shirt, including one that said "Toxic" in calligraphy.

This was Sinjin Fields. The topic of five minutes of my lunch conversation.

Standing in front of him, with his penetrating green eyes seeming to see right through me, I knew that whenever I thought of Your Toxic Sequel from now on, I would picture his face and not Lucas Wolfe's.

I dropped my phone back into my purse and pointed over my shoulder toward the center doors. "I should go and—"

"I don't bite." To give me room, he moved the book sitting in the center of the bench to his other side, but not before I caught a glimpse at what he was reading: *The Running Man*, which was on my own reading list. When he took in my thoughtful expression, he sneered up at me. "You don't have to run off just because I'm out here. Unless you're scared … if that's the case then go right ahead and take your skinny ass back inside."

He was skinnier than me, but I didn't point that out. He was also issuing me a challenge. Although I knew it was best that I did go back inside and wait in Suze's office, I decided to accept Sinjin's invitation.

Cautiously, I walked around the bench and sat as far as possible away from him on the edge. I heard my phone vibrating, indicating a new text, but I held my bag close to my chest instead of checking Norah's response. The side of my face tingled. Sinjin was still staring me down. But why? I turned my face to the side, meeting his amused expression head-on.

"What?" I asked in a small voice.

"I'm trying to figure out what you're in for, is all. After all, from the way you looked at me a couple minute ago, you know exactly who I am and why I'm here." He cocked his head to one side, squinting at me, dragging his green eyes from my legs, which are crossed at the ankles, to the stubby blonde ponytail at the nape of my neck. "So what is it? Adderall? Cocaine?"

"No, I—" But I stopped myself from informing him that I wasn't a patient and shook my head furiously. "Why would you assume either of those?"

Draping his tattooed arm over the back of the bench, Sinjin granted me a casual shrug. "Because you reek of overachievement."

Reek. Of. Overachievement. Focusing on one of the tattoos on his arm—a Mexican sugar skull inked strategically over his inner elbow—I let those three words settle into my brain. This wasn't the first time I'd heard something like that. Hadn't my ex-boyfriend said just about the same only weeks before I kicked him to the curb for cheating?

Still, either way, it was a load of bullshit.

"I'm not a patient here," I said pointedly, crossing my arms over my chest.

"Your folks doing the tour of shame then?" When I gave him a confused look, he drew in a deep breath, his nostrils flaring a little. "What I'm asking, Princess, is if your rich parents are interviewing centers to stick you in?"

This man was famous, no doubt *rich*, and yet scorn dripped from his words. I gave him a tight, cool smile. "I don't think I meet the prerequisites to enter the center."

A look of comprehension dawned on his face, and he smirked. "Then why the fuck are you here?"

"Because, I—" But as rude he was, there was something about Sinjin that made me want to tell him the truth. I uncrossed my ankles and leaned forward to rest my forearms on my knees. "I'm here to see my dad. I needed to talk to him about college stuff."

But Sinjin motioned his hand for me to keep going, and after a moment, I did. I told a complete stranger about falling out of love with playing music, and how I was exhausted. How I wanted the break from college and music to rekindle that desire to pick up my violin.

I told Sinjin how terrified I was of disappointing my dad after he spent years paying for my music lessons, new instruments, and then college.

When I was finished, Sinjin was quiet, and I looked down at the backs of my hands. His problems were so much bigger than mine that I was positive that he was thinking just how stupid I sounded.

Self-consciously, I tucked a loose blonde tendril behind my ear. "Now I feel like a brat whining about the small stuff."

"Mmm, I don't know about all that. I've heard shit that was so much smaller being blown to proportions you wouldn't imagine." Sinjin slid an inch or two closer to me, and I struggled to keep my breathing under control as his scent—Ivory soap—invaded my senses. "So, how'd it go with your father?" Once again, his voice held a hint of contempt.

It caught me off guard, and suddenly, I wanted to know even more about Sinjin Fields.

"I haven't actually had a chance to yet."

A laugh tumbled from the back of his throat. "Because you're not going to. Judging by your voice, your actions, you made up your mind not to before you even came out here."

My head popped up, and I simply stared at him in surprise. Was I that easy to read? Then, the irritation set in. "Why do you say I'm not?" I demanded through clenched teeth.

"You keep staring down at your thighs." The way he said thighs, almost teasingly, sent a shiver through me. "You're fidgeting. You—"

"I get it," I cut him off. Slinging my bag over my shoulder, I gave Sinjin the kindest smile I could muster. "Look, it was nice meeting you, Sinjin, but—"

"Yet another reason why I'm sure you'll keep playing your violin."

"What would that be?"

He shifted, moving his tall, lean body even closer. "Ten minutes. I've known you for ten minutes, and you've tried to run off on me twice."

Frustrated, I dragged my hands through my hair and gazed at him incredulously. "You called me an overachiever."

"Because you are. You want your father's blessing even though you're coming here of all places to visit him."

Again, he was assuming incorrectly. It was obviously a bad habit of Sinjin's, and I wondered how much trouble it's gotten him into in the past.

"Even if my father was—" I paused to reconsider what I was about to say. This was my opportunity to dive into Sinjin's head—to turn the tables on the man who had gotten me so flustered—and I doubted telling him that my dad's one of the therapists here would win me any points. "Do you think having a ... problem means someone isn't entitled to offering their opinion?"

He snorted. "That's what they're calling it now? A *problem*? Why don't you try again, Princess, but this time with a little more feeling."

"You're being evasive."

"You don't *want* my opinion—everything that comes out of my mouth is a mess." He tilted his head back and stared up at the clear sky. "If I'm lucky, I'll learn some self-control while I'm here. Figure out a way to make up for everything I said and done before I got put in here." For the first time since I sat down beside him, the calculated sarcasm has disappeared from his voice. It's been replaced by raw pain.

And I hated it for him.

"You could start with sorry," I suggested, ignoring the tightness building up in the back of my mouth.

"Sorry is just five letters of nothingness. It doesn't mean jack shit."

"It always worked for me."

"But I'm not you." Shaking his head, he sat up straight and dragged his gaze back to mine. "I don't hold anything back. If something is on my mind, I just say it. Maybe—" And then he stopped. He stopped talking just to stare at me. It was unnerving, but I wasn't about to let that end our conversation. Not quite yet.

"You're holding back now," I murmured. And I desperately wanted to know what he was going to say next. This time, I leaned in to him. "Maybe what?"

Without warning, he closed the space between us and placed his forehead against mine. I didn't pull away, even though common sense screamed for me to. "Maybe being a little more like me would be good for you and vice versa," he breathed.

He was right. And in a way, I felt like he was silently issuing me yet another challenge. Daring me to lose a little of my self-control—at least when it came to telling my dad how I felt.

I started to get up, but his hand closed around my wrist. Electricity raced through arm, twisting and curving through my body, shocking my senses. I jerked away from him, holding my wrist tightly against my chest. "I've got to go see my dad now."

He let go of my wrist and moved his own hand to the bench. I watched as he dragged his thumb over his fingers, like he was just as affected by my touch. "What will you tell him?"

I thought on it for a split second before saying, "That I'm sick of the violin."

"Good girl," he said appreciatively. As I walked through the garden, shoving my hands deep into the pockets of my tight jeans, he called after me. "You never told me your name."

I spun around to look at him, giving him a nervous smile that caused him to narrow his eyes in confusion. "Zoe Whitlow."

His green eyes widened for only a moment as he made the connection between my father and me. He mouthed something, but I was too far away to see what that was, and then the corner of his lip jerked into a knowing smile. "You let me think you were someone else."

"No." I shook my head. "I let you assume, Sinjin." Just before I disappeared into the building, I turned to give him one last look, but his nose was already buried in his book.

The End

About the Author

Emily Snow is The New York Times and USA Today bestselling author of the DEVOURED series (October 2012, January 2013), TIDAL (December 2012), and the SAVOR US series (June 2013, summer 2014). She loves books, sexy bad boys, and really loud rock music, so naturally, she writes stories about all three. Emily lives in Virginia with her family where she's currently working on her next novels, WRECKED (release date TBA). Visit her online at http://emilysnowbooks.blogspot.com or at www.emilysnowbooks.com.

Links
Blog: http://emilysnowbooks.blogspot.com
Website: emilysnowbooks.com
Twitter: https://twitter.com/EmilySnowBks
Facebook: https://www.facebook.com/pages/Emily-Snow/363370467075260

Seduction & Temptation

Sins, 0.5

Jessica Sorensen

Copyright © 2014 Jessica Sorensen
All rights reserved.

Chapter One

My day had been mellow for the most part, a rare but welcomed occasion. I'd woken up with no hangover, even after partying way too hard the night before. I went and put flowers on my mama's grave and had a nice long one-sided conversation with the engraved stone, something I'd been meaning to do for a few weeks now, ever since I'd found the letter. It was written by her to a man named Evan Milantes, divulging to him that I was his daughter, not the man who raised me for the last twenty-one years like I'd thought. The letter had changed my life in an instant and everything I'd ever thought about myself felt like it'd been erased, which is exactly what I told the gravestone.

After I'd finished saying what I needed to say, I'd taken a long walk in the park, to think, to decide, to work up the courage to finally do what I'd been wanting to do since I'd found the letter. Up and move. Leave everything behind. My life. My friends. My family and all the money and connections that come along with it. I'd lived a life of lies and deceit for too long and I wanted to start over and perhaps I'd go find this Evan person, if I felt daring enough, because quite honestly I was curious what he looked like, who he was, what kind of person he was. Was he like my father, good to his family but his morals and choices perhaps a little twisted and dangerous, or did he simply live a quiet, boring life?

I'd finally made the decision after about an hour of wandering around beneath the trees, but a little too late. Because about thirty seconds after I'd turned around to go pack up my shit and hit the road, a car had shown up. I knew something was off as soon as I saw it. Sleek and black, expensive, tinted windows, the way it crawled up to the curb beside me. I'd seen stuff like it in movies. Heard about it on the news. Been warned by my father about it. Kidnappings. I barely had time to react as two very large men wearing black suits and sunglasses, all very *Men in Black* like, jumped out of the car and grabbed me in broad daylight. Bodyguards for one of my dad's many enemies. The question is, which one?

I had hardly any time to come up with an answer while I struggled to get away from them. I did manage a few good screams, kicks, and one very good bite, before I was roughly forced into the backseat of the car. Then they placed a bag over my head, tied my hands behind my back, and sped off.

Twenty minutes later, I'm still sitting in the backseat of the car, squeezed between the two sweaty, smelly men. My heart's knocking inside my chest, despite how much I'm telling it to shut the hell up. That I'm tougher than this. That I've been taught better than to panic in alarming situations. Preparation when kidnapped. My dad taught me well for this, like he'd always thought it'd happen. "Lolita, nothing will ever conquer you if you don't show any fear," my daddy always used to say. "In our world, never show fear. Never let it own you. Always be strong or else you won't survive." He's right. Fear is the enemy in our world. Fear is making my head foggy. Making me think irrational ideas like throwing myself forward and trying to escape blind. Crying. Screaming. I need a level head if I'm going to accomplish anything.

I try to steady my breathing, stable my heart rate, inhale through my nose and exhale through my mouth. Let my muscles unravel. Think of something relaxing… drinking… shots… beating the shit out of the guy beside me… sex… hot, sweaty sex… that usually works. But not this time.

After I get about as calm as I can—still somewhat jittery though and with way too much adrenaline pumping through my bloodstream—I sink back in the seat and assess my surroundings. The engine is still humming and I can hear the sound of the wind, which means the car's still moving. I think about the weapons I have on me. Brass knuckles and mace in my purse, but I dropped my purse when the guys grabbed me. I do have my knife tucked in my boot—my father taught me to always carry one on me. But how the hell am I supposed to get it out when my hands are bound and I can't see anything?

Turning my head to the side, the sunlight sparkles through the thin fabric of the bag over my head and I can see the top of the guy's head beside me. I wonder if he's watching me? The pervert pretty much felt me up as he shoved me into the car and tied me up, looking as though he got his kicks off of bondage and helpless women. But I'm not helpless dammit! I'm strong—always have to be strong—otherwise I'll wind up dead.

As I'm evaluating my options—keep sitting, try to fight blind, cause a scene—the car comes to an abrupt halt. I hear the driver say something to someone, then a door opens and the guy to the side of me gets out. Then he either climbs back in or someone else takes his place.

Moments later, the scent of cologne and cigarettes touches my nostrils and I realize it's definitely someone else sitting next to me since the previous guy smelled like BO. There's something very familiar about the scent too… I know it. Somehow.

I feel them shift in the seat and I cringe as their warm breath caresses my cheek. "Just calm down, Lola," they whisper, brushing the inside of my wrist with their finger, a comforting gesture only one person in my life has ever used on me. "Everything will be okay."

I know that voice. Boy, oh, boy do I know that voice. And now I know just how much trouble I'm in. Who's behind the kidnapping and how slim things are looking for me ever seeing the light of day again.

"I should have known," I say venomously to Layton Everett, the guy sitting beside me and who used to be one of my best friends when we were younger, but now he works for my family's enemy, the Catlersons. Frankie, their leader, despises my father more than any other drug lord on the east coast. He's been trying to get my father arrested for his criminal activity and involvement with drug dealing, even though he's a drug lord himself. I think he even put a hit on him once, but it was quickly taken off when my father retaliated and a truce was made between the two of them. Of course, this isn't something I'm supposed to know, but the house I grew up in had cathedral ceilings that caused every conversation to carry throughout the rooms and hallways.

"Lola, don't start," Layton warns, his fingers leaving my wrist. "You're only going to get yourself into trouble if you get your mouth going."

"Fuck you." I lean into him and lifting my leg, move my foot around until find his shin and then I kick as hard as I can.

"Dammit, Lola," he curses, his leg moving away from mine. "What the hell's a matter with you?"

"What's the hell's a matter with me?" I'd gape at him, but it'd be pointless since he can't see my face beneath the bag. "I got picked up while I was innocently walking in the park, felt up by a middle aged man with the worst comb over I've ever seen, then bound and thrown into the back of a car. What's not wrong with me at the moment?"

"Innocently walking in the park," he says with sarcasm. "I highly doubt that."

He's right, but I'm not about to tell him that during my walk, I was plotting to run away from this life forever. "Where are you taking me?" I ask, slumping back in the seat, annoyed that I feel more relax about this situation now that he's sitting here beside me. "I'm assuming to Frankie, but I'm wondering why?"

"Keep her quiet, Layton," a deep voice advises from the front seat.

It takes Layton a second to answer, the rhythm of his breathing surprisingly unsteady for him. "It has to do with your father," he says in a quiet voice.

My entire body goes rigid, my already amped up adrenaline skyrocketing. "Yeah, but what does Frankie want with my father this time? Money? Drugs? Revenge? Usually he's more set on getting him arrested, not kidnapping his daughter." I'm trying to portray toughness, but my voice cracks at the end, revealing that I'm getting nervous.

Another maddening pause from Layton, then I feel him slant closer to me. "It's not what Frankie wants from your father, but what he wants from you, which is for you to pay your father's debt."

"Debt?" I'm thrown off by this revelation. "Since when does my dad owe Frankie anything?"

"Since he came to him to borrow money about six months ago." He pauses while I try to wrap my head around the idea, but it doesn't make sense to me.

"But we're wealthy…" I try to argue. "What did he need the money for?"

"I'm not sure exactly." He sighs heavy-heartedly. "Look, he's in real trouble, Lolita. And I mean really big trouble, worse than before. "

"Don't call me that," I mutter, loathing that he used my full name. "And what sort of trouble. Layton, tell me what's going on?"

"Keep her damn mouth shut, Layton," the same person warns again and this time I recognize the deep baritone voice. Tony Madman Makafee, one of Frankie's guards, the one's that do his "dirty work."

Shit. Am I his dirty work?

This is bad. Worse than what I originally thought. People who go with Tony, usually aren't ever seen again. God, is the sunlight slipping through the fabric the last I'll ever see of daylight?

"What do they want from me?" I whisper under my breath to

Layton, scooting closer to him on the seat.

Layton blows out a stressed breath and I can almost visualize him running his hands through his hair, like he used to do all the time whenever I was making him anxious. "Lolita please just be quiet and cooperate." He places a hand on my knee. "This will all be over soon."

"I told you to stop calling me that." I jerk my knee out from under his hand. "And what do you mean it'll be over soon… Are they going to kill me?"

"What? No." He sounds startled. "Lola, I would never let that happen to you."

"But you're letting me be here," I snap. "Bound and blindfolded in the backseat of the car. That's not too—"

"God fucking dammit, Layton. I told you to shut her the fuck up," Tony growls. I hear the sound of fabric brushing against leather, then the light through the mask dims.

"Tony, that's not necessary," Layton says with an edge to his voice. His body heat is suffocating as he slants nearer to me, our shoulders press together, his arm aligning with mine our fingers inches apart. If I didn't know better, I'd guess he was trying to comfort me. But I do know better. I won't make the same mistakes with Layton again, thinking he'll put me before his job and duty he feels toward his family. "She'll be quiet."

"I already gave her three chances," Tony replies then I hear him climb over the seat. Moments later he plops down beside me, so close his knee is crushing against mine. "This way's a lot easier."

"What way?" I incline back, trying to get away from Tony and closer to Layton. "Don't fucking touch me, douche bag, or I swear to God—"

Before I can finish the sentence, a needle pricks my forearm then enters my vein. Shit. Another thing Tony's known for. Sedation of his victims… this isn't… good…

"Layton… help…" I hate the plea in my voice, but I have no other option at the moment. I'm slipping out of consciousness. I'll be more helpless than I ever have… weak… "Please…. Do…. Something…"

And he does. He catches me as I fall back and black out.

Chapter Two

12 hours later...

I'm having one of those moments were I'm reflecting on every single bad thing I ever did in my past. Every bad decision I made. The path I followed that led me to this moment in time. Granted, this isn't entirely my fault, nor do I regret a lot of the things I've done—good and bad. Not yet, anyway.

My body still hurts from the sedation and the hijacking, my heart aching from what happened after the car stopped, my mind still trying to grasp what I have been ordered by Frankie to do. My pulse throbs, the music pounding deep inside my body. My skin is damp and my body is numb from the multiple drinks I've consumed. I have on a short, backless black dress with torn sides that shows off a flower tattoo on the side of my lower thigh and an intricate dandelion one in the center of my back. A pair of lace-up boots cover my feet and half of my legs and a thick leather collar is around my neck. My long, black hair's done up on the top of my head in waves and curls and I have three studs above my eyebrows. My lips are stained a fiery red to cover up the cut I got while being thrown in the backseat and the vamped color matches my painted nails. The real icing on the cake to my attire is the 9mm pistol strapped to my thigh. The metal is icy cold against my skin and sends goosebumps erupting all over my legs. I have a very intense urge to reach up my dress, pull it out, and throw it in the trashcan. But it would probably alarm the people in the club around me and bust the plan to shit. And a lot is riding on me not to screw this up.

"Would you relax?" Layton places a hand on my knee, trying to get me to stop bouncing it. "You used to be less jittery. What happened to you?"

"What happened to me that I'm here, not under my own freewill and all of this—what I'm about to do—all relies on something I don't want to do. And I hate doing things I don't want to do. Plus, I could easily end up getting caught, go to jail, get shot, get a hit put on me." I tear my eyes off the dance floor and focus on his hand that's on top of my knee. "And touching isn't part of the deal." I elevate my gaze to his silverish blue eyes. "So hands off." Quite honestly, during a different time in our lives, I would have loved to have his hand on my knee. Layton is sexy as hell; dark messy hair, a tattooed body, long, lean arms. And he used to be a good and nice person, at least to me, but not anymore. And being sexy can't make up for why we're here or what happened in the car.

His lips quirk as he removes his hand from my knee. "If that's what you want, Lolita," he says, restraining a smile as he picks up his glass filled with scotch. "Then I'll oblige."

I narrow my eyes at him as I reach for my own glass of scotch. I'm not usually this bitchy toward him. But that was back when we were teenagers and our life was school, fun, excitement. Hot summer nights where breaking curfew, stealing bottles of expensive scotch from our daddies' liquor cabinets, and the occasionally harmless brawl was the biggest risk we ever took. But we're not friends anymore and we're not teenagers. We're twenty one year old adults who are about to break the law for different reasons. He's doing it for his job and I'm doing it because otherwise his boss, Frankie, is going to kill my dad, something that was very bluntly told and shown to me after I woke up from the sedation. I was told either I can take out the Defontelles or he'll put my father in a safe alive and drop him in the lake to drown a slow, but very effective, death—Frankie's words, not mine. The real sick part is, I was actually momentarily conflicted about my choice. I'd never gotten a chance to talk to my father about this Evan man, so I'm not sure if he knows about him or not. But what if he has known all this time? What if he's been lying to me all my life, just like my mother? I'd selfishly hesitated over this factor, but seconds later, came to my senses. Lying or not, he still raised me and was good to me, more than most father's probably.

I shake the glass a little in a circular motion and the ice swishes around. "How many times do I have to tell you, it's Lola. No one's called me Lolita since—"

"Since you were fourteen years old and Billy Maders found out the meaning of Lolita is seductress and everyone started calling you a whore." He raises his glass to his lips and takes a long swallow before setting the glass down. "Yeah, I remember what happened."

He's actually wrong. I stopped wanting to be called Lolita the day my mother died, because she'd always called me that. But I never told anyone the real reason and blamed in on the Billy thing.

"Would you stop acting like we're friends?" I ask, irritated that he knows me so well. He's supposed to be the enemy, but it's hard to look at him like that when I've known him since we were being potty trained. "We're not anymore."

"And who's choice is that?" he questions with a crook of his brow.

"Yours," I reply then take a long sip of my drink, noting how he observes my neck muscles as I swallow. "When you decided to work for Frankie."

"I didn't decide to work for Frankie." His jaw tightens as he looks over at the bartender. "There were circumstances that led up to it."

"What circumstances?" I set the glass down on the countertop. "Because from what I heard, you went to Frankie looking for a job. Or was that just a rumor?" I eye over his stiff shoulders, tight jaw, the firm grasp he has on the drink. Tension is flowing off him. "Is there more to it? Are you in some kind of trouble?"

His eyes smolder as he looks back at me. "Drop it, Lola." He angles his hand back and knocks back the rest of his drink, then slams the glass down so hard, it cracks up the side. "You don't want to go sticking your nose around in Frankie or mine's business, especially with what's going on with your father."

"Is that a threat from Frankie? Or you?" I ask heatedly, crossing my legs. "Tell me Layton. Did you feel bad at all when Tony stabbed me with a needle? Or did you enjoy it?"

"I didn't like letting him do it, but I knew it had to me done." His voice is emotionless.

"Wow." It's all I can say, because quite honestly I'm hurt but I'll never admit it. "All those years of friendship and this is what we've turned into."

He frowns, but doesn't disagree with me, and it stings a little. "I wish things could be different," he mumbles.

I don't say anything, because I don't know what else to say. He's right. I wish things could be different too, but after this—especially after what I do tonight—I can't see that never happening. Unsettling silence takes over and thoughts of why I'm here at the club return to my mind. I try to think about anything else, but nothing works.

"This is depressing," I mumble, turning my knees inward as a group of guys come wandering by dressed in spikes, leather collars, gloves, dark clothes, chains. One even has horns tattooed on his head. Devils & Demons has a strict gothic dress code. Layton and I almost didn't get in because of his poor choice in clothing; leather pants and a fitted black shirt apparently aren't enough (although his ass does look amazing in the pants). But he was never into Goth. However, I went through a phase when I was around sixteen years old and saved a lot of my clothing. And the studs in my brows and tattoos are just me. I like to consider my body a canvas and paint it up whenever I can.

Layton tracks the guys from the corner of his eye and I can see the distaste in his expression. "They have some unique people around here," he says, shaking his head. "I honestly don't get why the Defontelles want to own a club like this."

Vomit burns at the back of my throat at the mention of the name Defontelles and what I'm about to do to one of them. The gun chills my leg and my muscles spasm. "Unique isn't bad," I say tersely. "In fact, I prefer unique over ordinary and who knows, maybe all those guys are really good people… They probably are… better than me." I reach for my drink again, the gun feeling like it weighs a thousand pounds, crushing my thigh. It's not like I'm a good girl. I'm not at all. But what I have to do to Anthony Defontelles, even if he's not necessarily good people, is wrong, but I don't have another choice, besides letting my father die.

"Hey." Layton touches my hand as my fingers wrap around the glass. I notice I'm notably shaking, which isn't good. The Defontelles have eyes everywhere. He takes the glass from my hand and sets it down. "You need to relax, Lola, otherwise you're going to blow this."

"I know, but it's hard to," I draw a line up the side of my thigh, "when I have this thing strapped onto me, reminding me what I'm about to do."

There's a twinkle in his eye. "It's not the first time you've had a gun strapped to your leg, Lola."

"Yeah, but the last time wasn't so I could…" I trail off, unable to say what I'm about to do.

He watches me intently for a while, his head slanting to the side. "We've probably got like another half an hour to an hour before Anthony Defontelles shows up," he finally says. "What can I do to help you relax?"

"Is that part of your job?" I ask dryly, devouring the rest of the scotch in one large searing gulp. "To keep me relaxed until the dirty work's over?"

"Yeah, but I'd do it anyway," he replies with a ghost smile on his face. "In case you don't remember, you and I used to be close friends."

"Used to be, being the key words." My blood burns thinking about all the used to be's. "Things are different now. You work for my family's enemy," I say bitterly. He starts to say something but I know what he's going to say—that I don't understand stuff. And he's right. I don't. But it doesn't matter. Even if I understood his reasons for working for Frankie, I'd still never be able to forgive him for tonight.

I end up cutting him off before he can say anything. "There are only three things that make me relax in tense situations. Scotch, which isn't helping at all tonight. Kickboxing. And sex. So either you can let me kick the shit out of you out back or fuck me in the bathroom."

There's no shock factor with Layton. He knows me enough to know how I am. I'm blunt. Forward. And usually say it how it is.

"We haven't fucked since junior year of high school," he remarks, his eyes sweeping across my body, then he presses his lips together.

"Yeah, the year you took my virginity. So what? You can't fuck me now because of that?" I ask and when he stays silent forever, I add, "I gave you another option, you know. Kicking might be easier for the both of us."

With his eyes locked on mine, he asks, "Do you still have that no kissing rule?"

"Of course. Kissing still makes things complicated." The one and only time I kissed a guy was when I was fourteen. Trayson Millony forced a kiss on me when I refused to kiss him during a game of spin the bottle and in return, I kneed him in the balls. No kissing is a rule my mother taught me, something she picked up during her escort days. No kissing. No strings attach. Until you've found the one, which I guess for her was my father, since they kissed all the time. Too much quite honestly.

"And what about the no falling in love rule?" he questions, his gaze relentless, daring me to comment on me breaking his heart. With anyone else I would crack a joke about him being weak sauce, but Layton... I care... cared for him once. And the day he told me he was in love with me and I told him I didn't feel the same, was the one and only day I ever felt my heart ache just a little over a guy.

"Yeah, the no falling in love rule still applies too," I manage to say calmly, even though I feel a flicker of pain recollecting the memory. "So are you going to help me relax?"

He stares at me a moment longer and I can't read him at all. Then with a quick swipe of his tongue across his lips, he rotates around in the barstool and raises his hand to get the bartender's attention. When the bartender comes over, he orders two double shots of Bacardi, then sits in silence while he waits.

I'm barely disappointed by his rejection. I have bigger problems at the moment than whether or not I get laid or get to take out my aggression issues on another person.

After the bartender sets the two shots down on the counter, Layton slides one toward me. "Drink this," he says.

"Why? I already told you drinking wasn't it doing for me tonight," I remind him as he retrieves his wallet from his pocket then tosses a twenty down on the countertop before guzzling his shot.

"Drink the shot." His voice is demanding as he sets the empty glass down, but I detect a hint of a tremble in his hand.

"Fine." I collect the large glass in my hand. Putting the rim up to my lips, I let the fiery liquid spill down my throat. It tastes like trouble, danger, and ecstasy all mixed up in one potent swallow.

"Now dance with me," he says, slipping his fingers through mine and pulling me to my feet after I've finished the shot.

"Dance?" There's doubt in my voice as we make our way to the crowded dance floor. "Seriously? Since when do you dance?"

He places a hand on the small of my back and guides me closer as we near the mob of people, drowning in sweat and the sensual throbbing base of the music. He pauses as he reaches the center, getting poked and prodded with stray elbows, knees, bulging body parts. "Just relax and trust me," he says, turning to face me.

"I don't trust anyone," I remind him, staring him down with reluctance. "And you know that."

He contemplates what I said then grabs me by the waist roughly. His touch makes my skin burn and my thighs erupt with heat and I blame it on the Bacardi, when I'm really not sure if it's the entire reason. "Okay, then just try to relax," he says, drawing me closer.

Despite how much I want to fight him on this one, because it's in my nature to want to defy, I give into him and dance. It's really the only option I have at the moment. In just about an hour, I'll be taking someone's life and I have a feeling that after that, the life I know now isn't going to exist anymore. That dancing or having any sort of relaxing moment isn't going to be in the cards for me.

Chapter Three

"Sex can be two things," my mama told me when I was about thirteen, the age she deemed vulnerable to male temptation. "A weapon and just plain fun and relaxation, if you'll let it. Don't always make it such a big deal, my Lolita. Don't let men own you because of it." She was what a lot of men called a promiscuous woman (which I'd always defended while growing up, but after the letter I'm wondering if maybe people were right.). My daddy met her when he hired her as an escort. She was twenty-one and he was thirty-five and after spending one night with her, he fell madly in love with her sporadic , mysterious, impulsive character, along with her beauty. One month later they were married and nine months later I was born. which means during the first month they were married, she'd had an affair with this Evan man.

I probably would have never have known the real life story of my parents if it wasn't for my mother's sister, Aunt Glady, who told me all of this right after my mom died when I was fourteen. Aunt Glady had been on the bottle for three days straight. She told me never to tell anyone that I knew the secret—that my daddy would cut her out of the will if she did. And being from a poor family from Cheyenne, Wyoming, she needed the money.

My dad is loaded with money and has a lot of power. Benny Big Bones was the name he was given when he was eight by Fast Draw Petey, a huge drug lord in the seventies. My dad was his protégé and his nickname has never left him. Although, I just call him daddy or dad if I'm angry with him. Despite the fact that my life has been more dangerous than the average one, I've never had bitter feelings toward my dad. He's a good father and I was allowed to grow up with pretty much any luxury that I wanted. I always felt loved, nurtured, cared for. But being in the kind of business that my dad's in, there was always that feeling of danger in the air, the sensation of insecurity. I had personal bodyguards up until I was eighteen that would escort me to and from school every day, but it's not like I needed it. I was taught to handle myself on my own; kickboxing, self-defense, I learned how to shoot my first gun when I was twelve, something my father ordered to have done despite my mama's protests. I'm strong. Independent. I don't take shit from anyone for the most part. And just like my mama taught me, sex doesn't own me. Men don't own me. I can hook up and have sex for fun, just to relax. And this has helped me survive the stressful lifestyle I grew up in, but I'm doubtful it can help me now—I don't think anything can. But I still want to try.

Twenty minutes after Layton pulled me out on the dance floor, sweat is beading my skin, as I rock my hips to the rhythm of the Ooh La La by *Goldfrap*. My feet hurt like hell along with where the needle entered my arm. But pain's never bothered me. I can handle pain.

As I move to the music, Layton's hands wander all over my body, cup my ass, grab my hips, his breath touches my neck. It feels so good. I want more. Want what I know awaits me if I can push us both further. A few minutes of bliss from this shitty night. I need it. Crave it. Hunger for it. Finally, I can't stand it anymore. The need and desire, mixed with a hell of a lot of Bacardi and Scotch is too much. I spin around and grind my body against him for a moment, while dipping my lips to his ear.

"Take me into the bathroom and fuck me," I whisper hotly against his ear while running my fingers through the back of his hair, while I rub my hips against his.

He pauses, breathing, in and out, in and out, driving my body mad. The feeling amplifies as he pulls back and his eyes are dark below the low lighting as he assesses me. The DJ starts saying something in the background. The crowd cheers. But neither of us look away from each other, our gazes and bodies welded together. Then without saying a word, he grabs my hand and shoves his way through the dance floor, pushing people out of the way. Excitement roars through my body and fleetingly erases the edge I've been feeling all night.

But then I spot one of Defontelles' bodyguards entering the bar area and I'm reminded of why I'm here. But I don't pull away from Layton. God dammit, I need this—need just one more moment of calmness before my whole entire world is turned upside down. I know things will never be the same after I go through with it. I've known a few people who have committed hits for various different reasons and they were never the same afterwards. Even if it's for a good reason and the person they kill is bad, it changes them forever. Darkens their soul. Hollows them out. They carry pain on their shoulders forever. Some even don't survive, ending their own lives later on.

Layton pushes through the bathroom door, startling a group of women putting lipstick and mascara on in front of the mirror. A couple of them holler at him to get out and the rest simply stare. Layton disregards them completely as he strides toward the end stall, towing me along with him. He shoves the door open and then tugs me in before letting my hand go then locks us in. By the time he turns around and faces me, I'm panting with need, my chest heaving ravenously.

"Pull your pants down," I say, relaxing back against the wall.

He shakes his head with a trace of a grin on his mouth. "You've gotten bossier since the last time we hooked up."

I bite my lip, telling my body to be patient, but it's difficult now that we've gotten this far. "I know."

He hesitates and it's frustrating. "Maybe we shouldn't do this."

I'm more insulted than hurt. "Why?"

"Because…" he struggles for words, gaze fixed on me, searching my eyes. "Because you're stressed. Drunk. Under a lot of pressure. A lot of different things."

I shake my head in frustration. "Oh would you knock it off. I'm fine." I unzip the zipper going down the side of my dress and let it fall to my ankles. Then I carefully step out of the dress and stand there in my lacey black bra and panties, gun strapped to my thigh. "Now your turn."

He leisurely scrolls over my body. "God, you're so fucking sexy," he mutters. Then with his eyes fastened on me, he slowly reaches for the button of his pants and undoes it. But then lets his fingers linger so long on his zipper that impatience gets the best of me. I stumble across the small amount of space between us, and jerk them down myself, along with his boxers.

"Shit, Lola." He practically groans as I drop to my knees and take him deep in my mouth without warning. His head bangs against the door as he falls back, continuing to make throaty sounds as I move my mouth up and down along his swollen cock. I can hear whispering on the other side of the door, something about me being a skank, but I don't care. I don't care about anything and that's sort of the point of all of this. Sex can be numbing. Invigorating. Distracting. So much so, that I can barely feel the gun on my leg anymore. The fear of what I'm about to do. The pain of knowing what's been done to my father. It's all gone and for a moment I'm simply Lolita and I'm okay with it.

"Lolita," Layton moans out my name as he threads his fingers through my hair, tugging out the pinned up curls, and yanking out at the roots.

I'm about to pull away and warn him not to call me that, when he guides my mouth away himself by softly pulling on my hair.

"What's wrong?" I ask as his fingers enfold around my arms and with one swift tug, he practically lifts me to my feet.

Once I'm standing up, his fingers leave my arms and drift under the hem of my panties. He jerks them down my legs and I eagerly help him out by stepping out of them and kicking them off to the side. Seconds later, his fingers are in me, feeling me thoroughly, in and out. I'm on the verge of combusting, losing sight of what's around me. My hands take on a life of their own and I rip his shirt off his head, feel his lean muscles, trace the dark lines of his tattoos as I collapse back against the cold wall and my eyelids drift shut.

"God, this is exactly what I needed," I moan, my fingers finding his cock again and I grasp it in my hand. We keep feeling each other, panting, sweaty, growing needier and needier until finally we can't take it anymore. He pulls his fingers out of me and I open my eyes to find him taking a condom out of his pocket. He tears it open and then I help him out, snatching it from his hand, and put it on him, slowly, making his eyes roll into the back of his head. Smiling at my power, I pull my hand away. His eyes come back into focus and he grabs my thighs forcefully and picks me up, slamming me against the wall as he backs us up. Then with one hard thrust, he sinks deep inside me.

My legs hitch around his waist. "Oh God," I gasp, starting to let my head fall back, but before I can, his lips come down on my mouth equally as hard. Before I can protest, he slips his tongue deep inside my mouth. For the briefest second—one based on confusion and Bacardi—I tangle my tongue with his, loving the taste of him. But then my common sense kicks in and I pull my tongue out and bite down on his bottom lip hard.

"No kissing," I warn, tracing my fingers up his chest as he pauses inside me, still holding onto me.

His eyes are glossed over and he looks completely out of it. "Fine… if that's what you want."

"Those are the rules," I say, slowly rolling my hips forward and he sucks in a sharp breath from the sensation. He reciprocates by rocking his hips forward, sliding inside me so gradually, it's almost painful, and I have to claw at his flesh as I teeter near the edge of losing it.

He does it again and again, grasping onto my thighs, fingertips delving into my skin. I clutch onto his shoulders, my nails piercing at his flesh as I move my hips in sync with his. The lights, music, voices—everything—fades around us. My body climbs higher and higher. I forget where I am. Who I am. I forget about everything as he drives my mind and body further away from reality until I completely come apart, crying out his name as my head falls back. He gives one last thrust inside me, then joins me, struggling to hold onto me as he comes.

After everything settles, he rests his face in the crook of my neck, completely stilling inside me. He starts placing light kisses on my damp skin and I don't even bother stopping him, too tired and content to speak.

This was good, I want to say. *Much better than the first time.* But by the time I work up the energy to say it, his phone starts ringing from inside the pocket of his pants. Blowing out a loud breath, he sets me down, then pushes away from me, his eyes on the floor as he pulls up his pants. He has scratches all over his chest, his hair disheveled, his lips swollen, I just had hot-as-hell sex is written all over him. I'm sure I look the same.

I collect my panties from the floor in silence and put them back on while he retrieves his phone. He checks his messages, his frown deepening the longer he stares at the screen. I try to put on my dress as calmly as I can, but the look on his face and the quietness is killing me. It's impending. Because deep down I know what the phone call is.

Seconds later, he confirms what I already knew. "It's time," he says quietly, still not looking at me. "I'll let you get dressed and then meet me outside the bathroom." Then he puts on his shirt, exits the stall, and leaves me alone, taking all my contentment along with him.

Chapter Four

I've never been a much of a worrier or a nervous person. The only time I came close was when I was twelve and one of my dad's enemies tried to kidnap me when I was playing in the park with one of my friends. It never got very far, partially because it was just a couple of crack addicts pissed off at my dad for the increase in money to feed their addiction. And partially because I had Dougie and Dominic, my two bodyguards who rarely left my side at the time. As soon as the crackheads approached me, they were taken out. Nothing major happened. But I did see a bigger picture at the moment that worried me a little. That all those times my dad had made me go practice shooting guns, all the self-defense classes, all the protection, was for a reason. That my life was a lot more full of risks than most.

But I quickly learned to deal with this revelation and for the most part lived a pretty content life, at least up until a few hours ago when I woke up in the warehouse. That took any contentment left away. I started realizing that this point in time was probably inevitable. That it probably had been set in my future since I was born, or at least something like it.

As I stand in the bathroom stall, the smell of sex all over me, half dressed, I can't help but reflect over the last few hours, the moments from when I got out of the car to this exact one.

After Tony drugged me, I'd woken up on the cold cement floor of a big empty warehouse with only a television and Frankie Catherlson in it. Suddenly, I knew those risks I'd realized briefly when I was twelve were about to take over and that I probably should have seen it coming a long time ago.

Frankie is a surprisingly a very short man. He's also stocky and has these bushy eyebrows that take over his face. But despite his lack in body features, he always dresses to impress. Designer suits. Gold jewelry. Ways to scream that despite his small demeanor he's still got his wealth and how he got his wealth makes him important. Don't under estimate him. He'll kill you if he gets a good chance.

He was wearing slacks and had a button down shirt with the sleeves rolled up, along with a holster, a gun on each side, warning me that he was in control of the situation. "Lolita, so nice to meet you again," he said as if we were going to soon be friends.

Layton had entered at that point and I'd given him the coldest glare I could muster up, feeling angrier than I ever had for bringing me into this situation instead of out of it, like he did so many times when we were kids. Take the time when I was fourteen and I'd beat the crap out of Manny Depler for grabbing my ass. Layton took the fall for it when the Delper clan had showed up for payback. They beat him up pretty good over it and when I'd asked him why he did it, he'd simply said, "Because I care more about you, Lola, then I do myself. I'd rather get hurt then see you get hurt." But I guess things change.

"It's Lola," I'd replied to Frankie, which I probably shouldn't have. I'd felt Layton tense as he walked up and stood in front of me, probably thinking oh shit, please watch it Lola.

Frankie had merely smiled, revealing two gold teeth. He didn't care if I was trying to be a pain in the ass. He had what he wanted—me, my father, the perfect blackmailing situation.

"You're so much like your mother," he said, pacing back and forth in front of the television with his hands behind his back. "So feisty and beautiful."

I wanted to clock him in the face—and probably would have too—but my hands were still bound. So instead I'd said, "Don't fucking talk about my mother. Ever. You didn't know her so don't pretend you did."

That'd made him laugh. "Everyone knew Lalana, Lola," he'd said, stopping and facing me. "Most better than you, probably."

I'd cringed, wondering what he knew about her. "Why am I here?" I asked through gritted teeth.

His smile had broadened as he continued to pace the floor, pointing his finger at me. "That's a very good question." Then instead of answering me, he'd turned on the television and showed me the video of my father being beaten.

After about five minutes, Frankie had shut off the television, and told me how things were going to work. "You're going to do a hit on Anthony Defontelles. In exchange for your father's freedom and life."

"No way," I'd argue, trying to wiggle my hands out of the ropes, my eyes scanning the warehouse for an easy exit. "I'm not a hit man."

"Are you sure about that?" He'd considered this for a while with a look on his face like he'd believed otherwise, and then ultimately shook his head. "This isn't an argument, Lolita." He'd strode toward me, eliminating the space between us. I'd felt Layton shift toward me, his arm brushing mine, as if he'd been contemplating protecting me. "You will do it or you'll never see your father again. Alive anyway."

"I don't know how to kill," I'd argued, my pulse so erratic and unsteady I was becoming dizzy. But I fought it. Stood my ground. Told myself I was strong, despite how weak I felt inside. Fear. It was potent. I was overwhelmed by it.

He's reached out and touched my cheek, stroked it as if I was a dog. Up close he was barely my height—five foot eight—and I could easily have leaned forward and head banged him. Thinking back, I should have.

"Do you know what happens to people who don't pay their debts to me?" he'd asked, his fingers lingering on my cheek. Even though it disgusted me, I refused to lean away and let him feel that power over me. "I put them in a safe and drop them alive in the lake, so they slowly drown and have a lot of time to reflect on their pathetic lives." His voice had deepened, carried warning and my stomach burned, along with my temper, but I kept my lips sealed. "So make the hit and this will all be over."

There wasn't much to say after that. I didn't verbally agree to do it, but I didn't have to. It wasn't really a choice in the end. Either way I was going to be responsible for a death so it might as well be someone that wasn't my father.

Chapter Five

After I get dressed and fix my hair and makeup, I meet Layton outside of the bathroom. He's there just like he said, leaning against the filthy wall, arms crossed, his hair back into place, clothes smooth of wrinkles, as if we hadn't just fucked the hell out of each other.

"You ready?" he asks when he spots me walking down the hall toward him.

Stopping in front of him, I shrug, blasé as I can be. "As ready as I'll ever be."

He nods his head once and then stands up straight, motioning me to follow him as he heads back down the hall toward the bar area and dance floor. The music slams against my chest and the lights sting at my eyes as I step out of the dim hallway and into the room. I don't have to ask him where he's going as he makes his way down the side of the bar and toward the back door. Frankie already told me step by step what I was going to do. The hefty bartender standing behind the counter is Big Dog Hankton and actually works for Frankie, but Anthony doesn't know that. He's supposed to give Layton the heads up when Anthony arrives, which I'm assuming was the phone call Layton got right after we fucked. After the go head from Hankton, Layton is supposed to take me to the back room where Anthony does a lot of his dirty work; beatings, dealings, whacks ect. Tonight he's going to be alone, at least according to Hankton, so it should be a clear hit and I shouldn't run into problems. Of course, if I do, then it's all going to fall back on my family, which is why Frankie's having me do this, at least that's what he said, although I'm not naïve enough to believe there's not more to it than that. Still, the last thing anyone wants to do is be at war with the Defontelles, the second most powerful drug lords on the east coast. I've heard stories about them; one's where they cut off head's of the people who cross them, then send them to the family members as a warning, pure torture—who knows for sure.

This is all I can think of by the time Layton and I reach the back door—my head being shipped to my father in a box with a big red bow on it. Is this where I'm going to end up after all of this? Beheaded? My stomach churns. *God, it seems like such a shitty way to go.*

"Are you going to be okay?" Layton's voice jerks me back to reality.

Blinking back into focus, I realize I'm trembling more than I ever have. I clear my throat and square my shoulders, try to suck it up and appear more confident than I am. "I'm fine." I start to step toward the door, but he captures my arm and stops me.

He leans in close to me, putting his lips right up beside my ear and cups my wrist in his hand, feeling my throbbing pulse. "You don't have to do this… this shouldn't be your problem. You can just walk away and let your father deal with it. It's his problem anyway," he whispers in my ear.

"No it's not," I say, refusing to look at him, because I don't want to see the look in his eyes—the one that either says he's just saying this to try and make me feel better or the one that says he really wants me to walk away, because I just might be tempted too. "I'm not just going to let Frankie kill my father, so unless you have a way to free him without me doing this, then let me go so I can get this over with."

He breathes against my ear for a few seconds longer then pulls his hand away from my wrist. Blowing out a breath, I stare at the door.

"So I'm just supposed to walk in, then?" I ask, stalling. "And then just… pull the trigger?"

Layton doesn't answer, instead stepping forward and grabbing the doorknob. "It'll be over quick. Just don't hesitate, okay?"

"Does Anthony have a gun on him?" I ask, avoiding eye contact with him.

Layton shakes his head, trying to catch my eye. "He shouldn't. Hankton says he puts it in a safe when he comes in here. I guess it's his sick way of showing that he thinks he's invincible or something."

"And what about you?" I ask, finally daring to look at him. For the briefest moment, I see the Layton I used to know. The one who cared about me—who'd do anything for me. And it makes this situation twenty times harder. "People have seen you here. Aren't they going to put two and two together?"

"I'll be fine," he says in a tight voice, the emotion in his eyes dissipating as he looks away from me and down the hall. "You need to worry about yourself at the moment."

There's something he's not telling me—I can tell—but I don't have time to press him right now. I need to focus. Think clearly. Do what I need to do—get it over with.

He steps away from the door and I reach forward to open it. "Just think of it as target practice," he says quietly, quickly brushing his fingers along the back of my neck. "Just pretend Anthony's a target."

I doubt that will work, but there's no point saying it. I need to be strong, remember why I'm doing this. For my father. The man who raised me, Took care of me. Gave me everything I wanted. *But what if he's not?* I shake the fleeting thought from my head. It doesn't matter. He's the only father I've known and that's what matters.

So with trembling fingers, I turn the doorknob and open the door quickly, giving myself no time to hesitate. Then taking another deep breath, I enter the room.

The first thing I notice is how bright the lights are and how musty the air is. It makes it difficult to see and breathe and I have to catch my breath and blink a few times. The room starts to come into focus and that's when I realize just how big of trouble I'm in. Anthony's not alone. He's got two really big guys beside him, his bodyguards I'm guessing. They're sitting at a square table with fold up chairs, with enough money and bags of cocaine to fill up an entire trunk of a car.

I'm debating whether or not to bail because this isn't how this is supposed to go down, but then Anthony glances up from the pile of cash and drugs in front of him and I know there's no turning back.

He's in his mid forties, tall, sturdy, and has a scar going all the way down his nose and to his lip. I'm not sure how he got it, but I've heard a lot of rumors; he did it to himself during a fit of rage, a woman he cheated on did it to him in his sleep, his father did it to him when he was younger.

"Who the fuck are you...." he starts to say, but then trails off as he recognizes who I am.

The sequences of events that happen after that move so quickly I barely have time to process them. The two bodyguards turn around and jump out of their chairs. I panic and start to turn around to run out the door, but I catch Anthony reaching for his jacket pocket and I see the silver handle of a gun. I react the only way I can think of. I quickly slide my hand up my dress and withdraw the 9mm. With one swift movement, I lift my hand and point the gun at him at the very exact moment he points his at me. My heart hammers in my chest. I can't breathe. Think. See straight.

Don't hesitate.

Don't hesitate.

Don't hesitate

But I do hesitate and Anthony grins, like he knows exactly what I'm thinking. Then his finger starts to press back on the trigger... at least I think it does. Seconds later, a gun goes off, but it's faint, quiet, the noise of the club outside washing it away. I see my life flash before my eyes. I wait to die, wait for the pain to arrive, but quickly realize I'm still, breathing, my heart beating deafeningly inside my chest.

"Get out of here," I hear Layton's voice from behind me, snapping me out of my trance.

Reality slaps me in the face. There's blood everywhere and Anthony is lying on the floor, bleeding profusely from his chest. The bodyguards have pulled out their guns and aiming at Layton and me. I still have my gun out in front of me, my hand unsteady, making any shot fired dangerous. Layton is beside me with his gun out, spots of Anthony's blood on his face, his hand steady as a rock as he holds his gun in front of him.

"Get out of here, Lola," he orders without taking his eyes off the men.

I could listen to him. Run away. Let him deal with this mess, that is if they didn't shoot me on the way out, which I'm sure they will. I'm not stupid enough to believe that I'll walk away from this.

"She's not going anywhere, Layton. Both of you aren't," one of the men says. I don't know his name, but he has this four-leaf clover tattooed on his scruffy cheek, along with the number 99 and the words Denny. I wonder what it means. If it's his lucky number or something more personal, like a year someone was born. Maybe his kid. Does he have kids? Am I about to see a father die? Am I about to see Layton die? Am I about to die?

My mind is racing with thoughts and the fear inside me is making me want to puke. Seconds later, I hear another fire go off. There's no warning. No time to react. It all happens so fast. And I get caught up the middle of it, making choices based on my fear, going against everything my father ever taught me. My gun goes off... I can't even remember pulling the trigger. But somehow I do and end up shooting the last man standing—the man with the four-leaf clover.

He goes down hard, a hole in his chest, blood everywhere. Just like that, it's all over. Everything's changed, just like I knew it would. Because I officially become a hit man and a murderer. Nothing will ever be the same again.

Chapter Six

Everything seems so much darker and colder.... I've never been so cold and I don't think I'll ever warm up again. The last few minutes keep replaying in my mind, like a nightmare, even though I'm awake. But it always ends the same, with blood on my hands and the haunting image of the name Denny branded in my head. I can't stop wondering who Denny is, if I killed a father. I'm not sure if it would matter either way. His blood would still be on my hands no matter who he was.

After the shots are fired, I go into shock, my body cold, numb, dead, just like the bodies on the floor. There's blood splattered all over my skin, my hair, the floor, the wall, my clothes, the ceiling. I'm still holding the gun—*why am I still holding the gun?*

I drop it like it's poison, then stagger back from the bodies and throw up in the corner of the room. Layton doesn't say a word as I empty my stomach then sink to my knees. He doesn't ask me to get up—I don't think I could if I tried. Instead he scoops me up in his arms and carries me out of the club through the back entrance where no one will see us. Then he puts me in his car, buckles me in, and gets into the driver seat.

It's still dark outside, the moon a sliver in the sky, stars twinkling. It's the middle of May, a warmer time of the year, yet it feels so cold.

"You have blood on your cheek," I say as I sit in the seat with my knees pulled up to my chest, shivering and chattering.

He reaches up and wipes away the blood, then glances over at me. He opens his mouth to say something, but then I guess decides against it, and instead starts up the car and drives out of the parking lot and onto the street.

"Where are you taking me?" I ask, shutting my eyes and turning forward in the seat. The heater blows over my body, but I can't stop shivering.

"Home," he utters quietly, gripping the steering wheel tightly.

"What about my father?" I ask, leaning my head against the window.

"I'll tell Frankie you did the job and to let him go. Everything will be fine, Lola." He's speaking to me, yet he's not at the same time.

I open my eyelids, even though they feel so heavy. "And what about you?"

"I already told you not to worry about me," he says, looking straight ahead at the road. "I can take care of myself."

I want to tell him that I am worried about him—that I do care about him—but I'm afraid to go there right now.

Layton and I don't speak until we reach my house, but there's not that much to say I don't think, other than we could talk about what happen. But I don't want to talk about it. Think about it. Remember it.

When he parks the car in front of my house's entryway, he gets out and opens the door for me and helps me out of the car. My legs are wobbly and I stumble to get my footing. He catches me in his arms and helps me get my balance, holding me against him. He still doesn't speak, instead smoothing his hand over the back of my head over and over again. All I want to do is sink into him, disappear, vanish forever.

He starts placing kisses on my head over and over and then he steps back from me and again I feel so cold. "Go inside and wait for your father to get home," he instructs, quickly brushing his finger down my cheekbone, looking torn over something.

I nod, getting my balance, then start to walk toward the front door. His hand stays on my arm, sliding down it to my wrist, then he lets me go. I wrap my arms around myself, wishing I could feel warm again, but it just keeps getting colder.

"Take care of yourself, Lola," Layton calls out.

It feels like he's saying farewell to me forever, as if he'll never see me again. I wonder if he has to go into hiding for killing Anthony. I want to ask him if he has to. I want to ask him a lot of things like why he stepped up and shot Anthony himself. If it was because I hesitated and he thought I was going to get shot or if maybe he was never going to let me shoot Anthony all along. If he does still care about me like he did when we were kids. I'll never know though, because I'm not sure I want to hear the answer, my fear owning me at the moment.

"Thank you," I call over my shoulder without turning around, knowing those are the last words I'll probably ever say to him. Whether he realizes it or not, I mean it more as a thanks for stepping in and not letting me get shot. Whatever the reason he did it for, I'm still alive because of him.

He doesn't say anything else and I go into the house. He waits until I'm inside and the door is locked before he speeds away, the tires screaming against the road. I can tell he's running. I wonder where too. If he'll get very far. I wonder a lot of things.

My heart feels about as empty as the house, so unfamiliar, so dead. I want to crumble in the emptiness and cry my heart out, but I'm not going to. Blood on my hands or not, I'm not going to be a weak girl. I'm stronger than that. So instead, I pull myself together, go straight up into bathroom to take a shower. I have to scrub so hard to get the blood off that my skin starts to bleed, but by the time I'm done, I feel a little cleaner.

After I get out, I get dressed and then take a pair of scissors to my hair. Chop it off. Erase who I am. I know better than to think that my father won't do everything he can to find me and probably Anthony's family will as well. If I don't want to be found, I have to be careful. Be smart. Go into survival mode. And I don't want to be found. I want to disappear. Forever. Carry out my plan I made in the park, pretend tonight never happened.

By the time I'm finished hacking my hair off, it'd is chin length and looks like shit, but I feel satisfied. I pack my stuff, along with the letter my mom wrote to Evan, then grab a stash of cash from under my mattress, the one my father gave me for emergencies. Then I get in my car and drive away, never looking back. As if the last fourteen hours haven't happened. I'll turn it all off—that is my goal as I drive down the road toward the bus station.

It's a pretty far drive since we live in the more rural, rich area of the town and by the time I pull into the parking lot, the sun is coming up. I leave my keys in the car because I won't need them, grab my suitcase from the trunk, and go inside. As I walk by people, I wonder if anyone can see what I am. What I've done. Do I look like a murderer now?

No one seems to be alarmed, but I still feel nervous as I walk up to the counter to buy a ticket. When the cashier asks me where I want to go, I say, "Anywhere."

He gives me a confused look, like he has no idea what to do. Sighing, I ask, "Where's the next bus going?"

The cashier guy turns to his computer, types something, and then reads over the screen, "Great Falls, Montana. It leaves in about an hour."

"Sold," I say without missing a beat. Montana is far. Rural. An unlikely place for me to pick.

After I pay for the ticket, I briefly consider asking the cashier guy if he'll come screw me in the bathroom. He's not bad looking at all, although a little preppy for my taste, but I need to relax somehow.

But after staring at him long enough that I make him uncomfortable, I end up walking away, for reasons I can barely grasp. I take a seat on one of the benches, waiting to get on the bus. While I'm watching people wander around, searching the crowd for signs of the Defontelles, my phone goes off in my pocket. It rings on and off for five minutes, but I ignore it until a text comes through. I check it and no surprise, it's from my father.

Dad: I'm okay, Lolita. On my way home. Stay there until I get there and please call me.

I read the message over five times and with each time, I grow angrier. I'm not even sure why. If it's because of what I had to do tonight, because he got me into a mess where I had to kill. Or is it something else.

Finally, I throw my phone into the trash bin. The last connection to my home gone. It gives me a little sense of peace. I wonder if Layton's doing the same thing. If he's erasing his identity. For the briefest moment, I think about pulling my phone out of the garbage and calling him, just to make sure he got away okay, but in the end I don't—can't bring myself to do so. I simply get up and get on the bus, leave everything behind, knowing I can never be Lola or Lolita again.

About the Author

The New York Times and *USA Today* bestselling author, Jessica Sorensen, lives in the snowy mountains of Wyoming. When she's not writing, she spends her time reading and hanging out with her family.

Connect with me online:
Jessicasorensen.com
http://jessicasorensensblog.blogspot.com/
http://www.facebook.com/#!/JessicaSorensensAdultContemporaryNovels?notif_t=page_new_likes
http://www.facebook.com/pages/Jessica-Sorensen/165335743524509
https://twitter.com/#!/jessFallenStar

Don't Close Your Eyes

Hilary Storm

Copyright © 2014 Hilary Storm
All rights reserved.

Chapter One

    These bags are extremely heavy. I should've asked Scott to help me, but I'd hate to inconvenience him and his new wife. There really isn't anyone else to call for help since they've all stepped out of my 'crazy' world; the sudden changes I made scared everyone off. I can still hear their comments about how unstable I am. 'Who quits their job to write a book?' Yeah, well bitches, I did. I've written five novels in a series and I have plans for so many more, but none of them know that. They seriously think I sit here in my apartment and grieve.

    I didn't become a New York Times bestselling author by crying myself to sleep at night. I don't have time for tears; there are places to go and people to meet. I'm headed to a book signing in New York City. It's a privilege to even be invited to this event. A part of me is excited and another is dreading this day.

    I just wish I could have one more day with him. I'd love to show him that I'm doing it, even though our friends and family have zero faith in me. He always believed in me and supported me in everything I set out to do. Very few people find a person who truly comes through for them when they have off the wall ideas. You know, like work as an accountant for six years and then one day decide you'd like to write a book. I guess it didn't help that I decided to do that exactly one month from the day he died.

    He would've been one hundred percent behind me, but he's not here, so I go it alone. Don't get me wrong, I miss him like crazy, but that won't bring him back to me. As for everyone else, they stepped away from me when I needed the support the most. They got off this crazy train and it doesn't circle back around to pick up passengers who jump ship. Scott's the only one who has had much to do with me since I 'went crazy'.

To be honest, my emotions were so out of control that it took me spilling it all onto paper for me to be able to cope with everything. I miss him so much and everyone wants me to 'talk' about it. I just can't and it's easier to work through my demons on my own.

I finally work my way past airport security after checking my luggage. Obviously, security isn't getting any easier to pass through because I had to be scanned separately from the others. It's probably because they sense the 'crazy' that the others speak of. This loneliness is partly my fault, but it would've been nice for them to believe in me a *little*.

The flight is full of people and should be interesting. I haven't been in a crowd of people since the funeral almost a year ago. This is a big step for me, though. A book signing in New York City is huge for an author to attend, never mind the fact that I've always wanted to go there. James and I talked about traveling there together many times.

I sit in my window seat and hope for the peace I need to stay focused on my inner strength to get through this weekend. My ear buds begin to blare one of my favorite Hinder songs and I pull my magazine out of my bag to stay entertained for the non-stop flight across the states.

The passengers keep piling in and I begin to wonder just how large this airplane is. I paid extra money to fly First Class in hopes of staying under the radar of any chatty passengers and kids that don't mind their parents.

I'm trying to stay focused on my article while someone is reaching over my head to load his luggage, completely distracting me. I really should've purchased the seat next to me. *Why didn't I think of that before now?* Even with the help of the flight attendant he has to force the bags into the compartment. *How the hell much stuff does he have?*

I purposely don't make eye contact with him after he flops into the seat right beside mine. His leg pushes against mine a few times and he seems extremely restless. I'm not sure it's intentional, but it seems that way.

We begin to prepare for take off so I pull out my ear buds to hear all of the safety information. Watching and listening to the flight attendant give her instructions kind of overwhelms me, but I'm sure it'll all come to me in case of a true emergency. It's not like we'll survive if this huge bird has a real emergency anyway.

I slip the buds back in for take off and begin to read again. It isn't until he presses his leg into mine again that I begin to get irritated. His posture is slouched and he's noticeably oblivious to the fact that he's invading my space with his legs spread open like that.

"Excuse me." I yank out an ear bud and let it fall against my chest while I use my hand to gesture toward his leg. I'm sure my face is telling him exactly how I feel, because it never lies. I have a very shitty poker face.

"No worries. You're not bothering me." The shock on my face from his audacity has him smiling.

"You're bothering me. So if you don't mind, please move your leg." I sit back in hopes of him doing as I ask and grab the ear bud to reposition.

"Nah. I don't mind. Sorry, ma'am." *Ah HELL NO. He did NOT just call me ma'am.* That makes me feel so damn old. I choose to attempt to ignore him and move to plug my ear again, but *hell* if it doesn't bother me. His stare begins to heat my skin—you know, like the weird feeling you get when you can tell someone is watching you. I shift so that I'm turned more toward the window and try to enjoy the view of the landscape below. The feel of his leg brushing up against mine again causes me to pull further away from him. I notice the touch of his finger on my shoulder and everything inside of me wants to stand up and scream for this creep to get off of me. My head whips around to glare at him when I notice the attendant staring at me in the aisle.

"Would you care for something to drink?"

"Yes, I'll take a water, please."

"One water, one Jack and Coke. I'll be right back." Why do I let it shock me that this character is drinking at 8:30 in the morning? It really shouldn't shock me at all.

"Don't you think it's kind of early to be drinking like that?"

"It's okay. I drink Coke any time of day!"

"Right... Well, good luck with that."

"You're pretty stiff. You could probably use a drink like that yourself!"

"I'm not stiff, so keep your comments to yourself, if you don't mind."

"I think you *are* stiff and you have to live a little, but I'll work on keeping that to myself." *Who does he think he is?* He doesn't get to judge me after only sitting beside me for a couple of minutes.

"You have no idea what I'm going through, so don't try to judge me based on the few minutes you've seen me today."

"Touché. Let me apologize and maybe we can start over." I wait for his actual apology and find myself waiting too long. My impatience grows wild and I can't believe I'm letting this guy really get to me. He enjoys my silence a little longer before he finally speaks.

"I'm truly sorry for calling you stiff. Please accept my apology and let me buy you a drink." He watches my face very closely and must finally get a clue that he's pissing on a ticking time bomb. He extends his hand in an introduction-like stance.

"Liam Brooks." The disgust on my face *has* to be obvious as I refuse to shake his hand or willingly touch anything of his. His sexy as hell grin flashes across his face and damn if my eyes don't betray me. Those lips are the kind you want to watch someone run their tongue over. There is an awkward silence before I begin to reach out to accept his introduction.

"Olivia Drake." My eyes get caught up in his gorgeous baby blues for a few seconds before I realize our hands are still touching. I pull back slowly and shift back in my seat.

"Olivia Drake, what has you headed to New York City?" Telling a stranger any more about myself is *completely* out of the question, so I quickly decide to be as vague as possible.

"Business trip."

"Me, too. Do you travel there often?"

"No, this is my first time."

The drinks arrive and he immediately asks for a second drink of the same. "The lady will have what I'm having." His persistence is such a pain in my ass. This flight is going to be torture if I continue to let him get to me so I send the flight attendant a smile in agreement.

He leans back in his seat in such a relaxed state next to my very straight, upright and uptight posture. Taking note of that makes me realize I *am* stiff and tense. I prefer to call it focused and driven, but those words don't really explain my posture.

I try to relax a bit by leaning the seat back and decide to prove to myself that I'm not *stiff*. He offers me the Jack and Coke just as I have this epiphany so I gladly accept his challenge.

Chapter Two

The smell reminds me of him. James loved Jack and Coke. I close my eyes and inhale the memorable scent before I swallow my first sip. The liquor is so strong that it causes me to cough. His laughter pulls my attention from the memories.

"Glad you find this funny."

"Your expressions are very dramatic and I can tell exactly what you're thinking."

"Really? What am I thinking right now?"

"You're thinking…. 'This jackass thinks he's fucking suave and he's nothing but a piece of shit on the bottom of my shoe… aren't you?"

"Well hell. You *can* read my mind!" His drink arrives and he turns to face me.

"To not forgetting to live life." I try to figure out how, less than an hour ago, I was fighting with my luggage by myself and now I'm drinking to *living life* with a stranger.

"To living life." This sip goes down a little better, probably because I get a little lost looking at him again. His dark, messy hair *does not* have me wanting to run my fingers through it. The sleeves of his tight t-shirt aren't so tight that I can see his muscles bulging and I sure as hell *don't* want to see what else is under that shirt. Not. At. All.

My eyes travel back up to his face just in time to see that he's enjoying the view as well. Sitting back quickly, I pull my shirt up a little to hide any cleavage that's showing. *What am I doing? Why am I reacting like this with a complete stranger?* Guilt reigns over me for the next few minutes. I try to process the reasons that I feel like this. It's been a long time for me and I know that's part of it. James and I had a very active sex life and I've really isolated myself since his death. I must be sex starved; that would explain why my thoughts are complete chaos right now.

What frustrates me a little is the fact that I know this guy knows he's affecting me like this. Really, what's the harm in flirting with this guy? It's not like I'll ever see him again. This drought could go on for a decade if I don't let myself feel every once in awhile. *What if?*

What if I let this guy into my life just long enough for some fun and he rocks my world just like I crave? What if he rocks it so hard that I forget my damn name and where I live, which is all totally possible. Writing romance novels really *does* get to a girl after a while.

What if I try to get somewhere with him and he rejects me? Can my ego take that right now? Being an author really messes with your self confidence and actually traveling to New York at this moment has me nervous if I think about it at all.

What if we have sex and he decides he wants to see me again? That can't happen. Listen to me! I'm already plotting how the story will go and I've hardly said a word to him.

What if I put my ear bud back in and ignore his pompous ass for the rest of the flight and write him into my next novel? I could kill him off in the first chapter just to prove a point. I'll make it gruesome and let it be at the hands of the strong female character.

"What kind of business in New York?" He attempts to strike up the conversation once again. I could tell him that I'm an author, but why tell a complete stranger how to actually find you if he chooses to search for you?

"I'm an accountant. There's a conference I have to attend." Neither of those statements are a lie, yet I think they *will* manage to keep my information private.

"Nice. I'm terrible with numbers."

"Yeah, luckily it comes easily to me. What about you?"

"Business as well. I'm doing research for a project that I'm working on."

"Oooooh. Intriguing. You have my attention now! What kind of project would have you traveling to the big city?"

"Family stuff. I promised a loved one that I'd follow up on something very important, and here I am doing what I promised."

"Man of your word, then."

"Most definitely." Okay, this is good for me. Honesty is very important to me, not that I'm looking for a relationship with him, though.

"So tell me, Miss Drake, did it hurt?" *Hurt? What is he talking about?*

"Not sure what you're asking."

"When you fell from heaven." Oh great! A corny ass pick up line. My laughter becomes obnoxious before I have a chance to stop myself.

"Don't be so sure that's where I'm from!"

"I can tell you're one of those good girls, straight out of the book. You don't get out much and you're okay with that. You probably stay home on the weekends and work." I really hate that I'm this transparent.

"Well, *I* can tell that you get around and probably use lame ass pick up lines on girls after getting them drunk, just so you can get laid."

"Damn. You see right through my plan!" My face lights up with a smile. Actually, it's one of the first smiles I've had in a very long time. "You have a very nice smile. You really should smile more often." His words make me stop and think about my life for a second. I really *don't* take the time to smile. My life revolves around being an author and living vicariously through my characters. My reason for smiling is gone and I can't really do anything to get that back.

"Yeah, well I'll try to work on that."

"I always try to find at least one thing every day that'll make me smile." I choose not to tell him how lonely my life is and that there really isn't a reason to smile outside of my success as an author. Our conversation stops for a few minutes while the attendants serve the complimentary snacks. I shove mine in my bag, knowing New York City is a big place and I'll probably opt out of leaving the hotel in search of food.

"So, Livi, tell me more about yourself." I pause in thought as my mind runs wild with reasons to shut him off from any actual information about myself, but my gut feelings about him win over. Livi as a nickname kind of grew on me when it came across his lips.

"I'm a single, hard working woman who stays at home on weekends and works. I live in Phoenix and I have a dream of traveling the world one day."

"Very nice! I knew I was right about you. Where would you like to travel?"

"Oh, you know, London, Paris, Australia, Canada. Really my list could go on forever. I just want to see places that I've heard so much about."

"Sounds like you need a bucket list."

"Yeah, I guess you could say I already have one. One day I'll be able to do some of the things I have planned."

"I hope so."

"How about you? I've shared a few of my secrets, now it's your turn."

"I'm a single, hard working guy who doesn't stay at home on weekends and I also live in Phoenix, but I'm originally from Denver. I've traveled quite a bit in my life, but not for enjoyment. Maybe one day I'll be able to travel for leisure. I have four brothers and we all work together."

"That's awesome! I wish I had a brother."

"There have been days where I would've let you have them. But all in all, I'd do anything for every single one of them." He's so serious now that he's talking about his family. His mind seems to wander for a brief second before he quickly returns to give me his full attention again.

"I'd give anything for a family." My statement is cut off by the announcement that our plane will soon be entering turbulence. The thought of a rough flight doesn't settle well with me. I start to look through my phone for another song to play. I'm so used to having music on all day.

"What are ya listening to?"

"I have a huge play list, I'm just scrolling through."

"Let me choose a song for you." His finger brushes over mine when he reaches for the phone. I glance down as he removes the phone from my hand and notice his leg bumped up against mine again, but this time it doesn't irritate me.

He scrolls through my music and I watch as he hesitates, but I can't see what he's looking at. "Okay. You ready?" The song begins and an instant rush of heat flows through my body. There is no mistaking that beat. I'm not sure where the grin on my face comes from, but it spreads across my lips. I begin to move my leg with the beat, closing my eyes and allowing the music move me. It's impossible not to move your body to this song. He really did just play 'Closer' by Nine Inch Nails to me. I'm going to take this as a sign that we will be pushing this a little further than conversation.

I listen to the entire song while he watches my every move. I can feel him adjust in his seat a few times while the music moves me. The pressure of his body leaning on mine gives me hope for what's to come.

When the song finishes, I don't really know how to react, so I begin to scroll again. The sexual tension is so damn tight right now I can hardly breathe and I know *he* feels it, too.

"What hotel are you staying at?" His whisper in my ear sends a chill straight through to my core.

"Downtown Marriott." My breathy answer proves to him that I'm game for anything. He hasn't pulled away from my face since whispering in my ear. I let my eyes move up his chest, over his lips and to his eyes. His close proximity has me holding my breath for sure. His eyes begin to move over my features right before he sits back in his seat. He's still leaning in my direction, but not right in my face so I can finally take a much needed breath of air.

The rest of the flight seems to go extremely fast and it isn't long before we land. I spend the remainder of the time contemplating what I'm about to do. It's been almost a year since James passed, but I still really miss him. I think knowing that this will be nothing more than a one-time hookup will work for me. Anything more than that and I know I'll have a hard time,

There really isn't any further conversation between us until I step into the airport. "I'll help you with your luggage and then we can get a cab to your hotel room." He stands right behind me while we are waiting for the luggage to arrive. I'm talking *right* behind me and I'm guessing it's to hide the bulge that I can feel against my ass. Shit, it's been a long time and I want to do this. I refuse to let myself begin to think about my past and reasons why this shouldn't happen.

Chapter Three

He carries all the luggage except one small bag and I'm not going to lie, it's nice to travel with someone. I slide in the back seat of the cab, scooting all the way over and he follows me, moving so that he's right up against my side. His hand slides across my knee and up my leg once the driver begins to move. The tingle of feeling someone touch me again has me shifting in my seat. He works his way up my leg and then between my legs. *Why didn't I wear a skirt today?*

He continues to move his hand all over until he eventually puts one arm behind me, pulling me in close. His fingers brush over my breast and I lean into his touch. I let my hand travel up his leg and over his bulging erection that is more than ready for attention, trying to stay under the radar of the cab driver noticing what's going on. I put extra pressure in my touch when I move across him one last time. I know I'm probably playing with fire, but I've realized I really want this right now.

"I'm going to fuck you the second we close the door to your room." *Damn.* The way he exhales when he talks in my ear has me nearly straddling him right here in public.

I manage to get checked in very quickly and the ride up the elevator seems to take forever. Apparently everyone is trying to go up at once and this car is packed tight. Standing this close to him has me even more eager to get into my room.

My fingers can't get the door open fast enough with his hands on my ass. The door slams open as we bust through it and begin to race for each other's zippers. My body is hyperaware of every single touch from him. I'm on fire and ready to ignite. There's not a doubt in my mind that my first orgasm will come quickly. His hand moves from my jeans to my hair where he grabs a handful. Pulling my hair into his grip and tugging it gets my attention real quick.

"This is going to be hard and fast. If you can't handle that, don't let this go any further." That should scare me, or at least make me doubt this entire situation, but it doesn't. Actually that's exactly what I need this to be. Zero emotions and just a hard fuck that is nothing more than exactly that.

"The harder the better." His grip tightens just slightly and my hair is deliciously, yet painfully being pulled away from my scalp. I meet his eyes and don't let his stare intimidate me from staring back. "You gonna' fuck me or just stare into my eyes?"

"Strip. Now." He drops my hair and leans back against the wall to watch my every move. My clothes seem to be working against me, but I refuse to lose the battle. I need this so bad.

"Get on the bed on all fours." His voice is very deep and there isn't any emotion coming through his words. I climb on to the bed and look over my shoulder at him to see if I can catch the smallest glimpse of what he's doing.

"Turn around. Face down." My heart actually skips a beat and the hitch in my breath escapes loudly throughout the room.

"Spread your legs a little further. I want to see everything." I can feel his eyes on me, traveling over my entire body like a kiss tickling my skin. I obey his every command and look forward to the next.

"Back that beautiful ass up to the edge." I move slowly and calculate the angle as I move back in hopes of him meeting me there. He doesn't disappoint me when his hands meet me and begin to travel between my legs, spreading my wetness all over. His fingers enter me and the feeling of sexual hunger overtakes my emotions. The magical way he rotates and moves his fingers has me near climax very quickly.

As soon as I moan he removes his hand, leaving me completely empty and vulnerable as I wait for him to attack again. I feel his breath between my legs and begin to sway, begging for contact. He blows slowly, tickling every bit of my aching clit. My inner muscles begin to clench with the anticipation of being filled with him. I let my brain begin to beg him. *Please touch me. I need to be touched. Please, hurry.*

The touch of his hands as he spreads them open over each of my ass cheeks sends chills all over my body. His hands roam up my back then back down again. He spends more time moving over my backside and I hear the sound of clothes rustling and a condom wrapper tearing. He removes his hands from me again.

My patience is being tested and I'm honestly not sure I can take much more of this. He finally brings his hips up to mine and I feel his very large erection as he rubs it all over my slit. His fingers make my skin tingle all the way up my back until he grabs a fist full of my hair, yanking my head up off the bed.

The pleasure-pain radiates through my entire being and the level of my awaiting orgasm has just been heightened beyond any level I can remember. I'm so damn hungry for this.

His first thrust is fast and deep, just as he warned. His cock fills me completely and he pauses just long enough for me to adjust before he pulls back only to slam forward immediately. He pulls my hair even harder and uses his other hand to grab onto my shoulder using it for leverage for the fuck he promised. Damn, this angle has him so deep inside of me that I'm ready to go on the third time he thrusts forward.

He continues to slam into me over and over, not slowing in the slightest when I scream through the hardest orgasm of my life. He shows no mercy and this is everything I'd hoped it would be. Meaningless and mind-blowing sex with a stranger is exactly what I need. It isn't until I feel the burn of his release that I feel completely satisfied.

My body collapses on the bed when he releases my hair and shoulder. He doesn't follow me onto the bed and I get irritated with myself that it bothers me. James would've wrapped me up in his arms until I fell asleep. The feeling of guilt begins to rush through my mind. How could I be so disrespectful to him by fucking someone I don't even know? The worst part of it all? How the stranger made me feel.

I hear him putting his clothes on and decide to move so that my nakedness is covered. Shame will make you hide under the covers very quickly.

"Livi. I have to go." I refuse to acknowledge that he's really pulling the wham-bam-thank-ya- ma'am on me. I can hear his movements in the room for a couple of minutes before the sound of the door opening startles me.

"I really did have a great time today. Livi, take care of yourself." And with that, he closes the door behind him and walks out of my hotel room. This makes me feel like a slut and it disturbs me that although I'm mostly ashamed of it, a part of me actually enjoyed it.

Chapter Four

There are author events going on this evening and I really don't want to leave my hotel room. This trip is supposed to be about me reaching out to fellow authors and meeting some people similar to me, but in this moment I don't care to see anyone. I need to work through some of this guilt so I'm doing what I do best when I need to release. Writing has become my escape and a chance to get away from reality. Somehow in the escape, I find a way to deal with the emotions I'm facing. This usually happens when I write in a character that goes through something similar. I've written over five thousand words since he left.

This new character is a whore who goes around having sex with anything that will look her way. Right now, the sex scenes are smoking hot and I'm sure I'll eventually come to some realization that deep down she's just a broken girl that needs to find the perfect someone to complete her. But for now, she has sex. Lots of dirty, nasty sex.

The sound of my phone going off pulls me out of my deep concentration of describing the best sex my character has ever had. I move to check my screen and see a text message from an unknown number, but when I see the message I know it's him.

Liam: I want to see you again.

I set the phone down and go right back into my story because I can't deal with him right now. *How did he even get my number?* He doesn't get to walk out after sex like that and then text me later. The sound of my phone interrupts my thoughts again shortly afterward.

Liam: Don't even think about ignoring me.

I think about not responding, but I have a feeling this will go on and on if I don't at least respond with something.

Olivia: We'll have to get together again someday.
Liam: Let's choose a time and place now, so I can look forward to it.
Olivia: I'll get back to you. I'm busy this weekend.
Liam: Surely you have a little time in your busy schedule.
Olivia: No, not really.
Liam: Okay.
Olivia: How'd you get my number?
Liam: I called myself from your phone.

So him walking out on me *wasn't* a plan to forever avoid the one-night-stand he hooked up with in New York City. He made it so that he could still reach me.

Olivia: Clever.
Liam: I'm not an idiot. Now when can I see you again?
Olivia: I am really busy this weekend, but I can see you back in Phoenix??
Liam: That'll have to work I guess.

His texts have completely distracted my flow of words and I find myself irritated that he's getting to me like this. I actually *want* to see him again. How do I let my mind wrap around what happened today and get to where he can be in my life back home? Our conversation throughout the day went from me being extremely pissed off to entirely turned on and ready to explode in both scenarios. He has a way of shifting my emotions all over the place and I'm positive every time we see each other it'll be the same.

I think really hard about my next text and debate whether to even send it but to be honest, I'd like to see him again *here* before bringing him into my personal space.

Olivia: You know where I'm staying if you decide it doesn't work.
Liam: It doesn't work. I'll be by later tonight.

The meaning behind his last statement is obvious and it actually jumpstarts me into action. I need to shower and go to the dinner while I can still make an appearance, but not before I'm dressed and ready to see *him* again.

****

I make my way into the large dining hall and try to locate anyone that seems friendly. There's a table toward the back of the room with a couple of seats available so I sit and try to fit in. There are four women sitting at the table talking and I begin to listen to them when I hear my name.

"I just *love* Olivia's series! She's supposed to be here! I'd love to meet her, but she is such a private person I don't even know what she looks like."

"We'll get to see her tomorrow during the signing! I'm going to have her sign my Kindle!"

"I can't *wait* for her next novel. Can you believe she killed Meagan off in the last book?"

I enjoy letting them go on and on about my stories, knowing in just a few minutes I'm going to shock the shit out of them. It means a lot to me to hear their true reaction to my series knowing it's genuine. I decide it's time to let them in on my secret.

"Hi guys! So I hear you ladies are looking to meet Olivia Drake!" They all turn their attention to me and begin to look around the room.

"Yes, do you see her?"

"Well, not exactly. I *am* her!" Watching the shock on their faces and listening to the excitement in their screams startles me. This is my first real life fan-girl moment and I'm just not sure how to take it all in. I smile and watch them until they all finish speaking at once.

"Oh my God! We are sitting with Olivia Drake! This is so badass!" Finally their excitement settles enough so we can start having actual conversations. I truly enjoy learning about these women. We enjoy dinner and a few drinks before the meet and greet starts to fizzle out. I leave wishing I had tried to mingle some, but spending quality time with true fans meant a lot to me. Of course, they all promise to come to the signing tomorrow to see me and get my autograph.

Chapter Five

On my way up to my hotel room, I start to think about Liam again. I begin to wonder what time he'll come by to see me and find myself hoping it's soon. The wine is making me feel slightly tipsy and horny as hell. The memories of this afternoon begin to surface and the delicious ache of my muscles reminds me just how great the sex was.

After my short ride up in the elevator, I turn the corner to the hall where my room is located. My eyes travel down the hall to the man leaning up against my door. *Damn if he isn't hot as hell.* The fact that he's waiting for me excites me beyond words. I choose to get the upper hand when I come face to face with his gorgeous features. I love that he has just the right amount of scruff and lips that I could suck on all night. I dive straight into kissing his lips and splay both of my hands on the wall out beside him, pinning him in.

His hands remain at his sides during our tongue battle and if it wasn't for the fact that he's having to lean his head down a little to kiss me, the effort would be all on me. *How can he have such discipline when I'm ready to climb his body and go for the ride of my life?*

Our kiss isn't romantic or sensual. It's hungry and carnal, quickly becoming the roughest kiss I've had in my life. I use my teeth to nibble on his bottom lip and start to pull away. We probably should get inside the room very soon if this kiss is any sign of where we're headed.

His hand stops me from separating us more than a few inches and his intense stare has me frozen in place. I notice our exaggerated breathing mirrors each other by watching the rise and fall of his chest.

"Did you enjoy yourself tonight?"

"Yes." It comes out barely a whisper and I witness my entire body betray me. I shouldn't want him *this* bad. Hell, I just met him today and now my nipples harden just by the sound of his voice.

"I can taste the wine on your lips." My chance to respond is minimal and he leans forward to sample the flavor again. The sudden movement of him flipping around me takes me by surprise. Then the pressure of him behind me forces me into the wall so tight that I can feel every ridge in his body.

"You like it rough, don't you?" I don't know how to answer him. This is all new to me and I've never experienced anything like it. My emotions are so all over the place that I don't want to respond. He runs his hand up my leg and under my dress only to find barely-there panties that are wet as a result of how much I want this.

"No need to say anything, your panties tell me what I need to know." I whimper when his finger slides between my folds and the heat of his breath hits my ear.

"Tell me you want this. Tell me you'll submit everything to me again." I nod in approval right before he pulls my mouth to meet his. He invades me with his tongue and he slips his finger covered with my juices into my mouth. I welcome his attack and my mind slips into the chaos of being impatient and hungry for more of his touch. Pulling at my purse to reach for my room card, I feel his hand move down my neck and into my bra. His other hand is full of my ass once he slides his fingers over my garter strap. I rush to get the card in my hand and start to move us toward the door. Here we are again, shoving on the door faster than I can get it open.

The room is dark and we don't bother flipping on the lights. He continues to walk me through the room until my legs bump the bed. This time he turns me to face him and begins running his tongue down my neck. The feeling of him traveling between my breasts, leaving a trail of chills, has me ready for anything he wants from me. His hands move up to the V-neck of my dress before he rips the material from my chest. He continues to rip the dress completely off of me and I'm at a complete loss for words. Something like this should really piss me off, but I find it very arousing and I'm looking forward to what he'll do to me next.

I stand there like a statue while he rains kisses and nibbles all down my torso. He pauses when he reaches my panties and I hear him inhale right between my legs.

"Mmmm. I love the smell of pussy." Those words would have offended me in any other time, but considering he has me very aroused and ready to sit on his face, I'll take it as a compliment.

He uses delicate fingers to remove my panties, leaving the garter belt in place and pulling my heels from my achy feet. His demeanor is so different than it was just moments ago and the difference has my curiosity piqued as I wait for his next move.

He stands up and connects with my lips while he starts removing his own shirt, one button at a time. I move to help him with his belt and he moves both hands to hold my head, entwining his fingers in my hair in the process. I wait for the tug, but it doesn't come. Our kiss is now passionate, almost like lifelong lovers who have all the time in the world to spend with each other.

He leans me back onto the bed and we both crawl further onto the mattress, never breaking our kiss. His hands become tender and his touch is perfect as it glides over every inch of my skin. We continue with the sensual movements for what seems like an hour. *Should I want to kiss a man this long? What happened to this being a one time fuck and then I move on?*

I've missed this. I didn't realize just how *much* I've missed this until his arms began to feel like James's. I let the tears forming in my eyes run down my cheeks, hoping he won't notice. *If I close my eyes and think about James, I can do this.* I'll just pretend it's him here with me because the thought of walking away from this feeling isn't an option. I need this.

He gently moves between my legs until he's poised at my entrance. He reaches for a condom that I didn't even know was near and I wait while he protects us both. My invitation is a slight shift of my hips letting him know I'm ready. He slides in slow and with great discipline as the movements between us become natural. This pace continues until I can feel the heat of his release deep inside me again. My orgasm follows right behind his and the tears flow just as hard as my release.

I let him wrap me up in his arms and hope he doesn't ask me about my tears. I'm not ready to share James with anyone and I should've never used Liam like this.

My mind tries to process why it was better to be handled like I was this afternoon over how he's holding me now. *Maybe it's because I'm not ready to face the fact that he's really gone forever.*

I roll over in hopes of evading the inevitable inquisition that's headed my way. He pulls me in for a spooning embrace and I let him hold me while my tears fall. He doesn't ask me anything, only holds me tighter when my sob escapes. I'm very thankful he just lets me cry.

Chapter Six

I wake the next morning to an empty bed, swollen eyes and the smell of sex. Rolling over, I notice my phone on the night stand. I only have about an hour to be downstairs for the signing so I begin to rush around. Makeup barely covers the mess I made of my eyes last night, but I do my best to hide the puffiness.

On my way out the door, I glance at my phone to see if he left me a message. I'm not going to lie and say it doesn't hurt a little when there isn't one.

The silence in the hall allows me to collect my thoughts about last night. His contradicting behavior has me confused and I hate that I fell apart. What I had with James was very special to me and to be honest, I'm lost without him. We were supposed to have forever together. Instead, I'm here living a life with fictional characters constantly running through my head, trying to move on. It's obvious by my behavior last night that I haven't. *How do you say goodbye to your everything?*

James and I met right after college. Our connection was immediate and we fell in love very quickly. I never had to question his love because he always made me feel it. I'll never forget the day Scott rang the doorbell to tell me the news. He didn't even get a word out before I was shaking my head 'no' over and over, falling to the floor just as my heart was exploding out of my chest. I really thought I had cried every tear possible for him over the next few days as it all became a blur. If it hadn't been for Scott being there, I'm not sure how I would've made it through the funeral arrangements even though the department handled most of them.

We'd been trying to start a family and I had just gotten the news from the doctor that the chance of me becoming pregnant was extremely unlikely. I remember thinking that was the worst news I could've ever received. I had no idea of the reality of what a true loss was.

The weeks following, I remained a shell of a person with zero emotion. Until one night I decided to write in a journal. I really haven't stopped writing since—my writing has just evolved into new characters. The first few stories I wrote will never be published. After all, they contain my happily ever after with the love of my life.

I never went back to work after James died. To be honest, I've avoided people at all costs, and the few times I've agreed to leave my house, I quickly wished I hadn't. Our friends and his family believe that I've gone crazy. I don't even answer their messages or the door anymore because I'm tired of trying to defend myself. What's the purpose? They might all be correct.

I found my escape in writing. It's easier to deal with fiction than reality. I decided to self publish a story a few months ago and somehow it became a best seller and everything has been complicated ever since. I begin to focus on setting up my table for the signing. I'm hoping to meet some new fans today and take my mind off of everything else.

Sitting like a zoo animal waiting for fans to approach you is odd to say the least. I put on my fake happy face and try to seem more approachable. The fans from last night's dinner walk over just a few minutes after the signing starts. I make sure to spend extra time with them and it isn't long before there's a line in front of my table. These fans have come from all over the nation to meet an author today—setting aside my chaotic emotions is the *least* I can do.

The day is long, yet rewarding. Words of encouragement give me hope to do even more with my writing career. When the day is over, I find myself back in the elevator and a small part of me hopes Liam is waiting for me again. I check my phone for the first time all day, but still nothing.

Turning toward the hallway to my room I notice he isn't there. Quickly entering the room, I move straight for my computer and begin to write. This asshole character likes to love em' and leave em'; leaving sluts all over the nation as he walks out on them after giving them the best fuck of their lives. I pause in thought and try to tell my mind not to kill off the character because there are good qualities somewhere deep within him.

I had hoped he'd be on the same flight the next day but he wasn't, making the trip long and uneventful. Somehow I manage to have an empty seat next to me, which is very nice. I just want to be left alone right now and I don't need anyone else fucking with my life.

****

The week goes by quickly and quietly. Tonight will be my weekly visit from Scott. He keeps tabs on me throughout the week by calling and texting, but insists on seeing me weekly. We both decided on a set time for him to stop by each week. It keeps him from randomly popping in to check on me and gives me the time to accept the fact that I have to let him in. I know he's just watching out for me and some weeks it's nice just to have the human contact.

He just recently married his girlfriend and I couldn't be happier for him. I don't think she's fond of me since he never brings her to dinner. I throw the lasagna in the oven and begin to prepare the salad just before he arrives.

When he walks in, I stop to greet him.

"Decide you can just walk in?"

"You gave me a key!"

"To take care of Sam when I'm gone, not to use when you visit."

"I knew you'd be busy. I rang the doorbell. I'm sorry, Olivia, I'll wait for you to answer in the future."

"I'm just teasing you. Where's Meg?"

"Oh, she went to see her parents."

"How do you like being a newlywed?"

"It's great. Not much different than when we lived together, but it's nice that it's official. We have some news, though."

I can feel the jealousy rising, so I turn to cut up the cucumber so he doesn't see my expression. Is it bad that I want what he has? Is it so much to ask to be happy? *I know what he's about to say. We're pregnant!* That would be their next step and something he would want to tell me like this.

"Oh yeah?"

"She's carrying my baby, Olivia. Karma is going to make me a father."

"Wow. I'm happy for you guys."

"Yeah, we are, too."

Our conversation continues while I move around in the kitchen.

He's made himself comfortable in his usual bar stool watching everything I do.

"So, how was your weekend?" I pause and try to decide whether or not to tell him about Liam. What do I really need to hide? I hooked up with a guy in New York City, why is this a horrible thing?

"It was great; I met so many fans at the signing and even managed to hook up." I purposely look at his reaction to see what kind of conversation I'm headed for.

"You *what*?"

"I hooked up with a guy I met while I was there." His loss for words brings a smile to my face and I decide right then that I need to keep this vague. Scott seems to be protective of me and I know he's just worried, but I'm a grown ass woman.

"Ok. What's his name and address?"

"Scott, I'm not telling you anything about him. It doesn't matter anyway; it was just a one night stand."

"In New York City? Are you *crazy*?" He knows he's said it the instant it comes out.

"That's what they say."

"I didn't mean that, Olivia. You know I'm just worried about you. I knew I should've gone with you on that trip."

"Uh…. no, you shouldn't have. I was fine and he was actually a really nice guy." I leave out the 'most of the time' from my sentence because Scott would never leave this alone if he knew the guy had treated me like the slut I am.

"You're not going to any more of these things by yourself."

"I don't have any others planned for a very long time, so it'll all be okay." He lets the topic drop and starts to talk about everyday stuff. I can't help but look at him like a big brother during these visits. We don't have anything of importance to talk about, but have no problems talking about nothing.

He doesn't stay long after he helps me clean up the dishes. I don't mind because I'm beat from the weekend and can use a long bath to relax in.

Chapter Seven

I plug my phone into the speaker inside the bathroom and grab a playlist that will be perfect. I'm barely in the bathtub when a notification comes through. I try to let my mind not focus on the curiosity of who would be messaging me. There are really only two people it could be.

Despite telling myself I need to ignore it, I step out of the tub and reach for my phone to see who it is.

Liam: Make it home okay?

Everything before this moment was just a random hookup on a business trip. If I answer this and let him into my personal space, this becomes something more. *Am I ready for more?*

I turn up the volume and set the phone back down before sliding back into the warmth of the water. *How could he be so cold and walk out on me without even a note? What is his deal with leaving after sex?* Shit like this could give a girl a complex. I'm not even in the tub five minutes before the next message comes through. *Who does he think he is?* What an impatient ass! What if I'm busy and don't have time to deal with his mood swings?

Of course I can't *not* look at the message the second I step out of the water again.

Liam: This is the last message I'll send you. If you want to reach me, you have my number.

Really? My temper begins to rise the more I think about his audacity. He walked away from me, *twice*. Then he acts like this when he literally left a message *minutes* before. Give a girl a fucking second to respond. I begin to pace my apartment in my robe thinking about everything. It's nice to have someone to look forward to seeing, but seriously, this guy has issues. I definitely enjoyed our time together, but can't have the walking out anymore. It's not like answering this message lets him into my house. I can choose to do that later if things actually go that far.

Olivia: My, aren't we impatient?
Liam: You telling me you weren't trying to decide whether to reply?
Olivia: Did you make it back to Phoenix?
Liam: Nice dodge. Yes.
Olivia: You expect me to drop everything if you text?
Liam: Yes.
Olivia: Good luck with that!
Liam: We'll see.
Olivia: Will we? I'm not really fond of your Houdini moves.
Liam: I'll work on that.
Olivia: What makes you think you'll get another chance to work on that?
Liam: We'll see.

I decide not to respond. It won't hurt him to be left hanging a little. This interaction is nice, I'm not going to lie, but he's pretty sure of himself. Cockiness has never been an attractive personality trait to me. I remove my robe and slide in between the sheets. I've always preferred to sleep naked and I didn't change that when James died. I move to turn off the light and hear my phone again.

Liam: Go on a date with me.
Olivia: What's your idea of a date?
Liam: Dinner and talking.
Olivia: Where?
Liam: I'll make it worth your while.
Olivia: When?
Liam: Tomorrow.
Olivia: I'll think about it.

Liam: I'll pick you up tomorrow at 7.
Olivia: I said I'd think about it.
Liam: Okay, go for it, but I'm going to be there at 7.
Olivia: You don't know where I live.
Liam: I could figure it out if you make me.

Why is there no doubt in my mind that he could find my address? What could dinner hurt? I should be open for a night on the town by now.

Olivia: 1425 Glendale Avenue, 7:30
Liam: See you then.

I toss and turn the whole night thinking about what I'm doing with Liam. It shouldn't be this hard to see someone. He's complicated, but so am I. I think about James and what he'd want me to do. He would have wanted me to be happy, but safe. Liam Brooks really is a complete stranger, but I just feel like he's a good guy beneath the demanding, impossibly sexy facade he portrays.

After tossing and turning for hours, I give in and pull out my laptop. Maybe if I switch my train of thought to my characters, I can quit worrying about my own drama.

****

It's afternoon before I wake from my deep sleep. The laptop is in its usual place on the bed beside me. I pop open the lid to check my emails and Facebook. There are literally hundreds of messages so I take the time to answer a few. I can never get through them all and still focus on writing.

I begin to think about my date tonight. I want to keep it simple and not go overboard trying to prepare for it, but my excitement has me eager to find the perfect outfit. Is it possible to be excited for something and equally dread it? Because that's what I'm feeling but it's nice to be feeling something *real* again.

I remember that I need to go to the bank today so I'm on a mission to make it a quick trip. I also stop to get milk and a few other things I need from the store. My cart has only a few items when I step up to the cashier. Glancing around at the people in the vicinity, I see Liam picking through the apples in the produce section. I pull my cart out of line and move to see him.

"Don't tell me we shop at the same grocery store?"

"I guess we do! Are you ready for your date tonight?"

"I will be if the guy shows up on time."

"I hope he's not an asshole."

"Yeah, me too." I watch the flirty smile on his face and can't help notice how it lights up my own. He begins to sort through the apples yet again, so I decide to leave him to his shopping.

"Well, I guess I'll see you tonight."

"Yes, tonight." I don't miss his eyes as they move down my body when I turn to walk away. It really does mess with my head that I feel like a teenager around him sometimes. I need to get a grip.

Making sure my house is straightened and my makeup and hair are perfect becomes my sole focus for the rest of the afternoon. I shave everything, hoping it won't all be for nothing. *Look at me. I get sex after a year and now I'm acting like this.* I slide on a new black dress that shows more than enough cleavage. I'm sure I'll get more than enough attention in it, but it's nice to put myself out there for a change.

Chapter Eight

He arrives exactly on time, just like I knew he would. I open the door to a very sexy man in a suit. His attire screams authority and I feel my breath hitch with the thought of that. His dark hair is messy, yet perfect and I watch as he looks around the neighborhood before he notices me. When his eyes finally come in contact with me he seems to have the same appreciative reaction to what I'm wearing. The chemistry is so thick when he's around and I'm sure he notices it, too.

"You look beautiful, Livi." It's been a long time since I've received a compliment that made me feel like it might actually be true.

"Thank you. You look gorgeous yourself! Let me get my purse." I purposely don't invite him in, but it doesn't surprise me when he comes in anyway.

"Your house is nice. Do you live here all by yourself?"

"Yes." Simple answer, but that's all I'm ready for. I grab my purse and pull out the keys to lock the door. He begins to move around the living room, looking at the pictures I have out. There is no doubt he is seeing James and me together, because that's what every picture is. I wait for him to ask, but he doesn't. He studies each one and it begins to bother me. He doesn't have any right to those memories.

"Are we doing this or not?" He senses my tone and quickly pulls his attention away from the pictures and back to me.

"Yes. I'm sorry, I was just appreciating your pictures."

"I wish you wouldn't."

"Okay. I didn't mean to overstep my boundaries." He closes in on me, looking directly into my eyes and I realize very quickly that I can't be angry with him when he's this close to me.

"It's alright. That's just a part of me that I'm not ready to share."

"I understand. Are you ready for a night out?"

"Yes, please." I turn to lead the way and I'm thankful he follows. The panic my heart feels with him near my photos of James is unexplainable and I'm definitely not ready to deal with this.

He waits while I lock up the house and then leads me to his Hummer waiting in the driveway. I wasn't prepared to climb into a vehicle this tall, but I manage to climb in with out any issues. He closes the door behind me and my eyes don't leave his body once as he walks around the vehicle. His stride is completely and utterly sexy and I can't stand myself for being this drawn to him even when he pushes my buttons.

He eases the tension on the drive to the restaurant by bringing up topics of conversation that are easy to navigate. We don't have any problems talking through dinner and I bite my tongue when he orders my meal for me. If he hadn't already asked me what I was getting, I would have walked away from the table. How can he be so domineering but sincere at the same time? His personality still has me on edge waiting to see what'll come next. Maybe this is why I'm enjoying myself so much. I like the surprise factor and I'm out of my element just being on a date.

I limit myself to two glasses of wine and let him lead in the conversation. I really enjoy hearing about his family; it sounds like they are very close. This is intriguing to me since I don't have any family left. I decide to share a few details of my life with him. Telling him about James is difficult, but I make it through it. He really eases me through my conversation about James by asking questions that bring up happy memories of our lives. I even go into the events following his death and what led up to me being an author. He genuinely seems interested in my stories.

It's so easy to talk to him and I notice myself realizing that I've been missing this. Someone who cares how my day is going and what has happened in my life to make me who I am today. This is him showing the sincere side of himself again.

We talk for hours and I lose track of time, forgetting that I was supposed to call Scott to check in. I pull out my phone and find that he's been trying to reach me.

Olivia: I'm sorry. Out on a date, I'll call you in the am.

I know this isn't going to appease him the second I hit the 'send' button. Maybe I should've thrown in something random to keep him from worrying about me.

Scott: Okay. I need his name, now. You can't go on a date and not tell me.
Olivia: Scott, I'm okay. I'll call you when I get home.
Scott: I'll put a damn tracker on your phone if you pull this shit again.
Olivia: I'll call you later.

That conversation is *far* from being over and I'll need to prepare for him to be 'checking in' on me even more. Liam looks at me with a questioning look and I know it's rude to be on the phone during a date.

"Sorry. That was Scott checking on me. He was James's partner on the force when he died and he's been watching out for me since I lost James."

"So Scott is pissed you're on a date?"

"No, it's more the fact that I didn't tell him about it and that I won't tell him your name. I know the minute I do, he'll be running a background check on you." Liam's face looks slightly shocked, but he seems to accept it pretty quickly because he continues our conversation right where we left off.

"I should probably get you home, now." I'm slightly disappointed this is how the date is going to end, but I appreciate the step back from how things went in New York. The drive home is a little quiet but he manages to make me laugh a few times. He parks in my driveway and I struggle with the idea of inviting him in. I decide there's no way I'm ready for that. This is James's house.

I reach for the handle and feel his hand touch my other arm. "Livi, I really enjoyed our date."

"Me, too."

"I want to call you sometime."

"I'd like that." I move again for the handle to open the door and hear him getting out of his side. The engine is still running, so I'm going to assume he's just walking me to the door. We reach the door and he waits for me to unlock the door before he moves in for a kiss. This time when he kisses me, I feel beautiful and respected. It's a soft kiss, not demanding and passionate like what we shared in New York. He pulls away and makes sure that I lock the door before he leaves. I watch out the peephole while he drives away, leaving me wanting him now more than ever.

I pick up my phone again to call Scott only to see he's left countless messages asking me to check in.

"Hello. You have got to chill."

"Olivia, I see the crazy fuckers every day. You need to at least check in if you're going on a date with someone." I really can't disagree with him about the 'crazy fuckers' and figure the best way to calm him is to agree.

"Okay. I promise IF I go on any other dates, I'll let you know."

"Are you going to tell me his name?"

"No, because you'll just investigate him and put him through the ringer."

"You're damn right I will!"

"Scott, just calm down. If I go on any more dates, I'll let you know and I'll even tell you his name then. There probably won't be another date anyway."

"Why, was he an ass to you?"

"No, he was a perfect gentleman. I just don't know if I'm ready."

"Okay. I can accept that. You have to be careful!"

"I will. I promise."

"James loved you, Olivia."

"I know he did. I'll call you tomorrow."

My brain begins to run on overtime as it replays the night. After analyzing and reanalyzing everything, I'm left feeling like there really *is* a connection with Liam and I need to decide if I can handle that. Luckily, this realization relaxes me a bit and I fall right to sleep.

Chapter Nine

I wake in the morning to the sound of my phone ringing. Liam has never called me, so I find it weird to see his name displayed across my screen.

"Hello."

"Good morning. Are you dressed?"

"Uh… Not exactly. Why?"

"Get dressed. I'm on my way to pick you up now."

"Where are we going?"

"I'm taking you out for the day. You'd better get a move on, because I'm almost there."

"I need to shower, so you'll have to wait on me."

"Call when you're ready."

I move quickly to get showered, shaved and dressed. I throw on makeup again, which isn't my usual routine, but required if I go out in public. Picking up the phone to dial him, I hear someone at the door.

I swing the door open to find Liam standing there in jeans and a t-shirt and I quickly decide this is my favorite look on him. I get to see the muscles in his arms this way.

"Hey there!"

"Hi. I'm ready. Do I need anything in particular?"

"No. Just yourself."

I'm not surprised when he helps me in again and the ease of the ride is nice.

"So, where are we going?"

"Family barbeque."

"You're taking me to meet your family?"

"Yeah."

"Turn around right now. Why would you do this without asking?"

"Calm down. It's not like you're thinking. There'll be hundreds of people and it's not like I'm taking you home to meet the parents." I'm more than a little panicked. This never crossed my mind as something he'd consider.

"I'm not sure about this."

"Too late now. I told Mom you'd be there."

"Great, Liam. How exactly did you announce that you'd be bringing your fuck buddy to the family function?" With my words, he pulls over onto the shoulder of the road and puts it in park.

"Do you really think you're just a fuck buddy to me?"

"I don't know *what* to think. You can't take me home to meet your family. I don't do large groups. I haven't been around any people in almost a year, with the exception of New York, and you're about to take me into a group of hundreds? What do you expect from me?"

"It's just an annual event they have to raise money for the schools. I didn't mean to upset you. We don't have to go." I feel like a bitch in hysterics right now. Is this something I can do? I take a deep breath and try to compose myself.

"It's okay. We can go somewhere else. You just tell me where you want to go and we'll go right now. I didn't mean to upset you."

"No, let's go, but keep in mind it might be something I need to work through." I should be honored to meet his family, from what he described last night they are outstanding people. I know they are all very special to him.

"I'll never leave your side."

He pulls back onto the road and we continue until he turns into a long driveway with cars littered everywhere. I know this is going to be a challenge the second I see all of the people.

"They do this every year?"

"Yeah. Mom and Dad are very big supporters of the school districts." I'm pretty sure I'm going to like his family. It's been a long time since I've been involved in the community and it's something I used to enjoy.

As we're walking up to the group, a younger version of Liam meets us. When I say younger version, I mean that you can tell these two are family and there is no mistaking them as brothers.

"Livi, meet my little brother, Mason." He extends his hand to shake mine and I watch his eyes focus on my cleavage.

"Very nice to meet you!" The staring is a little awkward so I turn and lean into Liam.

"Mason, you'd better back off real quick."

"I'm sorry. I don't mean anything by it; consider it a compliment that I appreciate the view. Not many women catch my attention like you just did." I feel like a scared kitty cat hiding against Liam's side, but this is helping.

"Please accept my apologies." I watch his face for sincerity and when I see it, I begin to ease up a bit. Another guy walks up and I wait for the introduction.

"Jace, this is Livi. Livi, this is my older brother, Jace." I begin to think exactly how this day will go. I'll be meeting very hot men that are all related to Liam by the looks of things. I know there are at least two more, but who knows if there'll be other family members with these genes.

"Nice to meet you, Livi."

"Thank you, same to you."

"Mom wanted to see you when you got here." Jace seems very laid back by the way he carries himself. I let Liam lead me through the crowd and into the house. The instant we hit the kitchen, I can tell who is in charge. I watch him as he goes to greet her with a hug and she stops everything to pull him in. It's as if the realization hits her that I should be here because she begins to search the room. Her eyes land on me and she moves from him straight over to me.

"Welcome, Livi! Liam has told me all about you." The surprise on my face must be obvious because she begins to speak to me as she walks back to work in the kitchen. "Liam seems very fond of you, my dear, so I know you'll fit in just fine today. Please make yourself at home."

I debate whether to follow Liam out into the backyard or move to help her. She's very busy and looks like she could use the help.

"Mrs. Brooks, how may I help you?" The smile on her face becomes enormous and she directs me to prep the lettuce. I work as fast as I can, but I'm in no way keeping up with her. She has a system and is boss in this kitchen. People come in constantly to take more food out. I can see Liam talking with a group of guys outside the window and kids playing all around them.

An older man walks in and smiles at me while sneaking up on Liam's mom. He holds his finger over his lips to shush me from warning her. I watch as he slides in behind her wrapping his arms around her.

"Bill, you know I'm busy!"

"I'd *like* to get busy." My laughter brings their attention to me and I wish I could've held that in.

"You, my dear, must be Livi. I'm Liam's dad and you can't blame a guy for trying!" He pauses at the counter to greet me and I have a feeling I'm going to like this guy. His fun personality is infectious. It's hard not to feel like you belong in this house when everyone welcomes you like they have.

The three of us grab the last of the food and go outside with everyone else. Liam is quick to pull me over to meet more family and I enjoy the conversations. Being locked up for nearly a year has really isolated me from companionship and it's in this moment that I realize that.

We spend the day helping with the event and I suggest we stay to help clean up afterward. His mom seems to really appreciate it and I'm not sure who enjoyed the company more.

"Livi, you are welcome here *any* day! You come back even if you're not with Liam. I'll be glad to see you!" She pulls me in for a hug and it feels nice for someone to appreciate me again.

When we pull out of the driveway, Liam turns down the radio and looks over at me. "Well done. You have my family eating out of your hands."

"What?"

"My family loves you!"

"Your family is nice. You're lucky."

"I know I am." His voice trails off and he changes the subject.

"So, where to now?"

"I guess you can take me to my house."

"What about my house?" I think about his proposed idea for a few seconds. I really do like Liam and if today is any indication, I need to step out of my cave and try to live again.

"I'd like that."

Chapter Ten

We drive for a while and I turn to watch him. He senses my stare and looks my way.

"What?"

"Just wondering where you came from."

"I came from Denver." I place my hand in his and leave it there until we pull into his garage.

****

The decor in his house is modern and I'm surprised at how everything is perfectly in its place. He invites me into the living area and we sit close to each other. His behavior is a little off, almost like he needs to get something off his chest. I wait for him to either initiate conversation or what he has planned. We both sit there for several moments before he finally speaks up.

"Liv, I need to know when we're together that you see *me*."

"I don't understand."

He hesitates for quite some time before he continues.

"The last time we were together, I know it was James you we're feeling. I want it to be *me* the next time we're together."

Does he know what he's asking?

"Liam, I can't promise you that I won't think about him. He was my life and I really miss him." I look down at my hands that are folded together in my lap and try to think of the right words to say. My mind doesn't find the right words, because I can't promise to give him what he wants.

"I know you can't promise anything, but I want you to be ready for it before we go there again. Your tears almost broke me that night."

"I know that I've enjoyed every moment with you. I know I really like you and want to see where this takes us and I'm not afraid to try with you." I turn to face him and try to express how I'm feeling. "And I can promise you I didn't think about James the first time we were together. You had my full attention."

"So you like it rough." His directness causes me to shy away from his face and sit back into the couch.

"I liked it that day. This is all new to me and I don't know what to think."

"That's why we need to slow things down until you have time to work through your feelings." He pulls me into his side, wraps his arm around me and we spend the entire evening together watching movies and talking. It's the personal time like this that I miss the most.

****

I wake to him lifting me in his arms. I let him carry me through the house and into his bed. He lays me in his bed and turns to walk out of the room.

"Where are you going?"

"I have to do some work, but I'll be back soon." I lay there and think about everything that's happened in the past week. How exactly one week ago we were in New York and he was spinning my world out of control. Now it seems like everything has settled and I really think I can try this. I can try to live again. He's a great guy and I love that he's not predictable.

I move to find the restroom and get a view of the master bedroom he left me in. The furniture is massive and the room *still* has a ton of space. The bathroom is just off the room and the shower is gorgeous. I pull off my clothes and start the water in the showerhead that's closest. I've never seen a shower this large and I actually feel tiny in the massive space.

The steam fills the space rather quickly and I let the water travel over my skin. I move my fingers across some of the beads of water that are running down the glass shower door and nearly scream when I see his shadow.

"Shit. You scared me!" He continues to watch me as I begin to lather soap over my body. He eventually starts to remove his pants and I decide that I'm okay with whatever happens. I really like him and it's good for me to be active in my life.

"I didn't mean to scare you. You're just so damn sexy in my shower." He slides into the shower with me and I let my eyes skate over his body. This is the first time I've actually been able to look and enjoy the view. His abs are defined and his arms are built but not bulging. His body is perfectly proportioned and this makes me want to run my tongue over every ripple of muscle.

I move into his arms and wrap mine around his waist. He's quite a bit taller than me, so we just fit together easily. He reaches for the soap and begins to lather my skin all over again. His touch on my skin feels so good so I let him continue to draw tingles to the surface. Grabbing the soap, I return the favor and enjoy exploring every bit of his body. I don't shy away from washing his erection, adding extra lather and spending a little extra time there. His moan of appreciation and continued growth let me know he's not objecting to my advances. I begin to move even faster with each small thrust of his hips.

"Shit, Livi." Not slowing down, I move around him so that my chest is against his back. His breathing gets louder and I can't help but place a small bite on his back while placing kisses in every direction. His release comes hard and fierce, hitting the shower wall and running down my hand. I curl my arms under his and lean into his back, just enjoying this moment.

He turns to face me and I let him wrap me up in his arms. His lips begin to travel and send even more sensation through my skin. I brace myself against the wall while he moves down my body until he's between my legs. He moves my right leg over his shoulder and begins to return the favor. My hips move toward his face when he nibbles just hard enough to bring my orgasm to the surface. The invasion of his fingers sends me over the edge and I struggle to stand on one leg through the entire thing.

Watching him rise to meet my face again is very real. His eyes are dark and hungry. I love having this effect on him. Our lips meet and we fight for air during the kiss that eventually leads to ice cold water. It's nice to have someone who likes to spend time kissing.

Once the water turns cold, we step out and towel dry. I watch him mess his hair up with the towel and smile at the thought of running my hands through it soon. We move into the bedroom and both climb into the bed. I wait for him to begin to push this further, but he doesn't. He pulls me in, wraps me up and we both fall asleep.

****

I wake in his arms. This is progress. *Of course, Livi, it's not like he can leave his own house.* My stomach is growling and I'm sure he'll be hungry once he wakes up. I slide out of bed, being careful not to wake him. His closet is full of T-shirts, so I throw one on. It's probably not a good idea to cook breakfast naked. I grab my phone so I can call Scott.

Quietly, I slip out of the room and down the hall. His house is much larger than I remember from last night, of course I didn't get a chance to get the tour since I passed out on his couch. I pass a few doors in the hall that are all open, noticing he has quite a few extra bedrooms for guests. I'm very intrigued with some of the decor he has throughout each of the rooms. The last door on the right is closed, so I turn the knob to take a peek.

This room is absolutely breathtaking. There are books from floor to ceiling on the one wall and a huge ornate desk in the center. The other walls are filled with more art. My phone vibrates as I begin to really look at each piece. It's Scott, who else would it be since Liam is here?

"Olivia, where are you?"

"I'm fine, Scott."

"I don't think you understand how ridiculous you're being. There are insane people and I worry about you. Hell, right now we have two women missing and you probably have no idea since you don't watch the news anymore."

"Scott, you're overreacting. I'm at Liam's. I stayed the night with him and I'm getting ready to make breakfast." I start to move through the room, admiring some of the novels on the shelves.

"Is it too much to ask that you let me know when you're going out and with whom?" I'm not really listening to him rant anymore. I begin to run my fingers around the edge of the desk and the gorgeous woodwork has my interest. Walking around the massive desk, I try again to calm him down.

"Look, Scott, I'm seeing Liam now. I don't go anywhere else. He's not a criminal and you're going to have to let me have some space on this." I let my fingers travel over the drawer handle, sliding it open as he continues to nag at me.

I'm confused by a picture of me that's on top of a folder. I pull the picture out for a closer look. *How did he get a picture of me during my signing?*

"Olivia, I need to meet him. What's his address?" I slide the drawer open further and lift the top of the folder. There are more pictures of me. I pull a few out and my confusion only gets worse. There's one of me at the airport, one of me getting my hair colored and one of me in my front yard. *What the hell?*

I reach in to pull the whole folder out, not responding to Scott due to the shock of what my eyes begin to see. Pictures of me in my house fill my hands. I'm just doing everyday things in my own living space and someone is invading my privacy by taking pictures. My shock only gets worse when I see one in my bedroom.

"Olivia. Did you hang up on me?" I set the folder on the desk and spread out all the pictures. My eyes move to the pictures where I'm changing or soaking in the bathtub and horror takes over my thoughts. *How did he get these pictures?*

The pictures range from right after James's death all the way up until this week. I begin to feel violated and my instinct is to scream, but I know he'll hear me.

I grab the phone tight and start to panic. "Scott, you have to come get me, *NOW*. Come right now." My voice is hysterical and my breathing is out of control. I can't think straight and I'm overwhelmed with repulsion that I just spent the night with someone who would do this to me. *Why would he have all of these pictures?*

I'm startled by a sound across the room and my insides scream in terror the second I see Liam standing in the doorway.

"What's the address? OLIVIA, TELL ME THE ADDRESS!"

TO BE CONTINUED
'Don't Close Your Eyes' ~ Summer 2014

Author's Note

It's an honor to be involved in an anthology dedicated to such an important charity. Thank you so much for including me and I hope you enjoy my contribution.

~Hilary

Website: http://www.hilarystormwrites.com
Facebook: https://www.facebook.com/pages/Hilary-Storm-Author/492152230844841?ref=hl
Amazon: http://www.amazon.com/Hilary-Storm/e/B00DH2J1VM/ref=sr_ntt_srch_lnk_3?qid=1391310194&sr=1-3
Twitter @Hilary_storm
Goodreads: https://www.goodreads.com/author/show/7123141.Hilary_Storm

Acknowledgements

I owe HUGE thanks to all of the amazing authors who donated their time and creativity to this fundraiser — J.L. Berg, JL Brooks, Dani Hart, Jade C. Jamison, Sloan Johnson, J.B. McGee, Maggi Myers, Tess Oliver, Julie Prestsater, CJ Roberts, Emily Snow, Jessica Sorensen and Hilary Storm. Thank you so much for meeting my tight deadline and being a part of Pink Shades of Words!

Shayne McClendon and Gretchen de la O — Thank you so much for not thinking I was a nut job when I first came to you about this idea. Thank you for answering every single one of my questions and guiding me through this whole process!

For my formatter — You saved me from formatting (when I had no clue how to do it)! Thank you for donating your services and formatting in such a quick turnaround. You rock!!! Thanks to you — I will even get to see Pink Shades of Words as a paperback!!!

Big shout outs to the amazing people at GotPrint.com for donating all of the postcards and business cards. I can't thank you enough for the promotional materials!

Kristen Karwan — Thank you for putting up with my tight deadlines & doing such an amazing job with all of the graphics. You made my vision of the cover into a reality! You have done an extraordinary job with all of the graphics for the cover, postcards and teasers.

Elizabeth Davis — Thank you Thank You Thank you for helping me with all of the edits!!!

FIFTY SHADES OF PINK team —

Karen Snyder- Six years ago, we met by chance when we were both doing the Avon Walk by ourselves. You have been an amazing teammate and support through all the years of doing this walk! We have come a long way now... I have gotten to see your daughters grow and you become a grandma (I still don't think you are old enough to be a grandma!)

Sharon Covington — You are truly my best friend. Even before you joined our team, you were always a huge support with my fundraising! I'm so happy that we get to add more memories to our friendship with the annual walks! But no more passing out in the medical triage unit — unless the doctor is single and really cute!

Maria Estrada — Thank you for joining our crazy team! You will be rocking Pink and Handcuffs for two days like no other!!!

Lets Rock This Bitch and Kicks Cancer's Ass!!!

Made in the USA
San Bernardino, CA
08 March 2014